Royal, Rich & Dirty

A ROYALLY RICH ROMANCE BOX SET

ROYALLY RICH
BOOK FOUR

VIVIAN WOOD

Author's Copyright

Cruel Heir

Chapter One

MARGOT

IF YOU'VE ALREADY READ THIS, YOU CAN SKIP TO PART II.

"WAIT!" I say, crouching down and peering through my camera's viewfinder. We're on a random side street in Brooklyn, so we're not in anybody's way. Both sides of the street are industrial and it's a definite look. It sparks my creativity. "Hold that pose."

Pippa rolls her eyes and grins, freezing in place. "Margot, you had better get a few good photos for Insta, at least. I'm only in New York for the weekend and we have soooo many places to go and things to see… boys to meet…"

Her sleek British accent makes her stand out; her outrageously gorgeous good looks are almost enough to make me envious. She should be on a stage somewhere, performing before an enraptured audience.

Instead, she went to NYU and majored in journalism, just like me.

Shaking my head, I sigh. Pippa is pretty boy crazy. She has been since college. I kneel down and frame my shot carefully. It's late and dark except for the light coming from the streetlamp. But there is something about that light, coming from behind Pippa… illuminating her willowy frame and filtering through her bright red hair…

I take a handful of shots, then stand up. "All right."

Pursing my lips, I press several buttons on the camera and review what I just shot. Pippa comes over to look over my shoulder. She's a good four or five inches taller than me so it works. At five foot one, I'm definitely used to being the shortest chick in the room.

"Scroll to the photos of both of us," she says, nudging me. "The ones that your friend took in the pizza place?"

Bobbing my head, I scroll through the various artsy shots of objects until I get to the pictures she means. The two of us beam at the camera, my petite stature, my black leather jacket, and my shoulder length pink hair seeming silly next to Pippa in her loose white dress.

She doesn't see it that way, though.

"Oh, we look absolutely smashing! Ugh, I just love your whole aesthetic. I'm all soft pinks and flowy garments and you're all like…" She gestures to me.

I look down at my RESIST t-shirt, my super short red tartan skirt, my torn fishnets, and my black Converse. I cock a brow. "I look like I'm either a rich kid from Columbia University that's experimenting with couch surfing or a genuine street rat with a drug problem. But the trouble is that you can't tell which," I joke.

Pippa rolls her eyes at my comment. "Yeah right. Everyone wishes they had a tenth of the style that you have and you know it."

My face heats. I change the subject as I loop my camera strap around my neck again and start moving down the sidewalk. "We're already going to be arriving at this spot pretty late."

She shrugs. "Who cares?" She looks up at the night sky, sighing. "That's one of the things I miss the most since my move to Copenhagen. People there care if you're late. Here, you just shrug and say that there was a crazy person on the subway. As if that's even a real excuse for anything."

I grin. "That is one of the things that is a unique charm of New York."

She slides me a glance as we hurry across the street and continue down the block. "I guess you'll just have to get used to it when you follow me to Copenhagen. Seriously, I've talked to my editor at *Politiken* and showed her some of your photographs and articles. She is receptive."

"Yeah?" I say, raising my brows. "I've always wanted to move to Europe for a job… It sounds funny though, just saying it aloud." I spot the distinctive bright green door ahead of us, standing out from the dreary surrounding buildings. "Oh, that's the door of the club. They have to move this place pretty often to keep it under wraps, but the door is always a bright color."

Pippa and I jog up to the door. I lean close, pulling out my phone, and knock on it forcefully. A slot slides open and a pair of eyes appear.

"Password?" a feminine voice asks.

I look at the e-vite on my phone, skimming for the password. "*Saluta regi*," I call out.

The slot slides closed with a metal thunk. A few seconds later the door creaks open, the door woman dressed head to toe in skintight black latex. "Come in."

We step into the tight, dark space. I can hear the thud of music, feel the vibrations coming up through the floor. She opens a second door and we're immersed in raucous sound and a low blue light.

I walk out into the back of the warehouse turned venue, pausing to look around and get my bearings. To my right is a very crowded, very small bar. To my far left is a stage, a cheering and raging crowd swelling around it. Two singers scream into a single microphone while the rest of the band plays loud post-punk music.

The speakers are shitty but loud, which is always a feature of these shows. Pippa leans close to me. "Want to get a drink?"

"God yes." I follow her to stand behind some other girls who are decked out in shiny silver lycra. My eyes wander across the stage and to the audience. I recognize some faces at the back; people that I know from Red-Green Party meetings, a socially liberal and anti-monarchal political movement.

The Red-Green party started in Copenhagen but it has since blossomed into a genuine political movement, almost anarchist at its core. The same people that used to show up at the Occupy Wall Street and Dakota Access Pipeline meetings often show up in support of the Red-Green party protests.

There is an energy to it, a grassroots anger about the clenched fist of capitalism that seems to drive the whole scene. I respect and admire any kind of rebellion against the system, so… I'm here for it, basically.

Pippa gets us each a beer and a shot of whiskey, as is the usual. We established this pattern in college of taking turns buying rounds for each other. I take the shot, wincing at the burn, and move out of the line.

I glance at Pippa, seeing her brighten. "Hey, I see some people I know. Come on, let's say hi."

She pulls me by the hand toward the opposite wall. There are three extraordinarily tall guys that are propped up against the wall, their heads turned toward the stage. They are probably in their mid twenties, just a few years older than my own twenty three. One of them turns and glances at me briefly. Our gazes snag and hold.

My breath leaves my lungs in a little whoosh. I don't say that lightly, but…

He is *beautiful*. Extremely tall, handsome, dark haired, with cheekbones that look like they could cut steel. Wearing a dark t-shirt, low-slung jeans, and dark shoes, he looks like he should be on a fashion runway, not in this grimy pop up club.

His eyes are an intense light blue. They skate over me and toward Pippa, but then come back to me. He frowns just a little, like there is something that he should know but can't quite figure out.

I step on a beer can and stumble, breaking my gaze away. When I look up again, I realize that the other guys he's with are equally handsome, one looking so similar to him that I almost can't tell them apart. The third guy has lighter hair and dark brown eyes. Upon looking closely, he's just slightly taller than his two friends.

It's this third guy that catches Pippa's gaze and stands up straighter. He says something to the other two, who nod. Then he pushes himself off the wall and steps out to greet Pippa.

"Pippa, hey," he yells. His accent is strange, Norwegian or Swedish or something. "What are you doing here?"

The band onstage stops playing abruptly and the crowd cheers. Pippa clears her throat, pulling me forward. "Hey. I'm just in town for the weekend. This is my friend, Margot. Margot, this is my friend Erik…"

The lighter haired guy nods at me, taking a second to take me in. "Hey. This is Lars," he points to one brother. "And this is Stellan."

He points to the other, the one I noticed first. The tall one, with the eyes that could melt steel. I blush under their collective inspection, tossing my hair back.

"Hi. I'm Margot." That's all I give them. Luckily Pippa is so extroverted that she just naturally fills in the gaps, making my aloofness seem okay.

God, I've missed her so much since she moved.

"Margot, these guys are from Copenhagen," she says. "They… umm…"

She seems at a loss for how to describe them.

Lars jumps in. "We're Danish. We are enjoying your city, seeing the sights."

Ah. I was close when I guessed at their accents, but not quite there. I sip my beer and keep watching all three of the men.

Stellan is silent and still, but I can tell from his keen gaze that he's drawing all kinds of conclusions. I just don't know what they might be…

Loud pre-recorded music comes over the speakers. Pippa looks around. "We should go dance!"

She heads off without so much as a glance back, just expecting that we will all follow her. Or maybe it's not that, maybe it's just that she knows she will find someone to dance with in the crush of the crowd.

Knowing Pippa, she is probably correct in that assumption.

"Are you staying here?" Erik asks Stellan.

"*Ja.*" Stellan nods. Erik glances at the dance floor. He clearly wants to go out there. Stellan jerks his head toward where Pippa went. "Go dance."

"*Jeg er lige i nærheden,*" Erik says quickly. He looks at me briefly, his gaze narrowing for a second. But then he heads out into the throng, bobbing his head to the music.

I sidle up to the wall beside Stellan, sliding him a gaze as I lean against it. He looks at me too, then shakes his head and looks away.

"What?" I ask. I take a sip of beer.

He shrugs. "I have to go to the bar." He pauses. "Do you like aquavit?"

I wrinkle my nose. "I have no idea what that is."

The corners of his lips lift ever so slightly. "It's like gin, a little."

His accent makes the way he pronounces the word gin a little funny.

I smirk. "Then I guess so."

Stellan pushes off the wall and heads toward the momentarily empty bar. "Come on. You'll like it, I think."

What makes him think that I, a person that he doesn't know from Adam, will like it… I do not know. But I follow him, my wariness of him easing for some reason.

It turns out, I don't hate aquavit. In fact, I kind of like it.

For the next hour we mostly drink and talk a little. We dance at one point. We flirt shamelessly. We dance some more, moving closer and closer together on the dance floor.

"You like this music?" he asks, getting closer to be heard over the music. I inhale his scent; most of the guys I encounter don't smell incredible like he does. Fresh bread and clean soap mixed with a certain maleness. It's kind of addictive. It's also unfair, when you add it to his height, his broad shoulders, his intense blue gaze, and his cheekbones.

I grin up at him, well aware that he's almost a foot and a half taller than I am. Leaning in so my lips brush his ear, I whisper. "Yes."

"It sounds like noise," he says. "There is a melody that is there, but it is under all these… other sounds. Does that make sense?"

My eyes twinkle. "Yes."

He chuckles. "I'm having a good time."

"Me too."

I realize that I'm working up the courage to ask him to come home with me. I have a little sixth floor walkup not far from here. I am drunk and having a good time. And I want to know what his body looks like without those clothes that cling to his muscular frame.

All night the pressure has been building inside me.

Just ask.

He can only say no.

The way he's looking at me, he won't say no.

I'm almost drunk enough to loosen my tongue. *Is that a good thing?* I wonder.

But suddenly Erik appears, whispering intently in Stellan's ear. Stellan frowns and whispers something back. Then he pulls a pen from the pocket of his jeans.

He grabs my arm, the first time we actually touch. It's erotic; for a second, I am aware only of the feeling of the current passing between us, of the goosebumps the electricity leaves in its wake.

He scribbles something on my arm, then points to it. "That is my number this weekend. Call us if you get up to anything fun before Sunday, *ja?*"

Looking up at him with wide eyes, I nod. He releases my arm and turns, following Erik as he heads to the door.

Pippa comes up behind me, a tiny wrinkle of worry set in her brow. "Where are they going?"

Shaking my head, I raise my arm. "I don't know. But I did get Stellan's phone number."

Pippa's brows jump up almost comically. "Really?"

I nod. "Yeah. He said to let him know what we get up tc tomorrow night."

Her lips twitch. "Well, well. I guess we are going out tomorrow then, huh?"

I roll my eyes. "We'll see."

"Come on, let's get one more drink before we call it a night." She grabs my arm and steers me away from the door, changing the subject.

My arm still tingles faintly where Stellan touched it.

All right, I can admit it… I'm excited about possibly seeing him tomorrow. And curious about where he went tonight…

Sighing, I stand in line and listen to Pippa talk, only partially paying attention.

Chapter Two

STELLAN

"SO, Stellan… what is it like to be the future king of Denmark?" the reporter asks, holding his pen at the ready. His American accent is bland and unremarkable.

I shift in my seat, glancing off the balcony of the Four Seasons. The skyline from the vantage point is absolutely stunning… but the afternoon heat is starting to get to me.

That and the fact that being interviewed by a nosy reporter is the very last thing I want to be doing right now. the reporter from the New York Times is named Mark; he and I have been working together for several hours today and yet we're still stiff and disjointed whenever we speak.

My head aches dully from too much partying last night. I take a sip of the coffee laid out on the low table that separates us, a silent sigh on my lips. "It's the only life I have ever known. I couldn't begin to guess at what it is like to live any other way." I crook a brow. "Please tell me that you intend to ask me something better than that?"

He looks up from his pad of paper, pushing his glasses up his nose. His cheeks stain just a bit with embarrassment. "Of course. I have a whole list of more in depth questions."

I study him. He's perhaps fifteen years older than my twenty six years, his gray hairs just beginning to overtake his blond ones. He's a little scruffy and dressed moderately hip in a dark gray button up and black jeans.

It's not that I'm usually a jerk to reporters. I don't mean to put this man on his back foot, although that's not out of the ordinary for a first meeting between me and a commoner.

Rather, it is more that I have my guard up as high as possible with anybody that is outside the royal family. Not just now, but always. And *especially* with the press.

My existence — how I live my life — is a source of curiosity for the rest of the world.

"The reason I agreed to this interview with the New York Times is simple. I am growing into my majority; that is to say, I am ready to take the crown in a few years. It will benefit Denmark to have a ruler that is well known to the American people, as my father King Göran has proven."

It's one of the answers that was provided to me in a nice packet of papers that was left on the royal family's private plane. Just one glance at the words, typed on royal stationery, gives off a whiff of my grandmother, the Queen Mother.

It was her idea to set this all up in the first place.

He nods. "*Ja*, King Göran and Queen Thora's love story is quite well known here. They still seem to be very much in love every time they come visit."

A corner of my mouth tips up. "They are quite the pair."

Mark takes a moment to consider his next question. "Your life is one of opulence and luxury. The finest schools, flashy cars, so many castles owned by your family to even name."

I bob my head, sipping my coffee. He licks his lips and continues.

"I think what people would like to know is how growing up in the spot-light with so much wealth and notoriety influenced you. How does it feel to have your life already laid out for you? Does it feel… mmm… restrictive?"

I want to roll my eyes at the question. It seems obvious that being the Royal Prince of Denmark is, in fact, beyond stifling. This golden mantle is heavy and it only grows more weighted the older I get. But I've been trained since birth to repress and hide my emotions.

So I just blink a few times. "It can be. But I choose to look beyond my duties and responsibilities and see it instead as an honor and a privilege."

Another quote that sounds false, mainly because I'm being puppeted by the Queen Mother. Mark narrows his eyes on my face, but I just stare back at him. I am not easy to embarrass and I've spent years learning how to control that response.

My phone vibrates on the table. I sit up, glancing at Mark as I reach forward. "This could be important."

No, it couldn't. Anything that's important passes through my best friend Erik, who is hovering just out of my eye line inside the glass doors that lead into our suite. There is a hierarchy of what information I need to receive.

Judging by the fact that his enormous shoulder isn't busting the door down, I don't think an affair of state is in question. Flipping over my phone, I see a text from an unknown number.

Tonight. After 9. 5930 Palmetto St. See you there?

It's unsigned, but I have no doubt that it's from *her*.

Margot.

Pink hair, a leather jacket, and Converse. So fucking sexy, so vibrant, so exactly the type of girl my grandmother would hate.

I almost took her home with me for the night, but Erik came and forced me to come back to the hotel. He's a bastard, but he was right.

I bite my lip and turn my phone over. I can't text her back right away, because then she will know that I've been waiting to hear from her.

I raise my eyes to the reporter once more. "Can we do the rest of this over email? I have a pressing engagement."

He pauses like I'm actually asking him whether or not it's possible. "I have a few questions that are more delicate in nature— "

I rise from my seat while he fumbles for an answer. The words *we're done here* might not have passed my lips, but I smile and act as though they did.

"It was a pleasure to meet you." Plastering a vague smile on my face, I hold out a hand for him to shake. Mark's brow pulls down but he shakes my hand.

At the same time, Erik steps onto the balcony. "Mark? I'll show you out…"

I keep that same expression until Mark hurries off, then collapse with a groan of aggravation. Throwing my arm over my eyes, I lay on the outdoor sofa until Erik returns from seeing the reporter to the front door.

"Don't be such a baby," Erik says, taking Mark's seat. His voice is low-pitched, almost a rumble. "I told you not to drink too much last night, did I not?"

I glance at him. He's a distant cousin of mine and you can tell by the way we are similarly built broad, tall, hair cropped close to our scalps. You could easily imagine Erik as a Viking warrior; he even has the light hair to pull it off.

"Aren't you supposed to make me more comfortable?" I grouse.

He rolls his eyes and sits back, kicking up his big booted feet. "*Rend mig i røven.*"

My lips curl upward. "Telling your crown prince to go fuck himself is not very nice, Erik."

He looks at me blankly. I think I'm pretty hardened and hard to read, but I've got nothing on Erik.

"We should have left that club earlier." His eyes narrow on my face. "But you wouldn't leave Pippa's friend…"

I grin at him. It's nice to be able to actually express myself, even if it's just between us two. "Her name was Margot. And you'll never guess where they've invited us to go tonight…"

The way his face tightens would be imperceptible to most people. But Erik and I have been friends since birth. I know that he is displeased… I just don't care.

After all, he's my keeper, not the other way around.

"Hey, you agreed to this," I say with a grin. "I said I didn't want to come to New York. You were the one who wanted me to comply with my grandmother's insane demand to come here and do a little positive publicity."

"The Queen Mother was not wrong."

I sit up and lean over the table, pouring myself a glass of sparkling water. "She thinks she can run everything for everyone infinitely. I can't wait until I'm not under her thumb anymore."

Erik pours himself a glass of water too, sipping it. "Be glad for these last years of freedom, Stel."

I snort. "*Ja.* I feel super free. Especially since the Queen Mother celebrated my birthday by giving me a list of the girls she considers marriageable." I pull a face. "Like I need to review. The same girls have been paraded in front of me for my whole entire life."

He lifts his shoulders. "You've dated about two thirds of them, too. You already know what they'll be like. If I were you— "

"Which you're not."

He gives me a look. "I would just pick a girl and settle down."

"Ah. If you were in my place, my grandmother would adore that. She'd get the rule follower that she always wanted. And I would be free of the royal curse."

Erik steeples his fingers. "Don't call it that."

"What should I call it, then?" I rise, heading to the balcony's edge. Far below, a small crowd of protestors are gathered. "The Red-Green Party people have followed me here again. Look."

He doesn't move. "I've seen them."

I turn, dangling my glass between two fingers. "They say that I am representative of the old world order and the patriarchy. Do you know that? If I were only allowed to express my true feelings once in a while…"

His expression smooths out and he looks off at the horizon. "You are ready for the crown. I get that. But you haven't done any of the steps that a prince traditionally does to show he's ready…"

"Like marry a good girl and produce a few heirs," I say, wrinkling my nose. "*Ja*, I know."

For just a second, an angry expression crosses his face. "Don't be in such a hurry for something to happen to your father."

For a second, his rebuke actually takes me aback. Erik usually doesn't like to talk about his father's death. My brows rise in surprise. "I'm sorry, Erik. I didn't mean that. My father doesn't actually have to die for me to ascend to the throne. He just has to relinquish the crown. You know that."

Erik shrugs, apparently no longer interested in the topic. He is usually moody, but this is something else altogether. I drain the rest of my water, my mind wandering back to my phone.

"So about tonight…" I say. "We should go party with Pippa."

His cool green gaze finds me. "And Margot?"

A smile curls my lips. "And Margot," I admit. "She had all the qualities that I love. She's young, she's wild, she's unbelievably hot… and there is something especially sexy about a girl who is clearly attracted to you but doesn't ask a lot of questions."

Tiny, with a heart shaped face and the sweetest, hottest little body I've ever seen. She's like a very feisty doll in sexy fishnets and a leather jacket. And that hair… perfect, bouncy curls that just happen to be neon pink.

There is something about her hair alone that makes me fucking hard.

He rolls his eyes briefly. "She was all over you last night, too."

"She seemed like she was absorbing everything around us, like a sponge. She was…" I squint. *"Hun har hovedet skruet godt på.* What is the English word?"

"Mmm…" He thinks for a moment. "Perceptive?"

"Ja. Perceptive."

He pushes himself to his feet. "I think I need a shower, a headache powder, and another cup of coffee before I can even think of going out. Christ. Maybe two litres of water, too."

"And ibuprofen," I add, nodding gravely. "Definitely add that to the list."

"Come on," he says, heading inside. "I'll call downstairs to room service. Then we can make a plan for the night."

Squinting into the sunset, I turn around and look off at the skyline once more. "You go ahead. I'll be inside soon."

Erik shrugs and goes in, leaving me to wonder what Margot and Pippa are doing at this very moment.

I pick up my phone and text Margot back.

See you there.

Smiling, I gaze off the rooftop once more.

Chapter Three

MARGOT

"I SWEAR, if Jeff shoots down one more of my articles, I'll scream. Just scream, in front of the whole entire office." Griping about my editor may not be the best or most helpful thing in the world, but it is satisfying.

Pippa glances at me, reaching out to straighten my pink and black negligee that I'm wearing over a pair of ripped fishnets. "Jeff is a ghoul. Not only that, but I heard he tried to put the moves on Marie during the staff Christmas party last year."

I grab a fistful of her filmy white dress. "Marie quit in January!"

Her expression turns pained. "I know. Jeff is really, really awful."

"Ugh!" I say. "Just ugh."

Pippa wrinkles her nose at the dank hallway we're in. We're definitely underground and the whole place smells like piss and a million stale cigarettes. "Are you sure we're in the right place?"

"Definitely. I've been here before. Come on." Pulling her down the hallway, I turn the corner and stop at a thick steel vault.

She eyes the doorway uncertainly. "If you're sure…"

Wrenching open the door; I slowly uncover a den of inequities. Loud pop music plays and the bass actually shakes me where I stand. There are few lights, mostly strobes here and there. As we head in, closing the door behind us, it's obvious just how crowded the dance floor is.

Everybody who's anybody is here right now. Excitement hums through my veins.

Pippa smiles at me, holding out a pill and a bottle of water. "Here."

Biting my lip, I giggle. I take the pill, a little MDMA mixed with a tiny bit of powdered mushrooms. Just enough to make everything pretty, shiny, and fun. Swallowing it with water, I pass the water back to her. She takes a pill too, grinning when she's done.

"Ready?" I ask.

"So ready." She grips my hand and pulls me into the crush of people. The song changes and a female singer comes on, her voice like a siren's call, pulling people onto the large dance floor. Around us, gorgeous people dance together and separately, some of them grinding on each other.

I let go and throw my hands in the air, celebrating my freedom and my body. Pippa and I garner male attention immediately. Everything is heady and pretty from the drugs: the lights seem a little brighter, everything much funnier than usual, and the cool beers that someone hands us seem to slide right down our throats.

I don't let anyone get too close, though. One guy in particular keeps trying his luck and putting his hands on me again and again despite the fact that I dance away each time. Finally I've had enough.

I get close to his ear. His arms envelop me. I whisper to him. "I have a knife hidden in my garter. I will cut you if you touch me or my friend again."

His eyes go big and he takes a staggered step back, raising his hands. I make a *go away* gesture with one hand and twirl, my negligee spinning out like a top when I do.

When I stop spinning, giggling and starting to feel the effects and the drugs pulsing their way through my system…

That's the moment that I lock eyes with Stellan. His gaze is smoldering. His eyes are light blue, but they are searingly hot. Possessive, almost.

I shiver as he strides over to me. He doesn't say a word. He just cups my face and pulls me close, leaning in for a kiss.

My breath freezes in my lungs.

My whole body tingles strangely.

It seems as though there is an odd electric current jumping between us, sparking as his lips draw closer to mine.

My eyes sink closed.

I push onto my tiptoes, needing his kiss like I need air to breathe.

Like a river running down to the sea, I rush to press my lips against his. And there is an immediate jolt of sensation. I clutch at Stellan's shirt and his hands tighten on my jaw and hip where they hold me.

It's perfect. A moment in time that is free of flaws.

Stellan crushes me against his body for a split second. I make a muffled sound, unable to speak. But if I could have, I would've said, yes.

More.

Please.

In the next second he seems to realize that he's a giant compared to me. He lets go and steps back, his eyes still shining with intensity. The music pounds in my ears and slides through my veins.

"Hi," he mouths.

I grin at him. "Hi."

He nods toward a side room that Pippa's distinctive red head is moving towards. I nod in agreement and he takes my hand, leading the way. As we sluice through the crowd, I marvel at the difference between our hands. His is a giant's paw; mine looks petite and pretty holding his hand.

Feeling feminine isn't usually something I'm interested in, but there is something about his sheer size that makes me blush. Is there a correlation between his massive height and the size of his cock?

That's really a dirty thing for me to think, but could it not actually be true?

I giggle to myself as Stellan pulls me into a small side room. The first thing I notice is that music is quieter in here; the second thing is that there are a bunch of old bench-style car seats strewn around. Stellan leads me over to where Pippa, Erik, and Lars have already made themselves comfortable.

He releases my hand and sits down. I bite my lip and sit next to him, unable to keep my blush under wraps. Pippa looks at me and flashes me a grin, then leans back against Lars.

Only Erik seems on edge, constantly looking over his shoulder. What he expects to happen, I couldn't say.

When Pippa pulls out her phone to snap a selfie of herself and Lars, Erik's eyes narrow on her. She just rolls her eyes.

"Don't worry," she says. "I know the rules about photos, okay?"

That gives me pause. Why are there rules? What are they protecting, exactly?

I'm not quick enough with my questions, though. I blame the mushrooms. I just feel too good right now to start quizzing anybody.

Stellan clears his throat uncomfortably. "There are a lot of people in this club for a weeknight."

Lars speaks up. "Especially for New York City. It seems like you all live to work."

Bobbing my head, I lay back on the couch. My flop lands my head on his thigh. He tenses beneath me for a second, a little surprised.

"Is this okay?" I ask, peering up at him.

"*Ja*," he says. He clears his throat again. "I thought that you Americans were all prudes, but I suppose I was wrong, eh?"

One corner of my mouth lifts in a mischievous smile. "I suppose you were."

Everyone sits and talks for a little while. I just let the conversation flow around me. At some point Stellan starts stroking my arm.

I butt my head against his chest. "Mmm. I like that. Do it more."

He obliges, running his hand up and down my arm and across my ribs. Somehow or other a beer appears in Stellan's hand, then another when the first is finished.

When I sit up, Pippa, Lars, and Erik are gone. I notice that Stellan is looking at me like I'm a puzzle he can't figure out.

"What?" I ask.

He mouth turns up a fraction and he shrugs. "I am just trying to figure you out."

Pulling the skirt of my negligee down so I'm not flashing anybody, I fold my legs up on the couch. "I'm not that much of a challenge, am I? New York City, born and raised. Put myself through college at NYU, which is how I know Pips." I stop for a second, pushing my cheek out with my tongue. "I'm a Cinderella story, where I'm both Cinderella and the prince." I grin. "I never had much of anything, which gave me a work ethic like no other. With tonight as being the exception, I guess. Pippa is here, so no work tonight."

He smiles at that. "No, I guess that would make you a bad host."

Eyeing him, I cock my head. "I don't know that much about Danish people. But if I had to guess, you've never had to think about where your next meal would come from."

Surprise looks good on Stellan. "*Ja*. You are right, Margot."

I nod my head. "Yeah. That's what I hope for, when I think about having kids someday. That they'll never have to think about finding food or shelter."

He looks a little taken aback, which is the only way I know that I've overshared. My face goes beet red. Before he can say anything, I pull out my phone, a handy distraction.

"Let's take a picture together," I suggest.

To my surprise, he's hesitant. "I don't think that's a very good idea."

I wrinkle my nose. "Come on. Just for me. I want something to remember you by after you go back to Copenhagen. *Ja?*"

I imitate his accent on the last word. He grins at that, rolling his eyes. "Alright. How do you want me to sit? Like this?"

He adopts a silly pose, which makes me dissolve in giggles.

"Wait, just hold that…" Dropping in the frame beside him, I pull a face. "Okay, now a serious one…"

The song shifts, changing to a young pop singer that I unabashedly love. I grin, standing up. "Dance with me."

Stellan stands too, glancing at the dance floor. "Are you sure you want to go out there?"

I step closer and pull at his shirt, looking up at him. "I wanna dance right here. Just the two of us."

He smiles, his hands sliding down to land on my hips. "Okay, Margot." He pulls me against his body, biting his lip as he looks down at me. His gaze is direct and intense; I almost get lost in his ice blue eyes.

"You are very pretty," he says, cupping my cheek. I blush furiously and yet, I can't look away. "Your hair…" His fingers move to stroke my hair. "And the way you dress…" He fingers the bottom of my negligee. "It's perfect. You seem to be put together just to please me. Do you know that?"

I can't even begin to figure out how I should answer that. A smile tugs at my lips. "Then there is just one thing you should do."

One of his hands slips down to my ass. Electricity crackles between us. "What's that, *skatter?*"

Skatter. I don't know what it means exactly, but the way he says it is enchanting. I lean my head back, presenting my mouth to him, whispering my words. "You should kiss me."

A dimple flashes in his cheek. He doesn't say anything, but his hand that's on my ass presses me closer. His cock presses into my belly.

My eyes widen just a bit at the sheer size of it. That can't be real, can it?

At the same time his face lowers, his breath teasing my lips when he stops just a hair's breadth shy of kissing me. It seems like the most natural thing in the world to close that gap, to push up on my toes and press my lips onto his.

His lips are hot and firm. There is an immediate sense of urgency, growing with every second. I curl my hands in his shirt, needing more. I want to sink into his mouth and never return.

I feel the roughness of his stubble against my smooth face. I feel the frantic beat of my heart against the loud bass beat of the club's music. I feel his arms tighten around me, a python with its prey in its grasp.

I feel all of it, and I want *more*.

He deepens the kiss, bending me back a little. His tongue invades the cavity of my mouth, dancing with my tongue. He tastes so good, like mint and beer and male, under it all.

Stellan starts moving with me, swaying against me, dominating my whole body. At the same time he presses his hips into my belly again, grinding. I suddenly have a flash of exactly what Stellan is going to be like when we go to bed together.

Rough. Dominant. Hard. But I have a feeling that he knows exactly how to make me come, how to make me scream his name, over and over again until my voice gives out.

I shiver and crush myself against him.

All my secret cravings for someone like Stellan will be fulfilled. And the best part? After this weekend, he will vanish into thin air.

Poof.

I can be as uninhibited with him as I want. He's the ultimate one night stand.

It's hard not to bite his earlobe when I whisper in his ear.

"Let's go somewhere private."

Stellan smirks, that dimple flashing in his cheek again. "Come on. We should go back to my hotel."

He takes my hand, leading the way. And I follow him, a rush of heady excitement sluicing through my veins.

Chapter Four

MARGOT

THE UBER RIDE to his hotel could take forever or it could be just a few short minutes. I don't actually know because Stellan has his tongue down my throat and his hand on my thigh. His fingers brush under my negligee and over my pussy a few times.

I'm in the grip of the mushrooms and the MDMA. But more importantly, I'm into *him*. My hands rove over Stellan's chest and back and clutch at his shirt. My eyes practically roll into the back of my head every time he touches my breasts or teases the silk-covered triangle between my clenched legs.

The lobby of the hotel seems fancy; I glimpse gold and marble as he hustles me to the elevators. Once the elevator doors glide closed, I gasp as he picks me up and backs me against the mirrored wall.

My eyes sink closed. I pant as he leaves hickeys all over my neck and breasts. His hot mouth is everywhere, his hands rucking up my negligee. He pushes my knees apart and presses between them. If it weren't for a little denim and silk, we would be fucking right now.

I wrap my legs around his back as the elevator rises. When the elevator chimes and the doors slide open, he carries me off and walks straight into the penthouse suite. I pause, my eyes opening.

"Holy shit," I say. Stellan doesn't stop moving, but I can't help but notice the floor to ceiling windows with their exquisite view of Manhattan.

"Jesus. What are you, rich? Or is it that you're a rebel? Hmm? Did you steal the keys to this place?"

No response to that from him, except for to suck on my neck extra hard. He keeps moving through the space, dodging the low gray modern furniture until he gets to the bedroom. I take that to mean that Stellan somehow *borrowed* the keys to this suite.

I'm not exactly worried about it; I like a little danger mixed with my fucking. As he lays me down on what has to be the softest mattress ever made, I grin. Such opulence should be used and shared by everyone; just a few hours ago I was wearing a ripped t-shirt that declares EAT THE RICH.

He backs off, pulling his dark t-shirt up over his head. My eyes widen at his well-built chest and muscular arms; he even has a taut six pack, which I didn't think actually existed outside of the movies. He's actually a giant, descended from the Vikings… that's what my overheated brain tells me, anyway.

I lean on my elbows, watching him strip his shoes and jeans off, leaving him in nothing but a pair of tight black boxer briefs. My gaze trails up and down his body, ravenous for his touch.

"Fuck. You're *hot*," I say. Tossing my hair, I bite my lush lower lip.

He grins, flashing me that dimple again in his cheek. "I take that as a compliment, coming from you."

I blush. "Thanks."

His eyes glint. "Now for the love of everything holy, get fucking naked. I can't believe I've waited this long to taste you."

My fingers shake as I sit up, pulling my negligee up and over my head. It falls to the side, forgotten. My tits are bare, my chest tightening and lifting under his inspection. Stellan drinks me in, his white teeth sinking into the pink flesh of his lower lip. His ice blue eyes rake over me, making my nipples pebble.

He reaches down and adjusts his cock in his boxer briefs. Then he grates out another command. "Take off your panties."

My lips twitch. I tilt my head. "Why don't you come over here and do it yourself?"

He smirks and then moves onto the bed very, very slowly. "You are defiant."

The breath leaves my lungs as his arms cage me in. "Until my last breath."

He considers me for a second. Then he reaches up and pushes my hair away from one side of my neck, the backs of his fingers touching my neck. "Someone should teach you a lesson, *ja?*"

My heartbeat pounds wildly in my own ears. I lift my head. "I've been waiting for a teacher."

His beautiful blue eyes glitter. He runs a single fingertip down my neck, over my collarbone, tracing a line between my bare breasts. I suck in a breath.

His touch trails down my ribs, across my navel, and ends at the top of my panties. I squeeze my thighs together, feeling myself grow wet, feeling the slide of my body growing ready for him.

Stellan glances at me. "I'm going to fuck you senseless. If you're going to tell me to stop, this is your last chance."

I bite my lip, smothering a grin. I shake my head. "Less talk. More action."

He smiles as he literally rips my panties off of my body. He kisses me on the hip, then on the top of my thigh. I can't hold back the sultry moan that rises in my throat. His fingers walk up to find my nipple and tweak it hard.

Gasping loudly, I arch into his touch.

"Good girl," he purrs. Stellan splays a big hand underneath my belly button, covering my pubic mound. He presses down firmly as he showers little bites and swift nibbles to my thighs, working his way closer and closer to my shaved pussy.

I watch as he runs the tip of one thick finger up the seam of my pussy, just barely touching. A twisted, angry grunt leaves my lips.

"Stellan," I reprimand him.

He looks up at me, grinning devilishly. He places the lightest of butterfly kisses over my pussy, making me writhe.

"Stellan, please!" I beg.

He shakes his head. "I don't think so, *skatter.* I'm not going to let you come just yet."

Instead, he pushes himself up onto his knees and grasps his cock through his boxers briefs. My lungs constrict as I watch him, looking down on me, naked and spread out.

Eyeing me, he bites his lip. "I think you need to taste me, *skatter.* I want to feel the tip of my cock in your fucking throat."

My entire body tightens with need. His lips form a naughty smile.

"Can you control your gag reflex?"

My cheeks color. "A little." I get to my knees, reaching for him, but he sneers at me.

"No. You lie on the edge of the bed, like this." He grabs me, positioning me so that my head is by the foot of the bed, dangling off just a little. "If it's too much, just tap my leg. *Ja?*"

Nodding, I watch as Stellan strips his black boxer briefs off. His cock bounces up, jutting straight out.

"Holy shit," I breathe, my eyes widening. I knew he was well endowed, but… he's absolutely *huge*. His cock is long, thick, and veiny in a way that male porn stars would be jealous of. He's also uncut, which honestly is a little unnerving.

I don't follow Judeo-Christian beliefs or anything, but it reinforces the fact that he is definitely not from here.

Stellan grins, grasping his cock and wiggling his eyebrows. Then he steps forward. "Open your mouth. Cover your teeth for me, *skatter.*"

My heart pound in my ears. *Relax,* I tell myself. *Whatever you do, don't gag.*

Licking my lips, I open my mouth. He steps closer and nudges the tip of his cock between my lips. I taste his cock, the deep earthy maleness and manly musk bursting across my tongue like fireworks.

He groans, closing his eyes for a brief moment. "Ah, fuck."

That's fucking sexy. The sound of his rumbled curse makes my breasts tighten. I relax a little, resting my hand on his inner thigh.

Then he starts very slowly working his length in and out of my lips. More rumbles of pleasure leave his lips. Not groans or moans, but *almost*.

Stellan stops and peers down at me after a few seconds. "Good?"

I nod, my mouth still full of his cock. He grips his cock and starts pumping in and out of my mouth, his eyes squeezing shut. I grab him and pull him closer, attempting to work my tongue against his cock.

His reaction is immediate. His whole body seizes up. There is an intense look of concentration on his face. "*Fuck*, Margot."

I slide my hand down to delicately cup his balls. His eyes actually roll back in his head as he starts to move again, jerking in and out of my lips roughly. "Fuck," he breathes. "*Skatter…*"

He stops suddenly, pulling out of my mouth. Before I can even react, he's covering the tip of his cock with his hand, cursing and clenching his eyes shut. He cums, shooting jets of milky white semen into his hand. The look of pleasure on his face, so intense and ecstatic it nearly borders on pain, makes me quiver.

When he's done, Stellan opens his eyes again. "That wasn't quite how I was supposed to finish… but your mouth felt too good. Too hot."

I lick the corner of my mouth. "My pleasure."

He chuckles, reaching across to the bedside table for the tissue box. He wipes his hand off and then pads over to the trashcan, disposing of the tissue. When he comes back, he kneels at the foot of the bed.

"Now it's your turn," he husks. "Come down here."

Feeling a little weird about it, I turn around. Stellan isn't interested in waiting, grabbing my knees and spreading them wide. I feel a little awkward being exposed like that, but he isn't too worried about my emotions just now.

"Cup your breasts," he commands, ducking his head low. I expect him to start flicking his tongue over my clit, but of course he doesn't.

He is always surprising, always keeping me on my toes.

Instead he starts kissing the inside of my thigh. His hands touch my inner thighs, sliding up as he trails his kisses toward my pussy. I moan softly, bucking just a little. He looks up at me, catching my eye.

His dark brow descends and he looks utterly sincere when he utters the next words. "You are so beautiful, Margot."

Then his head lowers again and he licks along my seam, causing my eyes to flutter closed. My brow wrinkles as he teases me, using two fingers to part my lower lips. When he finally seals his lips over my clit, sucking on it gently, a wave of pleasure washes through my whole body, rippling out from my pussy.

I grab my tits, shaping my nipples with hard pulls. He alternates between licking and sucking my clit. Stellan is going to drive me mad. He pulls unintelligible sounds of need from my lips, makes my hips thrust against that magical mouth of his.

When he's good and ready he tests my entrance with the tips of two thick fingers, working them in and out. My pussy is beyond wet and ready for him, but there is still some resistance as he slides his fingers home. I groan, ready to explode.

"Fuck. Fuck, right there," I whisper. "That's so good, Stellan…"

I feel him pause, wetting a finger from his free hand. Then he starts licking my clit again… while he pushes that fingertip against the tight balloon knot of my ass.

My eyes widen, but it doesn't feel bad. Actually, with my clit being stimulated and Stellan working his fingers slowly in and out of my pussy, it feels… naughty. But good.

I whimper, uncertain.

When he actually penetrates my ass with one finger, my eyes roll up in my head. "Oh god," I choke out. "Don't stop, Stellan. God, don't stop…"

For a second, it's quiet, aside from the sound of blood rushing in my head and my heart beating like a drum. I stop trying to breathe and thinking about anything at all.

I only exist for the pleasure that Stellan is giving me, right now, right here.

I come suddenly, the orgasm ripping through me, clenching and spasming. One moment I'm at the top of a cliff, looking down into the looming crevasse. The next I am in free fall, plummeting toward the bottom, praying that there will be a body of water to save me from certain death.

I'm pretty sure I scream. At some point Stellan withdraws, licking at his mouth. When I can focus my eyes and breathe again, I look at him, chuckling because I am so overwhelmed.

"What?" he asks. He lays down on the bed beside me, fisting his cock. He's hard again, which is impressive in itself.

"That was…" I trail off, shaking my head. I try to catch my breath. "Incredible."

"Mmm." He eyes me, carnal interest still lighting a fire in his eyes.

I turn on my side. Should I be this winded after sex? I'm too young for it, I feel like… "What now?"

His lips turn upward. He moves closer, pressing a kiss to my lips. He still tastes like me, a little metallic but also earthy with a hint of sweetness. He cups my tits, renewing my interest.

"*Skatter*… I want to have your mouth again," he whispers against my lips. "Give it to me, Margot."

I lick my lips, looking deep into his eyes. "For tonight… I'm all yours, Stellan."

That apparently amuses him, but he doesn't say anything. Instead he just kisses me again, so deeply that I forget that morning will ever come.

Chapter Five

STELLAN

IT'S EARLY in the morning when I wake. At first, I just open my eyes and stare at the ceiling. It takes my system a minute to boot up, to realize where exactly I am and that I am not alone. I roll over onto my side and see Margot sleeping there, her outrageous pink hair sticking out in every direction.

She sleeps on her side, her face drawn into her chest. It almost looks like she's trying to protect herself, even in her sleep. But from what?

I repress a sigh and look at her lovely face. Her skin is radiant, her cheekbones high, her eyes large and expressive. For Satan, but she is pretty.

There are faint circles under her eyes.

I am actually partially to blame for that. We stayed up most of the night fucking. Well, doing everything but fucking actually… she sucked my cock until my eyes rolled up in my head over and over. I fingered her and licked her until she came screaming. Her taste still lingers faintly on my lips and tongue.

I don't actually mind that. She tasted sweet and musky; there are far worse things to wake up smelling like.

The point is, I was exceedingly careful where my sperm went.

Even drunk, I know better than to actually spend my seed inside of random girls. If I accidentally got a girl pregnant and the press found out about it…

Ah, there it is. The faint pounding of my head, between my eyes. It's funny… for a minute, just brief window of time, I almost forgot that I was a royal.

Almost.

I hear a noise outside of the bedroom door. Cocking my head, I frown. Is that Erik, then? Where did he end up last night?

Pushing myself up into a sitting position, I sigh. I really need a glass of water and a headache powder to even begin dealing with today.

Erik slams the door open, holding up a phone. Margot stirs and panics a little, sitting up too.

"Erik—" I start.

He has eyes only for Margot, though. "You fucking bitch!"

My eyes narrow. Margot looks alarmed. "What? Don't call me a bitch…"

"Erik, don't call her that. What do you want?" My head pounds, less faintly this time and more like a jackhammer.

Erik looks at me, beyond aggravated. "She posted pictures of you two together to fucking Instagram, Stel. *Intimate* photos."

That gets my attention. "What?"

I have a vague memory of Margot snapping a couple of pictures with her phone last night. A cold fist of worry forms in my stomach.

I look at her, clutching the comforter to her chest. Always protecting herself. My eyes narrow.

"Is it true?" I ask.

Her delicate brows descend, making her eyes darker. "Well… yeah… I didn't realize that you guys had a weird hang up about Instagram or whatever…"

I flinch, then look at the ceiling. Scrubbing my hand over my face, I try to think. I want to scream at her. But that won't help anybody.

When I speak, my voice shakes with barely contained fury. "You have to take them down."

Erik hisses. "It's too late for that. Her post went viral."

"What?" Margot says, confused. "Why?" Her gaze darts to me, accusing. "What don't I know?"

I avoid her gaze, looking at Erik instead. "Can we shut it down? Have you already talked to the royal press office?"

"I called them first. They are working on it, but they don't know if they can squelch the info. Once it's out— "

"It's out." I bury my head in my hands. "Fuck."

"I'm sorry. What the fuck are you two talking about?" Margot clutches the comforter to her chest as she rises to stand beside the bed.

I don't fight her for it; I have plenty of things to be embarrassed about, but my body isn't one of them.

Instead I grab my boxer briefs from where they lay on the floor in a discarded heap. Stepping into them with a curse, I turn to Erik. "Grandmother is likely going to have two heart attacks at once when she hears about this. Give me five minutes… I will meet you out in the living room."

Erik gives a curt nod, shooting Margot one last glare before he stalks out of the room. I find a shirt and pull it on. I can't help but feel the dread growing in my belly, threatening to take over everything.

Margot starts putting on her clothes. Her face is drawn and she's muttering a little. "I don't have to stick around for this. You act like I'm not even here!"

I pull on a pair of pants, casting a dark look her way. "You don't even realize the shit storm you have managed to stir up, Margot."

She shoves her hair back out of her face, looking outraged. "Do you want to explain why? Or do you just want to go vent about it to Erik some more?"

I cross my arms. "I'm the crown prince of Denmark, Margot. The heir to the throne. And the last thing I needed was for you to run around telling people on the internet who I hook up with."

Her eyes go wide with shock. "What?"

"Didn't you notice Erik's reaction to having his photo taken? He knows the drill. Nothing on camera, *ever*. Because if it's on film somewhere, someone is going to find it." I spread my hands wide. "And once the press has it, they will run with it. Make up all kinds of things. You should know… aren't you friends with Pippa?"

Her expression is sheepish, but the second I turn it around on her, she glares at me. Going over to her purse, she grabs a laminated badge and waves it in my face.

"I'm member of the press," she says, her voice rising in pitch. "So maybe stop for a hot second before you malign my own organization to me, okay?"

Now it's my turn to be shocked. "*What?*"

I'm vaguely aware of my heart pounding loudly. Oh god.

She's one of *them?*

I really, really fucked up this time.

She stuffs her feet into her heels, glaring at me. Then Margot grabs her purse and tosses her hair. "I'm a photographer. And I think you are overreacting. Just because a couple of people reblogged my Instagram posts…"

I cross the bedroom, grabbing her by the elbow. "You don't understand. I'm a member of the royal family. These jackals have hunted my family down for centuries. And once they scent blood…"

I shudder. But I'm not prepared for the way she looks at me, like I just kicked her puppy or something. She jerks out of my hold.

"We are *human beings*," she grits out. "The only things separating you and your family from the rest of us are a few tiaras and a lot of fucking money. Money you didn't even earn!"

I glare at her. "I knew that you were bad news the second I laid eyes on you."

Margot tosses her hair and heads for the door. "I can't believe I spent the night with you."

"Wait!" I call.

She looks back at me. "I don't have the time or the emotional space for this."

I growl. "You don't want to leave now. Let Erik find a way to smuggle you out of the building. Maybe if we do that and you take your Instagram posts down—"

"You are unbelievable. You know that?"

Erik comes back in, standing in the doorway. He stares Margot. "This is all your fault."

Looking between us, she cocks her hip. "What, are you going to physically keep me here? I'm a hundred percent certain that there isn't any amount of money in the world that will keep me quiet if you resort to false imprisonment."

Erik and I make eye contact. I fidget. He starts toward her, a giant grizzly bear stalking his weak prey.

"Stop!" I call out. They both look at me. I square my jaw. "Let her go, Erik. If the story is out, it's out."

Erik pauses, but doesn't move. "It was only two weeks ago that the royal family was in the news, apologizing about your uncle Heinlein and those call girls of his." He looks back and forth between Margot and me. "The press will rip you both to shreds."

"I'll believe it when I see it," she sasses.

He rolls his eyes and moves clear of the doorway. Margot is out like a shot, not another word to either of us. In a few seconds I hear the elevator chime.

Flinging myself across the bed, I bury my face in the pillows. My whole bed still smells like sex and flowers, a remnant of her perfume maybe.

"Your grandmother is going to have your head on a spike," Erik says, sitting on the end of the bed.

I close my eyes. "I know."

"I told you to be careful with a commoner."

I grit my teeth. "*I know.*"

He sits there for a moment longer, then hoists himself to his feet. "I'm going to start arranging our trip home. I have to figure out where the fuck Lars is at the moment."

I open my eyes and glance at him. "If you can't find him, my brother can figure out how to get home on his own." I repress a sigh. "I think we should leave as soon as possible. Grandmother will want to see me soon, I expect."

He's quiet for a beat. "Maybe it won't be that bad."

Groaning, I roll over. "Have you checked downstairs, then? Are the press not swarming all over every entrance to the hotel?"

He looks away. "They are. I really wish your girl would've let me get her out without a fuss... because they are going to go nuts when they see her."

Shrugging, I think about Margot's soft curves. I think about how she jammed that press pass under my nose, sending me into shock.

God, how stupid could I be? "I have other things to worry about now."

"All right. Get your stuff together. I want to leave in thirty minutes." He heads out of the door, leaving it wide open.

I wallow in bed for another minute, inhaling the smell of our scents mixed together. It's funny; if none of this had happened, I could've really liked Margot.

Not that it would have done either of us much good… I'm still going to be saddled with some long-faced dullard from my grandmother's list. This little event will actually only speed up the process, I fear.

Going to the closet, I start pulling down the suits and jeans hanging inside, my core filling with dread.

Chapter Six

MARGOT

I UNBOLT the door of my tiny Bushwick apartment, opening the door. Instantly there are camera flashes and reporters shouting my name.

"Margot! Margot! Are you and Prince Stellan an item?"

"Do you plan to move into one of his castles?"

"Margot!"

I see a flash of red hair. Pippa edges through the crowd, throwing a few elbows. "Move, please! Move!" Her British accent makes her sound more polite, but I can tell from her expression that she's actually pretty fucking annoyed.

Welcome to my new life, Pippa. It's hell on earth.

She eventually makes it to the door and squeezes herself in. Then she shuts the door behind herself, giving her long mane of red hair a little shake. She smoothes her hands down her pristine pink floral dress and pulls her oversized white leather handbag onto her shoulder.

"That was insane!" she says, looking at me with wide eyes. She jogs a brown paper bag full of groceries on her hip. "I brought you bagels."

My eyes well up. I rush over and give her a tight squeeze, surprising her a little. "I'm so glad you are here."

Pippa hugs me back with her free arm. "I'm just glad I'm in town." She bites her lip, pulling back and looking at me. "Although I have to admit, if I wasn't visiting, you never would have met Stellan."

"None of this is your doing." I tug the paper bag out of her arms, heading over to the kitchen and setting it down on the counter. "It's one part my fault, one part Stellan's. He could've just told me who he was. Or maybe handled the aftermath a little better."

Pippa sighs, brushing a strand of her hair back. "Yeah. But really, it's the American press that's the problem. They're having a field day with the whole situation."

I wrinkle my nose. "I know. The tabloids are running all kinds of headlines about me. Mostly focusing on the idea of a rags to riches story, which is almost completely made up." I wince. "Well, they aren't wrong about where I came from. They're just making up lies about where I'm going."

She looks around my tiny apartment, screwing up her face. Walking over to my sofa, she sits down. "I'm guessing you haven't heard anything from Stellan, then?"

I snort. "No."

Pippa tosses her handbag down. "I think the whole royal family is on lockdown. It's been one scandal after another for them this year."

Sitting beside her on the couch, I look wistfully out my small living room window. "I don't particularly care. I just want the tabloids and the paparazzi to leave me alone." I glance at Pippa. "Did I tell you that I lost my job over this whole thing?"

Her jaw drops. "What?"

"Yep." I make a disgusted sound. "Jeff said that if I didn't come in yesterday, I could consider myself no longer employed. I can't even get out the front door without enacting a mob scene!"

She reaches over, placing a comforting hand on my arm. "I'm so sorry. I wish none of this had happened to you. Really I do."

I sort of shrug off her concern. We have been friends for a long time, but it's just hard for me to let people show concern for me like that. "I'm fine. Or I would be, if some scummy tabloid hadn't dug up a couple of people who knew me in high school. They've been running these clips of different people that say they spend time with me, when in fact I didn't even recognize their names until I looked them up in my yearbook."

Pippa bites her lip. "That sounds like bullshit."

"It is!" I growl.

"Well…" She flashes me a nervous smile. "I actually come bearing news on that front. *Politiken* is still very interested in you, perhaps even more so now that this little fiasco happened."

My eyebrows fly up. "Really?" Then I scowl. "I don't know. I don't want to be headhunted just because I posted some pictures online of myself with Stellan."

She scrunches her face up. "I'm sorry to be the one to tell you this, but... tough shit."

Her pronouncement actually makes me smile. It feels good to express something other than the anger and disappointment that's been consuming me for days. "Yeah?"

"Yeah!" she says. "Stuff happens. This *happened* already. It's sort of shattered your existence. All you can do now is figure out the best way out of this mess." She raises her eyebrows, with a hopeful smile on her face. "Plus, *Politiken* is offering to pay for your flight and basic moving expenses. You are getting an offer to move to Copenhagen, all expenses paid. What could be better than that?"

I bite my lip. "I... I'm not even sure what to say."

Pippa squints, then looks around. "You live in a space where you can almost fry an egg from your bed. Your bathroom is just a shower and a toilet, packed into a few square feet. You don't even own a mirror that I can see..." She makes a face. "So... what? You are afraid to give up all this opulence for a chance at adventure?" she teases me.

I can't help the bark of laughter that escapes my lips. "Hey, at least the heater works." Then I stop, admitting the truth. "Well, it works *sometimes*."

"So come work at *Politiken*. Stay with me. My roommate moved out last month so it's basically perfect." She gives me a cheesy grin. "It'll be like the NYU dorms all over again. But like, less marijuana smoke drifting through the halls."

I glance outside again. "I don't know. I've never lived anywhere that wasn't New York City."

Pippa rolls her eyes. "New York isn't going anywhere anytime soon. It'll still be here when you decide you're tired of Copenhagen. Besides, what will you miss?" She wiggles her brows. "Come on! Say yes!"

Outside, I can hear raised voices. Likely two of the paparazzos are bickering with each other. I release a long-suffering sigh. "You're right. I think I should go. At least for a few months until this whole thing blows over."

Her entire face brightens. "Really? I didn't actually expect you to accept…"

My heart seizes up. "The offer isn't real?"

"It is," she assures me. "*Politiken* definitely asked me to beg you to come. They'll be over the moon that you said yes. I just didn't foresee your answer, that's all."

I bite my lip. "Do you think it's the right choice?"

A loud thump comes from my front door, making us both jump. Pippa's eyes widen.

"Definitely."

I screw up my face. "In for a penny, in for a pound… How soon do you think I can leave?"

She stands up, pulling out her phone. "I can find out with one phone call… just give me a minute…"

She presses the phone to her ear and walks to the other side of my studio apartment, setting the wheels in motion. I start to pull out my two duffel bags, filling them with my clothes.

It doesn't feel real. Then again, nothing really does.

Nothing except for the fact that I'm still angry at Stellan.

It's only the work of an hour for Pippa to get us booked on a flight to Copenhagen. She keeps giving me the same comforting smile while she works on it, checking on me every so often.

But Pippa was right… there isn't anything holding me back. Nothing tying me to New York except that I was born here.

And that just isn't enough.

We pack up everything I could need to take in twenty minutes. Then I open the front door, looking out into the crowd of reporters. There are a million camera flashes and people jockeying to be close enough to me to ask me a question.

"Margot! Margot!"

"Are you joining the prince?"

"Will you become queen, Margot? Is that what this is about?"

I roll my eyes harder than they've ever been rolled in my life. There is a somewhat violent struggle between the paparazzi to get my attention. I stop, giving them the only sound bite that I will ever utter.

"It must be terrible for you to be so bound by the rules of the patriarchy," I tell one woman who keeps shoving her microphone in my face. "You should really work on that."

Pippa locks the door behind us and then steers me through the jostling crowd. We get into the waiting Lyft, jetting off toward Pippa's hotel, our only stop on the way to the airport.

I look out the back window as my flat disappears around a corner. Splaying my hand out against the glass, I say a silent goodbye to my shitty apartment.

Then I turn and face forward, wondering what Copenhagen will be like.

Chapter Seven

MARGOT

AT TWENTY THREE YEARS OLD, this is definitely not where I saw my life headed.

Exiled from New York.

Running away to Denmark.

Haunted by memories of a man that wasn't at all who I thought him to be.

A man whose fiercely good looks and skills in bed still wake me up at night, panting his name.

Stellan.

I close my eyes and lean my forehead against the smooth off-white plastic surrounding the window of the plane. I let myself drowse and drift. As the plane carries me across the Atlantic, I'm in the elusive space between wakefulness and sleep. My mind wanders, half-formed shapes rising out of the ether to remind me of what I'm running from.

"Margot! Margot!"

Dimly, I am aware of a round black microphone materializing out of the dull gray void, and being pushed toward my face.

"What was it like to sleep with Denmark's future king? Do you have royal aspirations? Are you and Prince Stellan declaring your intentions to marry?"

I flinch away, stirring a little. The microphone is shoved toward my mouth. Everyone is waiting for a response. I have no choice but to answer.

No, I think. *I don't want anything to do with him.*

Stellan's face takes shape in my mind. He is tall and broad, dark-haired with ice blue eyes and cheekbones for days. He is exceptionally gorgeous. It's clear as day that he descended directly from the Vikings and looking at his face makes me feel weak in the knees.

In fact, I would describe his features as being distinctly aristocratic. But along with that comes the aloofness that I have always associated with royalty.

He holds himself apart from everyone else, makes a distinction based solely on how much money his family has. And that makes me wish I had never slept with him, no matter how fuckable I find him.

"Margot!" the reporter says again, jostling me. "Margot?"

Why is the reporter suddenly speaking in a smooth English accent?

I open my eyes to find Pippa peering at me. Pippa is my best friend from college; she is taking me with her back to Copenhagen, to outrun the screaming mob of paparazzi that dogged my every step back in New York.

Well, that explains the accent. Pippa is British.

It takes me a moment to realize that we are still on the plane. Pippa brushes her fiery red hair out of her face and folds up her tray table.

"We're about to land," she says. She nods to something past me. "Look out the window."

I turn and look at the view. It's pitch black out as it is quite late here in Copenhagen. A million tiny points of light shine through the darkness, filtering up to me in the shape of a city. It isn't nearly as huge as New York City, the place that I'm running from.

But it shimmers and twinkles all the same. I place my hand against the glass as we start to descend. Copenhagen will be my home for the next few months.

As the plane lands and I rush to follow Pippa to customs, I am beyond nervous. We line up behind half a dozen other people, all waiting to have their passports examined and stamped. I flip open my brand new passport, creasing the book a bit, and peer at the picture inside.

A tiny, shell-shocked woman with pink hair glares back at me. I'm wearing a leather jacket in the photo and look like more of a badass than I actually feel like. I grew up with less than nothing; not only did I not have any money; I wasn't even sure from night to night where I would sleep or how I would eat.

I've definitely never been out of the country before now. Swallowing, I try to slow my heart rate, which soars higher with every step I take toward the plexiglass security booth.

Pippa leans in close, seeming to tower over me. Pippa is a good six inches taller than me and always dresses impeccably in long, flowy dresses. "Relax." She elbows me. "We'll be through this line in just a minute."

She winks at me. I wrinkle my nose but stay quiet. It's often best to stay silent if you only have negative things to say, I find.

We go through customs and security, arriving outside. New York City is hotter than this in the early summer. It's probably only about seventy five degrees outside right now, just warm enough to not be chilly.

As we get into a cab that Pippa flagged down, she yawns. "This time change thing is going to give me killer jet lag. Tomorrow we should sleep in if we can before we have to be at *Politiken*."

I look out at the blurry cityscape, feeling bleary. "*Politiken* is essentially the New York Times of Copenhagen. It's about as liberal as they come…"

I look at Pippa, who cocks a brow. "I know. You're telling me about a place that I work. And as of tomorrow, we will both work there."

Giving my head a shake, I roll my eyes at myself. "Sorry. I think the jet lag has somehow caught up with me already. I meant to ask whether you think that they'll want me to just write or to take pictures, too. My camera hasn't been used professionally for way too long."

Photography is very much my first love.

She shrugs. "I have no idea. My editor Anna just told me to get your butt to Copenhagen… she didn't say what kind of stuff she'll have you working on."

I lean my head back, closing my eyes. "Maybe this is the launch of my career and I don't even know it. Maybe it's a new opportunity that comes disguised as a torrent of paparazzi screaming questions."

It's true. When I left New York, it was under a black cloud. It seemed like every paparazzo had the same endless strings of questions for me every time I dared to open my door just to check the mail.

Margot, did your affair with Prince Stellan leave you star struck?

Are you going to Copenhagen to be with him?

What is it like being a real life Cinderella?

The last one really stung. The tabloids really concentrated on the rags to riches aspect of the whole salacious affair. Basically I didn't tell them anything, so they just jumped ahead without any kind of factual basis for the entire story.

Stellan has been radio silent ever since I walked out of his hotel to a mob of reporters. I met someone that I thought was my dream guy… tall, handsome, and witty… and then he vanished into a swirl of dust at the first camera flash. A low sinking feeling still lurks in the pit of my stomach a week later.

Pippa chuckles. "I know you must be tired, because that is way more optimistic than you usually are."

I grin. "Yeah, probably. Ask me how I feel tomorrow and I can guarantee it will be different."

The taxi stops downtown in front of a high rise and we get out. I carry my two duffel bags — the sum of all my worldly possessions — up to the fourth floor. Following Pippa into her apartment, I look around.

It's a cozy little apartment; the perfectly white kitchen is to my left, a living room set up to my right. There are stacks of magazines, newspapers, and junk mail piled haphazardly every place I look.

Pippa bares her teeth as she sweeps a pile into her arms and drops her suitcase on the couch. "Sorry it's such a mess. I didn't realize I would be returning from New York with a new roommate." She pauses. "I'll actually have to move some stuff out of your room. And make some room on the counter in the bathroom…" She pulls a face. "And you shouldn't open the refrigerator…"

My lips curl upward. "It's okay, Pips. We lived together during college. I remember it fondly."

She blushes. "I'll get a maid if my mess starts to affect you."

I shrug. "I've literally been homeless before. I'm sure I'll manage."

Pippa shows me down the hallway and into the second bedroom. There's a little futon set up in there that is literally covered with books. Other than a tall IKEA lamp and a mostly empty closet, the room is bare.

"We'll set it up way better," she promises. Then she yawns and stretches. "Come on. Help me get these books off the bed. I think I have some extra sheets in my room…"

Half an hour later I lay down on sheets that only smell like mildew a little bit, sighing as I close my eyes. It's almost two in the morning here now.

I toss and turn for a few minutes before I realize that I am used to a streetlight glowing just outside my window when I'm trying to sleep. My brain is just full of anxieties: my work, my address, and my social status have all changed in the last twenty four hours.

Rolling onto my side, I stare up at the ceiling. In the back of my mind, one paparazzo's question stands out in my mind still.

Margot! Aren't you glad that you won't have to work anymore now that Prince Stellan is your lover?

I grit my teeth. When it comes down do it, that is the problem. These tabloid hacks are allowed to make up whatever they want about my life. Not only that, but they reap rewards from lying.

I would never give up my dreams for a guy, no matter who he is. I don't know how I feel about love in general. Can it be trusted?

It doesn't matter in this case. No amount of insanely chiseled abs or dimples that make me swoon are worth that. Besides, giving up photojournalism for a man would make me extremely vulnerable.

Vulnerability isn't something I can afford, not when Stellan is around. One night together shattered my entire world… I hope I never have to be in that position ever again.

Blech! I make a face in the dark, though no one sees it except for my musty-smelling pillow.

No. No fucking way. I would rather die than be that dependent on any man.

I'm Margot fucking Keane, and I make my own way in the world. For better or for worse, I will always be independent. I've been at the ass end of society: on welfare, my parents MIA, uncertain where my next meal could come from. I've been homeless and I've was even in the foster care system for a while.

What I've learned in all that time is a fiercely held independence and a kind of stubbornness that can shame the devil. And no matter how hard they try, they can't take that away from me.

Rolling over, I bury my face into my pillow with a sigh.

Chapter Eight

STELLAN

SHE'S SO SMALL, *her features like that of a doll. Her head doesn't quite come up to my shoulder. Yet she is so...* perfect.

Soft pink hair like so much cotton candy, with dark blue eyes that follow me whenever I move. And her body... as she tugs her black negligee over her head, the sight of her full breasts makes my breath leave my lungs. Her nipples are the most alluring color of blush; they make my mouth water.

God damn, she's so beautiful.

I reach down and adjust my cock in my boxer briefs. Then I grate out a command. "Take off your panties."

Margot's gorgeous lips twitch. She tilts her head. "Why don't you come over here and do it yourself?"

I smirk and then move onto the bed very, very slowly. "You are defiant."

The breath leaves her lungs as my arms cage her in. "Until my last breath."

I consider her for a second. Then I reach up and push her hair away from one side of her neck, the backs of my fingers touching the slim white column of her throat. "Someone should teach you a lesson, ja?"

She lifts her head, her eyes full of need and want. "I've been waiting for a teacher."

I can feel her racing pulse. I run a single fingertip down her neck, over her collarbone, tracing a line between her bare breasts. She sucks in a breath.

My touch trails down her ribs, across her navel, and ends at the top of her panties. She squeezes her thighs together, biting her lower lip.

I smirk at her. "I'm going to fuck you senseless. If you're going to tell me to stop, this is your last chance."

Margot bites her lip, smothering a grin. She shakes her head. "Less talk. More action."

I smile as I literally rip her panties off of her body. I kiss her on the hip, then on the top of her thigh. She can't hold back the sultry moan that rises in her throat. My fingers wander up to find her nipple and tweak it hard.

Gasping loudly, she arches into my touch.

"Good girl," I purr. I splay a big hand underneath her belly button, covering her public mound. Pressing down firmly as I shower little bites and swift nibbles to her thighs, I work my way closer and closer to her shaved pussy.

She watches as I run the tip of one thick finger up the seam of her pussy, just barely touching. A twisted, angry grunt leaves her lips.

"Stellan!" she reprimands.

I look up at her, grinning devilishly. I place the lightest of butterfly kisses over her pussy, making her writhe.

"Stellan, please!" Margot begs.

I shake my head. "I don't think so, skatter. *I'm not going to let you come just yet."*

Instead, I push myself up onto my knees and grasp my cock through my boxer briefs. Her lungs constrict as she watches me. I'm looking down on her, naked and spread out.

Fuck. She's the most gorgeous little thing I've ever seen.

Eyeing her, I bite my lip. "I think I need to taste you, skatter. *But I also want to feel the tip of my cock in your fucking throat."*

Her entire body tightens with need. My lips twist into a naughty smile.

"Can you control your gag reflex?"

Her cheeks color. "A little." She gets to her knees, reaching for me, but I sneer at her.

"No. You lie on the edge of the bed, like this." I grab her, positioning her so that her head is by the foot of the bed, dangling off just a little. "If it's too much, just tap my leg. Ja?"

Nodding, she watches as I strip my black boxer briefs off. My cock bounces up, jutting straight out.

"Holy shit," she breathes, her eyes widening. My cock is long, thick, and veiny in a way that male porn stars would be jealous of. I'm also uncut, which honestly can be unnerving to the unprepared.

I grin, grasping my cock and wiggling my eyebrows. Then I step forward. "Open your mouth. Cover your teeth for me, skatter."

Licking her lips, she opens her mouth. I step closer and nudge the tip of my cock between her lips. It's hard to be still in that moment. I want to take her mouth, fucking it with abandon, and making myself come in a matter of seconds.

But I don't.

I groan, closing my eyes for a brief moment. "Ah, fuck."

She relaxes a little, resting her hand on my inner thigh.

Then I start to move, very slowly working my length in and out of her lips. A rumble of pleasure leaves my lips. Not groans or moans, but almost.

God, it's hard to be good right now.

I stop and peer down at her after a few seconds. "Good?"

She nods, her mouth still full of my cock. I can feel the slow slide of her tongue against the sensitive underside of the head.

Fuck. I had better start moving before I lose control.

I grip my cock and start pumping in and out of her mouth, my eyes squeezing shut. She grabs me and pulls me closer, attempting to work her tongue against my cock.

My reaction is immediate. My whole body seizes up. It feels so fucking good. "Fuck, Margot."

She slides her hand down to delicately cup my balls. My eyes actually roll back in my head as I start to move again, jerking in and out of her lips roughly.

"Fuck," I breathe. "Skatter..."

I know I'm going to come. There's no stopping it.

I halt suddenly, pulling out of her mouth. Before she can even react, I'm covering the tip of my cock with my hand, cursing and clenching my eyes shut. I come, shooting jets of milky white semen into my hand. The look of pleasure that was on Margot's face when I closed my eyes makes lust slither through my gut.

She likes watching her handiwork.

When I'm done, I open my eyes again. "That wasn't quite how I was supposed to finish… but your mouth felt too good. Too hot."

She lick the corner of her mouth. "My pleasure."

I chuckle, reaching across to the bedside table for the tissue box. I wipe my hand off and then pad over to the trashcan, disposing of the tissue. When I come back, I kneel at the foot of the bed.

Margot looks at me uncertainly, biting her lower lip.

"Now it's your turn," I husk. "Come down here."

She turn around, her movements a little awkward. I'm not interested in waiting, so I grab her knees and spread them wide. Her lower lips spread, giving me unbridled access to her most intimate parts. She squeaks softly, probably feeling a little awkward being exposed like this, but I'm not too worried about her emotions just now.

"Cup your breasts," I command, ducking my head low. She sucks in a breath and does as I ask, mmming at the sensation.

I start kissing my way up her pale, creamy skin, just inside her knee. My hands touch her inner thighs, sliding up as I trail my kisses toward her pussy. She moans softly and shivers, bucking just a little. I look up at her, catching her eye.

My dark brow descends. "You are so beautiful, Margot."

One second I'm about to go down on Margot, the next second I am awake and sweating.

Where am I, exactly?

I manage to focus my eyes and see that I'm in my bedroom at the palace, naked against the thousand dollar silk sheets of my bed.

"Fuck."

I close my eyes, trying to recapture the dream. But it's like trying to catch fog in my cupped hands; the dream slips away and I'm left feeling a twisting kind of loneliness.

Margot is gone.

I left her behind in New York.

And I'm here by myself, almost four thousand miles away, the scent of her perfume still teasing my senses. Groaning, I cover my face with a satiny pillow and try to go back to sleep.

Chapter Nine

STELLAN

DON'T REACT. *Just keep your facial expression smooth and untroubled.*

I'm sitting at one end of a very long dining room table, looking at the coffee cup in front of me. I am being lectured on responsibility for about the millionth time; I learned as a child to school my expression into a troubled frown and look at some object that's just out of reach.

God. Why am I even here? I know I messed up. But my mother and father, the queen and king of Denmark, are sticking to their world tour. They are busy; my four siblings are off doing god knows what with god knows who.

Why won't my grandmother just let this scandal die?

But I can answer my own question. As the oldest child of Goran and Thora Løve, I should expect to inherit the crown someday. There are endless expectations and responsibilities that I'm responsible for… things that even my closest family and friends don't know about.

"I don't even think he's listening!" Prime Minister Finley, the prime minister of Denmark, growls at me.

He stops to brush a fleck of lint off of his dark gray suit, shaking his head. He tsks and tuts; with his fake blond hair and his preening posture, reminding me of nothing so much as a prized cockatiel.

As of today, he's an angry cockatiel. He puts his hands behind his back, pacing back and forth. Several other members of my private cabinet have been brought to Amalienborg Castle to watch this act of Finley's. To watch and learn as Finley scolds the golden boy prince.

They sit at the opposite end of the table, looking at least as bored as I am. This isn't new, the summoning of multiple people to witness my dressing down.

My grandmother watches everything from her seat by the window, her keen blue eyes picking up on everything she sees. She clears her throat gently and picks at a phantom thread on her pink Chanel suit. A tendril of steel gray hair has escaped from her chignon. No one says anything about it, though. Just like no one is fooled by the fact that she isn't speaking.

We all know who really has the power in this country, and it isn't the absentminded king or the ridiculous prime minister.

"The entire reason you were sent to New York was to do one simple interview. And what do you do instead? You go and cause a scandal!"

He walks over to the table and points a long, pale finger at the tabloids that are spread out over it. My face is splashed on every last one, as is the same shot of a very harassed-looking Margot leaving my hotel.

PRINCE STELLAN HAS ONE NIGHT STAND
   ONE MAGICAL NIGHT WITH THE MAN WHO WOULD BE KING
   RAGS TO RICHES: BEFORE MARGOT MET STELLAN
   And my personal favorite…
SHE'S ALREADY PREGNANT WITH HIS ROYAL BABY

God, even in that picture of her scurrying away from my hotel, her face pinched, Margot looks incredible. She's a tiny person, yes. And she's wearing nothing but a dark-colored negligee and that shocking pink hair… I could've given up everything if only she had let me keep sleeping with her.

Instead, she ran away—

"Stellan!" my grandmother calls. I look up, my cheeks coloring slightly. She nods to Finley. "Prime Minister Finley isn't done."

I crease my brow but my expression stays… not placid, but fixed. Margot reached out to me after she fled my hotel. Several times, actually. I've obsessed over her messages but not returned any of them.

After all, I'm supposed to be on publicity lock down now. The last thing I need in the world is a spotlight.

"You see, that's the problem with your generation…" Finley says, puffing his chest out and pacing again. He pulls out his glasses and puts them on, blinking at me like an owl. "You don't have any privations or restrictions on what you can do. You have so much more freedom than our generation ever had…"

The feral beast inside my chest raises his head at that. He glares at Finley, showing his teeth.

What Finley knows about my personal freedom could fill a thimble. And the fact that he has the audacity to come here to my home and lecture me makes me fucking furious.

But I shove that anger down deep, trying to exude a vaguely repentant air. I want everyone in this room to know that I'm concerned about the scandal, but not *too* concerned. There is an art to wearing the right level of intensity on my face.

My grandmother Ida checks her tiny gold watch, silently sighing. Her gaze rises to take in the whole room with its vaulted ceilings and baby blue walls. Outside the gauzy drapes of immense windows, the summer sun is at its zenith.

Could that mean that Ida expects this to end soon? It's been going on for over an hour and it's the fourth time this week that I've been yelled at for…

Well, an *indiscretion*, to say the least. It's really not even my fault… I just looked into Margot's eyes and saw myself. Or not myself, exactly. But myself if I were not a royal.

If I weren't going to be king, how different my life would have been. How could I be so close to that reflection of my other self and not lean in a little?

She just had this quality that made me forget about everyone else around us, homing in on *her*. What is that, exactly? If I could, I would find out and bottle that essence for the future.

It made me fall for her, at least a little.

Besides, I can guarantee that one glance at Margot's incredible body and her unbelievable ass would have even old Finley howling like a wolf at a cresting moon.

"What do you have to say for yourself?" Finley's smug expression and cocky strut make me fucking angry.

I roll my neck, listening for a loud crack. When I speak, I try to show Finley and his government cronies not an ounce of genuine emotion. "It was a mistake." I grit my teeth. "It won't happen again, obviously."

"You're damned right it won't happen—" Finley starts.

Ida rises from her seat. As soon as she does, the room falls silent. Everyone is extremely afraid of her, the physically weakest one among all of us.

One day, I hope to wield that kind of power.

"I think that's quite enough, don't you?" she says. She gives Finley a smile that is as cool as ice. "As it happens, I have a solution."

Finley looks astonished. "A solution?"

The smirk is in her voice but not on her face. She just appears critical, as usual. "Yes. A solution. You may not be familiar with them as you are only prime minister, but in the royal family we require them from time to time." One of the cabinet members gasps quietly. Ida cocks her head and her lips curl up. "It appears that the girl has already moved here. All the royal family has to do now is find a way to silence her."

My eyebrows rise and I rock backward in my chair. "She moved here?" My brows hunch. "Why?"

My grandmother eyes me for a long moment before walking purposefully over to the table, looking down at the tabloids splashed out there. "It appears that Miss Margot Keane is a journalist. I used a contact at *Politiken* to lure her here." She frowns. "Not that I gather she will miss much about New York. From my understanding she doesn't own anything of value."

She shrugs, the movement barely raising her shoulders. What she isn't saying out loud is the second part of her sentence. *In comparison to us; we have all the castles and all the yachts that anyone could want.*

Ida raises a brow, looking down at me. She's very small and very fierce; she eats lesser men than me for breakfast. That's her unspoken communication sent to me, anyway.

I shift in my seat, struggling to keep my face assembled in a remotely pleasant expression. "And you think that Miss Keane will just… what, sign a nondisclosure agreement? I'm assuming that you believe that she will agree to lie for the royal family."

She scans the room, pretending at being thoughtful. "Prime Minister Finley, cabinet members… would you please leave us? I think my grandson and I should speak in private."

Finley bows, turning to usher the rest of the small group out of the room. Picking up my coffee cup, I take a sip and look at my grandmother. I would guess that she came up with whatever plan she's about to unveil days ago.

She comes up to me, pulling out a chair and sitting down. Ida looks at me, her blue eyes like two frozen pools of ice.

"Now then." She cants her head. "Perhaps we offer Miss Keane something… like an exclusive story with you, close up and personal. We could have her sign documents saying that you were working together in New York… and she won't be able to contradict us, because she will have signed a nondisclosure agreement. We will control the story, not the other way around."

Ida's lips quirk; she looks pleased with herself, from what I can tell. I narrow my eyes at her.

"*Momse*," I say, careful to use her pet name. "I don't think this is a good idea. Will Miss Keane just write an article based on nothing, then?"

My grandmother's lips flatten. "No. She will follow you around for a few weeks or a month to complete the charade."

I shake my head. "People don't like to be led around by the halter, *Momse*. I hate the press as much as anyone. You know that. I don't want or need anyone in my private business. But—"

She pushes herself to her feet with an anger that is born of ruling a kingdom with an iron fist for ages. "Enough! I expect more from you, Stellan. I pulled you out of the fire once already when you were wrapped up in drugs. I stepped in and made sure that other girl and her family stayed quiet." Her expression turns from disappointed to terrifying. My toes curl up in my shoes. Even though she's old and almost a third of my size, she's still domineering. She has been this way since I was born.

I lower my gaze. "I know, *Momse*."

She slams her hand down on the table, startling me. "I was willing to write that off as a youthful failure, *ja*? But this? This could be the end of the monarchy."

I stare at her for a second. Yes, she absolutely did have to save my fucking neck once. And she did so without question. But that was ages ago.

I feel defensive. Rising to my full height, I fold my arms across my chest. "That was a lifetime ago, *Momse*. And this little mistake with Miss Keane? It was just that. Why can't we just let it be?"

When Ida gets angry, she glares at me and her face puckers like a wrinkled apple. Her eyes flash, their blue icy enough to cut fucking steel.

"One day soon, I will be gone. Let's both face it; your father does not have the instincts that my husband had. So I am trying to instill those instincts in you." She pauses. "I think I've done a passable job. But I will not have this family brought down by some little girl. You understand? I won't allow it."

I soften a bit, reaching out to touch Ida's elbow. "I know, *Momse*. I don't want the monarchy abolished either. Okay?"

That's a lie. Or at least a partial truth… when I was a kid, I used to lie in bed at night and dream about the monarchy's downfall. I wanted to do normal things like go to school or have play dates with friends.

That was a long time ago, though. I squeeze my grandmother's arm in an attempt to make her feel better. She pats my hand a few times and then pulls away.

If anything ever defined our relationship perfectly, it's that moment right there.

"Miss Keane will follow you around for a month." She goes over to the chair that she previously occupied and presses a button to summon the staff. "And you'll be on your best behavior now that you know who she is. *Ja?*"

I incline my head. "*Ja.* Sure, *Momse.*"

She narrows her eyes at me. "There are half a dozen suitable girls just waiting for you to look their way, Stellan. I've given you my list of acceptable candidates. The next time you find yourself in need of company, call whichever one you want. It's long past time that you got married."

I shoot her a scowl just as a butler sweeps into the room. He bows. "Your purse and coat, your royal highness. The car is waiting for you downstairs."

She walks stiffly over to the door, then pauses just before she hits the threshold. "I'm off to Sønderborg to try to dig your brother Finn out of whatever mess he's in. Do try to stay out of trouble while I'm gone, won't you?"

I hesitate. She doesn't wait for an answer. She just glides out of the room, patting her perfectly coiffed gray hair.

I am left alone to stare out the window and curse the luck of being born royal.

Chapter Ten

MARGOT

THE BUILDINGS in Copenhagen are a kaleidoscope of different colors: the façades are white and brown and peach and brick red, the roofs green and orange and blue and black. Gammelholm, the prestigious downtown area where the offices of *Politiken* are located, is bustling at nine in the morning.

Businesspeople going to work, tourists meandering toward the nearby art museum, a stream of teens who rush into what can only be a school next door.

Sucking in a deep breath, I look through the viewfinder of my camera at the building that houses *Politiken*'s offices. I snap a couple of photos; I've been taking photos all morning, documenting my first morning in Denmark.

I love taking photos. I love the symmetry that can be found in a perfect picture of an everyday object. I love the pungent smell of the chemicals used to develop film. I'm definitely a nerd about photography.

As I stare up at the ancient cream-colored stone of the building, Pippa gently elbows me in the ribs.

"We're already late," she says, grabbing me by the arm. "Come on."

Everything inside appears to be marble. Eschewing the ancient elevators as she tows me up the stairs, Pippa jogs down a marble hallway until we reach the doors.

Politiken, the glass of one of the doors reads. *Nyheden kommer først.*

Pippa swings the door open and pulls me inside a big room with high ceilings and about thirty people working in cubicles. A standard newsroom, it wouldn't be out of place at any paper anywhere in the world. No one even looks up at us when we rush in; the reporters are too busy typing manically or talking quietly on the phone. Against the back wall are the glass-walled offices of people in positions of power here at the newspaper as well as a well-appointed conference room.

A tall blonde woman in her fifties stands across the office, watching us with an annoyed expression. Pippa curses under her breath and tugs at her pale pink dress.

"That's Anna," she says, picking up her pace as she makes a beeline toward the woman. I do a quick scan of Anna's person and take stock of her wrinkled light gray pants suit and the stain on her white dress shirt.

A woman after my own heart. I'm wearing one of three pairs of black dress pants I own and a black Violent Femmes t-shirt paired with an oversize yellow cardigan. Seeing Anna's disregard for dressing up bolsters my confidence.

Two seconds later, I stand in front of her and rethink my opinions.

"You two are quite late," Anna says, looking down her nose at us both. She looks at me, at the Nikon camera on its strap around my neck, and she rolls her eyes.

Pippa jumps in.

"Yes. Sorry. We had some trouble trying to leave the house." Pippa bites her lower lip, sliding her gaze to me. "But I brought Margot to you like you asked!"

Anna's gaze tightens on my face. "Yes. So you did." She spins, heading toward the back of the room. "Come to my office, both of you."

We head back to Anna's spacious office, sitting down in the chairs in front of her sleek chrome desk. She frowns as she types something into the computer at her side, then slides a drawer out.

"Margot!" she barks. I sit up, wide eyed.

"Ma'am?" I say.

She gives me a hard look before she hands over an employee badge. "This will get you in and out of the building. You'll need to fill out some tax paperwork at some point… Max will get you settled with that." She pushes back in her office chair, looking at Pippa and me. "We should talk about the story you will be covering."

I tilt my head. "Well... I came prepared with several ideas to pitch to you— "

"Enough," Anna says, cutting me off. "Your assignment has already been chosen for you."

I send Pippa a questioning glance. She shrugs and makes a quick *I don't know anything* face. Anna starts drumming her fingers on her desktop.

"You weren't aware of this already?" she asks.

It's hard to tell what she's thinking from her expression. Should I already know something?

Shaking my head, I feel my cheeks warm. "No."

Anna grunts, but I still don't have the slightest idea what she means by it. "I got the call late last night. You have been selected to work on a cover piece about Prince Stellan and his life."

My jaw drops.

No.

No way.

It's not possible.

One night together already made me flee New York. Any further contact between Stellan and me is just... a terrible, horrible, impossible idea.

Pippa, for her part, looks stunned.

"Oh, I can't do that," I blurt out, crossing my arms. "Give it to Pippa!"

Anna glares at me. "If I had my way, the most senior correspondent that usually gets her name on the most bylines would do the story. But obviously I had nothing to do with the choice, due to the fact that we had yet to meet."

My brow hunches. "Who decided that I would do the story, then?"

"Someone from the royal family, I gather." Anna scrunches up her face. "The question is, why?"

She puts her elbows on her desk, rubbing her lips. My cheeks immediately redden.

"I'm assuming that you are aware of the American tabloids and their... err... interest in me?" I tuck a strand of pink hair back behind my ear, chewing my bottom lip.

Anna glances at Pippa, then makes a show of pulling several brightly colored tabloid newspapers out of a drawer of her desk. Every single one features me on the cover, usually with an inset photo of Stellan.

She tosses them on her desk and then kicks back in her chair. "I'm familiar, yes."

I clear my throat, unwilling to be shamed. Not for this, at least.

"I think that this is a bad idea," I say. "I'm not sure why the order came from the royal family… but I have a bad feeling about it. Why sign up for something when I know out of the gate that I am going to be manipulated in some way?"

Anna glances at her watch and sighs. "This has honestly taken up more time than I care to devote to it. Either take the assignment or don't…" She smiles coolly. "But if you don't, you can kiss writing goodbye for a year. You can run research and get coffee for the office but bylines are saved for those who write whatever they are assigned."

My mouth falls open. "But… I mean…" I shoot to my feet, alarmed. "I… I don't mean to be picky…"

She stands up, folding her arms across her chest. "Yes or no?"

I quail. "Uhh…"

"Get out," she says, making a sour face. "I have to call the press office at the palace and tell them that you said no."

A gray-haired man appears in the doorway of Anna's office. He's older, maybe in his late sixties, and impeccably dressed. From the way that Anna and Pippa straighten when they see him, I gather that he's fairly important.

"Is this Margot?" he asks, smiling widely.

He sticks out his hand to me. I take it, not particularly understanding.

"Hi. Margot Keane."

"Margot, I am Emil Dall. I'm the managing editor here at *Politiken*. I was told you are going to be handling the profile of our royal prince!"

My face heats. "Well, I mean… Anna did bring it up, but I just told her that I don't want— "

He cuts me off, not even pretending to listen to my jabbering.

"Great! Anna will give you all the guidance you need. Not that we will be seeing much of you… From what I gather, you will be assigned to shadow Prince Stellan for a few weeks."

"But— "

"And did Anna tell you about what we are offering as incentive to finish this piece?"

My eyebrows go up. So do Anna's… which I think means she's as in the dark as I am.

"No…" I say slowly.

Emil smiles even more widely, showcasing his teeth. "We are looking for someone to run the arts and entertainment desk. If you take the job, you would be editing all the pieces and pitching your own ideas. It would be a huge thing for your career. You would be at the bottom of the editors food chain but above all the reporters. *Ja?*"

My eyes widen. Anna makes a choking sound, turning away and reaching for a glass of water on her desk. I glance at Pippa, who gives me a look that says *duh! take it!*

I clear my throat. "Thanks. I guess… I mean, how can I say no?"

"That's the spirit!" cheers Emil. "You will do great, I'm sure."

He turns to Anna, saying something pointed to her in Danish. Anna's face colors a little but she just nods and thanks him.

"It was nice to meet you, Margot." He smiles at everyone, puts his hands together, and bows. Then he marches out of Anna's office.

Pippa reaches out to me, her eyes wide. "He doesn't even know my name. And I've worked here for over a year!"

Anna glowers at us. "I'm glad that you changed your mind, Margot. You do realize that you will need to be *extremely* respectful when you are dealing with the royal family, *ja?*"

I wrinkle my nose. My heart still gallops against my ribs. "I know how to act. I wasn't raised by wolves or anything."

Anna's eyebrows lift a fraction. "I don't understand what you mean. What is *raised by wolves?*"

Yikes. Everyone I've encountered so far has spoken flawless English; clearly, I need to brush up on my Danish, not the other way around.

"I'm sorry, I— "

Anna flicks her hand at me impatiently. "Go set up your employee email and further instructions about this assignment will be sent soon. Now if you would kindly get out of my office, I've got an actual job to do."

She makes a shooing motion with her hands as she sits down again, pointedly looking at her computer instead of us. I beat Pippa in the rush to get out of her office and out of Anna's earshot.

Pippa pulls me over to her cubicle, still agog. "I can't believe this is happening. Emil is a *really* big deal in journalism here. There's an award with his name on it given out yearly to the best journalist."

I pull a chair over from an empty desk and sag into it. Pippa sits in her chair, biting her lip. I lean back, looking up at the ceiling as I let out a sigh.

"What in the world am I doing?" I wonder out loud. "Other than upsetting the natural order of things by getting orders from the royal palace or what the fuck ever."

Pippa sucks in a breath. "Oh god. Do you think…"

I glance at her. "What?"

"Do you think that Stellan asked for you?"

For a foolish second, my heart clatters around in my chest. Did he? Could it have been him?

Then I frown and shake that thought from my head. "I don't know. My guess would be no. But then again, I clearly have no idea who is pulling the strings around here."

"Hmm." She puffs out her cheeks. "I can try to find out whenever I talk to Lars next."

Her familiarity with the royal family makes me give her a crooked smile. "Sure, Pips."

She bites at her fingernail, swiveling toward her computer. "All right. In the meantime, let's get your email set up…"

I bob my head, sighing.

Chapter Eleven

STELLAN

"BUT WHAT IF instead of going to this factory and doing a tour, we all just commit suicide instead?" my little sister says, sighing as she looks out the window of the car we're being shuttled in. Annika is only eighteen and the baby of my family. She's also the weirdo.

I say that with love, as the twenty six year old black sheep of the family.

I cock a brow. "That doesn't sound particularly productive."

She brightens. "Maybe, as the royal family, we should declare that the nuclear threat to our nation is viable. And that we should, as a nation, move underground. We can all become mole people. Ooh! This factory can be the base from where we start the revolution!"

She wiggles her delicate blonde eyebrows and grins. She looks classically Danish: light blonde hair, bright blue eyes, with a smattering of freckles across the bridge of her nose. She's always full of her unique sense of humor, although it is a bit morbid.

"Mole people, huh?" I repress a sigh and look away, out the window as the city falls away behind us.

My best friend Erik looks back at both of us from the passenger seat of the SUV.

"Annika, we will be at this factory for a grand total of four hours, tops. I don't think we will have the time to overthrow the government." He runs a hand through his dirty blond, close cropped hair, shifting in the passenger seat. All six and a half feet of him is barely confined in the front seat and he doesn't look comfortable.

Coming in just an inch shorter than him, I can sympathize. Annika is tall for a girl, but when she walks between Erik and me, she looks downright dainty.

She throws Erik a grin. "You don't think that's enough time? Maybe you're just not as efficient as I am."

Erik rolls his eyes. "I'm much more efficient than any of you Løves. That's what being raised as a non-royal amongst royals does to a person."

I frown a little. "Erik, when we were growing up, you went to the same palace tutors as I did. You played the same sports. You even joined the same military regiment as me. Don't act like you're exactly a normal person."

He smiles coolly at me. "And yet... one of us will be a king and the other will not."

My neck heats. He has always had a funny knack for putting his finger right on the pulse of the issue.

Annika wrinkles her nose, looking at me. "All I know is that you both owe me big time. *Momse* wanted to send Lars or Finn along with you on this little trip, even after the disastrously bad way they handled things at the easter egg hunt. I convinced her that I am the superior choice." She grins, showing her teeth. "You're welcome."

I ignore that. Of my four siblings though, she is unquestionably my favorite. It doesn't hurt that Annika knows exactly when to put on the saccharide smile and when to keep her mouth shut.

Unlike Finn, Lars, and Anders...

"How are my little brothers doing these days?" I ask, looking at her out of the corner of my eye. "Is Anders back from Malaysia or Madagascar or wherever he went?"

"Morocco," Erik chimes in. "He's been in Casablanca."

"He's just come back." Annika looks bored. "Lars and Finn have been relatively quiet too. I think Finn is doing some survival fitness thing in the Swiss Alps... and you should know better than I where Lars is. Didn't he go to New York with you two?"

Erik chuckles, which earns him a glare from me.

"We had to leave him there in our rush to get back," I say evenly. "Duty called back here at home."

Annika smirks and rolls her eyes.

"Speaking of being the heir to the throne… I hear that we are going to meet Margot today." She purses her lips. "You remember Margot, don't you? Pink hair? An ass that won't quit? Hooked up with you and somehow *everybody* in the world found out about it?"

My eyes narrow to slits. "Yes, I remember."

Erik adjusts his mass in the front seat, sliding a look over at the driver. The driver doesn't even look at him, just keeps his eyes on the road. Erik shrugs.

"I would rather we deal with the situation like this than have some royal fixer have to go clean it up afterward."

He makes eye contact with me when he says the last bit. My neck heats again.

He's referencing the same thing that my grandmother did. The time when I was nineteen and acting out, drinking a lot and doing a lot of cocaine. I called Ida while I was strung out on drugs and desperate because I'd ended up in a motel with a girl who lost consciousness.

The royal fixers swept in and cleaned everything up. I was sent to dry out in Spain; Mathilde, a hard-core party girl and sometimes friend, ended up in a coma that lapsed into a vegetative state.

I look at the driver, my mouth twisting. There are a ton of things I feel on the topic of Mathilde, but I'm not willing to risk saying any of them out loud in front of the driver. Besides, Annika doesn't even know.

No one does, outside of my grandmother, Erik, and the royal fixers. I clear my throat and rub my temples.

"Are we almost there yet?" I grit out.

Erik sighs, looking at his phone. "*Ja*, we're only a minute away."

When we arrive at the large factory, I look up at the two-story slab of cement. I'm strangely nervous, though I would guess that has more to do with Margot being here than the public nature of my visit. "What does this place make again?"

Erik consults his phone. "Porcelain plates."

"Mole people will probably make porcelain plates their first form of currency," Annika says, straightening her aquamarine dress.

I shake my head as I stride up to the factory. I mirror her, shaking the wrinkles out from my light gray suit. Adjusting my powder blue tie, I shake hands with the owner of the plant and several other people that are deemed important.

"God morgen." I smile and shake hands with another man whose name I will not remember. *"Det er godt at være her. Ja tak, hvis det ikke er til besvær."*

Good morning. It is good to be here. Thank you so much for taking the time to show me around.

Smile, shake hands, repeat until I'm sick with it. Just part of being the crown prince, I guess.

All the while, I'm scanning the small crowd that has gathered by the front doors to meet me. Annika is all smiles and zero sarcastic comments as she shakes hands to my left. Erik is his usual brooding self as he hovers by my right side, shaking hands only when they are thrust at him.

As I am ushered inside, I spot Margot standing in the entryway there, just out of the way. Her hair is still pink and long, pulled up in a messy bun. She's still petite, her face still sweetly heart-shaped.

But this time instead of her short plaid skirt and a Hole t-shirt ripped in a dozen places, she's wearing a pair of sensible black dress pants and a black blazer. She still rocks her pink Converse and what looks like a band t-shirt under the blazer.

And looking at her still makes my heart lurch and stutter.

God, if she even hints at feeling the same way about me, I will be so completely, utterly fucked. All I have known up until now is duty.

But one look at Margot, at her beauty and her unbridled enthusiasm for life, and that all falls away. I can't ever let her know that she makes my heart race; if she has the slightest idea what is going on in my head right now, she could close her fist and crumple me like a sheet of paper.

It's time to put on my mask.

Tamping down on my facial expression, I turn my head away and pay closer attention to what the factory owner is saying to me now. Something about the plates his factory makes… something dull, no doubt.

But out of the corner of my eye, I watch Margot turn around and lay eyes on me properly. Time slows down. Her eyes widen, her breath catches.

There is something magical about the effect we have on each other, even from thirty paces away. Something *electric*. For just the briefest moment, we are the only two people in the whole world.

This, *this* is the reason that she had me teetering on the edge of falling for her.

"Stellan," Erik says, elbowing me. "The plant manager just asked if we would like a tour. I think we would, don't you?"

I pull my gaze away from Margot and zero in on the people I'm supposed to be talking to. "*Ja, ja. Hvis du venligst.*"

The plant manager beams like this is the most exciting thing that has ever happened in her whole career. She ushers us all down the hall and through a series of doors.

For the next half an hour I put on a thoughtful face, sometimes switching it up for an astonished one. Everyone's eyes are on me, making sure that I'm pleased with the porcelain plates.

I honestly couldn't give half a fuck, but I nod and smile. Annika nods and smiles too, and interjects questions where they are appropriate. We are more than just ourselves to these people, after all…

We are two members of the royal family and the rulers of Denmark. I don't even have to remind myself to keep up a cool and aloof veneer around normal people.

I think they are as alien to me as I am to them, honestly.

When we are done with the shaking hands and smiling portion of the morning, Erik wordlessly offers me a squirt of hand sanitizer. And I take it; this gesture is repeated so often on days like today that it's almost second nature for me.

Margot is at a table by herself, admiring a stack of plates. I clear my throat, adjust my tie, and walk over. When she looks up, she bites her lip. Her dark blue eyes are full of unanswered questions.

"*Haj,*" I greet her.

Her eyes tighten on my face. Then she actually curtsies, a tiny smirk on her perfectly pouty lips. "Your highness."

For some reason, that throws me off balance. I frown. "I take it you survived the media vultures that circled you, looking for any little scrap of information?"

She rolls her eyes. "Yeah. I mean, they drove me out of New York City, if that's what you mean by *survived.*" She tilts her head, her eerily blue eyes pinning me. "It would've been better if the whole situation hadn't ever happened though."

I push my tongue out into my cheek. Part of me wants to apologize for everything that happened. But the wiser part of me insists on being thorny. She won't get close if I am just a complete jerk to her.

"*Ja*, it would've been better. I like to keep my private life exactly that… private."

She turns to me, folding her arms across her chest. "You threw me to the wolves, Stellan. You packed up and fled New York and then I was just there, unable to leave my house." Her expression turns sour. "I guess that will teach me to go home with people who I don't know anything about."

She's right. Absolutely, completely right. But I've decided to go this direction, to throw up my walls. There is no stopping now.

I heave a silent sigh, my eyes wandering to the rest of the people at the factory. "I'm sorry. I did try to warn you…"

A laugh bubbles up from her chest. "Yeah, once the media already knew about me. You could've told me who you were when I met you."

A cold smile curls the corners of my mouth. "And you could've asked. But you didn't. And I had no choice but to turn tail and run. The paparazzi in your city are merciless. At least now that you are here, you are getting something in return for spending the night with me, *ja?*"

Her eyes widen and her mouth opens. "Are you serious? It's not like I did this for any kind of fame! And to accuse me of… of riding your coattails… it's ridiculous!" Her voice drops as she leans closer. "I made the best of a very *bad* situation. That's it."

My voice lowers. "Well, you signed a nondisclosure agreement. Which basically means that the royal family has complete control of anything you write and anything you say about me." I smirk. "So I would suggest that you keep it professional, okay?"

"Ugh!" she says, looking offended. "As if I would write about our… *fling*. You are so… so…. arrogant! And spoiled! And full of yourself to boot."

Drawing myself up to my full height, I scowl at her words. I'm not a monster, though of course she can't know that. But still… the fact that I have some sort of feelings for her only makes her barbs all the sharper.

I cock a brow, throwing it right back at her. "*Ja?* I bet you would do anything to get your name in the papers again."

Margot draws herself up to her full height, which isn't very tall at all. "You wish. I bet you have entire *fantasies* about being one of my conquests again."

She honestly has no idea how many fantasies I have that involve her.

Erik is approaching, so I just shake my head. "Keep dreaming big, Margot. That's the only way you'll ever see me naked again."

Margot's murderous expression is priceless. Turning away, I move toward Erik and raise my hands. "I think I'm ready to go. Can you have the car brought around?"

"Sure," Erik responds, his gaze sliding between me and Margot. "Come on."

Throwing a smirk over my shoulder at Margot, I stride off of the factory floor.

Chapter Twelve

MARGOT

THE NEXT MORNING I'm in the newsroom, leafing through the huge pile of documents the royal press secretary sent me. I signed my name to a simple two page nondisclosure agreement already, but I arrived this morning and found a whole stack of other documents and agreements on my desk.

Pippa peeks her head into my cubicle around lunch, scrunching her face up. "Hey Mags."

I shoot her a look. Mags is my nickname that only she is allowed to use; only Pippa is charming enough to outweigh the awfulness of that name. In return, I started calling her Pips, which she doesn't seem to mind a bit.

"Hey," I say.

"Almost done? I'm thinking of grabbing a kebab from the cart down the street."

I make a face at the pile of documents. Careful to dog ear at the page that I'm on, I set the papers down on top of my keyboard. "I'm not actually sure where I'm at. I think I should stay here and keep plowing through these documents, just to make sure I'm not signing my name to anything insane. Would you mind bringing me a kebab back?"

She wrinkles her nose. "Yeah, sure. But just so you know, there's a coffee cart right beside where I plan to go. And I know how you feel about coffee… but I can't carry coffee *and* a kebab back."

I brighten. "Ooh. You know I'm always in search of a decent cup of coffee."

Pippa bobs her head toward the door of the office. "I know. Come on."

"Okay, one sec." I stand up, putting the heavy sheaf of papers in a drawer of my desk and logging out on my staff computer. Then I grab my purse and hurry to catch up with Pippa.

As I'm about to leave, I hear Anna yell from her office. "Margot! Come in here, please."

I freeze in my tracks, then back up and walk to her office. "Did you want something?"

Her mouth thins. "Only for you to do your job. Will that be okay, Miss Keane?"

My eyes widen. "Yes. Of course."

She picks up a stack of papers from her desk, jogging them as she makes a sour face. "All right then. The palace press office just sent this over."

She hands me a piece of expensive card stock that is elegantly engraved with dark blue ink.

Your presence is requested tonight for a celebration honoring the 68th birthday of Her Royal Highness, The Queen Mother Josefine Ida Løve. The gathering will be held at Marselisborg Palace and require fancy dress.

No presents shall be accepted.

Kongevejen 100, 8000 Aarhus, Denmark

I look up at Anna, my eyes so wide that I'm worried about my future ability to blink. "A party?"

Anna makes a sound of disgust. "Yes. You have been given a stipend for renting dresses during your work with the palace. I really suggest you use it." Her eyes trail down my figure, taking in my clothes. "And when you get your first paycheck, I would seriously consider getting a whole new wardrobe."

My cheeks flush with embarrassment. I thought I had left the old sense of shame behind when I entered the job market… but here I am, trembling a little, trying to think of what to say.

Anna narrows her eyes at me. "You know, maybe I should do a piece about you. About how you came to be here, serving a function that no one thinks you can handle."

A look at her, puzzled. "Is that… some kind of weird threat?"

She folds her arms and surveys me. "Maybe I'm just intrigued by the flurry of excitement that followed you here from New York."

My eyebrows rise. "I'm sorry?"

"How you met Prince Stellan. I mean, you shouldn't be rubbing elbows with people of his class, *ja?* From my research, it appears that you are the kind of girl who needed several scholarships just to go to college. So how did you two meet?"

I grit my teeth. My hands ball into fists. "Are we done here? I have a thing to get ready for. You know, a royal gathering at a *palace*."

Her eyes narrow, confirming my suspicions. She's jealous. I have something that she wants, apparently.

If she only knew how tenuous my relationship with Stellan actually was…

Anna sweeps her hand out in a dismissive gesture. "Get out. And try not to horribly embarrass the paper while you're there, okay?"

"Yeah, I'll be sure to curtsy a ton when I'm off rubbing elbows with the whole royal family." I leave her office with a snort.

Bullies come in all shapes and sizes. They hang out on the playground, in cool kid cliques, in court rooms… basically anywhere that anyone can be vulnerable.

But one thing all bullies have in common? They might be able to dish it out but they can rarely take even the slightest criticism.

I make a beeline for the front door. Pippa appears at my side, wide eyed and ready for gossip. "What was that?"

Glancing back at Anna, who is still glaring at me from behind her glass-doored office, I shrug. "Not here, okay? Are you ready to go? I need to go shopping on my lunch hour."

"Yeah, sure. Just let me grab my coat."

It's less than a minute before we are bursting out of the front door of the building. I'm still processing everything, and I'm getting more annoyed by the second.

"Who does Anna think she is?" I say, grimacing.

"What happened?" Pippa asks, pushing a strand of her wild red hair out of her face. "And where are we going?"

Screwing my mouth to the side, I pull out my phone. "I need to find a place that rents fancy dresses."

"Oh! I know a place. And it's not far away. Come on. You can tell me what happened while we walk there."

I hand her the invitation while we walk and talk, doing a brief round of what happened upstairs. Pippa's eyes widen.

"Oh my god," she says, clutching her stomach. "What a bitch! She's never acted like that before."

I scrunch up my face. "She was jealous." I look at Pippa. "That's what it was, isn't it?"

She nods slowly. "That's what it sounds like, yes. I had no idea that Anna felt so strongly about getting close to the royal family."

I exhale, sliding her a glance as we rush across a crowded street. "It won't be like that with us though, will it? I mean, you know the royal family way better than I do. You've been hanging out with them for years."

She smiles at me. "No, it definitely won't. Even if you end up marrying Stellan— "

My jaw drops. "No way! That would never happen in like a million years!"

She shrugs off my protests. "We will see."

"No. No way. There are a million things about myself that I want to keep private… especially about my past run-ins with the law. The last thing that I should do is spend a hot second swooning over Stellan. Besides, he's an ass."

Pippa rolls her eyes and points across the street. "Look, there's the shop."

She points to a little display window with five elaborately dressed mannequins, each garment a totally different color, each one as fancy as the next. Pippa taps the glass over a peach taffeta ballgown with sweetheart neckline. It's embroidered with what must be a thousand pink and white and peach flowers. "That is gorgeous."

"Oh man. I was thinking of something more like… above the knee, black, and slinky." I make a face. "Come on, let's go inside."

Pippa opens the door and ushers me inside. I'm immediately overwhelmed by racks and racks of dresses in every color imaginable. Silk and taffeta and crinolines are all stuffed together in the little shop, piled so high that I can't even see to the back.

"Oh, I—" I start.

A short, balding man with the most stylish spectacles and a gray silk suit pokes his head through the stacks. *"Kan jeg hjælpe dig?"*

Pippa grabs me by the elbow, bowing her head. "English, if you please? We are here to get her a dress to wear tonight."

"Ah!" he says, waving us further in. "Come. We will find good dress." He looks at me, measuring with his gaze. "Where you go?"

"A royal function. I assume I need cocktail attire." I mimic a dress that falls above the knee. "Something black."

"Ah yes!" he cries. "Black cocktail. Black cocktail. Good, *ja*. Come, please."

He vanishes back behind a rack of dresses. When I hesitate, Pippa pushes me forward. "I've done this like a hundred times. Come on."

I shoot her a look and then wedge myself around a rack of dresses. I'm surprised to see a little changing room set up and a wooden counter holds an old fashioned cash register. A collage of brightly colored dresses cut from magazines adorns the wall behind the register.

"Hold please," the shopkeeper says, holding up a finger. While we stand there, still taking everything in the shop in, he disappears again. When he comes back, he has an armful of short black dresses.

"Black cocktail!" he cries, shooing me into the changing room. "Here, you look. You..." He thinks. "You pick."

He holds up each dress for my inspection. I wrinkle my nose. "How about... this one... this one..." I let him cycle through a couple more. "Ooh, and that one. That should be good."

"Now try." He points to the dressing room, which constructed of no more than a few pieces of dark velvet draped over a wire frame. "Then you come out, look in mirror."

He waves to a full length three way mirror that is stashed in the corner.

I step inside the little booth and strip down to try on the first dress. It's loose and unflattering, so I quickly move to the next. This one is a slinky little velvet number in a dark blue that reminds me of the cobalt sea, far from the safety of the shore.

Pulling back the curtain, I step out. Pippa squeals. "Omigosh! That dress on you is really everything."

I walk over to the mirror and my brows rise. The blue of the velvet matches my eyes perfectly. And the way the dress lays on my body is phenomenal. The neckline is a little daring, showing a hint of cleavage. But it doesn't show too much skin overall.

I do a twirl, thinking to myself that this dress fits like it was made for my body. Looking at the shopkeeper, I can't help but grin. "How much?"

"Three hundred *krone*."

Arching a brow at Pippa, I check with her. "Is that a good deal?"

She nods. "Indeed it is. It's about thirty five or forty dollars, I think. And I think I have a pair of heels to match back at the flat."

"Ah!" I turn to the shopkeeper. "You have yourself a sale."

I turn back to glance at my reflection once more. I imagine Stellan's smug face turning into wide-eyed disbelief when he sees me in this dress. Yeah, this is definitely a great choice for tonight, especially after yesterday went so poorly. Blushing a little, I retreat to the changing room.

I'm almost a little loathe to take the dress off, even though obviously I have to. When we are about to leave, the shopkeeper hands me a beautiful hair clip studded with gemstones.

"For you hair," he says with a wink. His English is a little broken, but I'm not in any position to criticize. He leans close to whisper to me. "You bring back, *ja?*"

I bow my head in gratitude. "*Ja*, of course. Thank you."

As I step outside of the shop, Pippa links arms with me. She looks more excited than I am about tonight. I wrinkle my nose.

Before I can say anything, she smiles. "We only have a few hours until it's time for you to leave. Luckily, I keep a full makeup bag at the office. Now your hair is a different matter altogether…"

She pulls me along, chattering about preparations. And I follow her, trying not to get too anxious about seeing Stellan again.

Chapter Thirteen

STELLAN

I'M LOST in a sea of tuxes and ballgowns. If one more old parliamentary representative comes up and orates to me about how I should fund his personal pet project the next time the parliament meets… I swear I will just open my mouth, look up, and scream *GET ME OUT OF HERE* as loud as I can.

All right, maybe not. But it's good to know I have that as a backup plan.

Erik is by my side, plucking a stray hair from the shoulder of his tux. His gaze roves around the ballroom, always on the lookout. For what exactly, I don't know.

"Are you looking for danger, political advantages, or hot girls?" I whisper out of the side of my mouth.

His eyes find me, crinkling with humor. "Who's to say I'm not looking for all three?"

"I hope for your sake that you're not expecting all three in one package…" I squint off into the corner of the ballroom. "Though I would very much like to meet her if you do manage to find someone that meets all your requirements."

He chuckles. "It's a deal."

I turn around slowly, looking for a waiter. What I spot is Prime Minister Finley bearing down on me from some distance away.

"Let's move," I say, whirling in the opposite direction.

That's when I almost trample Margot. There she is, with her heart shaped face, her pastel pink hair, and her little dark blue dress. My eyes widen a bit as I take in the flash of cleavage and the unabashed showing of her admittedly amazing legs.

With her hair pinned up, she looks like she could be a burlesque performer. God, she looks totally unlike anyone else here. And I do mean that in the best way possible.

"Margot," I say, trying not to let everyone else realize that I'm drooling over her.

She just looks at me, her steps faltering. I reach out and stabilize her, realizing that something is out of place. It's another second before it clicks.

She's underdressed for this party. Not just underdressed, but… every other lady here is puffed up in a full ballgown. Margot seems scantily clad by comparison.

And I am watching her realize it in real time. Her cheeks turn bright pink. She looks around, sucking in a breath.

"Oh. I think…" She bites her lip, swinging her dark blue gaze over to me. "I think I misjudged the dress code."

I snort. "You think?"

She flushes even further, her mouth screwing up. "How was I supposed to know? It just said fancy dress." She looks down at what she's wearing, a little shiver running down her spine. "Maybe I should go."

As she turns away, my hand snakes out and grabs her arm. I'm a little surprised at myself; it's definitely better for me if she fails and recedes into the wings of this little show we're putting on. But she looks back at me with something like suspicion in her lovely eyes, a frown making her pouty mouth turn down at the corners.

I refuse to let her just walk away from me. Even if it is cruel, considering the circumstances.

"Stay," I order her.

A mixture of uncertainty and derision is visible in Margot's eyes. It's strange; her elfin facial features show no hint of guise. Is she always so easy to read?

While she's still making up her mind, Prime Minister Finley appears, looking like a silvering, disgruntled parakeet. He takes one look at the body language between Margot and me… and a smile creeps over his face.

"Your highness, who is your companion?"

Margot stills, looking to me to explain her presence.

I swing my head around in both directions. "You already know Erik, Prime Minister Finley."

His eyes tighten on my face, which makes me happier than I can say. "I meant the young lady."

I smile indulgently. "This is Margot Keane. Margot, this is Denmark's prime minister."

She looks a bit taken aback. Pulling out of my grip, she offers Finley her hand. "A pleasure."

Finley shakes her hand for only a second. "Tell me, Margot. Was it your name that I read in the papers a few weeks ago? Something about being caught running away from Stellan's hotel, wasn't it?"

Erik clears his throat. "Prime minister, I have someone important for you to meet."

Finley looks over at him, then back at me. He frowns and smooths the bottom half of his tuxedo jacket. "Yes, all right. I'm looking forward to catching up with you later, Miss Keane."

He doesn't wait for her response. He merely waves at Erik. "Lead the way."

Margot releases the breath she's been holding loudly, looking at me. "That's the prime minister?"

"*Ja,*" I answer with a sigh.

She screws up her face. "He clearly sucks."

One corner of my mouth kicks up. "*Ja.* He was raised by wolves, maybe."

She huffs a laugh. "Don't blame his lack of manners on bad parenting. I was raised by a mom who was an addict and the American foster care system. If I don't get an excuse, neither does he."

I look at her, a little surprised. "You were?"

"Yep." She looks around, as if she's already decided to leave and just needs to pick a direction. "I believe each of us gets a family of our own choosing. So maybe my mom sucked. But I've got Pippa, and she's definitely more loving and accepting than my mom could ever be."

I snag two glasses of champagne off of a passing tray. When I hand one to Margot, she gives me a glare that is instantly suspicious. I chuckle.

"It's just wine." I take a swig, nodding to the exit. "Come on."

I head for the big double doors of the ballroom, keeping my gaze slightly downcast. I've long since mastered the art of being able to leave a room without talking to anyone. When I get out of the ballroom and into the hallway, I pause for a second to let Margot catch up.

She gives me a hard look. "Do you always expect that when you snap your fingers, other people will jump?"

Raising a single eyebrow, I give her a hard stare. "Yes."

She glares at me. "Look. You clearly have a..." She waves her hand over my body. "Like a whole thing going on here. Cocky, handsome, bad boy, brooding... whatever. To each his own. But I think we can dispense with the bullshit. Don't you?"

I don't give her an inch. Instead I just roll my eyes and casually head for another set of doors on the other side of the hallway. I call back as I fling the doors open. "So you think I'm handsome?"

She makes a strangled sound, following me into a darkened parlor. There is no furniture except for one couch, which I promptly fall on. Margot looks around the room, then opts to sort of lean against the back on the sofa.

"I clearly meant that... you were going for... that sort of thing," she bites off.

I can't help but notice the outline of her ass in that velvet dress. Just looking at her right now makes me thirsty. I have to say something, something to let her know she doesn't get to me.

Even though she so clearly does. She starts pacing, from her spot behind the couch to a spot right in front of me.

God, I have never wanted her more than right now. Her color is high, her dress is slutty, and she's stalking around the room in a fit of pique.

I frown, scanning Margot from head to toe. "God, you really are under-dressed. Are you even wearing panties?"

She turns bright red, standing up straight and avoiding my gaze. "Wouldn't you like to know," she snaps.

"Well... yes, actually." I smirk at her. "That's why I asked."

To my complete shock, she actually balls up her first, moves right up to me, and smacks me on the shoulder. "You are such a jerk!"

My eyes widen.

No one other than my brothers has ever dared to breathe too hard in my direction, much less actually *hit* me. I'm surprised a second time when I burst out laughing. I throw my hands up, playing innocent. "It's strictly for scientific observation!"

Margot scrunches up her face and hits me again. Only this time I grab her small hand in mine before she can land a blow.

She glares at me, tugging at her hand. "You really are the worst. Do other people get to witness this side of your personality, or am I just the luckiest girl in the world?"

I smirk, refusing to let her go. "You're a brat. Did you know that? Every single inch of you is just a spoiled little brat."

She yanks at her hand, which makes me grip it harder. "When did I have the chance to become spoiled? Hmm? Was it when I was growing up in that group home? No, maybe it was when I was busting my ass and working two jobs to put myself through college."

The way she's looking at me makes my blood sing. My heart starts hammering a staccato beat in my chest. My cock stirs, making its needs known. I give her a dry rumble of a laugh.

"I don't know, but you are. You're also rather defiant."

She tosses her head haughtily. "You know next to nothing about me. How can you stand there and judge me?"

Margot's eyes are throwing sparks as they burn into mine. Her chest heaves.

"We are not equals. I was born to the throne… I was born to rule. What were you born to do?" I tug on her hand hard and her small hips jerk against mine. The contact sears me through.

She actually laughs at that. My eyes stray from hers down to her mouth. Her lips are bewitching. "You're crazy."

I bring my hand up to grip the back of her head, barely aware of my intentions. Before I know it, I lean forward and press my lips to her lips. She only has a split second to respond; she turns her head just a little so that my mouth ends up only catching the corner of hers.

Margot's eyes widen.

For a moment, we are frozen just like that. Me, knowing I have made a huge mistake. Her, probably wondering how to get out of my embrace.

That second seems to stretch forever… but it shatters when she raises her hands to my chest and shoves me. She's smaller than I am so in effect she pushes herself away, sputtering.

"What are you doing? Are you insane?!"

I can't help but agree with her, honestly. What was I thinking? Taking a deep breath, I try to ease some of the tension that has been building between us. I shrug my shoulders and play it cool.

"It seemed like the thing to do."

She makes a disgusted sound and backs away from me. "It wasn't."

A narrow my eyes. "I won't apologize."

Margot gives me a bitter look. "Of course not. Why would you apologize about anything at all, ever?" Straightening her dress, she turns and starts to leave the room.

I stop her with a word. "Margot."

She stills, although she doesn't turn back toward me. When she answers, her words are tart. "Yes, your highness?"

My lips twitch. "You look good in that dress."

She whips her head around and glares at me, then leaves the room with a disgusted sound on her lips. I lean my head back and close my eyes.

For just a moment, I enjoy my solitude. Then I hear Erik.

"Stellan?"

I open my eyes to find him poking his head in the room.

"*Haj*," I greet him.

"You need to meet with the French ambassador. And there are also a whole entourage of people here from Morocco to meet with you."

I sigh. "*Ja*. I'm coming."

And just like that, I'm swept up in the royal machine again.

Chapter Fourteen

MARGOT

I TURN A CORNER, hurrying along the bright streets of Copenhagen. I'm wearing a set of headphones which are plugged into an ancient iPod. Hole is playing, the angsty, screechy guitars and rollicking drums paired perfectly with Courtney Love's violent wails.

I know, it's not for everybody. But for me, it's soothing. Sometimes it's nice to hear something that really matches how I feel on the inside. I cast my gaze over the city street in front of me.

Everything seems clean here. There is no trash on the ground. There are no homeless people milling around. The buildings that rise up on each side of me are white or tan or brick. They contrast nicely with the slate gray of the street and the black and orange and green roofs.

It's early morning and fog clings to the tops of the buildings. It's hard to see more than a few blocks in front of me, which is just as well. I try to keep my mind on the architecture as I cross the street. The second I turn a corner and the palace rises out of the mist like a graceful giant, my heart rate starts rising.

There are four buildings that make up the palace; four massive tan brick buildings all huddled in a circle, all saluting a rather large statue of a man on a horse. With their white-trimmed windows, dark roofs, and guards dressed in scarlet, the palaces definitely proudly exude *money*.

It's funny to think that the whole compound belongs to one family.

Wrapping my brain around it is hard. Every single instinct I have tells me to run away screaming. The dirt poor little girl from Brooklyn who still lives inside me is terrified of all this… this *wealth*.

It's just so… *conspicuous*. I've worked so long and so hard to fight against the idea of oligarchy, that a country should be run by the rich and not by the common man. I've protested with Occupy Wall Street; when Citizens United was handed down by the supreme court I marched in the streets.

And yet… here I am, staring up at the palaces with a sourness in the pit of my stomach.

How is this place Stellan's home?

And how did I end up spending a night in his bed?

I swallow against the strange knot of anxiety that forms in my throat as I walk up to the gates. The palaces seem to frown down at me as I present my press card at the security checkpoint.

I feel like a fraud just walking through these gates, even though I'm not perpetrating any kind of deceit. A stoic guard waves me inside the gates and instructs me to walk straight ahead to the giant door of the first building on my left.

Tossing my hair back over my shoulder and smoothing my hands down my blazer, I adjust my tote bag on my shoulder.

You can do this, I tell myself.

It takes a couple of minutes and two separate skeptical looking palace servants to gain access to the palace.

I'm led down a large hallway by one of the servants. I can't help the fact that my eyes bug out a little as we walk; the echoing hallway is made entirely of dark wood, adorned with a demure dark blue carpet runner, and lined with paintings of royalty.

I feel like every painting I pass stares down at me, somberly disapproving. Telling me I don't belong here. My palms start sweating.

The servant stops by a door, motioning me inside. I'm not expecting to see Stellan; I've seen enough royal movies to know that I should be content to wait.

But there he is, extraordinarily tall in a white button up shirt and dark suit pants, standing in a room with crisp white walls. He faces away from me, contemplating a photograph that is hung on the wall. The photograph is a black and white close up of a lion on the hunt in the savannah.

How appropriate for Stellan.

He turns a little when I approach his side. He stares down at me, brooding. The intensity in his ice blue eyes makes me repress a shiver.

Ah, yes… I forgot how compelling he is, here in the flesh.

He smirks a little. "You are a photographer, *ja?*"

My hand slides to my tote bag, where my camera rests. I raise my chin. "Yes."

He looks away, back to the photograph on the wall. It's a little like a spotlight has been taken off of me.

Why do I always feel like he is going to look right through me?

"What do you think?" he asks idly, nodding to the photo.

Frowning, I turn toward the photo in question. Tilting my head, I just stare at in for a second. "It has an interesting composition. The play of light around the lion lends the photo an intensity that I like. And the lion is very close up, and obviously fixated on something the audience can't see. It draws the audience to look just past the edge of the photograph."

"So you like it?"

Squinting, I shrug. "Yes. It's not the most interesting concept to me, but art is very subjective."

He nods, looking at the photo for another few seconds. Then he turns, pacing a few feet away to stare at the next photograph hung on the wall. I follow him, curious.

"What am I doing here, Stellan?"

He looks at me for a second, his expression telling me nothing. "I was told you were here to do an in-depth article about me. Is that not the case?"

My eyes tighten on his face. "I think you know that the reasons for the article are… well, to be polite, I would say that they are politically motivated."

One corner of his mouth curls up, making a dimple appear in his cheek. "And if you were not being polite? What would you say then?"

My mouth twists. "That buying my silence and covering your tracks by using *Politiken* is a form of government corruption."

His eyes pin me right where I stand. "I see. That's a harsh view of things, *ja?* As far as I am concerned, it just sort of…" He pauses, then shrugs. "It worked out to benefit both of us. Don't you think?"

I fold my arms across my chest. "It's just you and me here, Stellan. You don't need to lie to me. I've already signed your nondisclosure agreement. There is no illusion between the two of us."

He mirrors my gesture, wrapping his arms across his broad chest with a smirk on his face. "It's often like that when you are dealing with the aftermath of a royal scandal. Trust me. This isn't the first one I've seen."

My brow hunches. "That's it? That's your answer?"

He looks thoughtful for a moment. "That's about the scope of it, yes."

I shake my head, a little disgusted at him. "I don't know how I was ever attracted to you. Your…" I wave my hand to indicate his body. "Your body is so great, but your politics *suck*. Usually I hold myself to a higher standard than this."

His eyebrows lift in surprise. "You are saying that you learned that I'm a royal… and it made you *less* attracted to me?"

I let out a laugh. "Yes! I like to sleep with people who are actually from this planet. People who are dealing with the same kind of issues that I'm dealing with. That is…" I give another huff of laugher. "That's just not you."

He casts a skeptical gaze over me. "You're telling me that even as a little girl, you never had dreams of being Cinderella? Come on now, Margot. Be honest."

The image of me at age six flashes through my brain. A skinny, dark-haired little girl in an oversized hand-me-down dress. A little girl who had just realized that Santa wasn't real in the same month she found out what it meant when kids at school called her a welfare princess.

Bitterness threatens to overtake me. I screw up my face. "No, Stellan. You know what I dreamed of when I was a little girl?"

He pauses, his brow wrinkling. He cocks his head to the side. "No. What did you wish for?"

"I wished that my mom wasn't a junkie. I wished that the other kids in my elementary school wouldn't make fun of the old clothes that I wore. But most of all, I wished that I would always know where my next meal was going to come from."

His eyebrows rise. "Surely not. There had to be some sort of…" He splays his hand out in front of himself, gesturing. "Social safety net or something. I mean, no one in Denmark suffers that way."

My face tightens. My voice lowers. "A lot of people fall through the cracks, no matter how many safety nets there are in place. People like *me.*

That's just how life is. As the future king of Denmark, I hope you know that by now."

He scowls at me. "I don't believe it."

I give him an offended look. "What, that I was starving while you were living your best life? You are the top one percent of the top one percent. You're beyond rich. And me?" I thump my chest. "I'm poor. Even with a college degree, I will never earn a fraction of what you were just… *born with.*"

Stellan stares at me for a second, his ice blue gaze direct and intense. "You would correct the imbalance, I presume? Take my family wealth and distribute it differently?"

I make a face. "That's not really what I'm about. I want systematic change. Global change. The weakest and most vulnerable among us need to be taken care of. And places like this palace…" I gesture to the walls around me. "They should be repurposed. Made into museums and hospitals and schools. They shouldn't be held by one family that was chosen to rule Denmark centuries ago."

For several long seconds, Stellan actually looks like he might just leave the room. That or summon some guard to seize me. He stares at me with an icy glare.

When he finally speaks, his voice is low and gravelly, his expression stony. "The people of Denmark need their royals."

I give a soft chuckle. "Why? Why do you get to live such a lavish life just because you were born into a certain family?"

He takes a half a step forward. "We guide them in times of crisis. We celebrate when good things happen. We do a ton of charity work. But most importantly, we reflect the current state of affairs back at them. We serve as a touchstone for the entire Danish community!"

I cock a brow. "You deserve wealth because you are a mirror of the Danish people?"

He glares at me, smoothing a big hand over his stomach. "Among other things, yes."

"You keep telling yourself that, buddy. And I'll just be over here, working to right a small portion of the injustices that happen every single day." My mouth twists sourly.

He takes another step toward me, then another, then another. I gulp as he approaches, the difference in our heights never more apparent than now. Determined to show no fear, I raise my chin and glare at him, defiant.

He stops when he's almost on top of me. A hair's breadth away. The air between us seems to thin, making me drag in my breaths. Our gazes clash, him staring down at me as if I'm a bug, me giving him my best impression of the rebellious James Dean.

I can feel the heat radiating off of his big body. Scorn lights the fires raging in his ice blue eyes.

When he speaks, his voice is low and rough. "Just so you know, Margot. This little journalism assignment wasn't my idea. You being here doesn't exactly *please* me. And I am counting the days until you're out of my life forever. Do you understand?"

My gaze wanders down to his mouth for a second. I notice the dip of his cupid's bow, the press of his lips, the hint of his perfect teeth when he sneers at me. Am I stupid to bother arguing with someone that has obviously been bred for this kind of wealth?

I give my head a tiny shake. "I completely understand, *your highness*. In a month's time, I will be gone. You will move on with your life. Believe me, I fucking get that."

His laugh is deep and gravelly. "Good."

Then he moves past me, deliberately bumping my shoulder as he goes. I frown, watching Stellan stalk from the room.

That guy is definitely tightly wound.

The question is… will his behavior affect me? Because if it does, I could be well and truly fucked.

Chapter Fifteen

STELLAN

MY FINGERS ARE CRAMPING up from scrawling my signature on over eight hundred letters. Not only that, but I can feel Margot just behind me. Her eyes threaten to burn a hole in my upper back. I roll my neck until it makes a satisfying pop.

Tension still simmers in the room. It has ever since Margot walked in half an hour ago.

Arrogant. Spoiled. Full of yourself.

Those words still ring in my head, thrown at me by Margot herself. I'm cantankerous today and that's a big reason why.

I turn and face the windows of my study, a room as large and dimly lit as the rest of the palace. With the same high ceilings as the rest of the palace, this room manages to be as drafty as the others. The only difference here is that the walls are predominately dark wood, the only color a hint of blue in the curtains surrounding the floor-length windows.

The light filters through a gauzy curtained layer just before the windows. Dropping my fountain pen with a sigh, I push myself up out of my chair. Instantly Margot is on her feet.

"Where are you going?" she asks, her voice low.

I walk to the window, unwilling to look back at her no matter how badly I'm tempted. I already know what will happen.

I already know that she will look at me with those deep blue eyes, her expression as cutting as a blade. She's always just on the cusp of figuring me out, or at least that's what her expression indicates.

"Nowhere," I answer, gritting my teeth. As if I could just leave when I have a mountain of letters left to sign. It's all part of the deal, being a royal. "Just stretching."

I do take a minute to stretch, raising my arms over my head. I'm half dressed for the arts event that I have to leave for in half an hour; white button up with two buttons undone, sleeves rolled up, a pair of light gray trousers.

As I stretch, I'm aware of her eyes again. Those clever, piercing eyes. I usually feel like an animal in a zoo exhibit on my best day. But having her here, in the midst of my most mundane daily tasks, is almost too much to handle.

I hear paper rustling. "Can I ask you some questions while you're stretching?"

Looking back at Margot from the window, I see her opening a little notepad. It's almost cute, the way she is deadly serious about her job. Her pink hair is curly and hangs loose. Her heart shaped face puckers a little bit as she frowns down at her notepad. As usual, she wears the same black blazer and black pants, although this time she wears an old yellow Blondie t-shirt.

I lift one shoulder casually. "If you must. I don't imagine that you actually have to write a single word if you don't want to. You know that the royal press office would gladly write the whole damn article for you, don't you?"

Her eyes narrow. Her mouth twists. "I'm writing the article. It's going to have my byline slapped on it. I might as well make something of the experience."

Shaking my head, I turn back to the window. "Suit yourself."

I move the gauzy layer blocking the window aside and peer out across the perfectly manicured lawn. A gardener moves at the far end of my view, closing a wooden gate. He has a basket of flowers on one arm and he stops, wiping his head with a cloth from the pocket of his gray coveralls.

"When you think of Denmark and its future, what do you hope for?"

Hunching my brow, I drop the curtain and turn back to face her. I know the answer to this question by heart. "Stability, success, and growth." I give her my most deadpan expression. "Next question."

Her nose wrinkles. "You didn't even think about it."

I repress an eye roll, adjusting one of my shirt cuffs. "You do know that I'm constantly being asked the same questions, right? I'm on display a hundred percent of the time. I come prepared with the answers to fifty most commonly asked questions."

"Ah." She writes something down in her little notepad. "Well, I guess I'll have to ask a wider variety of questions, won't I?"

Instead of an answer, Margot gets a shrug in response. I return to the table where my letters are stacked, sitting down and picking up the pen once more. Dropping back into signing them is the work of ten seconds.

For fifteen minutes, I let myself fall into a trance. I relax my gaze. I think of nothing. I feel the pen moving across each piece of paper; I barely notice the fact that I have to move each piece of paper across the desk and into the finished pile. I am only barely aware of time moving.

It's not exactly a pleasant feeling to be able to lose myself so completely in a task. Nor is it bad… it simply *is*. It speaks to the fact that once a week, I do this exact same thing, in the same span of time. A thousand signatures on a thousand letters of reply. I've done it since I was old enough to hold a pen.

When I sign the last letter, I return to everyday life with a sigh. Standing, I stack all the letters neatly. Although I don't jog them; people that write me want their letters neat, without bent corners.

I do my best to give it to them.

When Margot speaks, I startle. I had forgotten that she was even here.

"What happens now?"

My head jerks to face her. I run a hand through my dark hair, standing up. "What?"

She nods to my work. "The letters. What happens to them?"

That gives me pause. "I don't know. I just leave them here when I am finished. They appear and disappear routinely." I frown. "I suppose someone in the press office comes to collect them." I shrug. "Why?"

Margot gives me a careful look. "Just trying to get a sense of what happens. There are probably a hundred thousand little tasks that get done without you ever knowing it."

My brow furrows. "I suppose so."

She flips her notebook closed. "So where do you go to now?"

I check my watch. "Oliver should be here any second to tell me I have to get ready to go. I think today I go to an art exhibit followed by a primary school."

Eyeing her, I start to roll down my sleeves. "Fetch me my tie from over by the door, will you?"

Her expression grows stormy. "Is there something keeping you from doing it?"

I raise my eyebrows. "No. You are just closer, that's all."

She folds her arms across her chest, cocking her hip. "Do it yourself."

I roll my eyes and saunter over to the tie, which has been placed on a coatrack with extreme caution by some unseen hand. As I put the tie on, I cast my eye over Margot's defiant stance.

My lips curve upward. "You're cute when you're being mutinous."

Her cheeks color, giving me a certain kind of satisfaction. She scowls. "You're a pig."

Chuckling, I nod. "I couldn't agree with you more. I'm right, though."

All that earns me is a glare.

Oliver's soft knock sounds at the door. I swing the door open, surprising him. He stands up a little straighter, his white hair and black suit looking dapper as always.

"*Deres Højhed,*" he says, bowing stiffly. He always calls me *your highness*, even when I ask him not to. It's just his way. "Your car is waiting."

I start out the door behind him, only stopping about halfway down the hall. I look back with a frown. "Oliver? Hold on a second, would you?"

I walk back to the doorway that I just left, finding Margot standing at my desk. She's not touching anything. But she is staring down at the stack of letters, her brow furrowed.

"Hey," I bark.

She looks up, eyes wide. Her pink tongue darts out to wet her bottom lip. "Yes?"

I cock my head. "Aren't you coming?"

"Oh." She frowns. "Yes. I just thought— "

I turn, leaving her to hurry after me, her explanation falling on deaf ears. She has to practically run to keep up with my natural stride. I see her looking at me, trying to figure me out again. I've done something that she didn't expect and now she's trying to pin her understanding of me down again.

I hurry downstairs and up to the back seat of the waiting Audi limousine. It's considered polite to help a woman into the back of a car first. I stop and stand stiffly by the back door, motioning her in. It's more of an automatic gesture than anything else, but Margot's face flushes as she accepts and climbs in first.

Once we're in the car, I roll up the partition between the driver and us. Margot buckles her seatbelt and frowns at the partition as it rises.

"What?" I ask.

She rolls her eyes. "Nothing. I just wanted to know who was driving us."

Shrugging, I sprawl out, taking up the majority of seat. "Who cares? We'll get where we're going."

Her eyes tighten on my face. I can tell that I've somehow said the wrong thing, but I don't particularly care. "Just sit back and enjoy the ride, *skatter*."

I grin. Her cheeks flare bright pink. She frowns and shakes her head, looking away.

"What does that mean? *Skatter*," she says, sounding the word out.

"It means the one I treasure. My sweetheart."

Her eyes widen and the bright pink blush on her cheeks turns into a beat red flush. All right, that was kind of fun. It's entertaining to watch her squirm.

When she looks back at me, there is an intensity in her expression that wasn't there before. "What does the palace expect from you, exactly?"

I cock a brow. "What do you mean?"

Her lips thin for a moment. "I mean… you are supposed to be a king someday. That position comes with a lot of expectations, I'd imagine. Along with being born with a silver spoon in your mouth, there have to be downsides. Personal sacrifices. What are they?"

I furrow my brow, looking out the window thoughtfully. "Every word I say is recorded. Somewhere, somehow. Everything I do is pulled apart and searched for motives." I wrinkle my nose briefly. "That's why I liked being a nobody in New York. It's nice to set aside the political correctness and the strict guidelines and just… be anonymous for a while."

When I glance back at her, I see her scribbling in that notepad of hers again. "I can see how that would be hard," she mumbles.

My lips twist. She has no idea.

Shaking my head, I sigh. "I've never been able to just do what I wanted.

When I was younger, I couldn't go to school with all the other kids. Instead, my friend Erik and I—" I stop for a second. "You know Erik, *ja?*"

She looks up at me, the blue of her eyes taking my breath away for a second. "Yes."

"Erik and I were tutored together here at the palace. He— "

"Wait, wait." She flips a page. "Okay. Is Erik a royal, then?"

I snort. "No. He's the son of the groundskeeper. My father got drunk with the groundskeeper one day; the next day, Erik was brought into my room to play." I smile wryly. "I think we were about four."

She nods. "So you weren't even allowed to choose your best friend, basically."

"Nope." I grin. "I'm lucky that he's not a fucking psychopath. And if you think that's bad, wait until you hear how my wife is being chosen for me."

That seems to actually shake her. She stops writing. "What?"

"Yep. I was presented with a list of young, eligible ladies. Each one with a pristine pedigree, each ready to produce as many heirs as I want, each one as boring as the next. I've been told to just point to one, or decide which flavor I want… a blonde, a brunette, a redhead…" I sigh. "And I'm assured that the rest will be taken care of. All I have to do is show up reasonably sober on my wedding day. Voila! Instantly, the perfect wife."

Margot scrunches up her face. "That sounds… *awful.*"

"It will be!" I say. "Add to that the fact that I basically live in a fish bowl, with no expectation that any part of my life will ever be private… and you get the royal experience in a nutshell."

She chews on her lower lip, scribbling a few notes to herself. "Is it worth it?"

I tilt my head to the side. "What do you mean?"

"Everyone thinks that being a royal is amazing. It is, obviously. But it sounds more complicated than that. I guess what I'm saying is… does having everything you've ever wanted make it worth not getting to make your own choices?"

I repress a sigh, turning my face away from her. "I don't know. This is the only life I've ever had. I don't know how to live any other way."

Margot makes a soft sound, a little *mmm.* I don't know what it means. I'm not willing to ask. I'm definitely not going to look over at her to see her expression.

It's better this way. I probably shouldn't have even told her all of that. I don't know why I let it slip.

Not only that, but I find myself irritable now. Margot has a way of making me open up, but I don't want to.

I have exactly zero interest in being vulnerable around her ever again.

Leaning forward, I press the button to lower the partition. When the driver looks back at me in the rearview mirror, I catch his eye. "Could you fucking hurry it up? I have places to be."

He bows his head. "*Selvfølgelig, deres højhed.*"

Despite what I said, he doesn't drive any faster. The palace drivers never do. They always drive five kilometers under the speed limit. It's in their training. After all, they are moving precious cargo.

Sighing to myself, I lean my head back and close my eyes.

Chapter Sixteen

STELLAN

I PAUSE FOR A MOMENT, making sure my weight is centered, making sure I have the right grip on the basketball. Then I jump, shooting the ball toward the hoop. It sails into the basket, runs around the rim, and then falls off the side.

"*Rend mig i røven!*" I shout, feeling sweat slide down my back.

Erik gives a bark of laughter. "You are terrible at this game, Stel."

He runs to catch the ball, dribbling it as he returns. I wipe my brow on my shirt, turning to look at Margot as I do. She sits on a set of bleachers on the other side of the gym, with her notepad open and her pen in her mouth. Her head is down, her hair spilling everywhere as she scrawls something to herself.

I can see that she's shed that terrible black blazer she usually wears, obviously feeling warm in the stifling gym. It sits beside her, thrown carelessly on one of the lower bleacher steps like a piece of driftwood left by the sea. She has on a short black dress and leggings, the neckline of her dress tantalizingly low.

As a matter of fact, when she sits in just this position, I can almost see her nipples.

Almost.

I stare for a second too long and she looks up, catching me. Her cheeks immediately turn pink and she sits up, adjusting her dress. I lift a brow at her, just in time to get a basketball right in the stomach.

The breath leaves my lungs in a whoosh. I catch the ball and glare at Erik.

"Quit that," I command. My order is met with an eye roll.

Erik has always been my closest friend and biggest rival, all at once. He's also the only person who is completely unafraid of telling me to go fuck myself.

"Stop staring at the pretty reporter," he says, grinning. "We're supposed to be playing a game here."

I roll my eyes and forcefully chuck the basketball back at him. He catches it, dribbles, and then makes a shot. The shot goes in the basket without even touching the rim. He does a celebratory dance.

Shaking my head, I run to catch the ball. "I'm a thousand percent certain that you aren't supposed to do a dance every single time you make a basket."

His grin only widens. "Says the guy that can't dunk. Do I detect a note of jealous bullshit?"

He's right, of course. It irks me beyond measure that I'm the future king of Denmark and the soon to be ruler of everything I see... and yet I just can't manage to master basketball.

I casually stride around the court, trying not to let my ego get the better of me. We could play some sport that I actually have a chance at scoring goals, like football or handball. But Erik likes to mix up our shared workouts to allay boredom.

So today, I'm playing basketball.

I line up another shot and jump, throwing the ball. This time the ball bounces off the backboard and then bounds away from me. My eyes tighten; I hate being so intensely bad at something that should be so easy.

I swing my gaze over to Margot, who is watching my every little movement. She tucks her pink hair back behind her ear, looking at me with an unreadable expression. As she tilts her head to the side thoughtfully, she comes off as analytical.

What is she thinking?

"Seriously?" Erik asks. I turn to him, my expression innocent, but he just rolls his eyes.

He cups his hand around his mouth and calls to her. "Hey! Margot!"

I glare at him, my pulse picking up. What is he going to say?

Margot looks at him, arching a brow. "Yes?"

"You can go. Stellan needs to concentrate on his workout and then he's going to bed early. We have to get up super early tomorrow for our hunt."

Her eyebrows rise. She glances at me but I refuse to meet her eyes. Instead I just go after the ball and dribble it, shooting it toward the basket. Margot gathers her coat and stands, coming over to me.

The way she looks at me feels strange; it's the work of half a minute to realize that this is the first time I've been dressed down since New York. Usually I wear my button ups and Briony dress slacks like they are a kind of armor, keeping my shields up and everyone else out.

But just now, as she's walking over, I realize that I'm only wearing a black t-shirt and black athletic shorts. It's weird, but I feel just the tiniest bit vulnerable.

She stops a few feet from me, jogging her tote bag on her hip, her coat over her arm. She scrunches up her face. "Am I needed tomorrow?"

I keep my eye on the ball as much as I can, catching it when Erik throws it to me. "I would rather you stayed at home, if that's what you are asking."

Her eyes narrow. "It isn't. When is super early? And what are you hunting?"

Shrugging, I shoot another basket. This time it goes in the hoop. Erik whoops.

"That's what I am talking about!" he crows. Then he turns to Margot, wearing a smirk. "Five thirty. That's what time we're going. If you're going to come, wear clothes you can get dirty."

Margot scrunches up her face, her gaze sliding to me. I lock down my emotions and keep my face smooth; it's almost second nature to me, even though Erik just flat out lied to Margot about what time we start.

"All right," she says at last. "I'll see you both bright and early, then."

She turns, heading out of the gym. I can't help but watch her ass sway in that short black dress; there is a hole in her leggings on the back of her thigh that gives me all kinds of dirty thoughts.

For instance, right now I'm thinking about slipping my fingers inside that hole and ripping the thin black fabric. Revealing the rest of her pale, creamy thigh to my view…

"Stel!" Erik barks.

I straighten, my neck heating, and look at him. "What?"

He looks back at her disappearing through the gym doors, waiting until they close. Then he cocks a brow. "Once wasn't enough for you?"

I shoot him a look. "What do you mean?"

He pushes his cheek out with his tongue. "I mean, does Margot have some kind of spell cast over you? Because you can have anyone in the world… anyone but her."

I stiffen. "I know that."

"Do you want me to call some ladies over? Maybe we should have a private party."

Shaking my head, I start walking over to the wall where a cooler full of water bottles is stashed. "Have I ever in our history wanted your help to get dates? If I wanted, I could have thirty women naked in a pit, fighting over me."

He shrugs. "It's just an offer. I just saw the way you looked at her. The same way that you looked at her back in New York."

Grabbing a bottle of water, I roll my eyes. "What, like a person I find interesting?"

"No." He folds his arms over his chest. "You look at her like she's a fucking filet mignon and you're starving to death."

"As long as I don't touch her, I can look at Margot any damn way I please." I uncap the bottle, taking a long pull of the chilled water.

Erik sighs. "I just don't want the press to start investigating who you're sleeping with again. You know that one wrong look at her in front of the wrong person could spark the rumor mill to start again."

I laugh. "You think I am not aware of that? Besides, of all the women in the world…" Thinking about Margot, I shake my head. "Trust me, she is the last one I would pick to sneak around with. She's the opposite of what I want."

That isn't exactly true. Even as I say it, it sounds flat and wrong leaving my mouth. And not just to me…

Erik gives me a funny look. "You don't have to lie to me, Stel. The bullshit with the press is one thing. But here, just between us, there do not need to be any secrets."

I grin at him. "Everything is fine, Erik. You are overreacting." Taking another swig from the bottle, I set it down on top of the cooler. "Come on. Let's go for another twenty minutes, then call it a day."

His eyes narrow, but he just shakes his head and runs to get the basketball. As we dribble and shoot, he stays quiet. That doesn't mean I don't feel his eyes on me, wondering just what I'm up to though…

I'd like to know as much myself.

When we're done, we head outside, Erik regaling me with the story of last Saturday night. I'm only partially paying attention, honestly.

I admit, I am wondering about what Margot said to me earlier.

Does having everything you've ever wanted make it worth not getting to make your own choices?

That question echoes in my head for longer than I would care to admit…

Chapter Seventeen

MARGOT

AT EIGHT THIRTY, I hear loud voices approaching me. Opening my eyes and straightening from where I was slumped over on a couch, I look up. Erik and Stellan are heading down the hallway where I'm at, both dressed in baggy paint-covered khaki shorts and scuzzy t-shirts.

And behind them is a group of maybe ten or twelve people that are all talking excitedly. Standing up, I brush off my old gray yoga pants and hole-filled Black Sabbath t-shirt. I try to school my expression to keep my annoyance off my face, but something tells me that I'm not very successful.

I showed up here before dawn and I've been waiting for three hours. A funny little prank for them to pull. It's a good thing I have slept much worse places than in this hallway on a stiff burgundy couch.

When Stellan sees me, he smirks. He strides up to me and then moves past my couch without stopping. I'm forced to gather up my tote bag and my jacket and run to catch up with him.

"So you are coming, then?" he asks casually.

I shoot him a glare. "Yup."

"Sorry we're a few minutes late," Erik chimes in, grinning like an idiot. I could smack them both in the face right this second, if they would only slow down to allow me to do it. They're both so tall; everyone in this damned country is tall, pretty much.

"You told me to be here three hours ago," I mutter. "You're just lucky that I know how to keep myself occupied."

Erik just shrugs. I speed walk down the hallway with them, taking a right down a staircase. The entire group takes a right and suddenly we are outside, queuing to load ourselves into a white passenger van.

Stellan and Erik are the first ones in. I hang back, climbing in last next to a willowy blonde young woman. She wrinkles her button nose at me.

"I'm Annika," she says, offering me her hand.

I shake it, sizing her up. "Margot."

Her delicate brows rise. My name apparently means something to her. "*Haj*. Did we already meet?"

"Yes. At the porcelain factory. It's nice to see you again." I smile, then I bite my lip, glancing back at the other people sitting in rows between us and Stellan. "How do you know everyone here?"

She laughs. "Well, I'm related to half of them. My last name is Løve."

"Oh! So you're Stellan's younger sister?" I ask. That makes sense; she has the same light-colored eyes as Stellan, and his ungodly cheekbones. I dig through my tote bag for my notepad and pen, making some quick short-hand notes.

"Yes, I'm the youngest of five kids. The only girl, too. Stellan is the oldest... and then there's Lars..."

She points out Lars, who is a dark-haired clone of Stellan's, if Stellan had two days' worth of stubble on his cheeks. I nod.

"I actually know him. He visited New York with Stellan and Erik."

"Oh, don't get me started on Erik. He is a pain in my ass... but you probably know that he's not actually related to the Løves, right?"

"I do."

She nods. "Over there, Anders is one of ours too..." She points to Anders, who wears his dark hair a bit longer and has a beard. He looks like Stellan, but he's younger and he looks as though he likes emo. "And then the rest are family friends."

"Wait, that's..." I stop, squinting as I count silently. "Yeah, that's only four Løve children."

She shrugs. "Finn is the missing link. And he's... out of town."

Her eye roll hints that there is more to the story. But before I can ask anything else, the van rolls to a stop. I crawl out, looking around what seems to be an abandoned children's playground. Jungle bars with half the bars rotted away, see saws that have seen better days, a long abandoned treehouse, and a geo-dome for climbing that appears very rusty and dangerous.

Don't get me wrong, it's all definitely overgrown and cool looking. But what exactly are we supposed to do here?

"What in the world?" I ask, wrinkling my nose.

Erik and Stellan climb out of the back of the van, sharing a grin between them. "Paintball."

My eyes widen. The driver starts handing out big airsoft guns with a few racks of various neon colored paintballs. I take one when it's handed to me, but I have zero idea how to get the paintballs in the gun.

Tilting my head at it doesn't seem to make the gun make more sense, either.

"I—" I stammer, looking around. Surely no one actually expects me to play, right?

"I'll team up with Stellan!" Erik says, grinning as he grips his gun.

"Oh, come on," Anders interjects. "Everyone here gets it, okay? You two are the ideal pairing. Why don't you make at least a little fun for the rest of us, *ja?* Spread some of that alpha male top dog bullshit around."

Stellan sighs, tugging on his t-shirt. "He's right."

"I think Stellan should be with Margot," Annika chimes in, sliding me a wink. "To help her really get a fuller picture. Erik, you can be with me."

My eyebrows rise. Erik gives her a stormy look but reluctantly agrees. "Fine."

Everybody else pairs up, heading into the middle of the playground. I tag along, watching Stellan. I thought maybe I was just drunk when I met him; I had convinced myself that it is just his usual button up and dark slacks that make him attractive.

But now I realize that I was wrong. As we all line up around the dome-shaped climbing structure, I look at Stellan's handsome features. His dark hair, his ice blue eyes, his cheekbones sent straight from heaven.

Those things are still a part of him when he's dressed down, apparently even when he wears an outfit that looks like a post-apocalyptic version of what college frat boys don.

He nods to me, leaning close. "When the driver blows the whistle, run for that big old tree right there." He nods to indicate it. "And whatever you do, do not stop."

The driver looks odd, following us in his formal black suit. He blows a little whistle. "On my signal! If you get hit, even a little, you must head back here."

I nod, trying to juggle my tote bag and my gun at the same time. The driver blows the whistle and everyone takes off in pairs; I run after Stellan as fast as I can, wondering how I'm even supposed to get the paintballs into the gun.

Surely it can't be that hard, right?

Stellan ducks behind the huge oak tree, looking around. I stop and he yanks me out of everyone else's line of sight just in time; three paintballs whiz by my head, making my heart skid to a halt.

Looking up at Stellan with wide eyes, I start to thank him. He shushes me, then takes my gun and feeds one of my tubes of paintballs into it with a loud *click*. He does the same for his gun, then holds a finger to his lips.

He leans down close. "Leave your bag here. No one will move it, I promise."

I bite my lip. The only thing in my tote bag worth stealing is my Nikon, which is worth so much that I will probably never own another like it ever again. I reach in my bag and pull out my camera, hanging it around my neck.

"Ready," I whisper.

He looks at me, his ice blue gaze seeking the answer to some question. "Why— "

Just then, a paintball whizzes by his head, landing on the tree with a hard splat. "Get down," he whispers, crouching. I mimic his movement, although I'm so much tinier than him that his version of crouching evens out with my actual height.

"Come on," he says, running full speed away from the direction that the paintball just came. I hurry after him, looking around with my senses on full alert.

One of the guys that was in the van with us pops out from behind a tree. He aims straight at me, firing but missing. I panic, shooting my gun off a couple of times. The paintballs soar into the air way over his head.

Stellan turns and sees what's going on. In one swift motion, he fires twice. The paintballs explode as they hit the man in the chest. Two giant blots of bright orange paint blossom over his heart.

"Ah, fuck!" he yells, turning to start walking toward the geo-dome.

Stellan hisses at me and I scurry over to him. He grabs my hand and pulls me behind another tree. For a few seconds, my heart rate picks up. I look up at him, at how fierce and protective he is at this moment.

I know that it's cheesy to find that appealing, but I do. Despite my resistance, I really, really do.

"You are terrible at this game," he says, scowling down at me.

Stellan releases my hand and sweeps the scope of his paintball gun in a semi-circle. I shrug a little, trying to keep the fact that I'm obviously turned on by this kind of behavior under wraps. It's just...

I can imagine that, in a scenario where the end of the world has arrived and everyone is out for their own interests, I would want to have this guy in my corner.

God, I need to say something. Anything to change the topic in my brain.

"I don't like guns!" I blurt out.

He gives me an odd look. "It's just a game, Margot."

My cheeks heat. "I know..."

Stellan's nose wrinkles. "You know what? I think you are a snob."

My jaw drops. "Me? How am I a snob? This whole thing is *your* event, your highness."

"So what? It's something new. And I think that something new totally scares you. So you turn your nose up at it without even trying it out. That makes you a snob."

I narrow my eyes at him. "Are we still talking about paintball? Or are you just taking what you feel about everything and projecting it onto this topic?"

He rolls his eyes. "Do you have to read into everything, Margot? Can this not just be about shooting people with paint?"

Adjusting my gun, I size him up. "I don't know. You tell me."

Stellan sighs, scrubbing his hand through his dark hair. "Why don't we declare a truce? Just for today. You and I will just be on the same side for long enough to dominate this game. Then we can go back to full out class warfare tomorrow. Okay?"

The corner of my mouth kicks up. I give him a sly glance. "Yeah, okay."

He looks a tiny bit surprised that I just agreed. "Okay," he repeats. "Okay, good. There's a spot that we want to get to over there." He nods.

"A… I don't know the right word. Where you are protected but you can shoot at targets?"

I scrunch up my face. "Um… I think that's called a blind, maybe?"

"All right. Let's run over to it. *Ja?*"

This time, he looks to me, waiting for my reply. I can't help but nod. He bolts toward the blind and I run after him. We make it there safely and peer out from behind the trees, sniping anything that moves.

I can admit it; I have kind of a good time, shooting people and yelling when unseen people shoot through the trees. While we have this truce going on it is easy to forget that he's Prince Stellan Løve, heir to the throne of the kingdom of Denmark. I'm not a commoner that he looks down on, either.

Just now, he grins at me in a way that makes me shiver. I bite my lip and grin back at him. We even high five when I duck and roll to narrowly avoid a paintball to the chest.

His gaze roves the world in front of us again. "Come on. Everybody knows where we are. We should make a run for it. And I think there is a good hiding spot this way."

He takes off at a crouched run. I'm left trying to follow, beaming at him. We reach a large oak tree and he slows to a stop. He glances at my face, putting a finger to his lips. Then he holds up a hand, gesturing for me to wait.

Just on the other side of the tree, the earth falls away, leaving a good deal of the roots exposed. I lean over and look down as he jumps about five feet to the bottom.

He's graceful, I'll give him that.

But I'm not expecting what he does next. He just turns to me, looking up at me expectantly. "Come on. I'll help you."

He holds his hands up, waiting. I definitely don't trust him not to just drop me. Biting my lip, I take his hands. But instead of jumping into his arms, I sort of awkwardly try to hit the ground beside him.

Stellan's eyes widen as I launch myself down toward the ground. He tries to correct the course of both of our bodies with the weight of his… but he fails.

Instead, he just staggers a little, catching me as I crumple of top of him.

Shit.

My chin hits his collarbone, my knees hit the hard flesh of his thighs. The breath is knocked out of me by running into the density of his chest.

"Oof," I squeak.

He grunts. Picking my head up, I realize that I'm face to face with him, close enough to kiss. I gaze into his stunning blue eyes, gulping. My eyes drop for just the barest second to his perfect mouth.

Should we… should I…

His mouth twists with a sour expression. When he whispers, his voice is low and intense. "You make things awkward. You know that?"

I catch my bottom lip between my teeth. "I've heard that, yes."

"Let's just…" He stops, shaking his head. "We just have to get through this month, okay? Then you are free to live your life. You'll never see me in person again."

That isn't what I wanted to hear, honestly. I don't want to spend time with Stellan, but no one wants to hear that they are bad company. "Just like that, huh? When we spent the night together— "

He shoves me away, taking a full step back. "We don't have to talk about that, Margot."

My face darkens. "You know what, Stellan? You— "

I hear the paintballs being fired only a second before my thigh bursts into flame. It hurts to be shot with a paintball! Looking down, I see the spread of neon pink paint on one leg of my yoga pants.

I make a strangled noise. Whatever argument I had planned falls away. I look back up and realize that Stellan and I both got pegged by someone who likely heard our arguing.

He grits his teeth, pinning me with an annoyed glare. "Great. Just great. Come on. We should go back to the center of the game and wait until we're reset." His expression is just short of a sneer. "I definitely want a different partner next time."

I roll my eyes. "Whatever."

And just like that, our truce is ended. He starts trudging around the bottom of the tree, letting me trail in his wake.

Chapter Eighteen

STELLAN

I'M SITTING at my desk, looking at a stack of financial papers that are awaiting my signature. Cracking each of my knuckles in turn, I look down at the figures presented to me. Each of these documents is important because they are from charities that I patronize; nearly every single one of them is asking for a significant raise in the money that is allocated to them this year.

Money doesn't grow on trees. I know that as well as anyone. So I'm trying to ascertain what monies go to which charities. The whole thing is enough to make my temple throb.

When a footman comes into my study, I'm relieved to be able to focus on anything else for a minute.

"Her Royal Highness," the footman announces, backing out of the way with a bow.

My grandmother sweeps into the room, looking prim and proper in a white skirt suit and sensible stockings. "Hello, darling."

I raise my brow, pushing up out of my seat. "*Momse*. What brings you here?"

She glances behind her, to where the footman still stands. "Get the door on your way out, please. I would like to talk to my grandson in private."

"Your highness," he responds, bowing and seeing himself out.

As the door closes, my grandmother gestures to the love seat and chair set up by the fireplace. "Join me, Stellan."

She perches on the edge of the loveseat, crossing her ankles. I walk over and plop myself into the overstuffed leather chair, tilting my head. "To what do I owe the pleasure? I mean, it's always nice to see you, *Momse*. But I assume that you are here for a reason."

She gives me a small smile. "I don't know if you know this, but I believe I have spent more time with you than I have with any other grandchild of mine."

That gives me pause. "Perhaps."

Her lips quirk. "No, not perhaps. Definitely. I've always been here for you. Your father hasn't..." She pauses, thoughtful. "He has been quite busy, running the kingdom of Denmark. He and your mother both are always on a world tour. I've made sure to be here at your beck and call. I wanted to make sure that you were growing up with the right ideals."

I narrow my gaze at Ida. "Yes, all right."

"In addition to that, I think you know that you are my favorite." She gives me another small smile. "You look very much like my own father, after all."

What is she getting at? I squint at her, trying to puzzle out what she is trying to say to me. "Yes, Momse."

She folds her hands in her lap. "I want you to consider that when I tell you what I came here to tell you."

A sinking feeling in the pit of my stomach tells me that her announcement is not going to be good news. I frown. "You're killing me. Just tell me already."

Her brow creases. "I know it's been a while since you've seen your parents."

"Yes. They've been on a tour of Australia and Africa for almost two months."

There is hesitation on Ida's face, which is unusual. She usually just says what she has to say, feelings be damned.

"Your father... your father's health has not been good over the past year."

My heart falters. "What?"

She inclines her head. "The king has been ill several times in the past twelve months. It's enough to make me worry, honestly. And when I start to worry, I start thinking of what I can do to prepare our country for any future… changes."

My eyebrows rise. "You think that I will have to take over?"

Her lips press into a firm line. "I think that it is not outside the realm of possibility. In my opinion, it is time to start preparing you to take the crown."

For several moments, I'm too shocked to respond.

"But…" I shake my head. "No. I'm only twenty six. I shouldn't even be thinking about the line of succession."

My grandmother stops me by leaning over and putting her hand on my knee. "I'm sorry, Stellan. But I'm afraid that you will have to begin preparing for something catastrophic to happen. And the very first step is finding a wife."

I draw myself back, frowning and shaking my head. "What? No. That should be the last thing I have to worry about right now."

Ida raises her hands, trying to calm me down. "Finding a wife now will make everything much easier. If you have to step up suddenly— "

I cut her off. "No."

Her eyes narrow. "It's not just me saying this, Stellan."

It takes everything I've got to keep my words civil. "Let me guess. You have Prime Minister Finley on your side?"

She tilts her head. "Yes. And others."

"Have you noticed that two of the names on your list of marriageable girls are related to Prime Minister Finley?" I cross my arms, my heartbeat sounding loud in my ears. "The list is only ten names long. That means, assuming that I actually go by your absurd list, I have a one out of five chance of being related to our good prime minister. Sure, I hate Prime Minister Finley and everything he stands for. But why not make him part of my family for the rest of my life? Hmm?"

She narrows her eyes at me. "There are eight other choices on that list."

I stand up, nearly trembling with repressed rage. "No. I'm not interested in having my life managed to that degree. I do everything else by the book, but I won't choose some insipid girl off a list of girls chosen by their heritage and willingness to breed. It's disgusting."

My grandmother climbs to her feet, giving me a tired look. "You have to, Stellan. Your father probably won't make it for another year in his current position."

"Well, I'll deal with that when he calls on me. And as for marriage… when it's the right time and the right girl, I'll let you know. But I don't want to hear another thing about it until I bring it up."

Her lips thin. "You can't give me orders, young man."

"And you can't dictate who and when I marry. So here we are, demanding things of the other we know will be ignored." I hold my hand out, gesturing to the door. "Now if you'll excuse me, I have this huge stack of papers to read through before my afternoon appointment at a children's hospital."

She gives her head a tiny shake and then moves gracefully toward the door. "I'm not dropping this subject, Stellan. We'll talk about it again as soon as your father is back from his trip."

I give her the most saccharine smile as I head back to my desk. "Have a nice afternoon, *Momse*."

She shoots me a glare, then opens the door and stalks out. The footman hovers at the door, looking anxious.

"Can I not be left alone?" I yell.

He goes pale, scurrying out of my sight. The throbbing headache I was getting earlier returns in full force. Rubbing my temples, I pace over to the window, looking out at the view absently.

I don't have control over so many things in my life. But this… picking a girl to marry… that is one of my few choices. I'm not insane enough to think that I will marry for love. But I'll be damned if I pick a random name off of a list that was approved by parliament.

I would rather stay unmarried forever than have marriage forced on me like that.

Turning my thoughts back to my father, I picture him in my mind's eye. He looks just like me, tall and dark haired with light blue eyes. Except there is a shock of silver in his hair, which mostly serves to make him seem even more refined.

Try as I might, I can't imagine him being ill. Distant? Sure. Quiet? Definitely.

But sick?

That thought just isn't compatible with the man I know. It just seems unlikely.

Which means that my grandmother is manipulating me. It's certainly far from the first time… but she was being honest about how much time she has devoted solely to me, to making sure I grow up as she wishes.

What would be the profit in driving me away with her endless questions of marriage unless… unless there really is something going on with my father?

A knock on the open door startles me from my morbid thoughts.

"Hey," Margot calls out softly.

I turn, narrowing my eyes. She's standing there, wearing her usual businesslike blazer and black work pants. Her pink hair is piled atop her head today, though several tendrils have already escaped to curl around her face.

Her mere presence makes my heart beat frantically against my ribs.

"Hey," I answer. I tilt my head. "Come here."

Her brows rise but she sets her ever-present tote bag down by the door and walks up to me. She stops when she's still two paces from me.

For some reason, that drives me fucking crazy.

Her tongue darts out to wet her lips as she peers up at me. Her eyes scan my face, trying to shuffle the puzzle pieces around, searching for some kind of explanation. "Are you okay?"

My lips tip up at the corners of my mouth. "I've been worse. I just had my grandmother here, reminding me of the plans she has made on my behalf."

Margot frowns. "What plans?"

I shrug. "Big life plans. It seems the closer I get to ruling this country, the less freedom I have in my own life. It's actually a bit funny."

She tucks a loose strand of her hair back behind her ear. "I see."

I give a dry chuckle. "No, I'm absolutely sure that you don't."

Her hand goes onto her hip, her eyes narrow. "There is no reason to be rude, Stellan. I thought we were getting along today."

Her posture is rebellious. There is something about the way she stands… no, the way she *is*… that calls out to me. My gaze slides down to her mouth.

A half-smile forms on my lips. "I like it when you're feisty. You know that?"

She gives a throaty laugh. "You've gone insane."

"No." I shake my head. "I'm just seeing the future in a certain light."

She gives me an odd look, wrinkling her nose. "What light? What are you— "

I stop her words by reaching a hand out and yanking her toward my body. Her eyes widen. Her palms fly up and land on my chest, resisting. Her lower body meets mine, pressing into me intimately.

It makes me crazed. I suck in a deep breath and catch her scent, honeysuckle and fresh laundry. My body responds without my brain; my cock grows hard, my skin tingles like it's about to catch fire.

"Stellan—"

I lean down, brushing my mouth against her gorgeously plump lips. I hear her sharp intake of breath, but I don't stop. No, I press my lips against hers, working my mouth in a delicate rhythm.

I can feel her heart beating beneath her skin.

For all her protests, she doesn't push me away. Quite the opposite. She pushes up onto her tiptoes and opens her mouth, letting her tongue dance with mine. She tastes so fucking good, like sugar and cinnamon and most of all, choice.

Kissing her is a kind of freedom, just in this moment. When she pulls away, her brow puckering, and looks up at me with those probing dark blue eyes…

I suddenly snap back to my senses, pushing her away roughly. "Fuck!"

"What was that?" she says, her fingertips going to trace her mouth.

I whirl, shaking my head and pacing back to the window. "Nothing. A moment of weakness."

My head pounds faintly. What exactly just happened between us?

"Should I—" she pauses, hesitating. "Maybe this is a bad time. Do you want me to come back?"

A laugh bubbles up from deep within. "I don't want anything from you, Margot."

A few seconds pass. "I should… I should come back later."

She turns and flees, her footsteps sounding as loud as gunshots on the hardwood floors. Grimacing, I rub my forehead.

Sensitivity to sound. I know all too well what that means. It's the first sign that I'm getting a migraine. Muttering a curse, I stalk from the room, heading to my private apartments to pull the shades and lie in silent misery.

Chapter Nineteen

MARGOT

IF THIS IS the palace's attempt to impress me by introducing me to the glitzy, glamorous side of royalty… I have to say, it's working. I glance around the palace's garden, taking in everything: men in dark tuxedos, women in light-colored ballgowns, servants swooping by the guests with silver platters full of champagne. Everything else is a bright, vibrant green that speaks of how many hours the palace gardeners put into their upkeep.

The high hedges in the distance are immaculately maintained. The sun is just beginning to set and a million little fairy lights twinkle from where they have been hidden amongst the leaves. As I move around, the topiaries and fountains sprinkled here and there hide and reveal different groups of people.

I produce my notepad out of the secret pocket of my dress, jotting a few notes to myself.

At least three hundred people here that I can see; I wonder how many more are walking around, ducking behind the hedges, out of my line of sight.

I pause, my pen poised. Then I sigh and put my notepad away.

Ever-present, rising high in the background, is the palace. The tan brick façades and squat dark roofs look austere in comparison to the lively party fanning out in the palace's wake.

I feel more than a little out of place, even though I'm in a rented ballgown just the color of my hair. Feeling like a huge piece of salt-water taffy, I look down at my carefully beaded taffeta gown. I stand out from the crowd. Normally that's a good thing, but here…

Here I feel like even more of an outsider than usual.

A young woman in servant dress comes up to me with a tray of drinks, smiling a bit. "Champagne?"

"*Ja*, thanks." I pick up a flute off of the tray. The servant smiles and swishes off to the next group of people she sees. I sip the wine, wrinkling my nose at the tiny bubbles that burst on my tongue. It tastes awfully sweet.

I look around for a friendly face. Someone to talk to. Pippa assured me that she would be here, but as I sweep my gaze around the hedges and fountains, she's nowhere to be seen.

I do see someone I know, though. My mouth turns down at the corners. Standing on the far side of the party, chatting to a bunch of other guests in tuxes and ballgowns, is Anna. She glances my way and shoots me a wry grin.

Oh god. I have to move. Whirling away before she gets the idea to come over and bother me, I look around, lost. A large group of people catches my eye. I stalk toward them, spying a lovely statue of what appears to be a nymph playing a lyre.

As soon as I get close, I see Stellan standing apart from the large group, a slight frown on his handsome face. As I approach, he loosens his bowtie and pulls it off, stuffing it in his black tuxedo pocket. When he notices me, he smirks.

Something about that light blue gaze of his makes me blush and squirm. I hesitate.

Should I keep going? Or should I pretend that I didn't see him and just go somewhere else? Before I can make up my mind, he makes it up for me.

"Margot!" he calls. "Come here."

Making a face, I sigh and continue walking until I'm about two feet away. Then I stop; this is close enough. If I get closer, he might think that I am inviting his attentions again.

And I'm definitely not.

…right?

No, definitely not.

He gestures to the garden around us. "Welcome to our little soiree."

I chew on my lower lip and scan the garden. "Shouldn't you be talking to… well… everyone? I'm sure that almost everybody here wants some alone time with the heir to the throne."

He looks over to the big group, then shrugs. "They do. And I've given them what they wanted for the past hour. Now it's time for me to do what I want." He tilts his head. "Do you want to go on an adventure?"

I step closer, looking at him with a mixture of curiosity and skepticism. "I thought I was supposed to be here, swooning over how glamorous this whole party is?"

Stellan grins, sweeping his gaze over the garden area. "Are you impressed by this little get together? This is just a regular Thursday night."

My lips curl up at the corners. "Even if that's true, I'm not exactly dressed for an adventure."

He arches a brow, his gaze wandering down to my dress. He gives me a knowing smirk. "We'll be all right." He jerks his head toward the tall hedges. "Come."

I huff out a laugh as he turns away toward the maze. He just expects me to follow him. Then again, if I were born into royalty, wouldn't I expect the same?

I trail after him, picking up my pace when he disappears behind a tall hedge. Grabbing my dress, I jog after Stellan as best I can. As soon as I turn the corner, I stumble right into him.

My hands land on his hard abs. My eyes widen. I look up at him, my breath constricting. From this close, his ice blue eyes crackle. He bites his bottom lip, smirking a little as he grabs my upper arms to steady me.

"Careful," he says, righting me. "We wouldn't want a repeat of yester-day, would we?"

My brow wrinkles. I take step back, shaking my head. "What, when you randomly kissed me out of the blue? I had nothing to do with that, honestly."

He smiles ruefully. "You didn't exactly resist though, did you?"

I take a step back, smoothing my hands down the length of my dress. "I don't understand what's happening here. You have been cold and distant to me since I got here. Now you have done a complete one eighty and you want to talk about how we kissed yesterday?" I fold my arms across my chest. "You have to stop. You're giving me whiplash."

He turns away quickly, before I can see his expression. "I'm not trying to, Margot. Honestly." He starts moving away, deeper into the maze formed by the hedges. He glances back, but doesn't quite stop. "Are you coming?"

I swallow, then start after him. On my short legs, catching up to him actually proves quite a challenge. When I finally pull even with him, I glance up into his face. "Can I ask you some questions for my article?"

Stellan's lips thin. "Must you?"

My lips quirk. "Yes."

He slides me a look, slowing his pace. "All right."

I pull out my notepad, flipping through a couple of pages until I find the list of questions I came up with while I was doing research. Skimming the list, I choose a light topic to start.

"Your mother and father seem to be fairly busy people. Obviously." I blush. "What I mean to ask is, who did you grow up around while they were running the country?"

He frowns. "I had a whole swarm of educators and caretakers. And my grandmother was around, making a lot of the day to day decisions regarding my care. She still is, actually. Just yesterday she was here, pressing me about my private life." His lips lift at the corners. "She's bossy, but I don't mind. I think I inherited that from her."

I scrunch my face up. "That still sounds kind of lonely. Didn't you go to school?"

He sighs. "No. I was tutored privately. But once Erik was around, I never wanted for a friend."

My lips curl. "Yes, I can see that. You two are inseparable."

He stops, turning to face me. "What about you? Tell me about your childhood living in the Big Apple. Or… did you move to New York later in life?"

I give him an annoyed look. "We made it through one question about you. *One*. How am I supposed to write this article if you won't cooperate?"

He shrugs a shoulder. "You're not supposed to bore me to death, I'm pretty sure. My whole life has been documented. Photos were taken to mark each little milestone of my life. It's a part of the public record." He gives me a hard look. "I'm just trying to keep things interesting. I regurgitate sound bites about my life. You give me some of your story in return."

"What if I said that I wasn't interested in the same sound bites that you've been giving for your entire life?" I cock my head, challenging him.

"I want the truth. Besides, if I write anything that is too sensitive, it will no doubt be caught by the press office."

A genuine smile plays across his mouth. "Fair enough. What I need to know is, will you be as honest in your answers as you are encouraging me to be?"

I roll my eyes. "Of course. I have nothing worth hiding."

A wrinkle of concern appears on his forehead. "So you say."

"Yes. So, to summarize: if I answer your questions, you'll answer mine."

He examines me for a moment, his eyes searching my face. "It's a deal."

Stellan holds out his hand. And I take it, shaking it firmly.

"Stellan!" a woman calls from the other side of the hedge. "Stellan, come tell everyone about your trip to Okinawa!"

He lets go of my hand and shakes his head. "I don't even know who that is." His lips curl down into a frown. "Tomorrow, we'll go somewhere private and try to get most of your questions out of the way."

My eyebrows lift. "Okay…"

But he's heading away, already turning around a corner in the hedge maze. I frown after him. What am I supposed to make of our agreement? I have absolutely no idea.

But I do know that this is entirely new territory for me. I'm in a foreign land, at a freaking palace, trying to puzzle out a tall, dark, handsome enigma.

Nothing is familiar here, not anymore.

My office mandated cell phone buzzes in my pocket. It's a brand new iPhone, so new that I haven't even taken the plastic film off the screen yet. I slip it out of my pocket, frowning at the unknown number.

INTERNATIONAL NUMBER is splashed across the screen.

That could be anyone. An old colleague. A friend from New York. Or it could be a member of the American press. I haven't given anyone this number yet, but that doesn't mean anything in this day and age.

I let it go to voicemail, biting my lower lip. Then as soon as I get a notification of a new voice message, I press play and put it to my ear. I'm only half listening as I turn and head back to the party.

Mostly, I'm really hoping that Pippa is around. I spent an hour and a half getting myself ready for this event... I'd hate to just go back to the party and skulk around, wasting all my efforts.

When the voice mail finally plays, I almost drop my phone in surprise.

"Hi. It's your mother calling." There is a sound on the line, like the crinkling of a bag of potato chips. "I just found out that not only did you move out of the state, you frigging moved all the way across the ocean. I thought you said the last time we talked that we were going to keep in better touch with each other. Guess that doesn't matter to you though, does it?"

I break into a sweat. My mom always makes me so nervous. Even though I'm well past the age of having to worry about when and if she would ever show her face at home... it's hard to overcome a lifetime of that.

"Anyway," she continues. "Your little friend called me. What's her name? Abby? No... Something with an A. She said she had a lot of questions about you."

I pale. About me? An uneasy feeling slithers through my gut.

"I said I'd have to talk to you first." Mom smacks her lips. "I think you and me should talk, baby girl. Give me a call back quick, else I think I'm going to have to talk to that nice lady." She hangs up.

As I lower the phone, I realize that my hands are shaking. I haven't actually heard from my mom in almost a year. The last time we talked, she hit me up for money. *Again.*

And now some idiot reporter has unearthed her somehow?

Pippa's face appears around the corner of the hedge maze. "Hey! I have looked everywhere for you. Come on, there are people that I want you to meet."

Scrunching my face up, I nod. "Okay..."

I head back toward the party, but my mother looms large in the back of my mind, a specter of ill omens.

Chapter Twenty

STELLAN

I **STAND** beside the gray gelding, petting him absently. Standing in this riding ring takes me back to my childhood days. The colors of the landscape, heather and green moss, dark colored earth and endless blue skies, all blending together seamlessly. The air here is full of strangely comforting scents: fresh cedar chips, sweet horse feed, the baser scent of horse dung.

I swear, nothing here has changed since I was a little boy, first learning to ride. The world around me back at the palace never seems to slow down. But out here, in the ivy-covered stables only a twenty minute helicopter ride from the palace?

It's just a whole different world. Time stands still. I think it's because everyone has to dress in riding gear. I'm currently wearing dark riding pants, a loose white button up, and knee-high boots almost shiny enough to see myself in.

Stroking Karl's muscular neck, I stare off into space and just… relax. Being who I am is not easy; everyone needs something from me, all the fucking time. Every minute of every day is jam-packed full of doing things to help other people.

I'm not complaining. But it's not often I get to zone out. Just… let my mind drift.

When Margot clears her throat gently, I tense up. My time is up, it seems.

I turn, eyeing her. My eyes widen a little bit. She's wearing the khaki jodhpurs and chestnut riding boots that were brought along for her… but on top, she wears a black t-shirt that reads The Smiths. Her riding pants are skintight. And her t-shirt is loose and full of holes, one especially large that shows off her neon pink bra.

God, why haven't I taken her riding before now?

She blushes under my inspection. "You are making me feel even more like an alien from another dimension than I did when I walked out of the changing room."

I shrug. "I can't help it if you look…" I pause, trying to think of how to word my thoughts diplomatically. "Eye catching."

Her eyes narrow to slits. "Cool it. Are we going riding or what?"

"*Ja, ja*. Look, the stable hand is bringing in the gentlest of our mares for you now." I point over to the fence, where a stable hand leads in a sleek-looking black horse. "Okay?"

Her expression remains full of uncertainty, especially when she's clambering on top of the horse. The stable hand helps her get into the saddle and then backs away, looking nervous. Not half as nervous as Margot looks, though…

Wide eyed, she clutches at the reins.

"You act as if you haven't ever been on a horse before," I chide her, mounting my horse.

Beneath her, the mare stands placidly. She looks at me as if I've grown a second head. "Of course I haven't!"

I raise my eyebrows. "Wait, really?"

"No! You think I'm joking about it?" Her expression darkens.

I guide my mount over to Margot, glancing over at her upright posture. "Relax your grip on the reins. Hold them like this."

I demonstrate, giving my horse a few inches of slack. She copies me, biting her lower lip. I reach over to her and correct her grip once, then smile. "There. Only pull back on the reins when you want the horse to slow or stop. And use your heels to encourage the horse to start moving. Like this."

I use my heels to nudge Karl forward. Using exaggerated motions, I demonstrate how I guide my horse. Margot's brow puckers, but she follows my movements. Soon, she guides the horse around the ring, successfully starting and stopping a few times.

"Come on." I jerk my head to the horizon. "Let's go out of the ring, into the wild. We'll go on a really easy ride, okay?"

She looks at me with terrified eyes, but she doesn't back down. She just swallows. "Okay."

Margot is clearly afraid but she's not going to let a little worry keep her from trying something new. God help me, but that's the most attractive thing she's done yet. I grin at her, nudging my horse toward the gate.

The stable hand opens the gate, standing aside to let both of us pass. I grin back at Margot as I ride. Her expression is really delightful, part suspicion, part fright, part determination. I lead her down a gentle hill, just as slow as the horses want to take it.

"Wouldn't Hunter S. Thompson be proud of you right now?" I tease.

She glances over at me, a puzzled frown on her face. "Who?"

"You know, the guy who wrote *Leaving Las Vegas*. He invented gonzo journalism. He rode with biker gangs, ran for office, and did a ton of drugs."

"Ah," she says, chuckling. "Yeah, I recognize the name now. I feel like he'd take one look at me right now and die laughing. This isn't exactly gonzo journalism."

"No?" I ask, grinning. "I don't know… You are obviously out of your element, but you're keeping your shit together."

She makes a face. "Maybe. We'll see." She looks out at the surrounding landscape, pursing her lips. "I have to say, it's quite pretty out here. What is that sort of gray plant with purplish blossoms that is growing everywhere here? It just looks like there are endless fields of it."

My lips twitch. "Heather."

Margot looks at me, her slender brows rising. "Really? It's awfully beautiful."

I nod, adjusting in my saddle. "*Ja*. There is a famous Danish song about seeing the waves of heather underneath the rolling blue skies…" Eyeing her, I shrug. "During the summer, it is so nice here."

She slides me a look. "What about during the winter?"

I wrinkle my nose. "The snow is very pretty. It can be breathtaking, in a brutal sort of way. But *ja*, the snow gets old after a few days."

"Same thing in New York. Except it is much hotter there during the summer. There's no air from July until nearly September. Stifling is the word, I think."

Pulling gently on Karl's reins, I drop back so that Margot and I can walk two abreast. She shoots me a hasty smile. "What? Am I doing something wrong?"

I shake my head. "No. I just want to be able to see your face while we're talking." I smirk. "You know that everything you are thinking is spelled out by your expressions, *ja?*"

She sends me a tiny scowl. "It is not."

"Yes, it is." I shrug. "When I was younger, maybe age seven or eight years old, I had acting classes. My instructor was a very old French man named Monsieur Bernard. And Monsieur Bernard would make us all dress up and stand in a line to be inspected." I smile, huffing a laugh. "Little kings and queens, he called us. Even Erik, though I think he knew that Erik was common. Monsieur Bernard always said that it is very important for the family of the king to learn to control their faces at all times."

Margot looks a little surprised at that. "Really? That's… interesting. Most parents would be afraid that their children might hide things from them, I would imagine."

I look out at the horizon, squinting. "You don't know my family, Margot. They are not like anyone else's family."

Her nose wrinkles a little. I fully expect her to ask when she will meet my father and mother, to say that it is an important part of her article or whatever. But she doesn't.

"No," she says, her full mouth flattening. "It would be weird to expect the royal family to function the same as everyone else, I guess."

I study her, wondering what she's thinking that makes her mouth turn down at the corners. "What about you?"

She looks up at me. "What?"

"You never answered my question yesterday. Did you grow up in New York City?"

"Ah." She looks down at the reins in her hands. "Yeah. I was born and raised in Brooklyn. It was…" She laughs to herself under her breath. "It was basically the opposite of growing up here, I think. That's what I'm gathering, anyway."

"What do you mean?" I ask casually.

Her resulting smile is a little bitter. "I didn't have anything as a kid. And I don't mean I didn't have a palace and a fleet of jets. I mean…" Her cheeks turn red. She pauses, then shakes her head. "I was just brought up differently, that's all."

I shrug. "Almost everyone grew up differently than I did."

She tilts her head, cocking an eyebrow. "Have you ever thought about finding someone who was raised in the same way? I mean, I know you are being pressured to pick someone to marry…"

Rolling my eyes, I shake my head. "Nope. Not interested."

"In talking about it, or doing it?"

I pin her with a stare. "Either. Now come on."

Digging my heels into my horse, I take off like a shot. And Margot isn't far behind, nudging her horse into a gallop and letting out a whoop of fear and excitement.

For just a moment, I let go of everything extraneous. Worries about my father's health, heavy thoughts about becoming the ruler of Denmark, constant needling about choosing a wife.

Right now, in just this moment, Margot and I are just two people flying far and fast, all the rest of Copenhagen and it's concerns be damned.

Chapter Twenty-One

MARGOT

"AND LET us not forget the children for whom we raise this money…" Stellan says, smiling into the microphone. He's in his usual dress of a richly-cut navy suit and a crisp white button up, standing behind a podium before a ballroom of people.

I'm staring at him from the sidelines, my cellphone in my hand, recording the whole thing. Still I look at him, at how he draws the attention of the entire room.

Elegant. Coiffed. Handsome.

You can say a great deal about his other attributes, including his often-oafish personality. But I look at his dark hair, his light blue eyes, his cheekbones chiseled from granite…

A person really can't find fault with his physical appearance, is what I am thinking. My cheeks warm, but I don't look away.

I watch him talking to the audience in his native tongue, something that is still foreign to me. He speaks quickly but assuredly, his voice honeyed as it glides over the alien-sounding syllables. I bite my lip, thinking to myself that I have to learn Danish sooner or later.

That is, if I stay here in Copenhagen after the article is published. All of that is a little too far into the future, murky at best.

My attention wanders: the ballroom we are in is in downtown Copenhagen, not owned by the royal family from what I can tell. The ceilings are soaring, the decoration ornate. Everything that I've seen so far in this hotel is done up in silver and black, in the style of jazz age era hotels. There's even an old gramophone; I saw it as I entered, segregated from the rest of the room with slinky red ropes.

"Thank you!" Stellan finishes his speech and the small crowd of businesspeople applaud wildly. As cameras flash, I roll my eyes just a bit.

No wonder he has such a huge ego. If everyone clapped every time I gave a speech about anything, I would probably have a big head too.

I see Stellan searching the crowd for me a second before his gaze meets mine. Blushing a little, I smooth my hands down yet another rented ballgown. This one is strapless and snow white, with a white length of taffeta meant to be worn as a wrap.

I slip my phone into my tote bag just as Stellan reaches me. He's riding high on the applause, his cheeks still pink, his smile still brilliant.

"What did you think of my speech?" he asks. His Danish accent is more pronounced just now, I suppose from speaking his mother tongue only moments ago.

I lick my lips, darting my eyes away from his face. "I think I still need to learn Danish."

He shakes his head at me, repressing an eye roll. Behind him, a five piece quartet starts playing jazz standards. "Want to see something cool?"

Clearing my throat, I manage a smile. "Always."

Stellan makes a pleased sound deep in his throat, almost a growl, but lacking the heat of anger. He grabs my elbow and starts towing me out of the ballroom. "Come. You're going to like this."

I bite my lower lip. "Am I going to be able to take notes?"

He pulls me out into the darkened marble hallway, shaking his head just a little. "I would rather you didn't. I'm celebrating tonight. You should be too."

I give a huffed laugh. "What are you celebrating, exactly?"

He shrugs. "What does it matter?"

My lips curve up. "Touché."

He guides me to the grand elevators, pressing the button to call it to our floor. I cock my head, looking at our reflection in the elevator doors. Stellan is so big and tall, so darkly handsome. I am so petite next to him; with my bubble gum pink hair and my white ball gown, I look as though I am made of marzipan candy.

What would he be, if we were both made of sugar? Perhaps some bitter black licorice, or some sort of molasses drops. Not the kind of candy most people would want to gorge themselves on, anyway…

I hear raised voices and turn my head. Stellan does too. Down the hall, Annika comes rushing out of some darkened room, her expression stormy. She says something cutting in Danish, holding her purple ball gown skirts up.

What is she running from?

My question is answered only a second later when Erik steps out into the hallway, reaching out and catching her by the arm. He spins her around to face him as if she weighs nothing.

She looks mad enough to spit at him. He leans his dirty blond head close to her ear. His words are too low to make out; from this distance, I only get the low grate of his voice.

"Erik!" Stellan shouts.

As one, Erik and Annika freeze, then turn to look at us. Annika steps away, wresting her arm from Erik's grip. Erik clears his throat and then calls down to us.

"We were just having a disagreement about…" He pauses. "Suitable choices."

Annika leans over and pushes his shoulder hard. "And I was telling him that he can't tell me what to do!"

She screws up her face and stalks away from all of us, vanishing around a corner. I see a look of concern slide between Stellan and Erik.

"*Er alt i orden?*" Stellan asks.

Erik shrugs. "*Ja. Vær ikke urolig.*"

Before I can ask Stellan to translate, Erik takes off down the hall after Annika. I watch Stellan's face and catch a suspicious look rippling across it, but in the next second he turns back toward the elevators. He presses the button again, impatient.

"What was that all about?" I ask. The elevator doors slide open and we step inside.

He presses the button for the top floor and shakes his head. "I have no idea. My sister has always been dramatic. Erik has always been… I don't know, whatever the opposite of that is."

The doors close. Stellan runs his hand through his hair, using his reflection in the elevator doors to groom himself. I fidget nervously, wondering where we are going.

As the elevator car rises, I look at Stellan. "What are we gathered here for? Tonight, I mean. All the fancy people downstairs in the ballroom."

He swings his gaze to me. "Is it going to end up in your article?"

Sighing, I give my head a gentle shake. "Not if you don't want it to."

The elevator slows. He brushes off his tux. "We raised several million krone for my homeless youth outreach program. I am pleased, to say the least."

The surprise must be evident on my face, because he looks at me with a chuckle. "Oh, come now. If there's one thing the royal family is good at, it's fundraising for charities."

The doors roll open to a little lobby. Stepping out, I see a luxurious restaurant to the right, people in their evening attire chatting and drinking, waiters circling with refills. I start to walk that way but Stellan stops me with a hand on my inner elbow.

"No, no." He pulls me the other way. "Come on."

He walks to a stairwell and opens the door for me. I head where he directs, up the stairs to where the stairwell dead ends at a dark metal door. When I look back at him, he jerks his head to the door.

"Open it."

I push the door open and step out into a little area no bigger than a closet. To my surprise I'm greeted by the night sky full of stars overhead. I move forward just a little to a railing. Looking down, I can't keep from gaping.

"You can see the entire city from here!" I gasp. I look back at Stellan, who grins at my reaction. "I can see the palace from here. Oh! And the *Politiken* offices are right over there… which means…" I consider the cityscape, then point. "I think Pippa's apartments are that direction."

He steps forward, pressing himself against the balcony railing. "I think her apartment is over that way, actually."

I shoot him a puzzled look. "Why would you know?"

He grins at me, his eyes dancing. "Because I know. Pippa's been friends with our family for years. Does that soothe the jealous monster within?"

Yes, a little. I stick out my tongue at him. "I'm not jealous, Jealousy is for the rich. Me? I'm just trying to figure out how I'm going to scrape by."

He smirks, running his gaze up and down my body. "You're doing all right, if I had to guess. Except that your top half seems to want to be free of your ballgown…"

My mouth opens. A little sound of displeasure comes out as I quickly adjust the top of my ballgown. "It's a rented gown, okay? My boobs don't stand a chance of actually fitting in this thing." I scowl at the grin that spreads across his face. "Quit looking at my tits!"

He leans a little closer, biting his lip. Only now do I realize that he's almost close enough to touch me. My pulse starts speeding up as I look up into his face.

"And what if I don't want to stop looking?" he taunts.

My mouth goes dry. I'm suddenly aware of my hands. What should I do with them? I slip them in my pockets as my gaze slips down from his ice blue eyes to his perfect, soft-looking lips.

He breathes a little harder than usual. When I look back up to his eyes, I can tell his pupils have dilated a bit.

He wants me. I can feel it. There is something in the air, something occupying the space between us.

Say something. Tell him you want him, I think.

"I— "

The moment is shattered by his phone ringing. His eyes widen and he straightens, giving himself a shake. He reaches into his pocket and looks at the screen, then shrugs one shoulder.

"I should take this. I'll see you later, maybe."

Stellan whirls and puts the phone to his ear, pulling the door open. *"Hej ja ja - nej du forstyrre ikk."*

I sigh, looking back out over the amazing cityscape, wondering *what if?*

Chapter Twenty-Two

STELLAN

AFTER A RECORD NUMBER of photo ops, meet and greets, and charity galas, I find myself fucking exhausted. Not just exhausted, actually… I feel like I'm on the verge of getting sick. I've done too much over too small of a window of time.

It's time to retreat from sight.

I text Erik letting him know that I am going to get away for the weekend. He should cancel all my plans, at least until Monday. He responds quickly.

I'll let Fredensborg Palace know that they should expect to see you. Will Margot be going with you as well?

My eyebrows rise. I hadn't thought to bring her… but I can't see the harm.

Yes, I answer. *Call her if you would. And send a car to pick her up. I'm going to drive myself.*

His response is instant. *Ja, okay.*

An hour later, when I pull up in Fredensborg's curved drive, Margot stands waiting. I take my helmet off and admire the way her pink hair looks against Fredensborg's white stucco walls and green metal roof. She gives me her most aloof look, running her hand over her short black dress.

She looks like a little pink meringue on a dessert plate. My mouth curves up. I stride over to her.

She looks less than pleased to see me. "Why am I here? I'm supposed to be having an evening off, according to the schedule your press office gave me."

I shrug. "You're here to keep me entertained."

Margot glances up at the darkening sky. "Why are we here, though? You could've asked me to come anywhere in Copenhagen. No need to drag me all the way out here." She wrinkles her nose and glances at the palace behind her. "Not that the scenery isn't majestic or anything…"

"Stop whining," I command. "Follow me."

Stalking straight ahead, I climb Fredensborg's stone steps, entering the palace itself. Two butlers and two maids await me in the grand foyer, curtsying low. I look back at Margot, who is following me with a frown.

"Hurry," I say, waving her on. "This way."

I turn right, down an echoing marble hallway. The butlers trail after Margot, as if they are unsure what I could be up to. No one will be left hanging for long, though.

I stop outside of two double doors, swinging them open to reveal my grandfather's rather large billiards room. There are three red felt pool tables by the far wall. Two long bookcases line the back wall. Standing guard by the fireplace are a taxidermized bear and panther, both posed as if they were about to attack.

As a little boy, those figures both terrified and delighted me in equal measure.

A distinguished bar made of polished cedar sits to my far left. And to my right, there are several couches and chaise recliners made out of red velvet. The walls of the room and the windows are draped in a dark green fabric.

It looks like the Great Gatsby threw up in here, but this room called my name when I thought about where I might spend some downtime. And when Margot steps inside, her eyes widen with awe.

"Oh my god," she breathes. She glances at me. "Is this place for real?"

"Yep." I take my leather jacket off and sling in onto an ottoman on my way to the bar. "Would you like a drink?"

She's not really listening. "Sure, whatever is fine," she murmurs. "God, it's like something out of a Hemingway novel in here."

She runs her hand over the smooth cedar bar top, taking it all in, her tone one of hushed awe.

Pulling a couple of glasses out from the little cabinet below the bar, I smile at her words. "I think my grandfather and Mr. Hemingway knew one another. In fact, I bet that if we went over to the library, there are some signed first editions in there."

She whirls, pinning me with a stare. "Shut. Up."

I cock a brow at her. "No."

"Ugh!" she says, throwing up her hands. As she turns away, looking at the bookshelves that are in here, I smile. She leans over and comes very close to showing me her panties. As a matter of fact, I think I catch a glimpse of them while I pop the cork on a bottle of champagne.

They're pink and lacy, just as I hoped they would be. If she knew that I could see them I doubt she would like it... so I bite my lip, not breathing a word about it. In fact, I think she'd yell at me for looking at her ass.

Why spoil such a good thing for myself?

"Who picked these books?" she asks. She straightens and turns, biting her lip as I walk over to her.

I hand her a coupe glass of champagne. "Here."

Margot accepts it, taking a sip. "Mm. Thanks."

I throw her a smile, then take my own glass of champagne over to one of the couches. I lie down on it, kicking my feet up. "I think my grandfather picked the books."

She comes over, sitting on the same couch, but at the other end. I take the liberty of putting my feet in her lap. She makes a face and slides my feet to the floor.

"Hey!" I protest. I can't suppress a grin though.

"Your grandfather had pretty strange taste. There's a whole section of transcendental poetry wedged in there."

My eyes find her face. "I have no idea what that means."

A huff of laughter escapes her. "Neither does anybody else, so don't feel bad."

I cock my head at her. "You're really smart, aren't you?"

She turns red and rolls her eyes. "Shut up."

"No. I mean it. Who the fuck has ever heard of transcendental poetry? And I've heard you call me privileged for growing up with private tutors, but you haven't exactly missed any references. You are actually, genuinely smart."

She covers her face with her hands. "Oh my god. A change of topic was needed like… *yesterday*."

Smirking, I shrug. "Okay. Tell me one thing I wouldn't guess about you just from looking at you."

Margot peeks out from behind her hands, then relents. She drops her hands, still blushing but looking thoughtful. "Umm… Ooh. I like pop music. I mean, not all pop music. But like… Billie Eilish? I know every single one of her songs by heart."

I chuckle. "I wouldn't have guessed that."

She sips her champagne, sneaking a look at me. "Now you."

I pull my feet up again, this time resting them on her thigh. She scrunches up her face but doesn't try to remove them. I consider that a win.

"I play polo."

"Ugh, I could've guessed that. I need something good."

I wag my finger at her. "You didn't let me finish. I play polo, but only because one of my charities asks me to every year. And every fucking year, I get my ass beat. I'm ridiculously bad at it."

She laughs. "All right, you win. At this game, not at polo. Because you apparently *suck* at polo."

I sigh dramatically. "You wouldn't understand. You're *common*."

Apparently, that was the wrong thing to say, because she stops laughing. Instead, she fixes me with a frown. "I don't like the way you say that. *Common*. Like there's something wrong with everyday people. Why don't you realize that we are what is normal? It's you guys, the top one percent of the one percent… you're fucking weird."

Taking several gulps out of my glass, I pin her with a stare. "Maybe. Then again, I'm not putting on airs. I'm not pretending to be something I'm not, hanging out with people I wouldn't normally meet. That's *you*."

Margot sits up straight, looking at me with a puzzled frown. "You get that I'm only here because my job told me to be, right? It's important to me that you understand that."

I roll my eyes and put my feet down on the floor. "This conversation has gotten very boring all of the sudden."

Standing up, I upend my glass of champagne into my mouth and slurp it down. When I look back at her, she has this wounded look on her face, like I'm the one who is being a bully.

I'm not.

Am I?

"Come on," I say, nodding my head to the door. "Let's explore the palace. I bet you I can count at least six blades hanging on various walls."

She wrinkles her nose but gets to her feet, following me around through room after room. She's gone quiet.

And that's no good, because I like it when she's a noisy rebel. Instead, she nods and soaks up information. No matter how I try to encourage her wild side to come out, she's retreated somewhere, put up walls that I haven't seen before.

"Come onnnnnnn," I prod her, walking down yet another marble hallway. Fat cherubs look down on me from the corners, seeming disappointed in me. "It's just a swimming pool. You don't need a suit…"

She stops in her tracks, whirling to face me. "What is your deal, Stellan?"

I pause, my mind turning over the possibilities of what she could mean. "My deal?"

"Hot or cold? Hmm? Which one do you want to be today? The friendly guy who teases me about skinny dipping in the palace pool? Or are you the jerk who likes rubbing my nose in the fact that I'm not royal?" She cocks her hip, fury written all over her face. "If you could just let me know, that would be great. It's nice to have some idea of when I should be strait-laced and when I should cut loose."

One corner of my mouth curls up. "I would love to see you cut loose. Is that an option?"

Her eyes narrow. "You know what? Hold that thought. Let's go somewhere that you don't have the home turf advantage."

I squint. "The what?"

She holds up a finger and stalks away, putting her phone out and fiddling with it.

And that's when it hits me. This big, huge wave of warmth, of happiness, of pleasure.

Oh god.

I like Margot.

I like her even more when she's a little bit cruel to me.

I *like* her when she's mean.

How did this happen to me?

She puts the phone to her ear, speaking softly into it. And all I can think is how fucked I am if she finds out how I feel. It's hard enough right now as it is…

Margot spins, her eyes lighting up. She hangs up the phone, practically bristling with excitement. "Get your coat. We're going out."

And I just nod like an idiot, trying to smash my feelings down into a hole deep inside. I can't act on them. So why does being with Margot make me so… well, *happy* isn't quite the right word, is it? I turn back toward where I left my coat, swallowing against the knot forming in my throat.

Chapter Twenty-Three

STELLAN

AS MARGOT LEADS the way past the bouncer and into the loud, crowded club, she looks back at me. The lights flash, illuminating streaks that splash across her glitter-covered face. I tug on the dark hooded sweatshirt she made me change into. She grins, reaching back and pulling my hood up a little further to better hide my distinctive features.

I grab her hand and frown. I lean close to her to make myself heard over the loud music. "Where are we?"

She pins me with her gaze. "Somewhere you won't be expected to be. Come on."

Turning, she leads me into the bar area. The bar top is made of thick plastic and lit up neon green. It casts a sickly light over all the patrons crowded around, waiting for their turn to order drinks. Ahead of us, I can see people pushing their way into what I assume is the main dance floor. The DJ booth is in the far corner; rock music plays so loudly that it reverberates through my bones.

This atmosphere is familiar to me. Grungy, underground, yet exceedingly packed with people. Just like New York, although maybe this club is a little bit cleaner.

A very little bit.

As we line up at the bar to wait for service, I brushes up against her. I leans down to her ear.

"Have you been here before?" I ask.

She shakes her head, looking up at me with a crooked smile. "Nope."

"And why are we here again?"

"The same reason you are concealing your identity. This is a neutral place. Your money doesn't mean anything here." She smirks.

I frown and open my mouth to respond, but she just turns away. The scruffy bartender comes over and she leans close to his ear, ordering drinks. He plops two beers on the counter and she pays for them.

She turns to me, plastic cups in each hand. "Here."

She hands me my beer and then heads away from the bar, elbowing her way through the crowd as she moves toward the main room. I take a sip of my beer and find it stale but cold. Shaking my head, I follow her as she weaves through the young, hip crowd. There are actually several people in this room with unnatural hair colors, but she's the only one with her unique frothy pink color.

Against her pale skin and dark little dress, it really pops.

When she finds a place that calls to her, she turns with a grin. She takes a long swig from her red solo cup, throwing up her free hand and swaying along to the insistent beat.

I take a long pull of my beer and shuffle my feet around, hoping she doesn't realize how much I feel like a fish out of water just now. She grins and grabs a fistful of my hooded sweatshirt, pulling me toward her.

I slide my free hand around the small of her back, touching my hips to hers. She bites her lip and sways against me, her eyes meeting mine. I see a teasing sort of amusement reflected there.

The song changes tempos, slowing down just a bit. I give her a smirk and lean down close to her ear.

"You are playing with fire," I tell her.

"Who, me?" she says, sliding her arms around my neck. "I don't know what you mean. Usually I'm so *cautious*."

I shake my head a little, smiling down at her. "You are dangerous."

All the while our bodies move together, almost grinding against each other, but not quite. Her small hips fit neatly against mine; my big hands splay out over her lower back. Our bellies press together but I'm hardly aware of that.

No, I'm sucked into her dark blue eyes, full of mischief and daring. We dance like that for another half a minute, then the DJ changes out music again, something faster this time.

Margot puts some space between us and rocks out, her hands going up, her movements rhythmic. Her eyes are closed, her pink hair glowing under the low light, the neckline of her dress dipping low to show off a scant quarter inch of her bright pink bra.

After another few songs, I'm staring at her like I'm a man dying of thirst and she's the only refreshing sip of water left in my canteen. I'll admit it; I'm starting to be obsessed with the way that she shakes her hips, the way that her chest rises when she breathes, the plump bow of her lips in relation to her heart shaped face. She slows down, jerking her head to the bar.

"I need another beer. Wanna come with?"

My lips lift. "Sure."

When she turns and walks away, I follow. I'm staring at her perfect ass and amazing legs as long as I can before it disappears behind other people who cross between us. Margot glances back at me, giving me a knowing smile.

God *damn*.

I find myself walking a little faster to catch up with her. She queues up, trying to pull out her wallet again. I make a face at her.

"Put your fucking wallet away," I grit out.

She wrinkles her nose. "I'm just trying to be egalitarian about getting us beers."

I lean in close, pushing the hood of my sweatshirt down off my head. "I'm the fucking crown prince of Denmark. The idea of you trying to get even with me by buying me beers is laughable."

Margot shrugs, rolling her eyes, but there is still a trace of a smile on her lips. "Whatever makes you happy, your highness."

A blonde girl in front of us overhears a little of our conversation. Turning her head, she checks out Margot, who absolutely looks like she belongs here in this club. When the blonde looks at me, her eyebrows go up. She does a double take, squinting, trying to place me.

Shit.

I turn away, raising my hood. The last thing I need tonight is getting spotted here, and with Margot to boot. Luckily, a few seconds later the bartender comes and asks for our orders. After we grab more beers, we head to an ill-lit corner away from the blaringly loud music.

There aren't any tables here as such. It's just a single long red leather booth that contours to the walls, worn and torn and covered in graffiti. Margot plops herself down on the seat beside a few young guys that look at her with wide eyes.

They probably think that their dream girl just came over to make their whole lives a little better. Shooting them a quelling glare, I find a seat beside her and stretch out my long legs.

Margot sizes me up, one corner of her mouth kicking up. She looks almost impish, sitting there so petite and so clearly amused.

"What?" I ask, sipping my beer.

She shrugs, smiling as she tastes her beer. "For an obscenely rich person, you're pretty okay, I guess."

I sputter, spitting some foam back inside my red solo cup. She grins at my reaction, wiggling her eyebrows.

"So you're saying I'm not horrible?" I laugh, wiping foam from my nose.

"I'm saying that you have your moments," she says, rolling her eyes. "You also have moments where you act like a rich spoiled brat."

"What? No way, I'm a lot more grounded than you think. I mean, considering my unique set of circumstances, the fact that I can hang out here is like… amazing."

She cocks a brow. "I admire you less for it because we're talking about it. Like I just lost maybe… five percent of the esteem that you gained in my eyes."

I chuckle. "That's good to know." I tilt my head to the side. "So not terrible and handsome. Is that all you think about me?"

She turns bright pink. "Who said I think you're handsome?"

Squinting at her, I set my beer by my feet. "Unless you've changed drastically since New York City, I would say that you did. It was implied when we fucked."

Margot shakes her head and rolls her eyes. "We didn't fuck. We did… other stuff."

I bite my lip, unprepared for the influx of mental images that spring to mind.

Margot giving me the naughtiest look as she drops to her knees. The way her hair felt against my fingers as she took me in her mouth. The way I spread her wide open and tongued her clit, over and over, soaking up every rich drop of pleasure that I could wring from her flesh.

I'm already hard for her. Leaning over, I brush her gossamer hair back. Then I lean in close so that my lips almost touch her ear.

"What, oral sex isn't fucking now?" I grate out.

She sips her beer coolly and glances away, but I can see her blush. "I stand behind my statement."

The second I lift up my hand to touch her, a static electricity starts to build in the air. Sliding my hand around to cup her jaw, I turn her to face me. I use my thumb to angle her head just so.

Margot looks back at me, her deep blue eyes pinning me in place. God, I could just look at her like this, in this moment, forever.

But her gaze slides down to my mouth. She sucks her bottom lip between her teeth, pink clashing with the white or her teeth. My ring finger slips over the pulse point in her neck.

Her heart races. I lean in, brushing my lips over hers. Her pulse jumps and she lifts her hand to my hoodie, fisting it tightly in her grip. I start to pull back, but she follows me, ghosting another kiss over my lips.

I growl into her mouth, my hands shifting Margot half out of her seat. She surges forward and I'm ready for her, kissing her. I slide my hand down between her legs, making her gasp. Then I fucking feast on her, dominating the exchange, groaning as I sweep the inside of her sweet fucking mouth with my tongue.

I groan. She tastes like stale beer laid over something indescribably delicate and sweet. Margot nips at my bottom lip when I give her the chance. I growl again, picturing exactly how she will look naked and writhing against my pillows.

God damn, she is so fucking hot.

But then she pulls back, breathing hard, her eyes darting back and forth across my face. "Stellan…" she whispers, biting her lip. "This? You and me? It's not a good idea."

I give my head a shake and try to kiss her again, but she shoves me off. "I said no. I know that's not something you're used to…"

"You want me," I say, trying to keep the accusations from my voice. I splay one big hand across her heart and pin her with my gaze. "I know you do. I can feel your heart race every time I fucking touch you."

Margot rises to her feet, surveying me as smoothly as any queen would look at a peasant groveling at her feet. "I think I'm going to go dance."

She picks up her beer from the floor and then walks off without so much as another word. I'm left sitting in the uncomfortable bench and scowling to myself.

Margot is being a total dick about this. She's probably right about it being a bad idea, but that doesn't make me feel any better.

As I lurch upward, heading after her, I catch the sneers that the young guys next to me are sending my way. I lean over, purposely using my height and sheer size.

"Fuck off," I growl.

Then I grab my beer and stomp off after Margot, my brain still doing cartwheels, trying to figure out what just happened between us.

Chapter Twenty-Four

MARGOT

I STEP off the luxurious private jet onto the tarmac, pulling my sunglasses onto my face. Kristiansund spills out beneath my view like an inky puddle; I can see the coastline spreading out a couple of miles down from where I'm standing, bright green grass meeting the cobalt blue sea. In the distance, I can make out yellow and red and white cottages.

This looks like a sleepy little fishing village.

I shiver against the wind. We're so far north in Norway that the weather is quite brisk. The flight attendant is right behind me with my bags. I try to take them at the bottom of the stairs.

"Here, let me help," I offer.

I can immediately tell from the puzzled look on his face that I'm not actually supposed to take my bags. When he speaks, his English sounds clipped. He's Finnish or Norwegian, maybe.

"Let me take them over to the car for you," he says, smiling despite his bafflement. In his tidy-looking steward's uniform, he is the very picture of propriety right now.

"Right," I mutter, trailing along behind him. Raising my eyes to the limousine that awaits me, I allow myself to be ushered into the back. "Thank you!" I manage to call to the steward.

He tilts his head and a vaguely disapproving expression appears on his face. He inclines his head. "Have a pleasant journey, Miss Keane."

I never even got his name.

That's what I think about while the limo takes me down into the village, down cobbled streets as little white and yellow houses zoom by my view. That, and how I got here.

The note is still in my tote bag.

Come with me for the weekend.
   Pack a bag. — S

Five hours later, feeling remarkably hassled even though I was just on a *private jet*, here I am. The limousine pulls to a halt outside of an adorable little red cottage and I get out, heaving a sigh.

Stellan called. He's my assignment.

That's the reason I came. The *only* reason. After parting ways the other night, I didn't hear from him for five days. Five interminably long days.

I wasn't entirely sure I would hear from him ever again, period. And yet here Stellan is, opening the door when I knock. He smiles coolly, stepping back and welcoming me in.

"Come on," he says, his lips carefully pursed. "Don't let all the heat out."

My nose twitches at the tone of his voice; he sounds commanding, not inviting. Heaving another sigh, I walk into a cozy, bright kitchen area. It's all done in teal and baby pink, a decorator after my own heart.

The driver leaves my bags by the door and leaves without a word. Stellan just skirts around the marble kitchen island and heads out of the room. I hate when he expects me to follow him without asking any questions.

Grinding my teeth, I trail his wake into a living area. Sunlight spills into the room from a window that stretches almost from one wall to the other. A bright white couch sits against the wall to my far right, piled high with cozy-looking afghans and soft pillows. To my left is a little table that doubles as a chess board and two chairs pulled up to it.

Straight ahead, I can see that there is a hallway, probably containing the bedrooms and the bathroom. Stellan is already throwing himself onto the couch, so I pull one of the chairs out. Sitting down, I cock my head at him. "So?"

He squints. "So what?"

A huffed laugh leaves me. "I'm here. You summoned me after putting me on the back burner for most of the week. Now what?"

He scrubs a hand through his hair. "Honestly? I don't have any plans. I just had a really busy week, so…" He shrugs one shoulder. "That's the only reason I didn't call you sooner."

I narrow my eyes and cross my arms. "So your sudden coolness has nothing to do with the fact that you kissed me last week?"

He looks tiredly out the window, sighing. "No, Margot. I don't understand you, really. You reject my advances… but still you expect me to treat you like a friend, as opposed to a nosy fucking reporter." He peers at me. "Which you are, by the way." He stands up suddenly, looking fierce. "That's what you want, isn't it? To be my friend?"

"Yes." I uncross my arms and sit forward, leaning my elbows on my knees. "Stellan…" When he looks over at me, I take a steadying breath. "You realize that I'm just trying to keep us both safe, right? I'm attracted to you. You are attracted to me. And that would be good enough if you were anyone else. But… you're not. You're the crown prince of fucking Denmark."

Stellan looks at me, his ice blue eyes threatening to pierce me through to the core. "You don't think I know that? You don't think I'm aware of that every fucking second of every single day? No one will let me forget it."

I falter. He seems to be in pain. Or maybe it's just a weariness that comes with carrying the burden of being the prince. I don't know which.

"I'm sorry, Stellan. I really am." Sitting back in the wooden chair, I watch him recompose his facial expression. He wipes away all the traces of sadness. What's left is a face I recognize all too well.

He looks remote. Withdrawn. Untouchable.

My fingers itch with the need to touch him, to tell him that things will be okay. Even though I know that saying that might just be a pretty, comforting lie.

I have less control over this situation than anybody else, honestly.

He turns to me, changing the subject as if the entire conversation before now simply never happened. "Do you want to go for a walk? Maybe we could go down by the shoreline. There is a little restaurant there that I always patronize whenever I am here."

"Are you sure you wouldn't rather stay here and talk some more?" I ask.

He pins me with his gaze. "I couldn't be more certain." He heads to the hallway in the back, leaving me to bite my lip and wonder what exactly is going on in his head. Is he still upset about the other night?

Or is he really just switching tracks like he changed subjects?

Stellan reappears, zipping a light raincoat up over his dark wool sweater. He eyes me in my dark leather jacket, short black skirt, and neon pink tights. "Are you going to be warm enough?"

I scowl at his question. "I'm fine."

"Okay." He shrugs. "Come on, then."

He strides out of the room and through the kitchen, making me scurry to keep up with him. He's out of the door and into the cool air in seconds. I follow, shivering a little at the shock of going from the warmth of the house out into the chilly atmosphere.

Stellan turns back and sees me shiver. His eyes narrow. "I told you."

I grit my teeth and stick my hands in my pockets. "It's fine. Keep leading the way, like you always do."

He squints at me, then casts a look around the cobblestone street we are on. "Yeah, all right. Whatever that means. Come on, will you?"

I start marching downhill and Stellan falls in beside me. His eyes are on the horizon as we walk. I look at the green grass and the brown shoreline, only a quarter of a mile away. They are fitted so snugly with the blue-black ocean, each affecting the other's shaping.

At length, I scrunch my face up and look at him. "So is this how it usually works? You do five intense days of hand shaking and autograph signing, then you are allowed to jet off to one of the royal family's getaways for the weekend?"

He sighs. "*Ja*, more or less. Usually Erik is with me when I escape."

I nod slowly. "And where is he this time?"

His shoulders lift in a shrug. "No idea. He said he had something he wanted to do. I didn't press him for details. Besides… it's nice to be alone once in a while."

I look at him oddly. "You're not alone, Stellan. You're with me." I scrunch up my nose. "I guess you are used to having a staff at your beck and call, Erik reminding you of appointments, a hundred people always wanting to shake hands with you. I'm starting to think that you have no real idea of what being alone is like."

He looks unamused. "Maybe I don't. Or maybe this weekend is about me, inviting you into my solitude."

My eyebrows lift. "Oh. I hadn't thought of that."

He lifts his head, nodding to a building in the distance. "I want to stop in there for a second. Wait for me."

Stellan jogs off toward it, leaving me alone to think about what he said. My mouth twists. I guess there is a wealth of things I don't understand about his life, just the same way as he can't possibly fathom every single thing about mine.

No, it's not just that, actually. It's more that I won't let him in to find out all the secrets about my past that I've buried. I don't want him to know just how poor I used to be. I don't want anyone to realize how fucking sad I am deep down either.

My cell phone beeps in the pocket of my leather coat. Shaking my head, I pull it out and read the screen. It's from an unknown number, but I have no doubt that Anna sent it.

I just got off the phone with a friend of a friend who says that you and Stellan were kissing at a club last week. That's interesting, isn't it?

Before I can respond, she sends another message.

I think that warrants a more thorough search of your background. After all, you are cozying up to the crown prince... What do you think I will find?

My face heats. I block the unknown number, furious.

How dare Anna imply that I'm out to seduce Stellan for financial reasons? The whole idea is so wrong that it takes every ounce of willpower not to throw a tantrum right here and now.

For all the good that would do...

Stellan emerges from the shop, each hand holding a little white pastry bag. He hands one to me and continues his walk down to the shore.

"Umm…" The bag is warm in my hands. I get a whiff of vanilla and sweet baked bread. "Thanks?"

I hurry to follow him, peeling away the pastry bag to reveal a sort of creamy yellow custard overflowing it's donut container. He takes a bite and moans.

"It's so good." He chews for a moment. "They are called skolebrød and they are the best thing to come out of Norway, period."

I take a small bite, managing to get custard and powdered sugar absolutely everywhere. It's yeasty and sugary, custardy but light. My eyes light up. "Oh, that is good."

He smirks at me. "Don't say I never bought you anything."

And with that comment he starts walking faster, leaving me and my short legs woefully behind. I smile ruefully at his comment, then savor another bite of the pastry.

Chapter Twenty-Five

STELLAN

"YOU ACTUALLY MANAGED to make this on your own?" Margot asks. I can't tell if she's teasing or not, but I did make this popcorn on the stove with no assistance.

I roll my eyes and hand her the huge bowl, plopping myself on the couch beside her. "I can make popcorn," I say, a little defensive. "I'm not a complete idiot."

Her lips curl up at the corners. "I'll be the judge of that."

She takes a few pieces and puts them in her mouth, chewing. Then she nods. "Someone exceedingly smart made this. I can tell."

I make a face and reach for some of the popcorn. "What kind of wine do you think goes with popcorn? A chardonnay, maybe?"

Margot pulls a face. "Maybe, I'm not much of a wine drinker."

Settling back on the couch, I give her a measuring look. "You're missing out."

She grins. "Really? I don't feel like I am. I feel like I'm just fine over here, with my beer sipping and whiskey guzzling. It turns out, you don't need money to have a pretty good time."

That's the tenth time that she's brought up money since she got here. I wonder if she realizes that she wears her apparent poverty like a nationalist drapes himself in his flag. It's all she seems to want people to see when they look at her. It's almost like a suit of armor that she puts on.

Doesn't that protective shield grow heavy sometimes?

I watch her rummage around in a box of board games. "Hey, do you want to play cards or something?"

My lips twitch. "Not a chance."

Margot sighs, setting the box aside and munching on popcorn. She slides her gaze to me, smirking. "Okay. What do you want to do? Play twenty questions? Or let's go even more mature… truth or dare?"

My brow creases. "What is that?"

She rolls her eyes. "It's a game that teenagers play. I ask you to choose between answering a question truthfully, or doing something crazy that I ask of you. It's stupid, really."

Repositioning myself in a more comfortable spot, I shrug my shoulders. "It doesn't sound stupid. Let's play."

"Oh god. No," she says, shaking her head.

I cover her hand with mine, pinning her with my gaze. Her cheeks turn pink, reinforcing the idea in my mind.

I know exactly what I'm doing. Playing with Margot's feelings, pursuing her even though I know it will end up with us being in a mess.

I'm just so tired of doing what is right, what is beneficial in the long term. I don't want to make every single choice based on the specter of the future.

So I tease her a little. "*Ja,* we can play. Can I go first?"

She glances at me, then ducks her head. "If that makes you happy."

I grin at her. "Truth or dare, Margot?"

Her cheeks turn from pink to red. "Umm… truth, I guess."

Leaning forward, I snag the popcorn bowl from her and launch a few kernels into my mouth. "I was hoping that you would choose dare," I admit. "I was going to ask you to strip."

She pins me with a probing stare. "Too bad."

There is a hint of humor around her mouth, though. I squint at her, formulating my question. Mostly I'm trying to decide if I should start with something easy, or ask her something hard. I puff out my cheeks.

"Stellan, ask already!" she protests.

I tilt my head. "*Ja, ja.* Okay. When is your birthday?"

Her eyebrows rise. "October 20th. I'm a libra."

I nod. "That makes sense. Mine is April 28th."

Her lips curve upward. "That makes you… what, a Taurus? God, never in my life have I met someone who fits that bullish description so perfectly."

"I choose to take that as a compliment." I grin.

She rolls her eyes. "I've got a question. What do you like to do for fun in your downtime?"

I narrow my eyes at her. "This is my downtime. What little I get of it, anyway."

She raises her eyebrows. "Oh."

"Okay, now it's your turn, right?" When she nods, I squint at her.

Her eyes almost close for a second. "I'll go with truth. I don't want to strip down to my underwear or call the royal palace with a fake accent and demand to speak with the prime minister."

My eyebrows go up. "What?"

She blushes. "That's the kind of stupid stuff that you get dared to do in this game."

"Ah!" I chuckle. "Noted. You chose truth though, so…" I pause, thinking for a second. "In your childhood, what do you think was the most memorable experience? No, not memorable…" I struggle to translate the word. *Gribende* is what I keep thinking, but language limits me. "What could you draw a line to from the person you are now and say, that is why I am who I am?"

She gives me a funny look. "I thought for sure you were going to ask me something about sex."

I smirk. "I'm full of surprises."

She wrinkles up her face. "I see that. Umm… I have no idea, really. I just… I'll say that I do remember being maybe seven or eight years old. My mom was on a bender, she was… just off, wherever. And I was supposed to do this project at school that required me to look stuff up. So after school, I went to the public library to use their computers. And I couldn't quite figure out how to use it. You know, the New York public libraries don't exactly get funding for the latest software."

"No?" I ask.

She chuckles. "No. Anyway, when I eventually found my way to the New York Times site… I was totally blown away. Just riveted! I remember thinking that I couldn't believe that people were telling other people the news. It just… it really gave me that sort of… light bulb moment, where something lit up inside of me. I spent like three hours reading every single word I could, until one of the librarians shooed me off the computer."

I tilt my head to the side, taking in her slow smile and hand gestures as she tells the story. "Let me guess. That was the moment when you decided that you wanted to be a journalist?"

Two pink spots appear in her cheeks. "Yeah, something like that. Although I'm not actually as much of a journalist as I am a photographer."

I nod a little bit. "So you've said. Where is your camera now?"

Margot grins sheepishly. "In my tote bag, less than thirty feet away."

"You'll have to show me some of your photos sometime."

Her flush intensifies, creeping down her neck. She looks away. "Maybe some time." She clears her throat and shakes her head. "But not now. We're in the middle of a game, aren't we?"

I nod my head slowly, enjoying the nearness of her. What would it take to get her in my lap, I wonder? My head cocks to the side as I picture that particular image.

She looks at me, her lips twitching. "I have a good question. If there was no such thing as money, and you could do anything you wanted, what would you devote your life to?"

"Wait. You didn't ask me whether I prefer to tell the truth or perform a dare."

Her eyes roll. "All right. Truth or dare, I guess."

Eyeing Margot, I bite my lip. Then I move closer to her until my thigh touches hers. She looks down at the spot where our bodies meet, making some kind of calculations.

I wish I could read her mind, just for a moment.

"Truth," I say.

Her gaze flicks up to my face. She licks her lips. "I already asked you my question."

I sprawl out on the couch, laying both of my arms on the back. I'm already close enough to Margot that I could put my arm around her with ease; if I moved my right arm another half inch, I would be hugging her. I can feel the heat from her body against my skin.

Her eyes grow large. Her pupils dilate just a little.

I'm careful not to move again. After the last week of almost kissing her, of almost seducing her, I'm okay with just teasing her for a bit. It's impossible not to smirk as I answer her question.

I lean my head back, forcing myself to focus. "Hmm. If money were no object?"

She nods, leaning back. Her head rests against my arm and she doesn't jerk away.

I bite my lip, giving her another smirk. She looks at me, only a few inches away. We are so close that I can see a few faint freckles on her nose, can make out her the dark shadow of her lashes against her skimmed cream cheeks.

"I was trained as a pilot when I was in the Navy," I tell her. "I did two years there, and I have to say, I quite liked it. I enjoyed being up in the air, in charge of everything that I saw. Everything else… when the ground fell away from the plane, so did everything else."

She wrinkles her nose. "Do you think you could ever be happy living like that? I mean… not living as a royal."

I shrug, resting my head back and looking up at the ceiling again. "Who's to say? I don't plan on finding out." I suck in a deep breath. "I'm a member of the royal family, Margot. I owe certain things to my country. And one of them is my life…" I shake my head just a little. "I will always be a prince, first and foremost. I will always have my obligations. It's just… it's part of the whole package, for better or worse."

When she speaks, her voice is a mere whisper. "I know, Stellan."

I roll my head to the side, flashing her a half-hearted smile. "God, my grandmother would love to know that those words just came out of my mouth. She's always on my back about how I owe the country this and that… My honor and… whatever else." I exhale. "It's hard not to want to be different, though. It's really damned hard."

I look right in Margot's eyes as I say the last line.

The grate of her voice stirs me. "There are… there are rules you have to abide by. Right? Rules you can never, ever think about breaking?"

My throat works as I swallow my sudden burst of anger. Anger at the fact that I'm royal, anger at what is expected of me. "Yes." I reach out to cup her face, my fingers trailing over her jawline. That contact is electric, charging the air, lighting me up inside. "My life is not my own. I can't live however I want. In many ways, I have less freedom than anyone else." I suck in another breath, my gaze dipping down to her mouth. "The crown comes before all else. Especially my own wishes."

She leans in, pressing her lips ever so lightly over mine. I close my eyes, struggling not to give in. I want to kiss her back so badly that my hands are shaking.

But I know where that leads. That's the exact way that we ended up in this mess, isn't it?

Margot's hand comes up to sink into my hair. She kisses me again, her lips soft and warm. She shifts her body to touch mine; her breasts brush up against my chest, her free hand grazes my knee.

When she kisses me a third time, the touch of her lips and against mine so light and gentle that it's almost painful not to respond. I finally give in.

I kiss her back, my hand slipping from her jaw and knotting in her hair. Angling her head just so, I tease her lips with the tip of my tongue. She opens her mouth and I sweep my tongue against hers, moaning at the sweet taste. Cinnamon, mint, and a sultry hint of something deeper.

A sweet, feminine musk. I've been dreaming of that flavor; I know that I can taste more of it if I spread her thighs and feast on her damp pussy.

God, if only.

I pull away from her lips, gasping for breath. Bowing my head, I close my eyes and struggle to pull air into my lungs.

"Fucking hell," I mutter. "What the fuck is wrong with me?"

Margot doesn't say anything. She just leans her forehead against mine for a long moment. Then she kisses my cheek, the gesture perfectly chaste.

I open my eyes in time to see her stand up. I meet her deep blue eyes, which are so full of sorrow that it's almost heartbreaking to see.

"I'm sorry, Stellan," she says. She looks away and pulls at the hem of her skirt.

I stand up, straightening to my full height. That only makes the air between us crackle with some strange electricity, but I just frown. "I meant it when I said the crown comes before everything else. It comes before me. It comes before you." I shrug, feeling a sense of helplessness. "And whatever this is? This… desire? It comes before that, too."

She tosses her hair, her mouth curving into a frown to match my own. "I know."

I pause, drinking the sight of her in. Then I turn toward my bedroom, seeking solitude. "Goodnight, Margot."

If she says anything else, I don't hear it before I'm out of the room.

Chapter Twenty-Six

MARGOT

WHEN I GET up the next morning, the late morning sun pours in through the window. Lying in bed, I think about last night. The memory of the way that Stellan looked at me, so soulful and direct, even as he told me why we shouldn't kiss… It warms me in my bed, makes my whole body tighten and flash hot.

It's funny… I think the mere illicitness of the relationship makes Stellan more desirable. I want what has been explicitly forbidden to me… the specter of what a kiss could turn into makes my desire twice as intense.

Groaning into my pillows, I know that it really doesn't matter what I want. Isn't that the point Stellan was trying to make?

I get up and go to the kitchen, looking around for him. He's nowhere to be found. So I just spend a couple of hours getting dressed and feeding myself a toasted bagel. I start a jigsaw puzzle on the floor of the living room.

That's where Stellan finds me when he comes in from his run. I look up at him as he enters the room and my eyes widen. He's wearing a t-shirt and running shorts, and his whole body is damp with sweat. He pulls out his earbuds, still out of breath.

"*Haj*," he says.

"Hey." I put my arms behind me and size him up. "Are we in a fight?"

He looks a little surprised. "I don't think so." He pauses, taking a deep breath and exhaling loudly. "Do you want to go for a walk? There's a water-fall that's only about two miles from here. I'd like to go see it, spend a little more time communing with nature before I have to return to civilization tomorrow."

My lips lift in the ghost of a smile. "Sure."

"Great. Let me get changed. We'll leave in five minutes, *ja?*"

I nod, putting the pieces of the puzzle back in the box. I toss my black leather jacket on over my dark jeans and black tank top. By the time I get my Converse on my feet, Stellan is rearing to go.

"You ready?" he asks. He seems… distracted.

"Yep." I follow him outside, zipping up my jacket against the cold.

I take a second to give him a once over. He's wearing dark jeans, an off-white Henley shirt, and a cobalt blue jacket. He's also nearly vibrating with a restless kind of energy that keeps his eyes on the horizon. They rove around the countryside as we stroll, looking everywhere but where I'm at.

Ah, that's it. He's trying not to look at me. I suppose I should do the same, then.

I stuff my hands into the pockets of my jacket, looking around me. We walk up the steep cobblestone road, emerging onto a road outside of the village pretty quickly. On either side of the road is the greenest pasture land, contrasting with the seemingly endless skies, a fat swath of white just barely tinged with blue.

We start veering left; in the distance I can see the shore of the land looming near. As we walk, the road only grows steeper. We don't have to talk; we each struggle to draw in breath as we continue to climb. I can't help but sneak looks at Stellan.

Two spots of red ride high in his cheeks. His dark hair ruffles in a gust of wind. He's handsome and brooding and everything I never thought I would want.

Stellan eventually notices me looking at him.

"It's not much farther," he says gruffly. "I promise."

I merely shrug, stuffing a quip about how he always keeps his promises deep down inside myself. He turns out to be right, though. As he leads me up a little hill, I can hear the water rushing. It gets louder with every step I take, though I can't see the source of it at all.

We are getting closer and closer to where the land drops off dramatically, ending on a cliff that overlooks the dark blue, restless sea. Close enough that I can feel the salt spray in the air, feel the rush of the air whipping around my face. By the time I see the waterfall, I'm right on top of it.

Right on the edge of the cliff.

I lean over to look at the waterfall as it spits torrents down the craggy cliff face to fall into the ocean. Stellan pulls me back, his hand gripping my upper arm. "Careful."

Frowning at him, I shake off his hold on me. "I'm fine."

Heading along the edge of the cliff, I find a spot with a full view of the waterfall. It's majestic if a little loud. Then I sit down, dangling my feet over the edge.

Stellan comes to sit beside me, squinting at the horizon. "It's beautiful out here," he murmurs.

I glance at him, at how close he is. His hand nearly touches mine; our thighs are only a few inches apart.

I wish he were closer. Why do I spend so much time longing for this man? I could pick anyone else to have this terrible crush on… but I pick the one person who can't return my affections.

What does that say about me?

He turns and looks at me, his ice blue eyes actually making my heart skip a beat. His gaze drops to my lips, then he heaves a sigh.

"What am I doing, Margot?" he asks. "Why is there this… this heat between us?"

Blushing a little, I duck my head. "I don't know," I admit. "But I feel it too."

He blows out a slow breath. "I like you."

Wrinkling up my face, I nod. "I know."

He looks at me, a little surprised. "You do?"

I roll my eyes, a smile on my lips. "Yes. Something about all the kissing tipped me off to the fact that you might have feelings of some kind for me."

He squints at me. "I am so fucking tired of all the expectations that are heaped on me. I just…"

I cut him off with a kiss. Stellan brings up his hand and cups my jaw, returning my kiss with a passion and a vigor that surprises me. I slide my hand around his neck and bury it in his short hair.

The entire time he's touching me, my whole body is awakening. Tingling, flashing hot, aching. He finds the seam of my mouth. I open to him eagerly, unable to bridle my reaction. His tongue sweeps the inside of my mouth and dances with mine.

He tastes like the way I imagine the earth feels right after a rainstorm; fresh, sharp, wet, and clean. I moan into his mouth as he pushes me down onto the ground, his mouth leaving mine to trail kisses down my jaw.

He pauses for a second, his eyes finding mine. "I want you so badly, Margot. But I won't make any promises about what the future holds—"

I kiss him again. "I don't care. Take me if you want me," I whisper against his lips. "I'm yours."

He brushes my hair away from the column of my neck, kissing and nipping the sensitive skin he finds there, sucking at my pulse point. I slip my free hand around his back, beneath his jacket and shirt. Finding a hot, smooth expanse of skin there, I rake my nails delicately across his lower back.

He growls at me, moving his mouth down to explore my collarbone, the top of my breasts. His mouth is delightfully hot and wet. Unzipping my leather jacket, he kisses my breasts through my dark tank top, shaping them with his hands. I can feel the wet heat of his mouth even through the fabric.

"Fuck," I murmur. "That feels so good."

I toss my head back and bite my lip, moving my hand around to feel the sharp lines of his hip and Adonis belt. He growls and pulls back, stripping off his jacket and pulling his shirt over his head.

My eyes widen. He is perfect, from his muscular arms and rippling abs to his clenched jaw and the sheer need in his eyes. It's like someone has just given me a hit of something strong, and now I'm in free fall.

When he starts pulling off my leather jacket and hiking my shirt up, I groan and reach for the zipper on his fly. I unzip his jeans and get my hand inside, wrapping it around his long, thick, hot cock.

Stellan groans and lets me work my hand up and down his length briefly. The skin of his cock feels velvety soft in my hand, hot and veiny. I bite my lip and watch his face, monitoring his reactions.

His eyes roll back in his skull for a minute, but soon he loses patience with my hand. He pushes me onto my back and tugs my shirt up over my head, kissing my newly bared breasts with such enthusiasm that I laugh a little, my head tipping back as I arch into his kisses. His tongue feels a little bit raspy on my nipples, as though he were part cat.

I open my legs and urge him to lie between them, guiding him with only my feet. He reaches between us and unzips my jeans, pushing them down a little.

He groans with frustration when he realizes that it's impossible for him to touch me like that. He rolls us both over so that I'm on top, then starts pushing my jeans down.

"Get these off," he orders. "Panties, too."

I'm only too happy to oblige him. It's the work of half a minute to strip myself completely. When I return to his embrace, I find him looking at me like I'm a prize fucking mare.

"God, you're so beautiful," he murmurs, running his hands down both my sides.

I blush bright pink. "Thank you," I whisper. "You're not so bad yourself."

Stellan pulls me back down to kiss me. I push down his jeans, anxious to have him inside of me. His cock touches the inside of my thigh and we both groan.

God, this needs to happen right fucking now.

Reaching down, I grab his cock and position the blunt head to press against my pussy lips. I'm more than ready for him, wet with excitement.

"Hey," he whispers, looking into my eyes. I pause, biting my lip. He moves his hand up to my face, pushing back a strand of hair that is caught against the wetness of my lips. "Go slowly for me, *skatter*. I'm close enough already and I'm not even inside of you."

I lean down, kissing him gently. At the same time, I push myself down ever so slowly, impaling myself on his cock. The fingers of one of his hands slip into my hair and knot there.

He grunts as my pussy stretches to take his whole cock. His free hand wanders down to my breasts, shaping them and pinching a nipple. Then his hand pushes me back and meanders down to my pussy, his fingers finding my clit.

"Fuck!" bursts from my lips. My pussy feels so incredibly full; his fingers tap out a rhythm against my clit that makes me writhe.

And then he starts to bounce my whole body up and down on his cock. I look up at the sky, my mouth opening, sensation blossoming. It flows from my pussy up to my tits. My whole body tightens.

Stellan stops suddenly, making me hit him with my balled up fists. "Don't stop!"

He growls and uses all his strength to flip our positions, his weight settling against my core. "Be good for a minute, *skatter*."

He starts to withdraw and plunge back inside my pussy, moving so slowly that I could scream. I writhe underneath him, needing more. "Faster, Stellan. *Please.*"

He picks up my legs and puts them over his shoulders, moving faster just like I begged him to. My hand slips up around the nape of his neck into his hair.

I close my eyes, the sensations driving me ever closer toward the edge. "Stellan, yes…" I whisper. "God, that's it. Right there. Don't stop…"

He kisses me, a breathless affair. And then he starts fucking me with short, staccato movements, jackhammering his cock into my pussy.

"Oh god," I breathe. I make noises but I'm not sure what I say. I am only aware of the friction between our bodies, of the spring deep inside of me that tightens and tightens, slowly, bit by bit, until I burst.

I come without warning, shaking, screaming, gripping Stellan with my legs. Inside I'm falling off the edge of a precipice into a canyon of sensation, crashing toward the shore like a tsunami.

Stellan stiffens and cries out something I don't understand in Danish, pumping into my body, his semen feeling hot as it enters my pussy in long lashes.

"Fuck, *skatter*," he mumbles, slowing at last. "Christ."

A note of laughter bubbles to my lips. I'm high, I think; high on him. Stellan leans down and kisses my lips so passionately and forcefully that I lose my breath all over again.

When he pulls out of my pussy and lies down beside me, he's still struggling to breathe. A shiver runs up my spine and he gives me a guilty look.

"*Ja*, I know." He pulls his pants up and then starts dressing me, which is a little weird. "I should've just fucked you last night instead of dragging you out here to a waterfall to fuck."

My lips curl upward. "I didn't say anything."

He purses his lips and tries to pull my shirt down over my head. I laugh and grab the shirts from him. "I can dress myself."

Then he kisses me deeply, until I almost forget that I am cold. "Come on. Let's go back to the house."

Pulling on my pants, I arch a brow. "Are you ready to go home already?"

He pulls his shirt on over his head, wrinkling his nose at me. "No. I can think of about ten different ways I would like to fuck you, if I'm honest. I just don't want to get caught with my pants down out here."

Biting my lip, I give him a daring look. "I'll race you back to the house."

Stellan takes off without warning, apparently taking my challenge to heart. I laugh as I start running after him, feeling more playful than I have since I was a kid.

Chapter Twenty-Seven

MARGOT

WE BARELY MAKE it inside the house before Stellan is on me again. He stops me at the kitchen island, turns me around, and lifts me onto the smooth marble counter. Bending his head just a little, he kisses me hard, then leaves a stinging bite on my throat.

I suck in an audible breath. "Oh…"

He pauses to look at me, his eyes scanning my face to gauge my reaction. "I want to play rough."

A shiver runs down my spine. "By all means. Don't let me stop you…"

He looks at me like a kid who's just been given a lifetime supply of candy; like he can't believe that I actually gave him permission to be rough. "*Ja?*"

When I nod, he slides his hand through my hair and grips it hard, pulling my head back a fraction of an inch. "You have only to say stop, *skatter.*"

I give him a slow smile. "Why would I tell you to stop doing what makes me hot?"

Stellan groans a little, pulling at my leather jacket. "We need to go somewhere with a bed so I can fuck you in it. I need your body, *skatter.*"

My face heats. "Oh?"

He's already moving me backward through the house, kissing me and groping me. I love every minute of it too, getting wet just knowing that he *needs* me. He backs me into a bedroom, throwing me on the bed.

"Take your pants off. Actually, I want all of it gone. I need you bare before me."

It only takes a second for me to ditch my clothes. When I'm naked before his gaze, he looks at my mouth, my tits, the apex of my thighs.

He moves back to look at me, and I see the fire raging in his eyes. A fire that I feel too, a fire that could consume us both for all I care. His gaze drops to my lips, and I lean forward, lips parting. He moves to kiss me, his lips firm and demanding.

This is no peck on the lips. His tongue invades my mouth, sweeping and exploring. My tongue dances with his as I sigh and sink into it.

Curling my hand around the back of his neck, I reach out boldly with my free hand and grasp his hip. He allows it for a second, then breaks off the kiss and pushes me back onto the bed.

"Stay there," he orders me.

He begins to undress, taking off his shoes, pulling his tee shirt off over his head. His torso ripples as he does, and I admire his light dusting of dark chest hair. He's also got a trail of hair that leads down from his belly button and disappears into his waistband. His arms flex as he unzips his jeans, but he stops there.

I get a tantalizing peek into his unbuttoned pants as he comes closer, just for a second.

He moves onto the bed, kneeling at the end. He considers me for a moment, like he's trying to decide what to do with me. "Come here."

I shiver as I move closer, feeling like I'm under a microscope. He narrows his eyes and runs a single fingertip across my collarbone, down under the remaining strap of my slip. He draws the strap off of my shoulder, and then rolls the top of the slip down until my pink nipples are exposed to the air.

"I've imagined this a hundred times," he says absently, his eyes fixed on my nipples. "But there is no comparison to the way you actually taste."

He leans down, cupping one breast and pulling the nipple to his mouth. I immediately groan at the sensation of his hot, wet mouth on my flesh. He rolls it around with his tongue, then bites it very carefully, almost like he's testing me.

"Ahh!" I gasp. "You can do it harder."

He smirks, looking up at me. "Permission noted."

Then he elbows me aside, lying down. I look at him a little quizzically, but in the next second he lifts me onto his body, so that I'm straddling him. He angles me so that he's planted face first between my breasts, and my bare ass is in the air. I'm a little shocked at how easily he picked me up, but he clearly has other things on his mind.

He licks the skin between my breasts with his tongue, then pulls one nipple into his mouth. I moan as he bites it and sucks it, alternating pain and pleasure for me. His hands wander down to my hips, bunching up my slip. He runs his hands over my ass, groaning when he finds that I am bare underneath the slip.

He releases my breast with a wet pop, looking up at me. "*Fuck*. You're not wearing any panties. Do you know how much that turns me on?"

I blush, slowly shaking my head. "Uh uh."

He pushes my hips down until my pussy is pressed directly against his cock through his unbuttoned jeans. We both groan as he bucks up against me. He runs his hand through my hair, fisting it, and uses his hand on my hip to guide me just where he wants me.

I gasp silently as he lifts his hips and bears down on me, his denim-clad cock almost touching my clit. He starts kissing and licking my neck, using my hair as a tool to move my head to his liking. He sucks the spot where my neck meets my shoulder, bucking his hips up, and my eyes roll back into my head.

"Ahh!" I cry. "Stellan—"

He's not satisfied with that, though. He releases me, pushing me off of his lap. I'm left breathing hard. He gets up and starts to peel his jeans off.

I'm taken aback for a moment by the image of Stellan, completely naked. I've seen it before, but it's every bit as stunning to see him nude this time as it was the last. He's all muscle, his cock juts proud out… and right now, he's looking at me like he's going to consume me.

He climbs onto the bed, dragging me down to lie beneath him, and he starts kissing my neck again. I wrap my arms and legs around him, pulling him closer. I can feel his hardness against my thigh, long and hot and throbbing. He sucks at my neck, my breasts, and then he moves lower.

I don't know if I can even handle his mouth on my clit, but he passionately kisses my thighs and my knees. His scruff tickles in the best way. I open my legs wide for him, spreading my thighs. He makes a growling sound as he kisses my clit, and my whole body is suddenly alive with electric sensation.

"Oh my god!" I cry out, my hands burying in his hair.

Already, I'm bucking my hips against his mouth, desperate for more. He closed his mouth around my clit and sucks on it in long pulls, each one sending ripples of sensation up my spine. My toes curl as he brings his hand up to my pussy and introduces one thick finger. He ever so slowly pushes his finger inside as he circles my clit with his tongue.

I come suddenly, clenching and crying out. His tongue slows, helping me ride out my orgasm. Soon though, he climbs up my body, kissing me hard. I taste the faint flavor of my own juices on his tongue and shudder.

He pulls back a little bit, grasping his cock and positioning himself just so. The blunt tip of his cock presses against my pussy, and I still for just a second. I'm busy looking at his cock, trying to understand how the hell it ever fits inside me. He pushes inside the barest inch. I cry out from pleasure and pain all at once.

Stellan glances down at me, biting his lip. "You're so tight, *skatter.*"

I'm honestly not sure if that's a good thing or not, judging by his face alone. He looks like he's trying to defuse a bomb or something. I wrap my legs around his hips, pulling at him a little, urging him onward.

He closes his eyes and pushes himself inside, inch by slow inch. I feel like he's stretching me out, little by little, filling me up and touching every single part of me. It's uncomfortable, even though I'm wet.

When he is finally inside me to the hilt, he opens his eyes, staring down at me with the most intense black-brown gaze I've ever experienced.

I look him right in the eye, realizing in that moment that I'm in love with him. I don't care that his dick is so big that it hurts a little; I'm too busy being stupidly, dumbly in love with Stellan.

I reach up to pull his mouth down to mine, tenderly kissing him. He kisses me back, starting to move his body, withdrawing his cock and then thrusting back in.

"Ahhh, that's so good," he mutters, raising himself up so that he can see our bodies joined together. "Fuck, Margot. God, you're so damned beautiful."

He grabs my wrists and pulls them up above my head, working his thick cock in and out. I dig my heels into his upper back as he starts kissing and biting my neck again. I start to forget the discomfort, focusing instead on the pleasure of his lips on my skin, the wonderful weight of his body against mine.

I moan as he releases my hands in order to palm my breasts. It feels natural to wrap my arms around him to lightly rake my fingernails down his back.

Stellan suddenly withdraws from me, flipping me over. He guides me to my hands and knees, positioning his cock at my entrance before he plunges back inside.

"Ohhh!" I cry out, feeling my innermost muscles clench.

"Your pussy feels so good," he grits out. He takes my hand and guides it down to my clit, rubbing it in gentle circles. "I want you to come again. Show me what a good girl you are. Make yourself come for me."

His words send a shudder of pleasure down my spine. He lets go of my hand and grabs my hips, thrusting his cock into me again and again, as hard as he can. I call out, an insensible sound, as I start to touch myself.

The way he is fucking me now is rougher, coarser than before… but for some reason I like it more. A lot more. I close my eyes, rubbing my clit, and feeling the brutal way he handles me, ramming into me over and over again.

An invisible spring tightens deep inside me with every thrust, feeding my craving. My fingers help me along, but it's really Stellan's cock that makes little ripples of pleasure swell and burst across my body.

He's touching some spot deep inside me, a spot that I seem to be able to angle my body just so to encourage him to hit over and over again.

"Yes," I groan desperately. "Yes, right there… I…"

And then I'm calling out his name, screaming it, as I go over the edge, falling into a deep ocean of pleasure. He stiffens and growls, filling me with three single, brutal thrusts. I can feel him pulsing inside my pussy.

He slows at last, half-collapsing on the bed with me. He turns me over, kissing me tenderly. I cling to him, feeling…

Loved? Freshly fucked? Overwhelmed?

I lay on his chest, listening to his rapid heartbeat as it begins to slow. My eyelids begin to droop, and my breathing evens out. I'm not asleep per se, but I'm not far from it. When he speaks, it startles me.

"Ready to go again?" he asks, his voice barely more than a rumble in his chest.

I open my eyes and squint at him. "Again?"

He chuckles, brushing my hair back from my neck. He places a long, lazy kiss on my bare skin. "You want me, don't you?"

I bite my lip, but we both already know my answer.

It's yes. It will always be yes, for him.

Chapter Twenty-Eight

STELLAN

GOING BACK to real life after a full weekend of Margot seems like the world twisting a cruel knife in my gut. And yet here I am, back in the palace, going through my schedule for the next month with Erik and a young woman from the royal press office.

I try not to look completely disinterested as Nora pushes a piece of paper to me across the dining room table.

"These are the schools you are engaged to speak at this month," she says, looking down at the stack of papers on the table in front of her.

"Mm," I say vaguely.

Erik clears his throat, looking up from where he's seated beside me. "Is that a '*mm, I approve*' or a '*mm, I don't approve*'? Send a smoke signal. Help us out here."

I consider him, frowning. Then I look at Nora. "I approve of everything you have to present me with today. I think we should wrap this up, don't you?"

Nora flushes, rising and clearing her throat. She gathers her papers and bobs me a curtsy. "Your highness."

I follow her to the door of the dining room, peeking my head out into the hall to make sure that no one is lurking around. Then I close the door.

Erik kicks his feet up on the table, scanning me critically. "What's up with you? You usually tell the press office to cancel at least half of your engagements."

I walk to the window, looking out over the gardens. "I'm distracted today, I guess."

He's quiet for a few beats. "Does this have to do with Margot?"

I swivel my head toward him, shooting him a glare. "What?"

He looks unruffled. "I know that you flew her up to meet you in Norway over the weekend. People talk."

I look back out the window, my face contorting. "*Pis,*" I curse. I heave a sigh.

Erik stands up, stretching. "So? Did you two finally fuck?"

"*Ja,*" I admit. Then I think about what he just said and turn to give him a hard stare. "And what do you mean, finally?"

He rolls his eyes. "Please. You two were always going to fuck. I saw the future written all over your face when you first told me that Margot was going to be coming here."

I snort. "You can't have known that."

"We've been best friends for twenty years. I've never seen you as far gone for a girl as you were when we left New York. If you think I didn't pick up on the sparks between you two, you're crazy."

I consider that for a second and then nod slowly. "You're right. I won't deny it. We did fuck like two rabbits. On every surface, multiple times. Four times in the shower."

A grin spreads across his face. "I knew it!"

"*Ja, ja.* You're psychic." I screw up my face. "I'm not sure what is wrong with me, though. Usually after I fuck a girl, I don't think about her again. Margot is still in my system, I guess."

I crack my knuckles, brooding. Erik walks over to where I'm standing, leaning his shoulder against the window's frame. He looks at me carefully.

"Are you in love with her?"

Shooting him a dark look, I cross my arms. "What? No. I only recently decided that I don't hate her, honestly."

He smirks at me. "You know what they say about there only being a thin line between love and hate…"

I scowl at him, opening my mouth to retort. But I don't get a chance. The heavy door to the room flies open, a butler hurrying to get inside the room.

"We're having a private conversation," Erik starts calling.

That's when my grandmother steps into the room, her eyes narrowing at us. She looks as polished as ever in her white woolen skirt suit. "Mr. Moen. Your services are no longer needed. Take the rest of the day off."

Erik's eyebrows fly upward. He understands that my grandmother has way more power than he does; he bows to her, sliding a quick look my way. "Your majesty."

"I'll catch up with you tonight," I tell him, waving him away. Then I turn to my grandmother. "You look lovely today, *Momse*."

She gives me a look that is nothing short of withering. "Get your jacket. We both have an engagement at the *Rigshospitalet*, the children's hospital."

My eyebrows rise slightly. "I think I'm supposed to be at some kind of children's puppetry thing in an hour."

Ida stares at me coolly. "Meet me downstairs at the car in five minutes. Don't keep me waiting."

"*Ja*, of course" I say, but she's already turned and is marching out of the room.

As I gather my dark suit jacket and add a dark blue tie, I try to figure out just what she wants with me. My fingers freeze as a stray thought crossed my mind: what if Ida somehow knows about Margot and I fucking?

Surely not... right? I mean, she would have to have spies everywhere for that to be the case. Trying to recount to myself the handful of people who would know *and* could've told her, I head down to the limo that is pulled up downstairs.

My palms are a little sweaty as I reach the car. She's already inside. She's small and frail, and yet... she carries herself with the kind of poise that a supermodel would kill for.

When I slide in, Ida waits until we start moving to eye me. "May I be frank with you, Stellan?"

I incline my head. "Please, *Momse*."

She looks away, out her window. "Your grandfather was a mighty king. He was fair and just, but he was first and foremost Denmark's king. Before me. Before his children." She pauses, drawing a breath and pushing it out. "Having such a remote father figure had an undesirable effect on his children."

My eyebrows rise. "On my father?"

Ida clears her throat, swinging her gaze around to me. "It was a personal failing, as I see it. I felt responsible. And I was determined that the next generation... that's you, dear... I was determined that you should grow up with a strong sense of duty. And I hoped that your grandfather would be able to carry the crown until you were ready for it. But... that obviously wasn't meant to be."

I am more than a little surprised that my grandmother is being so forthcoming.

"I'm sorry about grandad passing." I reach out and touch her forearm. She gives me a resigned smile and pats my hand a few times.

"Thank you. But that's not really the point I am trying to make. I am trying to say that I am not omniscient. I don't see everything. I can't always catch every little mistake and correct it before other people see it."

Fuck. So she does want to talk about Margot. A solid mass of angst rises in the pit of my stomach.

"*Momse...*" I begin, trying to decide. Should I deny the allegations she's about to lay against me? Or maybe it would be better to explain. "Let me—"

She cuts me off. "Stop." She draws a line in the air with her hand. "Listen to what I'm saying."

I settle back, looking at her with a blank expression.

"I need you to really take what I'm telling you seriously." She pauses. "It's time that you settled on a wife."

I shake my head. "I don't—"

"Stop talking for a moment!" she cries, her hands balling into fists. "You are not listening! We are out of time. Your father is not well. Do you hear me? He's ill. He may need to be replaced at any time."

My mouth opens and closes. My eyes are fixed on her small figure. "... what?"

"Your father is ill, Stellan. The doctors aren't sure what is wrong with him, but he's been forgetting things for a long time. And then last week he just fainted. We revived him but he had trouble with his vision... He was blind for almost a day." She draws in a shaky breath. "I learned about it from a phone call. Gorän says it wasn't a big deal, but I know he is wrong."

A million questions race around my head, half of which Ida probably doesn't have the answer to. I try to marshal my thoughts.

"Where is he? When are my parents arriving back home?"

My grandmother looks upset. "Your father is insistent that he and your mother continue on their world tour. I tried every argument I could think of… he will not hear anything different."

"That's…" I search for the word. "That's *absurd*. He needs to come home and be checked into the hospital."

Ida shrugs. "I quite agree. Do you think I would be here with you if I had the option of being by my own son's bedside? But it's not in your father's nature to be told what to do or where to go. That leaves me in the rather precarious position of getting you ready for coronation. And the first step of that process is to find a suitable marriage partner."

"It's not like I have to be married," I fire back.

She glares at me. "It's what has always been done."

"So?" I ask, defensive.

I blow out a breath, looking out the window. We're driving through downtown Copenhagen and many beautiful multicolored building fly past my view. But I can't even take that in; I'm just floored by my father's illness and my grandmother's demands.

"Stellan," she says sharply. I look at her, trying like all hell to keep my emotions off my face. The last thing I need right now is for all my secrets to come out. And I swear, Ida has a way of just looking at me and knowing what is in my soul.

It's time to chance the subject.

"I'm worried about father," I say, hedging a little. Yes, I am worried about him… but there are other things, bigger secrets, that are in the forefront of my mind just now.

"Are you going to make me pick a girl for you?"

Startled, I frown at her. "Do you really think I would let you do that?"

She folds her hands in her lap and favors me with a hard look. "It's not really an issue of what you'll allow. I don't want to select a mate for you. But if you don't, I will."

"Momse," I say, my voice gone to grit. She looks at me, her eyes tightening. "I'm telling you right now. If you do that, if you so much as bring a single girl around with the purpose of getting me engaged, I will freeze you out. Don't make me do that."

We pull up to the children's hospital just then. My grandmother doesn't take her eyes off of me, though.

"Decide for yourself if you want to. You've got a month. Then I will start to make plans on your behalf." The driver opens her door and helps her out, leaving me scowling after her.

"Your highness?" the driver says, looking in the car.

I don't want to go inside, not after what Ida just said. But I'm finding that what I want rarely factors into any decisions when it comes to the royal family. So I just get out of the limo, rearranging my scowl into a pleasant smile.

There are a few photographers, and I raise my hand to them, waving politely. But inside, I'm a seething mass of anger.

Chapter Twenty-Nine

MARGOT

"I'M SORRY, MADAME." The butler bows his head. "His royal highness Prince Stellan has stepped out rather unexpectedly."

I wrinkle my nose, unsurprised. Of course Stellan doesn't show up the day after we fucked each other's brains out. *Of course.*

"Ah. Thank you." I lift my camera from my tote bag. "Would it be okay with you guys if I just took some photographs? Just you know, the dining room and the salons…"

"Of course, madame. We have been instructed by the press office that you are to be given full access to the upper half of the palace. Will you need anything else?"

"No, no." I shake my head and give him a halfhearted smile. "I'm fine."

The butler bows and retreats, leaving me alone in the corridor just outside Stellan's study. Biting my lip, I look around. I try the study… but of course, it is locked.

What could I have hoped to find in there anyway? Stellan's private diary with all his innermost thoughts jotted down just for me?

Unlikely.

Besides, he's made enough of a statement by just not showing up than anything I could've read.

I just wander the halls, opening doors at random. Mostly I find the rooms empty or filled with the ghostly shapes of furniture with the dust covers on. Climbing the stairs, I am drawn to the elegantly draped window that dominates the end of the hall.

I snap a few photos of it, and then draw the see-through curtain aside. Aiming my camera lens down onto the street, I catch an unexpected sight.

A flash of a familiar hair color. It's bright red, like a candy apple.

Yeah, that's got to be Pippa. And she's wearing a loose white romper and beaming at a man. She says something and he picks her up, whirling her around. When he stops, she kisses him. Then he glances my way, laughing.

My eyebrows fly up. It's Lars Løve, Stellan's younger brother.

Whoa. That is a hell of a secret to keep, especially for someone as chatty as Pippa.

Pippa bats at his arm. He puts her down and then heads off at a loping run. Pippa turns like she is going to walk somewhere, maybe to our apartment or the offices of *Politiken*.

I stuff my camera in my bag and sprint downstairs, catching up with her in less than a minute. She looks at me, her blue eyes widening.

"Margot!" she squeaks. "I haven't even seen you since Thursday night. Where have you been?"

I chuckle. "Do you really think you're just going to distract me with a question like that?"

A hint of pink lights up her cheeks. "What?"

"Did I just see you kiss Lars on the lips just a minute ago? You two looked pretty comfortable..."

She tosses her fiery hair, glancing around. The blush spreads further across her cheeks and darkens to a red hue. "Shh." She pulls me further away from the palace. "It was just a one time thing. No need to announce it, okay?"

I grin at her. "Umm, wow. I had no idea that you were sucked into the royal family like *that*."

She throws up her hands in front of her face, hiding. "It's... complicated. Lars and I go way, way back."

My eyebrows rise. "What? Tell me everything!"

She peeks at me from behind her hands. "How about I tell you everything over a cup of coffee? I haven't had any caffeine today and I'm dying."

"It's a deal," I say, putting my arm around her. "There's a coffee shop around the corner. Come on, let's hurry so you can spill your guts all over the place."

Pippa rolls her eyes but doesn't resist as I pull her along. I wasn't kidding about the cafe being really close; when we turn a corner, there it is, all glass and pastel colors inside. We order and then take our seats outside.

I lean forward eagerly. "Tell me everything," I demand.

Pippa wrinkles her nose. "I met Lars when I went to St. Malo, a prestigious boarding school in Switzerland. And before you even start, I want you to know that I only went to a school that the Danish royal family would send their child to because I was offered a full scholarship."

I shrug. "I wasn't judging."

Her shoulders relax a fraction. "Oh. Well… yeah. I've known Lars since we were both just kids. He was a year older than me at school… and he was also my first kiss."

"Whoa. That sounds like a relationship."

She glances at me sharply. "It is definitely *not* a relationship. It's just… a friendship that has lasted a long time. It's complicated."

I stare her down. Is she for real? It seems like she really believes it, but I'm not sure where I stand.

The barista brings our drinks out and Pippa makes a big deal of thanking her and sipping her latte. I level her with a long look.

"So if you're just friends, what happened between you last night?"

She flushes. "Too much wine. We just… fell into old patterns."

"Old patterns like sleeping together?" I ask, scoffing.

Pippa looks down at her latte, running her finger over the white cup's handle. Her mouth twists with humor, but I see a faint echo of sadness on her face too. "Yes."

I take a sip of my latte, savoring the creaminess of it while I look at her. "Why are you two not dating?"

She looks up, a little bit of alarm on her face. "Well, for one thing, neither of us is interested in being tied down. Also, not to put too fine a point on it, but there are a million expectations of anyone who openly dates a royal. Not the least of them being the you are well bred and well behaved… and looking for a ring."

I swallow, looking down at my latte. "That does sound like a sticky wicket."

She smirks at me. "You are actually the only person who probably knows better than I do, Margot. Tell me, has anything come of your insane crush on Stellan yet?"

My eyes widen. I blush furiously. "I'm not sure what you mean."

She shakes her head at me. "Oh, please. Ever since the second you laid eyes on him, you've been making this face at him. Like this."

She angles her face and flutters her lashes. I make a disgruntled sound.

"Uh! No. I am not like that!" I protest.

"Oooh, you are too!" she cries, laughing. "Talk about a couple that just seems like they are bound to slip up and end up banging the hell out of each other…"

I feel my face heat. "Pippa…"

She studies me for a second, then grins. "Oh. Oh! I think you already did slip up! You did, didn't you?" She throws her head back and cackles. "I was right!"

"Oh my god," I say, rolling my eyes. "Okay, so Stellan and I finally did it. So what?"

"Umm… yeah, that's not good enough. I'm going to need details. Was it great? Where did you do it? And how did you guys leave things?" She spreads her hands out over the table. "Tell me everything."

I groan. "Please don't make me."

She snots. "Dish."

"Ugh." I run my fingers through the curls in my hair. "Okay. Umm… yes, it was great. We went to a little coastal house in Norway for the weekend and we…" I pause, screwing up my face. "We did everything we wanted to do for a full twenty four hours, on every conceivable surface. And then…" I shake my head. "I thought we left things on a good note, but then he just stood me up today, so…"

I throw my hands up in the air. "Who knows?"

Pippa leans forward. "Do you think he got in his own head? In my experience with Stellan, duty is his weakness. If he spends too long thinking about how he wants to do something but is duty bound to do something else… he ends up doing the un-fun thing. It's just how he is."

"Well… it doesn't really matter. I am not exactly chomping at the bit to get involved with all the crap that comes along with trying to date Stellan. He is great, but…" I shake my head. "The whole 'requirements to date a royal' thing doesn't sound like I'll like it. I'm all about smashing the patriarchy and breaking through glass ceilings, not reinforcing them."

Pippa gives me a look. "You might say that. But what does your heart have to say?"

I give a humorless chuckle. "My heart says what I tell it to say, period. End of story."

"Does it? Tell me, how do you get your heart to listen? That's one of the things that I struggle with constantly." She pouts.

I shift in my seat, not entirely comfortable. "I don't know. You just do."

Her lips lift. She raises her latte to her lips, sipping it coolly. When she sets it down, she eyes me.

"I think you are full of shit."

"What? Why?"

She shrugs. "I think you just haven't given yourself enough time to consider whether you are a complete lovesick fool or whether you're just dabbling. Dipping a toe into Stellan's pool to test the waters." She smirks. "I'm willing to bet you're the former."

"Well, I call bullshit on you not being in love with Lars! It's complicated? I just bet it is, Miss Welch. I think you love him and you're just not willing to say it out loud."

"Ah!" she says, making an outraged sound. "I could say the same for you!"

"No, no. You and Lars share a history. Stellan and I were born under two totally different moons in two completely different solar systems. Okay?"

Pippa's eyes narrow. "I don't think so."

My phone buzzes. I reach for it, checking the screen. Then a warm feeling rushes over me when I read the words.

Sorry about today. Got held up. Meet me at seven tonight? Wear cocktail attire.

There is no signature, but I know who it's from. I smile as I respond.

Just give me an address.

. . .

When I look up, Pippa is surveying me knowingly.

I turn red. "What?" I ask, putting my phone away.

She rolls her eyes. "Don't pretend like that wasn't Stellan. You are so easy to read, it's crazy."

I sigh. "All right, it was Stellan. Happy?"

She reaches across the table, catching my hand. She looks me in the eye. "Yes. I am."

I pull a face. "Do you want to walk with me back to that dress shop? I need something to wear tonight."

She grins. "I can't think of anything that would make me happier. We need to put you in something that is so hot, it'll melt Stellan's tie right off his body."

Giggling at Pippa's description, I down the rest of my latte and then head to do some shopping.

Chapter Thirty

STELLAN

I PULL AT MY TIE, wishing like anything that I could loosen it. But this little gallery opening is as fancy as they come. My black suit and tie just make me one of the crowd.

I take a sip of the old fashioned I ordered at the bar earlier, scanning the gallery for the hundredth time. Margot is running late.

If she's coming at all, that is.

And I'm standing here, uncomfortable in my suit jacket, fending off the general public. I sigh aloud and make myself focus on a large framed photo photograph that's displayed on the wall.

Somehow she sneaks up to stand beside me. When I notice her standing there, looking thoughtfully at the art, I take a step back.

"Jesus christ," I mumble. "You look…"

I trail off. She's wearing a short-sleeved, floor-length dress that is just a shade or two darker than her neon pink hair. Although the dress doesn't show any cleavage or legs, it's so tight that it looks like she was sewn into the damn dress.

She runs a hand through her hair, giving me an uncertain smile. "I hope that sentence ends well."

I nod slowly, trying to unglue my eyes from her tits and ass. "Uh huh."

She cocks her head. "I'm guessing you're not secretly mad at me, then?"

"What?" I glance up and meet her deep blue eyes, puzzled. "Why would I be?"

She shrugs one shoulder, coming close to me. One corner of her mouth turns up. "I didn't know what to think when you didn't show up today."

Casting my gaze out over the gallery, I squint. "*Ja*. My grandmother changed my itinerary unexpectedly. Apparently, no one thought to inform the press office."

"Ah. Is everything okay?"

Her eyes are on me. Probing me. I glance down.

"*Ja*. My grandmother is just reminding me of my duty to the country, I guess. Nothing for you to be concerned about, Margot." I sigh, smoothing my face into a pleasant expression. "Let us talk about other things. The art, for example. I thought you would like the exhibition."

She arches a brow, then swings her gaze to the wall. A large photo of a busy Bombay market hangs in front of us, the image colorful and busy. While she looks at it, taking a little step toward the canvas, I look at her.

Margot really does look beautiful this evening. Her dress rustles a little as she leans forward, then she looks at me, her dark blue eyes crinkling with humor.

"Do you have any idea who this photographer is?"

I screw up my face. "No. This is a benefit for the Copenhagen Contemporary Museum. I just thought that you would appreciate this particular room, that's all. You know. It's the same kind of art that you do."

Her lips curve up. "It's very nice."

I cock a brow. "There seems to be a *but* waiting in the wings."

"But nothing." She comes closer, standing beside me and sliding her hand into the crook of my arm. "Is this okay?"

I look down into her face, my mouth kicking up. I hope that no one looks at the two of us standing so close and assumes that we are guilty of exactly what we are doing… but then again, I don't really care. Not when she's so close.

"*Ja*," I say softly. Bending down, I whisper in her ear. "Your dress is really killing me right now. I'm imagining that it would look so nice on my bedroom floor."

"Stellan!" she admonishes me. Then her lips twitch. "I guess you really aren't mad at me."

"You wouldn't be here if I was." I straighten up as one of my father's cabinet comes into view. "Ah, shit. There is a man over there that I would rather avoid, if I can. Let's keep moving."

Margot lets me guide her into the next room, which is just more of the same thing. Light gray walls, with photographs centered ten feet apart. I flag down a waitress and get her a glass of champagne.

For her part, she seems to pay less attention to the art hanging on the walls than the glamorous people in fancy dresses and swanky suits strolling around. She's unusually closemouthed, which makes me even more curious.

"I can't help but wonder what you're thinking," I say.

She breaks away from her hawk-eyed gaze over the gallery patrons and flushes. "I guess I'm just… absorbing. I had never considered before today that maybe people just live like this. The parties and galas, the freshly pressed suits and fancy dresses…"

"You realize that you are wearing a ballgown, do you not? You're actually a little bit better dressed than almost everyone else here."

She gives me a tiny glare. "This is a rented dress, Stellan. I'm definitely Cinderella in this scenario, trying to fit in at the ball."

I smirk. "Do you have singing mice to dress you?"

"No, but I've got Pippa." She rolls her eyes. "I just… I'm wondering if all billionaires and millionaires are so… hands off. That's what I was thinking, to answer your question."

"Ah. Well… in my family, the answer is definitely no. My mother is very active in her charitable work, most of which involves spending a lot of time with HIV and AIDS patients. My sister Annika is really devoted to working with the NATO peacekeepers. She's gone for a month at a time, advocating on their behalf. Finn spends a good deal of time working with refugees in Spain and Portugal. Anders is worried about feeding the entire world…" I shake my head. "Everyone that I know has their causes that they support and work toward."

She frowns. "But not you?"

"Uhh, no. I mean, I have events like this. I'm a major patron of so many museums and I sit on the board of tons of charities… but when it comes down to it, I just have the crown to worry about. Trust me, it's plenty."

Her eyes meet mine briefly before she glances away. "I see."

I tilt my head to the side. "Do you?"

She nods, screwing up her face briefly. "Actually, yeah. I can imagine that it's an all-encompassing thing. As it should be, I guess. I mean… in the

United States, we have the president. And they have to be on call twenty four hours a day, seven days a week while they're in office. I can't imagine that being the king of Denmark is any different… and that's *for life*."

Making a face, I nod. "*Ja*, that's about the size of it."

She squeezes my arm. "Wanna get out of here for a while? I mean, as long as you are avoiding people…"

I smirk. "I can give you about half an hour. Then people will start to notice my absence, I think."

She grins, mischief lighting her eyes. "Take a walk on the wild side, Prince Stellan. Be bad."

I roll my eyes. "Please. Nobody does bad the way royals do it, okay?"

"Mm." Her eyes dart around the room, spying a partially hidden door. "Let's see where that one goes."

I let her pull me along after her, slipping out the door and into the shadows of the museum after nightfall. Margot slides her small hand into mine and pulls me down the hall.

I would be lying if I said that feeling her warm skin against mine wasn't as exciting as our escape from the gallery benefit. I try to remind myself that I can't actually like this girl… I shouldn't even be here, letting her pull me into a darkened gallery.

But I don't do anything to stop her. I'm not entirely sure I could if I wanted to. She turns the light switches on, a spotlight falling on her and throwing her into profile.

She glances at me, her eyes sparkling with mischief. "Pick a painting." She motions to a couple of paintings. "And look at it for a minute. Then tell me how it makes you *feel*."

"You had me sneak away from the party to critique art?" I ask.

Margot cocks her head, tugging at my elbow. "It's important to look at things and process how we feel about them. Art is all about making that process happen in a safe space. Sometimes what you see intentionally invokes emotion; sometimes it's a more…" She pauses to find the right word. "Internal process, I guess."

She pulls me over to one painting. It looks vaguely familiar. It's small, probably only two feet by three. Hanging in a simple silver frame, it's an enormous field of what looks like wheat, all in oranges and yellows. There is a lone figure cutting the wheat in the far corner. Overhead, a light green sky overshadows the mountains.

"It's… nice, I guess?" I say, tilting my head to take it in from another angle.

Her lips curve upward. "I recognize the painting. It's called *Wheat Field With Reaper*. Look, look how everything is yellow, yellow-green, orange-yellow, gold… There is a man working over here. And he is just surrounded by these dry, *thirsty* colors. I look at all that and I wonder at how hot it is… I can't quite make out the detail of the man's face, but I see him laboring all alone. It's sort of serene, I think."

I nod slowly, glancing down at her. "I can see that."

She gives me a half smile. "It's by Van Gogh, for what it's worth. He said it was about death and how he wasn't scared of dying."

"Ah! For some reason, I find that sort of worrisome."

Margot shrugs a slender shoulder. "I think the next painting is a Van Gogh too. I don't know what it's called, though."

We walk over to look at the painting, which is several trees painted against a field of little white flowers. In the back, a river or a road meanders past.

"Hm." I study the painting.

"What does it make you feel?" she asks delicately. "The mishmash of colors on the trees. The oddly… sort of curvy and pointy bark of the trees. The white and yellow and green of this field of flowers… Back here, you see some blue flowers as well."

She gestures, wiggling her fingers over the painting. I make a face.

"I'm really terrible at this game."

"Just look for another minute. Let that particular bright shade of green soak into your senses. What does it make you think?"

I give her a long look, then glance at the painting. "I don't know. The green is… fresh? Sort of… it has an energy?"

She lights up. "Yes! It definitely does."

Scrunching half my face up, I sigh. "It's spring, obviously. So it kind of makes me wonder what the same place would be like in other seasons."

"It most certainly does." She grins. "That wasn't so bad, was it?"

She looks up at me, her eyes so deep blue, her hair so perfectly pink. Grabbing her by the waist, I pull her against my body and kiss her. I pull in deep lungfuls of her scent, making me horny as fuck and plastering a stupid smile over my face.

When I release her, she turns pink and bites her lip. "Thanks." She giggles. "For the kiss, I mean."

"Oh, that was strictly for my personal pleasure."

Margot rolls her eyes but she has a grin on her lips. "Should we get back?"

I let her go, following her back into the darkened hallway. But as I go, there's something in the pit of my stomach… a sensation I can't quite name.

It sticks with me for the rest of the night, floating around in my head. I don't want to name it, so I pretend it isn't there.

But it definitely is…

Chapter Thirty-One

MARGOT

I HAVE A LONG WEEK. At the newspaper, I have to explain to Anna why I'm not almost done with my article… I haven't even started writing it, but she doesn't need to know that.

Add that to the monotony of the royal routine finally setting in. I arrive in the morning. I spend an hour with Stellan at the palace, more likely than not having intense, gymnastic sex. And then we spend a full day visiting factories, schools, children's hospitals…

It's fun for a few days. And then… it's *work*. By the time I get home at night, I'm dead on my feet.

I can see Stellan getting tired as the week winds down. To myself, I can admit that I'm fairly exhausted too. And yet this is only my third full week of keeping pace with the royal schedule.

I have no idea how all the Løve family do it forever.

Luckily, Stellan proposes the perfect antidote to my exhaustion. A whole weekend at a house on the coast, a two hour drive from Copenhagen. We'll be by ourselves in a mansion…

Yeah, it doesn't sound too shabby. I just have to shove down all my *working class girl* judgments to enjoy it. Without really taking any time to think it through, I tell Stellan yes.

Two hours later, we are so close to the ocean that I can actually smell the salt in the air. As we pull through the trees, the ocean is just right there, down a sandy beach. I sit up as we pull around to a gray, three story mansion house.

The second we stop, Stellan is out of the driver's side. "Look at it!" He points to the gray sea, grinning as he opens the car's trunk. "I could stare at that all day."

I climb out of the car, squinting at the coastline. A gust of wind takes me by surprise and blows up the back of my short black dress. I squeal and smooth my dress down.

Stellan grins at me. "You might as well get naked, because I plan on being au naturel all weekend."

A shiver of excitement runs down my spine at his words. I don't want him to just assume that I am game for anything, although I mostly am. I shoot him a look. "We'll see."

He grabs me and hauls me up against his frame, kissing me hard until I'm just a little breathless. Then he lets me go and picks up the suitcases. "Come on. Wait until you see the inside of this house."

I follow Stellan up the neatly manicured tan brick path into the house. As I step inside, my eyes widen. I look around at the foyer, which is painted with the most amazing mural of a river with nymphs playing around it. There is no furniture here, just this delicate and detailed portrayal painted on the walls.

"What... what is this?" I say, noticing something new every second I keep staring around.

He grins. "Apparently one of my relatives holed themselves up in this house for several years. This was the result."

"Whoa." I move closer to the wall, squinting to make out the detail in one of the nymphs. "This is amazing."

"Wait until you see the living room," he says, nodding his head toward it. "I'm going to go upstairs and drop our things in the master bedroom."

He heads off up a staircase. Nodding absently, I follow the hallway back, taking the first doorway that opens to the left. Inside I find no furniture to speak of. Instead there is light that pours in from the floor length windows, illuminating another breathtakingly detailed painting.

It depicts a plain-looking building, maybe Greek or Roman in design. A robed woman who carries a basket of bread is in the center of the painting. A burst of sunlight shines down on her, signifying that perhaps she is chosen by god. She hands pieces of bread to a flock of ratty looking children, some of whom are crying upon receiving their ration. And the look on the woman's gently lined face… it is so sorrowful, it actually makes my chest seize up.

Stellan comes to lean against the doorframe, ducking a little as he enters the room. "Amazing, isn't it?"

I move closer to the wall, in awe. "It's so lifelike. And her expression… you can tell that whoever did this has felt exactly that kind of sadness before."

"*Ja.* Apparently it is St. Agathe, feeding the children of Carthage." He wrinkles up his face. "After the museum, I got the idea to come here. There are loads more paintings in every room. But this one is really good."

"Who did this painting?" I murmur.

He shrugs. "I think a great aunt, several times removed? I don't know. Someone crazy."

I frown at him over my shoulder. "That's a cruel thing to say."

He rolls his eyes just a little and shrugs again. "Come. Let's go into the kitchen. There is a happier painting in there. It's gold and jeweled, apparently inspired by a Fabergé egg."

He turns and heads down the hallway, expecting me to follow. And I do… but I cast a glance over my shoulder as I leave the room. St. Agathe looks back at me, her eyes so full of sadness that it makes my heart break.

That will stay with me for a good long while, I think.

Stellan shows me a few more paintings, then takes me upstairs to the master bedroom. To my surprise there is no mural waiting for us in here. The walls are robin's egg blue, the room dominated by a giant four poster bed with crisp linens.

He pulls me onto the bed, his blue eyes lit with lust and hunger. He kisses me passionately, already tugging my dress up and over my head. He tosses it to the side without a second thought. I toe my shoes off, sighing as he kisses my neck.

"Fuck," he mutters, sliding his gaze up to meet my own. "Do you realize how fucking beautiful you are, *skatter?*"

My cheeks turn pink. Under his relentless gaze, I feel so *seen*, the opposite of invisible.

"No," I breathe. His look is so direct and frank, so honest. It sears me from the inside out.

When he speaks again, it's as much a worshipful promise as it is a compliment.

"I do." He sucks in a ragged breath. "You are so damn beautiful. And I don't just mean physically."

My eyes widen at that. He means… he likes my personality? It's a little hard to believe him, but it's even harder not to counter that with the earnestness written across his face.

In the next second, Stellan buries his face in the space between my breasts. I'm not wearing a bra, so I'm bare before him.

"Fuck," he mutters again, looking at my breasts. My hard pink nipples demand attention. My whole body tingles in anticipation of his mouth on my skin.

"Yes," I moan. "Touch me. Taste me. You can have all of me."

He puts his hands on my breasts, pushing them together, licking and kissing them both. My back bows, thrusting my nipples out and pushing my head back. This is too much, the sensations are so pleasurable that I fear for my sanity.

I feel that familiar connection in my body, between my neck and my breasts, my nipples and my pussy. He touches my breasts and I feel it in my pussy, feel my body readying itself, feel myself growing wetter. I roll my hips against his, my mouth opening to release a soft moan.

I need more. This is everything. This moment, these sensations, that passionate expression on his face. But I can't wait until he's inside me.

"Stellan..." I whisper. "I need you. *All* of you."

I push eagerly onward, rolling my hips again. Stellan has what I lack. He is going to fuck me, filling a chasm deep inside of me that I never even knew was there with his magnificent cock.

Burying my fingers in the short hair at his nape, I gasp as he kisses me. There's an impatient moment where he tries to get his shirt off. But as soon as he does I run my hands over his abs and sides, my breath catching as I look at the skin he exposes.

"You're so *hot*, " I marvel.

"I can't wait anymore." He groans, looking at me. "It's not enough, *skatter*. It's never enough. I want you naked, wet, and ready for me," he grits out.

His gaze is direct and scorching. He is a ravenous fire, threatening to burn me alive. And I am the kindling, stacked and ready, welcoming his spark to my dry tinder. We are so very close to combusting, all we need is a match to light our fire and raze us to the ground.

"I'm ready," I whisper, tugging on his jeans. "I need you, Stellan. I need you to fuck me."

He presses his kiss down on me like he's drowning and I'm the only oxygen in the whole entire world.

I work at the zipper on his jeans, undoing it and then sliding my hands around to his ass. His skin is hot and smooth under my touch. I slip my hands down the strong muscles I find there, pulling him against my body again. I slide his jeans down his hips, kissing him again.

Our tongues dance for several beats, as if we are fighting one another. God, yes.

He frames my breasts with his touch, skating one of his hands down my

ribs, down my belly, to the fine thatch of dark hair that grows between my legs. I close my eyes and moan as his fingers trace the lips of my pussy. It's all I can do not to spread my legs and beg for him to touch me. I'm like a bitch in heat, out of control, only for him. And I don't care at all.

I'm shameless and needy and wanting what only he can give me.

In the next second though, he nips at my earlobe and lays me down on the bed.

"Scoot back," he urges, voice gone to gravel. "Open your legs for me, *skatter*. Let me see your creamy pussy. Let me see what is *mine* for the taking."

Dropping my head and moving a couple of inches further back on the bed, I obey, opening my legs a little. My thighs shake with need and excitement; I can feel myself creaming at the very idea of him tasting me. I moan as his clever fingers find my clit.

"That's it," he coaxes, looking down. He puts a little space between our bodies, urging me onto my back. He repositions himself, rubbing his long, hard cock when it pops out of his jeans. "Spread your knees wide for me, skatter. I want to see all of you."

Feeling a weird combination of shameless and embarrassed, I spread my legs as far as they will go, knowing that he could crush me or reject me.

If he did that right now, I swear I would die. If anybody else saw me like this, so naked and utterly desperate, I would cry. But I look at Stellan and the desire in his ice blue eyes emboldens me.

I want to be wanton with him, to show him how hungry I am for whatever he will give me. I've waited for this moment for what feels like forever, so I might as well be brazen right now.

"Looking at you like this, spread out and waiting for me to touch you... it's the hottest thing I've ever seen." Stellan puts two fingers in his mouth, then drops those fingers down to massage my clit. I stiffen at his touch. It feels so good and all he's doing is gently massaging my clit.

I am not a choir girl; I've definitely rubbed my clit before. But when he does it, it feels wholly different. It feels so damned good, like I'm stretching and reaching for something explosive that is just outside of my grasp.

I suck in a breath. He kisses my lips, looking deep in my eyes and controls me with his touch. I'm spread open and wet, my heart pounding, my blood singing in my veins.

"It feels so good," I whimper.

He massages my breast with his free hand, shaping the nipple with clever fingers. I lean back a little, biting my lip and staring at him. I want to remember this moment, this moment of being connected to him so intimately.

Stellan gets this little smirk on his lips as he looks at me.

"What?" I ask, flushing at his probing gaze.

His smirk becomes a sly grin. His fingers dip from my clit to my core, circling and teasing. Bringing some of the moisture from my slit up to massage my aching clit in slow movements. I gasp and arch my back.

"I'm just watching you. Waiting to see you come apart." He slides one finger into my core, making my pussy ache to be filled.

I shiver against the sensation, desperate for more. "Stellan..." I gasp.

He sinks down to his knees. My thighs tense and my knees start to close, but he tuts at me. "What are you going to do? Are you going to stop me from tasting you? You want this, I promise you."

Biting my lip, I relax my thighs.

Pulling both hands out to push my knees wide again, Stellan starts kissing the inside of my thigh, making his way down to my pussy. I squirm, aching for what I know is coming. He's gone down on me before and I remember exactly how fucking good it felt. I can feel the excitement building, feel myself growing hotter and wetter every second.

His nose tickles the inside of my thigh, just an inch from my soaking wet slit. I can't help the moan that escapes my lips when he parts my pussy lips with two fingers, blowing delicately on the glistening pink flesh he finds there.

Stellan glances up at me, still smirking. "Make noise for me, *skatter*. I need to hear it."

My breath leaves me all at once, like someone punched me in the stomach. I nod slowly. "Yes, Stellan," I whisper.

As he teases me with slow kisses to my pussy, I hold my breath and bury my fingers in his hair. When his tongue circles my clit, a moan bursts from my throat.

"Oh god," I gasp. "Oh, please don't stop... *please...* "

He chuckles against my flesh. It seems natural to voice what I'm feeling, so I just go for it. As he sucks on my clit, I writhe against his mouth.

"Stellan, please! You make me so hot... I can barely look at you eating my pussy..."

He sets up a rhythm, licking and sucking, making me as hot as fire. It feels good to rock my hips against his mouth, to whisper *yes* when he hits the right spot, to throw my head back and let soft sounds leave my throat.

All the while, he keeps leading me down a path, driving me wilder and wilder with desire. He makes me crazy, playing my body like a violin, driving me insane with want.

"Please, baby..." I moan, my eyes closing. "I'm right there..."

I climax suddenly, violently. Choking, I feel the vibrations deep within my body ripple out to my breasts, my collarbone, my legs, my fingertips, my toes. God, it feels so amazing. I never want it to end.

Stellan is already kissing his way up my body, getting to his feet. I can't speak so I just turn my flushed face up to him, offering him my mouth.

He takes it greedily, kissing me hard, his mouth tasting deep and earthy and charged, the flavor a little like putting my tongue on a battery. It's my taste, I realize with a start.

How could I not have known that I have a flavor of my very own? I gasp, finding it unspeakably sexy that he still tastes like me.

His hands are everywhere, sliding from my shoulders down to grab my ass, then back up to my breasts. Although I just orgasmed, already I can feel my body preparing for more. There is no question; I still want him.

I cling to his shoulders with one arm as I begin to fumble with his jeans with the other, smoothing my fingers down his back, clutching at his bare ass. I've lost some of my shyness, exploring the shape of his ass, the way his lower back and legs feed into it. It's dense muscle, lean and smooth just like every other place on his body that I've touched. I slide my touch down the back of his legs, finding the exact spot that hair begins to grow.

He doesn't seem to mind my explorations or my curiosity in the least.

Stellan moves back an inch, pushing his jeans down to reveal his cock. Thick and long and gloriously pink, it jumps at my touch. His cock has a number of veins that seem worth exploring. I trail my fingers down his length, shuddering when it feels like hot velvet. Curious, I feel the weight of it in my palm, looking at his face.

He bites his lower lip, his eyes hooded, and allows my inquisitive touch for a moment. When I curl my fingers around his cock and give it an experimental stroke, he groans and reaches out to stop my hand.

"Not this time, *skatter* ," he manages, looking a little strangled. "I've waited too long. If you keep touching me, and keep looking at me with those innocent eyes, I'm going to come right away." Stellan leans down and kisses me passionately. "I really want to know what it feels like to come inside that pretty pussy of yours."

My eyes widen and I lick my lips. "I want that too."

He pushes me back on the bed and eases his cock out of my grip, pressing the blunt tip against the inside of my thigh. I pull him in with my legs, making him readjust a little until he settles the tip of his length against my soaking wet slit.

Stellan closes his eyes, his breathing growing heavy.

"Fuck me," I plead with him. "Please, Stellan. Don't make me wait any more."

We both groan in unison as he pushes inside, stretching me out with each inch. My whole body is alive with sensation, my breasts tingling.

"You're so big," I whisper.

I grip his shoulders, my nails digging into his flesh. His brow furrows in concentration as he works his length all the way in. It's a little uncomfortable for me, if I'm honest. Having so much weight crushed against me and being so intimately stretched out is awkward and almost painful.

But I trust Stellan; he has only brought me pleasure so far.

"God *damn*, " he murmurs. He closes his eyes for a moment, then opens them and pins me with his icy gaze. "You are so fucking tight, Margot."

The reverent look on his face excites me, makes me squirm, grinding on his cock.

"Keep going," I urge him. "You told me you would fuck me, so do it."

He looks up at me, a sheen of sweat beginning to break across his forehead. He moves then, slowly pumping his cock in and out of me. I start to feel ripples of pleasure, tentative at first, then more and more certain.

I moan, loving the feel of him, of his big body smacking against mine. I run my hands down his muscular back, feeling the power that coils within him. It's addictive.

Stellan takes my breast in one hand, pinching the nipple. I start to move in time with him, rolling my hips. Little licks of flame start to unfurl themselves deep inside of me, stealing my breath away.

"Ohh," I moan. "More," I beg. Tossing my head back, I meet his cautious thrusts by snapping my hips again and again. He's being careful with me, but I don't want that. I want him to have all of me; I want to feel scorched by him, ruined by his every movement. "Stop being careful. I want... *more*. Fuck me harder, Stellan. Do it like you mean it."

He stiffens for just a moment, then grabs my hips and pulls me up a few inches. He forgets his hesitant rhythm and starts hammering himself in and out of my pussy. My eyes widen for a second.

"Shit," I swear. My pussy clamps down on his cock in the position we are in. Suddenly, I feel everything a thousand times more, every single nerve ending on fire. "Oh god. Yes. Yes!"

He starts sweating in earnest, his sweat mixing with my own. Looking at his fierce expression, I'm unsure what I've unleashed in him, more beast than man. He looms over me, his thrusts nearly violent, every single one of his muscles working toward one goal.

Fucking me. I know I can touch myself, make this come to an end for me. I don't want to, though. It's so good, feeling stretched out by his giant cock, his sweat dripping off his face and landing on my chest. But at the same time, the ripples of my inner pond are growing in size, becoming chaotic.

I can't hold it in forever.

It feels unbelievably good to move my hips in time with each thrust. I focus on that, squeezing my eyes closed, my fingers grasping my own nipple. Stellan groans, slowing his pace down and slipping his hand down between us.

"I need you to focus," he whispers. "I can't come until you do and I'm getting close."

He brushes my clit, the sensation like a live wire. I suddenly feel electrified, moaning and clutching at his shoulders.

"Yes," I breathe. "Yes! Faster!"

He speeds up his thrusts and punctuates each one by thrumming my clit. Sounds pour from my throat; I clutch at his shoulders, ready to burst. "Come for me," he whispers, his words a plea and a command at once.

I clench my eyes shut, stretching, reaching for what I know is about to happen. I can feel the strings of desire tightening... I just need them to break. "Stellan... I..."

I reach a sudden cliff, running up one side and launching myself off. I howl my pleasure skyward. That's what coming feels like — falling down a

deep, dark crevasse. My lungs seizing up, my whole body shaking and clamping down. My pussy spasms, clenching his cock. A million tiny jolts of sensation overwhelm my entire system, all at once, threatening to burn me alive.

Stellan doesn't need to ask if I climaxed. He seems to know my body already, that all I need right now is for him to finally come. I open my eyes and keep my hips moving, trying desperately to breathe. He hammers his cock home at a blistering pace, his movements freezes as he approaches his own peak.

"God damn," he whispers, pumping his hips madly. He pushes me back down, his fingers tightening around my throat. Not actually choking me, just dominating me completely.

And I love every second of it.

I raise my chin, sliding my fingers over his and pressing down. "I'm yours, Stellan. I'm fucking yours."

That seems to trigger his orgasm. His eyes widen, his thrusts growing erratic. He slams his body against me, filling me with his cock. "Fuck, Margot, you're making me come..."

Then he roars, thrusting hard and raggedly a half dozen times. I feel him coming, feel his semen fill me in hot pulses. He closes his eyes and shudders as he comes, gasping in breaths. I can only turn my lips up to his once more.

Chapter Thirty-Two

STELLAN

WHEN I WAKE up late the next morning, I find myself alone in the big bed. We fucked four times, each time a little different. The first time was about exploration, the second time I dominated her, the third time was sort of breathless and quick. And the fourth time… the fourth time lasted all fucking night into the early morning.

Margot drained all the energy from my body and I fell asleep with her head on my chest.

And yet here I am, waking with my cock already hard for her. There is some kind of spell she has woven around me, with her sly smiles and breathy moans. She tugs the ends close so that I'm stuck in a strait jacket of my own desire; I can't help but want her.

Only her.

My chest feels tight as I get up and throw on my jeans. I pad downstairs to the kitchen, where I drink water straight from the tap and then put a pot of coffee on to brew.

I lean against the kitchen counter, closing my eyes and thinking of the last couple of weeks. The main bright spots were times when I got to sneak away with Margot.

Time we spent together, alone.

It feels like that means something, but I'm unsure what. Scrubbing a hand over my face, I sigh. A delicious aroma fills the kitchen and draws a sleepy looking Margot in.

"Hey," she says.

"*Haj*," I greet her.

She wears one of my dark t-shirts and presumably nothing else. That idea excites me, although I should probably at least refill my body's energy supply before I strip that shirt off her body. Sliding her phone onto the marble countertop that stands between us, she gives me a feeble smile.

Fuck. Now that I look at her face, she looks as though she's been crying. Her eyes are puffy and her nose reddened. My hands curl into angry fists.

"What happened?" I ask.

She glances at me and shakes her head. "Nothing."

"That's bullshit." I place a mug of coffee before her, then start filling my own mug. "Tell me."

She wrinkles her face. "I just talked to my mom, that's all. We argued. It has nothing to do with you."

I lift my mug with a frown. "I'm assuming this is the same mother who caused you to be put into the foster care system?"

She looks up at me, startled. For a second I think she's about to fire back a retort. I cock a brow as she stares at me with those gorgeous dark blue eyes.

And then her face crumples. She whirls and takes off through the house, a sob escaping her as she flees.

My eyes widen. What just happened, exactly?

"Fuck," I mutter, putting down my mug. I hurry around the kitchen island and go after her, calling her name. "Margot! Margot, wait…"

Chasing her into a small room crowded with dust cloth-draped couches, I watch as she falls onto one of them and curls into a ball. The room is lit only by a window at one end. I follow her to the couch, watching as she buries her head and stifles another sob.

Royal life prepared me for so many things, but this is just not one of them. I sit down on the couch as gingerly as I can, reaching out a hand to touch her shoulder. She shudders under my touch but doesn't look at me.

"Margot," I say, feeling helpless. "What's going on?"

She inhales a shaky breath and then turns her head toward me. I frown as I take in her red-rimmed eyes and the tears on her cheeks. She studies me, sucking her pink lower lip between the whiteness of her teeth.

God, that look of hers skewers me, sears me right through.

"*Skatter*," I murmur, reaching out to cup her tear stained face. "Talk to me."

She sits up, wiping at her face. When she responds, her voice is watery and tight. "I wasn't supposed to cry in front of you. That is definitely not how I saw the weekend going."

I shrug lightly. "A month ago, I didn't plan to be here with you at all. Things change."

Margot bites her lip, looking at me carefully. "Back there, in the kitchen? The way that you talked about my mom and my time in the foster system. You were just so casual about something that you have no way of knowing anything about. And that... that *hurt*."

My brows rise. For a moment, I am genuinely without words. I made her cry? Her tears were my doing?

How do I even respond to that? I'm so out of my depth here and drowning quickly. She frowns a bit as she watches me.

"I... I'm sorry," I say, looking at her earnestly. "I didn't mean to hurt you."

She nods and looks down to her lap, wiping her cheeks again. "I know," she mumbles.

I move closer to her, putting my arm around her. It feels a little awkward but I do it anyway. Cupping her jaw, I tilt her face up to look at me. Then I sweep my thumb across her cheek, collecting the remnants of moisture I find there.

"I really am sorry," I say, my eyes darting back and forth as I try to read her face. "You always mention it so casually. I just thought... I mean... I never realized that you were sensitive about your mother."

She gives me a watery smile. "It probably doesn't help that I just got off the phone with her. She had the usual horrible things to say."

"Like what?"

Her cheeks stain pink. "She's been talking to several reporters about me. More like baiting them, it sounds like. She hasn't decided which reporter she wants to spill my life story to..." Her mouth twists bitterly. "Which means, I assume, that no one has said that they will pay her as much as she thinks she deserves." She wrinkles her nose. "My mom has always been that way."

"She's going to sell your story to some paparazzo?" I ask, baffled. "Why on earth would she do that?"

Margot sighs, shaking her head. "According to her, I still owe her big time. If she hadn't gotten pregnant with me, she says she would've quote 'been a real beauty'. Having me ruined her body I guess."

I squint. "What? You didn't choose to be born. How could any of that be your fault?"

She shrugs a shoulder. "That's only the beginning of what mom says I owe her. My mom has a running tally of my debts that goes all the way back to when she had to buy me diapers and pacifiers." She bites her lower lip for a second. "Don't even get her started about how I drained her resources anytime that I lived with her. Funny, because any time I was in foster care, she railed and ranted about how the government shouldn't interfere in our lives."

I glance away, struggling to keep a lid on my temper. "Your mother sounds..." I trail off, searching for the right word. I don't want to upset Margot, but it's clear that her mother has some mental issues that predate Margot's birth.

She sniffs, breaking my hold. Putting a few inches between us, she looks down at her hands. "Go ahead. You know you want to say it."

Her voice is distant. I think I almost made a very bad misstep, twice in a row.

"She sounds hard to deal with," I finish, touching Margot's knee. "It sounds like you had a lot of stuff piled on top of being... financially unstable. That's what I am hearing you say."

She looks up at me, sucking in a shaky breath. "Yeah. That's just the very surface of it, honestly. The tip of the iceberg."

Standing, I pull her to her feet. She comes naturally into the shelter of my arms, looking up into my face. I don't have the words to describe how it feels, just holding her like this. "I want you to tell me more. You say I don't know about it. So I want you to tell me. But... not in here. This room is weird and creepy."

Margot pushes up on her tiptoes and cups my jaw, then kisses me lightly on the lips. My heart thuds painfully against my ribs; I'm relieved at the fact that I finally did something right, but it's more than that.

Her scent is in my nose. Her warmth seems to invade me, my whole being. My fingers curl around her waist, digging into her skin. What is this feeling?

Possession. That's it. This is the first time I've really ever felt like she was *mine*. And for the life of me, I can't see how I'm just going to let her go. Not yet.

She lets me go and steps back, turning around and leaving. I trail after her, trying to get a firm hold on what I'm feeling. But of course, she doesn't give me the chance.

She walks into the kitchen, bites her lower lip, and gives me a once over. "You don't really want to hear about my background, do you?"

I stop a few inches away from her, looking at her sweetly curved face. "I meant what I said."

Margot wrinkles her nose and presses up on her tiptoes to kiss me. Then she takes a seat at the kitchen bar and inhales slowly. "Okay." She grabs her mug of coffee, running a finger around the rim. "I was born in Brooklyn. Which sounds like it was hip and funky… but it wasn't. My mom was a stripper for most of my childhood, and that job… well, I don't know if it led her to drugs or if drugs led to her stripping. Either way, my mom was too busy living her life to give me much thought."

She smiles sadly at her coffee mug. "Yeah. It's always been just my mom and me, no dad in the picture. As soon as I was out of diapers, she stopped paying for a babysitter. She just left me for days on end. So I found ways to keep myself busy… like the story I told you about discovering my passion for journalism at the library." She sucks in a deep breath. "But there were other things that I did, too. Bad things. I ran with a really awful crowd for a while."

My eyebrows lift. "I was wondering where you got your sense of style."

She looks up at me, smiling sheepishly. "Yeah, I guess I always idolized the punks of the 1980s. They just seemed so cool. Like they were living their grubby little lives out loud and not shutting up about how miserable and downtrodden they were." She makes a face. "Plus their music was just noisy and riotous and fun to dance to."

"No disagreement here." I slide my mug of coffee across the counter, taking a sip. It's tepid, but it's still coffee. "So… your mother didn't always take care of you."

"She did what she could do, I guess." Margot shrugs a shoulder. "I was in and out of foster care, usually in group homes. I did really well in school, but I was an outcast for sure. Nobody wanted to be friend with the weird kid who wore the same clothes all the time and never brought any cake on their birthday."

I nod. "Yeah, children can be cruel-hearted."

She sighs. "Yeah. Luckily, I got myself into NYU. And that's where I met Pippa." She drums her fingers against the counter. "That was a huge turning point for me. She was also into journalism and she sort of opened a doorway to that world."

Tilting my head, I try to imagine Pippa and Margot back then. Margot looks at my expression and laughs.

"What?" she asks.

"Nothing. I'm just trying to imagine a world without this rebellious, punk rock-loving version of you in it." I shake my head. "I think I'm glad that you are you."

Her lips curve upward and she rolls her eyes a little. "Thanks, I guess."

Standing up, I drag her chair towards me. Then I bend down and kiss her. Margot turns her head up, digging her fingers into the short hair at the back of my head.

When I pull back, I lean my forehead against hers. I whisper lulling words to Margot. "Thank you for opening up to me."

Her smile turns into a slow grin. "Of course." She twists and pushes the chair she is sitting on away and leans her small frame against mine, hips touching hips, her breasts against the hardness of my chest. "Take me to bed, Stellan."

I've never wanted anything more. I sweep her up in my arms and carry her toward the bedroom, my lips on her lips, my heart beating in time with hers.

Chapter Thirty-Three

STELLAN

I RISE EARLY, the habit ingrained from my time in the military. After I shower and dress myself, Margot is still soundly asleep. I sit down on the bed beside her, looking down at her. Some women I've spent the night with have been like sleeping beauty in their slumber; placid and peaceful, unresisting and serene.

Margot isn't like that. She hugs a pillow to her bare chest, a tiny pucker of emotion creasing her brow, her mouth set in the echo of a frown. Her cotton candy curls spill backwards from her head like a dash of ink spilled in water. Her hands are tight little fists, looking like she's ready to fight.

And yet, I still find her incredibly beautiful. Not despite.

Because she is rebellious to her very core. Even in sleep, she doesn't lose her edge.

But the best thing is when I lean over, dropping a kiss to her bare shoulder. She stirs, opening her sapphire eyes a crack. And then she smiles at me. Big and bright, sleepy but all the more meaningful for it.

"Hey," she rasps.

One corner of my mouth lifts. "*Haj.*"

She wrinkles her nose. "Were you watching me sleep?"

I shrug a shoulder. "Just for a second. I was actually coming to wake you up."

She sits up, stretching and yawning. "What for?"

"A surprise. Come on." I stand up. "And wear a bathing suit. There should be a bunch in the closet. We're going somewhere that I want you to see."

She makes a face at me but gets out of bed. An hour later, she joins me in the kitchen. I'm leaning against the island, sipping my coffee.

One look at her makes me do a double take and choke on my coffee just a bit. She's wearing nothing but a tiny black bikini under a filmy white robe. And her Converse, as per the usual.

I bite my lip. "You look..." I search for the right word. "*Edible*. Maybe we shouldn't even leave the house."

That earns me a scornful sound from her lips.

"This bathing suit is scandalous," she complains, indicating her outfit. "There were so many of them hanging in the closet, but this is the only one that was my size."

I give her a smirk. "You are just lucky that we carry sizes suitable for tiny people. You are elf-sized."

She rolls her eyes. "Are we going out to the beach or what?"

"We are. Here, I made you a coffee to go."

Her eyes widen with glee as she accepts the mug. "You're really getting to the core of who I am as a person," she jokes. "Coffee first, then literally everything else."

The beach is only a short walk from the house. As soon as we step outside into the salty air, I take a huge breath. The sun beams down on us as we stroll to the beach. I came out here earlier and set things up, so my footprints are already in the sand.

Margot makes a silly face as she steps in one of my footprints. "A giant has already been here, apparently."

That makes me grin. "He's giant all over, if you know what I mean." I lean close to stage whisper. "I'm saying that I have a huge cock."

That makes her cackle. "Yes, I'm aware. It's not for nothing that I'm walking a little stiff-legged today."

Pure male satisfaction fills me. "If you're lucky, I'll show it to you again later."

She shakes her head at me but she can't stop grinning. "Shut up."

We walk down to the pebble-strewn shore, sand clinging to our feet. I've left two paddle boards there, their matching paddles sticking up out of the sand.

"What is this?" Margot asks, pulling her hair back into a bun.

"Paddle boarding." I wiggle my eyebrows at her. "I've done it before. I'm *practiced*, you could say. So I'll mostly just be here to watch you fail at it." I arch my brows. "It should be a good diversion."

She squints at me, then turns her gaze out to the green-blue sea. "Twenty dollars says I'll be good at it by the time we finish." She pauses. "No, wait. Money doesn't matter to you. How about you pose for my camera tomorrow if I can get good today. And if I don't..."

I grin wickedly. "If you don't, I get to put my cock anywhere I want tonight."

Her brows fly up and she turns red as a beet. "You want to do *anal?*"

"*Ja*. Of course. I have just been waiting until the moment is right."

Her eyes tighten a little. "Well, it doesn't matter anyway. Because I'm going to win."

I rub my hands together and lick my lower lip. "I really hope you lose, *skatter*."

She flushes and looks down at the paddle boards. "You're going to get your ass kicked. Let's go."

I hold up my hands. "Slow down. First I need to know if you've ever surfed."

Margot's brows knit. "I'm from the city. And even though the water is right by us, it's safe to say that I have never surfed anywhere."

"Okay. Starting from the end of the board, yeah?" I point to the end of one of the surf boards. "You grab the sides, and then move onto your stomach. Then you lift yourself upward..."

"Oh, right." She moves onto the board. "Like this?"

"*Ja*. Then you sort of turn your leg..." I show her on my board. "And slide your other foot forward. Then the hard part, which is having enough balance to stand on the paddle board."

"Right. Got it." She scrunches her face up. "I mean, I think I do."

"Good. Let's paddle out, then."

We pad out to the sea, the sand stiff and crunchy, breaking away under our feet. When I step into the ocean and feel it swirl around my feet, I suck in a deep lungful of salty air.

Glancing at Margot to make sure she's still with me, I put my paddle board down on the water.

"Don't forget to attach your leash to your ankle," I say. Balancing awkwardly for a second, I do as I said.

I look at her as she does the same, biting her lip as she attaches the leash. I can't help the way my eyes dip down to her lush mouth, or the way they slide down to her tits. She's taken off her cover up and is just wearing that little black bikini now.

I realize that I am as bad as a horny fucking teenager, filling in what I can't see. But I don't bother to jerk my gaze away this time.

She looks up and colors when she sees me looking at her. She tucks a strand of hair behind her ear. "What?"

I grin. "Nothing. Are you ready to try to surf?"

She starts to move out into the water. "Ahhh. The water is cold!"

She jumps back, glaring at me like I've just endangered her well being somehow.

I pull a face. "It's warmer than room temperature."

"It's so cold!" she disagrees. "You should've warned me."

"So you give up, then? Because I count that as a forfeit."

She wrinkles her nose at me. "No."

She stomps back into the water, her movements obviously irritated. She likes to win; I should make a note of that. I wade out after her, carrying the paddles, and watch as her body disappears into the ocean. I shiver a little as I submerge myself up to my shoulders.

We both paddle out a little ways. The wind picks up a bit. I can feel the ocean sweeping us aside, which is unusual. When I have paddle boarded before, the sea was calm and placid.

That doesn't stop us from trying to paddle board today, though. She flounders a little bit trying to get on top of the board and then pops up… only to fall back into the water. When she resurfaces, gasping, I can't help but grin.

"You can give up any time you feel like it, you know."

She splashes me and I laugh. She grabs her board. "I'm ready to go again. But I want to see you do it."

A wave crashes just behind us, distracting me. I look over my shoulder and see dark gray clouds on the horizon. "Shit. Those weren't there before, were they?"

When I turn back to look at Margot, she's eyeing me suspiciously. "I don't think you can do it."

I roll my eyes. "Of course I can. We'll do it at the same time, *ja*?" And look over my shoulder again. "I'd say we have about thirty minutes before we probably should get off the beach."

She jerks her chin up at me. "Bring it on, Hagrid."

"Who is Hagrid?"

"Less talking, more paddle boarding." She grabs her board and steadies herself, struggling to get on the board.

I balance my own board, climbing on and standing up. I use the paddles that I'm holding to help keep myself from tipping over either way. Grinning, I turn to Margot.

Just in time to see her fall again, hitting the water with a loud smack. I make a face; that had to hurt. A wave crashes right on top of where we are swimming, distracting me for a second.

When she doesn't resurface immediately, I look around for her board.

Fuck.

I can't see it anywhere.

Turning myself around, I keep looking.

Fuck, where can he have gone?

"Margot?" I call, panicking.

I sense movement about ten feet away. I see a flash of pink right before she surfaces in a spray of white water, coughing and choking. She flails a little bit, pushing the wet hair out of her eyes, going under for another second.

I don't think. I start swimming towards her, calling out her name. "Margot!"

She comes back up just as I reach her. We make eye contact but she looks like she's a little confused and disconcerted.

"You're okay," I promise. "You're okay. Come with me." I tug her into my arms and swim for shore, although it is a struggle to hold onto her and swim with one arm. When my feet hit the sandy bottom of the ocean, I feel a strange sense of relief.

Margot coughs a few more times as I pull her onto the shore and put her down just out of the water's reach. "Hey. Are you okay? Look at me."

She nods, sucking in deep breaths. Her voice is pure gravel. "Yeah."

Untethering myself from my board, I sit down beside her and pull her into my arms. She's cold, much colder than me. She barely weighs anything. I press a kiss to her forehead, only just now feeling the weight of the adrenaline that kicked in.

My heart pounds. I'm sweating even though I'm not hot.

But Margot is safe. She's right here, in my arms

"Fuck," I mutter into her hair. "Jesus, that was scary."

She raises her head and I see tears in her eyes. She clears her throat. "Sorry."

I shake my head. "There is nothing to apologize for. It's just... for a second, I thought I had lost you. And that thought almost killed me."

Her eyes well up and she nods, falling against my chest. "Sorry."

"We need to get you warmed up. You're freezing." Pulling back from her, I stand up and help her to her feet. "Let's go back to the house."

Above us, the first lick of lightning splits the sky in two. A few fat droplets of rain fall onto us. Margot covers her face and takes off toward the house at a run.

I follow a little slower, weighed down by my thoughts.

What if something bad had happened to her?

What would I have done?

My chest tightens.

I realize, in that moment, that I'm in love with Margot. I love her so, so much. I can't even think about all the things that could have happened to her today.

Fuck. Just considering what almost happened makes my heart wrench in my chest.

She stops just before she reaches the door, shivering and looking back at me. And I pick up my pace without thinking about it, because she might need me.

And that's more important to me just now.

Chapter Thirty-Four

MARGOT

AFTER MAKING sure that I'm okay, Stellan kisses me with so much passion that it leaves me shaking. I want more, so I kiss him again.

We quickly devolve into two creatures born of need. The kissing turns to fucking, the fucking turns to shouting each other's names as we come. And then we do the whole thing again and again, until we are exhausted.

Stellan is splayed out on the bed, his eyes closed. I'm lying beside him, my leg thrown over his. I delicately trace the lines of his chest with my fingertips.

Looking up at his face, his dark hair all askew, his five o'clock shadow becoming more pronounced, I sigh silently. He is so damned beautiful, with a strength of character that drives me to distraction.

In the early evening light, shadows cling to his face in a way that I think is perfect. If I don't get a picture of this moment, I'll regret it. I want to suspend us in this moment in time, so that I can always return back to it.

Even after he's gone. Even after I don't have any right to touch him.

"Are you awake?" I whisper.

Stellan opens his eyes a crack. When he speaks, it's a gravelly purr. "Sort of."

"I want to get my camera and take some photos of you. The light is just perfect."

He closes his eyes again and raises his fingers to press the bridge of his nose for a moment. "Photographs for your article?"

"No. Just… photos for me. I want to remember this exact moment. I swear to you, I'm the only one that will ever see them."

His eyes open a slit and focus on me. I get the feeling that he's trying to decide if I'm being truthful or not. My cheeks heat.

But he just closes his eyes again. "Sure, *ja*."

I let out a squeak of excitement, bouncing up to retrieve my Nikon from inside my tote bag. I lie back down, a little farther back this time, and take the lens cap off. After fiddling with the camera setting for a second, I look through the viewfinder.

There Stellan is, seeming so much larger than life. His raked torso makes my mouth water. He shifts a little, putting his arm behind his head.

God, does he even realize how tantalizing he is in this moment? He's a perfect specimen. He's not just rich. Not just obscenely privileged. Not just attractive. Not just well-endowed.

He is all those things. And yet, there's so much more underneath. Compassion, kindness, curiosity about the world around him… all supported by a backbone made of steel.

I squint and snap several photos, then move to my knees and try for a different angle. For a few minutes the room is silent except for the sound of my shutter clicking.

Stellan opens his eyes and gives me a knowing look. "Did you capture the perfect image of me?"

My lips curve upward and I wrinkle my nose. "Want to see?"

He arches a brow. "If you are offering, yes."

I flip a switch on my camera and the screen below the viewfinder comes to life. Moving over to Stellan's side, I show him the first photo. His brow draws down and he frowns ever so slightly, but he doesn't say a word.

I silently toggle through the thirty or so shots I've taken. His face never changes; he shows a little interest and an equal amount of skepticism.

"Well?" I ask gently. "What do you think?"

He purses his lips and shrugs. "I understand why the outside world is so fascinated with me. I'm a member of the royal family. A curiosity. A zoo animal, at times." He screws up his face. "But I don't quite understand why you are interested in capturing me like this."

Tilting my head a fraction, I turn the camera off. "Like what?"

He hesitates then shrugs. "Naked. Resting." He squints. "Why would anyone want to see that particular side of me?"

"Do you mean while you are vulnerable?" I ask.

Stellan frowns and shrugs again. "Sort of. Maybe."

I take half a minute before I respond. "Doesn't everyone want to catch a glimpse of Atlas at rest?"

He huffs out a chuckle. "Is that who I am now? Do I carry the weight of the world on my shoulders?"

My answer is instantaneous. "Yes. In my opinion, a large part of who you are is wrapped up in your duty."

He seems to give that some thought. "I guess you are right. It's sort of impossible to be anything other than the king-to-be. I don't... if my life changed suddenly, I wouldn't know who to *be*."

I smile at that. "Oh, I don't know. I think you would figure it out very quickly. Your personality is more than your sense of honor." I turn my head to the side. "I could see you as a royal air force pilot. You'd eventually become... a commander, or whatever. And you'd live in a very fancy house downtown with your perfect wife and three gorgeous children."

His lips lift at the corners. "Sometimes I really, really wish that was possible. I wish I could have an ordinary life. My brothers have a normal life. My sister has one too, sort of." He sighs. "I'm not the only one who has to worry about appearances, but..."

I scrunch up my face, finishing his sentence. "But you're the only one that will be inheriting the crown. So everything really counts for you, and you alone."

He chuckles. "Basically, yes."

Putting my camera aside, I lay down beside Stellan once more. Running my hand across the smooth skin of his chest, I bite my lip. "I know that this is the only time we'll ever really get together. I just..." I lower my gaze, unable to meet his eyes. "I want you to know that I am trying to make the most of it. To... to cherish it, I guess. It means a lot to me."

His hand comes down to cover mine, pressing my fingers against the wall of his chest. "It means a lot to me too."

My eyes threaten to fill with tears. Suddenly, all I can think about is next week. "My article is supposed to be done by now. I haven't even started it, but... how will I... how do I begin to write it?"

He tips my chin up so that I'm looking at him. "I don't have an answer for that. But…" He hesitates. "I don't want this to end."

My lips tremble. I blink away a sheen of tears. "No?"

He shakes his head slowly. He has never looked so serious before this moment. "No. Do you?"

I blurt out every dumb thing in my mind without even thinking it through. "I love you, Stellan."

As soon as I say it, my eyes go wide and my cheeks turn bright red. The reaction is instantaneous; I close my eyes, my heart lurching in my chest.

What the fuck did I just say?

Did I admit to being in love with him *out loud?*

Am I a fucking idiot?

"I shouldn't—" I start, but he cuts me off.

"You do?"

I open my eyes, cringing. "Yes. I didn't mean to… I mean, I just blurted it out. It wasn't very elegant— "

He cuts me off again with a press of his lips against mine. Crushing, insistent, I hear him take a breath against my mouth. "I love you too, *skatter.*"

I freeze. Surely I didn't hear that right. "What?"

Stellan cups my jaw with his hand, his ice blue eyes burning into mine. "I'm in love with you. I know it's only been a little over a month. I know it feels like it's too soon. But I've never felt this way about anyone before in my life."

My brain feels like it's tumbling down a set of stairs. My mouth opens and words fall out. "You… you feel this way too?"

He draws my hand up over his heart and laces his fingers with mine. "Yes, *skatter.*"

"Oh." I stare at him for a second, giving him time to tell me he's joking. But he doesn't.

I scramble up onto all fours, climbing on top of his body and kissing him so fiercely that I can't quite think straight. He groans and sinks his fingers into my hair. His cock is already hard for me, long and thick and stiff as steel.

I reach down between us and position his cock so that it is flush with my entrance. Already I can feel my pussy growing slick with my excitement. When I push the crown of his cock inside me, he murmurs my name.

"Margot."

I bite my lip and look down into his face, already feeling stretched out by his cock. He draws my head down and kisses me slowly as I push my body down to meet his, taking him in inch by inch. When he releases me again, he moans.

"Look at me," he says. "Keep your eyes on me."

We fuck slowly, my hips working to raise me up and down on his hot cock, his hands roving all over my body. He tweaks one of my nipples and I cry out, increasing my pace.

The whole while our gazes are locked.

"I really fucking love you," he grits out.

I smile, breathless. "I love you too."

His hands anchor my hips in place as he starts to thrust up. When he moves like that his cock touches a spot deep inside me that makes my eyes roll up in my head and my toes curl. I can feel tendrils of excitement reaching through my body, up from where we are joined to my tits, my neck, my mouth.

It's like he's touching me everywhere at once.

"Look at me!" he commands.

I open my eyes and focus on his face as he thrusts up into me again and again, his movements growing rougher with every passing second. And I love it; I would take him any way I can get him, but when he's rough it's just that much better.

"Touch your clit for me. I want to watch you unravel," he whispers, ramming me with his rapid-fire thrusts.

I bite my lip and slip my hand down, two fingers searching for my clit. The second I find it and begin to circle it with slow strokes, my eyes drift closed.

"Open your eyes, *skatter*," he says, his voice gone to gravel. "Let me watch you fall apart."

I force my eyelids open just as I start to peak. "Oh my god. Oh my god… Stellan…"

My hips jerk as I climb the last few steps to plummet over the edge. As I watch his beautiful face, I come harder than ever, my pussy spasming, my hips lurching, my entire body on fire.

"Fuck," he whispers. He comes all at once, his cock filling my pussy with long lashes of his seed. I can feel him twitching inside my body and right now, it's the sexiest thing I think I've ever experienced.

Stellan reaches up and cups my face in his hands, tugging me down for a breathless kiss. I collapse on top of him, kissing him lazily and loving the damp, hot skin of his naked torso pressed against mine.

He gives a husky chuckle. "Damn."

I give him an exhausted grin. "I know. I didn't think that the sex could get any hotter between us... and then there was *this*."

He kisses the corner of my lips, then my cheek, then my jaw, working his way down to my neck. I inhale suddenly, still sensitive on every inch of my body.

"What are you doing?" I ask, giggling and squirming.

"I want you to remember this day forever," he murmurs, pressing lips against my throat. "And I'll use every tool at my disposal to do it."

He finds a spot just at the juncture of my throat and neck. Then he bites down pretty hard, hard enough to make me gasp. Just when I start to react, to push him away, he releases me and kisses away the pain.

"Why did you do that?" I protest.

Stellan's lips curve upward. He looks me dead in the eye. "Because now I can be sure that you'll remember. Every time you look in the mirror. Every time something touches your skin just here." He traces a light touch over the bite mark. "You'll remember that I said I loved you, won't you?"

The rush of tears that fill my eyes are unexpected. I nod slowly. "Yes, Stellan. I will."

He smirks. "Good."

Then he kisses me on the lips again, distracting me. But I will never forget that stinging pain at the base of my neck or the man that caused it. He is right. I will always remember why he did it, too.

Shivering, I embrace him and open my mouth against his, ready for more.

Chapter Thirty-Five

STELLAN

THE NEXT DAY, I push the morning's plan of packing up and leaving for Copenhagen into the evening. I'm a little desperate for more time before I have to be Prince Stellan again.

More time to spend with her, time I can be free. Time I can be *myself.*

Margot accepts the news of the extra day with a slow smile. "I agree to it on the condition that we leave this bed. I swear, you take me to these little coastal retreats and we hardly do anything but have sex. Not that I'm complaining about the sex, but…" She wrinkles her nose. "My body is pretty sore from fucking for like twelve hours in a row yesterday."

I smirk. "I like pushing your boundaries. How else will I know what the limit is?"

She rolls her eyes. "In hindsight, it was about two times less than we fucked yesterday. I should've had some more water or something because my arms and legs and abdominal muscles are a hot mess today. And that's not even talking about how much you…" She pauses, blushing. "Stretched me out."

I give her a wicked grin. "Good to know. I'll admit to being pretty sore myself. Maybe next time we should be prepared with bananas and coconut water."

She scrunches up her face. "Next time? What next time? My excuse for being in your life was officially over at the start of business today."

My heart starts hammering in my chest. God, I hadn't even thought of that. Tiny blades of turmoil slide through my gut and slice me to ribbons.

I don't know how I'm supposed to answer, so I just play it off like her question was no big deal. Even though in reality the thought of not seeing Margot again kills me.

I smile as if nothing happened. "The idea that we're not going to absolutely ruin each other's bodies later today is pretty laughable. But... I think there is a restaurant within walking distance. Do you fancy a stroll down the beach?"

She wrinkles her nose at my awkward phrasing. "Sure."

We get dressed, me in dark jeans and a white t-shirt, her in the short black dress that she wears so often. And then we walk down to the beach.

It's beautiful and sunny out, though windy enough that the day is pleasant rather than burning. I offer her my hand and she takes it, sliding her small palm against my own. She glances up at me, tucking a wild curl of her pink hair behind her ear. In the wind it's pointless though.

She sticks her tongue out at me and I laugh. "What is that for?"

She shrugs. "When you get too in your head, you get like... physically locked up. Your muscles are noticeably tighter, you're just all..."

She playacts jerky, blocky movements.

I shake my head. "Who says I'm in my head?"

She puffs out her cheeks. "You've been awkward ever since I said that we might not be able to see each other anymore."

I stumble in the sand and her eyes widen. "See? You are in your head."

I roll my eyes and shake my head. She's completely right, but she could at least do me the courtesy of ignoring it like I'm doing.

"So get my mind off of it," I challenge her. "Tell me a story."

"No." She wrinkles her nose. "We spent time on my story yesterday. I want to hear more about you, Stellan. And not the junk that you tell every other newspaper." Margot pulls my hand to her chest, holding it against her heart. "I want to know more about who you are as a person."

I make a face. "Like what? You want to hear my favorite bands?"

She shrugs a shoulder. "If that's what you want me to know, then sure. Who is your favorite band?"

Grinning, I slow our walking pace to a crawl. "The Rolling Stones."

Her eyebrows rise. "That... is not what I expected you to say."

"I live to surprise you, Margot," I tease.

"You just seem too buttoned up for that." Color springs forth in her cheeks. "No offense."

"*Ja?* Well. I'll have you know that I was once arrested."

Her eyes widen. "Wait, you were? What happened?"

"It was… I'll call it a youthful lapse. I partied a little too hard, did too many drugs. Got sick all over myself. Resisted the police when they were only trying to help. You know, all the usual embarrassing things."

She winces. "You didn't!"

"Oh, I really did."

"Oh, your parents must have been so angry!"

I exhale a slow breath. "Sort of. They knew, they were just… busy. My grandmother kept a keen eye out for all of her grandchildren, so she got the call instead of my father." I chuckle, shaking my head. "If you think I am stoic, wait until you see my grandmother receive bad news. But that night when the police brought me to the palace… the door shut, and it was just the two of us… It was the only time I can ever remember her being openly furious."

"That sounds terrifying."

"What, my grandmother? *Ja*, it wasn't great. You have to imagine someone about your size wagging her finger in my face and telling me how I wasn't living up to the family name. My grandmother was worried that her voice would carry and so she whispered and yelled at me, all at once. After about four hours of that, most people would go crazy."

She cracks a smile. "She sounds intimidating."

I squint off toward the place where the sky, sea, and land all seem to blend together. "You should meet her."

Margot pulls a face. "Uh… yeah, right."

My heart pounds in my chest. "No, I'm serious."

She stops, pulling her hand from my grip. I turn and look at her, my eyebrows lifting. She shoots me a confused look. "What?"

"I love you. You love me. So— "

"So we should *get married?!*" she says, horrified.

I give her a funny look. "No. I'm just saying… maybe we should… I don't know… *date.*"

She crosses her arms and cocks her hips. "Stellan… we both know that's a terrible idea. You have a list of girls to choose from— "

I reach out and grab her by the waist, tugging her up against my hips.

Then I cup her heart-shaped face, tucking a strand of those pink cotton candy curls behind her ear. "But I am not in love with any of them. I'm in love with *you*."

She bites her full lower lip and pins me with her intensely blue gaze. When she speaks, her voice is a mere whisper. "I know."

"So? I want you here. Stay with me." I draw in a deep breath, feeling more naked before her than ever before. "I've never felt like this about anyone before. And I'm not willing to just throw that away because it might upset some people."

She shakes her head, taking in what I said. Her brow hunches. "I don't even know how we would make that happen. Are you going to come up with a lie to tell your family? Am I going to lie to my editor?"

I take her hand, pulling it against my chest and trapping in beneath mine. "Is that what you want?"

Margot looks at me for a moment, as if trying to decide something. Then she shakes her head again. "No," she replies softly.

"So date me. We'll just show up holding hands and let everyone else deal with the fallout."

One corner of her mouth turns down. "That's not the best attitude to have, Stellan. Besides… dating you… I would assume that it comes with certain… *expectations*."

"It doesn't have to." I mean the words, but even as they leave my lips, I sense that they're not the fullest truth. "Look. I'm saying… this is all new to me. It's all new to you. Let's just… forge a path together."

She sighs, looking away. For several moments, I can hear nothing but the sea in the background and the hammering of my own heart.

Is she really going to turn me down?

When she swings her gaze back to my face, I can see the torment that is going on behind those beautiful blue eyes. "I want to say yes. I really do, Stellan."

My lips curl upward. "So do it, *skatter*."

Margot presses up onto her tiptoes, seeking out my mouth. I lean down and kiss her, pressing my lips to hers. She drops back down, biting her lower lip.

"Okay," she whispers. "I won't go anywhere, as long as you still want me to stay."

Wrapping my arms around her, I hug her. She settles against my chest, her arms slipping around my waist to hold me tightly.

I close my eyes and try to memorize every detail of this moment. To store this memory, keep it safe for a rainy day. Because I won't always be this happy. She won't always get to say yes.

But just now, it's enough.

Chapter Thirty-Six

STELLAN

IN THE DRIVER'S seat of my car, I look over at Margot. She looks anxious, chewing her lip and bouncing her knee.

"We are almost back to the palace," I say. "Have you thought of what you're going to say to your bosses?"

She looks over at me with a worried smile. "It's all I've thought about since we got in the car. Yet I haven't come up with anything good. What do I say? *Sorry about the story, but I've decided to date the crown prince?*"

I shrug. "Tell them the truth. They can't be mad at you for that."

She gives a huff of laughter. "Yes they can. They have every right to fire me. If I lose my job, I might get a call from immigration, wondering what I'm still doing here."

I fix her with a long look. "You won't. I'll have Erik make some calls."

Sighing, she looks away. "I wish I didn't need you to call in any favors. But thank you for doing it."

I pull the car up the long driveway in front of the palace, putting it in park. Glancing over at Margot, I tug her hand into my lap. She turns her head toward me, biting her lip.

I reach up and tuck a strand of her hair back behind her ear. "I have to go in and tell my grandmother that I'm defying her. You have to go tell your editor the same thing, basically." I inhale deeply. "If it helps, I'm still in love with you."

She laughs. "It definitely doesn't hurt."

I pull her in, kissing her fully on the mouth. Then I turn her loose with a sigh. "All right. I'm ready to face the firing squad."

Margot nods, opening the car door. "Yeah. Text me later and let me know how it went."

I climb out of the car and lean against the roof briefly. As she stands and grabs her bag, I stand there, looking at her ass and her bare legs in her super short dress.

God damn. After a weekend like we just had, where we fucked until we were too exhausted to move every single day… I should have found the saturation point with Margot. I should be content and fulfilled. And yet… I'm not.

I don't know that I'll ever be, to be completely honest.

I bite my lip, smiling. "I will."

She wrinkles her nose and then walks away, heading for the *Politiken* offices. I take a deep breath and look up at the palace. Then I stride toward the main entrance, jogging up the steps.

As I enter a few people are waiting for me. A butler, several maids… and Erik, standing tall, looking especially Scandinavian with his blond hair and enormous stature.

"Erik," I greet him. "How are things?"

Just from the way his lips thin, I can tell that he is irritated with me. He just turns and heads toward the carpeted stairs in front of us. "You were missed yesterday."

I follow him up the stairs and into the grand hall, heading toward my study. He bursts through the door and strides past the leather armchairs and the fireplace, throwing himself down in the leather couch with a loud sigh.

"Well?" he demands. I close the door and sit on a corner of my oak desk, crossing my arms and pursing my lips.

"Well what?" I ask.

"You cancelled your appearances yesterday."

Cocking my head, I squint at him. "So?"

"So… you missed the board meeting regarding the children's cancer center to be named after Anton. You knew that was important to me!"

That gives me pause. Anton was Erik's little brother; he died of childhood lymphoma. The board meeting was a meeting of the royal family, in which they voted on which projects to fund.

"Ahh. Shit." I wince. "Did the family really vote against a children's cancer center?"

"It got funded, but barely. That's not really the point, Stellan. You promised me that you would be there to champion Anton's name!"

I blow out a breath. In the back of my mind, I knew that coming back to Copenhagen was going to be like this. I knew that I would be disappointing someone and letting someone down. I always am, I guess.

It's just usually not Erik.

"I'm sorry."

"That's it? That's all you have to say?"

Puffing out my cheeks, I sigh. "I spent the weekend with Margot."

Erik stills, his eyes tightening on my face. "What do you mean, you spent the weekend with her?"

At that moment, the door to the study swings open. I turn and watch as my grandmother glides in wearing a light gray pantsuit.

I paste on my coolest smile. "Ah, *Momse*. Good, I can tell both of you at once."

My grandmother arches a brow. "I hope you are about to tell me why you felt like shirking your duties yesterday. It was very difficult to get enough royals to cover all your engagements."

I want to roll my eyes, but instead I just continue to smile. "I'm dating Margot Keane."

Her nostrils flare. Erik shakes his head, glaring at me.

"That's a bad idea," he mutters.

I shoot him a glare.

Ida raises her chin and looks me square in the eye. "Is that the journalist from America?"

"Yes."

She brushes a bit of invisible lint from her jacket sleeve. "You know that you can't marry her."

I hold up a hand. "No one said anything about marriage. I haven't even looked into that possibility yet."

She eyes me. "Stellan, you were raised to hold yourself to high standards. Certainly higher than a poor American reporter. I mean, really! I'm not even sure that our constitution will allow the crown prince to marry a foreigner, much less someone of such a different class than our family."

My lips thin. I draw myself up to my full height. "I know that Margot isn't your choice, *Momse*. But for now, she is mine. So you can either deal with it or you can find someone else to be your well-behaved little pet prince."

Ida's hand goes to her chest. She opens her mouth to retort, but I'm already turning my attention to Erik.

"And you." I glare at him. "I am sorry that I missed the vote yesterday. That was wrong of me. But I'll tell you now… I won't tolerate anyone telling me how to live my life. You need to get comfortable with the fact that I'm dating Margot." I look at Ida. "Both of you do."

Erik looks angry. "You don't even know any of her past, Stel. Trust me, she has plenty to hide."

"Really?" I ask, crossing my arms. "Tell me. Go ahead. Get it out of your system now."

Ida clears her throat. "I had someone look into her background. It isn't pretty."

I make a disgusted sound. "So what? Unless one of you is willing to tell me what kind of mysterious things Margot has done that I don't know about…"

There is a silent moment where Ida and Erik look at each other, their frowns heavy. I shake my head.

"I didn't think so," I say.

A butler hovers in the doorway and clears his throat. "Pardon me, but the crown prince has a number of engagements to prepare for today…"

"Thank you," I say to the butler. Swinging back to Erik and Ida, I shrug one shoulder. "Being the prince never ends."

Then I turn and stride out of the room, following the butler.

Chapter Thirty-Seven

MARGOT

GETTING out of the limo with twenty pounds of ballerina pink tulle zippered snugly around my body is a real struggle. I push myself up against the doorframe, cursing my own decision to wear this delicate, strapless ball-gown. When I finally find my feet, I pat my hair discretely.

Are we really about to do this? My heart pounds. I look up at the fancy hotel we are at, praying that I don't sweat in this dress.

Stellan is right by my side, offering his arm. He's at his most dazzling dressed in a dapper tuxedo and his smile as he looks me up and down gives me chills.

"You look amazing in that dress," he intones, his eyes taking me in. "You're going to be perfect tonight."

I place my hand on the inner elbow of his tuxedo jacket, exhaling. "Thank you. I won't even bother to compliment you, because you always look perfect."

He smirks. "Come on, then."

He leads me past the bowing bellhops and valets, through the perfect pink granite lobby, and up a gorgeous pink granite grand staircase. We emerge onto the second floor and hear the party before we see it; strains of a string quartet escape from the ballroom to our right. He sweeps right past the people crowded around a set of wide double doors. I try to play it cool, lifting my head high like I belong here, but I don't.

I am just pulled along with *him*.

As we enter the ballroom, I notice people bowing. They're definitely bowing to Stellan and not to me, but it still makes me uncomfortable. The party is already in full swing, the women in extravagant gowns, the men stunning in their tuxes.

It's a Wednesday night, for god's sake. Don't these rich people have better places to be than here? Especially tonight, the night that Stellan and I are stepping out together as a couple.

My heartbeat gallops away in my chest. I suck in a breath.

"There's Pippa," Stellan says, nudging me.

I glance in the direction he nods. Pippa is right there, wearing the most amazing bright pink ballgown topped with an enormous bow. She turns and spots me, grinning.

I look up at Stellan, then go still. I want to go see Pippa, but I definitely don't want to let Stellan down.

He leans in so close to my ear that his words are a kind of tease. "I'm afraid we have to say hello to a number of important people first. I promise you, the second we are through, you can go see Pippa."

I grin, slipping my hand down to find his. "Is this okay?"

His lips twitch. "Very." He kisses me on the lips and tucks a strand of hair behind my ear. I can feel the gazes of the people around us turning curious.

I blush red as a ripe summer strawberry, straightening his lapel. "You can take me around to as many people as you want. At the end of the day, I get to be here with you."

He smirks then leans down to whisper in my ear again. "Good girls get rewarded. Just something for you to think about."

My blush deepens, going all the way down my neck. "You are wicked. A truly wicked prince."

He winks. "You're fucking right I am."

Stellan guides me over to an older couple. He says hello, chats with them for a moment, then introduces me.

"This is Margot Keane, my girlfriend."

My eyes widen a little. I glance at him with a startled look. We definitely didn't talk about labeling this thing between us. The older couple look at me curiously as we shake hands.

"Hi," I say, because I have no idea what else to say.

"You're American!" the woman says, a little taken back. "How... interesting!"

My cheeks burn sixteen shades of red. She just made it clear as day that I am the weirdo, standing here in a dress I don't own, on the arm of a man who isn't mine. I nod dumbly, feeling like I want to crawl under a rock and never come out again.

This was such a bad idea. I watch Stellan's face anxiously, trying to figure out when he's going to pull the ripcord and bail out of this disaster.

It's only a minute before Stellan excuses us, pulling me by the elbow as he moves away. He looks down at me, but never stops moving. "If we keep circling, it will look like we are on the way to talk to someone," he confides.

"Should I leave?" I whisper.

That causes him to stop. "What? Why?" Then he glances back where we just were. "Oh, because of the Eldins? God no. I picked them as the first people because they will hate you no matter what you do. They hate me, to be perfectly honest."

My jaw drops. "What?"

"*Ja*. I just wanted you to cut your teeth on them. Because it doesn't matter if you are the most charming person ever or if you're a nervous wreck... they are so old and so conservative that they won't approve of you either way." He slides his palm up my back, his smile genuine. "It wasn't that bad, actually."

A surprised huff of laughter leaves my lips. "It was terrible! Not to mention the fact that you sprang the whole girlfriend thing on me..."

He smirks. "What? You're going to say that you don't desperately want to be my girlfriend?"

I blush and roll my eyes. "You know what I mean."

"I do." His eyes shine with a mischievous light. "Are you ready to meet people who aren't an absolute waste of space?"

I suck in a deep breath. "Okay. I'm ready."

For the first ten people I am introduced to — as Stellan's girlfriend, no less — I'm nervous. The next thirty or so go by in a blur. And after the next thirty, my head starts to spin.

"I need a break," I whisper to Stellan.

He raises his brow. "Now? We are almost done." he wrinkles his nose. "We just have to greet my grandmother and Prime Minister Finley. Don't worry, they are almost always together at these things. My grandmother thrives when she feels like she's important. Finley does his part by following her around and kissing her ass."

I color faintly. "Okay. I just… I don't know how you do it. Smile for everybody, remember mundane details about their lives…"

He shrugs. "I've had years of practice. Trust me, you get better at it the longer you do it."

Taking a deep breath, I close my eyes briefly. "Okay. I can do one more."

When I open my eyes, I find him looking around the ballroom. "I think my grandmother and Prime Minister Finley are holding court all the way over there."

He takes my hand and leads me through the densely crowded ballroom. It's weird to watch people realize that they are in the path that Stellan intends to take. They jump out of the way, apologizing profusely for having done exactly nothing.

We pass Pippa again, who is slow dancing with Lars. Her head is on his shoulder, her eyes are tightly closed. He holds her as carefully as if she were made of the most delicate glass. As if he is afraid to shatter her.

I tug on Stellan's hand. When he looks back, I nod at them.

He doesn't look the least bit surprised. "That's been going on for years. They're best friends. Or maybe they are lovers. Who can keep track anymore?"

He turns away and keeps going, and I force myself to turn my gaze toward the far corner of the ballroom. We pass by more people and then the path we are on clears. There in the corner of the room is a huddle of people, centered around the most petite figure, that of Stellan's grandmother.

She is elegance personified. She's wearing a dress made of ivory silk and she looks as perfect as a wedding cake topper.

"What do I call your grandmother?" I whisper.

"Her Royal Highness," Stellan whispers.

He leads me right up to the people gathered in the circle. Without a word, the circle widens, leaving a gap for us to step through. Her Royal Highness is just finishing a story and several people laugh.

She looks right at me, her face creasing ever so slightly. I can feel her gaze as it traces down to where I cling to her grandson's hand. She cocks an eyebrow, looking at Stellan.

"Should we go somewhere more private?" she asks him.

Stellan grips my hand harder. "Why would we? I just wanted to introduce you all formally." He turns to me. "Margot Keane, this is Her Royal Highness, the Queen Dowager. And right beside her is Prime Minister Finley, the Prime Minster." They each lower their heads for the barest second. "Everyone, this is Margot. My girlfriend."

Every pair of eyes within hearing distance is suddenly on me. Every drop of blood in my whole body rushes to my cheeks.

"Hello," I say softly. "It's a pleasure."

Prime Minister Finley clears his throat. "Girlfriend, you say?"

Her Royal Highness fastens her gaze on me. "I suggest we withdraw to somewhere we can speak alone, Stellan."

Stellan gives everyone a bland smile. "We are perfectly fine, *Momse*. Thank you. Actually, I promised Margot that we could head to another engagement as soon as she had formally met you."

The expression of astonishment mixed with a frosty anger looks right at home on her face. "I would speak with you in private— "

That's the moment that I hear the first angry shout. I whip my head around and see a few of people wearing all red coming into the ballroom.

"*Danmark ønsker frihed!*" one cries, raising a fist in the air. The others shout in support.

"*Frihed fra tyranni!*"

"*Frihed!*"

My eyes widen and my jaw drops. They are protesting. Worse, they are protesting *us*.

I look at Stellan, who instinctively steps in front of me. "What are they saying?"

"*Afskaffe monarkiet!*" another one screams.

Stellan's face is stony as he watches the protestors as a swarm of security guards moves in to surround them. "They're calling for freedom from tyranny. I assume that they are Red-Green Party protestors, calling for the abolishment of the monarchy."

I turn back and look at the protestors, my face going beet red. Though I've been too wrapped up in Stellan lately to be a rabble-rouser, I have been in their shoes. I've even been to Red-Green Party meetings.

How am I on the other side of the issue now? My heart starts beating at a frenzied pace.

Am I turning my back on the issues I once so cared about?

A bodyguard materializes out of nowhere. *"Vi må flytte dig et andet sted, Prins Stellan."*

He starts to corral Stellan, who has a good four inches on him. *"Vi tager afsted,"* Stellan says. "Come on, Margot."

I allow myself to be hustled out of the ballroom while the protestors are being herded out the opposite side. One of the protestors throws a balloon filled with red paint, which bursts against the doorway just as I pass under it.

Red paint falls on my head and the back of my dress, but Stellan shelters me from most of the fallout.

"Rend mig i røven!" he mutters. "Fuck! We have to go. Come on, let's get out of here before the press gets wind of the protest."

Still stunned, I let him lead me down the back stairway and to a waiting car.

Chapter Thirty-Eight

STELLAN

A FEW DAYS LATER, I'm escorting Margot down a long hallway at Winthrop Manor, the house in which my parents have finally come home to rest. I slow my pace, stopping her for a second. She looks up at me, her face worried.

"What?" she asks. "Did you forget something?"

My brow creases. "Are you okay?"

She nods slowly, pressing her hands down over the full skirts of her light blue ballgown. "Why wouldn't I be?"

I shrug. "You've been quiet ever since we went to that ball."

She bites her lip, her face heating. "I know. Just… I'm still a little shaken by the fact that the protestors were protesting you. I'm trying to figure out how to feel about being a part of the problem and not part of the solution."

My eyebrows rise. "I didn't realize you felt that way."

She bows her head and shrugs. "It's just… stuff I need to get over, I guess. I'll figure it out. Don't worry."

I reach out, grabbing her hand and hauling it against my chest. "Are you sure you're still okay with meeting my parents? It's a big step, I know." I pause. "Is it too soon?"

There is a moment of hesitation. I see in her eyes that she's still not a thousand percent sure. But Margot raises her chin, looking at me proudly.

"I'm ready," she affirms. "I promise."

I lean down and kiss her, reassuring myself as much as her. She tastes sweet and perfect, just like she did the last ten thousand times I've kissed her. I squeeze her hand, then lead her to the doorway of the dining room.

"Your highness," the servant at the door says, bowing low. "Please."

He waves us into the room. Everyone else in my family is already here, and my late joining doesn't exactly go unnoticed. The entire table turns to me, as if they are collectively waiting for something.

I reach behind myself and find Margot's hand. She's gone pale as we approach the two empty seats, situated between my father and my little sister Annika.

"Speak of the devil," my brother Lars announces.

"Yes, we were waiting for you two," Annika says, looking amused. "Join the party."

My father looks jovial as usual, a huge dark-haired giant with bright red cheeks. "Ah, our firstborn has finally deigned to join us."

My mother gets to her feet, rushing over to hug me. She's a tiny person, and when she embraces me tightly, several strands of her dark hair escape the chignon at her nape. "Ach, *min son!*"

I let myself be hugged for a second, then chuckle. "Okay, okay." My mother lets go and I draw Margot closer. "Mother. Father… this is Margot. Margot, meet the king and queen."

Margot curtsies awkwardly. "Your highnesses."

"Oh!" my mother says, beaming at Margot. "Please, call me Thora. And that's Göran."

My mother then proceeds to be her charming self, embracing Margot and pulling out her chair. Margot turns red and hurries to sit down. I see Annika tug on her arm and whisper something into her ear. Judging by the smile that appears on Margot's lips, I would guess that Annika just told her something whimsical.

"Sit, sit," my father says. "Join the rest of us."

I take my seat next to him, looking around the table. Lars and Finn are in attendance, though Finn looks bored.

"Where's Anders?" I wonder.

My mother clears her throat. "We should talk about that later," she says, smiling. "We are all here to meet your new friend, Stellan."

I reach for Margot's hand under the table, glancing at her. "Girlfriend. She's my girlfriend."

My father looks surprised. "You didn't tell my mother that, I hope? She would have a stroke."

"Oh, quit," my mother answers, rolling her eyes. "She'll be just fine. Your mother gets so hysterical over everything."

I look at my siblings to gauge their reactions to that. Annika wrinkles her nose, Finn looks at his glass of red wine, and Lars looks somber. No help there, I guess.

Not that I really expected it.

"I did tell her," I reply. "In fact…" I grip Margot's hand. "I was hoping that you could give me guidance about announcing the relationship to the cabinet and the parliament."

Margot squeezes my hand. I glance at her and she gives me a wide-eyed look that says *we didn't talk about that!*

I wink at her. "When the time is right, I mean."

Annika interjects. "Isn't that like… a step away from announcing that you're engaged?"

Between us, Margot goes pale and shrinks down in her seat an inch. My father sizes us up, then gives his head a shake. "Your sister is right. Telling parliament is quite serious."

My mother actually tears up. "I'm so happy for both of you! Now Margot… I learned you are from New York City. Is that correct?"

Clearing her throat, Margot nods. "Yes, ma'am. Born and raised."

"That's fascinating." My mother looks at my father. "Isn't it?"

"Very," he says. "Tell me though, aren't you a journalist?"

Margot goes red as a beet. "Yes, sir."

He waves his hand. "Göran, please. And you realize that being my son's girlfriend will probably mean you won't get the best stories assigned to you any longer, correct?"

Margot looks at me, wetting her lower lip with her tongue. "Yes sir… I mean… yes, Göran."

I sit forward, eager to defend her. "Margot isn't dating me for access to the royal family."

"Oh! Göran is not suggesting that!" my mother says, eying my father. "Is he?"

My father, ever the wise man, knows when he should stop talking. So he just smiles. "No, of course not."

I sit back and let Margot take over the answering, making eye contact with my father once more. His lips tip upward and he gives me a nearly imperceptible head tilt.

I take that to mean that he approves of Margot. Then again, how could anyone not be pro-Margot when my mother is so obviously over the moon about her?

We get through dinner just fine. Between Annika and my mother peppering her with questions, Margot talks almost the entire time. She is bashful at first but in the end, I feel like she charmed the hell out of my parents.

Now there is just the rest of the fucking world to go, I guess.

When it's time to go, my mother hugs both me and Margot so hard that it's almost painful.

I shake hands with my father, who is still seated at the table. "Talk soon?"

His lips tip upward. "Yes."

There's something hanging between us, a moment of hesitation on my part. Should I bring up what my grandmother told me? "I'm glad you are doing well."

He frowns but says nothing. He just nods his head.

Then I squire a talked-out Margot down to the waiting limo, where she crawls in the back seat and closes her eyes.

"Oh my god," she moans as I climb in beside her. "I'm so tired! How do you do that all day, every day and manage not to go insane?"

I give her a look. "That was just my family. That was the easy part."

She wrinkles her nose. "The easy part of what?"

"You have to know that being my girlfriend is..." I stop, trying to decide what I'm going to say. My mouth turns down at the corners. "My sister wasn't wrong. Let's say our next step is declaring our relationship to parliament. That's as good as telling everyone that they should expect a royal wedding in the next year."

Her eyes widen. Her throat works as she swallows. "I didn't realize that."

I puff out my cheeks, exhaling slowly. "Well... now you do. What do you think?"

She screws up her mouth. "I think that's asking a lot of us."

"So you would say no?" I ask, my brow descending.

Margot pins me with a surprised gaze. "What are you asking, exactly?"

I rake a hand through my hair, growing agitated. "I'm not asking you to marry me yet. But… are you at least open to getting married? I mean, you had to give this *some* thought when you agreed to date me."

She sucks her lower lip in between her teeth, her gaze lowering. "A little. I…" She pauses, taking a deep breath. "I'm not against getting married. I just didn't think… I mean… I thought we would have more time to get comfortable with the idea."

"Royals are born ready to marry. It's one of our duties to the country." I exhale, waiting a beat. "Historically, the royal family marries people who are wealthy and titled. People who may or may not be royals in their own right. People with the same expectations that my family has." I reach out for her hand, holding it gently. "I thought… I just thought that we were lucky, because we happen to be in love with each other."

She looks at me, grasping my hand. "I do love you, Stellan. You know that. I just wasn't prepared for all the bullshit that other people are forcing on us. But I realize that you don't really have a choice in the matter, do you?"

My mouth lifts at that corners. "No, I don't have a choice. In the grand scheme of things though… I can imagine much worse things than having you as my wife."

She gives me a tiny smile. "I feel the same as you do. It's just a lot at once. I have so many questions… Where would we live? What would happen to my job?"

I push my cheek out with my tongue. "There's only one question that matters, in my opinion. When I ask, will you say yes? Because everything else is flexible."

She blushes six shades of red, but she doesn't look away. "Yes. When you ask me someday, I will say yes?"

I shrug, a smile tugging at my lips. "Then that's settled."

Margot slides her palm along my jaw, drawing me close for a tender kiss. I let my eyes sink closed, let my thoughts only hover on this moment.

This moment in which she said *yes*.

Chapter Thirty-Nine

MARGOT

I WAKE SO EARLY that dawn has yet to break. I'm still not used to sleeping beside Stellan, especially not here in the palace. His bedroom here is beyond ridiculous, featuring a massive four poster bed and floor length windows wrapped in gauzy white.

I settle on my side and watch him in his sleep. Without his piercing ice blue gaze he seems softer, though his body is still every bit as rugged. My fingers itch to reach out and touch him.

I love him so, so much. My heart twists in my chest. I shouldn't wake him, but it is hard.

Rolling onto my back, I repress a sigh. My mind goes back to yesterday evening, to the all but proposal he sprung on me in the backseat of the car.

Honestly, I haven't really thought of much else since he asked me.

When I ask, will you say yes?

I thought I had died then and there when he asked, and I wasn't sure if I was in heaven or hell.

I mean, on one hand… Stellan and I have just fallen in love. It feels real… but there is so much more that's yet to be seen. Why rush into things?

And then on the other hand… he just basically asked me to be his *princess.*

Never in a million years did I ever actually think that someone as hot as

Stellan would ever look at me like he does. Like we're in the desert, and I'm the only glass of cool water for a hundred miles around.

I've never felt that kind of connection with anyone else. And I never expected to, either. I think that what Stellan and I have is so special.

But the whole royal thing really ratchets up our mutual expectations like a million degrees.

I'm not just agreeing to be his girlfriend. I'm agreeing to be the future queen.

And that thought terrifies me to the depths of my soul.

Heaving a silent sigh, I realize that there's no way I'm going to go back to sleep. I get up, moving stealthily to grab my pink silk robe from where it's hanging by the door. Then I pad out of the bedroom and into the adjoining living room.

A footman is just pulling back the drapes on the windows, revealing the new dawn just now breaking. I see the table, on which he has already laid out an assortment of waters and juices with fresh croissants and jam.

He bows to me and leaves without saying a word. Something I'm trying to get used to still.

I suck in a breath and wander over to the table, pausing when I see the newspapers spread out beside our breakfast. My own young face stares back at me, shell-shocked.

My mugshot.

Oh fuck.

PRINCE STELLAN'S LOVER HAS DARK PAST

My heart starts hammering in my ears. I snatch the paper up with trembling fingers and unfold it. I only have to scan the first few lines to realize that my own mother ratted me out.

Not only that, but she somehow dug up this old photo of me and gave it to the newspaper.

Fuck!

I stare at the picture. At sixteen years old, I was nothing but trouble. My hair is dark brown, I'm wearing oversized men's clothes, and worst of all… I hold my hand down low, but you can clearly tell that I am flipping off the camera.

I ball up the paper in my hands and release a scream. "Fuck! Where is my phone?"

"What's going on?"

I whirl and find a sleepy Stellan standing in the doorway, completely unashamed of his nudity. My eyes widen and my heart seizes. I can feel myself turning red.

I wasn't even thinking about him yet... What will he think about my teenage lawbreaking?

"I... I..."

He walks over to where I dropped the crumpled piece of newspaper, smoothing it out. His eyes widen and he looks up at me expectantly.

"What the fuck is this?"

The boom of his voice makes me jump out of my skin. I can't even look at him when I answer.

"I had two arrests when I was only sixteen. One for criminal trespassing and one for shoplifting. I guess... I guess that The New York Post must have paid my mother a lot for this story, because they have pictures and everything."

He points to a chair next to the table, his voice shaking. "Sit. Tell me everything that happened." His eyes pin me in place. "Do not leave anything out this time, Margot."

I scurry over to the chair, taking a seat. Stellan sits across from me, folding his arms across his chest and scowling at me in a way that makes my stomach do flips.

"Um. So..." I blow out a breath. "When I was sixteen, I ran with a bad crowd. There were a bunch of us, guys and girls, all about the same age. All homeless or in-between homes at the time. All angry. I didn't actually think my mom remembered any of this because she was on a bender at the time..."

"Margot!" he growls. "What happened?"

I suck in a breath. "Right. Sorry. I got arrested twice, like I said. Once for criminal trespass, because a bunch of us were squatting in a house together. And then I got busted like three weeks later for trying to shoplift stuff to eat."

I'm so humiliated at saying it out loud. My face is red, my ears are ringing, and I can't sit still.

"Why didn't you think to tell me about this when I asked about your background?" he asks, seeming mystified.

I glance at Stellan, biting my lip. "I didn't realize that you were looking for anything in particular. I was just... trying to tell you about my life," I say, growing defensive. "I didn't realize that you were asking for a full background check. I usually don't tell people I date about it for the first six months, if ever."

He looks so confused and angry. "Why not?"

"Because it isn't really anyone's business!" I shout. I shake my head. "When I got arrested the second time, I did a diversion program. When I turned eighteen without getting arrested again, my record was expunged. And I happen to think that my being a reformed bad girl isn't really the most interesting thing about me, if we're being perfectly honest."

Stellan shakes his head slowly, exhaling as he scrubs a hand over his face. "This is fucked up, Margot." He glances at me. "I mean, I won't lie. I was attracted to your rebellious streak. I love it sometimes, but other times… like now for example…"

I take a deep breath. "I wasn't trying to keep it from you Stellan. Honestly, I wasn't. It just didn't occur to me."

He studies me for a long moment, then nods. "I believe you."

My heart starts thrashing around in my chest. "You do?"

His face creases. "*Ja*. I don't think you are a dishonest person, Margot."

I launch myself on top on him, surprising him with a hug. Burrowing my head down against his chest, I let out a joyful sound. His arms close around me. He brushes my hair back, kissing the top of my head.

I've never been loved like this. Not ever.

My tiny brain gets totally overloaded and my eyes tear up. I hug him hard, blinking back tears.

"I'm sorry, Stellan." My voice breaks.

"Oh, *skatter*," he murmurs. "What am I going to do with you, huh?"

Wiping at my face, I lean back and look at him. "Will we have to tell your family?"

He looks at me like I might be simple. "Yes. My grandmother will have heart palpitations."

Ducking my head, I hide against the solid wall of his chest. "I'm so embarrassed."

"Mm. Not only that, but you have to tell me everything else. Any dirt, any secrets you have… spill them right now. It's better just to know where you might be vulnerable."

I frown. There isn't anything… is there?

"Well… I don't think that I have any other secrets…" I say.

"Really? Nothing else the press will get their hands on? Nothing that would make them salivate? Because I'm basically going to introduce you to the world as my better half. Soon to be a princess, one day to be queen."

That thought makes me heart seize. "Hearing you say that… it seems unreal."

Stellan pushes me back a couple of inches, his ice blue eyes pinning me. "I'm sorry to bring this back around to the point, but… what is the press going to find, Margot?"

An image swims up from deep down. "The only thing I can think of…" I wince. "There may be some footage of me protesting."

He frowns deeply. "Protesting what?"

My face heats. Occupy Wall Street. The Dakota Access Pipeline. The Red-Green party had a demonstration…"

Stellan makes a displeased noise. "Tell me you didn't sneak off and protest with the Red-Green party while you were here. Please, Margot."

I put a calming hand on his chest. "I didn't. They might be an actual political force over here, but in New York they are just people making noise. I went to one of their protests originally because a band I liked was going to be there."

He squints at me. "Has anyone ever told you that you are lucky you're beautiful, Margot?"

My blush depends. "I've heard that before, yes."

He cups my jaw and pulls me in for a deep kiss. When we break apart again, he sighs. "You are trouble, you know."

I wrinkle my nose. "I know. I don't want to be troublesome to you, though."

He cracks his knuckles. "I know, *skatter*. I really do."

I bite my lower lip. "Is there any way to contain this news story? Like… do you have any pull with the royal press office?"

He glances off at the window, through which the dawn has finally broken. "Some. It kind of depends." He hesitates. "You're probably going to have to apologize to someone about something."

My eyes widen. "To who? About what?"

Stellan shrugs. "I have no idea. But as soon as I tell the press office, I can bet you that they are going to tell you to apologize to everyone for everything." He scrunches up his face. "It's their advice about every scandal."

I make a face. "Do I have to?"

He smirks. "No. But it will make things easier if you intend to eventually make this your home and make me your husband."

I wince. "I love you so much, Stellan. I really do. That's the only reason that I'm okay with this."

He pulls me close for one last kiss, then sighs. "I had better get dressed. I'm going to have to try to get out in front of this."

I get up, biting my lip. "I'm just going to tell you this one more time. I'm sorry, Stellan."

The ghost of a smile crosses his face. "I know, *skatter*."

Then he leaves the living room, heading into the bedroom to get dressed. And I'm left standing in my silken robe, hugging myself and feeling bereft.

Chapter Forty

STELLAN

JUST AS I finish getting dressed to go over to Marselisborg Palace to see Ida, my phone buzzes. It's a message from Erik.

Your grandmother is here to see you and she is in a mood.

Fuck! Running out into the living room, I find Margot there, frowning at her phone.

"Come get dressed," I say, my eyes skating over her little silk robe. "My grandmother is on her way up here."

She stands up, slipping her phone into her pocket and swallowing. "Oh!"

She rushes past me into the bedroom and I close the door to give her privacy. A butler knocks on the living room door and I clear my throat. I won't lie, I'm a little nervous, going to bat for my girl.

"Come in!" I call out.

The door swings open and the butler steps in. "Her royal highness," he says, bowing as he escorts my grandmother in the room. Impeccably put together as always, my grandmother is wearing a light blue linen skirt and a modest white silk top.

"*Momse*," I greet her. "I was just coming to see you."

Ida looks at me strangely and then turns to dismiss the butler. "Please make sure we are not disturbed."

The butler bows and closes the door. Ida hesitates, then walks over to the sofas. She perches on one. "Take a seat, my dear."

Shit. What does she know? Could there be more in Margot's past that she wasn't honest about?

The thought is like an icy knife twisting in my gut. Composing myself sternly, I take a seat on the couch opposite her.

"It really isn't that big of a deal," I say.

Ida's eyes narrow on my face. "I don't know what you are talking about, Stellan. It doesn't matter." She clears her throat, looking me in the eye. "Your father has had an accident."

That news, completely unexpected, comes out of nowhere and hits me like a freight train.

"What?" I blink repeatedly.

"He is fine. He just walked off the middle of a stage yesterday. But I asked him what happened… and he admitted that he felt confused right before it happened."

My eyebrows lift. "What?"

Ida makes a conciliatory expression. "I've been telling you to be ready for this, Stellan. And now it's here."

"Wait." I shake my head, trying to understand. "Is my father hurt?"

She exhales, picking at a loose thread on her skirt. "Just some bruises and scrapes. But after talking to your father and several doctors, it has been decided that Goran needs to step down."

I have to lean back, letting that sink in. My father has always been so big and so strong. To think of him as… a confused man who fell off a stage…

"Stellan." My grandmother crosses her ankles, looking concerned. "You realize what I'm saying, do you not? Your father has to give up the crown. And you will have to step up and take it from him."

My eyes widen. "I'm sorry?"

"You are going to be coronated. And I'm afraid it will be soon." A wrinkle appears on her forehead. "Your father is ill. I'm sorry to put this so bluntly, but it's time to dispense with your little girlfriend and bring your focus back where it ought to be. On your country, my dear. Your life is about to become extremely complicated and I don't think you will have time for any… distractions."

I hear Margot gasp from behind me. I whirl, finding her in the doorway. She looks prim and proper in an expensive ivory silk dress, but her face has lost all its color.

"Is the king okay?" she asks, neatly ignoring her part in my grandmother's wishes. She looks at me, imploring.

My heart flip flops. I reach out my hand and Margot instantly picks up her dress and runs to sit down beside me, taking my hand. She looks at my grandmother.

"Please tell me he's going to be okay," she says again.

Ida clears her throat and narrows her gaze on where Margot touches me. "My son will be fine, thank you. It's my grandson I have to worry about, it seems."

Twining my fingers with Margot's, I pull her hand into my lap. "Tell me what you need, *Momse*. I will do what I can."

Her look of displeasure is cold as ice. "Very well." She lifts her head. "After I leave here, you will never be without protection again. Your guard will be right outside your door for the rest of your life."

I swallow. When I speak, it sounds as nervous as I feel. This is just a lot to take in. First my father, then the loss of my last little bit of freedom.

"Okay." I pause a beat. "What else?"

My grandmother looks at Margot, then purses her lips. "You're the heir to the throne, Stellan. You can't be dating. You can't let everyone see how vulnerable you are, especially not right now." She smiles coolly. "You have to either declare your intentions publicly or stop seeing one another."

I tighten my grip on Margot's hand. "Let me worry about dealing with my relationship, Momse."

Ida arches a brow and gives me a chilling look. "Fine." She stands up. "There are a thousand different documents for you to sign before you ascend to the throne. There's a ceremony to be planned out. You'll have to meet with all the lords and ladies that support us, and parliament besides. You'll have to decide who's going to be in your cabinet, who stays, who goes."

"I'll do what is needed," I promise her.

She levels a glare at Margot. "And you might want to see your father, because I'm sure that he will have thoughts on…" She waves her hand at me and Margot. "Whatever is going on here."

I rise, bringing myself to my full height and peering down at my grandmother. "That's enough. I've heard you."

Ida looks back at me, nothing on her face but sincerity. "I really hope you have, Stellan. The time for playing at being king has come and gone. Now you must show the entire world who you really are. I can only hope I've prepared you for the role."

She reaches out for me, touching my face briefly. Then she spins and heads out of the room, her head held high. I stare after her, trying desperately to take all the things she said in.

"Stellan?"

I look back and realize that I'm still gripping Margot's hand so hard that it's probably painful for her. I drop it apologetically. "Sorry, *skatter*. I'm just…"

She steps in front of me, pressing me down with two gentle hands on my shoulders. "It's okay. Sit down, Stellan."

I bury my face in my hands, feeling like a fool. "God damn it."

"I'll be right back. I'm just going to get your phone, okay?"

She disappears and then reappears, holding my phone up. "Here. When you're ready, you can text somebody to get in touch with your father."

"Thanks." I exhale, pushing myself backward into the pillows. "Fuck!"

Margot doesn't say anything. She just sits down beside me and runs her hand over my knee, looking distraught.

After a minute, I look at her.

"My grandmother was right about one thing."

She arches a brow. "Which thing? She said several."

I pin her in place with my gaze. "My life is about to become very complicated, Margot."

"I know," she says softly.

I stare into her dark blue eyes. "Are you still willing to run the gamut with me?"

"Of course," she says. "I'll do whatever you want."

"But what do *you* want? That's what I am really asking here."

She nods a little, taking a deep breath. "We should keep seeing each other, obviously. And I don't have any real objection toward you making things between us more…" She pauses and takes another gulp of air. "More official. I just want to be in the background."

I sigh. "I don't think that the press will let you just hang out in the background, Margot."

She nods again, looking down. "I know. But you asked what I wanted, not what's realistic."

She looks so sad that I can't help but pull her closer, pressing her small body against my larger one. My head rests on hers. My heart beat drums against my chest.

I close my eyes, inhaling. The sweet scent of Margot fills my nose.

"I want that too," I admit.

My heart aches. For my father, who I have yet to see. For my grandmother, who is just trying her best, though it may not seem that way.

For Margot, who is coping with the change in my status way better than I am.

And for this, this closeness. I have a very real sense that these moments are under threat now… though I swear I will do what I can to protect them.

My phone chirps. I open my eyes, sighing before I even read the words on the screen. They're from Lars.

He wants to see all of us right away.

I shoot off a reply before flinging my phone down.

Be there soon.

Then I look at Margot. She looks so anxious; I almost can't stand to look into her sweetly heart shaped face.

"I really fucking love you," I tell her.

She grabs my hand, pulling it over her heart. "I love you too. I always will."

Giving her a kiss, I reluctantly let her go and rise from the couch. "I'm going to go see my father."

She gives me a small smile. "I'll be here, waiting for you when you get back."

With a heavy heart, I turn and start moving away. When I step into the hallway, three suited guards turn to look at me.

"*Prime Ministerr*," I say, nodding to them. "*Lad os gå.*"

I head down the hall, feeling my invisible golden collar tighten just that much more.

Chapter Forty-One

MARGOT

I STAND IN THE DARKNESS, silhouetted by the enormous palace windows, just staring out into the moonlit night. I'm wearing a beautiful light gray ballgown but my shoes are abandoned by the door of the living room. I press my hands to my face, feeling the heat that rushed to my cheeks a few minutes ago.

I snuck away from the rest of the dinner party and ran up here as soon as I could. That's only after I made a complete fool of myself by talking over Stellan, though.

It didn't seem like that big of a deal to me. It's just a normal part of the conversational flow, at least in America. But apparently it was enough to stop every other conversation and draw all eyes my way.

My cheeks still burn just thinking about it.

"*Haj.*"

I turn a little, seeing Stellan standing there, filling up the doorframe. His face is mostly in shadow but I would recognize his tall frame anywhere. My mouth turns up at the corners.

"Think his name and he shall appear."

Stellan moves forward, his face emerging from the shadows. "I noticed that you were gone and I came to check on you."

I walk across the room to the couches, falling onto one of them.

Keeping my tone light, I look at him as he walks over. "You found me. Hiding upstairs from my own shame."

His lips twitch. "It wasn't that bad."

I roll my eyes. "Everyone at the dinner thought I was raised in a barn."

He gives me a funny look as he sits across from me. "What?"

"They thought I was lacking in manners."

"Ah! I wouldn't worry about what they think, honestly." He sits back, steeling his fingers.

"Well, I am worried. I'm worried from the second I wake up until the second I'm asleep. I don't want to embarrass myself... but more importantly, I don't want to embarrass you."

Stellan shrugs a shoulder. "I wouldn't worry about it."

I squint off toward the window. "I wasn't cut out for this... this caring about what everyone thinks. I just want to be able to wear my ratty old t-shirts and listen to my loud punk music and walk around taking photos. I don't want everyone else's opinions about how I walk funny and who I should be associating with."

I stick out my tongue to make a disgusted face. My expectation is that he will laugh, or make some funny remark. But to my surprise he leans forward, his face looking serious as the original sin.

"Margot. If you don't want this lifestyle, please tell me right now. There is still time to turn the car around."

My eyes widen. "I'm sorry. I didn't mean to complain..."

He shakes his head. "No, I'm serious. Can you be a royal? Can you deal with the invasion of privacy and the world judging your every move?" He stops, then exhales a long breath. "I know it isn't very romantic to have this conversation. But I really need you to think about your answer. You'd have to give up any kind of job. You'd have to put down roots here. I will move heaven and earth to make you my wife... but you have to meet me halfway."

For a second, I can only blink. For Stellan to say these things to me, so bluntly and without pretense or the disguise of humor... it's unusual, to say the least.

"Stellan— "

He holds up a hand. "I want you to consider what I am saying, Margot. There is an escape option for you... but that window is growing smaller by the day. Do you understand?"

I flush, sitting up and looking at my hands in my lap. "I do."

He put my conundrum into words, which is more than I have been willing or able to do. As I sit there, his words swirl against me and wash over me again and again.

Can I be the queen that Stellan needs? Am I dignified enough? Humble enough? Resilient enough?

Simply put, do I have what it takes?

Half a minute of silence lapses before I realize that he's waiting for an answer. I glance up at his darkly handsome face, biting my lower lip.

"I don't know," I confess. "I'm sorry. I wish I did."

Stellan sits back on the couch, looking upset. "I thought that you wanted this."

"I love you. That part has never been in doubt. But… you're asking me to make a major decision that will affect the rest of my life. And it's just… it's hard." Screwing up my face, I sigh. "If you were anyone else, I would just say yes right now. But… your honor, your sense of duty… they are a part of you. And I'm trying to figure out whether I can put honor and duty first like you do."

He frowns. "You make me sound selfless. I'm anything but that. If I really only cared about duty, I would've just picked a wealthy Danish girl to marry and sired an heir by now."

I wrinkle my nose. In my head, I can just picture Stellan and some willowy blonde standing in a royal portrait, holding a baby. The question is, can I put myself in the place of the blonde?

"I know," I say with a shrug. "I'm trying my best to figure out whether I can commit to the royal lifestyle. You already know that I'd commit to you in a heartbeat."

His smile is a little heartbreaking. "I know, *skatter*. We are just running out of time. A decision has to be made."

I suck in a breath and nod. "I know."

Stellan stands up, holding out his hand to me. "Come."

Getting to my feet, I slip my hand into his, relishing how warm his skin is. "Back to the dinner?"

His mouth curves up. "No. It's been two days since I've even seen you naked. I'm starving for your body, *skatter*."

My heart beat drums a staccato rhythm against my ribs. Pressing myself closer to Stellan, I pull his head down, kissing his mouth. He growls and sweeps me off my feet, carrying me to his bedroom.

He strips me naked and tosses me on the bed, then undresses himself. When he comes after me, his touch tender and brutal, I can't get enough.

He takes me from behind, pulling my hair and caging my body in with his. He fucks me, slowly at first, his thrusts growing more and more rough. He soon has me calling out his name, panting breathlessly, as he drives me closer and closer to the brink. And I've never felt so free as I do in the midst of our sweaty, mind-blowing sex.

Trapped under him, pinned like this, is exactly where I want to be. It's all the rest that has me questioning whether I can commit to being his.

Later, when we are done, our sweat cooling as we suck in hasty breaths, I cling to Stellan.

"I love you so much," I whisper against his chest. "I always will."

He just pulls me closer, still struggling to pull air into his lungs. The way he holds me, like I'm some fragile thing that is too precious to break… it almost makes me cry.

As I drift off to sleep, the last thing on my mind is a question.

Am I really going to let this wonderful man slip away just because I can't stand being scrutinized by strangers?

I really, really hope not.

Chapter Forty-Two

STELLAN

A COUPLE OF DAYS LATER, it is clear that word of my relationship with Margot has gotten to the press. Normally I am not bothered by a few reporters that might turn up here and there. But they've been growing in number over the last few days, showing up at every event I have, elbowing each other in order to get to within earshot of me.

"Prince Stellan! Is Margot your lover?"

"Stellan! Stellan! Will you marry her?"

"Will the wedding be soon?"

I ignore them as I get out of the back of the limo and hurry into the palace. Looking back at the swarm of reporters and paparazzi, I'm nearly blinded by a flashbulb going off to the right of the palace doorway.

Shaking my head to clear my vision, I turn and trot inside the darkened palace. Running up the grand staircase, I make my way down the echoing hallway to my living room.

When I open the door to find Margot wiping away a tear and trying to hide that she's been crying, I feel my heart twist in my chest. She sniffles and sits up straighter in the hard backed chair by the table, running her hand over her black cotton dress.

"*Haj,*" she greets me.

My heart twists again. She's trying to learn Danish for me.

"*Haj*," I say, walking over and giving her a hug. "I am guessing that you saw the reporters?"

Margot wipes at her face bashfully. "Yeah. I was going to go out to meet the personal shopper you suggested for me... but I couldn't even manage to leave the palace."

She sucks in a deep breath. "It's especially hard because I don't even have any answers for them."

I pull away, shaking my head. "That isn't anything I can help with, Margot."

Pulling out the chair opposite her, I sit down and glance out the window. She wrinkles her nose delicately.

"I know," she says. "I was just... telling you how I feel."

I drum my fingertips on the table. When I speak, my words come out sharper than I intended. "The prime minister came to see me today. He asked about you. How do you think I felt, telling him I don't have any more answers about our current predicament than you?"

I can actually hear her inhale. She narrows her eyes at me. "I'm sorry that you are feeling the pressure. It must be terrible to feel like you don't have much control of things."

I shoot her a glare. "It's not that hard to make up your mind, Margot. You either want me, and can accept all that comes along with me... or you can't."

She ducks her head, her jaw tensing. "You make it sound so easy."

I grind my teeth. "It might not be easy for you. For me, there was never a choice. I didn't get that kind of freedom."

She shoots to her feet, pacing over to the window. "Yes. I know that you had a hard childhood, Stellan. Just like you know that mine wasn't any easier." She hisses out a breath. "I feel like we could go around and around in circles over this for a thousand more years."

I try to take a calming breath. "We're out of time, Margot. I think you know that."

She leans against the window, scrunching up her face. "I just need more time."

"Time for what?" I ask, raising my hands. "What will a few more days get you that you don't already have?"

"I don't know," she says mournfully, her gaze still fixed on something out the window. "Clarity?"

I try a different tack. "When I came in here, you were crying."

Margot glances at me, uncertain. "So?"

"So… you had one run in with the press. And you… you cracked under the pressure! Not even very much pressure, I might add." I pin her with my gaze. "If that's the way you handle a tense moment, I worry about you being able to handle the everyday scrutinies that accompany royal life. Like… if you can't cope with this, how are you going to handle it when the paparazzi find out that we're engaged? How are you going to deal with being pregnant?"

Margot's eyes go wide. Her retort is immediate and biting. "I don't know, Stellan! This is all new to me! I can't fathom how I'll deal with anything, let alone being pregnant with your child!"

There has been a tenuous thread between her and me. But her outraged tone, her angry gestures… they cause me to pull on that thread until it snaps.

I get to my feet, my voice gone to gravel. "Maybe we should both do ourselves a favor and stop trying. Maybe we are just not suited."

She stares at me for a second, her mouth opening. "What are you saying, Stellan? Are you saying that this…" She gestures to the air between us both. "Isn't worth it?"

"Maybe I am," I say, my gut twisting.

A fresh sheen of tears in her eyes tells me that I've hit her in a soft spot. "I've been daydreaming. I've been living a lie. Pretending… pretending that if I tried hard enough, I could make people forget that I'm a foreigner. Make them forget that I come from nothing." She looks deathly serious, her little hands forming fists. When she speaks again, her voice is watery and rough. "I thought that I could make you forget. But that's not quite possible, is it?"

I spread my hands wide. "Maybe not, Margot. Maybe we are just… two people that should have been together. Maybe in another life, if we were a little more similar…"

A tear breaks loose and runs down her face. She swipes at it angrily. "We are fundamentally different, Stellan. That's what makes us… us."

I close my eyes for a second. "So… what? We're different. I'm still a royal. I'll always be a royal."

She crosses her arms. "And I'll always be common, no matter if you marry me or not. You could bestow a thousand titles on me and I'll still be..."

She trails off, unable to finish her thought. She looks down, ducking her head and wiping at her face.

My fingers itch to touch her. I ball my hands into fists. "All you have to do is leave," I grate out. "All you have to say is that you can't do it. If you don't want me to chase after you, I won't. I love you, but..."

Margot looks up at me, her dark blue eyes agonized. Her words leave her in a huff of breath. "But maybe love isn't enough."

Her words ring out, settling between us like shattered glass. I suck in a breath.

"Margot— "

"No!" she says, shaking her head fiercely. "No. I won't ever be the perfect, quiet, submissive little wife you all expect me to be! You want me to quit my job... and be just... completely dependent on you..."

She breaks down in tears, a silent sob rippling through her whole body.

I don't know what to say. I don't know how to make this better. My heart is frozen in my chest; my lungs feel brittle when I draw a breath.

"So go then," I utter. Margot looks up at me, tears running down her face. "Go!" I yell.

A final twist of the knife, cutting both of us to the bone. Her face goes white.

"If I leave—" she whispers.

"Fucking go. Be done with it already," I toss the words out, turning away from her. "This is over."

I start to walk away. Behind me, I hear her gasped breath. And then she lets a sob escape her as she turns and runs away, out the door faster than I can draw a breath.

When I turn back to look, all I see is an empty doorframe.

"Fuck!" I shout, reaching out blindly to overturn a plain wooden chair. Then I angrily tip the whole table on its side, making a noise that isn't half of the fury that I feel.

I storm toward the bedroom, needing to brood in silence.

Chapter Forty-Three

STELLAN

FIVE DAYS.

It has been five days since Margot and I fell apart. Four sleepless nights, five agonizing, drudgery-filled days.

I sit in the backseat of another limo, my eyes closed, wishing… well, I don't know exactly what I want. I want Margot to reappear, to explain why she was so wrong before when she said she couldn't live like I do.

"Stellan."

I crack open my eyes, sliding a look at Erik. He's sitting beside my against the black leather seats, looking concerned.

"I'm here," I say, adjusting my big body in the car.

He looks at me, scrubbing a hand through his blond hair. "We're almost back at the palace."

I loosen my tie, feeling miserable. "*Ja*, okay."

Glancing out the window as Copenhagen flies by, I flutter my eyes closed again. Erik clears his throat.

"What can I do to make you less…" He pauses. "Whatever you are right now? It's hard to watch you be so… listless. Is this still about Margot?"

I laugh and look at him again. "It's about everything and nothing, all at once."

He cocks his head. "Who rejected whom?"

His question puts a scowl on my lips. "That's unclear. I laid out an ultimatum… and she backed away from it." I sigh, shaking my head. "I just want to move on already. I want to be done with all of this."

Erik squints. "You look like you haven't slept in weeks. Maybe you need to talk to a doctor or something."

I shoot him a glare. "It's not that bad."

"Today you kept calling the minister of health Prime Minister Kelley, even after you had been corrected numerous times. Yesterday, at the gala, you were totally distracted and got drunk in public. I could go on."

I roll my eyes. "So?"

"So, you need to shake this off. You're the fucking crown prince of Denmark. If you want to drown your sorrows in women, all you have to do is say so. If you want to do something daring and dangerous, I have like five activities up my sleeve, waiting for you to say the word. But you've got to pull it together."

I clamp my mouth shut, glaring at the front of limo. When I don't respond, Erik shifts his weight.

"I'm sorry that Margot hurt you."

I look at him funny. My heart squeezes in my chest. "She didn't hurt me."

He slides me a skeptical look. "No? You wouldn't call this behavior you've been displaying heartbreak?"

If I could kill with a look, Erik would be bleeding out right now. "No. It's not heartbreak. It's… disappointment. It turns out that all my initial biases about Margot were right on target… I just allowed myself to get distracted by the nice ass and pretty blue eyes that those things accompanied."

He doesn't seem to know what to say to that. Furrowing his brow, he shakes his head. "It still sucks to go through a breakup. I mean… you've never really had to go through one before. Because of who you are, girls just flock to you. And you've never really spent any time with a girl who didn't want the crown."

I roll my eyes. He's right about one thing: Margot definitely didn't want the crown or anything attached to it.

Outside my window, the palace looms close. The second we stop, I bolt out of the back seat, not waiting around for Erik. He has to jog to catch up with me as I head inside, taking the stairs two by two.

I come to a halt when I reach the landing, squinting at the circus that awaits me there. No less than twenty young girls stroll up and down the hall, which is set up with a runway like a fashion show. The girls model barely-there dresses for my little sister, who sits at one end of the runway, her head cocked. Loud, upbeat music blares from a single speaker.

As soon as Erik and I walk over, suddenly the models are far more interested at making sexy faces in our direction than whatever Annika has them doing.

Annika turns around, spots us, and heaves a sigh.

"Girls, please!" Annika says, clapping her hands to get the models. "Take a five minute break, then we are all going again."

"What are you doing?" I ask her, annoyed. "This is my private hallway, Nika."

She scrunches up her face, standing up. I realize now that she's also wearing a sparkly silver dress similar to those the models have on; if Momse saw Annika right now, she would have a heart attack.

Annika gives me a cool smile. "Hello, big brother. It's nice to see you too." She wrinkles her nose. "This hallway has the best light. I need tons of good natural light for the fashion show I'm working on. Don't worry, it's for charity."

I grit my teeth. "Annika, take your models and your… party… somewhere else. I'm not in the mood."

Annika pulls a face. "You suck." She turns, cupping her hands to her mouth. "Turn the music off! We're moving to another floor!"

I glance at Erik, who is staring at Annika's barely covered ass so hard that it's a miracle it's not on fire. The look of longing on his face is an emotion I know all too well. It's the exact look I used to give Margot, before we fell into bed together.

I reach out and shove him. "What the fuck is wrong with you?"

He glances at me, his eyes widening. "Nothing. Let's go."

Erik starts pushing his way past the models and the runway, trying to get to the door of my study. I'm right on his heels, shoving him again once we make it into the study.

"On top of all the shit that I'm dealing with right now, the breakup with Margot and the upcoming coronation… I have to worry about you trying to fuck Annika?"

He pins me with a hard gaze. "Jesus. No. I swear. It's just been too long since I've gotten any pussy, that's all."

I glare at him. "That had better be all. You know better than to fuck around with Annika. She's only eighteen. Barely an adult."

"Stel, come on. Even if I was tempted — and I'm not saying that I am — I'm not stupid. Our friendship is more important than any crazy ideas my libido might have."

Getting very close to Erik's face, I stare him down. "It has better be. Twenty years we've been friends. Longer than Annika has even been alive."

"*Ja.* I know. I wouldn't do anything to mess that up, okay?"

I scan his face for signs of deception, but I come up empty handed. Shaking my head, I push past him. "You'd better remember that."

He gives me an odd look. "You really are fucked up right now, you know that? You should be more focused on making some kind of decision."

I throw myself down into one of the overstuffed leather chairs. "A decision about what, Erik?"

He takes a seat on the corner of my highly polished desk, looking down his nose at me. "It seems like you either need to call Margot, or you need to find some other way to deal with the breakup."

I scowl at him. "I'm not calling Margot. Things between us are done and dusted."

He shrugs a shoulder. "Okay. So let me throw a party. I'll invite a ton of girls and we'll all have a great time. You can have this weekend to party and recover, then be on your feet again by Monday."

This idea of throwing a huge party leaves a bad taste in my mouth. "I'll pass."

Erik checks his watch, then stands and wanders over to the bar setup that we always have on hand. He pours two glasses of whiskey, sauntering over to hand one to me.

I take a sip, though it can't be past two in the afternoon.

He drinks a little, looking at me. "You need to relax."

"I don't want to relax," I fire back, feeling prickly.

"What do you want to do, then? Huh? You can't spend any more time brooding."

Sitting back, I stare at the whiskey in my glass. "I don't know. I just don't want to feel like this anymore," I admit to him.

"Great." He walks over to my desk and sets his tumbler down, pulling out his phone. I watch him texting for a minute.

"Who are you texting?" I ask.

He looks up at me. "You said you don't want a huge party. So I am arranging for something more private and intimate. You, me, a couple of girls, a discreet evening."

Draining the contents of my glass, I stand and put the glass next to his. "Just give me a few days by myself, okay? I just… I need time."

His eyes narrow on my face. "To heal?"

"One more comment about how Margot broke my heart and I am going to punch you right in the nose."

He grins. "That's the spirit. No woman can keep you down!"

Rubbing my temple, I turn toward the door. "You are impossible. And on that note, I'm going to go lie down."

Leaving my study, I head down the hall toward my bedroom. But Erik's voice still echoes in my head.

And that's not heartbreak you're experiencing?

I don't know what it is, but I'm ready for it to be over, and soon.

Chapter Forty-Four

MARGOT

MY LEAST FAVORITE place to be in the whole entire world has got to be my current one: in Anna's office at *Politiken*, listening to her vent about how useless I am.

"I got a call early this morning," she shouts, pacing back and forth over the small office's length. "And would you believe it, it was from His Majesty's Press Office, calling to officially axe the article that you were apparently, supposedly, theoretically writing for us."

I slide an inch lower in my chair, my face turning neon pink. My input is not required for Anne's critique so I just swallow and try to ride it out.

As if I need another reminder that Stellan and I are over. Just thinking about it makes my eyes watery — and I swore that today, six days after we broke up, I wouldn't dissolve into tears in front of everybody.

Anne turns, pinning me with her dark gaze. "Well? Do you have anything to say for yourself, Margot?"

I suck my lower lip between my teeth and bite down. "No, ma'am."

She paces the tiny space for a half a minute, her face contorting with anger. "Of course not. You know, the press office refused to explain why they pulled the plug on this project… but the young woman that called said it was not their idea." She stops, turning to glare at me again. "That means that it was your idea, Margot. Is that right?"

I look down at my lap. "It's very complicated, Anna."

She laughs coldly. "You know what? Get out of my office before I fire you. As a matter of fact, take some time before you even think about coming back here."

I think she expects me to stay, to fight with her over my job. But I'm up and out of her office as soon as she says that. I can feel her eyes burning holes in my body as I gather my things.

As I barrel out of the front door, I repress a sob.

No Stellan.

No job.

Paparazzi mobbing the doorway of Pippa's apartment.

Will I even last here in Copenhagen? Because it sure feels like I have ruined Denmark for myself. Aside from Pippa, I'm essentially alone in a foreign country.

My eyes well up and I dash away my tears as I head toward the river.

"Margot! Wait!"

I turn to see Pippa rushing toward me, looking concerned. She catches up to me and throws her arms around me as I try not to cry.

"This place sucks!" I moan into her hair.

"Oh." She pets me as one would a cherished dog, caressing my hair. "I'm sorry. You should know that Guy asked me to come down and fetch you. Apparently, he didn't like the way that Anna handled you at all."

I allow myself one more whimper, then put some space between us. Pippa offers me a leather satchel, smiling a bit.

"It's a laptop. He thought you might have an interesting perspective on the royal family, if you feel up to it."

I take the satchel, adding it to the burden I already carry on my shoulder, including my tote bag. "Thanks."

She cocks her head, rubbing my shoulder. "Have you eaten anything?"

I nod. "A whole pint of gelato, straight from the container." My cheeks go pink. "And a cupcake." I pause. "And a whole loaf of French bread with butter."

She arches a brow. "I see. Heartbreak apparently makes you eat."

I nod. "I couldn't sleep again last night so I just stared at the ceiling and ate a whole block of cheese."

She grins. "Sadness-induced insomnia coupled with a little fridge binge. Got it. Honestly, I've heard of worse things."

I scrunch up my face. "My stomach hurts."

"Come over here," she says, marching me over to a bench and sitting me down. She sits beside me, squinting up into the bright blue sky. "Have you heard anything from him?"

Her question knocks the breath out of my lungs, so I just shake my head. She heaves a sigh.

"Stellan is quick tempered, as I'm sure you've found out. But he's also fair minded. I'm sure if you called him, he would take you back in a heartbeat."

I pucker up my face like I'm tasting something sour. "That will solve exactly nothing."

Pippa looks at me out of the corner of an eye, pushing her cheek out with her tongue. "Can I be really blunt?"

I raise my eyebrows. "I thought you already were."

She makes a face. "I think that this was your first fight."

I give her my most dubious look. "We fought all the time when I first moved to Copenhagen, Pippa."

She rolls her eyes. "That doesn't count at all. Since you guys have been all lovey dovey, you haven't been cross with each other. Then when you did get frustrated with each other, there was so much pressure on him to settle down… and on you to say yes to being a royal…" She wrinkles her nose. "It was a powder keg, just waiting for a match to be struck."

I suck a deep breath in, struggling not to start crying again. "I love him, Pippa. I really do."

Her hand lands on my knee, rubbing little comforting circles in my flesh. "I know, Mags. I know."

"It was just an insane amount of pressure," I admit, putting my bags down on the ground. "I wanted to say yes to him. I really did. But the time-line was all kinds of fucked up."

"Yes," Pippa says with a nod. "I think if you two didn't have to face his upcoming coronation so soon…"

"God!" I cry out, looking heavenward. "That really put a rush on things. I was trying to tell him to slow down… that things were going too fast for me… but I think that he just had so much pressure from his grandmother and his family that he couldn't hear what I was saying."

She sighs. "You're not going to like what I'm about to say."

I look at her for several long beats. "What?"

"If you really love Stellan, I think you should try to reach out to him."

"What?" My cheeks heat. "No way! No. He told me not to come back."

She rolls her shoulders. "Call it the heat of the moment. Wouldn't it just be tragic if he feels the same way and you never know because you're both so damn stubborn?"

I make a disgruntled sound. "What if I were to show up at the palace and he doesn't want to see me? That would be so embarrassing, I don't even have the words."

She smirks. "So you do want to try?"

"I didn't say that!" I protest.

"Okay, but let's just say that you decide you are willing to give it a go." She puts up a hand to stop my complaint. "We are just brainstorming here. No harm, no foul. Yes?"

I tuck a strand of hair behind my ear. "Just brainstorming," I reiterate. "Just… in case."

A dimple flashes in Pippa's cheek. "What if you made like… a grand romantic gesture?"

I scoff. "Like showing up at the airport at the last moment? Isn't the guy supposed to do that?"

Pippa shrugs a shoulder. "Maybe for other people, yeah. But you? You're Margot Keane. You're a rebel. You live by your own rules. And if you want to make a grand gesture, then by god, you can do it!"

I stare at Pippa for a second. "I just realized that you actually believe in me. You are a really good friend, you know that?"

She beams at me. "Duh. I've always believed in you, Mags."

I hug her, sudden and hard. She makes a funny noise at first, but then she relaxes and claps me on the back. When I pull back, Pippa arches a brow.

"So. Shall we make a list of romantic grand gesture ideas?"

I shake my head slowly. "No."

Her eyebrows rise. "No?"

"I just realized that we work at the main newspaper in the country. Millions of people see whatever gets onto our front page."

Pippa looks shocked for a second. "Are you suggesting what I think you are?"

I squint at her. "Maybe. I mean, my words will almost definitely reach Stellan. And if it works, I am sure the *Politiken* editors will forgive me." I wrinkle my nose. "Right?"

She looks a little unsure. "If it doesn't work, Margot... if you publish a personal letter addressed to Stellan in a public paper..."

I wince. "I would have to leave the country."

"Yeah, that would be the least of your worries."

"So... I'll have to make my letter really good," I say, taking a deep breath. "Oh god. Am I really going to do this? Agh! Where would I even begin?"

Pippa's lips curve upward and she slides me a knowing glance. "Start at the beginning."

She picks up the leather satchel, opening it to reveal the laptop inside. Then she stands, tucking her glorious red hair behind her ears.

"I should get back to my own work," she says with a sigh. "Good luck. Call me when you need help."

"Thank you, Pippa." I crack open the laptop and open a blank word processing document. "Start at the beginning. I can do that..."

Typing out the first line, I start the scariest letter I will probably ever write.

Chapter Forty-Five

STELLAN

MY FATHER CLEARS his throat and adjusts his seat at the table. We're having breakfast on the vast veranda of Gråsten Palace, where he and my mother are currently staying.

He pushes his mostly full plate away. I want to ply him with a million questions about how he is feeling, but I have a feeling that he won't like that. It's normally fairly awkward between us, but today… it's tense.

"So. Have you heard anything conclusive from the doctors?"

My father scratches his dark beard. "No."

I sigh silently. "May I speak openly?"

"I wish you would." He looks off into the distance at the verdant gardens below the terrace. I can't read him; I think I know exactly where I inherited my remoteness.

I take a deep breath. "Are you still stepping down? Because if not… I have a number of loose ends still that need to be tied up. If you are going to keep the throne— "

"No. You are still on track to be king."

My expression tightens. "Ah."

My father looks at me for several long beats. "You don't desire the crown?"

I give a dry chuckle. "No."

"Mm. I didn't either." He looks down at the glass of orange juice in front of him, turning it slowly by the rim. "What would you do if you had more time?"

Margot's face flashes in my mind. Frowning, I shake my head. "I don't know. I made some decisions recently that may have been hasty…"

I trail off and drum my fingers on the tabletop. My father spears me with his frosty blue gaze.

"You are talking about Margot?"

I can feel my neck heat. "Among other things. But yes, I would do things differently if I had more time." I scrunch my face up. "And if I had a time machine, I guess."

My father's eyebrows lift slightly. "How so?"

I shrug, uncomfortable. "I don't know. I would put less pressure on her to accept my marriage proposal, I guess."

He looks surprised. "I didn't realize that you had asked."

Pursing my lips, I shrug again. "I didn't ask her officially. I asked her what her answer would be… and she took weeks to reply to it."

He looks dubious. "Her reply was no?"

Heat creeps up my neck, coloring my cheeks. "Her reply was just that she needed more time."

"And you felt that you were running out of that resource," he comments, fixing his gaze on his orange juice glass again.

"Well… yes," I admit. "If I had it to do over again, I would do it differently."

My father sighs. "Stellan. Let me give you some advice. If you find a woman to share your life with, and you're sure that she's the one, you don't halfway ask her to marry you. You grab onto her and you don't ever let go." He coughs. "I consider myself insanely lucky to have found your mother. She is passionate. She is loyal. She fights for the causes she believes in. But most of all, I know that she'll stick by my side. No matter what. That's worth more than all the gold in the world."

I'm a little taken back by his words. My father and mother obviously love each other, but I have never heard my father talk about her for any length of time.

Letting that sink in, I take a deep breath. "I'm glad that you found Maman."

He snorts. "You'd better be. I never planned on having a bunch of children. That was all your mother. She wanted a big brood. And what your mother wants, she tends to get."

"That's… bordering on being too much information." I wrinkle my nose.

My father rolls his eyes. "That is neither here nor there. What is certain is that you need to contact Margot. If she is your great love, she will be glad to hear from you."

I give him a skeptical look. "Has Erik been talking to you about this? Because he said exactly the same thing."

My father sighs. "No. But there must be something there if we both have the same advice for you, Stellan."

Sitting back in my chair, I shrug. "I don't know."

"Do you love her?" My father cocks his head.

"Of course."

His gaze narrows on my face. "I don't understand. What is the issue?"

I grow embraced. "I don't know. What if she can't accept my lifestyle? I mean, the media scrutiny is already intense and we aren't even publicly a couple. What if she says yes and then changes her mind in a couple of months?"

He shakes his head. "If that happens, you can deal with it together. Don't be a fool. Take this risk, son."

I look down at my lap. He's right, of course. I have been a fucking idiot. I love Margot so deeply that she haunts my dreams.

"It's a big risk," I say, my voice growing rough. "But you are right… I have to put it all on the line. Otherwise she might leave Denmark altogether. And that… that would just crush me."

My father smiles. "Good. In that case… I think you are ready to read today's issue of *Politiken*." He pushes his chair back and stands, gesturing to a servant. "Bring him the newspaper, will you?"

The servant scuttles forward, offering me the newspaper on a platter. I frown and accept it, noticing the photo on the main page a few seconds later.

It's a gorgeous portrait of Margot, her expression sad. A tear tracks down her face as she contemplates her hands.

The headline is simple. Dear Stellan, I love you.

My heart starts pounding. "What is this?"

My father touches my shoulder as he heads inside. "I'll leave you to read it by yourself."

"Thanks," I murmur, unfolding the newspaper. Margot's letter is printed just below the fold. Not quite believing what I'm seeing, I start to read.

Dear Stellan,

We met one warm summer night in New York City. The attraction was instant, the chemistry between us so potent that a few sparks grew into a raging, untenable fire.

I knew from that moment — you were special somehow.

When I arrived in Copenhagen, I hated you. Or at least I thought I did. The news of us being tied together — me as the journalist, you as the subject of my research — hit us both hard.

I come from nothing. You come from the kind of privilege and wealth that makes my head spin. And yet... we found common ground.

You let me in. I dropped my shields, became vulnerable with you.

And somewhere deep inside, a begrudging respect turned into a breathless, wild, restless kind of love. It wasn't my choice.

I couldn't help but fall in love with you, my wicked prince. The world tried to turn us against each other... wanted us to dance to its beat.

I thought I couldn't do it. I ran, I hid. But in my heart of hearts, I know one thing is absolutely true: I will move mountains for you. I will walk across endless deserts, dive into the deepest oceans.

My love for you knows no bounds.

Now I stand here waiting, holding my breath, hoping desperately that you will read this... and you will meet me at Fredericksberg Gardens today. I'll be there at three in the afternoon, and I'll wait all day for you.

I hope to see you there, Stellan.

With undying love,

Margot

I sit back, floored. If there was ever a doubt about anything related to Margot, now I know exactly how she feels. She's assumed so much of the risk without realizing that I was only steps behind her.

God, I love her so much, it makes me feel sick. It is almost overwhelming in the entirety of it, hitting me like a tidal wave on an otherwise perfectly calm day at the beach.

I stand up, tucking the newspaper by my side.

"Well?"

I turn to find my father and my mother standing at the doorway of the terrace, looking expectant. My neck heats.

"I didn't realize you were there."

My mother stomps her foot. "Tell me your reaction to reading Margot's letter! I am dying over here."

"I… I'm going to go meet her," I say, swallowing. "Papa was right… no half measures this time. I'm going to the gardens alone and leaving with a fiancée, come what may."

My mother throws her hands up, squealing with glee, and bounds over to me for a hug. "That's so wonderful, Stellan!"

My father digs in his pocket and pulls out a ring box. "You will probably need one of these."

My eyebrows fly up. "A ring?"

He coughs. "Your mother dragged me along to the Copenhagen treasury after we met Margot for the first time. Your mother knew that you would need a ring."

"Ohh, and it's so perfect! It was your great grandmother's ring. Sparkly and pretty. It will look great on her delicate little hand, *ja*?"

Pulling me over to my father, my mother opens the ring box. I look at the ring with wide eyes.

"This is really happening," I say.

"Yes!" my mother sings, beaming so wide that it's hard not to get caught up in her happiness. "I'm so happy for you, my Stellan."

She cups my face, kissing me on the cheek. I smile, rolling my eyes a little.

"She hasn't said yes yet."

My father smiles softly. "I think we all know just what she'll say."

Shaking my head, I tuck the ring box in my pocket and wish my parents goodbye.

Chapter Forty-Six

MARGOT

THERE IS something tranquil about standing just where I am with my eyes tightly closed. The scent of gently blooming jasmine rises to my nose. Birds chirp from the perfectly manicured greenery all around me.

I exhale slowly, my hands still trembling. Opening my eyes, I take in the beauty of the romantic gardens with the soft pink wild roses growing up and around the natural wood gazebo.

I'm so nervous that I can't think straight. What if Stellan never saw my letter? Worse, what if he did and still doesn't show up?

This whole idea was really romantic in my head, but now... standing here in the same outfit I was wearing when we met, sweating through my clothes...

It seems destined to fail. Biting at my thumbnail, I pace the gazebo. Eight steps one way, eight steps the other.

This plan was not well thought through.

I hear a rustle and whirl around. The rose garden just beyond the gazebo is still. The tree lined path leading away is long, empty, and all but silent.

I check the time on my phone. 3:15.

God, Stellan isn't coming. I signed myself up for waiting all night for him... but I am as sure that he's not coming now than I have been about anything in my whole entire life.

I head to the steps, sitting down and burying my face in my hands. I suck in a shaky breath.

"What are you doing on the ground, *skatter*?"

My heart pounds. I look up and my eyes widen. Stellan strolls down the path, looking as dapper as he's ever looked in a tuxedo and a crisp white shirt.

One of my hands clutches my chest over my heart. "You came," I whisper.

He covers the last few steps, stopping right in front of me. "I saw your letter. You asked me to meet you. How could I say no to you?"

His eyes sparkle with humor. I'm still petrified. I make a promise to myself that I wouldn't cry.

Instead, I climb to my feet, looking up at him. "I should've written a speech. I didn't get past the point of you showing up."

He smirks. "I think we'll manage."

Reaching out a hand, he gently touches my shoulder. I don't know what comes over me, but I jump onto him, climbing his big body like a tree.

Stellan chuckles, the reverberations vibrating his chest. "I guess it wouldn't be real if you didn't make it awkward, would it?"

He slides his hand along my cheek and cups the back of my head, lowering his mouth to mine. I make a soft sound as his lips touch mine; he tastes sweet and clean, like fresh mint. When his mouth opens and his tongue touches mine, sweeping the inside of my mouth, I put my arms around his neck and plow my hands into the back of his hair.

I've missed this so badly.

He groans against my mouth. "I've missed your scent."

My lips curve upwards. "Is that all?"

He pulls back, brushing a stray strand of hair from my face. "No," he says quietly. "I've missed everything about you. Your smile. Your sense of humor. Your moral outrage. My body craves yours, *skatter*."

I'm left breathless and wide eyed at his openness, his vulnerability in this moment. His ice blue eyes are so earnest that it almost makes me cry.

"Stellan..." I whisper, my voice breaking. "I love you so fucking much."

He presses his lips to mine with such passion and intensity that I feel stunned. "I love you too, Margot. I know that my life is complicated, but I don't think I can go on without you."

I draw in a breath that turns into a hiccup. "I meant what I wrote to you. If you need me to, I'll move heaven and earth to be yours."

He exhales a shaky breath. "I think you know what I have to do, right?"

I arch a brow. "What?"

Pushing me back a step with gentle hands, he clears his throat and digs in his pocket. Then he kneels down on one knee. My hands fly up to my mouth.

He pauses for a second, lowering his dark head. When Stellan looks up at me, he gives me a tense smile.

"Fuck, I'm so nervous," he admits.

My eyes well up at that. I brush my hand against his shoulder. "Don't be."

He bites his lip and holds up his offering, a small dark blue velvet box. When he cracks it open, a dazzling diamond and sapphire ring sits cushioned there.

Oh god. Is this really happening?

Stellan reaches for my hand. "Margot Keane. You are the most challenging, most wonderful, most amazing woman I've ever met. When I think of the future, the only one I can see clearly is one with you by my side. Will you please do me the enormous honor of being my wife?"

My heart beat drums its rhythm in my ears. I dash away tears from my eyes, nodding. "I will."

His expression is glorious. He beams as he pries the ring from the box. Setting the box aside, he takes my hand and slides the ring onto my finger.

I reach down for him as he stands up. He kisses me and slips his arms around me, lifting me up in his arms. He's marking me for the whole world to see: I'm his now.

His, and his alone, until the end of time.

I finally pull away with a giggle. "Is this real?" I wonder. "I feel like I'm high on something."

He sets me on my feet, grinning. "I was just thinking the same thing."

My cheeks hurt from how hard I grin. I definitely look like a lunatic but I don't care. I glance at my hand and the ring takes my breath away again.

"Who do we tell first?" I wonder aloud.

He scrunches up his face. "My parents already know that I was planning to propose. They encouraged it, actually."

A hand flies up to cover my heart. "They did?"

He nods. "*Ja*. And Erik told me to quit being so stubborn and call you." He squints. "Everyone in my circle is very pro-Margot, it seems."

I smile at that, but I suck in a breath. "Everyone but your grandmother."

Stellan shrugs. "When she finds out that I have proposed to you and you said yes, she will change her mind. She wants the best for me. And you are what's best for me, *skatter*."

I grin. "Yeah?"

He pulls me against his hard body, smirking. "*Ja*."

I put my arms around his neck and press my lips to his again, inhaling that clean masculine scent that is purely him. When he finally pulls away, he takes me by the hand.

"Are you ready to be my princess now? Because the second we leave this spot, the press will be all over us. The Gardens kept them outside just because I asked but you know they'll be waiting just past the gates. They'll have a million questions and generally be pretty invasive."

I smile up at him. "As long as you're by my side, I can face them. I can face anything."

He twines his fingers with mine, kissing my hand. "Okay. I promise not to leave your side. You have my word on that, *skatter*."

I blush. "I love you, Stellan."

He gives me a wicked grin. "I love you too. Just wait until we get back to the palace, where I can show you just how much…"

My heartbeat thrums. "I can't wait."

Stellan winks at me, leading me out of the gazebo and down the tree lined path toward our future.

Chapter Forty-Seven

MARGOT

MY FEET ACHE in these staggeringly tall high heels. But that's what you get when you give your own fabulous designer free reign. I'm wearing what has to be the biggest, goofiest strapless ball gown ever created, dressed in head to toe pink crinoline. I looked in the mirror and gasped about how I look like Barbie threw up everywhere…

But when Stellan saw me in this dress, the way his eyes lit up told me I was wrong.

I lift my head, trying to look poised. A thousand faces stare back at me from the ballroom floor, making me want to squirm. I shift my weight onto one foot, prompting Stellan to look down at me.

"What are you doing?" he whispers. "You're thinking of running away, are you? This whole engagement party was your idea."

I wrinkle my nose at him. "You're stuck with me now. Sorry."

Even though we are on a dais, with probably a thousand people looking right at us, Stellan kisses me on the lips. Several cameras flash and I blush.

There is really no way of getting used to being watched every second that we are in public. At least I have Stellan here to keep me from lunging at reporters who ask me obnoxious questions.

Prime Minister Finley, who is front and center at the podium, clears his throat. "So I am quite proud to be here at the announcement of the engagement of our own Prince Stellan and his bride-to-be, Margot Keane. After the Prince's coronation next week, Miss Keane will officially set to marry the king…"

It's the hardest thing ever not to look down and hide my face from the cameras that go absolutely mad just now, flashing brightly for a full minute. I put my hand into Stellan's and he gives it a squeeze. Prime Minister Finley drones on for another minute but I don't hear much of what he has to say.

I'm being tested. And by god, I will pass muster.

"And lastly, I would like to make an announcement that comes straight from Prince Stellan and the future Duchess herself. This gala is open to the public. Everyone is welcome, of every race, sexuality, ability, and economic status. The couple hopes…"

He pauses, frowning ever so briefly. "That everyone will mix, mingle, and find their next charitable cause right here tonight. And toast the happy couple as they…" Finley fights a disdainful look. "Begin their lives in an act of service, forming a line of people serving hot food to all who come." Prime Minister Finley looks up, clearing his throat. "Hear hear."

The audience applauds, some more wildly than others. I look up at my husband-to-be.

"That's our cue," I say, wiggling my eyebrows. "Let's stop by the bathroom on the way downstairs so I can take off these heels, okay?"

His smile is warm. "As you wish, Princess Margot."

Turning around, I am immediately brought up short by the Queen Mother, Lady Ida. I almost trample her and then step back so fast that Stellan has to catch me to keep my balance.

"Queen Mother!" I blurt. "It's a pleasure to see you again, ma'am."

She smiles wanly. "Hello, Margot." She looks between me and Stellan. "I hope you two are doing well?"

Stellan slides his arm around my waist. "We are, thank you."

The Queen Mother seems pleased. "Wonderful. Margot, I wanted to borrow you sometime this week to talk about the wedding. There are so many Danish royal traditions to consider. Would you mind if my secretary reached out to…" She pauses, cocking her head. "Well, whomever is in charge of your schedule."

My heart thuds against my ribs. "Of course. I would be honored, ma'am."

She gives me an odd little smile. "You are going to treat Stellan well, won't you?"

Blushing, I nod. "I will, ma'am."

She nods back, looking at Stellan.

"Very well. Run along now, the press are probably foaming at the mouth to ask you questions."

She turns and heads off toward the prime minister. Stellan guides me toward the door, but of course his grandmother was right.

It's an absolute mob scene. Flashes go off. Questions are hurled at us.

"Margot! Margot!"

"Stellan, when is the wedding?"

"Margot, who are you wearing?"

"Are you two happy to be engaged?"

I close one eye, raising my hand against the bright camera lights. "We're thrilled."

A young man steps close to me, thrusting a microphone is my face. "Margot, your letter in *Politiken* has made you insanely popular with the whole of Denmark. How does it feel to be so universally loved?"

I burst out laughing. "Are you planted by the royal press office?"

He looks a little confused. "No. I'm from the Daily Tribune."

Stellan steps in. "Alright, alright. Move back a little and give us some space. Margot is unused to being so popular, *ja*? She is adjusting quite well."

His answer makes me want to kiss him. Instead I just pull at his hand. "Everyone, could we all start to move downstairs? You can ask your questions while we serve everyone food."

With a little bit of tussling, we make it down off the dais and into the hallway. A nameless assistant is there to hand me a change of shoes. I slip away from Stellan and push the door of the bathroom open.

There is no one inside, so I hurry into the fancy bathroom. As I sink onto the embroidered, overstuffed ottoman, I let out a sigh.

It's blissfully silent.

Taking off my heels with a clatter, I rub my feet for a second. "God damned beautiful heels. You are absolute murder on my feet but you look so pretty."

The bathroom door opens and I look up, a little startled. There is Anna, looking sleek and sophisticated in her knee-length black cocktail dress.

"Ah. There you are, Margot. I was hoping to catch you alone."

My eyes narrow. "What? Don't tell me you've come to yell at me some more about the newspaper? I don't know if anyone told you, but I quit two weeks ago."

Anna cocks her head and gives me the most saccharide smile. "I came to apologize."

I squint at her. "What?" I look around. "Who made you do that?"

Her smile widens and when she talks, it's through her teeth. "No one. I just realized… that I was wrong. And I should have been much nicer to you. If I had realized who you were— "

Standing up, I shake my head. "No. No way."

Her smile goes flat. "I think you should listen, Margot."

I slip my flats on my feet, picking up my heels. "You shouldn't treat people the way you treated me, Anna. And you definitely shouldn't be here apologizing to me now."

Anna clears her throat. "Yes, I am coming to understand that. I was hoping that we could work together because… you know, I know you…"

I give her a funny look. "And you don't think Pippa knows me better?"

She looks down at her hands. "Well, I just thought since I am an editor and Pippa is a bottom level journalist, you would want to speak with me."

I let out a sharp bark of laughter. "Yeah. No thanks. It was… interesting… running into you. I'm due to serve food to whoever wants it." I pause. "Maybe you should do some shelter work. It teaches you to be humble and kind. That would be my advice to you, take it or leave it."

Striding out of the room has never felt quite so good. To my surprise, Stellan is standing just beyond, waiting.

When he sees me, his smile lights me up inside.

"Ready?" he asks, offering me his arm.

I surprise him with a kiss. "I really, really love you. Don't forget that."

He kisses me, smoothing his hand down my back. "I love you too, *skatter*. That's what my ring on your finger symbolizes. It means that I will love you until the end of my days."

My lips curl up. "Forever?"

He chuckles. "Forever."

I link hands with him and let him lead me downstairs, toward whatever lies ahead. I know in my heart that I will get through anything as long as he holds my hand.

. . .

THE END

Want to get a little more of Stellan and Margot? You are cordially invited to their private wedding ceremony… sign up for my mailing list and get this exclusive scene right now.

Chapter Forty-Eight

ANNIKA

DUSK HAS JUST FALLEN over the beach, coating everything in sight in a dusting of shadow. The ocean looks dark and intense as the last rays of light disappear over the horizon. Our enormous beach house is the only structure around for miles and its back patio spills right out onto the dunes of sand that lead down to the water.

Other than the twinkle of tea lights on the patio, it's quickly growing dark. I open my arms to the unbelievable spread of the night sky. The stars wink down at me.

Maybe tonight is the night.

My best friend Kalindi looks over at me from her beach blanket, looking beautiful as ever. She has light brown skin and dark eyes, with hair as thick and lustrous as a raven's wing. She leans back, adjusting her pink bikini.

"What would you think about me snagging your brother?" she asks. Her accent is a mix of British and Indian influences, and her voice is melodic. But her words make me pull a face.

"Which one?" I ask. "Don't say Stellan. All my life, my friends have been asking me whether he is single."

She shakes her head with a soft smile. "No, Annika. I'm talking about Finn."

My eyebrows rise. "Finn?" I glance back toward the house, at the picnic

tables where the older guys and their friends are sitting, Finn included. "Are you sure you mean him and not Anders?"

Kalindi wrinkles her nose. "What's wrong with Finn?"

I scrunch my face up. "Nothing. He's just... odd. Remote. You are a beautiful ray of sunlight and I wouldn't want him to dim your vibrancy, that's all."

She rolls her eyes. "I just mean a casual make out, nothing serious." She turns and looks at the group again, wrinkling her nose as they get up and head for the house. "I think I'm going to go inside and change my clothes. This bathing suit is cute but itchy."

"Okay." I sit back, noticing that a lone figure walks by us out toward where the water laps at the beach. With his ruggedly good looks and his blond hair, I can spot Erik easily though it's dark. "I'm going to stay for a while."

Kalindi shakes her head. "You shouldn't like him, Nika. He's almost ten years older than us."

Pouting, I look down at my sun-kissed skin in my tiny black bikini. "Erik is only eight years older than me, first of all. And second of all..." I look up at her. "It's just snagging, as you say."

She shakes her head. "You are crazy. He doesn't even know you're alive."

That stings. I make a face. "I know."

She smiles. "Okay. As long as you realize. I'll be inside, scavenging for food."

I nod, letting her leave. My eyes find Erik again, silhouetted against the darkened beach. He wears jeans and a plain white t-shirt, his sleeves rolled up in a way that shows his bulging biceps. He bends over and rolls his jeans up to mid-calf. He keeps walking down a little further, submerging his bare feet in the foam left by the lapping sea. Without realizing it, I stand up, brushing myself off. It's only when I've pulled my shorts and black t-shirt on that I realize that I'm going to go talk to him.

I shiver. Maybe tonight will really be the night. The night that I'll remember for the rest of my life... The night that Erik takes my virginity.

I've only been waiting for him for five whole years. It's time.

Brushing my blonde hair back, I take a deep breath. As I pad barefoot through the sand, I give myself a mini-pep talk.

Just be casual.

Don't be an awkward weirdo.

Play it cool!

A few feet away, Erik turns and notices me. His expression hardens for a split second and then he turns away.

"What do you want, Annika?"

I freeze. This is not the reception I anticipated. Far from it, actually.

Walking forward to pull even with him, I take a deep breath. But when I speak, my tone is petulant.

"I didn't realize that you had the whole entire beach booked up," I say, gesturing to the vast darkness surrounding us.

He looks at me sharply, but doesn't respond right away. I take a moment to drink him in. He's extremely tall, taller even than my older brother Stellan's massive height. His body is perfect and muscular without being too bulky. He has a face that is made for movies, with high cheekbones and long eyelashes, and these deep hazel eyes that make me melt.

Erik grunts. "Stellan is a fucking asshole."

I squint, wrinkle my whole face. "It must be hard to be best friends with the future king of Denmark. Especially when it means you basically get a free ride, wherever you go."

As soon as I say it, I wish I could take it back. There is something about Erik that makes me mean and petty when I really want to be sweet.

He lets out a bark of laughter. "You are a brat, Annika. A spoiled little brat. You know that?"

My face heats. Of course I know that.

"No," I say, sticking my tongue out at him.

He scans me head to toe and then shakes his head. "Yes. You are."

He turns around, walking back toward the house. My heart wrenches; this was my chance to finally tell Erik that I've wanted him for longer than he could possibly know. Now that chance is ruined.

I curse my mouth, which operates on its own sometimes. When Erik stops a few feet away and picks up a bottle of liquor, I raise my brows.

He uncaps it and takes a long pull, letting out a gasping sound when he's done. He turns back to me, holding the bottle out to me.

"Whiskey?"

A breeze blows, making me shiver as I jog the couple of steps toward him, taking the bottle from his hand. He casts another glance at me as I uncork the bottle.

"You should be inside," he murmurs. "Where it's warm and safe."

I take a sip of the whiskey and wince as it burns its way down my esophagus. It's half a minute before I can speak. "Safe? Safe from what?"

Erik looks at me, smirking a little and shrugging. "I don't know. Give me the bottle back, brat."

I narrow my eyes at him, handing it over. Our fingers brush, our gazes collide. His hazel eyes are shadowed so I can't read his expression exactly, but for a split-second I swear there is a carnal interest there.

That, or I'm just imagining what I want to see.

Erik's eyes dart away. He takes another long slug from the bottle. "This whiskey is bullshit."

I wipe a couple of drops from the corner of my mouth, not really knowing how to respond. I'm eighteen; it's not like I have a ton of whiskey tasting experience.

"It's better than some," I come up with at last.

He eyes me skeptically. "*Ja*. It will get you drunk, which I guess is what counts."

I study him. "Are you? Drunk, I mean."

He turns to stare stonily out at the waves. "Maybe." He squints. "I'm on vacation. I almost never get to relax."

He sounds defensive. I shrug my shoulders.

"I'm not judging. I was just curious. I don't think I've ever seen you drunk."

He looks at me again, screwing his handsome face up. "*Ja, okay.*"

When he offers me the bottle again, I shake my head. "No. I like champagne, not whiskey."

He lifts a shoulder. "Suit yourself." Tipping his head back, he drinks.

I watch his neck as he gulps the liquor down. I notice his lips then, looking plump and perfectly kissable. Licking my own lips, I let my gaze wander down his body. His arms are both bare and impressively muscular. I can see the definition of his abs in his tight white t-shirt.

Before I realize it, words are leaving my mouth. "I changed my mind. I want some."

Erik raises his brow. "All right."

He takes a step toward me, handing me the bottle. I let the bottle drop to the ground, putting my arms around his neck. He gives me a startled look.

"Wait— "

I am too close to finding out what his lips taste like to stop now. I push up on my tiptoes and press my mouth against his, hesitating once my lips touch his. He seems frozen for a second, his brain taking a moment to catch up to reality. His eyes sink closed.

Then his hands find my lower back, drawing me against the firmness of his body. At the same time Erik deepens the kiss. No more peck on the mouth; his kiss is rough and dominant, his lips working against mine.

I open my mouth to him and he takes every inch I give him, sweeping his tongue inside my mouth like a man staking his claim on unchartered territory for the very first time.

A rugged rumble leaves his chest. If I weren't kissing him, I would have missed it. But it spurs me on, makes my hands spear into the back of his short blond hair.

That's all it takes to make him push me back a step. His eyes fly open, shocked.

"Fuck," he says. "Oh, fuck. That… that should not have happened."

My cheeks go pink. "Erik— "

He shakes his head, cutting me off. "No no no. That… I mean, you're barely eighteen! You're my best friend's baby sister."

I shrug. "So?"

He looks horrified. "So? So, your brother will kill me if he ever finds out. It doesn't matter that I'm drunk…"

I bite my lower lip, looking at him. "I won't tell. It'll be just between us."

Erik shakes his head. "This is bad. This… this can't happen again."

And with that, he picks up the whiskey bottle and starts running back to our beach house. I stare after him, touching my still-warm lips with my fingers.

Despite everything that Erik just said, my lips still curve upward.

He may think that he can resist me. But I haven't even tried anything yet. Not really.

I stand amongst the sand dunes, as the moon comes out to light the night with its soft glow, and make a silent resolution to myself.

Erik will be the one to take my virginity. I just have to convince him that he wants to fuck me as badly as I want him.

A smile plays on my lips. It shouldn't be that hard.

Shivering against the breeze, I stroll back toward the house, plotting my next move.

WANT TO FIND OUT WHAT HAPPENS NEXT? OF COURSE YOU DO! FIND OUT IN HIS FORBIDDEN PRINCESS!

Cruel Heir Extended Epilogue

Chapter One

MARGOT

OPENING THE DOORS JUST A CRACK, I peek inside the tiny church, biting my lower lip. My wedding dress — a simple garment made of ivory silk with spaghetti straps — rustles quietly. Looking around, I spy all of Stellan's family sitting on one side of the pews. My gaze travels to the other side, taking in the difference in size between the two groups. Stellan has everyone he could possibly want here in the pews; I flew a few old coworkers out, along with my favorite foster father.

My mouth turns down.

"Margot!" comes the whisper.

I turn around, widening my eyes. Pippa comes bearing down on me, a look of admonishment on her face. Closing the doors to the chapel oh so quietly, I give her a guilty look.

"I was just checking to see how full the church is," I say, blushing.

Pippa looks absolutely amazing in her bright pink babydoll dress. Her red hair is piled high on her head and she looks as glamorous as she ever has. She pulls me away from the doors with a soft hiss.

"You're supposed to wait where Stellan won't see you. Come back with me." She halfway drags me back into a little side room that we have commandeered for a bridal suite. It's nothing but a standing mirror and a couple of overstuffed couches.

Then again, I said I didn't want anything too fancy for today.

I sit down on one of the couches with a huff. "I'm too nervous to be cooped up in such a tiny space for so long."

Pippa closes the door behind herself and gives me a soft smile. "You've got less than fifteen minutes to wait now. I promise."

I wrinkle my nose. "Today is supposed to be about Stellan and I committing to each other before our friends and family. That way when the big day comes, when we have to stand in the cathedral downtown with the world watching, I don't lose my cool. I didn't factor in how anxious I would be now, though."

Pippa's eyebrows rise. "Do I need to steal a getaway car? Is that where you're going with this?"

The idea of Pippa driving as fast as she can away from the church while I stuff my fancy white dress inside the glove compartment of a car flashes in my mind. It makes me giggle.

"No," I say with a grin. "It's definitely just wedding jitters. I know that the second I step in that chapel, Stellan will be there, waiting at the end of the aisle."

I actually get choked up, just thinking about it. I fan my eyes. "Shoot. I can not cry. My emotions are just all over the damn place today."

She comes over and sits down next to me, giving me a hug. "That's perfectly acceptable. I would think you were weird if you weren't acting a little bit strange. After all, you will become Margot Love today. It's a huge change!"

I exhale slowly, fanning my eyes again. "Pippa, please don't make me cry."

She bites her lip. "So no speeches about how you are my best friend and I'm so damn glad that you found someone to share your life with?"

I tear up, hugging Pippa hard. "After the ceremony, okay?"

She wipes at her own eyes and laughs a little. "Deal."

Someone knocks on the door, sending a bolt through me. "Omigod."

She stands up, holding out her hand. "Come on. Let's not keep the man of your dreams waiting."

I navigate the next couple of minutes as though moving through a fog. I don't quite know how I get to the doors, but suddenly they are opening, revealing the tiny church inside.

I freeze up when people turn and look at me, rising from the pews. Pippa gives me a little push and I start walking down the aisle. Inside my head, I hear the distinct sound of a thousand sets of fake teeth chattering away. I swallow and search for Stellan's face.

My gaze catches his. He looks so smart standing at the end of the aisle in his navy slacks and his white button up, the cuffs rolled up and the top button undone. I giggle; looking at him makes me proud that I'm marrying him. His ice blue eyes pin me, but instead of making me wary, they drive me forward.

I run the last couple of steps, right into Stellan's arms. He catches me, grinning.

"You look..." He bites his lower lip. "Smoke."

I blush. "Take," I thank him. Thank you is one of the few Danish words that I know by heart.

He smirks down at me, then leans close to whisper in my ear. "You should probably step back. Everyone is waiting."

Turning a vibrant pink, I step back. Erik stands between Stellan and I, looking at both of us with something like pride.

"Are you ready to begin?"

I nod, eager to have the ceremony bit over with. Erik clears his throat.

"We are gathered here today to witness the union of Stellan and Margot. Today is the beginning of a remarkable journey for this couple. Drawing on their mutual admiration, respect, and trust, they are ready to embark on the next chapter in their lives."

He pauses for a second, then continues.

"I will now invite the couple to share their vows with one another. Stellan and Margot, the promises you make today are sacred; they are the groundwork from which your marriage will grow and blossom over time."

I beam at Stellan. It's hard to tell, but there is definitely an undercurrent of emotion running through his eyes.

"Stellan, would you like to begin first?" Erik asks.

Stellan clears his throat. When he speaks, his voice is rough.

"Margot, today you will become my wife. I promise to love you with all my heart, from now until eternity. I cannot wait to begin building our life together."

I start crying sometime during that statement. My heartbeat races and it's all I can do not to hide my face and sob. Erik smiles at me.

"Margot, your turn."

I suck in a wavering breath. "Stellan, today you will become my husband. I promise to love you with all my heart, from now until eternity. I cannot wait to begin building our life together."

Erik grins. "Stellan and Margot, it's time to join hands."

We join hands, clutching at one another, gazing at each other. For me, Stellan is the only star in the night sky. Erik's voice floats down to my ears, disembodied.

"Stellan, before your family and friends, do you take Margot as your beloved wife, to have and to hold, through laughter and in sadness, through challenges and successes, so long as you both shall live?"

Stellan's gaze bores into mine. I swear, I see a hint of tears when he utters his oath. "I do."

"Margot, before your family and friends, do you take Stellan as your beloved husband, to have and to hold, through laughter and in sadness, through challenges and successes, so long as you both shall live?"

"I do!" I squeak, wishing madly that I wasn't crying in front of Stellan's whole family. They'll have to forgive me though, because Stellan is mine. Now and forever.

Erik pulls out the rings, each in one of his hands.

"Wedding rings are a traditional symbol of the strength of the bond between two soulmates. This bond is never broken, and continues in a perpetual circle, glowing with the warmth and eternal light of two souls in a perfect union. By wearing these rings, you will be always reminded of the connection you share and the vows you have made today."

Stellan and I both nod enthusiastically. Erik waits a moment, then continues.

"Please repeat after me: I, Stellan, present you, Margot, with this ring as a symbol of our everlasting love. Let it never lose its luster, just as my love for you will never fade."

Stellan's eyes shine as he slides my ring up my finger. "I, Stellan, present you, Margot, with this ring as a symbol of our everlasting love. Let it never lose its luster, just as my love for you will never fade."

"Thank you. Now Margot. Please repeat after me: I, Margot, present you, Stellan, with this ring as a symbol of our everlasting love. Let it never lose its luster, just as my love for you will never fade."

I get choked up trying to say it. "I, Margot, present you, Stellan…" I pause, taking a calming breath. "…with this ring as a symbol of our everlasting love. Let it never lose its luster, just as my love for you will never fade."

Erik grins. He holds up his hands, shouting. "Stellan and Margot, I happily pronounce you husband and wife! Stellan, you may now kiss the bride."

Stellan slides his hand along my cheek and cups the back of my head, lowering his mouth to mine. I make a soft sound as his lips touch mine; he tastes sweet and clean, like fresh mint. When his mouth opens and his tongue touches mine, sweeping the inside of my mouth, I put my arms around his neck and plow my hands into the back of his hair.

He sweeps me off my feet, kissing me all the while, as all our friends and family rise and cheer. And I feel safe in the knowledge that I'm in his arms, right where I should be, right where I will be for the rest of my life.

Chapter Two

ANNIKA

DUSK HAS JUST FALLEN over the beach, coating everything in sight in a dusting of shadow. The ocean looks dark and intense as the last rays of light disappear over the horizon. Our enormous beach house is the only structure around for miles and its back patio spills right out onto the dunes of sand that lead down to the water.

Other than the twinkle of tea lights on the patio, it's quickly growing dark. I open my arms to the unbelievable spread of the night sky. The stars wink down at me.

Maybe tonight is the night.

My best friend Kalindi looks over at me from her beach blanket, looking beautiful as ever. She has light brown skin and dark eyes, with hair as thick and lustrous as a raven's wing. She leans back, adjusting her pink bikini.

"What would you think about me snagging your brother?" she asks. Her accent is a mix of British and Indian influences, and her voice is melodic. But her words make me pull a face.

"Which one?" I ask. "Don't say Stellan. All my life, my friends have been asking me whether he is single."

She shakes her head with a soft smile. "No, Annika. I'm talking about Finn."

My eyebrows rise. "Finn?" I glance back toward the house, at the picnic

tables where the older guys and their friends are sitting, Finn included. "Are you sure you mean him and not Anders?"

Kalindi wrinkles her nose. "What's wrong with Finn?"

I scrunch my face up. "Nothing. He's just... odd. Remote. You are a beautiful ray of sunlight and I wouldn't want him to dim your vibrancy, that's all."

She rolls her eyes. "I just mean a casual make out, nothing serious." She turns and looks at the group again, wrinkling her nose as they get up and head for the house. "I think I'm going to go inside and change my clothes. This bathing suit is cute but itchy."

"Okay." I sit back, noticing that a lone figure walks by us out toward where the water laps at the beach. With his ruggedly good looks and his blond hair, I can spot Erik easily though it's dark. "I'm going to stay for a while."

Kalindi shakes her head. "You shouldn't like him, Nika. He's almost ten years older than us."

Pouting, I look down at my sun-kissed skin in my tiny black bikini. "Erik is only eight years older than me, first of all. And second of all..." I look up at her. "It's just snagging, as you say."

She shakes her head. "You are crazy. He doesn't even know you're alive."

That stings. I make a face. "I know."

She smiles. "Okay. As long as you realize. I'll be inside, scavenging for food."

I nod, letting her leave. My eyes find Erik again, silhouetted against the darkened beach. He wears jeans and a plain white t-shirt, his sleeves rolled up in a way that shows his bulging biceps. He bends over and rolls his jeans up to mid-calf. He keeps walking down a little further, submerging his bare feet in the foam left by the lapping sea. Without realizing it, I stand up, brushing myself off. It's only when I've pulled my shorts and black t-shirt on that I realize that I'm going to go talk to him.

I shiver. Maybe tonight will really be the night. The night that I'll remember for the rest of my life... The night that Erik takes my virginity.

I've only been waiting for him for five whole years. It's time.

Brushing my blonde hair back, I take a deep breath. As I pad barefoot through the sand, I give myself a mini-pep talk.

Just be casual.

Don't be an awkward weirdo.

Play it cool!

A few feet away, Erik turns and notices me. His expression hardens for a split second and then he turns away.

"What do you want, Annika?"

I freeze. This is not the reception I anticipated. Far from it, actually.

Walking forward to pull even with him, I take a deep breath. But when I speak, my tone is petulant.

"I didn't realize that you had the whole entire beach booked up," I say, gesturing to the vast darkness surrounding us.

He looks at me sharply, but doesn't respond right away. I take a moment to drink him in. He's extremely tall, taller even than my older brother Stellan's massive height. His body is perfect and muscular without being too bulky. He has a face that is made for movies, with high cheekbones and long eyelashes, and these deep hazel eyes that make me melt.

Erik grunts. "Stellan is a fucking asshole."

I squint, wrinkle my whole face. "It must be hard to be best friends with the future king of Denmark. Especially when it means you basically get a free ride, wherever you go."

As soon as I say it, I wish I could take it back. There is something about Erik that makes me mean and petty when I really want to be sweet.

He lets out a bark of laughter. "You are a brat, Annika. A spoiled little brat. You know that?"

My face heats. Of course I know that.

"No," I say, sticking my tongue out at him.

He scans me head to toe and then shakes his head. "Yes. You are."

He turns around, walking back toward the house. My heart wrenches; this was my chance to finally tell Erik that I've wanted him for longer than he could possibly know. Now that chance is ruined.

I curse my mouth, which operates on its own sometimes. When Erik stops a few feet away and picks up a bottle of liquor, I raise my brows.

He uncaps it and takes a long pull, letting out a gasping sound when he's done. He turns back to me, holding the bottle out to me.

"Whiskey?"

A breeze blows, making me shiver as I jog the couple of steps toward him, taking the bottle from his hand. He casts another glance at me as I uncork the bottle.

"You should be inside," he murmurs. "Where it's warm and safe."

I take a sip of the whiskey and wince as it burns its way down my esophagus. It's half a minute before I can speak. "Safe? Safe from what?"

Erik looks at me, smirking a little and shrugging. "I don't know. Give me the bottle back, brat."

I narrow my eyes at him, handing it over. Our fingers brush, our gazes collide. His hazel eyes are shadowed so I can't read his expression exactly, but for a split-second I swear there is a carnal interest there.

That, or I'm just imagining what I want to see.

Erik's eyes dart away. He takes another long slug from the bottle. "This whiskey is bullshit."

I wipe a couple of drops from the corner of my mouth, not really knowing how to respond. I'm eighteen; it's not like I have a ton of whiskey tasting experience.

"It's better than some," I come up with at last.

He eyes me skeptically. "*Ja.* It will get you drunk, which I guess is what counts."

I study him. "Are you? Drunk, I mean."

He turns to stare stonily out at the waves. "Maybe." He squints. "I'm on vacation. I almost never get to relax."

He sounds defensive. I shrug my shoulders.

"I'm not judging. I was just curious. I don't think I've ever seen you drunk."

He looks at me again, screwing his handsome face up. "*Ja,* okay."

When he offers me the bottle again, I shake my head. "No. I like champagne, not whiskey."

He lifts a shoulder. "Suit yourself." Tipping his head back, he drinks.

I watch his neck as he gulps the liquor down. I notice his lips then, looking plump and perfectly kissable. Licking my own lips, I let my gaze wander down his body. His arms are both bare and impressively muscular. I can see the definition of his abs in his tight white t-shirt.

Before I realize it, words are leaving my mouth. "I changed my mind. I want some."

Erik raises his brow. "All right."

He takes a step toward me, handing me the bottle. I let the bottle drop to the ground, putting my arms around his neck. He gives me a startled look.

"Wait— "

I am too close to finding out what his lips taste like to stop now. I push up on my tiptoes and press my mouth against his, hesitating once my lips touch his. He seems frozen for a second, his brain taking a moment to catch up to reality. His eyes sink closed.

Then his hands find my lower back, drawing me against the firmness of his body. At the same time Erik deepens the kiss. No more peck on the mouth; his kiss is rough and dominant, his lips working against mine.

I open my mouth to him and he takes every inch I give him, sweeping his tongue inside my mouth like a man staking his claim on unchartered territory for the very first time.

A rugged rumble leaves his chest. If I weren't kissing him, I would have missed it. But it spurs me on, makes my hands spear into the back of his short blond hair.

That's all it takes to make him push me back a step. His eyes fly open, shocked.

"Fuck," he says. "Oh, fuck. That… that should not have happened."

My cheeks go pink. "Erik— "

He shakes his head, cutting me off. "No no no. That… I mean, you're barely eighteen! You're my best friend's baby sister."

I shrug. "So?"

He looks horrified. "So? So, your brother will kill me if he ever finds out. It doesn't matter that I'm drunk…"

I bite my lower lip, looking at him. "I won't tell. It'll be just between us."

Erik shakes his head. "This is bad. This… this can't happen again."

And with that, he picks up the whiskey bottle and starts running back to our beach house. I stare after him, touching my still-warm lips with my fingers.

Despite everything that Erik just said, my lips still curve upward.

He may think that he can resist me. But I haven't even tried anything yet. Not really.

I stand amongst the sand dunes, as the moon comes out to light the night with its soft glow, and make a silent resolution to myself.

Erik will be the one to take my virginity. I just have to convince him that he wants to fuck me as badly as I want him.

A smile plays on my lips. It shouldn't be that hard.

Shivering against the breeze, I stroll back toward the house, plotting my next move.

293

WANT TO FIND OUT WHAT HAPPENS NEXT? OF COURSE YOU DO! GET HIS FORBIDDEN PRINCESS RIGHT NOW…

Sinful Princess

Chapter One

ERIK

"FOR FUCK'S SAKE," I grumble to myself. "Tonight will never end."

My eyes travel over the crowd and to the ceiling of the event space; for the King's engagement announcement party, the ballroom has been decorated lavishly. The walls are adorned with trailing ivy and beautiful cascades of white blooms. Every table has a cluster of white flowers as the centerpiece. Waiters swish by me with trays of colorful cocktails named after Stellan and Margot. And overhead, a thousand glass orbs hang, each flickering with a white candle.

Everyone Stellan has ever known is packed into the large space, milling about and talking in little clumps. I notice a few waiters discreetly pulling discarded plates off tables. The time for eating has long since come and gone; soon Stellan and Margot will leave the party and then I can depart too.

Running a finger underneath my bowtie, I sigh. I can't wait for this royal party to be over so I can be anywhere but here.

I keep my eyes on Stellan's dark head, trying to gauge how much longer he will remain here. This party is to celebrate the announcement of his engagement to his beautiful pink-haired fiancée Margot. Right now, they stand in the middle of an adoring crowd looking like nothing so much as a wedding cake topper. Even now, I can see Stellan and Margot as they move through the crowd.

He's tall, dark, and handsome in his tuxedo. She's a tiny fairy of a person, pink-haired and wearing a pink dress. Her hand rests on his arm, his hand curls protectively around her waist. They keep looking at each other with these sneaky little grins. They are the center of their own blissful little universe.

And the way they gaze at each other and smile as they trade touches…

It makes me sort of wistful and a little bit jealous. I want someone to look at me the way that Margot looks at Stellan. I see hope and excitement and jubilance on her face.

It would be disgusting if it weren't so damn wholesome.

I'm over it. And this party… Everyone who is anyone here in Denmark turned out dressed to the nines, all to kiss the rings of the King and his future Queen.

Standing in the corner of the ballroom, I lean against the wall and clutch a tumbler of scotch. The expansive room is packed, everyone milling around, waiting for a chance to shake the new King Stellan's hand. Everywhere I look, symbols of opulent wealth are practically shoved down my throat.

The swish of expensive fabric. Men in their bespoke tuxedos, women in glittering ballgowns. Towering high heels, glittering jewelry, the floral scent of incredibly expensive perfume. The flush of young women when their randy husbands lean in to tell them just what's planned for their private afterparties.

There is unimaginable privilege is in this room tonight. Almost everyone present was just born into the lap of luxury. They've never had to struggle for a damn thing.

After so many years, it still makes me silently seethe.

I wasn't born to this life. I've lived it secondhand, mostly because King Stellan needed a confidante and I was deemed *good enough*.

As the newly crowned King's best friend and private secretary, I'm watching the crowd as they mix and mingle. Stellan has had his head in the clouds lately, living in an alternate reality from the rest of the world. One where his new fiancée Margot is his sun and stars… and everything else is just not worthy of his attention.

Stellan looks back at Margot, his expression enraptured. He isn't worried about anything else going on around him. But just because Stellan is on semi-permanent vacation from being the new king doesn't mean I get to slack off.

I drain the last of my glass and try not to look as bored as I feel.

Lars Løve comes ambling over to me, looking like a crooked photocopy of Stellan. He's Stellan's brother, one of the five Løve siblings. His dark hair is messy and a little too long. The collar of his tux is open at the throat, his bowtie nowhere to be seen. "There you are. We missed you at dinner."

Leaning over to a table, I set down my empty glass. "We?"

He squints. "You know. Me, Pippa… other people."

Pippa is his beautiful, elegant *will-they-or-won't-they* girl. It's always been that way, ever since he and the gorgeous redhead met in eighth grade.

I cast an eye over him. "I was in here, being lectured by Sarah from the royal press office. She didn't like it when I told her that Stellan was going to have to cut down his daily engagements."

Lars makes a face. "That sounds wretched."

I nod. "It was, mostly." Glancing around, my brow furrows. "Where's Pippa?"

He grunts. "Damned if I know. The last time I saw her, she was flirting with some loser in an overpriced tux."

I narrow my eyes at his comment. "Are you talking about yourself? Because you wear easily twenty thousand pounds more than anybody else in the room. You and all your siblings have that in common, my friend."

"Shut up. You act like you're not wearing a bespoke tux yourself." Lars snags a glass of champagne off a tray, sipping it coolly. He nods across the room to a group of people surrounding Stellan and Margot. "They seem very happy."

I look at Stellan, who keeps grinning at Margot like a total fool. It makes me happy for him, even as it turns my stomach.

That kind of love is not for me, just like so many aspects of Stellan's life. I'm the dutiful best friend, not actual royalty. That has been made crystal clear to me time and time again, ever since we were children.

"They do look happy," I say.

Lars's lips twitch. "So, do you think they will last?"

I look at him with a surprised expression. "Why would it not?"

He shrugs, pursing his lips. "It's just fast, that's all."

I roll my eyes. "Says the man that met the perfect girl before he was even in high school."

Lars frowns. "Pippa and I are friends. Nothing more than that."

I chuckle. "*Ja*, okay. Whatever you have to tell yourself. I've seen you two together, Lars."

He shoots me a glare. "My love life is private. I don't see you parading any new relationships around either, my friend."

My lips curve up. "No. I'm not Stellan. I'm the stable hand's son. I can't break the rules about class and date whoever I want. I can't just think that everything will be fine. I'm not royalty." My lips curl. "But I spend all my time with you lot, so I don't meet a ton of girls that are actually attainable."

His brows rise as he looks at me. "What does class have to do with anything? You're practically one of the royal family. I bet there are a dozen girls here tonight that would kill to get into your bed."

I press my lips together to avoid frowning. Instead of responding to that, I just look away. His comment was well-meant… but it was also naive. It just goes to show that he is definitely privileged in a way that few others could ever be.

A flash of movement catches my eye. A beautiful young blonde in an extravagant red ballgown storms into the room, her light blue eyes fixed on something out of my line of sight.

Annika.

I stare at her for a second, taking in her haughty posture and bright red lips. She's obscenely beautiful, with her waif-like figure and her elegantly pinned up hair.

The tiniest shudder runs through me.

It's important to remind myself that she's also Stellan's little sister, just nineteen years old. She makes me feel old and decrepit at twenty six. But my body and my brain are not on the same page here. They're not even reading the same book.

My body finds every little thing that Princess Annika does to be *extremely* attractive.

"Are you fucking serious?" Lars asks, interrupting my train of thought.

I tear my eyes away from Annika. "What?"

He slowly shakes his head and rakes his fingers through his messy dark hair. "You can't really think that ogling Annika openly is a good idea."

My neck heats. "What? No. I wasn't ogling her. I was just trying to see what she's throwing a fit about." I squint. "Probably some dramatic nonsense, knowing your sister."

Lars snorts. "I see your mouth moving, but I don't trust anything you're saying right now."

I roll my eyes. "Even if I found Annika the slightest bit attractive — which I don't — there are a thousand reasons why I would never, ever touch her. Not the least of which is Stellan." I squint into the distance.

He laughs. "No fucking kidding. That's pretty much the only reason I can think of, aside from you being way too old to date her."

I slide him a look. "There's also a great deal of income disparity between us."

Leaning against the wall, he sips his champagne. "She would find that with almost anyone she tries to date. And besides, aren't you some kind of secret day trading wizard? Last time we talked about it, you were making the stock market your bitch."

My lips twitch. "I shouldn't have told you that. I was drunk, as I remember."

Annika materializes, eyeing both of us as she stalks over. I push off the wall, straightening.

Lars gives me a look out of the corner of his eye. I button my tuxedo jacket as Annika arrives, looking flushed.

"Ugh!" she declares, looking around. She flags down a waiter and grabs a glass of champagne. "Momse is such a piece of work."

I clear my throat, looking over at Lars. He seems unconcerned by Annika's complaint, sipping his drink. So, I step in.

"What happened now?"

Annika flaps her hand impatiently. "Nothing. I just had an argument with Momse. It's so ridiculous."

She's referring to the Queen Mother, or Momse for short. The Queen Mother is the one that pulls all the strings in this royal Danish puppet show. Her son, the former king, and her daughter-in-law are...

What's a polite way to say that they've never shown much aptitude for parenting their five children? Maybe... disinclined to be in the state of Denmark, much less spend any time with Stellan and his siblings?

That still sounds harsh but it's true.

"What did the old girl do now?" Lars asks.

Annika's mouth turns down. "She says that I have to figure out what

I'm doing with my life. And I'm like…" She makes a strangled gesture. "I'm *trying*. Momse is always in such a hurry to make decisions. God."

She finishes her statement by swallowing half her glass of wine.

"Easy with the champagne, Nika," Lars says, surveying her critically. "You're toeing the line with Momse as it is. The last thing you need is to get drunk and misbehave while at an event like this. The place is packed with the press. And we both know that the press already has you pegged as a troublemaker."

She makes a wounded sound, scrunching up her face. "I thought you would be on my side, Lars."

He pushes off the wall with a shrug. "I'm on my own side. Always have been, always will be."

With that, he strolls off toward the door. I catch a glimpse of bright red hair moving out of the ballroom; he must be going after Pippa.

Annika puts her hand on her hip and shakes her head at him. Then she makes a moue of displeasure as she looks me up and down. "Isn't it past your bedtime, old man?"

I glare at her, checking my watch. "I'm here for as long as your brother is here, little girl. I go wherever he goes. I'm hoping that he'll leave soon… but I've already heard whispers of an afterparty."

She looks at Stellan, tilting her head thoughtfully. "Stellan is pretty damn victorious tonight. I can't believe my big brother is engaged."

I slide her a glance. "No?"

She shrugs. "I mean, it's not like Stellan and I are very close. I've only been back from Swiss boarding school for a year. Stellan always looks surprised to see me, like he forgot that I was here or something. But still." She scrunches up her face. "I have to say, I do like Margot."

I tug on my tie. "Yes. She's very… American. Very brash. But she's a good egg anyway."

She makes a face at me. "What will you do once my brother gets married? Huh? That's sure to open up a lot of free time."

My neck heats. I cock my head. "Oh, Annika. The things you say. You have truly been a shining gem since you've returned from boarding school."

Her lips twitch, her eyes on me. "I'm so glad I can perform that service for you. Really fill a niche. You must love me for that."

My lips curve upwards even as my eyes narrow on her face. "You are a brat, Annika."

She runs her fingers around the rim of her champagne flute, her eyes sparkling and sparking. "So, I've been told. I wonder, will you take me over your knee and spank me?"

My expression goes from shocked to disapproving almost instantly. "Annika, what the fuck!"

She dips her fingertip into her wine, then pops it in her mouth, sucking off the remnants. "What? You can admit it to me right now. There is no one listening."

Shaking my head, I give her a baffled face. "Admit what?"

She arches a brow. "That you totally want to sleep with me."

"What?!" I ask, my voice choked. "Annika, I could never... *That's unthinkable*. And I don't want you to go around telling people that, either."

She gives me a pout. "Ouch. It's lucky that I realize that you're full of shit." She grins. "Everyone wants me. Or a facsimile of who they think that I am." She rolls her eyes. "Haven't you heard? I'm the only princess and I'm almost old enough to marry. The boys flock around me like bees swarm around a rose."

My fists clench. "You are so full of yourself, Annika. Christ."

She blushes but keeps grinning. "Nah, not really. I just like to goad you because it gets you all tongue tied. Nobody else sees my wicked side."

Shaking my head, I adjust my stance. "Lucky me."

"I know, right?" Annika winks and then looks over her shoulder. "I don't see Stellan... I think I'm going to leave."

Arching a brow, I cross my arms. "What, you have somewhere better to be?"

She turns, pinning me with her gaze. "Wouldn't you like to know." She lifts up her voluminous skirts and tosses her head. "Goodnight, Erik."

And with that, she heads out of the ballroom, strutting like she's on a runway. I stare at her retreating figure, wondering why I find her so compelling.

She's too young, too wealthy, too privileged... and that's not even counting the fact that her brother is my best friend. She is the very definition of taboo and off-limits.

I heave a sigh and start searching the crowd for Stellan.

Chapter Two

ANNIKA

I **LOOK** out the rear window of the chauffeured car, pressing a hand to the cool glass of the window. The sun has slunk behind the horizon now and the last rays of light are slowly disappearing on this June night. I stare at the bright flashes of Copenhagen's stately skyline as we drive.

As the manor comes into view, I gaze at it out the window. My eyes widen as the car swings around the long, perfectly landscaped driveway. Every light is on in the house, every door thrown open. There are people spilling out of the house and across the lawn.

Straining to look out the window, I can hear the techno being pumped through the unseen sound system. I start laughing, looking over at my best friend Kalindi. She glances at the looming mansion, tucking a few strands of her long, shiny, black-brown hair behind her ear. A blush creeps into her cheeks, pink tinging her tawny skin just in the apples of her cheeks.

"I can't believe that Stellan sent us here," she mutters. Her accent is a melting pot of cultures: a little Indian, overlaid with British and Swiss, and finally finished off with just a dash of Danish. She turns her head to look at me. "Annika, are you listening to me?"

I wiggle my eyebrows at her. "Yes. You were saying that you are surprised that my big brother is supporting this enormous party. And my response is that it's a whole new world out there. Stellan and Margot just told us as much by announcing their engagement tonight."

She frowns just a bit. "Surely you support their marriage. Even though Margot is an American and a *commoner*." She makes a sound of distaste. "I actually hate that term. It's rather colonial, isn't it?"

I sigh. "I have no problem with them. Margot is nicer than most of the girls who tried to date Stellan. And I have to love her fire." I smooth out my skirt. "I'm just apprehensive about the press. They've been following me absolutely everywhere lately. If the paparazzi get one more photo of me that they can splash across the headlines of their papers, the royal press office may have a collective heart attack."

She wrinkles her nose daintily. "We don't have to go to this party, Nika. I mean… it is totally okay to tap out after… you know…"

My cheeks go pink and I look down into my lap. "My latest and greatest brush with being admitted to a psychiatric ward?"

"Well… yes," she admits. "The doctors said that you just had a panic attack but…" She grabs my hand, looking at me with serious eyes. "I was there, Nika. And it was scary. You never had panic attacks before we came back to Copenhagen. Playing the royal princess and having the spotlight on you isn't doing you any favors."

I sigh, squeezing her hand. "Kal, you are sweet to worry. But I feel fine. I just…" I look out the window again, biting my lower lip. "I need to stay out of the newspapers. Stellan asked me to 'cool it' until the wedding so…"

She nods. "Got it. We should be able to stay off their radar." She turns to look out the window, eyeing the scene with some skepticism. "I mean, this mansion looks like someone's house."

I lean forward, excited. "This afterparty is going to be wild. I doubt if Stellan even knew that, because he's such a fun vampire. This night just got interesting."

Kalindi looks at me, scrunching her nose as the driver pulls the car to a halt. "I hate it when you say that. It inevitably turns out insane rather than interesting."

I grin, opening my door. Loud music pours into the car, thudding so hard that I can feel it in my bones. "Come on!"

I scoot out, straightening my white linen dress. It's super short and strappy, showing a rather daring amount of cleavage.

Well, what little I have, anyway.

"Princess Annika!" A couple of giggling teenaged girls call to me. "Can we have your autograph? Please?"

They wave a piece of paper and a pen in front of my face. I take a deep breath, then give them my most dazzling smile. "Of course. Tell me your names!"

One girl squeals. The other tells me their names.

"Sofia and Agnes," she says. "I don't have the words to tell you how much this means to me. God, I have to call my mother and tell her. She'll be so jealous that I got to meet you!"

I shift from foot to foot, my perfect princess smile unwavering. "*Tak*, ladies. It is awfully nice to meet you as well."

I spend a full minute chatting with them and signing their piece of paper. When we're done, they run off into the deepening darkness, excited beyond words.

Kalindi favors me with a look. "You are so nice to everyone you meet. If I were you and I were accosted here, I would tell them to take a hike."

I roll my eyes. "It's a part of my job, Kal."

"Is it?" she asks. "Have you figured out what you're doing with your life, other than being an actual princess?"

My mouth pulls down. "No. I haven't, thank you very much. Now if you don't mind… there's all kinds of excitement waiting right here."

I squint out at the party raging in front of us. The mansion itself is quaint, red brick and covered in ivy. There are probably nearly a hundred party guests on the lawn alone, drinking and talking, tapping a keg in the far corner. The front door is open like a hungry mouth, inviting us in.

I grab Kalindi by the hand and halfway drag her up across the manicured lawn. She allows it too, her free hand fluttering over her conservative, preppy outfit. Her white blouse is tucked into a light blue skirt, topped off with a herringbone tweed jacket.

I slide her a look as we climb the steps of the front porch. "Expecting to see someone?"

She looks at me, blushing. "No." I narrow my gaze at her, and she lifts her chin. "I'm not. I'm just… being prepared. You should try it some time."

I grin, pulling her deeper inside the house.

Taking a deep breath, I reach in my purse for a piece of hard candy wrapped in a shiny gold colored wrapper. I pop it in my mouth and let it start to melt onto my tongue. The creamy toffee flavor instantly brightens my mood.

I can admit it; I'm more than a little addicted to these hard candies. And because they are low in sugar, I pop four or five of them in my mouth a day. Just whenever I need a little boost.

Once we get past the doorway everything is harder to make out. If there are any lights on in here, I don't see them; I continue straight down the main hallway, bumping into at least a dozen people, squeezing past a whole clump of girls gathered at the foot of the grand staircase.

Once we are past them, we make it into the kitchen. There I find Stellan and Margot, holding court in one corner, leaning against the kitchen counter. A dozen people I don't recognize are gathered around them. The music is a fraction quieter in here, so when Stellan sees me, he raises a plastic cup.

"Annika is here!" he calls.

My lips twitch. He and Margot are clearly drunk; poor little Margot doesn't look like she can stand on her own. It's a little cute how she leans on Stellan. She looks at my ridiculously hardheaded brother like he's the reason for her very existence. He slips his arm around her and pulls her closer.

I roll my eyes and ignore their handsy, drunken PDA. "Kalindi is here too. Where can we get something to drink?"

Margot hiccups. "Can someone please give them some punch?"

Just like that, we are each handed a plastic cup filled with a dark red punch. Kalindi looks into her cup with a frown. But I'm not put off by the alcohol and fruit scents floating up off of the cup's contents.

"To Stellan and Margot!" I cry, lifting my cup.

Everyone cheers. I take a sip, wincing a little bit. It tastes just like it smells, a ton of fruit flavors layered with a lot of aquavit.

Kalindi tries some and coughs a little, her free hand moving up to cover her mouth. "What is in this?!"

I grin at her. "Bottoms up?"

She wrinkles her nose. "Fine. But only because I'm just catching up…"

I'm already tipping the cup up and letting the alcohol pour down my throat. After a couple more drinks, I'm loose and warm and ready to dance. I lead the way to the dance floor, which was at some earlier point a dining room slash living room.

The hardwood table and matching chairs have been pushed against one wall; the other walls have the white plush couches and chairs seated by them. People are dancing and making out on the couches as I tug Kalindi into the dark space.

We start to dance, feeling the beat of the baseline. I shoot Kalindi a grin. "Keep your eyes peeled for hot guys, okay?"

She laughs. "Hot guys for you. I'm not kissing a stranger tonight."

"Oh, we'll see about that!" I yell.

She pulls a face. "I have to find the bathroom. Will you be okay here by yourself?"

I stick my tongue out at her. "I'm obviously completely fine."

She heads off the dance floor, weaving around a group of particularly exuberant dancers. I watch her go, realizing only after she's been gone for a minute that I don't feel like dancing without a partner.

Swiveling my head around, I look for a replacement. What I find though…

A tall, broadly shaped man in the corner is looking right at me. I take a step closer and a grin spreads across my face.

Blond hair, green-brown eyes, tanned skin, and more muscles than he even knows what to do with. It's none other than Erik, my brother's stoic best friend. He is still wearing his tux, but he's ditched the jacket and rolled up his sleeves to reveal his hot as fuck forearms. His gaze is fixed on me, his expression unreadable.

In the nine months that I have been back in Copenhagen, being able to torment Erik is really one of the only bright spots. I mean, I'm glad to have Kal, but she's so busy with university stuff.

Erik is always around, perpetually insanely handsome, and always so freaking stiff when I talk to him. It's impossible not to rib him a little.

Or a lot, as the case may be.

I sway my hips as I saunter right up to him. "I didn't expect to see you here. How have you not turned into a pumpkin, Cinderella?"

His handsome face twitches for just a moment, then he sighs. "I was just about to ask you the same thing, little girl."

My mouth makes a moue of displeasure. "Don't hate me for my youth and beauty, you joy kill."

He scans the room casually, shrugging. "One man's joy kill is another man's savior from the brink."

I roll my eyes. He's so starched and polished, even here in this room full of drunk idiots making out. "Do you tell yourself that when you go to bed alone every night?"

His greenish-brown eyes rake over me. "Don't you have a boy your age to torture?"

A sharp laugh is pulled from my lips. "Why would I do that when you're so much more fun? Taking the starch out of you is so much more… pleasurable."

He shakes his head at me, turning to move away. It's instinct to reach out and catch his wrist.

But when he rounds on me, his eyes snapping and crackling with an unexpectedly fierce energy, I gulp. He shakes off my touch like one would a burning brand, glaring at me.

I see his hand flex, tightening to a fist and then relaxing. How he had such an emotional reaction to something so simple as a touch astounds me.

He growls at me. "What are you doing, Annika?"

I pout. "I wasn't done talking to you."

He steps up to me, leaning down and getting in my face. "I don't think that I left it up to you, princess."

My eyes widen. I'm pretty tall for a girl, almost five foot eight. But he dwarfs my size, his muscular body much more immense than mine could ever be. It's kind of nice to feel like the fragile one for just a second, even though I'm definitely playing with fire.

My heart starts pounding. If Erik could wound me with those fiery eyes of his, I'd be skewered through.

When I finally find the words, they leave me in a mere whisper. "Now who's the killer of joy?"

He snorts angrily, turning and storming off. I am left with a frantically beating heart and trembling hands. A few moments later Kalindi returns, looking over her shoulder.

"The bathroom line is so long that I can't stand in it anymore." She looks back, then senses my mood. "What? Did I miss something?"

My lips twist sourly. "Not really, no. You just missed The Ghost of Christmas Past, stirring up trouble."

Kalindi looks puzzled. "I'm sorry, what?"

I pull a face. "I'm talking about Erik."

"Erik… Erik Moen?"

"The very one."

Kalindi cocks her head. "Why isn't he in bed already?"

I burst out laughing. "I said as much to him and he did not take it very well."

She shrugs. "He is tall and blond and unbelievably handsome… but he has a steel beam lodged up his you know what."

I grin, rolling my eyes. "Kalindi, you are old enough to say ass."

I hear a shrill scream from a nearby room. Everybody seems to freeze up, turning toward the sound. Then a loud male voice booms out.

"*Politibetjente!*"

"Shit," I mutter. I'm drunk, too drunk to deal with any police.

Without really thinking it through, I grab Kalindi's hand and start running. Everybody else has the same idea, running out of the house and into the manicured back yard.

What I did not anticipate was the flash of cameras as soon as I step out onto the lawn. I'm blind for a moment as I throw up an arm to guard my eyes.

"What the fuck?" I say, blinking rapidly. When I can see again, I see several paparazzi there about twenty yards away, going crazy taking pictures of me while I'm disoriented. "Fuck!" I shout, trying to shield my face from the paparazzi as best as I can. Kalindi is right there, shielding my face from their view with her tweed jacket.

"Come on," she cries, tugging me toward the front yard. "Let's get out of here."

We run across the spongey green grass to the smoothly paved driveway. My mind is all over the place, mostly focusing on what just happened.

I don't see any police cars… which means that this was just a paparazzi ploy.

Oh, god. They must have gotten some good pictures of me, standing there with my mouth hanging open, looking totally dazed.

As we climb into the first car we see, I sink down in my seat. Because already, I can hear Stellan's voice.

Can you just cool it until the wedding?

I close my eyes. "Take me to the palace, please."

Back to my upcoming punishment…

Chapter Three

ERIK

MY OFFICE IS a cramped space in the basement of Amalienborg palace. It's really confined, the space no bigger than one of Stellan's walk-in closets.

Not that I'm exactly jealous of my best friend, the King of Denmark. He has some big fish to fry, especially with his upcoming nuptials to his American journalist Margot.

But my office is really rather ridiculous. It's musty. It's dark. It's always freezing. It's only large enough to hold a desk and three chairs. It has a single window placed far above my head through which sunlight only streams in during the earliest hours of the day.

It's a little depressing, frankly.

I'm rarely in it anyway, preferring to always be on the go. But just now, it serves its purpose. It is cool and quiet, exactly what I need today.

My head pounds. Why did I drink so much last night?

I stretch out and kick my feet up on my desk, upset that I still have to wear my suit. Stellan is still in bed with Margot, but me… I am working.

I am always working. I squint and then unbutton the top button of my shirt. Loosening my tie a little bit brings an unimaginable kind of relief.

I think it also summons *her*.

When the Queen Mother sweeps into the drab little room that I call an office, I shoot to my feet and shut down my iPad screen. I'm still extremely hungover and trying to cover it up with an astounding volume of coffee and breakfast pastries. The leftovers of my breakfast are still on my desk but there's nothing to be done about it now.

I clear my throat, trying to appear presentable. I bow, wishing that I hadn't just loosened my tie. "Your Royal Highness."

The Queen Mother looks me up and down, as if examining me for flaws. She's a tiny person, probably only five feet tall. But what she lacks in physicality she more than makes up for in formidability.

She tucks a strand of her iron-gray hair back, looking above reproach in her modestly chic white dress. I stare at her blankly.

God, she makes me so nervous. No one else has this effect on me.

"Did we have a meeting that I forgot about?" I blurt out.

Her eyes narrow on my face. "No, Erik." She glances behind herself at the doorway, then looks back at me. She smiles tightly. "Do you mind if I sit down?"

I look down at my desk and the couple of chairs that have been crammed into this tiny space, intended for theoretical guests. "Of course. Make yourself comfortable."

As she squeezes herself into the chair furthest from the door, I find my seat again. A second after she sits down, I hear the clatter of high heels approaching very quickly.

Annika pokes her head into the room, making a face. "This is where your office is? God, could they make it any harder to find?"

"Annika!" the Queen Mother scolds. "You are late. Come in here."

Annika steps into my office. My eyes widen at the lavender minidress she's wearing, her long wavy hair covering a full third of the dress's skimpy length. Her long, tanned legs are bare and dazzling; they make my brain short circuit for a second.

The Queen Mother's expression turns thunderous. "You cannot wear that dress, Annika! If anyone sees you dressed like a street walker it'll shame the entire royal family."

Annika rolls her eyes, putting her hands on her hips. She purses her lips, looking at me.

"I'm too hungover for this. Are you feeling the same way?"

I favor her with a glower. "No."

I'm lying; I absolutely am hungover as fuck, but I'll be damned if I'm going to let Annika embarrass me in front of the Queen Mother.

The Queen Mother frowns. "Erik wasn't stupid enough to let a bunch of paparazzi snap his picture, Annika. That was you. And you did it after I specifically told you not to cause any commotion."

Annika scrunches up her face, pulling the remaining chair out and plopping down. "It wasn't my fault. The photographers used trickery to force us to run out of the house."

The Queen Mother arches a brow. "So? How can you not expect something terrible to happen when there is such an easy opportunity?"

Annika looks offended, her button nose wrinkling up. "I'm sorry, what? Are you saying that you expect me to suspect everyone at all times?"

The Queen Mother's expression grows pinched. She turns to me, smiling coolly. "I've decided that until Stellan's wedding, you should be pulled off of your duties as Stellan's private secretary. Instead, you will be in charge of making sure that Annika stays out of the newspapers."

Annika makes an outraged noise. "No way!"

My heart thumps hard against the wall of my chest. My eyes widen slightly. I must've heard her wrong. "I'm sorry. Say that again?"

The Queen Mother shoots me a glare. "The royal family needs you to help make sure she stays below the radar." Her lips thin. "If it makes it any more appealing, we could perhaps attach a title to it. Let's say... if you are able to successfully keep her out of the papers for three months, you'll get..." She pauses, thinking. "A duchy or something like that. Doesn't that sound good?"

I'm stunned. It's a generous offer, to be sure. My neck grows hot when I think about never working for Stellan again...

We wouldn't be equals, but we would both be titled gentry. My hands form fists as I think it over.

"Umm, excuse me!" Annika waves her hands. "You can't be serious right now. I do not need a babysitter. And I especially don't need... him."

Her whiny tone would hurt, if I actually gave a fuck about her feelings. Lucky for me, I don't.

I scoot forward in my chair. "Tell me more about what you are asking. I would only have to keep the princess under control until the wedding?"

The Queen Mother shifts her position. "Yes. For three months. Keep her from creating any new drama of any sort. Let the media focus their attentions where they should be, on the King and Margot."

I consider her words for a moment. "I see."

Annika shoots to her feet. "You can't really be thinking about taking Momse up on her offer, Erik."

I cock a brow at her, frowning. "You don't control what I do or say, Annika."

She makes a frustrated noise, throwing herself back into her chair. "For fuck's sake."

"Annika!" the Queen Mother scolds.

I sigh. "She's not wrong though, Your Royal Highness. I know I don't have a lot of say in the matter, but if I have any sway at all… I don't want this assignment."

Annika's brow pulls down. She huffs.

The Queen Mother levels me with an icy glare. "I don't care what you want, Mr. Moen. You might have been raised as Stellan's equal, but you are not. You are, at best, a step above the maid that cleans my rooms."

Annika goes silent, her brows rising. For a moment, I'm stunned too.

I glower at the Queen Mother. "If you don't mind me saying, that is a very simplistic view of the world you have."

That earns me a nasty glare from her. "It's honest. And it's not as though I was asking you to do it for free. I'll pay you quite handsomely, if that is indeed your issue."

I grind my teeth. "It's not."

Annika looks between us. "Momse, you have to realize that this is a bad idea. I mean, Erik is just… so stuffy and boring! He's a control freak. You can't expect me to just go along with this scheme."

The Queen Mother stands, running a hand down the skirt of her white dress. "Annika, my dear. You have been disappointing my expectations for most of your life. You would do best to sit down, keep your mouth closed, and be a little more demure. That's good life advice for you generally, but in the next few months? It's not an option." She slides a glance at me. "For either of you."

Annika crosses her arms, wearing a pout on her glossy pink lips. "I think you're being ridiculous, Momse."

The Queen Mother scoots past Annika, heading for the door. "I don't care." She pauses in the doorway, looking back. "This is what the royal family needs right now. It has given you both so much… so try not to disappoint my expectations."

With that, the Queen Mother exits, her head thrown back regally. I raise my brows, unsure how to respond to that.

Sure, the royal family has done a lot for me. They fed me, put me through the finest schools. I served as a major in the military because that was the rank assigned to Stellan. And for the past three years, it has allowed me to slowly amass my personal wealth while acting as Stellan's right hand.

But also… fuck that.

Annika looks at me, scrunching up her face. "She is such a bitch. Momse acts like Stellan walks on frigging water… meanwhile, she is so high-handed when she deals with literally anybody else. I can't stand it."

Leaning my elbows on my desk, I rub my temples. My headache has only intensified since Annika and the Queen Mother stepped into my office, that's for sure.

"I have a very bad feeling about how the next three months are going to go," I murmur.

Annika stands up, surveying my desk. She picks up my coffee cup and takes a sip out of it. Then she wrinkles her nose.

"Ugh! That coffee has turned to ice."

I stand up, pissed off, and pluck the coffee cup from her grip. "Jesus, Annika. Learn some fucking boundaries."

She heaves a sigh. "You're just going to have to accept me for who I am. Get used to it."

Glaring at her, I put my feet back up on my desk. "You know what? I've been treating you like a princess. But I think from now on I'll treat you like the brat that you are."

Her eye roll is unmistakable. "Great, then join the club. The rest of my family treats me like either I'm impossible to control or I don't exist at all. So… welcome. Get cozy. Because no matter what happens in the next few months, I'll still be the only princess of Denmark."

Then she turns on her sky-high heels, strutting like a model on the runway. I watch her walk away, biting my bottom lip.

I can't help but look at her legs and ass as she goes, which I know is exactly what she intended. But the fact that I grow hard at the sight of her tanned inner thighs…

That definitely makes me feel like a fucking pervert. I'm too old, too common-born, and too sensible for this… this *attraction* that I feel.

I close my eyes and sit back in my desk chair, sighing.

The next three months are going to be dark. I'm as sure of that fact as I've ever been of anything, ever.

Chapter Four

ANNIKA

I MEASURE most days by the number of toffee hard candies I need to get through the day. Some days are good; they only register as a four-candy day. That's the sweet spot, no pun intended.

But today? Today is definitely a ten-candy day. I unwrap another piece and pop it in my mouth, savoring the sweet caramel flavor of the toffee. I try not to focus on the fact that every piece of candy is a few extra carbohydrates as well as surplus calories.

I have bigger issues today.

"I can't believe this is happening," I mutter, glaring out the window of the SUV. The city has long since fallen away; now I look out at the coastline, little bits of scrub brush clinging to the sandy ground. Below that I get glimpses of a seemingly endless beach and restless ocean waves.

Erik looks at me from the driver's side seat. "This beach vacation has been on the books for three months. Stellan has been going on and on about it. Were we supposed to stay in Copenhagen just because you can't behave yourself?"

I glance back at Kalindi, who is asleep in the back seat, sprawled out with her mouth open. Lucky her; she doesn't have a frigging babysitter on this trip.

I scowl, scrunching down in my leather seat. "Lower your voice," I

317

whisper. "Kalindi is asleep. And for your information, this is not about me behaving myself. I think you know that, though."

He snorts. "*Ja,* okay."

I scrunch my face up. "Aside from being an uptight stuffed shirt, you are also a total jerk. Just in case you were wondering how I feel about you."

He gives his head a slow shake. "I wasn't… and now that I know, I still don't care."

I glare at him, crossing my arms. "Fine."

He looks unimpressed. "We are almost to the beach house. Can you just shut up until we arrive?"

I direct my glare out the window. "Sure thing, oh Benevolent and Great Dictator."

He just shakes his head but doesn't comment. I stare out my window and watch the massive mansion that we are heading to appear over the horizon. It is extremely Scandinavian in design, appearing as a sleek black block. When I can make out the details, I see a lot of chrome and glass, with almost a third of the house taken up by soaring windows and skylights.

Most importantly, there is a whole huge patio set between the house and the beach. It's an outdoor barbecue, a number of wicker chairs, and picnic tables. All surrounded by tall posts, from which twinkly lights and colorful lanterns are strung.

It actually makes me smile and lifts my mood a little. We have been coming to this particular beach house since I can remember. I will have a good time here, hell or high water.

Kalindi stirs just as Erik pulls up to the front of the beach house. She yawns. "How did we get here so fast?"

I glance and her, wrinkling my nose. "You slept through most of the drive. That's how."

Her cheeks glow pink. "Ah. I guess I needed to catch up on my sleep. Being on the medical track at university is slowly but surely draining my life force. I pulled four all-nighters this week alone."

I scrunch my face up sympathetically. "I'm glad you got some rest, then."

Erik gets out of the SUV, stretching his big arms out over his head. I get out too, my gaze taking in the mansion again. Three stories and excitedly modern looking, I see the brick fireplace running through the entire house.

Erik is unloading the bags from the back of the SUV and piling them on the ground.

Kalindi yawns again and takes a few steps toward the dark wood front porch. I take a step toward the house.

"Hey!" Erik calls out.

Kalinda and I both look back at him, surprised.

"I'm not your manservant," he says in an irritable voice. "Get your own bags."

Shoving a hand through his sandy hair, he picks up his duffel and stalks past me.

Rolling my eyes, I head to grab my own bag. Kalindi trails after me as I follow Erik up to the front door and inside.

Everything is hushed inside the neatly decorated house. The clean, modern lines of the main living room are to my right. To my left is the formal dining room, it's light oak furniture somehow still looking right.

Erik disappears down the hall and I can hear him clattering up the stairs. I follow him, hoping that a room that overlooks the ocean is still available.

"Are we the first ones here?" Kalindi asks as we climb the stairs.

"No. I think we are the last, actually. Stellan and Margot got here yesterday. The rest of my brothers and their guests came in earlier today."

I sprint all the way upstairs and down the hall, pleased to find the room I wanted still open. I call down the hallway. "Come in here! There are two beds."

Tossing my suitcase on an empty double bed, I go over to the floor to ceiling window and push the heavy privacy drapes aside.

The whole beach is right there below me, the patio the only thing separating me from the beach.

I see a clump of Løve boys down on the beach. Stellan stands and stretches. Margot's bright pink hair bobs around next to him as she sits on a beach blanket.

"Whoa," Kalindi says.

I turn to her with a frown. "You've been here before, Kal."

She tosses her suitcase on the second bed, admiring the view. "That doesn't make the view any less spectacular though, does it?"

A smile tugs at my lips. "No. You're right about that."

She tilts her head at me, an empath to her very core. "Are you still trying to figure out what cause to champion?"

I give her a rueful smile. "Yes. Everybody just expects me to know what charity to back. But none of them really make sense to me. Not even the fashion-based charities. Like… okay, your whole marketing thing is about how everything you make is made out of recycled plastic bottles. Good for you. But I'm not your shill."

Her brow wrinkles. "I can point you in the direction of some great medical causes."

Heaving a sigh, I turn back to the beach. "Maybe later. You know, it's too bad we came down so late. The sun is already beginning to set."

"Yeah. Wait… did you take your little green pill?"

I shoot Kal a look. "Yes, mother. I took my crazy pills this morning. No burgeoning mental breakdown on the horizon today. Besides, I'm at a lower risk for having panic attacks way out here. The press isn't around."

She smiles. "I'm just checking up on you. You know me. I'm a mother hen until my last breath."

I shoot her a rueful smile. "Thanks. I mean it. But you can hang up your stethoscope for the weekend, Dr. Kal. It's time to have fun and kick back."

She wiggles her arched brows at me. "There is a hot tub, if I remember correctly. We should definitely get in that thing as soon as we possibly can."

"Umm… we should definitely go do that, right now." I change into my barely-there bright pink bikini and head downstairs. The hot tub is on the tiny back porch and currently unoccupied.

I lean down and turn on the levers controlling the hot tub. As I do, Erik strolls by on his way out to the beach.

Our gazes catch. His eyes widen a fraction as they slide down my body. He stumbles for a second, taking me in. Then he yanks his gaze away from me, scowls, and trots off.

My mouth opens. Of course, Kalindi wasn't here to see what just happened, so there isn't an easy way to know… but I'm pretty sure that Erik was just attracted to me. He may not like my personality, but my body appeals to him on some level.

I look after him, watching his tautly muscled frame. He's wearing a sleeveless gray t-shirt and swim trunks that are clearly designed for men with normal proportions. His tanned knees and hairy, toned thighs are on full display.

I cock my head, thinking about it. I guess I feel the same way about him, now that sexual attraction bubbles to the surface. I know I like to tease him about it… but I think there might be a real spark between us, somehow.

I get the distinct feeling that he would rather die than admit it to me, though.

Kalindi comes out onto the back porch, two flutes of sparkling rosé clasped in one hand, a bag of snack chips in the other.

I take one of the glasses from her, taking a grateful sip. "Mm. Oh, this is just what I needed."

She dips a toe in the now bubble-filled jacuzzi, letting out a loud sigh of pleasure. "Oh, that's nice. I'm getting in."

I climb in too, taking another sip of my wine. Copying Kalindi, I sit down facing the beach. My gaze slides over to the figures on the beach, finding Erik again without even really meaning to.

He stands away from the crowd, watching Stellan and Margot with a blank expression. I can't help but wonder what is going on behind that placid mask he always puts on.

I lean back, enjoying the heat and the bubbles that surround me.

"What do you think of Erik?" I ask. It just sort of pops out of my mouth, unheeded.

Kalindi frowns as she opens the bag of chips. "What?"

I feel myself redden slightly. "I mean… you know. Do you think he's attractive?"

She arches a slim eyebrow. "Do I? Of course. I'm not blind. He's a true Scandinavian. That fetching hair of his. Well, he doesn't have blue eyes. But his eyes are certainly interesting. They're piercing. He has Viking blood, I'm sure of it."

I push my cheek out with my tongue, setting my glass of wine on the deck. "I always wonder what he is thinking about."

Kal looks thoughtful, turning her gaze to the beach. "Yeah, he is definitely hard to read. But that's part of what makes him attractive, I think. He's handsome and mysterious."

She munches on a chip. I reach for one, crunching down on it. It's salty and tangy and delicious, dissolving on my tongue.

"Hey, remember what we were talking about last weekend?" I ask.

She squints. "You're going to have to be more specific."

I bite my lower lip. "About… my… issue? I've been so coddled and protected my whole life that…"

Kalindi's brows rise. "Are you talking about how you are still a virgin?"

I blush to the roots of my hair. "*Ja.*"

She sighs. "I've told you this a dozen times. I'm a virgin too. There is literally nothing wrong with it. I'm… saving myself."

I pull a face. "For whom?"

She rolls her eyes. "I don't know. For marriage, I guess. Anyway, that is not the point. The point is obviously that you shouldn't be in a hurry to lose your virginity."

I roll my shoulders, loosening some knots. "I wouldn't say that I'm in a hurry… but don't you think Erik would be sort of perfect? He's hot. And I get the feeling that he's been with enough women to do it right. Omigod, and can you imagine the look on Momse's face if she found out?"

Just picturing how sour she would look fills me with glee. My mouth curls up at the corners. "She would die. After all, it would be because of her meddling. Sort of, anyway. And she secretly like… can't stand him. It would be so funny."

"You are terrible!" Kalindi says, wrinkling her nose. She laughs though.

On the beach, Erik strips off his shirt. I nudge Kal, nodding. "Just look. That man is literally a hundred and forty percent muscles. Abs… delta… triceps…" I squint. "Okay, I'm not sure why I started naming actual muscle groups, because I don't have any idea of what the rest of them are."

Kalindi lights up. "Ooh! Call on me. You just tell me what area of the body you're trying to compliment, and I'll try to fill in the blanks. We just learned all the muscles in human biology."

My lips lift. "Umm, pass. That's work. We're here to play."

She shakes her head and drinks the rest of her wine in a couple of swallows. "I'm going to bring the bottle out here."

She gets out of the hot tub, dripping wet, and runs inside. I'm left to sip my wine and watch as Erik disappears into the water down on the beach.

Chapter Five

ANNIKA

DUSK HAS JUST FALLEN over the beach, coating everything in sight in a dusting of shadow. The ocean looks dark and intense as the last rays of light disappear over the horizon. Our enormous beach house is the only structure around for miles and its back patio spills right out onto the dunes of sand that lead down to the water.

Other than the twinkle of fairy lights on the patio, it's quickly growing dark. I open my arms to the unbelievable spread of the night sky. The stars wink down at me.

Maybe tonight is the night.

My best friend Kalindi looks over at me from her beach blanket, looking beautiful as ever. She has light brown skin and dark eyes, with hair as thick and lustrous as a raven's wing. She leans back, adjusting her pink bikini.

"What would you think about me snogging your brother?" she asks. Her accent is a mix of British and Indian influences, and her voice is melodic. But her words make me pull a face.

"Which one?" I ask. "Don't say Stellan. All my life, my friends have been asking me whether he is single."

She shakes her head with a soft smile. "No, Annika. I'm talking about Finn."

My eyebrows rise. "Finn?" I glance back toward the house, at the picnic

tables where the older guys and their friends are sitting, Finn included. "Are you sure you mean him and not Anders?"

Kalindi cocks her head. "What's wrong with Finn?"

I scrunch my face up. "Nothing. He's just… odd. Remote. You are a beautiful ray of sunlight and I wouldn't want him to dim your vibrancy, that's all."

She rolls her eyes. "I just mean a casual make out, nothing serious." She turns and looks at the group again, wrinkling her nose as they get up and head for the house. "I think I'm going to go inside and take a shower. This bathing suit is cute but itchy."

"Okay." I sit back, noticing that a lone figure walks by us out toward where the water laps at the beach. With his ruggedly good looks and his pushed-back hair, I can spot Erik easily though it's dark. "I'm going to stay for a while."

Kalindi shakes her head. "You shouldn't like him, Nika. He's almost ten years older than us."

Pouting, I look down at my sun-kissed skin in my tiny black bikini. "Erik is only seven years older than me, first of all. And second of all…" I look up at her. "It's just snogging, as you say."

She shakes her head. "You are crazy. He doesn't even know you're alive."

That stings. I make a face. "I know."

She smiles. "Okay. As long as you realize. I'll be inside, cleaning all this sandy goodness off of my limbs."

I nod, not watching her leave. My eyes find Erik again, silhouetted against the darkened beach. He wears jeans and a plain white button-up, his sleeves rolled up in a way that shows his bulging biceps. He bends over and rolls his jeans up to mid-calf. He keeps walking down a little further, submerging his bare feet in the foam left by the lapping sea. Without realizing it, I stand up, brushing myself off. It's only when I've pulled my shorts and black t-shirt on that I realize that I'm going to go talk to him.

I shiver. I have a half-hearted plan. A plan that involves me, Erik, and a hell of a lot of writhing and heavy breathing. If I can just talk to Erik about taking my virginity, I feel like a weight will be lifted from my shoulders.

The subject of my innocence, of being the perfect and pure princess that Denmark expects… it has caused almost as many panic attacks as seeing my face in the tabloids ever has. I can't hope to live up to the sterling standard that has been set out for me.

So I will shed my virtue. Make it less of an issue. I just need someone to take my virginity.

Someone who I find attractive. But more important, I need someone *kind*. Erik may be stuffy… but the last thing that I think when I look at him is that he is cruel.

It just doesn't exist in him. I can tell.

Shoving my fingers through my hair, I take a deep breath. As I pad barefoot through the sand, I give myself a mini-pep talk.

Just be casual.

Don't be an awkward weirdo.

Play it cool!

A few feet away, Erik turns and notices me. His expression hardens for a split second and then he turns away.

"What do you want, Annika?"

I freeze. This is not the reception I anticipated. Far from it, actually.

Walking forward to pull even with him, I take a deep breath. But when I speak, my tone is pouty.

"I didn't realize that you had the whole entire beach booked up," I say, gesturing to the vast darkness surrounding us.

He looks at me sharply but doesn't respond right away. I take a moment to drink him in. He's extremely tall, taller even than my older brother Stellan's massive height. His body is perfect and muscular without being too bulky. He has a face that is made for movies, with high cheekbones and long eyelashes, and these deep green-brown eyes that make me melt.

Erik grunts. Half a minute goes by, with me looking at his gorgeous face and him gazing out at the horizon. He finally says, "Stellan is a fucking asshole."

I squint, crinkling my whole face. "It must be so *hard* to be best friends with the king of Denmark. Especially when it means you basically get a free ride wherever you go."

As soon as I say it, I wish I could take it back. There is something about Erik that makes me mean and petty when I really want to be sweet.

He lets out a bark of laughter. "You are a brat, Annika. A spoiled little brat. You know that?"

My face heats. Of course, I know that.

"No," I say, sticking my tongue out at him.

He scans me head to toe and then shakes his head. "Yes. You are."

He turns around, walking back toward the house. My heart wrenches; this was my chance to sweet talk Erik a little. Maybe tell him that I think he's dreamy. Ask him to take my virginity. If all else fails, I can probably seduce him.

Now that chance is ruined.

I curse my mouth, which operates on its own sometimes. When Erik stops a few feet away and picks up a bottle of liquor, I raise my brows.

He uncaps it and takes a long pull, letting out a gasping sound when he's done. He turns back to me, holding the bottle out to me.

"Whiskey?"

A breeze blows, making me shiver as I jog the couple of steps toward him, taking the bottle from his hand. He casts another glance at me as I uncork the bottle.

"You should be inside," he murmurs. "Where it's warm and safe."

I take a sip of the whiskey and wince as it burns its way down my esophagus. It's half a minute before I can speak. "Safe? Safe from what?"

Erik looks at me, smirking a little and shrugging. "I don't know. Give me the bottle back, little girl."

I narrow my eyes at him, handing it over. Our fingers brush, our gazes collide. His serious eyes are shadowed so I can't read his expression exactly, but for a split-second I swear there is a carnal interest there.

That, or I'm just imagining what I want to see.

Erik's eyes dart away. He takes another long slug from the bottle. Then he pulls a face. "This whiskey is bullshit."

I wipe a couple of drops from the corner of my mouth, not really knowing how to respond. I'm nineteen; it's not like I have a ton of whiskey tasting experience.

"It's better than some," I come up with at last.

He eyes me skeptically. "*Ja*. It will get you drunk, which I guess is what counts."

I study him. "Are you? Drunk, I mean."

He turns to stare stonily out at the waves. "Maybe." He squints. "I'm on vacation. I almost never get to relax."

He sounds defensive. I shrug my shoulders.

"I'm not judging. I was just curious. I don't think I've ever seen you drunk."

He looks at me again, screwing his handsome face up. "*Ja*, okay."

When he offers me the bottle again, I shake my head. "No. I like champagne, not whiskey."

He lifts a shoulder. "Suit yourself." Tipping his head back, he drinks.

I watch his neck as he gulps the liquor down. I notice his lips then, looking plump and perfectly kissable. Licking my own lips, I let my gaze wander down his body. His arms are both bare and impressively muscular. I can see a hint of the definition of his abs in his tight white t-shirt.

Before I realize it, words are leaving my mouth. "I changed my mind. I want some."

Erik raises his brow. "All right."

He takes a step toward me, handing me the bottle. I let the bottle drop to the ground, putting my arms around his neck. He gives me a startled look.

"Wait— "

I am too close to finding out what his lips taste like to stop now. I push up on my tiptoes and press my mouth against his, hesitating once my lips touch his. He seems frozen for a second, his brain taking a moment to catch up to reality. His eyes sink closed.

Then his hands find my lower back, drawing me against the firmness of his body. At the same time Erik deepens the kiss. No more peck on the mouth; his kiss is rough and dominant, his lips working against mine.

I open my mouth to him, and he takes every inch I give him, sweeping his tongue inside my mouth like a man staking his claim on unchartered territory for the very first time.

A rugged rumble leaves his chest. If I weren't kissing him, I would have missed it. But it spurs me on, makes me spear my hands into the back of his short flaxen hair.

That's all it takes to make him push me back a step. His eyes fly open, shocked.

"Fuck," he grits out. "Oh, fuck. That… that should not have happened."

My cheeks go pink. "Erik— "

He shakes his head, cutting me off. "No, no, no. That… I mean, you're barely nineteen! You're my best friend's baby sister."

I shrug. "So?"

He looks horrified. "So? So, your brother will kill me if he ever finds out. It doesn't matter that I'm drunk…"

I bite my lower lip, looking at him. "I won't tell. It'll be just between us."

Erik shakes his head. "This is bad. This… this can't happen again."

And with that, he picks up the whiskey bottle and starts a slow jog back to our beach house. I stare after him, touching my still-warm lips with my fingers.

Despite everything that Erik just said, my lips still curve upward.

I stand amongst the sand dunes, as the moon comes out to light the night with its soft glow. It's my only comfort as I watch Erik's figure walk away.

Chapter Six

ERIK

ANNIKA IS THE DEVIL. That's the simplest explanation for the torture that she's been inflicting on me.

That kiss… that brief moment where I lost control and just took what I wanted from her. Her soft lips hot against mine, a little hesitant once they brushed my suddenly sensitive skin.

Fuck.

My hands clenched as they slid around her waist. My cock instantly hardened. She made this sound… this soft moan… And she tasted like cotton candy with whiskey overlaid, somehow at the same time.

It doesn't get much more erotic than that. I guess I can't let my guard down around Annika… although she found me at the beach while I was drinking.

She kissed *me*.

I just shouldn't have liked it so fucking much. What in the hell is wrong with me?

Two days later when I'm stonily staring at my little desk in my bleak little office, I'm still thinking about it. I can still feel the weight of her in my hands.

This… this insanity… has to stop. A young brunette from the royal press office pokes her head into my office and I sit up straight as an arrow.

"*Haj*," she says. "I have your altered schedule here."

She holds a sheaf of paper out toward me and I beckon her forward. "I'll take it now. Thanks."

She hands me the schedule. I leaf through it, a sigh on my lips. Every single engagement that I set up for Stellan is now wiped clean from my schedule. Even the things that I personally lobbied for, like a meeting with the local high school students interested in technology.

Gone.

What a bunch of bullshit. Instead my schedule now contains more galas and soirees, plus luncheons for Annika's preferred charities. It looks like she has a lot of art museums and a ton of meetings with fashion designers on her upcoming schedule. Great, two things I couldn't give a quarter of a fuck about.

Rereading the first page, I check my watch. Shit, if I don't hurry, I'm going to be late. I don't even know where I should meet Annika to leave for this luncheon.

Grabbing my dark wool suit jacket, I put it on as I rush upstairs to Annika's quarters. When she returned from boarding school last year, it was decided that Annika was too young to live on her own. So, she's still on the top floor of the palace, in a suite of rooms that would be otherwise unoccupied.

I head up the staircase and down a hallway which is a perfect replica of Stellan's hallway, except done in hushed royal navy tones. Dark blue carpet, soft blue drapes, demure blue upholstered chairs at ten-foot intervals. The walls are hung with the same gilded mirrors and paintings of long-past relatives.

When I knock on Annika's door, her response is immediate, as though she were waiting for me. "Enter!"

I open the heavy dark wood door suspiciously. When I step in, I find Annika in the sitting room. The room looks totally unlike any other in the palace, though... it's like she emptied the room of all its furniture and replaced it with an eclectic blend of expensive, modern pieces.

In the corner, I see that she's set up an area dedicated to a three-way mirror and several lights. All the lights are turned on and focused on a single spot before the mirror.

What a waste of resources.

Annika herself is seated on a low gray tweed couch near the window. A blond male hairdresser is standing behind her, holding a can of hairspray and a comb, pursing his lips. Her hair is long and lustrous as per usual; I'm not sure what if anything he is even here for.

"It's done," he announces.

Annika turns, taking me in. She looks amazing in a stylish light pink dress, but then again, she always looks like that. Her lips twitch and her eyes shine with something akin to mischief.

"Thank you," she tells the hairdresser. "I'll see you again in the morning."

He walks out, casting a dour look over me as he goes. I look at my watch again.

"We're already late to your first appointment," I say, adjusting my cuff. "We should leave immediately."

She stands up, rolling her eyes. "Oh, that's a little trick that the royal press office tries to pull. They write down everything two hours earlier on my schedule in a blatant attempt to manipulate me into showing up early for events. I just ignore it and show up later."

I hunch my brow at that. "I see."

She walks over to a full-length mirror, stepping into the first of four pairs of heels that are laid out for her. She looks at her reflection and then kicks the shoes off, leaving them haphazardly on the floor. Then she slips on another pair, looks in the mirror, and poses.

I stand near the doorway, wondering if I should bring up what happened over the weekend. She doesn't seem troubled by the incident... but maybe I should be worried about that.

After all, the kiss felt earth shattering when it happened. For me, anyway...

Annika turns, pursing her lips. "Which pair of shoes makes me look the most fuckable?"

She sticks out her leg, modeling a shoe for me. I stare at her for a second.

Yeah, we definitely need to talk.

"I don't know," I say, adjusting the knot in my tie. "But I think we need to lay down some boundaries, Annika."

She looks up at me, her eyes dancing with merriment. "Like safe words? Mine will be *forage*. Or do you mean a list of sex acts that are labeled red, yellow, and green?"

I shoot her a look. "That kind of humor is not allowed, for one thing."

She rolls her eyes. "You really are a drag, you know that?"

I fold my arms across my chest and narrow my eyes at her. "I think it's important that we talk candidly to prevent any confusion between us. What happened at the beach the other day— "

She grins, interrupting me. "Are you trying to tell me that it was super hot?"

I flush. Did I fantasize about that moment later when I was drunk and alone? Yes. Did I think about her when I was stroking my cock? Definitely.

But I'm not proud of it… and she doesn't need to know about it, either.

"It was out of line. It's the reason that we need boundaries. A very firm set of rules of engagement, so that nothing untoward ever happens again."

Annika pulls a face. "Untoward? What are you, my grandmother?"

I glower at her. "I'm serious, Annika."

She favors me with a long look. "Things happen, Erik. We're both pretty people. We were both in the same place at the same time. So what? So, we kissed. Big deal."

She turns away, kicking off her heels and slipping her feet into another pair. I take a moment to absorb her words.

"I think we should have some rules, just in case."

She rolls her eyes, turning sideways to look at her slight frame in the mirror. When she doesn't disagree, I clear my throat and continue.

"No touching," I say, ticking items off on my fingers. "No talking about sensitive topics. No questions about my private life. And no discussion of anything that you wouldn't talk to the Queen Mother about."

Annika turns to me with a glare. "Don't tell me what I can or cannot do, Erik. I'm a part of the royal family. Like it or not, you technically work for me."

I huff out a laugh. "I work for your brother, not you. And if you have a problem with any of my conditions, you can go tell someone about it. Anyone, really. I'd love to see the look on your grandmother's face when you tell her that you're upset because you can't ask me about who I've fucked lately."

Her brows rise at that. "Who have you slept with? It must've been a while ago. Because you were so needy back there on the beach…"

"I was drunk!" I thunder. The words burst forth, so vehement and sudden and loud that Annika widens her eyes and goes still.

My words aren't a good excuse; alcohol is never a decent reason for anything. If anyone should know that, it's me. But I think I've wanted to shout at her for a good long while now.

Sadly, it's not very satisfying. Especially not when I can see that she's a little shaken by my tone.

"Annika," I say, shaking my head and looking off toward the window. "Jesus. You bring out the worst in me, you know that?"

She bites her lip and shrugs a single shoulder, looking very young all the sudden. "No."

I can't stand her sudden vulnerability, how it lurks behind her fullness and bratty attitude. It's a sword sharp enough to shred me into a million tiny ribbons.

"Stop it," I grit out.

She looks at me sharply. "Stop what?"

"That little innocent, wide-eyed ingenue thing you're doing. It's not working on me."

Her brow furrows. "What? I'm not doing anything."

"Maybe you're not trying, but you definitely are," I grate. My fists clench. "And it's not playing fair, okay? Just… behave yourself."

Her eyes narrow. Her expression cools. "So, you are just like everyone else, then. You make assumptions about my behavior. And then when my actions don't line up perfectly, you shake your finger at me and scold me." She lifts her head, tossing her hair back. "I'm done with that. I've had plenty of that in my life already. So, if you don't mind, get the hell out of my rooms. I'll meet you by the limousine in two hours."

She turns and marches to the doorway that leads to her bedroom. She opens it and slams it after herself hard enough that a painting shifts on the wall, skewing slightly.

I glare after her, shaking my head as I exit the room into the hallway.

Annika is a mess. One minute she's joking, the next she's on the verge of tears. Defiant, then charming, and then vulnerable. How am I supposed to handle someone like that?

I won't be drawn into her insane world of high drama and petty bullshit, that's for sure. With that reaffirmed in my mind, I head downstairs to my office to brood in peace.

Chapter Seven

ANNIKA

AS I SIT down in the very front row of the Greta von Grissel fashion show, I smile wanly at the big names that are present to support the show. I suck on my hard candy discreetly and try not to wonder how some of the people around me get so *thin*. A couple of actresses, a celebrity blogger, a fairly famous rocker… they're all stuffed around me, arranged like dolls for the cameras.

One of the actresses shyly asks me for a selfie. I smile and comply, not because I'm particularly in the mood. But because it's expected of the princess of Denmark.

I'm playing the part, being the perfect Danish princess. Short black velvet dress, sky high black heels, and a tiara to top it all off.

Normally I would relish a Grissel fashion show. After all, being here is paying tribute to my primary hobby. Change the world through using fashion to raise money for charitable causes. But the reason I'm in a sour mood is heading my way… and he looks like he just walked off the pages of a fashion magazine.

Tall, elegant, with sandy-colored hair and those cutting green-brown eyes. He's dressed simply but stylishly in a slim cut navy wool suit, a pristine white shirt, a crisp black tie, and spit-shined black leather Oxford shoes.

I watch the crowd notice him as he approaches me. The gorgeous women attending this fashion show arch their eyebrows and aim their pouts at him. The handsome men cock their heads and wonder who he is.

And Erik doesn't even know that he's being measured. His gaze locks on to me and narrows a little. Even from a distance, he appears brooding.

The lights start to dim. Behind Erik, the runway is lit while the area given over to the guests darkens. He walks right up to me, looking at the people carefully arranged around me on the white marble bench.

"Do you mind if I move you down?" he asks the young actress seated beside me.

She flushes prettily. "*Ja, ja*. Let's see..."

My mouth thins. She stands up and motions to everybody to move down. My gaze slides to the event planner, who is staring at us as though we've just ruined her life.

Erik sits down beside me. "Your highness," he says, nodding to me.

I narrow my eyes at him and adjust my dress. I continue to smile as there are camera flashes about every five seconds. But inside, I'm seriously pissed off at Erik. He is definitely high up on my shit list for the things he said yesterday.

I freeze him out, turning ever so slightly away from him. He casts a skeptical glance over me.

Then I hear the actress on his other side introduce herself in a whisper. I force myself to continue smiling and lean forward so that I can see her around Erik.

"He's in trouble," I say, smiling brightly. "Please don't talk to him."

The starlet's eyes go wide but she just nods. Erik shoots me a glare. But before he can say anything, the music starts blaring.

He shifts in his seat, watching as the models begin to work their way down the runway. I keep up my end of the bargain, applauding politely at every single model.

Privately, I'm not paying a single bit of attention to what's going down the runway in front of my face. But Grissel doesn't need to know that. And I still want her to make me ten designer dresses for next season...

A few minutes into the fashion show, Erik shifts his weight, pressing his thigh up against mine. My eyes widen just a bit.

It's probably an unknowing move on his part, but holy hell. The warmth of his big body radiates, heating my exposed skin.

I look down at where our bodies are pressed together, distracted beyond reason. Why is this the most erotic thing that's happened to me all week?

I stare at the spot where we touch. For some odd reason, all I can think of just now is Erik moving his hand to my thigh and inching up my dress.

I lick my suddenly parched lips, a rush of memory hitting me. Now I can remember exactly why I wanted him to be the one to take my virginity.

Suddenly the house lights go up. Everyone around my is rising and applauding Greta von Grissel, who traipses down the runway looking like a mythical goddess in a flowing dress of her own design.

I rise and clap too, wondering where the last twenty minutes went. Did I really spend them fixating on how good Erik's thigh felt when it was pressed against mine?

The designer bows. The paparazzi swoop in, shooting photos of us famous people.

"Can we get a shot with you and Greta, your highness?" one man calls.

"Who is your escort, your highness?" a woman asks.

I blanch. "Thank you, everyone! I have to go, unfortunately." I lock eyes with the designer, gesturing to mimic a phone. "Greta, I'll call you!"

And with that, I turn, raise my head, and sweep out of the room. Bodyguards fall in around me once I step outside of the ballroom.

Another of Erik's decisions, I bet.

By the time I climb into the back seat of the limousine, I'm furious. I pluck the tiara from my hair and run my hands through my strands, pulling out bobby pins and wrecking an entire morning's worth of effort.

Erik climbs into the backseat beside me, glancing at me as I irritably pull bobby pins from my sinuous mane.

I avoid his green-brown gaze, my brow hunched as I glare at the seat in front of me.

"What is wrong with you?" he asks.

I snort. "Believe it or not, I'm still pretty damn mad at you."

He exhales loudly. "Is this about yesterday?"

I glare at him. "Yes."

I gather all the bobby pins into a fat bundle, toying with them.

Erik grunts. "I'm sorry I said… whatever is making you upset."

"Agh!" I moan, sinking down in my seat. "The fact that you don't even know what made me mad, but you apologized anyway… that makes me angrier."

He laughs, a humorless sound. "This is insane. I can't keep up with you." He shakes his head. "You know what? I think this is still about how I rejected you on the beach."

I roll my eyes. "Oh, please. Like I can't have whatever or whoever I want, whenever it pleases me. I am the only fucking princess of Denmark, you know."

He glares at me. "Maybe that isn't good enough for you. Maybe you have some… some fixation on me. Forbidden fruit and all that."

I look at him, shaking my head. "Actually, you aren't explicitly taboo to me. This whole forbidden fruit thing only really works from your perspective."

He narrows his gaze on me, eyeing me up and down. "No. I think you are infatuated with me."

I open my mouth, hitting him on the arm repeatedly. "I am not, you pompous… arrogant… jerk! I could never be interested in somebody so self-righteous and buttoned up! Ugh!"

His lips curve upward. "You seemed to think differently on the beach last week."

I turn straight ahead, blushing deeply. "That was just a physical thing. I was there, you were there…" The lie feels a little forced, but I just keep on anyway. "I could never, ever, ever actually feel romantically attracted to you." I laugh at the very idea of it. "Like… no. Ew."

Erik frowns, crossing his arms and adjusting his position against the seat. "It's nice of you to lay it out there so that even I can understand it, princess."

I shoot him an annoyed glance. "I'm just expression my feelings, Erik. You may be hot, but you are essentially a walking suit. Just… there's no substance to you except doing what you're told and minding your p's and q's."

He rolls his eyes, looking at his watch. "I suppose you dream of falling in love with a man every bit as dramatic and shallow as you are. Maybe an actor, hmm?"

I scoff. "You don't get to tell me who to date, thank you very much."

He smiles and stretches out, dominating the space in the back of the limo. "We should talk about your next engagement, shouldn't we?"

I scrunch up my face, still annoyed with him. "The press office lies about how soon I need to be there, remember? It's so hopelessly stupid. How long of a gap is there on the schedule for today?"

He gives me a measured look then pulls his phone out and scrolls for a second. "Three hours."

Throwing my hands up, I pull a face. "There's no telling how long of a gap there actually is between events. Everything gets very distorted very quickly."

He considers that for a moment. "I can try to talk to someone in the press office about it, if that would please her highness."

I look at him sharply. What he said sounded sarcastic, but his words were meant to be helpful… at least, I think so.

"I thought you told Momse that the press office has blacklisted you."

He looks startled for a second. "Oh. Well… I did, but I can still see if I have any pull." His eyes narrow. "How did you know that?"

Blushing, I turn my head away and look out the window. "You mentioned it in passing two months ago. I remember everything. It's…" I think for a moment. "It's just something that I do."

I notice and memorize insignificant details of everyone else's lives. Well, actually… only the people who really matter to me.

Does my subconscious believe that Erik is somehow important?

"I see," Erik says. He seems to get lost in thought.

Sinking down a couple more inches, I shade my eyes and pray for our car ride to end.

ERIK

"IS this a rare glimpse into the master working in his studio?"

I glance up from a stack of tedious papers to find Stellan leaning in the doorway. Throwing my pen down, I lean back in my chair with a grin.

"You surfaced for air! Tell me, how is it being suctioned to Margot's side?"

His lips twitch. He strolls over and plops down in one of my chairs, running a hand through his dark hair. "Not as tough as being king, it turns out. Especially when my best friend and right-hand man vanishes on some mundane task."

I roll my eyes and fold my hands behind my head. "Hey, don't complain to me about it. Complain to your grandmother. She's the one that thought that Annika needed such close supervision."

Stellan sighs, looking around my tiny office. "We should really get you a better place to work, Erik. This place is too dark and too small for someone of your stature."

He's referring to the fact that I'm taller than everyone I meet, himself included. I shrug.

"It works for me. I don't need anything grand. It's sort of apt, don't you think?" I glance around my cramped office.

Stellan squints. "It's okay for now. But you are going to be titled gentry soon. Isn't that what my grandmother offered you for dealing with Annika?"

I stare at Stellan for few moments, studying his face for a hint at what he could possibly mean. He gives me nothing, his face a perfectly blank slate. Finally, I just shrug.

"Yes, she did offer that. But that's not the reason I'm minding Annika. Or at least not the only reason. I consider it to be a personal favor to you, Stellan."

His brows rise. "Oh?"

"Your royal highness! There you are." A red headed young man appears in the doorway, flustered and overexcited. "I've been looking for you everywhere!"

Stellan gives me a look. "Erik, this is Thor. He's your replacement until after my wedding."

Thor raises his head a little. "Your royal highness, you are going to be quite late— "

"Oh, god. Do calm down, Thor." Stellan rises, giving me another look. "I'd best be on my way. I just wanted to make sure you weren't just languishing down here."

I give him a tight smile. "Not too much, no."

Stellan smirks. "All right, then. I'll see you soon. Next week, I think we have some sort of family dinner or something?"

I nod. "You know where to find me in the meantime."

Stellan looks around my office once more. "That I do."

He heads out of my office, his footsteps echoing down the hall as he rushes off toward his next engagement. After he's gone, I try to focus on the papers in front of me again.

But it's no use. Glancing at my watch, I wonder what my father is doing. It's been almost a month since I've seen him. And Annika is locked in her rooms with her friend Kalindi, whispering and giggling like a couple of little girls.

With a sigh, I rise. If there is a better time to go visit my father, I don't know of it.

It's the work of a couple of minutes to exit the palace through the gardens. I roll up my sleeves and shove my hands through my hair as I walk. It feels silly but if I walk into my father's house looking like I have my shit together, my father will lose his temper.

And he will undoubtedly aim his anger at me.

The stables are only a few minutes further travel down a narrow, paved path. The birds are chirping in the trees, the sun is high in a perpetually blue sky, it's about as nice as Denmark can get.

But as I skirt the stables and head to my father's cottage, my mood darkens with every step. Bracing myself, I knock on the door of the charming, well-maintained little cottage.

I hear my father cough first, long and ragged. "Who is it?" he calls out.

I close my eyes briefly. "It's Erik."

The door swings open and I look into a very real image of my future. My father is my height, thin as a whip, with his hair gone completely gray. He's dressed in a pair of fresh khaki overalls and a button up shirt with the cuffs rolled and shot up as far as they will go.

He doesn't look happy to see me. "Haj, son."

He backs up and lumbers back into the kitchen, taking a seat at the heavy old table. Before him are a bunch of horse bits, a bucket of soapy water, and a rag. And the ever-present schnapps bottle, of course.

Blanking my expression, I close the door and circle the table, taking a seat at the long bench.

My father takes a quick nip from the bottle of schnapps, wincing. Then he picks up a bit and the rag and starts cleaning.

I try not to look around too much; there are memories in this cottage, and not pleasant ones. Memories of my beautiful blonde mom. Memories of my father, drunkenly screaming at her. A memory of her crying and wishing me goodbye, then slamming the front door one last time.

"Well?" my father demands. "What are you here for, Erik?"

Blowing out a breath, I eye him. "How are you?"

He glowers down at the bit in his hands. "Does it really matter to you? *Herre* High and Mighty." He makes a sour face and looks at my shirt. Then he shakes his head, setting the bit aside and picking up the bottle again. "You look like a poor man masquerading as one of them royals."

My neck heats. I want to fuss with my shirt, but I don't. Instead I paste on a smile. "You made that choice for me, far. I was barely out of diapers. You'd driven *mor* away…"

My father grinds his teeth. "It's not my fault that your mother left, okay? And I was just trying to scrape by."

I level a look at him. "You made enough money. That's never been the issue between us."

My father takes a swig from the bottle and narrows his eyes at me. "I'm not saying you was at fault then. You was little. But when I told my troubles to King Goran… and he offered to take you off me hands… well, I never expected him to turn you into that little prince's shadow. I thought…"

He trails off, wiping his chin with the rag. I fold my arms across my chest. "I didn't come here for this."

My father looks up at me, his hazel eyes pinning me in place. "What did you deign to come all the way down here for? The royal palace is only five minutes away, but it must be too comfortable to leave. Even to visit your own flesh and blood…"

Taking a deep breath, I brace my fingers around the bridge of my nose. "And why would I not visit more? I can never get enough of your gruffness."

My father narrows his eyes at me. "I'm just telling the truth."

My hands form fists. I want to hiss with rage and turn this fucking table over on its side. But I don't.

Instead I school my expression into a bland mask. "Let's change the subject, *dar*."

He shakes his head, looking down at the bit in his hands. "I imagine when you find a girl and settle down, you two will just move away and leave me here. Won't you? Better to start over, without an old man weighing you down."

His tone is self-pitying, an abrupt switch from his accusations just moments ago. I am ready for it, though. He usually vacillates between the two the entire time I visit.

I turn my head, stretching my neck. "I don't know, *dar*. That's years down the road, if ever."

What I don't say is that I'm absolutely certain that he screwed me up so badly that I'll never be able to love another person. At least not anyone other than Stellan, who I feel a bittersweet mix of love and envy toward.

He grunts. "Is this when you tell you're a fairy, boy? I'll tell you this right now, there's no use in you pining away over that prince of yours."

My muscles tense. "We've had this conversation. I'm not gay. I am not in love with Stellan. End of story."

My father throws down the bit and the rag with a *thunk*. "Then why haven't you got a girl? Hmm? When I was your age, I was already married. Come to think of it, you had already arrived."

I notice that he just avoids talking about my mother altogether, as though I simply appeared on his doorstep one morning.

I force a hard smile. "Romantic love just seems… messy. You should understand. You and *mor* couldn't make it work— "

He shoots to his feet. "Her leaving was your fault, Erik. Before you came along, she was happy. It wasn't until you were born that she… she…"

I stand up. "What? She couldn't stand to be in this house, belittled by you day and night. I'm not surprised that she left, *dar*."

He turns red. "Get out of here, Erik. You don't want to be here anyway. According to you, I treat you and everybody else so terrible. So, I'll say it again, get the fuck out of here."

Shaking my head, I walk toward the door. "Gladly, old man."

He sits down, picking up the horse bit and resuming polishing. "No son of mine would treat me so bad, I'll tell you that much."

I shake my head, pushing out the door of the cottage with a bang. This. This feeling right here, this ball of black hate right where my heart should be?

This is why I don't visit my father, even though he's so close. Even though he's the only family that I have left.

As I storm up the little lane, the birds chirp and the sun still shines. But I'm far too wrapped up in my angst for them to make me feel any better.

Chapter Nine

ANNIKA

I STARE at the tabloid newspapers spread out on the table before me, horrified. The headlines are a variation on the same theme.

PRINCESS ANNIKA PIGS OUT (AGAIN)!

Followed by pictures of me in an unflattering royal blue dress, about to take a bite of dessert. My eyes gleam like that bite of dessert is the apple of my eye. In the insets are half a dozen other photos from the same event, with me trying different desserts.

What they don't mention, of course, is that I was the royal assigned to attend a dessert competition. They also neglected to mention the fact that I went hungry for two days leading up to that to save up a bank of calories just for that event.

All I had for forty-eight hours was unlimited water and a handful of my favorite hard candies. I wish I could scream that fact at the paparazzi that snap my photos… but they don't really care.

No one cares about the work that I put into being perfect except *me*.

I tilt my head, surveying the photo closest to me. I'm wearing a shapeless dress with bell shaped sleeves in the picture, which isn't really even that unflattering. I just look like a person who's eaten thirty bites of cake, which is exactly what I was at that moment.

Standing up, I grab a waste bin and sweep all the papers into it. Then I stomp to the door of my parlor, putting the waste bin outside of it.

I breathe, trying to get the image of me and the words PRINCESS PIGGIE out of my head. But I just can't. Later when I'm done getting dressed in my room, I still hear the words to a particularly cruel song in my head.

A small choir of children happily croon: Princess Piggie, Princess Piggie. Eats her weight in toast smeared with figgie...

Kids used to sing that old nursery rhyme when I was in earshot, knowing full well that it would make me die inside. Like everyone else in the world, I went through an awkward stage from age ten to fourteen. But unlike the rest of humanity, my awkward stage was caught on film and celebrated throughout Denmark.

I can picture myself now, being twelve and trying not to eat in front of anyone, because I would feel judged later. My expression hardens as I march out to the huge three-way mirror in the corner of the parlor.

Standing as straight as I can, lifting my ribcage and posing just so, I look at myself. The girl that looks back at me isn't fat. If anything, she's a little bit too skinny to really be what anyone would call beautiful. I turn and angle my body this way and that, reposing my arms dozens of times.

If only I could control what people saw when they looked at me... but I've long since learned that I can't.

It doesn't matter that I have a designer white lace dress on. It doesn't matter when the last time was that I actually ate a full meal. It doesn't matter to the paparazzi that I'm a real person with tender feelings.

I take a deep breath in, my eyes filling with tears.

A knock on the door sounds. I whirl, cursing my emotions for running wild. Carefully swiping at my eyes, I call out.

"Just a moment!"

I check the mirror, telling myself to lock those damn emotions away for now. After making sure that I look okay, I call out again. "Come in!"

The door opens and Erik enters, his expression stormier than usual. He is wearing a dark suit that fits him like a glove. as though he was just called down off of a runway. He shoots his cuffs, running a hand through his neatly combed hair.

"What is this?" he asks, waving a tabloid paper at me. He tosses the newspaper onto the table, pinning me with a glare. "When did this happen?"

I flush but raise my head a little, running my hands down the front of my dress. "Months ago. It must've been a slow news day."

He folds his arms across his chest, starting to prowl the room. "This isn't good, Annika. You aren't supposed to be covering any papers. What did you do to get the attention of the paparazzi?"

I give his words a little huff of disbelief. "I was born into the royal family, for starters. Do you know that when I was only two years old, a paper published photos of me and called me chunky?"

He stills. "No."

I shake my head, turning back to the mirror to put my earrings in. "I have had a contentious relationship with the press since I had the gall to draw breath. The Danish people claim to love me. But they also buy every single paper that says nasty things about me so…"

I shrug helplessly.

Erik's tawny green-brown gaze spears me when I turn around. He's closer than I thought he was… almost close enough to touch.

My gaze dips down from his face to his impressive physique, exceptionally showcased in that tight white button-up and his tautly fitted black wool jacket. He's dreamy, I'll give him that.

"You can't be doing anything to capture the attention of the paparazzi," he says solemnly.

I roll my eyes. "Like you know anything about it. You just got here. Give yourself a minute to settle in and see how insane it all is."

I walk past him, bumping his shoulder intentionally. But I don't expect his reflexes to be so good that he catches me just as I brush against him.

Erik's hands clamp around my arms. Eyes widening, I look up into his elegant face with its savage expression. His body presses against mine tightly. His hands control my every movement.

This close, he could kiss me. He could ravage me. He could even really hurt me. When he speaks, his deep voice slides down my spine like a chill.

"I don't think you understand the implications of what we're dealing with," he grates out.

My gaze drops to his mouth. I bite my lip. "Oh, no?" I ask. My mouth curves upward, unbidden.

He gives me a little shake. "Be serious, Annika."

I look him in the eye, raising a brow. "And if I am not?" I ask quietly. "What will you do with me then?"

He bristles. His hands press into the flesh of my arms so hard that they may leave me bruised. It's obvious from this close that Erik is so much bigger than I am, that his height and weight mean he can haul me around with ease or even genuinely hurt me if he really wants to.

And though I don't want to admit it, I think that's what really turns me on about him. Lurking underneath that calm surface is something sleek and dangerous and calculating. It's a little like going for a swim in a placid sea, knowing that just under the surface, a shark waits for his next meal.

"You should be punished." His voice is gone to gravel. The anger in his expression and the volatility in his eyes is nearly frenetic; there is something *almost* violent mirrored in his eyes.

I open my mouth, my core clenching. "What will you do, Erik?" I look him square in the eye and toss off a haughty laugh. "What *can* you even do?"

If my goal is to goad him into action, to push him to a breaking point, I get exactly what I wish for. He glares down at me, sliding a hand into my mane of fair-colored hair. Fisting my hair, he tugs my head back, exposing my throat to him. My eyes widen and I stop breathing for several seconds.

"Someone should have taught you a lesson years ago," he rasps, a cruel smile on his perfect lips. Then Erik bends his head down, placing a searing kiss on my throat.

I gasp at the feeling of his lips against my skin. But when he moves up an inch and bites my neck hard, I just shudder. I'm turned on, confused, and a little scared all at once.

Yes. Do it as hard as you want, I think.

But I don't say that. I find myself strangely tongue tied around this furious, sexual version of Erik. He's so uptight and controlled that seeing this side of him is fascinating and frightening and arousing all at once.

My hands come up to clutch at his arms, but he knocks them away. "Uh uh."

His lips touch shoulder, my collarbone. Flexing his hips into me, he leaves me with no doubt that his cock is rigid. Pressed against my belly, every time he moves his hips, his cock thrusts against me *hard.*

I shiver as he trails hot, rough, wet kisses inward toward my breasts. He releases one of my arms and tweaks my nipple through my dress, pulling another gasp from my lips. It hurts… but there is a corresponding throb low in my body after he releases my flesh.

My body wants his. Between my tightly pressed thighs I can feel a slither of moisture slipping from my core, preparing me for him.

Erik lifts my head up, his eyes glittering. "It's what you deserve, princess."

I bite my lower lip, swallowing heavily. "Erik…" I manage.

His hazel eyes lock on mine. "Let's see."

Maintaining his brutal grip on my hair, he uses his free hand to begin rucking up my skirt. My eyes widen and I start struggling. Erik just lifts his fist clutching my hair and I wince, stilling.

"Stop resisting, Annika."

His hand touches the inside of my thighs which is a shock to me. I feel burned, scorched by his touch. How dare he touch me like this? I push at his torso uselessly, my mouth twisting with bitter bile.

Then he looks down at my body, my white lace thong bared to his gaze. He brushes the apex of my thighs, his fingers arching in toward my core. He delves into the folds of my pussy and finds a pool of sticky moisture there. I stiffen, feeling both aroused and like I've been caught doing something naughty.

An involuntary shudder and a huff of breath leaves my lips. "Erik!"

He looks me in the eye, lifting a single brow. He wiggles the fingers he has pressed against me so intimately. "Don't try to lie to me, princess. Your mouth says no, but your body says yes."

I shake my head, trying to argue with him. "No, you don't— "

Erik pulls my head toward his face for a brutal, devastating kiss. It leaves my lips feeling bruised and my pride feeling dimmed. At the same time, a part of me wants… more.

It makes my body *ache*.

He releases me suddenly, stepping back. "Before you try to fucking rattle my cage again, you'll remember what happened here."

Then he whirls and stalks out of the room, slamming the door behind him so loudly that it actually makes me jump. One of my hands runs across my lips. The other one is already pulling down my skirt, returning things to normal.

But things aren't normal… things may never be normal again.

Shivering and trembling, I sink onto the couch and try to stop my thoughts from spinning out of control.

Chapter Ten

ERIK

CLEARING MY THROAT, I stand ramrod straight as I hold the door to the ballroom open for a crowd of ladies. My face creases as I peer inside the ballroom. The walls are draped in a light pink velvet. The many tables are each covered in spring green or off white or baby pink. The tables are set with gleaming silver tiered trays of macaroons and sandwiches, polished water glasses, and white porcelain teacups.

Looking at how intricately decorated the room is for high tea makes me tense.

Doubly so when my glance trips over Annika. She's breathtaking just now in her baby blue dress, her blonde hair swept off her neck in a fashionable knot.

I escorted her here of course, because apparently, I'm a very expensive and very glorified babysitter. But she didn't so much as speak a word to me in the car on the way here. Instead I just stewed in the icy tension brewing between us.

And tried not to relive every second of the evening before, when I grabbed her. When I pulled her close, dug a hand into her hair, and kissed her neck. When I ran my hand up the soft skin of her inner thigh.

When I touched her pussy, finding it hot and wet and ready for me.

A fine shudder runs through me, remembering the sensation. I know that

I misbehaved. The fact that I completely lost my mind for a moment and laid my hands on Stellan's little sister makes me so deeply ashamed.

I just don't know what to do about it. And it's clear that Annika doesn't either.

I move inside the ballroom, smoothing a hand down my navy tie and black suit jacket. Everywhere I look there are fancy ladies in sleek light pink or white dresses, gathering at tables to sit down. I see that Annika is standing awkwardly by her mother the former queen and her grandmother, waiting. for them to take their seats. She looks like she's about to drown in this sea of older women.

My attentions aren't needed there. Like many times in my life, I think that it would be best if I were to just wait downstairs near the cars.

I turn around and am brought up short when I almost knock over a young brunette in a skintight pink lace dress. Her upturned nose and severely plucked eyebrows look familiar but I can't immediately place her. She grins and latches onto my arm.

"Erik!" she crows. Her voice is loud and high-pitched, and it brings me back to last summer. She's a royal hanger-on, one of those girls that used to flutter around Stellan, hoping he would look their way.

"Dalia," I summon her name out of my memory. "Right?"

She beams at me, leaning close and hanging on my arm. "Of course, you remembered my name. How gentlemanly."

My eyes narrow. "I was just leaving."

Dalia widens her eyes. "But why? When I heard that you were going to be at our table, I got all starry eyed. You can't leave me all alone at the Queen Mother's table!"

I blanch, glancing behind me. The Queen Mother and Annika are just now taking their seats, Annika with a scowl on her face.

"Yeah, I don't think—" I start.

"Shh. Come on," Dalia says sternly. She starts towing me toward the table in question,

I resist. "Seriously, Dalia— "

But Dalia is already making a scene, waving to the Queen Mother. "We're coming!"

I release a sigh, allowing myself to be pulled over to the table of honor. There are six women already seated and just two seats left on opposite sides of the table. One is next to Annika; I can see from the place cards that it's intended for me.

I shake off Dalia's grip. "This is my spot."

Dalia pouts as she slinks to the other side. I slide into my seat, trying not to call too much attention to myself. Annika gives me the cold shoulder, tossing her hair and turning away.

Just as well and fine with me, honestly.

"Dalia! Who have you found?" an older brunette asks, indicating me.

Dalia smirks and makes the introduction. "*Mor*, this is Erik. He's one of Stellan's friends. Erik, this is my mother, Lady Shane." She pauses, eyeing me. "As you can see, the Shanes and the royal family are very close."

I repress an eye roll, bowing my head briefly. "It's a pleasure, Lady Shane."

The Queen, who is usually noticeably absent, clears her throat politely. It's obvious that Annika and her mother share the same gene pool; they have the exact same aristocratic nose, the same impossibly high cheekbones, the same pouty lips. I can tell exactly what Annika will look like in twenty years' time just by glancing at her mother.

And I have to say, she will still be undeniably beautiful.

"Erik, it's so nice to see you here," the Queen says.

I incline my head again, deeper this time. "Thank you, your highness. His Royal Highness is feeling well, I hope?"

Without even thinking about it, I just casually mentioned her husband the former king. Until a recent Alzheimer's diagnosis, he reigned as king for my entire life.

A flush comes to the Queen's cheeks. Annika kicks me under the table, shooting me a frown.

The Queen recovers gracefully though. "He is very well. Thank you for asking. And thank you for taking care of Annika." She smiles at her daughter, patting her hand. "She does need a little extra attention. Right, darling?"

Annika's cheeks turn scarlet. I expect her to say something sarcastic. But to my surprise, she doesn't. She just looks down at her lap and mumbles, "Yes, mar."

My eyebrows rise a fraction. Looking back and forth between the Queen and her very unhappy daughter, I think that I'm missing some important info. I have no idea what, just that there is something about the Queen that makes proud, reckless Annika… submissive.

What is that, exactly? I wonder about it while several waiters come around our table, filling our teacups with dark, fragrant tea. The Queen looks at me. "How have you been, Erik?"

I raise my gaze from my teacup, feeling a little put on the spot. "Very well, your royal highness."

She smiles. "Please, call me Thora. We are practically family, after all. And besides, I feel like Margot and Stellan have really shaken things up in the royal family. I stepped down as Queen, Margot will take my place later this year…"

Annika gives her mother a small smile. "That's a good view to take."

Her mother tilts her head and sighs. "I was just talking to Stellan yesterday, and he said the same thing. Which of course meant the world to me…"

Annika flinches at Stellan's name, looking back down at her lap. The Queen doesn't notice her daughter's distress; she goes on to tell a long, rather uninteresting story about how as a child, Stellan would bring her flowers and brighten up her day.

Dalia narrows her eyes at Annika, smirking just a bit. "That's so wonderful. I'm glad one of your children only brings you joy. What do the others bring, I wonder?" She pretends to think about it for a second. "Nothing but news headlines, I suppose?"

The Queen smiles and reaches out her hand to Annika's. "My other children bring me joy. And occasionally, they are the thorns in my bouquet of roses. But they still make me proud."

Lady Shane clears her throat, sensing tension bubbling between Dalia and the Queen. "Of course. I am certain that Dalia only meant to tease. Didn't you, dear?"

Dalia beams. "Oh yes. Certainly. I didn't mean to bring up those ugly headlines about Annika stuffing herself— "

Annika shoots to her feet, her face contorting with rage. "That's enough from you, Dalia. And FYI? You'll never be a member of the royal family. My brothers all hate you— "

"Okay!" I jump up, cutting her off. I laugh a little as I slip my arm around Annika. "You know, I think Annika is tired. Poor girl, we had a late event last night…"

I see Annika's chin start to wobble; a telltale sign of tears sure to come. The Queen folds her arms across her chest and looks displeased.

"I see," is all she has to say.

"Ladies, if you'll excuse us," I say, bowing my head.

Annika wrenches herself out of my grasp and storms off, leaving me to chase after her. It's a little dicey because there are still waitstaff circling and serving the many other tables. Annika manages to slip through the crowd, something someone of my stature can't do nearly as easily. But after dodging several tea-wielding servers, I catch up with Annika outside the ballroom.

"Annika," I try.

"Don't," she warns, barely repressed fury in her tone. She dashes away a welling of tears from her eyes.

She looks angry as she stalks down the hotel's grand white marble hallway.

"Annika—" I say, trying to grab her.

She suddenly stops, squaring off with me. Her head tips back, her face is flushed, and she glares at me utterly defiantly.

"I won't…" Her eyes suddenly shine with unshed tears, her voice growing strained. "I won't… apologize."

I step closer, my hands coming up to brace her arms. Not a hug, exactly. But I can't very well stand here and be a stone wall.

"I wouldn't ask you to," I say, searching her face. She peers up at me, guileless, her blue eyes shimmering.

"I know that you don't want to be here," she says, her voice breaking. "I know that you're just doing as you're told. The good little soldier. God, what must you think of me?"

I grip her arms, frowning down at her. "I don't know, Annika. I can't seem to decide what to think."

Annika hangs her head. "If you read the newspapers, you'd have an opinion. Did you know they call me Princess Piggie?"

A muscle ticks in my jaw. "That's not how I see you."

"No?" She flexes her hands, looking down at them. "My hands feel weird." She wheezes the next few breaths, looking back up at me with a distinct note of worry. "I… I can't breathe. My chest is…" She shakes off my touch, clawing at her chest. She continues to struggle for breath. "I think… I feel like I'm dying."

My brow hunches. I glance around the hallway, feeling like a fish out of water. When Annika grips my arm hard, I glance back at her, feeling helpless.

Fuck. Is she going to be okay? Do I need to get a doctor?

"Get me…" she pauses, wheezing. "Get me somewhere quiet."

I can hear her struggle to breathe. I can feel the waves of anxiety coming off of her.

"Okay." I look around, spotting a door only a few paces away. "Come on."

I guide her to the door, opening it to find that it's just an empty closet. I hesitate for a moment. But Annika breaks out of my hold, going straight inside and huddling in a corner.

Leaving the door open a sliver, I get down on the floor beside her and try to offer some kind of comfort. She sits down and puts her head between her knees, leaning against my body.

"It's okay," I say, looking down at the top of her golden head. "Everything is okay."

She wheezes, pulling oxygen into her lungs. She's trembling, clenching and unclenching her fists. And I am just sitting here beside her, completely out of my depth.

"Should I do something? Should I get someone to help?" I ask.

Annika just shakes her head. She reaches out a hand to me. After a moment of staring at it, I take her hand and grip it in both of mine.

I feel like a fucking idiot. Putting my arm around her shoulders, I wait for a few minutes. Her breathing relaxes a little. Her trembling subsides. She finally sits up, leaning her head back against the wall.

"Fuck," she says. "For a good ten minutes, I really felt like I was going to die."

I frown. "You should go to a doctor, Annika."

She chuckles humorlessly and glances at me out of the corner of her eye. "Believe me, I did. It was just a panic attack. I've had them for years."

She tugs at her hand, which I have forgotten that I'm still holding onto. I let go, my neck heating.

"I see," is all I can manage.

Annika gives her head a little shake. "I think that I'll call it a day. Surely the royal press office can't say anything if I'm sick. Help me up?"

Narrowing my eyes, I climb to my feet. I offer her a hand, which she takes. As I hoist her up, she squeezes my hand. She pins me with her powder blue gaze and cocks her head.

"Thanks," she says softly. There is a moment, just a few beats of my heart, where something shimmers in the air between us.

A sensation of emotional openness.

Then she drops my hand, whirls toward the closet door, and bolts away. I'm left to follow her, my heart squeezing in my chest, a million questions crowding into my brain.

ERIK

OUR CHAUFFEUR PULLS the limousine around the entrance of Amalienborg castle. I take a moment to look at the majesty of the place. Made of light-colored brick, the four massive tan brick buildings all huddle in a circle, all saluting a rather large statue of a man on a horse. With their white-trimmed windows, dark roofs, and guards dressed in scarlet, the palaces definitely proudly exude *money*. It's truly a sight to behold.

I glance over at Annika. Her expensive black designer heels are on the seat between us. She has hiked up her floor length blue velvet dress to mid-thigh. The delicate silver tiara that adorned her upswept hair is tossed carelessly next to the shoes, and she's run her fingers through her wavy mane. She is slumped against her door, scrolling through her phone with a glazed expression.

For a second, my lips curl. She reminds me of nothing more than a big cat right now. Resting, yes, but still monitoring what is going on with a jaundiced eye.

The second the limo pulls to a stop, she is in motion. She flings the door open and vaults herself out of the cool leather seats. She doesn't wait for anyone to open the doors for her… and she completely ignores the tiara and shoes that she's discarded.

I frown and scoop them up, following her out of the car. Annika is already disappearing inside the palace, the tail of her long blue dress carelessly crumpled in one hand.

I follow her inside and up the grand staircase with a sigh. "Annika!"

She doesn't even pause. She's been acting oddly all night, as if she isn't wasn't aware of my presence. We went from a school opening in the morning to an afternoon at a water polo match and ended the evening at some charity gala or another.

And the whole time, I never once saw her smile in my direction or even acknowledge my existence. So, when I enter her private living area, I am not really in any mood for her drama and hysterics.

"Annika!" I call again, trying to project my voice into the open doorway across the room. She has disappeared into her bedroom but left the door ajar. "You forgot your fucking tiara and your goddamn shoes!"

Her golden head appears in the doorway, her guileless eyes piercing me through and through. "Could you help me with the zipper to this dress? It's stuck."

Squinting at her, I nod. "Yes, your highness. Whatever my mistress desires."

Arching a brow, Annika steps back through the doorway, a smirk on her lips. "You're very salty tonight, Erik. My grandmother would hate that you're talking to me in such an insubordinate manner."

My eyes travel down the length of her body. Midnight blue velvet clings to all the right places. Her tits look amazing. The curve of her hips is alluring. And her tight little ass in that dress?

It looks more expensive than all the money and jewels in this house, combined.

Annika walks over to me, turning around. She holds her long platinum hair up and flashes me the back of her neck and her sleek upper back.

My heart starts to pound. How Annika always does that to me, I have no idea. All I know is that being so close to her, reaching out to touch her... it's definitely filling my head with perverted thoughts.

I move closer, seeking the hidden zipper that runs along the column of her spine. As my fingers brush the back of her dress, all I can think about is the feel of her lips pressed against mine and the little sounds she made when I kissed her.

Swallowing, I manage to unzip her dress, baring her sun kissed bare skin to my eyes. I blink, forcing myself to step back. "I'm done," I say, averting my eyes.

I feel like such a fucking predator right now, preying on someone so much younger and more inexperienced than I am. Yet Annika turns around, a mischievous glint in her eye.

"Thanks. Pour me a drink, will you? I have to change out of this dress." She points to the bar cart near the floor to ceiling window.

I narrow my eyes at her as she vanishes through the doorway leading to her bedroom once more. "Annika..." I husk out, shaking my head.

She has no answer for that, it seems. I turn toward the door but can't seem to make myself walk out of this room.

What is it with this girl? Why do I feel so much... lighter when I'm around her?

Heaving a sigh, I walk over to the bar cart. There are only those funny-looking prohibition-era coupe glasses on top. It pairs well with the little fridge filled with several bottles of expensive champagne.

Shaking my head, I pop one of the bottles of champagne and fill two glasses with the aromatic bubbles.

When I find a seat on the gray tweed couch, sipping the champagne, Annika reappears. I almost do a spit take at the slinky little white silk robe she's wearing.

"Ah, thanks," she says, tossing her hair and taking the coupe glass from my hand. She sits down beside me.

I swallow and stare. Just six inches of couch sit between me and her silky-looking, bare knees and thighs. She sips at her champagne.

"That hits the spot."

I drag my eyes back to my glass and make a noncommittal noise. "Mm."

She leans back on the couch and scrunches up her face. "That charity event was boring with a capital b."

I swirl the contents of my glass and glance at her. "I wasn't even sure what it was to raise money for, actually. But it seemed to be in poor taste to ask."

She throws back her head and laughs. The sound is low and throaty. "Hah! It was for school lunches or something."

"Yeah. I mean... there were ladies that stood in front of the whole audience and talked. But I'll be damned if I can remember what they talked about. My mind definitely wandered."

Annika tilts her head to the side, sizing me up. "What did you think about? You're always so mysterious. Just a huge, brooding question mark to me at all times."

My neck heats. I definitely spent no less than thirty percent of that time wondering what exactly Annika had on beneath her slinky dress. And fantasizing about what I would do with her if she were anyone else in the world...

I clear my throat. "I was plotting my next move on the stock market."

Her eyes widen; her expression turns questioning. "What do you mean?"

I give her an odd look, a teasing smile on my lips. "Do you need me to speak more slowly? How can I be clearer about what I just said?"

She bats my shoulder. "I meant... like... are you trading stocks or something?"

I roll my eyes a little. "Yes, princess."

A little line of worry forms in her brow. "Are you any good at it? Like... do you make money doing it?"

I shrug. "I do all right."

She nods slowly. "I had no idea."

"No one does." I chuckle, sipping my drink. The bubbles burst on my tongue, almost too sweet to even drink. I roll the wine around my mouth.

"This is really terrible champagne." I set my glass on the floor.

Annika glance at her coupe, shrugging. "I don't know. It's whatever the sommelier buys for the palace."

"So, it's fancy and terrible. Good to know." I sigh, sitting back against the rough tweed of the couch. "Buying that wine was a decision... but that isn't the worst advice I've ever received. Actually, it's not even the worst thing that has been pitched to me today."

Annika's lips turn upwards. "No?"

"Nope. This morning, a professor cornered me at the event and told me all about how solar cells are really going to power everything in two years' time."

She wrinkles her nose. "If it makes you feel any better, some woman at the gala caught me in the line for the bathroom. She told me about how she feels for me every time she sees me in the newspapers. And then she started talking about some kind of radical self-love movement…" She shudders. "She was one of those ladies that doesn't wear a bra but needs to."

I roll my eyes. "Did she have a pamphlet? I hate when they have pamphlets to show me."

She flashes me a dimple. "No. She did tell me to look up radical self-love on Instagram, though."

I laugh. "You'll have to report back when you've learned what that is. Unless it's just… you know, masturbating a lot."

She crows with laughter, batting me on the arm again. "Shut up. You think it could be?"

I lean closer to her, lured by her laugh. "I think the probability is high."

She grins, wrinkling her nose. "Ah, I needed to laugh. This… this is nice."

"What?"

It's only then that I realize how close we are sitting. I kept moving closer, charmed by her smile. But I see now that we are probably too close.

Okay, definitely too close.

I clear my throat, moving back a few inches. "Sorry. I forgot that."

I trail off, not really wanting to finish that sentence.

That we need way more space between us?

That I'm just here to babysit you?

That if there weren't a title on the line I wouldn't even be here right now?

She scrunches up her face. "Don't be so weird. You were just starting to be a normal person, Erik."

I shoot her a glare. "And what was I before, Annika?"

She puts a hand on my arm. I freeze.

Her casual touch shouldn't feel like a burning brand… but it does. It's the simplest thing and yet… I would do almost anything to find out what it feels like when she grips me, pulls me closer.

My eyes widen at the thought and I dart my gaze over to the window, feeling guilty.

She's not for you.

She's a literal princess.

And she's your best friend's little sister.

I bite my lip.

She just smiles and crinkles her face. "Call me Nika. Okay? We can be friends while you keep an eye on me. But only if you stop calling me Annika. You sound so matronly when you say my name like that."

I stand up, shaking off her touch. Awkward is my middle name right now. "Sure. Whatever you want."

She arches a brow. "Are you going to be okay, Erik?"

My neck heats. "Yeah. I just realized that I'm late. For… a date."

That's a lie. I'm not late for anything but lying in my bed alone, touching myself and fantasizing about the beautiful girl right before me.

Her eyes narrow on my face. "Oh. Well… don't let me keep you."

Committing fully to my escape plan, I start stalking toward the hallway. "Goodnight, Annika."

As I get to the doorway, she calls after me. "It's Nika!"

I give her a backwards wave and flee the room, feeling like a complete ass.

Chapter Twelve

ANNIKA

WHAT DO *the terms radical self-love and self-acceptance even mean, anyway?*

I furrow my gaze, rocking back on the flimsy plastic chair I'm sitting in. I scroll down the screen of my phone, trying to figure that exact question out for myself. The ballroom I'm sitting in is dank and musty with disuse, the overhead lights flipped off and the floor to ceiling green velvet curtains pulled shut.

Faintly I hear laughter coming from the other ballroom of this hotel. Someone has obviously said something funny at the gala. But I couldn't suffer through another minute of smiling and laughing politely so I snuck in here to do a little reading.

Plucking at my white chenille dress, I screw up my face.

Radical self-acceptance is a philosophy that means that you are enough. More than that, you are doing fine…

A door creaks open, the lights overhead flicker on. Erik is illuminated, looking mouthwatering as ever in his dark blue suit and black tie. He cuts quite a figure, tall and light-haired and muscular.

He crosses his arms, pushing out his cheek with his tongue. When he speaks, he doesn't sound happy. "Why are you hiding in here?"

Sighing, I turn off the screen to my phone. "If I have to hear one more old rich man tell one more story about the good old days before the immigrant problem, I'm going to snap. I'm not here to make rich guys feel like they are winning the war against progressivism or whatever."

Erik cocks his head. "We can't leave. We just got here. And we were two hours late for this event because you had a hair emergency."

I stand up, brushing at my skirts. Strolling toward him casually, I come to a halt less than a foot away from where he stands. "If I have learned anything from my grandmother, it is that a princess's beauty is far more important than whether she is always precisely on time."

He gives me a dubious look. "I doubt that very much, An—," He catches himself. "Nika."

I smile at him slyly. "If you really believe that, you don't know Momse at all."

He scowls. "Let's go. All you a required to do is smile and nod for the next…" He extends his arm, checking his watch. "Thirty minutes."

A light bulb goes off in my head. My smile widens. "Orrr… we could be bad and sneak off to do something fun. No one will probably even notice that we're gone. It's not as if either of us is as important as Stellan, right?"

His eyes narrow on my face. "We're still required to do our jobs, Nika."

Biting my lower lip, I scrunch my face up. And then I grab his hand, giving it a tug. "Please? Come on, you know that you're dying of boredom out there. Have a little fun for once in your life, Erik."

For a moment, I can almost feel his critical gaze as he locks me up and down. I expect him to say no. I expect him to give me a stern talking-to about how we're here to represent the royal family.

But to my surprise and delight, he glances behind him and then shrugs. "Where do you want to go, princess?"

My eyes widen. I beam at him, pulling on his hand. "I actually have a place in mind. Come on."

Erik gives me a funny look and pulls his hand from my grip, looking like he might already regret saying yes. But when I run across the ballroom, kicking up little dusty whirlwinds in my wake, he trudges after me. I open a door that lets out into a quiet, brightly lit corridor. Hiking up my white skirts feels natural. Sneaking down the corridor and down a back staircase is less so, but still fun as hell. When I finally push my way out into a breezy Copenhagen evening, I grin back at Erik. The block we're on has giant buildings everywhere I can see. There are a ton of lit up signs and a lot of foot traffic.

I make a sweeping gesture. "What did I tell you? Freedom."

Erik rolls his eyes a little bit, but his lips tug upward too. I count that a victory. "Lead the way," he says, stuffing his hands into his pants pockets.

I shake my head at that and lead him down the block, trying to blend in. People passing by do double takes when I scurry past them. I'm more than used to it by now.

Looking at the signs on the tall buildings, I spot exactly what I want.

A faded light up sign, white with yellow lettering that says, "The King's Ransom Games".

"Here we are," I say, pushing inside the steel double doors. As soon I step in, I'm transported to somewhere else entirely.

The room is dark and warm, the lights and noises from the old school arcade machines instantly comforting. At the far end of the single room shop, a bored looking teenage boy scrolls through his cell phone.

"Oh my god," Erik says, suddenly beside me. I notice Erik's height because he's only an inch or two shorter than the ceiling. I hadn't actually thought about it, but I guess the ceilings are pretty low in here.

Erik grins. "I… I thought you were going to take me to another bar or something. This is…" He looks around with wide eyes. "This is awesome!"

He heads into the lion's den with no fear at all. I follow him, grinning at his reaction. There are machines with joysticks and names like Ultimate Fighter Four. There are a few racer games, a Ms. Packman game, and an air hockey table. The arcade has a few customers who don't pay us the least bit of attention.

That's one of the reasons my father would bring us all here when we were little kids.

I bite my lip, wiggling my eyebrows. "This is my top-secret place. No one ever hassles me here. Everyone is absorbed in their games. I can just… kick back and play some Skee-Ball." I lean in and whisper the last bit. "If I had a choice in the matter, I would never leave this place."

Erik nods, looking me up and down. "That makes sense. This arcade is a weird place that I would never expect to find you in."

He is already pulling out his wallet and approaching the prize counter. He waves at the oblivious teenage boy. "How do we play?"

Without even looking up from his screen, the gawky teen points to a row of vending machines. "Right there."

Erik smirks a little at me, making change. He ends up with a big handful of silver tokens. He glances at me.

"I don't actually know how games are priced," he says, looking around the crowded room. "What should we try first?"

I glance at the Dance Dance Revolution game where two players are challenged to see who dances better to Japanese music. "Maybe that?"

Erik pulls a face. "Something easier."

I crinkle my nose and look around. My gaze lands on two decrepit Skee-Ball machines. The object of the game is to roll a heavy wooden ball up a sloping incline, managing to sink the ball in one of the holes cut in a slanted wall.

I wiggle my eyebrows at him, heading over to the game. "I used to be so good at this game. I bet I can kick your ass."

He follows me over, slapping down a few tokens on my machine. "I'm willing to take that bet, princess."

I grin. "You should probably take your tie off because this competition is about to get serious."

He takes his tie off, stuffs it in his jacket pocket, then unbuttons the very top button of his shirt. I kick my impractical heels off even though the floor is cheap, old, sticky carpet.

"It's on," I say, grinning. A game behind me beeps triumphantly, a sign that someone has won.

But I hardly notice the sticky floor or the noises going on around me… because Erik laughs, looking like an overgrown kid.

He puts two of his tokens in the machine and balls roll down a slot, making a noise that I've never heard anywhere else.

Shaking my head, I do the same. Then I face the inclined ramp and pick up a ball. The *thunk* of the wooden ball when I wind up and release it underhanded is so satisfying.

So is the way that the ball climbs the ramp effortlessly, dropping into the nearest hole.

"Yes!" I cheer.

Erik rolls his eyes. "Calm down, that was a twenty-point shot. Watch this."

Thunk. I watch his ball sail up the ramp and up the wall, coming close to the upper left hole. That one is worth a hundred points… but it doesn't matter, because the ball rolls down into the gutter.

"Hah!" I say, pointing at Erik's machine. "Take that."

"Whatever," he says, rolling and stretching his neck. "That was only the first one. Let's see you land one of the top holes, Nika."

I wiggle my eyebrows, grabbing another ball and rolling it up the incline. We both do it over and over again, twelve times total, until we are out of balls. The machines start beeping and trilling, pushing out some tickets.

I end up winning by twenty five points, which I rub in Erik's face. "I told you I was the master of Skee-Ball, didn't I?"

He takes off his jacket. "Let's go again. I'm sure that the jacket was just holding me back."

I throw my head back, laughing so hard I'm honestly afraid for the seams of this expressive dress. "You must be dreaming!"

A throat clears behind me. I whirl, expecting an adult. But I find a red-cheeked little boy, probably about ten years old. He clutches a pen and a piece of paper.

"Princess Annika?" he says, blushing. "Would you mind if I got your autograph, please?"

I beam at him. "Of course not. What is your name?"

"Paul," he says, turning an even brighter red. I take the pen and piece of paper, chatting with him for a second and then signing it.

And then I end by offering him a hug. He agrees and hugs me surprisingly hard around the middle, for so long that Erik clears his throat and steps toward us.

Paul squeals and takes his autograph with him as he flees back into the wall of beeping and ringing machines. Erik's lips twitch.

"You just earned yourself a fan for life." He screws up his face. "He's too young to be creepy, right?"

I laugh. "I think so."

He leads me back toward the Skee-Ball machines. "That was the first time I've ever seen you being the princess of Denmark. I mean, I'm sure you do it plenty. But that was the first time I've ever been around when it happened." He puts two tokens in his machine, making the balls roll down. "You were very natural with him."

I put my tokens in, eyeing the machine before me. "I should be. I've had nineteen years worth of practice."

He chuckles. "I just meant that you were good with kids. That surprises me for some reason."

I pick up a ball, rolling it up the incline. "I don't know why. I love children. I plan to have at least four when I get older."

The ball sinks into the gutter, causing me to pout. "Damn it."

He's looking at me. I can feel his eyes on my figure. I frown, trying to concentrate.

"What?" I ask.

Erik shrugs a shoulder. "Nothing. It's just… I didn't realize you were so…" He pauses. "Complicated, I guess."

I roll another ball, which also goes straight into the gutter. "Damn it!"

I whirl to him, frowning. "Everyone is much more complicated than they seem, Erik. Even the most seemingly boring person has multiple facets to their personality."

He reaches out and grabs my arm, giving me a squeeze. "Okay, okay. I'll make a mental note."

For a second, the breath leaves my lungs. Our gazes connect. The warmth of his fingers against my skin makes me shiver.

I swear, I see some forbidden emotion lurking there in his eyes.

Desire, maybe. Or is it just lust?

I lick my lower lip, my mouth opening.

And then he gives himself a shake, dropping my arm and stepping back. When he smiles at me again, it seems faded and plasticine.

"Throw another ball," he says, jerking his head toward my machine. "See if you can beat me again."

Then he looks down at his own machine, concentrating on his first ball. When he rolls the ball again, he hits the top right hole. The Skee-Ball machine goes nuts, ringing and announcing that he is a winner.

He grins and pulls a long strand of tickets from the machine. "Come on. Help me choose what prize to take home."

"Here." I giggle, handing him all the tickets from my machine. As he leads me over to the prize counter, I scrunch my face up. There is a whole wall of prizes, everything from stuffed animals and remote-controlled helicopters to smaller prizes in bins behind a glass counter.

Cellophane wrapped candies. Tiny, brightly colored cars. Shiny silver stars. Fake mustaches in different colors. Bouncy balls that look like little planets.

Erik looks at the tickets in his hand thoughtfully. "I don't think we have enough tickets for any of the stuffed animals. It looks like we are stuck picking a couple of these trinkets."

Looking at the goods behind the counter, I grin. "Well, you need that one."

I point to a pair of Groucho Marx-style glasses that have a fake nose and moustache attached. Erik rolls his eyes, handing his tickets to the disinterested teenaged boy. The guy doesn't even count them. He just grabs the glasses and hands them over silently.

"Hmm," Erik says, bending down to see a second shelf of plastic jewelry. "Oh! Can I get that one too?"

The boy looks bored as he fishes the piece of plastic out.

"No, no. The ring. It's for her," Erik corrects.

The attendant pulls it from the case and slaps it on top of the counter. It's gaudy, looking like a solid pink piece of bubblegum made into a ring with a multifaceted surface.

"Oh yes," Erik says, picking it up. "That's the one."

I laugh as he slides the ring on my finger, just like a wedding ring. "Oh darling, it is so thoughtful. You must have put so much thought into picking this out."

"Hold on." He picks up the glasses, fitting the fake nose and frames on his face. "There! Now we are perfect for each other in every conceivable way." He sticks out his elbow. "Come on, Ms. Potato Head. Let's go back to the Barbie Dream Mansion and race our Hot Wheels against each other."

I can't hold back a grin. "You know, you kind of look like Ken."

He shakes his head, leading me to the exit. And I look up at him adoringly, wishing that we could always be the people we were tonight.

Chapter Thirteen

ERIK

ANNIKA CROSSES her arms as we walk up to St. Mark's preparatory school. It's the sister school to the boarding school all of the younger Løve siblings were sent to and it is right in the middle of downtown Copenhagen.

Annika raises her head and schools her expression. I glance at her stylish wide legged black trousers and white top with an oversized pale blue flower on the shoulder. With her hair pulled back into a crisp bun and her understated makeup, she looks every bit the princess she is supposed to be.

But that in itself makes me worried. It's like Nika is making herself smaller somehow, less noticeable. I should be glad…

But all I feel in the pit of my stomach is acid.

She's been quiet this morning on the way here. Too quiet, in my opinion.

Just before we climb the steps to enter, I cast my gaze over Nika. "What's going on with you?"

She glances at me, arching a brow. "What do you mean?"

I glance around, then grab her elbow and pull her aside. "We're here to promote your boarding school to prospective new students. I assume that you agreed to this… so why are you so…" I squint at her face. "Subdued?"

She lifts her chin an inch, her cool blue eyes expressionless. "I am only trying to be who they expect me to be today. That's all."

She fingers the pearls strung around her neck, her gaze flitting to the ornate door that leads inside.

I grip her elbow harder, drawing her gaze back to my face. "Do you want to leave?"

She arches a brow. "No. My grandmother expects me to show up here and wow the applicants with my presence. So, I'm here. Let the wowing commence."

I stare down at her for a few more seconds. The heavy doors behind us open, a priest sticking his head out. "Ah! You're here! Come in…"

Annika gives me a strange look, twisting her lips and rolling her eyes. But then she pushes past me, heading toward the black-frocked priest.

"It's lovely to be here," she murmurs.

The priest absolutely beams, offering her his elbow. "It is so nice to meet you, princess Annika. I'm Father Jean. Come, meet some of the parents and potential future St. Xavier's students…"

I follow them through the set of doors, into a long hallway that is lined with beige lockers that match the tan floors. The air here smells slightly astringent, like someone has only just wiped down everything in the hallway.

I look around, wondering where everyone is. It is, after all, a school day.

Father Jean steers Nika through a set of wooden double doors to the left. I am right behind them, my eyes opening as I step into the huge room.

WELCOME FUTURE ST. XAVIER'S STUDENTS AND PARENTS is hung on bunting at one end of the room. In between, there are a number of priests speaking with several dozen pleased-looking parents and their bored or nervous looking children. A table is set up by the window offering coffee, tea, croissants, and fruit.

They all turn to look at Nika when we walk in, bursting into a light smattering of applause. I notice that Nika's free hand makes a fist, clench-ing. But when I move around to her side, she is smiling pleasantly.

There is obviously some cognitive dissonance going on here.

Father Jean raises his voice. "Everyone, if you would gather around. Princess Annika is here today to talk to you all about how important her education at St. Xavier's was. Annika, if you would just say a few words? Why did you decide to go all the way to a Swiss boarding school?"

Her fist clenches again. "Thank you, everyone. If you don't mind, I have written down some of my thoughts…"

I step forward, handing her a piece of paper straight from the royal press office. She clears her throat and begins to read it aloud.

"My time at St. Xavier's was the most fulfilling experience…" she reads.

I move to the other side of the room, trying to figure out just what is going on with her. She smiles on cue. She laughs at the father's jokes. She answers a few questions from the audience.

She even signs some autographs.

But her vibrancy, her almost catty sense of humor… it's just missing. It's almost like she's been sedated or something.

I frown, keeping a close eye on her. And as soon as the questions have been wrapped up and the autographs signed, I get her the fuck out of there.

I tuck her into the backseat of the limousine myself, feeling strangely protective. When the limo pulls out, I look at her.

"What is going on?" I demand to know.

Nika looks at me with a little yawn. "Nothing. My psychiatrist gave me something to calm my nerves in situations like this. I think it worked well, don't you?"

"What situation? Will you please just tell me why the hell you hated St. Xavier's so much? Because it's obvious to me that you did."

She closes her eyes, leaning back into the cream-colored leather of her seat. "I did hate it. You are right about that much. But my grandmother made it clear to me that I shouldn't talk about my feelings. It's bad for the royal brand."

A strange feeling blooms in my chest. "Did… did somebody at the school hurt you?"

She opens her eyes and chuckles. "No. Nothing like that, Erik."

I sigh, letting out a breath I didn't know I held. "What's your issue, then?"

She rolls her eyes over to me, then turns her body toward me, shifting her knees up onto the seat. "Being Princess Annika is great. Except for rare instances… like being trapped at a Swiss boarding school with seventy other twelve-year-old girls. Almost everyone had pedigrees, lineage, and all of them had already decided before they even met me what I was like. They read the tabloids and they decided that I was cold and aloof. So, they treated me like an outsider." She crinkles her upturned nose. "Except Kal, of course. If there is a god, I seriously have to thank him for assigning us to live together. She was my refuge."

I tilt my head. "But everyone else… didn't warm up to you?"

A bubble of laughter escapes Nika's lips. "That would be putting it mildly. The whole time I was there was wretched. My locker and gym clothes were trashed once a week. I would find huge blown up pictures of myself eating pasted all over the school, with and without pig ears and a pig snout. I've lost count of how many times I was intentionally locked out of my dorm building or came back to my room find that all of my clothes were gone."

I give my head a soft shake. "So, you are saying… your classmates bullied you? You're the princess of Denmark, Nika. You should've been able to snap your fingers and put them all in their place."

She sighs, looking away from me. "The girls at St. Xavier's were cruel. And no amount of adult attention or intervention did anything to put a stop to it. I figured out quickly that when I went crying to the house mother or even the dean, that just told everyone that their tactics worked."

Her hands close into fists. I look at her, at how angry she still is. And that anger echoes around inside of me, finding the darkness in my heart.

I know what being told that you're not good enough is. I have been told that practically my whole life, although it was more subtle than what Nika is describing.

I want very badly to touch her. Embrace her, tell her I'm sorry. Tell her that it's over.

But I don't know that I can do that and still maintain the distance between us.

"I'm sorry," I grit out. "That shouldn't have happened to you. And you shouldn't have to sell the school after the experience you had."

She gives me a humorless smile. "I couldn't get out of there fast enough. But I did get out. And now I'm just trying to look forward."

Her eyes sink closed. It's just as well, because I'm not sure what to say.

Annika being bullied for simply existing? That doesn't sit right with me. It makes me wish that I could draw her close and protect her.

That's not my job, of course. But it has to be someone's duty to look out for her… doesn't it?

I look at Annika as she falls asleep. Her wavy hair is coiled like a mass of snakes. Her long, dark lashes rest on her cheeks, her skin looking as smooth and clear as skimmed cream. Her button nose is sprinkled with a few freckles. Her lush lips are just below, begging to be touched.

Not by me. I know that. We are from two different worlds, just by virtue of being born. But someone will come along someday...

Someone worthy of her.

Someone that's not me.

I try not to think about the vague unsettled feeling that stirs within me at that notion.

Annika's head falls down, gravity doing what it does best. And I can't help but catch her as she slides toward me, cradling her like I've just been handed a delicate bird.

Nika's eyes open for the merest second, their innocence pinning me in place. Then she stretches out in my lap, closing her eyes once more. She murmurs something.

It might be, "I hoped it was you."

I go stiff and frozen, feeling very much like the new owner of a kitten who has fallen asleep in their owner's hands. I shouldn't be touching her like this, nor should she be touching me. And yet... I can't wake her up.

Not just yet.

Even though her body is warm and pliant, pressed against mine. And it's giving me ideas.

Very, very bad ideas. Flashbacks to the afternoon that she sassed me, and I lashed out at her. I kissed her and touched her hot, wet pussy...

For that moment, she belonged to me. She was mine to do with as I wanted.

She murmurs again, snuggling against my lap. I have an erection the size of the Eiffel fucking tower that she presses against, causing me pleasure and pain all at once.

That can't be comfortable to lean against. But she doesn't seem to notice or mind. I lean my head back, blowing out a breath and blanking my mind.

Still, it's a long ride back to the palace... and Nika being curled up on top of my cock doesn't make it any shorter.

Chapter Fourteen

ANNIKA

FRIDAY MORNING, I am stuck inside while outside, the weather is glorious. I am listening to a much older man with a purple striped bowtie tell me that there are important things that his generation can pass to mine.

"You see, it's just a matter of you young people paying attention." He tuts, winding up for what seems like a long diatribe. "If you would put down your phones and your internet for just a few minutes, you would really be able to learn."

I smile, not quite understanding how I became this man's unwilling prey.

More than anything, I wish I had brought the entire bag of hard candies with me. I feel no shame in front of this old man, who is lecturing me rather than trying to engage me in conversation. My attention wanders to the other people that are milling around at this charity luncheon. I am the youngest person that's here by a mile, although Erik is a close second. My gaze trips over him.

Tall, fair haired, and handsome as all get out. I can just make out the shape of his muscles beneath his tightly fitted sleeves. That light gray tweed suit he's wearing ought to be outlawed. It's unfair to me, especially when his green-brown gaze wanders over my way.

His eyes lock on me. I feel my cheeks growing warm. He cocks a brow, as if to ask if I need to be rescued.

God yes. I nod subtly, then refocus my attention on the man in front of me. "You know, when I was a young man, we had principles!" he wheezes.

Erik cuts in, taking my elbow. "I'm sorry. May I borrow the princess for just a moment?"

The older man's face darkens. "Bring her back when you've finished, young man. I could tell you both a thing or two about common decency— "

Erik just pulls me away from the older man, tucking me beneath his arm and escorting me out of yet another bland gymnasium. My heart beats a little faster at Erik's touch.

As soon as we escape into the hallway, I look around. Spotting an exit door, I take his hand and tug him toward it.

"Nika," he warns. "We have only been at this engagement for half an hour…"

But there is a distinct lack of concern in his voice. I look up at him, wrinkling my nose. "You know you want to come outside with me. Just do it for once, rather than putting up a front."

His gaze tightens on my face and his lips turn down a fraction, but he just shrugs. "Whatever you say, princess."

Grinning wickedly, I push out of the doors. I exit into sunshine and immediately start beaming. I raise my hands up high toward the sun, not caring that the hem of my short white silk dress might show off more than I had planned.

"Yesss," I say. "This is already so much better than inside the gymnasium, don't you think?"

His gaze is heavy on me as he smirks. "I can't disagree with you there."

I grin over my shoulder at him, wiggling my eyebrows. "Where should we go?"

His lips quirk. As he scans the fields just outside the doors, he tilts his head. "There is a playground over there, way to the left." He points it out. "It probably has benches. Or we can just walk…"

My eyes widen. "Umm, or we can swing." I grin at him, unrepentant. "That's my vote."

He rolls his eyes, but he can't stifle the smallest smile that appears ever so briefly on his lips. "Okay. Lead the way."

I take a moment, leaning against Erik's muscular form, to take off my six inch heels. Standing next to him barefoot is a little funny; without my heels, I'm basically tiny compared to him.

Holding my stilettos in one hand, I skip along toward the little park that Erik pointed out. It turns out to be pretty nice. There are several big, shady trees. Underneath those is an oversized swing set, a seesaw, and a large dark wooden jungle gym complete with a bright blue plastic slide. All of it is enclosed in a giant sandbox, well-tended yet vacant.

I jog over to the swings, dropping my shoes behind me in the sand. I perch on one of the swings, giving Erik a huge grin. He hangs back, watching me.

It's a little frustrating sometimes, seeing Erik not just dive into things. He's so careful about everything. Then again, I could learn a little restraint, I guess.

"Come on!" I urge him. "At least come over here and push me."

His eyes tighten on mine. For a second, I think that he's going to say no. But eventually he shrugs and comes into the swings area.

I smile as he awkwardly makes his way around me. "Hey." I stop him. "Here."

I stand up, reaching to ease the knot of his tie. He goes still and expressionless under my hands. But his eyes study me intently, the green brown standing out to me just now.

I smile up at him. "What are you thinking?"

He shakes his head. "Nothing."

I unknot his tie, slipping it off. I scoff. "Seriously? I'm willing to bet that isn't true."

He tilts his head. "Maybe it's just private. Ever think of that?"

My expression turns teasing. My fingers undo the top button of his shirt. "I definitely have thought about that. It only makes me more curious. What does Erik Moen think about that is private? Hm?"

He stills my fingers by grabbing my hand. "Most of my thoughts are private, Nika."

My lips quirk. "Even from me?"

He releases me, letting out a bark of laughter. "Especially from you."

I shoot him a pouty face. He just rolls his eyes and walks around the swings. "Sit down."

I seat myself against the black rubber of the swing, gripping the silver chains that rise all the way up to meet the top of the swings. Erik grips the chains too, just a little below where my hands are. He pulls me back gently and lets go of the chains.

I glide forward gently.

I send Erik a look over my shoulder. "You're terrible at this. Push me harder!"

He smirks at me. "That's your response to everything."

I laugh, leaning my head back. He does push me harder though, making me glide a little higher each time his warm hands touch my back.

I beam at him. "Admit it. This is way better than talking to people about serious issues back there at the school."

"I will never concede to it," he says, feigning seriousness. "You know that's my motto. Never admit to anything so that no one can be mad at me."

I put down a foot, slowing my swing by dragging it along the ground. "And how would you say that's going, Erik?"

He flashes a smile. "Perfectly okay. Absolutely bland."

I stop the swing, leaning back to look at him. "Want to sit on the jungle gym for a little while?"

He offers me a small smile. "Your wish is my command, princess."

Rolling my eyes, I stand up and bite my lip. "Race you there."

I take off at a sprint, not waiting for him to catch up. I head for the solid wood structure only thirty yards away.

"No fair!" he cries.

As it turns out, I don't need to wait for him. He's so tall and has such long legs that he has no problem catching up to me.

I give him a glinting look as I climb up to the top of the jungle gym. The floor beneath me is made of sturdy slabs of wood and there is a view of the school from here that is actually quite charming.

Erik climbs right up beside me. I sprawl out on the slab, patting an invisible seat. He sits down more carefully than I did; he's all knees and elbows for a second before he settles down beside me.

He heaves a sigh. I arch a brow.

"What?" I ask.

He shrugs. "I don't know. Don't you ever get tired of being a princess on parade? I'm sick of it and it's only been a few weeks."

My lips lift at the corners. "Of course."

His eyebrows lift. "Really?"

I nod. "Yeah, definitely. I just don't know how else I am expected to behave. If I just went by Momse's set of moral codes, I would just do this cheerfully. Every single day for a couple of years. Then I'd marry some suitable boy, pop out a couple of great-grandchildren, and sort of fade away."

Erik frowns. "That's what you think is expected of you?"

Shrugging a single shoulder, I pull a face. "I know that it is. It's what my dad's sisters did. And the generation before that… and the generation before that…"

"But you don't want that, I'm guessing."

I smile a little ruefully. "No. I mean… do I want kids someday? Yes, absolutely. And I don't want to sacrifice my life for theirs. But I also don't want to be…" I pause, hesitating. "I don't mean to sound selfish. I just don't want to repeat either my mother or my grandmother's mistakes."

His eyes narrow. "What do you mean by that?"

"I just mean I don't want to raise children that are complete strangers to me. But I also have no desire to control every single aspect of my unborn children's lives. I'd like to find a balance, I guess."

"Ah." He nods, looking off. "Yeah. It's hard to even think about being a parent right now. Like… how do you know for sure that you're not completely screwing them up?"

I try to think of the best way to phrase my question. "Is that what you think your father did? Screwed you up?"

He scrunches up his face ever so briefly. "It's hard to say," he says, avoiding the subject neatly. When he looks back at me, he smiles. "It's time for a change of topics."

I look at him, at his golden hair and bewitchingly fiery eyes, at his cheekbones and jawline carved of rock. Raising a hand to his face, I gently trace my fingers along the length of his jaw, up the side of his face to feather along his temple.

He allows my light touches, closing his eyes briefly. God, he is insanely gorgeous just now.

"You're not at all what I imagined," I murmur.

He opens his hazel eyes, smiling a little. God, I would do anything for him to keep looking at me with that expression on his face.

"Is that so?" he asks.

I trace my touch back down to his jaw, trailing it along the skin outside his mouth. Shaking my head, I smile. "No."

He bites his lower lip for just a second. "Nika," he rasps. "What are you doing to me right now?"

I move closer to him, pressing the gentlest of kisses against the very corner of his mouth. He stiffens, going still.

I grab his hand and put it around my waist. "Kiss me, Erik," I beg him softly.

I can feel his fingers flex against my back. "Nika…"

When I close my eyes and lift my mouth to his once more, a hungry little growl escapes his lips. He pulls me closer and sets his too-hot lips against mine. I draw him in, running my hand up into his short hair.

Erik nips my lower lip hard, making me gasp. Then he bends me back, spearing his free hand in my hair. He kisses me again, so deeply and with so much passion that it takes my breath away. I curl my fist in the collar of his suit jacket.

He closes his hand in my hair into a fist and draws my head back, making me gasp more loudly.

He could do anything with me. He holds all the power now and we both know it. His lips traverse down the narrow column of my neck and leave fire in their wake.

But when he kisses his way down between my breasts, that's when I actually lose my breath. He buries his face in my cleavage, then turns his face and places a hot, stinging, hard hickey on my left breast. It hurts… but it also makes me want more.

My eyes widen. My hand tightens in his hair.

Erik breaks away to kiss my lips again, as brutal and as punishing and as real as anything I've ever experienced. I moan and open my mouth to him, making a soft sound as he sweeps the sweetness of his tongue against mine. My hand clutches at his suit, trying to pull him closer. I would bring him inside of me just now if that were physically possible.

I want him. My breasts ache. My pussy drips. I'm as ready as I have ever been.

If only we weren't out here in the open, where anybody at all could see us. I don't have much self-control, but I don't want my first time to be so… exposed.

Or do I? Because the longer he touches me, the quieter the voice of reason is in my head.

When Erik finally pulls away, we are both struggling for breath. He looks deep into my eyes, passion and anger and frustration all playing across his face.

And I understand him perfectly, for once in my life.

He gives his head the tiniest shake. When he speaks, his voice is gone to gravel.

"Annika… we can't," he says. He doesn't move away, but I can feel him begin to withdraw. "We just can't. We shouldn't have ever even touched."

I bite my lower lip, dropping my gaze from his. "I know."

He raises my head with a finger underneath my chin. "It's my fault. Okay? It's… god, it's not fucking you. You're perfect."

And just like that, my eyes fill with tears. I pull out of his grasp, standing up suddenly. "I think we should go back. Don't you think?"

Erik blows out a breath. "Sure, Nika."

I jump down off the jungle gym, running to scoop up my heels from where they lie in the sand. Then I take off at jog, heading back to the school.

Tears prick my eyes, but I refuse to let them fall.

"Annika!" Erik calls.

I wave behind me, not interested in whatever he has to say. After all, he's already said everything I'm meant to hear.

"See you at the school!" I call out, picking up my pace.

And gentleman that he is, Erik lets me go.

Chapter Fifteen

ERIK

STRIDING into Nika's living room, I find her curled up on the couch in high-waisted jeans and a white crop top. When I enter, she looks up, flushing when she sees me. Her eyes are the same fiery color that goes right through me.

This is the third day since I kissed her on the playground. And it's the third day that she's been avoiding me.

But no more.

"Come on," I say. "Grab some riding boots and meet me in the stables in five minutes."

Her brow rises delicately. "Why?"

I cross my arms, favoring her with a serious look. "Because we still have to work together for another two and a half months. So, this thing where we don't talk? It won't work." I give her a sharp stare. "Five minutes. Hurry up."

I turn, leaving her rooms. I just have to hope that she actually follows me. Heading down to the stables is a short enough walk through the bright mid-morning sun.

It's just starting to get hot. I eye the verdant landscape as I trot toward the stables. All I can see is the fresh green pasture lands and the soaring blue sky overhead. There is nothing for several miles here. It's just untamed wilderness owned by the royal family.

I straighten the cuff of my hooded sweatshirt. It feels odd to be dressed down in a black hoodie and dark gray sweatpants. It's as if I'm going to work out, but I don't own any clothes just for this purpose.

Why would I?

I stalk into the stables, smelling the unique mix of clean horses, sweet horse feed, and the tang of horse shit. It smells incredibly nostalgic to me, harkening back to my earliest days.

Spotting a groom, I order two horses to be saddled. I know my father has the day off. I made sure of that before I hatched this plan.

It's unlikely that I'll see him. He's surely already drunk.

But there is still a vague unease in the pit of my stomach. It stays with me as I watch the groom saddle a black gelding for me and a smaller dappled gray mare for Annika.

When Nika actually shows up, looking uncertain about why she is here, that feeling grows even stronger. The groom leads our horses outside, holding them as we mount up.

"You know how to ride, right?" I ask, getting settled in the saddle.

Her gaze narrows on me as she adjusts her seat, petting her mount's neck. "Yes. I'm surprised that you do."

I take my reins from the groom, thanking him. "It's been a while since I've had to ride," I admit. "But I grew up in these stables. My father used to be in charge around here."

She looks down at her horse, nudging her into a slow walk. "I think I knew that. Your father is not here now though, is he?"

I squint against the sunlight. "No. He still works here though. I think he's off today."

I use my heels to urge my horse forward, breaking into a trot. Annika keeps pace with me but doesn't say another word.

I look over at her. She's pulled her hair back into a messy bun and there are two blotches of color on her cheeks. Her bare-faced beauty is especially stunning against the ruggedness of the landscape.

We turn down a wide dusty path that cuts through the greenery. I know that I shouldn't even be thinking about her in this way. But I can't help it.

What I can help is how I act.

I clear my throat, slowing my horse to a walk again. "Do we need to talk about the other day?"

A hint of a smile ghosts over her lips. "What is there to talk about? You've made your level of interest quite clear."

I grit my teeth, adjusting in the saddle. "I told you. It's not personal. I'm… I… find you… pretty." My neck heats. "But there are reasons why we shouldn't… be close."

She tosses her head. "Stellan isn't a good enough reason. He's defying the rules to marry Margot."

"He's my best fucking friend!" I bark.

Nika looks at me, pausing. I'm pinned by her ice blue stare, so intense just now that it's almost electric. Then she returns her gaze back to the path in front of us.

"I appreciate your loyalty to Stellan," she says softly. "But does he even notice? From what I can see, you follow him around and he just expects you to do his bidding."

I glower at the reins clutched in my hands. "I can't help it if you don't like my friendship with Stellan. Like it or not, he is the king. So, what he says goes."

She arches a brow. "And he said that I'm off limits?" She slides me a sour look. "I bet you haven't even tried to discuss it with him."

I shoot her my blackest of looks. Nika is perfectly right in that regard, of course. But that's not entirely the point.

I roll my shoulders back. "Even if Stellan was okay with it, which he is very much not, other people wouldn't smile upon it."

She cocks her head at me. "Why do you care so much what other people think?" she asks, frustrated.

I squint at her. "Why do you?"

She flushes. "I don't."

"You do. You care very much about how everyone perceives you. Don't try to hide it from me."

"Ugh!" she declares. She urges her horse forward all the sudden, quickly shooting out and leaving me to try to catch up.

I spur my horse onward, knowing that I messed up. The plan was to come out of this on better terms than before but now I'm worried about Nika even talking to me.

"Nika!" I call. I nudge my horse more urgently, until I'm riding hard. We thunder down the little path, the dusty road disappearing beneath the horse's hooves.

I close the distance eventually. "Annika!" I try again when I know she can hear me.

She throws a look over her shoulder, slowing down once more. Lifting her chin, she says, "It's always Annika when you're angry with me. But this time, I haven't done anything wrong."

I school my expression. "No. You haven't."

Nika makes a face. "What if we just… did what we wanted to do and kept it hush hush?"

My neck heats. I've thought about this very subject at great length for the last few nights. I look down, toying with the reins.

"That wouldn't be fair. One of us might… develop feelings. Only to have them dashed the very first time that we had to attend a function with a date."

She tilts her head, her eyes narrowing. "You're expecting me to be the one with feelings, then?"

I glance away with a shrug. "I didn't say that."

Her lips twist and she rolls her eyes. "You thought it, though."

I give her a small smile. "Not even once."

She eyes me with a sigh. "So, what do you propose? Hm?"

I lift my shoulders. "It's just a summer. Surely, we can both just… resist. It'll just call for a little willpower."

Nika looks at me very frankly. "I'm a virgin, Erik. No one has ever accused me of not being able to keep my hormones under control. I just… I'm ready to lose it. How will you feel if I give my virginity away to some other guy?"

I grip my reins tightly and try not to scowl. Of course I want to be the one she chooses. If I had my way, we would stop right now and fuck right here, in the middle of the goddamned road.

But that's not the way that Nika needs it to be. She deserves a hell of a lot more than a quick fuck on a dirty path behind the palace. She's worth so much more than I can ever give her.

It's time to lie my ass off.

"It would be better than the alternative," I bluff. "We couldn't keep it quiet forever. Eventually someone would find out. And I don't want there to be any consequences over what is essentially just a very bad crush."

I can see her open her mouth to argue. I hold me hand up to stop her. "Can you not just believe me when I tell that that's what this is?"

Her lips twist again. "I'm just supposed to listen to you, huh?"

I slide her the tiniest of smiles. "I am your elder, after all."

Amusement flickers across her expressive face. "So I hear." She glances up at the sky and screws up her face. "I should turn around and head back. I'm supposed to meet my personal shopper at noon."

I raise a brow. "You are going to be cutting it awfully close, princess."

She flashes me a grin. "She'll wait for me. Or didn't you hear? I am royalty."

With that she pulls the reins she's holding, turning the horse around. Then Nika starts galloping away from me, riding fast for the stables.

I stop my horse and watch her go, acid beginning to wash around in the pit of my stomach.

Chapter Sixteen

ANNIKA

I STOP JUST outside the CRAVE nightclub, brushing back a strand of my immaculately. blown out, gleaming hair. Kalindi comes to a stop just behind me, eyeing my itty bitty shiny black dress.

"One wrong move and you're going to show every single club patron your whole butt," she says. She wrinkles her nose. "I'm not judging you, but I am very concerned about a wardrobe malfunction happening."

I roll me eyes, looking critically at her outfit. "I would say something about that white romper, but honestly? You're rocking it."

She beams at me. "Thanks!"

Behind us, Erik approaches in his same dark suit that he wore all day today. I glance back at him, a frown tugging at my lips.

Things between us have been decidedly frosty for the last two days. He says that I should find someone else to focus my attentions on.

So that's what I'm going to do tonight. Find someone else… anyone else will do.

"Come on," I urge Kal, heading toward the door. "Let's go."

When we approach the door, the bouncer looks at me. I see him dismiss me and then look again. His eyes widen and he hurries to open the door.

"Welcome, princess," he says.

We strut right into the big space. Loud dance music thrums through my blood. It takes my eyes a minute to adjust to the near darkness, punctuated by spotlights flashing high above the club. In those moments of light, I can make out the dance floor. It's packed with nameless and faceless bodies that grind and gyrate to the low, insistent beat.

"Oh," Kal says, her mouth open.

I wiggle my eyebrows at her. "Come on. Let's start with a drink."

Pulling her along by the hand, I head straight for the bar. I know Erik is right behind us, his usual scowl in full effect tonight. But I refuse to glance back at him.

Tonight is about me and what I want. And just now? I can't wait to slam down a couple shots of tequila and hit the dance floor.

Kal leans across the bar and orders us drinks, flirting a little with the hot bartender. I turn and watch the dance floor again, shivering with anticipation.

I can't wait to lose myself in between the rhythmic beats.

Erik ruins my view, stepping into my eye line. The scowl that I imagined is in place on his perfect lips. He narrows his green-brown eyes at me.

"Nika, what are we doing here?"

His voice is rough and gravelly. He looks around the nightclub, as if he's searching for answers.

I shrug. "I'm trying to meet some eligible young men. I have no idea what you are here for."

He narrows his eyes on my face. "Be careful, Annika. You're coming very close to pushing my buttons."

Kal turns around from the bar, two shots in each hand. She arches a brow at Erik and hands me my shots. "Here you go. Bottoms up."

I tap the shot glasses against hers and then throw my head back, swallowing one shot and then the next. It snakes its way down my esophagus, burning as it goes.

"Blech!" Kal says, making a face. "Tequila is terrible." She looks at Erik apologetically. "Sorry, I didn't get you a shot."

Erik just crosses his arms and looks like he would rather be anywhere but here right now. His seeming detachment makes me want to punch him. But instead, I turn to Kal.

"The dance floor is calling to me!" I say, pulling at her arm. "Come dance."

I don't have to ask her twice. She grins and grabs my arm as I head out to the dance floor, sliding between people to get to the center.

Erik doesn't follow us, which is unbelievably fine with me. I throw my hands over my head and shake my ass, gyrating hypnotically to the booming bass. Kal is right beside me, giggling at the men that suddenly appear out of nowhere.

Two classically handsome Scandinavian-looking men start dancing with us. I grin up at the one I'm closest to, but I don't bother to introduce myself. If they somehow don't recognize me, I'm not about to ruin the night by telling them who I am.

I grin and keep dancing, working up a sweat. Kal seems to be hitting it off with her dance partner; he holds her by the waist as she shimmies and shakes. I grin.

This is great. Why don't we do this more often?

I glance up and realize with a note of surprise that there is an upper balcony tucked discreetly above the dance floor of this club. It's so dark that I probably wouldn't ever be able to see it…

Except that Erik is standing there, glaring at me, his expression a sullen pout. When our gazes meet, it stops me dead in my tracks.

I arch a brow, stepping closer to the guy who is dancing right beside me. The stranger puts his hands around my waist and pulls me against his body, which I could have honestly done without. But hey, I'm not a giant control freak, unlike Erik.

I put my hand around the stranger's neck, realizing that he lack's Erik's unusual height. Why that puts me off, I don't know.

Erik shakes his head and turns around, putting his back to the dance floor. I dance for another minute in my partner's grip. But when Erik isn't watching, it just seems less fun.

I turn to see Kalindi laughing as her partner whispers something in her ear. I make a 'I'm going to the bar to get a drink' gesture at her. She's so wrapped up in whatever that guy is saying that she just nods at me.

I head off the dance floor abruptly, leaving the man that I was dancing with behind. My mood is mercurial just now. I'm on the cusp of being pissed off.

Erik's black mood is contagious, it seems. Maybe if I just splash some water on my face, it'll help reset my frame of mind. Heading toward the back of the club, I find the bathrooms in a long black hallway. I push into the first bathroom, wincing at the low light. It's a single person bathroom; I start closing the door.

But someone stops me. My eyes widen.

Erik pushes the door open, glaring at me. He fills the entire doorway, his expression dark as I've ever seen it. "And just where do you think that you're going? Hm?"

I gulp, raising my chin. "What's it to you, Erik? You're just supposed to be my babysitter."

He steps inside the little room, eating up the small space. He takes a moment to close the door behind himself. The quiet snick of the lock engaging sounds loud to me.

Then again, I am used to listening to the thunderous sound my own beating heart makes. Erik rubs a hand over his mouth, looking at me like I'm his to judge. He takes a step, then another, so that he's only a few inches away from me. "What must you think of me?"

I back up until I hit the wall. He just steps forward again, his gaze dropping to my mouth.

I lick my suddenly dry lips. "What do you mean?"

He smirks, flashing me a dimple. "Do you think that I want to be here? Hmm? Do you think that I like standing guard while some other man puts his hands all over you?"

I bite my lower lip, glancing away from him with a shrug. "How should I know?"

He braces his hand against the wall next to my head, moving so close to me that we are a hair's breadth apart. Not touching… but almost.

My heart hammers in my chest. His serious eyes pierce right through me as he licks his perfect lips.

"I fucking hate it, Nika," he grates. "I hate that I'm just supposed to sit back and watch while you dance with another guy." He brings his other hand up, closing me in. And then he leans against me, tormenting me with the press of his body.

I tilt my head at him. "No one is making you do anything, Erik."

He looks down at my skimpy black dress, biting his lip. He traces a fingertip up my arm, touching a few strands of my hair.

"I think we both know that isn't true," he murmurs. He runs those same fingertips across my clavicle and down the line of my cleavage.

I squirm. "Erik—"

He interrupts me. "Are you even wearing anything under this dress?"

I swallow heavily and blush, looking up at him. It takes all the sass I can muster to say, "Wouldn't you like to know."

His lips twitch. He stares down at me for a few seconds, his expression unreadable. He leans down to my lips, placing the lightest kiss to the very corner of my mouth. He's playing with me, tormenting me.

And my response? My whole body aches. My breasts lift and tighten. My clit throbs. My pussy is damp and getting wetter by the second.

My mouth actually waters and I turn my head, trying to catch his lips with my own. But he's not interested in that.

Erik drops to his knees, making my eyes go wide with surprise. He makes eye contact with me as he touches my outer thighs, skimming his hands up the bare skin exposed by my dress. Erik presses a hand against my belly, pushing me back against the wall.

"Stay still," he warns me. "Be a good girl."

His words, spoken in such a deep and gravelly voice, make me suck in a breath. The anticipation builds as he slides his hands up my thighs.

He rucks the dress up around my hips, sucking his lower lip in briefly as he looks me dead in the eyes. I am naked before him, my whole entire pussy aching for his touch.

I've never seen anything so erotic in my damned life as seeing this man on his knees before me, bending his head toward my lower body. He raises one of my knees and exposes my most intimate parts to his view. I keep my pussy shaved completely, so I'm bare before his eyes.

I feel like if he doesn't touch me soon, I'm going to die. He licks his lips, sending a shiver up my spine.

God, he's about to eat my pussy. How long have I dreamed of this moment? I'm torn between closing my eyes and watching his every movement.

I rake my fingernails through his sandy hair, my heartbeat pounding in my ears. Erik places a single, scalding hot kiss to my inner thigh. When he nips the same soft skin, I startle, shifting my body a little.

His hands tighten on my hips. "I thought I already told you to be still." He looks up at me, his eyes promising to do dirty things to me. "I won't tell you again, Nika."

I swallow, nodding. "I'll be good," I manage.

He smirks, then hikes my knee over his shoulder. I squirm when he returns his lips to my inner thigh, kissing and gently biting his way toward my shaved pussy.

Erik splays a big hand out against my mons, gently pulling my pussy lips up and using his fingers to spread me fully. Moisture leaks from my slit. My clit throbs. Every part of me is so sensitive right now. I can feel myself beginning to tremble with need, the delicate muscles of my inner thigh shaking.

He leans in close and feathers a hot, wet kiss against the hood of my clit. I make a strangled noise, trying to tamp down my response.

He murmurs against my flesh. "I like hearing you moan for me, princess. Make all the noise you want."

He places another kiss just outside my pussy lips. I groan, shifting my weight. He just chuckles and puts another kiss below that, but still not close enough to my clit. I need more; more stimulation, more of his tongue on my clit. My hands run through his short flaxen hair, pressing him closer.

He continues trailing kisses around my pussy lips, always just outside where I want his mouth to be. I groan, whining a little.

"Erik," I whisper. "Please?"

His fingers trace the edges of my pussy, intensifying the teasing. "Please what?" he says.

He toys with the entrance to my slit, spreading around the moisture he finds there. Then he feathers a kiss over my clit once more, making my inner muscles clench with need. At the same time, he presses a single thick finger inside my pussy, pulling a hissing sound from my lips.

It feels so goddamned good.

I rock my hips against his finger, moaning when he withdraws. But before I can get too upset, he pushes a second finger inside my slit. I throw my head back and moan as he stretches me out.

Then he takes things up a notch by sealing his lips over my hot, aching clit. He sucks on it and then presses his wet tongue over it, making me cry out when he begins to lick it.

"Oh god," I whisper. "Fuck, Erik… that feels so good…"

He starts moving his fingers in and out of my slit, fingering me as he sucks on my clit. I struggle for breath as I tilt my pelvis against his mouth, moving it back and forth, experimenting with the sensations he's pulling from me body. A coil tightens somewhere deep inside me; I'm aware of my innermost muscles shaking as I climb some invisible mountain, desperate to reach the peak.

Erik flexes his fingers inside of me, moving his hand more forcefully. He hits a spot inside of me repeatedly that makes me weak in the knees.

I make an inarticulate noise, my eyes closing. Clutching at his hair, my nails rake his scalp. I'm no longer fully aware of what is going on.

My vision tunnels down to what feels good right this second. The press of his mouth against my clit. The movement of his fingers in my slit, stretching me and touching that same spot that makes me gasp out loud every time.

Erik pulls back. "Come for me, princess. Show me how good I make you feel."

His words drive me over the edge of the precipice. My entire body tenses, ready.

"Erik…" I cry out. "I—"

I come suddenly, shattering into a million pieces. My pussy clenches around his fingers. My head hits the wall. I spasm wildly, riding an unbelievable wave of sensation. Erik moans, still working his long fingers and his clever tongue until I pull away, too sensitive to be touched.

I feel wonderful. But I also feel like crying. I keep my eyes closed as my heartbeat thunders in my ears, slowly drifting down.

Erik kisses my inner thighs, drops my knee from his shoulder, and pulls my dress back down. Then he stands up.

I open my eyes and put my hands around his neck, pulling him down for a kiss. His mouth tastes like me; my eyes fill with tears though I am not sure why. He presses himself against my body, his hardened cock poking me in the belly.

For a minute he just kisses me, exploring my mouth with his own. I exalt in his touch and his taste, feeling… cherished.

For just this space in time, we are just Annika and Erik. Not princess and minder. Not rich and poor. There are no divisions between us, no age differences, no expectations.

But then he pulls away, stepping back. His eyes are full of sorrow and anger. "I shouldn't have done that."

I bite my lower lip, stepping close to him again. I reach out and grab at him, pouting. "Why?"

His expression darkens. He pulls away again, shaking his head. "You know why."

I draw a breath, cocking my head. "I know, yes. But I don't care. I want you to take my virginity, Erik."

He shakes his head, avoiding my eyes. "No. You don't know what you want."

I step closer. "I think I do. I like you. Erik."

"Damn it!" he curses loudly, looking at me. "No. You have no idea what you want or what you like. If you did, you would know that you and I have no future. None."

He turns away, fiddling with the lock on the door. I open my mouth to argue with him, but he just throws open the door.

"Can we just leave?" he asks, sounding angry. "Or do you have to find some more strange men to rub up against?"

I narrow my eyes. "It worked, didn't it? You couldn't stand seeing me touching another man."

His jaw clenches. "Annika— "

I shake my head, pushing past him. "Don't. If you're just going to keep telling me all the reasons why we can't fuck, I don't want to hear it."

He reaches out and catches me in the doorway, his eyes hard on mine. "I wish things were different. You have to know that."

I look up at him, at his tortured expression. "Wishing something could be different doesn't make it so."

Then I stalk out of the bathroom, intent on finding Kal and getting out of this club.

Chapter Seventeen

ERIK

I CAN'T SLEEP when I get home. I'm too aggravated. By Nika, yes. But even more than that I'm just mad as hell at my circumstances.

And yeah, later when I stroke my cock, I can feel the heat of her pussy pressed against my eager mouth.

I know I can't have her. Not really.

But the fantasy of being her first, of taking her virginity, is too real… and it feels too good to stop.

That translates into a sleepless night for me, accompanied by being extremely tense and cranky the following day. I walk around with the shortest of fuses, dreading what is to come…

Family dinner.

That's right. Me, Annika, Stellan, and all the other Løve kids together with the former King and Queen. I make sure that I'm presentable - my tie straightened, my cufflinks buttoned - before I step through the door to the grand dining room.

I'm the last to arrive, by no coincidence. The room is majestic; high ceilings, plenty of natural light from the windows, a table that can seat forty people comfortably. Tonight, the table is set for eight. Goran, the former King, and Stellan, the current King, are sitting at the far end of the table. Looking as alike as a set of matching bookends, they are deep in conversation. All the men at the table look like photocopies of each other; tall, dark hair, blue eyes, exceedingly rich.

Everyone except me, of course.

To my surprise Margot sits beside Stellan, appearing as uncomfortable as possible. Her hair seems less pink than it usually is, her roots growing out.

I wonder if that's a sign of her changing style or if she caved to the Queen Mother's persistent reminders that pink hair is not ladylike.

I flash her a smile as I approach the table. She pulls a face. Good, I'm not the only one who doesn't want to be here.

Thora, the former Queen, is sitting on her husband's other side and talking to Annika. Nika is a perfect, elegant reflection of Thora's stately beauty. But for a second, as she notices my entry into the dining room, she shoots me a glare.

Then she turns up her nose at me and engages Margot in conversation. The only empty seat is next to Nika, so I slide into the seat left vacant for me. I see Nika's hand clench the glittery gold skirt of her full-length dress. It's hard not to stare at her, especially right now when she's wearing such a provocative dress. Two golden triangles of cloth cover her breasts, connected by a slinky gold chain.

I can almost see her stiff, puffy nipples through the barely-there garment. Nika wears her risqué dress as though it's not a big deal. As though there is no one that wants simultaneously to rip that dress off of her and also to cover her up with one of my jackets.

Maybe I'm the only one that feels that way, but I don't think so.

I clear my throat and jerk my gaze away, looking at Lars sitting beside me. Finn is across from me, frowning. Both of the younger brothers look like they want to leave.

I lean over to Lars. "Am I crazy or is everyone here except Anders?"

Lars' lips lift. "No, you're not crazy. No one really knows where our brother even is. Asking where he is seems to be useless. Even *Mor* doesn't remember the last time Anders touched base."

I nod, looking around the table. A servant appears over my shoulder. "Would you care for wine, sir?"

I glance up at him. "No, thank you. Water will be fine."

Finn leans across the table. "Are you living a booze-less existence, Erik?"

I narrow my gaze. "No, Finn. I just have a long day tomorrow. Annika is expected to show at a red carpet event for some fashion charity that she sponsors." I squint.

"Erik!" Thora declares. "I didn't see you sneak in. Are you excited about tomorrow's red carpet? Annika told me that it's going to be broadcast on basically every network. You're going to have to be a good escort."

I lift my head, swallowing. The former Queen never paid me much attention at all. Having her spotlight on me now is more than a little uncomfortable.

"I am," I bluff. "Although as I was just telling Finn, it's going to be a very long day."

Goran clears his throat, joining our conversation from his seat at the end of the table. "You're walking Annika down the red carpet tomorrow, I assume?"

I feel heat creep up my neck. "Actually, no. I wasn't invited to be in front of the cameras. The reporters aren't interested in anyone who doesn't have a title or isn't already independently famous."

Goran lifts a brow. "Is that so? I had no idea that the organizers even cared who walks down the red carpet."

Of course he doesn't. The former king lives in a bubble, surrounded by only the best and the finest things in life. Until he got sick and gave up the crown to Stellan, he was almost always on an expensive, amenity-filled trip to some far-flung locale under the excuse that he was spreading peace.

Stellan jumps in. "You know, Erik is going to be titled this year."

Thora's eyebrows lift. She looks over to me. "Have we not managed to find you a title already? How thoughtless of us."

I look down with a shrug. What am I supposed to say to that, exactly?

Goran coughs a few times, bringing a meaty fist up to his face. Then he starts wheezing and turning red, sputtering and coughing much more forcefully. In a flash, the focus is on the former King.

Thora gets up and presses a glass of water into Goran's hand. Annika stands, her brow drawn down as she watches her father like a hawk.

"Is there anything that I can get you?" Stellan asks his father, a concerned expression on his face.

Goran just shakes his head, his coughing beginning to subside. "No."

He takes a sip of water. Thora rubs his shoulder, looking worried.

"It would help if your father's doctors would settle on a diagnosis.

We've been told that he might have multiple sclerosis or ALS… but other doctors are sure it's early onset Alzheimer's disease…"

I sneak a glance at Nika. She sinks back into her seat, her fists balled up like she's ready to fight someone. Her expression is unreadable, but I have the sense that just beneath the surface lies an endless well of sadness and rage.

Before I even realize what I'm doing, I reach out a steadying hand to cover one of her fists. Her eyes go wide as she turns her innocent gaze on me. She jerks away from my touch, her gaze sliding across the table to Stellan and Margot.

"Don't," she whispers, so quietly that I almost don't hear it.

I quickly withdraw my touch, my neck heating with embarrassment. My hand burns and I clench my fist.

What was I thinking, touching her here? It's almost like I want to get caught.

I clear my throat and look across the table. Luckily Stellan is still talking to his father. Margot meets my gaze head on though, arching a brow. She doesn't say anything, but her gaze slips back and forth between me and Annika.

I can only guess at the conclusions she's drawing.

Lars looks around. "If *dar* is going to be all right, can we eat? I'm starving."

Finn pushes his wineglass away and glances toward the doorway. "I smell meat."

As soon as he says it, servants come into the room with still-sizzling lamb shanks hot from the grill, brabant potatoes, and a cool selection of shaved brussels sprouts with slivered almonds and pecorino romano cheese. Plates are placed in front of each of us, the food artfully arranged.

I didn't even realize that I was hungry until I smelled that lamb shank. Thora reclaims her seat, and everyone digs in. The brabant potatoes and the lamb melt on my tongue. I forget sometimes that Goran and Thora have one of the world's best chefs at their disposal. The rest of the palace is served amazing food, but this… this reminds me that even within the palace walls, there are different classes.

Thora glances at Annika in between bites of food. "Annika, how are things in your world? When did you get back from boarding school? I'm afraid I'm sort of out of the loop when it comes to knowing the day to day.

It's been impossible to keep up with the world while my husband has felt ill."

Around the table, all of Thora's children raise their brows. No one dares to tell Thora that her lack of parental guidance didn't start when Goran feel ill. For most of my life, I've watched Stellan and his siblings struggle with having two parents that were rarely at home with their children.

It's understandable to some degree… but also sort of laughable for Thora to even say something so out of touch with reality.

Annika clears her throat and raises her fork, gesturing with it. "I've been back for the better part of a year, mor. And…" A muscle flexes in her jaw. "I'm feeling very smothered by being a royal at this moment in time."

Thora's brows arch up. "Oh? Well, that's no good. At least you have Erik, though. That's certainly better than having some bodyguards on your tail every moment of the day."

She just glossed over the fact that she didn't know how long Annika had been back here at the palace. Typical of Thora and Goran, though. The crown just allowed them to parent from a distance, it seems.

Nika looks down at her plate with a murderous expression. "I think that Momse would agree with you on that count, mor."

I clear my throat. "Everything is running smoothly. Isn't that right, Annika?"

She shoots me a glare and takes a big bite of her food, chewing it. I send her my stoniest look. But Thora's attention has already wandered over to her other children. "And Lars, what about you? How is… what's her name? That lovely redhead that you are always running around with?"

I glance over at Lars, who frowns down at his plate. "I assume you mean Pippa. And she's fine. She's actually just taken a new job with a fashion magazine."

Margot finally pipes up. "Yes, Pippa is going to be a junior editor with a fashion magazine. It's a huge step forward in her career."

Thora smiles. "Well isn't that nice. You know, Lars, it's really too bad that your Pippa is commonly born. She would make an ideal partner for you otherwise."

My eyebrows lift. Margot's face goes a deep shade of crimson. Thora seems unaware of the fact that two of her dinner guests were not born into her same world of wealth and privilege.

Goran clears his throat. "Thora, darling. You're making Margot uncomfortable. Let's change the subject."

I don't even factor into the conversation. I keep my expression carefully blank, but inside I'm wondering why I'm even here. Finn shoots me an uneasy glance and lifts a shoulder in a shrug. Nika looks at me, her mouth tugging down into a frown.

That's the worst feeling, in my opinion. Pity for being born poor, coming my way from a fucking princess.

No, not just a princess.

A princess whose hot little body I've felt under my hands, whose perfect pouty lips I've crushed with my kiss. I can't stand the fact that she feels pity for me now.

It makes me so angry that I can't even look at her right now.

"Well… this has been nice…" Lars rolls his eyes, clearly still upset over how his mother talked about Pippa. "But I do have to get up early tomorrow."

He rises, saying goodbye to everyone before he heads out. For a minute, there is an awkward vacuum of silence. I'm focused on keeping my emotions internal and silent.

Perhaps Nika does have a point with her teasing about my strait-laced, buttoned up personality. I look around the table uncertainly.

Stellan pushes himself up from the table. "I think we should call it a night."

He and Margot say their goodbyes. I eye Annika, trying to work out my own excuse.

Thora pouts a little bit. "All my children leave me. Stay for a bit, those of you that are still here." Silence reigns for several seconds, then Thora turns to her daughter. "Tell me Annika, who are you seeing right now? Is there anyone worth mentioning to me?"

Annika eyes widen. She goes still, looking extremely nervous. Her eyes dart to me for the briefest of moments. Then she controls herself, looking at her mother.

"No, mor. There is no one." Her mouth twists to the side. "I mean, there was someone, but he ruined it."

She doesn't even so much as glance at me, but I feel my neck heat anyway. I'm a thousand percent certain that she is talking about me.

"Oh, that's too bad." Thora pulls a face. "What did he do?"

Nika tilts her head. "He was obsessed with wealth and class and status… and because of our differences in how much money we were born with, he messed things up with me too many times." She licks her lips, darting her gaze my way. "You could say that I'm taking some personal space from dating now."

"That sounds like a good idea," Goran says, nodding.

I stand up abruptly. "I think I'm going to call it a night. Thank you for inviting me, your highnesses."

Annika shoots to her feet. "Me too! I mean… I should be getting to bed early tonight."

I glare at her, but Thora just smiles. "Okay. That's all right… I wanted to speak with Finn alone anyway."

Finn's face twitches almost comically. I feel more than a little bad for him, but I've already excused myself.

"Goodnight, everyone." I bow and then stalk out of the room, feeling immense relief when I am out of the formal dining room.

Chapter Eighteen

ANNIKA

I FOLLOW Erik out of the dining room, waiting until we are in the hush of the hallway to eye him critically. He stops for a moment, throwing his head back and sighing.

"Fuck," he mutters, bringing his hands up to cover his face.

"What?" I ask, irritated with him.

He lowers his hands and looks at me for a long moment. I can feel his eyes drop to my mouth, to my barely clad breasts, to the thigh high slits in my floor length gown. Then Erik starts down the hallway, shaking his head a little. I have to hurry to keep pace with his long strides.

"You are unbelievable," he says, looking straight ahead down the long hallway.

A derisive snort leaves my mouth without me really thinking about it. "Me? How about you? Why were you even at dinner?"

He slides me a look as we reach the other end of the hallway and take a sharp right into a small, mostly disused staircase. "I was invited by the king. It's not something that I could turn down, no matter how annoyed I am with you."

He steps out of the hallway and stops. We should part ways here, me going upstairs to my rooms, Erik going… wherever he sleeps.

The fact that I don't actually know where that is sticks in my head.

He nods. "Let's go. I'll walk you back to your rooms."

Shaking my head and rolling my eyes, I head into the service elevator. Erik ducks in after me, pulling closed the steel grating and pressing the button for the top floor. The elevator lurches upward, yanking us along with it.

I bite my lower lip and tilt my head at him. "You know, I thought we were in a good place. Then before I know it, you're telling my entire family about what it's like to… to desire me."

I blush a little as he pins me with his green-brown gaze, but I don't look away. He steps a little closer, lowering his voice.

"Do you think it was any easier for me to hear you tell your mother about me?" His lips twist. "It wasn't. It made me feel like a villain."

He moves a little closer so that we are separated by only a few inches of air. I arch a brow, looking up into his gorgeous face.

A little voice in the back of my head tells me to sass him. I feel the tension simmering, bubbling just below his surface. Something deep inside me is excited by the idea of seeing him lose him cool.

I smirk. "Aren't you the villain of this story, Erik?"

A muscle flexes in his jaw. His gaze drops to my lips, making my stomach flutter. He very carefully splays one big hand out against my waist, dropping his voice to a whisper. "Is that what you want, Nika? Do you need a villain to complete your fairytale?"

His green-brown eyes bore into mine.

I bite my lip suggestively. "How will I know unless we try?"

Erik presses me back against the elevator wall, a soft growl deep in his throat. "Don't do that. It isn't fair."

I reach my hands up to curl around his neck. His leans against me, his cock pressing into my lower belly. My pulse pounds. My eyes close.

I don't know if he kissed me first or if my lips found his, but somehow his hot mouth presses down onto mine. I moan as he slips his tongue inside my mouth, curling it against my own. The elevator jerks to a stop.

In the back of my mind, I know that I have to pull the trigger now. The moment is right. If I don't make a move now to declare my intentions, we might never get this close to having sex again.

I slide my fingers through the straps of my dress, tugging at them suggestively. Then I break off our kiss, throw my head back, and draw one of the straps down my arm. I can feel his breathing constrict as I expose my right breast. My nipple pebbles in the cool air.

Erik drags in a heavy breath, his eyes glued to my nipple. Trailing my fingers across my chest, I swirl my fingertips around the pouty, rose colored peak.

I expected him to make a noise or maybe to kiss my neck. But he shocks me by picking me up and holding me in place against the wall. I wrap my legs around him. He puts his incredibly hot, wet mouth against the pink tip of my breast, sucking and groaning loudly. The noise is hungry and needy, resonating with me on a soul-deep level.

Erik sucks and bites my nipple, causing heat to ripple outward, gathering and concentrating low in my body. My pussy throbs. He brackets my breast with a hand and takes another pull, forcing strange sounds to come from my throat.

I writhe against him, flexing my hips. He answers by rocking his own hips against me, his rigid cock making its presence known.

His free hand comes up to my bare thigh, skimming upward from my knee to my hip. When his fingers reach around to shape my ass, he grunts.

"No panties?" he husks.

I bite my lip, shaking my head.

He smirks. "You are such a bad girl, Nika."

I tilt my head. "Are you just going to tell me about it? Or are you actually going to fucking do something this time?"

His gaze narrows on my face, almost heated enough to be called a glare. He skims his hand up my arm, catching the strap of my dress and pulling it up. My breath catches.

Erik puts both of his hands on my kneecaps and lowers me to the ground. I stand on shaky legs, not really understanding what he is doing. Then he spins, sliding the elevator grate wide and pressing the button to open the door.

For a moment, I'm crushed. Is this his way of shutting the door on the growing heat between us?

But when the door slides open, he grasps my arm and starts hauling me out of the elevator. I look at him with a bewildered expression.

He grits out. "If you don't want to lose your virginity standing upright in a shabby elevator, start walking. You have exactly one minute to get in your bedroom and get this fucking dress off. Then I call the shots, wherever we are."

My eyes widen. I hurry along the hallway toward my rooms, trying to keep up with his decisive pace. As soon as I hit the doorway to my living room, I start thinking of just how I'm going to get out of this dress. Truth be told, putting it on was kind of an elaborate production.

I glance up at Erik, swallowing. He doesn't look at me; his gaze is fixed on my bedroom door. The second we walk through it, he slams the door closed behind me and pushes me toward my elegant four poster bed. I stumble toward the crisp white linens, kicking off my shoes as I go. He grabs me from behind, nuzzling my ear.

"Time's up," he whispers. He draws my hair back from the side of my neck and bites me hard.

It feels so good, having him dominate me like this. The breath leaves my lungs. My eyes roll up in my head.

I hear a loud moan, but it's several seconds before I put it together that the sound comes from somewhere deep inside me. He walks me over to the side of the bed, taking a step back and ripping my dress down the back. I shudder at the feel of my sudden nakedness, especially when he roughly strips the dress from my body. He shoves his knee between my legs and bends me over the bed. The sheets feel coarse against my face and my sensitive breasts.

When he grips my hips and grinds into me, I moan. "Erik…"

He flips my golden mane off of my neck, running his hand from my nape down my upper back. "Mm. Do you know how long I've wanted this, princess?"

I tremble, shaking my head. Turning my head to the side, I can just make him out. "No."

His lips lift at the corners. "Longer than I would like to admit." He skims his touch down my spine ever so slowly, drinking the sight of me in. "And now, here you are." Both of his hands shape the curve of my ass. "All naked and spread for me."

He thrusts his hips against me roughly, letting me feel his hardened cock. Then he steps back. He starts unbuttoning his shirt.

"Get on your knees, princess. Face down, ass up. Let me see your pretty pussy."

My face instantly starts to glow as red as a hot coal. While he undresses behind me, I crawl onto the bed and present myself to him.

He climbs on the bed, only wearing his boxer briefs. He slaps my ass, which surprises me and makes me squeal. I can feel the stinging outline of his palm on my ass.

Then he bends down, kissing and nibbling the back of my right thigh. I make a strangled squeaking sound. He doesn't pause for a second, though.

Pushing my backbone down to bow my back, he brushes his clever fingers over my slit. I gasp, feeling a fresh wave of moisture leak from my slit.

He looks at my ass and my pussy, waiting and ready for him to touch them. "Your pussy is getting ready for me, princess." His fingers brush my slit again. "I'm going to fucking stretch you out and make you call my name. That is, if you'll be a good girl."

I shudder. *Yes*, I think. *I'll do anything you ask.*

He dips a finger the barest inch inside my entrance, making my whole body tighten with need. He moves down, trailing his kisses down my left ass cheek to the back of my thigh. I clench subconsciously as he showers kisses over my thighs, my ass, and the very outside of my pussy lips. It feels incredible, but… I know that there is more.

Hell, after he shocked me by going down on me at CURVE. I have been waiting for this exact moment. It's just… he's killing me with his slow kisses on every single place except my dripping wet slit.

Finally, I moan out of frustration. "Erik… please?"

He pauses, his lips on my inner thigh. When he speaks, I can feel his lips move against my flesh. "What do you want, Annika? I want you to tell me."

I tremble, feeling very exposed. "I—" My face burns. I close my eyes. "Eat my pussy, Erik."

He chuckles and I feel the reverberations against my skin. He grabs my hips and presses his face in, licking my slit up and down. It feels so damn good, but I want more.

I can just tell him that… right?

"Erik? Please do that more," I whisper. My face burns anew at the begging tone of my voice. But he did say that I should be vocal…

He immediately starts licking and sucking my clit, making me give a pleasured hiss.

I grab onto my comforter, needing something to hold onto.

. . .

I FREEZE up a little but before I can protest, he slides his hands over my thighs. Holding me down, he licks my clit in slow, lazy circles.

I am desperate for him, moaning and clenching my hands into fists in the sheets. He takes full advantage, easing his fingertips against my lower lips. I am so wet and excited that I don't need any lube. As he presses his fingertips against my pussy, entering me with a shallow thrust, I make a sound, a kind of whimper, and he takes his mouth away again.

I can feel my body weeping for him, feel the sheets beneath my body growing damp, clinging to my knees.

"Are you going to be a good girl and be quiet so that I can finish eating your pussy?" he murmurs against my bare flesh. "I really hope you are, because I can't wait to hear you call out my name."

I nod, feeling my face grow hot pink. I shut my mouth and go still, willing him to continue.

He presses against my pussy lips again with his fingertips. Then he kisses my pussy again, withdrawing himself from the bed. To my surprise, he grabs a robe and puts it on, leaving the room. He's gone for a while, a couple of minutes at the very least.

I frown and sit up, not quite knowing where he's gone. Then he returns, holding a small black silk drawstring bag and looking immensely pleased with himself.

He sheds the robe again and comes to kneel on the bed, a knowing smirk on his features. He reaches inside the bag and brandishes a six-inch-long piece of smooth, polished glass. It is the size and shape of a cock.

My eyes widen. "What... is that a dildo?"

Erik gives me a heated smile. "Lay back. Let me pleasure you, Nika."

I'm so hot for him that I bite my lip, relaxing to lie down on my back. He teases me by touching the outside of my thighs with the cold glass. I gasp, shivering. But the dildo soon warms up in his hands. He eases my legs to open again, widening them until he has a perfect view of my pussy.

He looks at me, his excitement evident as he bites his lip. "God, you are so beautiful, Annika."

Erik drops a kiss to my inner thigh as he presses the tip of the dildo to my pussy lips. I am so wet; it slides in partially with no resistance. God, the pressure of the dildo feels good, almost like his cock.

He withdraws it, kissing my clit once more. I couldn't be quiet, so I groaned softly. He doesn't pause, he just moves the dildo in again, licking my clit.

"Oh god," I gasp. "Fuck!"

I grab the sheets, knowing that I am going to come soon. I feel my thighs shake as he French kisses my clit. As he moves his tongue, he gently pulls the dildo out of my pussy, and moves it to my ass instead.

I am shocked enough by the contact to make a noise, but luckily this time he doesn't stop licking. He turns up the intensity of his French kiss as he gently presses the dildo against my ass.

Erik pauses, and I groan. When he returns, he moves the little dildo against my rear entrance once more, and I feel the slipperiness of the lube he has added. I bite my lower lip and close my eyes.

It feels so naughty but so fucking good. He slips the dildo into my ass while he kisses my clit. The sensation of being very full and very fucking ready to come washes over me.

"Oh god… please…" I beg him.

He chuckles. That is enough for me. My eyes roll back in my head, and I clench and shake. I feel enraptured, but even as I am drifting down, he is already preparing for more. He sheds his boxers, his expression intense. I shiver with anticipation as I look at his nudity, biting my lip.

He gets up, putting the dildo aside. Flipping me over on my hands and knees, he smacks my ass once. A chill runs down my spine, unbidden,

Erik actually growls his excitement, which only increases my sense of anticipation. He pushes my thighs apart and presses his thick cock against the entrance to my pussy. He feels so huge from this angle, impossibly big.

He uses a little of my lubrication to push himself halfway in. We both groan. He wraps my long platinum hair in his fist, withdraws slightly, and then hammers himself home.

I cry out, the pleasure bordering on pain. He is so big, filling every single inch of me, touching every secret spot inside.

He grasps one of my hips and starts thrusting slowly. I shudder as he withdraws and then fills me completely, again and again. Erik increases his speed, gripping my hair and fucking me harder.

I moan, feeling him filling every inch of my pussy. He shifts a little, and suddenly he is hitting my g-spot. I tighten and clench instinctively around his cock.

"Ah!" I call. "God, right there!"

"You like that?" he growls. "I want you to come so hard. I want to feel you cream all over my cock."

I groan as he hits my g-spot over and over, his thrusts as rapid as gunfire. Everything inside my body tightens.

"Oh god… oh god, Erik, I'm— I'm—" I cry, clenching around his cock. I feel like I am exploding, my eyes rolling back in my head.

He groans as he comes, finishing with a final thrust. I can actually feel his cock twitching, hot spurts of come releasing as he buries himself deep in my pussy.

"Fuck," he mumbles, struggling for breath.

He loosens his hold on my hair, leaning forward to kiss my lower back.

When we are both lying on our backs, struggling for breath, his expression contorts. He puts his hand over his eyes, making a quiet sound of distress. I look over at him, pulling in a breath.

"What?" I ask.

Erik rolls onto his side, sliding his legs off of the bed, and then sits up. "Nothing."

I arch a brow as he stands. "Where are you going?"

A pained expression crosses his face. "To my bed. This was…" He squints, stretching. "We can't do this again, Nika. This was a one-time thing."

I sit up, tilting my head. "We both wanted it. There's no issue of consent or anything, if that's what you're worried about."

He grabs his dress pants, hauling them up his legs. He doesn't meet my gaze. "It's not."

I'm a little taken aback by how dismissive his tone is. "Did I do something wrong? Did I… not…"

His expression darkens. He looks at me, his eyes filled with so much guilt and regret and shame that the breath freezes in my lungs.

Erik sits on the bed, looking me in the eye. He takes my hand. "You were perfect, Annika. Really. You blew my mind. I feel lucky to have shared your bed."

I bite my lip, my brow furrowing. "So, what is the problem, then?"

A muscle ticks in his jaw. He glances away, taking a deep breath. "When I'm with you, nothing ever seems forced or contrived. It all just seems so natural. But as soon as I take a step back, I see all the cracks in our foundation."

My lips twist. "Are you talking about Stellan?"

His hazel eyes swing around to pin me in place. "Annika. That might be the biggest reason that we shouldn't be together. But that's not the only one. I'm too old for you. I'm too poor. I was born in a different world. My father— "

Furious, I shake my head. "If you repeat that you weren't born a royal one more time, I swear I will scream."

He lifts a single shoulder in a shrug. "Okay. But just because I don't say it doesn't mean that it isn't true."

I can feel angry tears beginning to prick my eyes. I'm frustrated by his rejection and angry at his reason for it.

There is nothing I want less than to cry in front of Erik, but it seems like it's about to happen. I stand up, grabbing my robe from the back of a chair that I keep by my bedside table. I can feel Erik's probing glance as he just stares at me.

I head for my bathroom, hoping like hell he will get the message and make himself scarce.

"Where are you going?" he demands to know.

I inhale a shaky breath, but I don't look at him. "I'm going to take a bath and sulk."

He looks mildly offended. "What? Are we just done then?"

I stop, my body tensing, my hands clenching into fists. My jaw tightens as I whirl around on him. "Erik, get out of my room. You don't want me, and you don't want to be here… so just leave!"

My voice gives out on the last word and I turn, shaking my head. I feel so ashamed and unwanted. Tears prick my eyes. I just need to be alone. I run the last few steps toward the bathroom, ignoring the way that Erik calls my name.

Entering the cool white marble bathroom, I slam the door behind me. A sob escapes my lips as tears start to pour down my face. Covering my eyes with my hands, I lean against the door and sink to the floor in despair.

I'm officially in full meltdown mode, crying on the floor like a lovesick little girl. What has this guy brought me to?

I hear Erik as he taps against the bathroom door. "Nika…"

His voice is muffled but I can sense the frustration there too. I don't answer. Or maybe I can't, I don't know. I hiccup and continue to ugly cry.

Crying feels almost relieving at the same time as it feels like a knife twisting in my guts.

I hear him just on the other side of the door, his discomfort complete and obvious. He stands there for several beats. Then I hear him step back.

"I'm sorry," he says. "I'm the one that allowed things to go this far. It won't happen again, Nika. I swear."

It feels like he is physically shredding my heart. But the worst thing is the leaden feeling in my chest when I hear his footsteps receding, his presence vanishing in the blink of an eye.

My heart sinks. Closing my eyes, I let the tears stream down my face.

This.

This is what anguish feels like.

I need to remember this the next time that I am feeling flirtatious.

Chapter Nineteen

ERIK

I SIGH and run my hand down the front of my tux, glancing around the press junket. It is a madhouse right now. There is a large white backdrop set up across from where I stand, complete with designer logos of the companies that are providing support for this charity event. Before the backdrop is a red carpet, laid out like an offering from the gods.

Women in barely-there, skimpy black dresses teeter on sky high heels down the red carpet. Men in tuxes just like this one I'm wearing walk beside the women, doing their best to keep the women upright and steady.

It's always a little surreal to be invited to one of these events. On television, it's so seamless and glamorous. But in person, you can see how frantic everyone is behind the scenes. There is a chaotic energy as assistants and reporters hustle back and forth, preparing for the red carpet event to take place.

Usually the royal press office politely declines. But this event is for one of Annika's favorite fashion-related charities. So here we are, me watching with anxious eyes as a camera crew begins setting up to my right.

Nika took a separate car to get here, presumably because she doesn't want to be around me at all. And I don't blame her for that, not in the least.

After I left her chamber last night, I laid awake in my bed, restless. I tossed and turned the whole entire night, unable to get the sound of Annika's muffled tears out of my fucking head.

Even sobbing and messy, she was so damn beautiful. I swear, I started to crack.

Today, in the cold light of day, I feel like an empty vessel, poured out and left to lie on its side. All that is left over is a little bit of anguish on the very bottom, amplifying whatever emotions I've been feeling the last few days.

It's an empty hollowness more than anything, a numbness which I am fairly sure that I didn't intend to feel.

Hell, I didn't plan to feel any of this.

I fuss with my bow tie and look at my cell phone. For someone that got exactly what he said he wanted last night, I'm acting like I am dying. I don't know what to do about that but it's still a fact.

I hear her arrive before she even gets out of the car.

I know that Nika has just arrived because a hush falls over the entire red carpet and the press pit. There are people whispering about it from this distance. The red carpet runs all the way down the steps to where the celebrities are supposed to get out of their cars. And the second that Annika gets out and looks around, a hush falls over the people around me.

I turned my head, looking at her. My eyes widen the little bit. If her grandmother sees just what she is wearing, that beautiful hot mess is a dead woman walking. She wears a short length of gold chain which has somehow been converted into a dress. It shows off her collarbone, her breasts, everything from her thighs down. And when she turns around for just a second, I get a glance at the back of the dress, if it can even be called that. The dress is fastened at the back with gold chain and a barely there bit of fabric covers her ass. That's it.

My breath leaves me in a huff. The guy to my right adjusts his bow tie and gives me a look. "I know, right? Who would've known that the princess was so…" He bites his lip. "Well, you can see for yourself."

I shoot him a glare and hurry out of the line of press that I've been hiding behind. I should stop Nika before she even steps on the carpet. That's the only way to make sure that her grandmother doesn't lose her mind afterwards.

Elbowing my way through the crowd, I keep my eyes fixated on Annika's long flaxen hair. She seems to notice me only at the last moment that I push towards her. Her guileless eyes take me in and coolly dismiss me. I grab her elbow, pulling her closer.

She turns towards me, opening her mouth as if to argue. That's when I smell the whiskey on her breath. Leaning closer to her, I narrow my gaze on her face. "Are you insane? Just what do you think you're doing?"

She pulls her elbow from my grip, her expression unreadable. "I'm walking the red carpet."

I growl under my breath. "Annika, I swear to god…"

Her head swivels as she searches the crowd. She lands on a tall, dark-haired man in a tux. He turns and brightens; he begins to nudge his way through the crowd to get to her.

She points her long arm at him. She teeters, her balance thrown off. Clearly, she is even more drunk than I gave her credit for. When she speaks, she slurs her words. "There he is now. He's my date. If you will excuse me?"

I grab her arm before she can walk away. "You think that I'm going to just let you drunkenly wander around here? You may be a princess, but I am your minder. And if you think that I am going to just let you embarrass the royal family by appearing on television right now in your current state, you've got another thing coming."

Gritting my teeth, I start to pull her back toward the limousine that she just left. The chauffeured car has long since pulled away from the curb, but I can still make it out, stuck in traffic.

Nika pulls herself from my grip once again, this time hissing at me. "What are you doing? Let me go!"

I don't even look at her. I just use my overwhelming size to push her through the crowd, trying to ignore that people are definitely turning their heads to see what the fuss is about. Honestly, it wouldn't even be that big of a deal, except that Nika is so well known.

I'm man handling the country's princess, after all.

So, while I'm doing my best to shield her from prying eyes, everyone is probably whispering about the fact that the Princess is being forcefully removed from this event. That isn't what I want per se. But if it comes down to deciding between making Annika angrier with me or protecting the royal family from embarrassment, I know what I will choose.

I make it down to the street, all but carrying Nika. She doesn't even try to resist, really. She just looks mad and flushed as she glares up at me. Her mouth is screwed up like she's just bitten down on a lemon.

A hand lands on my shoulder, pulling at me. I glower, turning my head to see that Nika's dark-haired date has followed me. He is looking between me and Annika, a little bewildered.

This close, I realize that he's actually taller than me. I raise a brow.

"Could you fuck off?" I bite off.

He flushes, looking at Nika beseechingly.

"Princess Annika. Do you need help?" he asks, his voice unusually high and grating for someone so big.

I shrug out of his grip and step backward, pulling Nika into my body protectively. The last thing I want is to cause a scene here where everybody can see us. But I don't have time or the inclination to explain myself to this random dark-haired stranger.

Annika looks at me, arching a brow. "I don't know. Do I need assistance, Erik? Or do you want to just let me go right now? Because I will cause a scene. That much I assure you of."

A man wearing a tuxedo, a headset, and a clipboard cuts into our argument. "Excuse me, Princess Annika? We need you to walk the red carpet now so that we can prevent the back up of celebrities as we begin our event. We want to go ahead and get you seated in the front of the room, at the table of honor."

Annika looks at me with a little smirk and wrests her elbow from my grasp. Then she straightens her dress and looks at the dark-haired man she's chosen as her date. She holds her arm out and smiles, showing off her teeth. "But of course. Let's go, David."

Her date takes her arm, leaning close to whisper in her ear. "It's Ben."

She pats his arm and starts walking back towards the red carpet, climbing the stairs once more. She doesn't spare a second look for me. I am left to follow in her wake, having the depressing realization that this is what babysitting royalty is all about.

If it weren't for Annika being so interested in flirting with me, this is exactly what it would have been like the entire time that I had been tasked with this duty.

I suck in a breath and hold it as I trail after Annika and Ben down the red carpet. No one is interested in me, which is not surprising at all. Everyone is interested in Annika, taking their microphones out for a comment and peppering her with questions. She smiles in a way that does not seem genuine and somehow manages to walk down the red carpet, despite the fact that she is drunk and those gold heels that she is wearing look like torture devices.

Sexy, yes. But they definitely look like she could die at any moment.

She pauses on the carpet, posing with Ben at her side. Her saccharine smile never leaves her face. And if there were no questions from reporters, I think that maybe Annika would've gotten away with the next incident. But unfortunately for her, they are still pressing in on her with a thousand questions.

One pretty female reporter steps forward out of the line and pushes her microphone close to Annika's face. "Princess Annika, who are you wearing? And who is your date?"

Annika leans against Ben and licks her lips apprehensively. "I'm wearing Greta von Grissel and my date is my lovely friend…" She pauses. It's clear to me that she has forgotten her date's name. She blushes a bit. "You can just call him my friend. That's okay."

The dark-haired reporter raises her brows slightly. She steps a little closer to the Princess. She must get a whiff of the booze on Annika's breath. I can see a split-second decision being made on the woman's face. She smiles at Annika, her expression turning a little cruel.

"Princess Annika, are you drunk right now?"

The crowd falls under a hush, heads turning. Everyone strains to see Annika's response. Annika's eyebrows go up, and her mouth tightening a fraction.

I see her shake her head, frowning just a little bit. "No. Why would you ask me that?"

The reporter presses closer, pushing her microphone into Annika's face. Annika reacts, stepping backward. But those gold heels betrayed her. She tips over and trips over the carpet. It's only a moment of quick thinking on my part that saves her from total disaster.

I move forward, neatly catching Annika by the elbows and hauling her up against my chest. She shoots me a glare and tries to shake off my touch. But I lean in close to her ear, pressing my lips close. "Are you really going to make this worse than it already is? This clearly isn't going to go your way. So, let me just take you home."

Annika bares her teeth at me. Her eyes lose focus for just a second, reinforcing the fact that she is drunk as hell. "Yeah, like I'm going to let you take me anywhere. That's just not going to happen," she hisses.

In the next second I step back from her. Letting her go so suddenly removes some kind of stability that she relied on, apparently. Because when I take my hands off of her arms, she goes down like a lead filled balloon.

And there is no stopping her from falling.

I belatedly realize what is already happening when Annika is looking at me with a bewildered expression, slumping helplessly to the ground. My eyes widen as she collapses.

Ben is right behind her, picking her up off the ground. But the damage is already done. Reporters crowd around her in a circle, shouting questions and fighting to be the closest one to the disaster.

That's it.

I go into auto mode, grabbing Annika and hauling her back toward the limousines. I grit my teeth and let my expression do most of the talking.

It's simple math. I'm much bigger than most of these reporters… and way more determined, too. I just haul Annika along, wishing like anything that it wouldn't be untoward to scoop her up and carry her.

But honestly, I'm not even sure that she's wearing anything underneath that tiny gold dress. Besides, I don't want to risk showing the world her privates any more than I want there to be pictures of me and Annika together.

Rumors have been started over the last couple and all I need right now is for this event to start them up again.

Reporters press in from all sides, seeming to circle like sharks. Right now, it's Annika's blood that they're tasting in the water and they move forward as I do, eager to get their stories.

"Annika! Annika! Who is your handsome savior?"

"Princess Annika! Are you going to a rehab program? Are you relapsing? Princess…"

"Annika, why do you keep embarrassing the royal family?"

Gritting my teeth, I keep moving, ignoring the camera flashes and shouts. By the time I get down to the cars, I open the back of the first limo that I see and shove Annika in. I don't even say anything to the reporters trying to push in and ask their questions. I just wrestle the door shut, closing it on them. Then I order the limo driver to pull away from the curb. I don't even care that it's not our car, either.

As soon as we begin to move away, I glance at Annika, my expression stern. She looks at me for a second, then her expression crumples and her eyes begin to shine with tears.

"I hate you," she whispers tearfully. She balls up her fists and hides her face behind them. She can't seem to decide between hatred, fury, and sadness when she delivers the killing blow. "I fucking hate you, Erik."

Her words are like a knife twisting in my guts. My heart sinks.

Do I deserve that? Yes. I deserve everything she could ever give me, every slur and barb she could ever throw.

Absolutely, without reservation. I never should have touched her. And now I'm just stuck between a rock and a hard place. Damn if it doesn't feel like my stomach is filled with lead.

Nika's body goes rigid for a second. Her eyes widen. She tenses.

Then she suddenly grabs the ice bucket from its resting place, hanging her head over it. She gags for half a minute.

I'm frozen for a second. I don't know what to do. My hand hovers on her back and she retches, throwing up into the ice bucket.

Then some instinct kicks in, some foreign knowledge of what to do in this exact situation though I've never even come close in practice. I lean forward and tuck her hair back out of her face, smoothing my hand over the bare skin of her back.

God, this is all wrong. Once, Stellan was the only one of the Løve siblings I had to worry about. But now Nika has had too much whiskey to drink and she's vomiting it all up. And though I have resisted taking care of her for so long, I rise to the occasion presented to me.

"It's going to be okay," I murmur to her. Raising my chin, I call out to the driver. "Do you feel like taking a ride? Because I think it would be best if we got out of the city for a bit…"

Chapter Twenty

ANNIKA

FOR A WHOLE DAY and a whole night, I just sleep.

I'm exhausted from just being myself.

From having so many damn feelings.

From trying to put on my smiling public mask and not let anybody see the cracks that have formed in it.

From being one thing to my adoring fans and another to my mess of a family and still another thing entirely to Erik.

Erik, who rejected me. He did it as soundly as a person can be told that they are not good enough or pretty enough or… well, enough.

I wake up with the realization that I have apparently been quite busy while I was passed out. There is a trashcan beside the couch that I'm sleeping on. It smells like the stench of alcohol and gastric juices. It's a very unique smell, one that makes me gag a little.

Pushing myself up on my arms, I try to breathe in deeply and not throw up the contents of my stomach, which by now are surely just acid and bile.

My head throbs as I look around. I haven't seen this room before. Where am I exactly?

I move to the other end of the couch and stand up shakily, wishing like all hell that I had not done quite so many shots of whiskey the night before. Or the day before…

I squint around the room, but there are no windows. Nothing to tell me if it is night or day. I feel like I've been asleep for a while, but I have no idea where or even when I am.

One thing that the room I'm in does boast aside from the couch is a small bathroom. I drag myself into it, peeing and brushing my teeth with a brand new toothbrush and a tube of toothpaste. I look down to find myself wearing a rolled up old button up and nothing else. I frown at that.

What happened to my dress that I wore earlier? What happened to the heels that I strapped on?

Then I clean myself up, running a damp washcloth over my armpits and privates. It's not the classiest thing I have ever done, but it's not the least classy either.

God, my head aches. How did I come to be here?

It's only then that I think of Erik. I get a flashback of the last time I saw him. In the back of a limo, patiently holding my hair back as I vomited.

Oh, god.

Erik is the last person I want to be vulnerable in front of. And yet, I have a vague memory of him lifting me from the backseat and carrying me into a house.

The sharp scent of saltwater overlays my hazy memory. The tang of saltwater, the cool breeze on my back, light wood a dark room.

A puzzle piece clicks into place. I go to the windows and throw the heavy curtains open, revealing the beach splayed out below me. Crisp, clean, all but virgin sands. In the distance, the blue-black sea spreads out as far as I can see. The waves crash on the beach, hissing as they retreat.

It's not quite the same view as the last time I was here but there is the neatly kept patio, leading out to the beach.

Erik brought me here.

He could've taken me anywhere in the world and yet…

Here I am. I can't think of why he would bring me here. I can't actually think of anything at all, not without my head aching.

Desperate for water, I venture to the doorway.

I heave open the door and stick my head out, nearly blinded by the golden daylight that pours in on me. If I had to guess, I would say that it was seven or eight in the evening. Not super late, but not nearly the time that I last remembered it being.

I squint around, looking back and forth down the hallway. It's lined with wood, ceiling to floor. I can see the huge plate glass window at the end of the hall, the sand and light green grass blending in with the décor of the house.

I press the heels my hands against my eyes, wishing like anything that this would all go away. But after leaning against the doorframe for half a minute, I realized that nothing is going to be resolved by me just hiding up here. So, I take the next step and wander down the hall, going downstairs. I find the downstairs living area airy and full of white furniture and the same light wood as I found upstairs. Everything is still and silent.

Water is still calling my name, so I venture into the kitchen, where I find Erik at last.

His back is turned to me. He has a radio on that plays some classic rock very quietly. And he is frying something, I can hear the sizzle and smell the butter as he hums to himself gently and agitates the frying pan. It's only when I step into the open area between the kitchen island and the countertop that he even looks up.

He bites his lip and looks me up and down, a little frown appearing on his face.

His gaze on my legs makes me realize that he probably undressed me and put me in his button up. There's something so intimate and personal about that, while at the same time it makes me a little sad. It also makes me think of the fact that I am naked beneath this oversized shirt and he knows it.

I don't know quite what to think about that. My head aches and I press my palm to my temple. He continues to look at me, finally making a comment.

"I see that you made it. I was starting to wonder."

He turns back to the stove and flips the sandwich he's making in the pan. I take a deep whiff of the smell of cheese and bread toasting. My stomach lurches and I take a step backwards. Not knowing quite what to say, I go around Erik, giving him plenty of space. I retrieve a bottle of mineral water from the refrigerator.

Then I sit down at the kitchen island, watching him. His light-colored hair is slightly askew, as if he has styled it by shoving his hands through it. He wears a T-shirt and dark jeans, slung low at the hips and looking quite like an advertisement for designer jeans. His mood seems lighter too, although you can never tell quite what is going on behind Erik's eyes.

I guess that being here, away from the city and closer to the beach, makes him more relaxed.

If I'm honest, it is a look that really suits him. He essentially ignores me and hums along with the song playing on the radio.

I sit in silence and drink my water. He transfers the grilled cheese sandwich from the pan to a plate, turning to look at me. "Do you want one?"

Just looking at that sandwich makes me feel queasy all over again. I swallow and shake my head. "No thanks. I have a rule about eating after I have vomited. It's usually not a good idea."

Erik looks at me for a long second and then sets the sandwich down on the counter. He leaves the room for half a minute, returning with a can of coconut water and a couple of aspirin. He leans over the counter and puts them in front of me, then goes back to his sandwich.

I take the aspirin and the chilled coconut water, washing one down with the other. He doesn't look at me, just takes a big bite out of his sandwich.

We sit like that for several minutes until I finish the coconut water and the bottle of mineral water. And then I scrunch my face up and look at him. "Where's my phone?"

He doesn't look at me. He doesn't make a face exactly, but I have an idea of what exactly he is thinking. He squints off into the distance, looking out the large windows toward the beach. "You don't need to check your phone. I called the press office and canceled your upcoming engagements. I think you should just relax and take it easy."

I blanch a little. He wouldn't say that unless the press was really swarming. "It's that bad, is it?"

He raises a single shoulder in a Gallic shrug, his expression unreadable. He looks down at his plate for a moment and I have to wonder what in the world he is thinking.

"I think we should stay here for a while. Maybe a month. Maybe more. I think…" He looks up, his tawny eyes pinning me in place. "I don't think that the spotlight is really a good place for you, Nika. I know you grew up with the press outside your window. I know you've always felt like you were on display. But I don't think that has served you very well, so far."

My mouth puckers. "What? What are you saying?"

He shrugs again and looks me dead in the eye. "I think it would be a good idea if you took a break from being in the public eye, that's all."

My cheeks flush. I toy with the rim of my water bottle, trying to guess at what he is really saying. I definitely blacked out earlier when I was at that red carpet event... How bad was my behavior that Erik is now advising me to retreat from public life?

The fact that I don't know what happened really puts things in perspective for me. I should never feel this way, not because of something that I did. That much is clear.

The real question is whether or not I am actually stuck here with Erik babysitting me or if he's just watching me temporarily. Biting my lip, I look up at him.

"How bad was it? Like are we talking about something that I should make the daily rounds on TV and do an apology tour? Or..."

He shakes his head, looking somber. "I don't think we should talk about how the press perceives you, Nika. We both know that when you live your life under a microscope, things can get distorted and blown out of proportion so easily."

My head pounds. I lean my face on my hands, shutting my eyes for a second. "So... what are you suggesting? We just take a break from the outside world for a while? We just... hole up in this house and don't listen to any outside news?"

He cocks his head, studying me. "Doesn't that sound... I don't know... like a kind of relief?"

I pull a face. "You are ignoring the fact that I would rather be trapped with a pack of wild dogs than spend time with you. I pretty much hate you."

In the next moment, Erik grabs me and shocks me by pulling me close and giving me a shake. "Don't say that," he growls. "Don't you dare start in on that again. You know you don't hate me. Apologize to me, right now."

I blink up at him, startled. A flush begins creeping up my cheeks. "Again? When did I say I hated you?"

His gaze narrows on my face. "What, you don't remember?"

The flush that has been creeping up my neck slowly turned into a full on blush. My cheeks heat and I bite my lip, looking away as I try to remember. Maybe it was something that I said when I was blacked out. "I..."

He gives me another sharp shake. "Of course you don't remember. That's your whole life, isn't it? You're so used to being a princess and getting everything you desire. You don't even realize that the things you say and do have effects in the real world to real people." He pushes me away from him, shaking his head with a disgusted look on his face. "You know what the worst part of it is? I'm not even that surprised. I just… It's always two steps forward one step back with you. And I am getting tired of this little dance."

He storms out of the kitchen, turning right and heading outside. I watch him go, my mouth opening a little with surprise.

What just happened? Somehow, it seems like I've managed to hurt the feelings that I didn't even think he had.

So what am I supposed to do about that?

Sinking back into my chair, I stare at the doorway that he disappeared through, my eyes welling with tears. I'm frustrated. With myself, first of all. But also with this situation in general.

First Erik and I sleep together. Then he tells me that it was all a mistake, that his feelings for me don't run that deeply.

And now this?

This… whatever this is.

It feels almost self-indulgent to cry right now, but that's exactly what I do. Laying my head down on my arms, I have a good long cry.

Unfortunately, I end up feeling like I am dehydrated by the end of my little crying jag. When my tears slow, I help myself to another can of coconut water before heading upstairs.

I try to think of how I should console myself, how a healthy person would do it. I have a choice of sorts. I could either dig myself deeper into this hole and spend hours looking at the internet, reading all of the comments about my appearance and my behavior.

Or… I can try to use one of the… what are they called again?

That book about radical self-love called them coping strategies, I think. One of the main coping strategies is self-care. Taking a bath, taking time to do my nails, or maybe doing some yoga.

Baby steps. I decide that before I do anything else, I need to take a bath and consider all my options.

That's the only way that I can see forward and out of this mess at this particular moment. Sucking in a deep breath, I raise my chin and head towards my favorite bathroom in the house.

ERIK

I STALK out of the house at sunset, my whole body vibrating from tension. I swear, one of these days, Nika will finally do or say the wrong thing… And I will just completely fucking lose it.

I'm so mad right now that I'm shaking as I storm out across the sandy beach. The sun is low in the sky but still present enough to make me shade my eyes as I trudge toward the horizon. I have to get away from Nika and away from that house. I don't know exactly where I'm going but anywhere is better than there.

I break into a run, just now realizing that I am barefoot. The grains of sand are a little coarse underneath my feet. When I go farther out, toward the water line, it seems like a good place to stop.

I turn and look back at the house, only now realizing that I have actually left the house quite a way behind. It looks very small in my peripheral vision, just a black, squat blip on my radar.

I suck in a breath and close my eyes, turning back toward the setting sun and the coolness of the sea. I wade out just a bit. I stand and let the waves lap against my feet. For some reason, it helps sooth the angry, injured being that lives deep inside me.

I take another breath and let it out very slowly.

It doesn't help that thoughts are pounding at my head, relentless as the waves themselves.

I hate you.

Nika said that yesterday, over and over again. I feel like that was just her way of saying what she couldn't when I left her bed that night... She might've been huddled and crying on the floor of her bathroom, but in my heart, I knew that she harbored black thoughts about me.

Hearing them said to me out loud is something I hope never to hear again. When she said that she pretty much hates me just a few minutes ago, it was the straw that broke the camel's back.

I just snapped. And rather than unload all of my anger and resentment and the confusing amalgamation of sadness and sorrow onto her... I just left. Which is how I came to be standing here just now.

But God, even hung over as she was, she looks so damn good that I nearly lost control of myself. Especially wearing nothing but my wrinkled white button up.

She was angelic for a moment there.

But in the next second, her smart mouth reminded me of exactly why I wanted to avoid all of this in the first place.

Because she's essentially a spoiled little brat. Yeah, maybe she has her own reasons. But nothing really overwhelms the fact that she has had everything in her life handed to her and has lived without repercussions.

In fact, I think I'm part of the problem...

Instead of making her stay in Copenhagen and face her colossal mistakes... She could have owned up to the fact that she made a complete fool of herself in front of the press. But instead I'm helping her hide out here.

Hell, I even thought of it myself. There is no one that made me do any of this. I just did it on my own, for her benefit.

And I would probably do it again if given the same situation. Because I have definitely developed some sort of crush on Nika...

Maybe crush isn't even the word. I guess a crush is something unrequited. What happens when a crush is returned, and you get exactly what you have longed for?

Man, I am starting to have this sinking feeling in the pit of my stomach. Do I have feelings for Nika?

Surely that can't be the case... Right?

But the fact that I'm standing out here, all angsty and brooding, indicates that I do have something to be worried about.

I grind my teeth and take another step into the shallow water that swirls then washes around my feet. I raise my head to the sky and bring my arms out, yelling wordlessly. It's the only way that I can express all the things that I am feeling.

My phone begins to buzz in my pocket. I'm irritated as I pull it out because I have almost everyone on silent. The only person that my phone would even notify me for is Stellan...

I swallow as I realize that that is exactly who is calling. Gritting my teeth, I answer the video call.

"Hello?"

Stellan's face appears, his dark eyebrows drawn down quite severely. It looks like he's at the palace, though with the low lighting behind him it's hard to be sure. He tilts his head to the side and looks at me quite seriously.

"Hey. I was just calling to check in on you and Nika. I'm wondering if we need to start talking about some kind of alcohol treatment program. Maybe somewhere far away on the beach?"

I sigh. "She's just young. That's all it is. I don't think that we have anything to worry about in the alcoholism department."

He pins me with his deep blue gaze. "Did something set her off? Because we can't have a reckless princess out there, running around and representing the royal family so poorly. It's just not something that is going to work."

My neck feels hot all the sudden. I squint off into the distance and try to think of how to explain it without telling Stellan that I definitely banged his sister. I feel a little queasy having to lie to him.

Maybe I should just tell him the truth and get off this babysitting duty. Of course, it would most likely have way more ramifications than that.

How do you tell your best friend that you have developed feelings for his little sister? How do you say that she is acting out because of something that you did?

"Erik. Pay attention."

I look at him, his white button up rumpled, his shirt sleeves rolled up. "Sorry. I just think that Annika needs some time out of the spotlight. From what she's been telling me, it sounds like every time she has to interact with the press, something goes wrong. So, my solution would be just, don't interact with the press."

Stellan looks tired, rubbing his face and sighing. "That isn't a permanent solution. That's temporary at best."

I nod absolutely. "Yeah, I know. It just isn't fair. If she were anyone else on earth, I would tell her to just walk away from the royal family. She would be happier if she did. But I know that that's not an option in real life."

"Nope. It's not." He pauses, screwing up his face. "You really don't think that she needs to be in rehab?"

My lips lift a little at the corners. "No, I don't think so. I just think we're going to have to find a way to distract her. Maybe there's some kind of retirement from public life or something…" I pause, though occurring to me. "You know who would know?"

He perks a brow. "Momse?"

"That's the one. She has knowledge of what the royal family has done in the past. I mean, there has to have been someone somewhere that opted out of the spotlight."

A thoughtful look appears on Stellan's handsome face. He runs a hand through his short, dark hair and exhales. "I'm sure that Momse does have some opinions about Annika. But honestly, I don't even want to give my grandmother that kind of power. I just finished setting some boundaries with her over the whole Margot debacle. I hate to take steps backward at this point."

I scrunched up my face. "Very true. Right now, it is a bit of a strange time for Momse. She is going through something, not being allowed to pull all the strings anymore. It's got to be an adjustment for her."

The corners of Stellan's lips quirk a little. "I'm sure. But I think that my parents let her run the kingdom of Denmark, essentially. And the fact that I'm taking control back is a rather prickly subject for her. I might be her favorite grandchild but I'm still her competition, in a sense. She's held the strings too tightly for too long."

I bite my lip. Somehow, we've drifted onto Stellan's favorite topic again. He loves to think about how the power dynamics are shifting in Denmark with his succession to the throne. But that's not why he called.

Did he just forget about Nika entirely? I press my lips together and sigh. He gives me a sharp look. "Am I boring you, Erik?"

I roll my eyes and give him a light smile. "Not at all. I was just wondering how we ventured on to this topic. I remember you calling about your little sister. That's all."

I hear a woman in the background, asking Stellan a question. He looks away from the phone. When he looks back, his expression seems distracted. "I have to go. Margot needs my attention. Are you guys going to be okay out there for now?"

I nod. The sun is all but set and I start walking back toward the house. "Yeah. We're fine. As long as I keep Annika away from the press, I think she will be content."

I hear Margot's voice again, clearly calling for Stellan. He rolls his eyes and says goodbye. "I have to go. If you need to get a hold of me, you can always call my new secretary. I'll talk to you later."

I think about how I should answer that. But Stellan has already hung up the phone. A blinking red icon on my screen indicates that the line has been disconnected.

I glare at the screen and shake my head, shoving my phone in my pocket. I'm not even mad or that surprised at his behavior. That's what you get when your best friend is the King of Denmark, apparently.

As I walked back to the house, that little quip about how I should get in touch with him through his new secretary rings in my head. I think he was joking… But in all seriousness, if I'm going to leave the service entirely, this could be my future. I could be facing a lifetime of missed calls whenever I try to actually talk to Stellan.

That fact has not escaped my worried thoughts. All the way back to the house, I walk over the sandy beach and feel the weight of that knowledge in the pit of my stomach. It is heavy and bitter, and it leaves me feeling more uncertain than usual.

I walk up to the house, heading through the French doors that I left open. To my surprise, I find Nika right where I left her. Although she has a bowl of cereal in front of her now. I glance at her and she takes a bite of her cereal, shrugging a shoulder. Through a mouthful of cereal, she apologizes, which takes me back.

"You were right," she says. She chews the bite of cereal and then swallows. "I shouldn't have said that I hate you. That was unfair. I'm sorry."

Exhaling loudly, I meander into the kitchen, stopping when I am opposite where she sits on the counter. Leaning back against the counter behind me, I fold my arms across my chest and look at her somberly. "Thanks for that."

She wrinkles her nose and pushes her bowl away, stretching her arms over her head. I can't help the fact that her movement draws my eye down to her breasts. They look particularly amazing under that loose white button-up shirt she is wearing. If I stare hard enough, I'm pretty sure that I can even make out her nipples. I lick my lips and yank my gaze back up to her face.

I find her giving me a flat stare. "Do I need to go put on real clothes? Because that kind of staring is not allowed. If we are just friends or I am just a babysitting assignment for you, that's fine. But don't stare at me like I am the juiciest steak and you haven't eaten in a year. It's not fair."

I feel my neck get hot. Tucking my head, I shrug a shoulder. "I'm trying. But we both know that the other is attractive. There's no denying that. It's just a matter of doing what is right as opposed to what I might want at this moment."

She pushes her cheek out with her tongue and looks annoyed. Nika stands up, grabbing her cereal bowl and stalking to the sink that is right behind me. I slide over a little to make room, looking down as she puts her bowl in the sink. When she's done, she looks up at me, her pale eyes narrowing.

"I don't understand how you think that the two of us can just coexist like this." She pulls her arms over her chest, framing and emphasizing her breasts. That isn't helping anything at all as far as I'm concerned.

I shouldn't lean closer. I shouldn't use my intimidating height as a weapon. I shouldn't play with fire by using the electric current that runs between us like this.

And yet, I do exactly that. I step closer to her until we are toe to toe, gazing down at her with a stormy expression.

"We only have to stay in the same place and stare at each other for three more weeks. Then it will be Stellan's wedding. And then you and I can quit this little babysitting routine. As far as I'm concerned, I'm only accountable for you until then. After that, you can do whatever you like."

Nika's head falls back and she looks up at me defiantly. "Oh yes. I haven't forgotten that you accepted the bribe that my grandmother offered."

I smile at her evenly, showing all my teeth. "If you weren't such a problem child, she wouldn't have offered anything at all. So, I guess I can thank you for my title-to-be. Without you, I would be a commoner for the rest of my life. Luckily, you're such a pain in the ass that no one wants to deal with it…"

She laughs coolly. "Gold digger."

She just tosses that accusation out like it's nothing. Like her words don't mean anything at all. It makes me angry. But the curl of her lip also turns me the fuck on.

I lean in very close to her, so that there are only a few inches between our lips. "Troublemaker."

"Opportunist."

One corner of my mouth hitches up in a smile. "Spoiled little rich girl."

Her nostrils flare and her eyes widen. I can smell her excitement perfuming the air. "How dare you."

I can't seem to stop myself from kissing those gorgeous, pouty, mouthy lips. I pull her against my body and stop her talking with my mouth, making a soft noise at the taste of her as it bursts across my tongue.

God, I can never get enough of her.

Her hands clutch my shirt, balling into fists and then relaxing just for a second. Then she suddenly shoves me away, taking a shaky step back and drawing in a breath.

Her eyes shine with lust, but she looks so distraught and angry. "Erik, we know where this leads. And I for one have had enough rejection in the last few days. So, if you don't mind, fuck off and leave me alone."

With that she spins on her heel and heads toward the staircase, trotting up towards her bedroom. And I just stand here, feeling the heat from her body and her mouth, knowing that she is right but wishing that she was dead wrong.

ERIK

IT'S BEEN a week since I took Annika from Copenhagen to hide out from the press. A very long week full of heated glances and angsty looks. The only bright side is that I completely forgot about the trip to Santorini until literally hours before we were supposed to leave.

It's Lars's birthday and I dropped a ton of money almost a year ago to get just the right spot to celebrate.

And the private plane ride to the Greek Isles is as awkward as can be. Silent. Angry. Full of her annoyed sighs.

But now… we're here. And we're not alone. Lars, Finn, Kalindi, and Pippa now stand between me and Nika, thankfully letting some of the tension out of the situation.

"Oh…" Lars says as he climbs the ramp and steps onto the gleaming white deck of the palatial estate I've rented in the Greek isles for the weekend.

Our mansion is made of perfectly sun-bleached white stone and topped with a brilliant copper dome. Heat snakes up from the perfect sapphire and cerulean water as it glistens all around us. A servant appears, taking our small party's bags into the house.

"Man, this is seriously swanky," Lars says, looking out at the small village of sun-bleached white buildings and rounded copper roofs.

He looks back at me, his grin bright. "You organized this for my birthday?"

I can't scowl, which is the only thing I feel like doing. So I keep my expression neutral. "I did."

I planned this almost a year ago, back when I was still Stellan's private secretary. Back before I realized that dragging a very uncomfortable Annika on this overnight trip would be so... tense.

To put it mildly.

I slide my gaze over to Annika now. She catches my gaze and whirls away, her cheeks turning a dusky rose color.

The color looks good on her. But it's also been her only reaction to me for days and I'm really starting to wonder just how far over the line I took things the other day.

I could've easily taken it so much further... just thinking about it makes my body harden.

Pippa tosses her red hair, looking stately. "Annika, Kalindi, do you want to go sun ourselves on the front deck?" She points to where she means, but Annika already has an answer.

"Yes!" Annika says. She glances at me, flushing prettily, and then hurries away.

Kalindi casts a dour look at me and follows her friend. Pippa looks around at Lars, Finn, and I. She shrugs and then moves off after them.

Oblivious to the tension simmering between Annika and me, Lars claps me on the back and points to the house. "I think I see a bar set up just inside the window there. Let's go check it out."

He takes off. Finn follows, always the darkest, quietest one of the Løve siblings. I don't think of Finn very often or really ask him to things. I'm not even sure who invited to this trip, but I'm glad he's here. One more person between me and Annika can't hurt anything.

Then again, you could put a whole country between us, and somehow things would still be stifling. With a sigh on my lips, I start heading after them.

The second we step into what appears to be a rather extravagant library, a servant hurries to pour us each a glass of bourbon.

"Thank you," I murmur. The servant bows his head. I turn to Lars, toasting. "To Lars, the reason for this little getaway."

Finn merely cocks his dark head and raises his glass. "Hear, hear."

We all sip what I am sure is remarkably fine bourbon, wandering back out onto the broad terrace. I look down at the private dock, which is only probably a hundred feet down from where I'm standing.

It's beautiful outside today with azure waves and little white peaks as far as the eye can see. There isn't a cloud in the sky either.

If I wanted to be here, it would be perfect weather for sailing. I look at the all-white power boats bobbing at their docks, calling to me.

Lars looks at the boats too, turning toward me. "We're going to race those, right?"

I wiggle my eyebrows. "I was only waiting for you to suggest it."

Finn chuckles and Lars grins, sipping his whiskey.

I love boat racing. Actually, I love any kind of adrenaline-pumping, action-packed sport. The idea of taking one of those boats out and pushing it full throttle excites me beyond reason.

Finn finishes his tumbler of bourbon first. "I'm ready. I should get the girls, *ja?*"

Lars laughs. "Definitely at least offer to take one of them in the boat with me. I don't know if any of you have seen Pippa or Kalindi in a bikini, but the idea of having one of them clinging to my arm while I win the race— "

I snort. "Dream on, Lars. You'll still have to race against me… and I don't usually lose."

Lars rolls his eyes. "Get ready to eat your words, Erik."

A smile tugs at my lips. "We'll see about that. I do like a challenge."

We head down to the docks, Finn lagging behind to get the girls on board. Each of the boats already has the keys in the ignition. I'm standing behind the steering wheel and gunning the engine when I realize that Annika is standing on the dock, glaring at me. She looks particularly fierce just now, with her long wavy hair falling to her waist and her very skimpy black bikini. She wears a white sarong around her waist, but almost every other inch of sun-kissed skin is on full display.

A shudder runs down my spine just looking at her. I raise my brows, turning to check on the other guys. Both of them are helping a girl onto their boat… leaving me with their little sister.

"Shit," I mutter. Looking back to Annika, I step to the side and offer her a hand up. "Come on."

Her mouth twists a little, but she accepts my help, her warm palms slipping beneath mine. She weighs virtually nothing as I help her aboard; when she makes the jump onto the deck, I steady her with a hand on her waist.

There is a split second where I hold her, staring down into those guileless eyes.

For just a second, I see something in her eyes… some kind of carnal interest that makes my hands tighten on her waist.

But then in the next second she brushes off my touch and tosses her hair. "Can I drive?"

My eyes narrow on her as she turns and walks over to the steering wheel. She walks right up to the wheel and turns around, a pout already on her lips.

"I don't think so," I say, rolling my eyes.

"Hey!" Lars calls. "Are you guys ready? The last boat to reach… twenty miles? The loser makes drinks tonight, ja?"

I jog a few paces until I stand right behind Annika. "*Ja!*"

Annika turns around, pinning me with her fiery gaze. Her full lips smirk. "Don't just say no. I need you to teach me how, Erik."

My heart stutters. My mind goes blank, short-circuiting. I can tell that she's teasing me. She definitely intended to get exactly this reaction from me.

As soon as I regain some amount of control over myself, I scowl. The other boats pull out, so there really isn't time to argue.

Stepping up to the helm, I just shake my head. "Fine. You steer, okay?"

Annika shoots me the most mischievous look ever over her shoulder. Putting the boat into gear, I move my hand under her arm to the throttle, which is to the left side of the steering wheel.

As the boat shoots forward out of its slip, Annika's lithe body pushes back against mine. I'm already hard for her and I grind against her ass. She freezes up for a second and her muscles lock up… but after a second she relaxes, leaning her head back against my chest. She grins as we take off and gives an excited whoop.

God, she feels so good right now. Her scent is everywhere for a second as we speed up, her hair blowing in every direction too.

Using one hand to steady the wheel, I keep the other on the throttle, pinning her in place.

I try to keep my eyes on the horizon, or at least the other two boats which are the best part of a mile ahead. But with Annika pressed against my torso like this, all I can think of is her incredibly soft skin.

It's as smooth and soft as silk, as warm and gently scented as fresh honey. I'm so close to burying my whole face into her shoulder, to biting and teasing her flesh until she pleads for me to touch her…

She turns her head, shouting for her words to be heard over the rush of air all around us. "Are we still in a fight, Erik?"

It takes all my self-restraint not to nuzzle her neck and nip at her ear. I frown, having to actively work at not letting my eyes stray down to her tits. I mean, they are right there.

Just waiting for me to fondle them, to cup them and pinch her nipples.

"No, Nika," I grate out.

She grins. "Okay. That's good, I guess."

She shifts her weight against my torso, pressing against my cock. My eyes close briefly. My face screws up. I let out a soft sound of interest that she probably can't even hear.

When I open my eyes though, I see her biting her lower lip and looking at me like…

Well, her expression is one of pure want. She's giving me these fuck me eyes and I literally can't think about anything else.

"Annika… we can't," I say, slowing our boat.

She narrows her eyes. "Why, because you're the king's best friend and I'm just his emptyheaded little sister?"

Shaking my head, I separate our bodies. "That's one reason. There are about a million more. Now if you don't mind?"

Annika's expression screws up. I can tell that the next thing out of her mouth is going to be a protest. Pulling her by the arm, I push her behind me. "Sit down and be quiet."

Her expression turns stormy. But before she can say anything, I stop her with a begging look and two simple words. "Please, Annika."

Her eyebrows lift. Then she gives in, stops pushing against me.

I turn around so that I can't see her anymore as I start to re-engage the throttle. But she doesn't utter another word of protest. She just sits down behind me and glares at my back so hard that I swear a hole starts to form between my shoulder blades.

All I can think is that when we get off of this boat, I'm probably going to get a fucking earful from her. Pushing the boat's throttle all the way, I shake my head and try to focus on the task at hand.

Chapter Twenty-Three

ANNIKA

LOOKING out over the moonlit shore, I tilt my head. The sea is so beautiful and calm just now, a great black mass that seems utterly still. The rocky white coast cuts into it at the edge and bleeds as far as the eye can see. The whole village of Santorini is asleep, the white buildings seeming like nothing so much as jumbled teeth jutting out, reaching toward the night sky.

I stand on my private balcony and shiver just a bit though it isn't cold. I'm wearing nothing but a filmy white négligée and feeling as though I nearly blend in with the white sandstone mansion behind me.

"What are you still doing up?"

Erik's deep voice nearly gives me a heart attack. I whirl, backing up against the little balcony railing. He appears out of the shadows in my room, stepping into the moonlit-drenched doorway.

God, he's handsome. His flaxen hair is messed up just a little bit. His hazel eyes and aristocratic nose war with his too-expressive lips. All that on top of a mountain of a man… a mountain elegantly carved from the richest stone, his muscles making him a true work of art.

And he's shirtless at the moment, clad only in a pair of low-slung jeans that show off his chest hair and his entrancing happy trail.

"What are you doing in here?" I ask, frowning. "And why aren't you wearing a shirt?"

He shrugs a muscular shoulder, the very picture of grace and power. "I'm not sure."

I bite my lower lip. "I can't sleep," I say. My head falls to the side as I look him up and down. "I mean, I usually struggle to fall asleep at the palace. But here, far away from all the noise, I find it too quiet."

He steps out onto the balcony and looks out toward the sea. "Me too," he admits. "I thought the sound of the sea so close by would lull me, but instead it just makes me…"

I exhale, knowing just how he feels. "Restless?"

That serious gaze finds me, narrowing on my face. He nods slowly. "Yes."

I toss my head, scrunching my nose. "Same here."

He is quiet for a moment, scanning the beach below. "I thought you would still be fuming about what happened between us on the boat."

I arch a brow. "Would that help either of us?"

A smile tugs at Erik's lips. "Definitely not."

Shrugging, I perch on the edge of the railing, carefully tucking the ends of my silky négligée beneath me. "I have to say, I'm sort of baffled."

He looks at me, surprised. "About what?"

I pluck at the hem of my nighty. "Well… you said there are a million reasons why you can't… *be* with me again. I was wondering what those are, exactly."

His brows rise. "You still need me to list them?"

I stare at the hem of my négligée. "Well… yes. I think I do."

He chuckles. "Okay…"

Wrapping his arms across his chest, he leans against the railing, just an arm's length away. "God, where do I even begin? Aside from you being the little sister to my best friend in the world, of course."

I tilt my head, considering him. "Naturally."

Erik sighs. "You're also so young."

"I'm almost twenty." I straighten my spine, trying to seem… old enough, I guess.

A rumble bursts from somewhere low in his chest. "You make me feel old, Annika."

I roll my eyes. "We're not even a decade apart in age."

He slides me a disgruntled look. "There is the fact that you are the only Danish princess. And I'm a commoner."

I push out my cheek with my tongue. "At least you are Danish. Stellan fell for an American journalist."

He squints. "Yes, but he is the king."

"And I am, as you pointed out, the only princess. Besides, you're practically one of us."

Erik cocks his head, looking at me. "I'm very far away from that and we both know it. And anyway, shouldn't we both be disgusted by the fact that we essentially grew up together?"

I press my lips together into a thin line. "Hah! Very funny. You didn't even acknowledge my existence until I returned from boarding school. I hardly think that qualifies."

Erik's gaze focuses on my face. "What do I have to say to make myself perfectly clear? Nothing will happen between us. I mean, nothing *more*. Even if none of those things were the truth, there would still be a fundamental difference between us."

I tilt my head. "Are you talking about our personalities?"

His lips twist. "Yes. You're off playing fashionista and preening while I'm just— "

"Being boring?" I suggest, cocking a brow.

He rolls his eyes and shakes his head. "You're attracted to me. Either you have bad taste or I'm not as stiff as you claim."

I bite my lip, trying to hide my smile. A blush creeps up my cheeks, warming me. "Oh? You're not stiff? Is that really what you want to claim?"

Wiggling my eyebrows at Erik makes color rise in his cheeks, setting off the jade in his eyes.

He glares at me. "That's not what I meant, and you know it. But yes, there are some fatal flaws in our… attraction to one another."

"I see. You want to just break everything down into simple thoughts. Black and white. Cats and dogs. Either it is raining or it's not. X or Y. It must be frustrating to live in that kind of a codified world."

He raises his eyebrows at me. "Do you think that I'm wrong?"

I suck in a deep breath and let it out, taking a second with my answer. "I'm saying that there are lots of things in between black and white. There is a whole world of colors and you have limited it down to just the two. So yes, I do you think you're wrong."

I turn toward the French doors that are open behind me. He reaches out and grabs my arm as I start moving in that direction. I give him a hard look. "Easy. I'm just getting a drink. Do you want some champagne?"

His fingers tighten on my arm and I bite my lip, looking up into his face. His eyes sparkle like twin tiger's eye gemstones, making me feel more seen then I ever have in my life.

He's angry, I can tell.

For second, I think he is going to break, to sweep me off my feet and kiss me.

But he doesn't. Erik releases me and I give him a smirk, shaking my head as I head inside. Once I go in the living room area, I look around and find the bar.

It's the work of a minute to find a suitable bottle of champagne and two glasses. As I pop the bottle, Erik saunters in the house behind me, making a striking silhouette against the bright moonlit night sky behind him. I smile and pour the champagne, handing him a glass.

He accepts the flute with two fingers, watching me carefully as he prowls around the living room. I take a sip of my champagne and crinkle my nose in surprise at the bubbly, acidic flavor. Erik swirls the champagne around in his glass, looking at me while he takes a sip.

I brush past him, smiling and shaking my head. He follows me out to the patio again, looking at me while I take a seat on the white wicker patio furniture. I glance up at him and pat the seat beside me. "Join me on the couch. Come on, the view is very nice."

After a second, he moves around to sit on the couch beside me. He looks out at the beach, the rolling sea relentless as ever in its pursuit of reaching the beach.

Erik doesn't say a word. He just sips his champagne and looks off into the horizon. I bite my lip and put my feet into his lap, stretching out. He looks down at my feet and then looks at me, his expression one of surprise.

I shrug shoulder. "What? I'm just being comfortable. I'm comfortable around you. Is that okay?"

He stares at my feet again and only and then smooths the top palm of his hand over the top of my foot. Even this slight touch warms me from inside out. He glances up at me, our gazes connecting. And then he just keeps stroking my foot, my ankle, my lower leg. All the while, he seems like a caged tiger ready to pounce.

I've driven him to this, I know it. There's no question that tension has been right in the air between the two of us for some time. If I am honest about it, the tension started to build the second he walked out on me after we fucked.

This is overdue.

I smirk at him and finish my wine, setting my glass aside. His gaze drops to my legs, where the silky fabric of my négligée meets my bare thighs. It's a powerful thing to be looked at in that way by a man like Erik.

He glances up at me, licking his lips, his expression tortured.

"Nika…" he whispers. "I meant what I said before. All the reasons that I listed for why we shouldn't even be touching right now… They are still real. If we slip up and fuck each other's brains out, the reasons will still be between us when we wake up in the morning."

I bite my lip. I know that he is just waiting for a sign, something urging him on. So, I open my knees a little wider, using two fingers to draw up the silky white négligée up my leg. Inch by creamy bare inch, my thighs are exposed to his view. Soon I reach the apex of my thighs, but I don't stop. I draw all the négligée up until my pussy lips are bare before him and widen my knees a little more.

Erik looks at me, swallowing. His gaze is so brooding and intense that meeting his eyes is more difficult than it should be. But I don't look away.

When I speak, my voice shakes more than it ought to. It's only then that I realize how badly I want him, how badly I want to feel his touch and all the things that come along with it. I want to feel the pleasure that I know that only he can give me.

A whisper leaves my lips. "If you want me, I am here for you. All you have to do to get me is just reach out your hand and take what is on offer."

He reaches out his hand and glides it up the inside of my thigh. He licks his lips, his gaze focused on my pussy. Then he reaches out a single finger and runs it up my wet slit, biting his lip as he gathers my moisture.

Shudders of electricity run up and down my spine. My breasts feel like they are achy and throbbing, just like my clit. I let my head fall backward and release the breathiest little moan, my lips parting.

He glances up at me and brings his finger up to his lips, popping it in his mouth and moaning at the taste of me. I swear, I've never seen anything sexier than a man who is that turned on by the way I taste.

When Erik sits back, pushes my feet out of his lap, and stands up, I don't know exactly what's going on. He offers me his hand and I take it, my heart going crazy in my chest.

I lick my lips and allow him to pull me to my feet. He gives me a little tug and I come into his arms so easily, like a choreographed dance move executed perfectly. I press up against the shelter of his hard body and I look up at him with wide eyes. He looks back at me with nothing but desire. It's all over his face, written so clearly that I could scream.

"I do want you, princess. I always want you, even when I shouldn't. That's my secret." He tucks a strand of my hair back behind my ear and tips my head up, leaning down and brushing his lips over mine. His kiss is burning, his touch so rough that I'm sure it will leave marks. But it lights a fire deep inside me, a burning inferno that I can't deny even if I wanted to.

"Yes," I say against his lips. "Please, Erik. Please…"

And just like that, he scoops me up in his arms and heads inside, leaving me shivering in his arms while he finds the bed.

Chapter Twenty-Four

ERIK

I STRIP WITHOUT THOUGHT. With one hand, I cup her chin upward towards my mouth. The other pulls her close against me. My hardness slips with ease between the heat of her soft thighs.

That little négligée teases me, looking so perfect against Nika's tanned skin.

I need more, want more, and by the way Nika responds, I know she does, too. I start to walk her backward, through the open bedroom door. When the back of her knees hit the bed frame, she sits down, her cherry red lips inches from my cock.

Before she can react, I lift her négligée over her head. I take a long moment to admire her, all that naked skin bare before my hungry eyes. I bend her back and bite my lip. Her pink nipples are already hard, her pussy damp, and my length hardens more, desperate for her.

But I am not about to give in yet. Instead, I twist the silky white négligée around her wrists like makeshift handcuffs. Slowly, I lower her bound hands and gently push her onto her back. Nika lifts her head to watch while I lower my lips to the full breasts I'd fantasized about non-stop since the last time I got her naked.

As I begin to nibble on one nipple, I pinch and squeeze the other. Nika lets out faint gasps and wriggles against her cuffs, which hold her captive.

My cock presses against one of her thighs, covering her skin in a thin coat of wetness.

"Please," she whimpers. She begins to whip her head from side to side while I move down her stomach with soft kisses. When I get down to her glistening pussy lips, I place a single light kiss on her clit. She lets out a loud groan, spreads her legs wide, and presses herself to my mouth. I smile up at her, though her eyes are screwed shut.

God, I love the way she makes me feel. This? This moment?

This is everything.

I kiss her again, deeper, using just a little flick of my tongue. Her clit is swollen and plump. With my every touch, she responds. I trace my tongue up the inside of her thighs and across the crest of her mound. Nika pants my name when I come close to her glistening clit, but I tease her mercilessly. Instead of the kisses and licks she clearly craves, I blow across her clit and order her to open her legs wider.

She calls out my name. It has never sounded sweeter than when it trips off her tongue.

She is so ready, her juices already starting to drip from her opening. I test her with a finger, which she pushes against greedily. As my finger enters her, ever so slowly, I taste her clit and feel her muscles tighten around my knuckle. I pull my finger out, though she does her best to press against my hand and keep me inside.

My index finger is covered in her clinging wetness. I hold my hand up to her and press my thumb and forefinger together so she could see just how wet she is. Nika leans up to suck my hand, but I pull away and trace her areola with her sweetness.

"More," she murmurs.

"More what?" I ask. I tighten my grip on the négligée as she starts to struggle again. At the same time, I tease her opening with two fingers and kiss her clit.

"Erik… Please, give me more," she demands breathlessly.

I slide two fingers into her. Nika cries out as I begin to work her clit, licking and sucking. When she begins to fuck my hand, writhing her hips against me, I let her. I match her rhythm with my mouth. Her inner muscles begin the tremble. When I can tell she is close, I make her slow down. I raise my head, switch my mouth for my thumb, and let my eyes feast on the glorious sight of Nika about to come.

With her head tossed back, eyes shut, and mouth open, she is an absolute vision. "Are you going to come for me?" I ask as I start to fuck her faster with my hand.

"Yes," she says. Nika opens her eyes and looks at me. I release her wrists just enough so she can prop herself onto her elbows and watch. "I'm close," she says.

"I want you to come in my mouth," I command. "I want to taste you."

"I can't—"

"Come in my mouth, Nika," I repeat. My tongue returns to her clit. I explore every crevice of her. When I can tell she was close to coming, I slow down again. I remove my finger from her even as she cries out in frustration—only to begin to moan when my tongue dives into her center.

"Please," she says when I trail my tongue from her opening to her wet clit.

"Come for me, Nika," I whisper. "Come right now."

Immediately, she weaves her fingers into my hair and pulls my lips against her center. I grip her hips on either side of my face and meet her furious pace. She fucks my face, my mouth, like it is all she'd ever wanted. Every time she cries out my name it makes me harder, makes me want her more. "I'm coming," she says. "Oh, fuck, right now."

I ready myself for the flood of her sweetness, but what she gave me I'd never have expected. Along with the gush of her coming, the juices that pour onto my tongue, I feel the stream of her squirting across my lower face. It drizzles along my throat and to my chest.

Holy *fuck*. That was surprising in the best way.

She is wetter than anyone I have seen before. Carefully, I lick up every last drop of her moisture. When I kiss her clit one last time, she shivers.

As I raise my head, I saw that she is flushed. Nika clutches the balled-up négligée to her face. "I'm sorry," she says. "That's never happened before… It just feels so damn amazing and—"

"Sorry?" I interrupt. "For what? That was the hottest fucking thing I've ever seen."

"Really?" she asks. Nika chews at her lower lip and gives me a half smile. I get up from my knees and she looks down my body. "You're still hard," she says, almost surprised.

"After making you come with my mouth and feeling you squirt? I'm harder than I've ever been in my whole life," I say with a laugh.

She brings a hand to my package, caressing it, but I catch her wrist. She looks up at me, piercing me with her gaze.

"Please?" she asks.

I smile at her. "I need you to tell me what you want," I say. "Please, what?"

"Please… let me have your cock," she says. She reaches for me with her other hand, but I catch it, too.

"I don't know," I say. "What do you want to do with it?"

"You'll see," she purrs. "Please."

Nika leans forward and takes my tip between her lips. I can't resist anymore. I drop her wrists and comb her hair back with my fingers so I can watch her swallowing my cock. Those lips I've dreamt of for the past two weeks are finally on me and feel better than I could imagine.

Nika licks the full length of my shaft and sucks gently on my tip. With her hand at my base, she takes me slowly all the way to the back of her throat. "Jesus," I mutter, unable to resist the urge to hold her head and guide her.

She makes satisfied little sounds in the back of her throat as she licks and sucks. "You're going to make me come," I warn her, my fingers twisting in her long hair.

Nika releases me. "Come in me," she says as she strokes me with a hand slick with saliva.

I pause. "What?"

"Come in me," she repeats. "Please. I need you to fuck me." She pushes herself back along the bed and opens her thighs to me. One of her hands pulls at her nipple while the other circles her clit.

"Say it again," I demand as I crawl toward her.

"Please fuck me," she whispers into my ear.

Positioning myself between her legs, I slide into her with ease and exhale at how fucking good she feels. Tight, wet, and warm.

Nika digs her nails into my lower back to keep me deep inside her. "Slow," she says. "I want to feel you."

I start to fuck her, slow and controlled, while I kiss and suck at her neck.

"Stay," she says suddenly as she pulls me as tight as she could against her. "Fuck… damn, I'm already coming again."

I feel the waves of her orgasm squeezing against me, stroking my cock rhythmically. It feels so intense that I can feel the edge approaching.

"Nika," I say. "Jesus, you're going to make me come right now."

"Come in me," she pants through her waves of pleasure. "Please, I need it."

I release myself into her with a cry, pumping my orgasm into her willing body. Nika calls my name as another wave of orgasm hits her.

"Oh my God," she repeats over and over. "Oh, Erik…"

I feel the aftershock of orgasms roll through her, each one squeezing out another drop of my cum.

As the sweat cools on my body, I just stretch out beside Nika and look at her. Her blonde hair is messy, her cheeks are flushed the loveliest pink I've ever seen. She pulls the soft-looking white sheet up from where we managed to kick it off and tucks it around her body. She seems a little embarrassed to have me look at her naked now that we are not actually having sex.

Turning on my side, I reach out a lazy hand and trail it down her hip, tugging the sheet down as I go. She looks at me, her pale eyes suspicious.

"What are you doing, Erik?"

My lips twitch. "I just like to look at you. Is that so wrong?"

Her cheeks turn bright red for a second. "I think you just like to wind me up."

I think that she expects me to crack a joke or maybe say something dirty. But instead I move little closer and brush a few strands of hair back behind her ear, cupping her jaw tenderly. I brush a kiss over her lips, thinking how much I like her.

"I like looking at you. I like the way that you have little freckles all over your body. I like your breasts and ass. I like your face. And when you aren't busy being mad at me, I really like your sense of humor and lack of pretentiousness. I think it's a shame that you try to hide things that are so magnificent. That's all."

She looks me deep in the eyes and swallows a little nervously. "I think you are handsome too."

I smiled a little and kissed her good. "I wasn't fishing for compliments. It just seems like there are so many parts of you that are beautiful and yet, you don't even seem to notice. That seems wrong."

Her eyebrows lift an inch. Her cheeks flame. If she could squirm out of the bed and hide herself, I'm pretty sure she would take that option. "Well… thanks, I guess."

I brush one more kiss over her luscious lips and then settle back on my side, studying her. She looks away for a moment and then pulls the sheet back up, tucking it in around her body.

I exhale deeply and prop my head up on my hand. She doesn't look at me, can't meet my gaze. I reach out to touch her sheet-covered hip again, moving my hand along the neat line created by the piece of fabric.

I'm not sure why she is so shy. She's gorgeous and I think you would have to be crazy to not realize it. Maybe it's just because she's so young. In the back of my mind, I rebuke myself again for being attracted to her, for sleeping with her. But I can't help what I feel.

And I definitely don't regret having made the decision to bring her into my bed. At least, not now. Not while I am still in her thrall.

I run my hand up her arm, just enjoying the feeling of touching her soft skin. It feels luxurious, lying in bed with her in this mansion in the Greek Isles. My whole life is pretty decadent… But this takes the cake.

I glance up and catch her staring at me as if she is trying to puzzle something out. "What?"

She bites her lip, hesitating for a second before she speaks. Her voice is husky, reminding me of the fact that we just had sex. She shrugs a shoulder. "Nothing. I just… I think I just realize how much I like you. And I'm trying to figure out if saying that aloud will make me look like a little girl or not."

I flash her a smirk. "I like you too, Nika."

She blushes bright pink. "Yeah?"

I pull her closer with the hand to her lower back. Just touching her like this, pulling her close to my body once more, I can already feel myself getting hard for her again.

"Yes, I think it's fair to say that we are on the same page. I can't go five minutes without thinking about you. If that's not some kind of infatuation, I don't know what is."

Nika rubs her hips against mine and presses her lips up against my mouth. "Will I ruin it if I tell you I've never felt this way about anyone else before?"

God, she's looking at me with those pretty, innocent eyes and touching me with those dainty little hands. It's enough to make a lesser man tremble.

"No," I whisper. I kiss her again. "God. If I never stopped kissing you, it wouldn't be enough for me. I just can't get enough of you."

Wrapping her arms around my neck, she smiles into my kiss. "It feels like this is…"

She trails off, an echo of uncertainty crossing her face. I reach out and brush some of her hair back, looking at her amazing features.

"Don't censor yourself for me."

She pins me with her gaze. "I was just going to say… This feels like more than a one night stand. I mean, I could be wrong. I've never been with anybody else. But…"

I look her dead in the eye, completely serious. "It can be more than that, if you want it to be. I'm having trouble imagining how I'm supposed to just let you walk away after what we just did."

Her smile is slow, but it definitely grows on her face. "Really?"

I nod, flashing her a dimpled smile. "I'm serious as a heart attack. We can't be together in a long-term sense, but that doesn't mean that we can't… explore each other, I guess."

She kisses me then, so eager and so hot that I nearly forget what I just said.

We can't be together in a long-term sense.

That bit is vital to keeping my life plan on track. Though just now, with Annika in my arms, it's unbelievably hard to focus on that fact.

I deepen the kiss and we are quickly swept away in a storm of our own passion.

Chapter Twenty-Five

ANNIKA

AT THE END of the weekend, everyone is packing to say goodbye. I stand next to Pippa, folding a barely-there bikini and giving her side eye. She tucks a strand of her red hair behind her ear and straightens her giant flouncy skirt, shooting me a questioning look.

"What?" she asks.

I turn my head, checking that the door to the sunny bedroom that we are in is mostly closed. Then I shrug. "I was wondering when you and Lars were going to come out and admit that you're a couple."

Her eyes widen and she looks up, a bit surprised. "What? We're not a couple. We're just friends. I thought that you of all people would not fall into the trap that everyone else does. You have guy friends, don't you?"

I scrunch up my face. "Not really."

Pippa up rolls her eyes and straightens her spine. In the strappy black tank top and the long black skirt she is wearing, she looks like a model. She even has a couple of inches on me and I fancy myself unusually tall for a girl.

"Sure you do. What about Erik?"

A laugh bubbles up from inside my chest. "I don't think of him as being a friend. He is…" I pause, trying to figure out exactly how to phrase it. What is Erik, anyway?

My lover? My babysitter? My mouth twists. "He's just working with me and keeping watch over me until Stellan gets married. That's the deal. My grandmother has worked out a plan with Erik in which he will get a title for doing her bidding." I roll my eyes. "It's all very upper crust royalty stuff."

Pippa looks down at her skirt, picking a piece of lint off and biting her lip. Her British accent is particularly strong just now. "I have eyes too, you know. I saw you and Erik kissing yesterday when you thought no one was looking. It's all very cloak and dagger but you can't think that it will go unnoticed by anyone for too long. That's just not the way that things work."

Kalindi comes to the door, knocking before nudging it open. "Are you guys ready? Because the cars are waiting outside to take us to the airport."

I shoot Pippa a smile and pick up my linen-covered suitcase, setting it down on its dark wheels. "I think we're ready. Right, Pippa?"

Pippa smiles and then nods. She picks up her suitcase and rolls it out of the room. When I go to follow her, Kalindi stops me with an arm across the doorway. I look at her, raising an eyebrow. "Yes? Is there something that you want to talk about?"

Kalindi's eyes narrow. "I saw you and Erik together this morning. How could you keep this from me?"

I look at her, my cheeks flushing. This is the second time I've been called out on this exact thing in this exact room. God, Erik and I are really doing a terrible job of hooking up in secret. I blow out a breath.

"It just happened. I just… I didn't tell you because it's all still very new. We don't even know what this is yet."

Kalindi opens her mouth to say something, but then Lars comes clattering down the hall, looking like he means business. "Are you guys kidding right now? We're all waiting on you. Let's go."

He points down the hall, ushering both of us toward the front of the house. Kal gives me a look that says that we are definitely going to talk about this later. But I just give her a soft smile and don't feel any need to continue the conversation.

As I pull my suitcase along behind me, I find Erik in the kitchen, his phone pressed to his ear. His expression looks intense and he's pacing back and forth. He spots me and puts his hand over the phone's speaker.

"Do you mind waiting for just another few minutes? Let the others go. They are on a different flight anyway." He doesn't even wait for me to nod or say anything, he just goes back to arguing with someone on the other end of the phone. "Yes, I'm still here. I'm trying to talk to someone about my father..."

His father? My eyes widen a little. I've met his father once, which was enough for me. I was 12 and his father dressed me down for what he called inappropriate riding gear, whatever *that* means.

How Erik managed to escape that man without ending up with a nasty temper of his own, I have no idea.

Leaving my suitcase by the door, I shoot Erik a single backward glance and then head out to say goodbye to my brothers and my friends. It's a relatively quick affair; as soon as I say my goodbyes, they are hustled into the back of a big white limousine and then the vehicle trundles out, heading down the steep driveway.

I stay put for a second, squinting out towards the ocean. It's looking especially blue today, just an azure hue that makes all the white buildings and tan sand of the beach stand out.

I hear Erik shouting into the phone. "Why not?" He pauses. "Then get him back on the phone!"

I turn, surprised. He is quiet for a second. I'm aware of the hot Grecian sun on my shoulders as I float back toward the front door.

"Are you kidding me? He's an old man. Make him do it! He— "

Erik falls silent. I can't stay away now, not without knowing more of what is going on.

When I follow his angry voice back inside, I find Erik furiously tossing his phone down on the counter. He walks away, pressing his fingertips to his golden hair just beyond his temples.

I bite my lip, hesitating to say anything. Erik gets upset like anyone else. But I have rarely ever heard him yell at someone... and never on the phone. He is just radiating this angry, frustrated energy right now and it's freaking me out.

I frown as I approach him.

He looks up at me with an irritated expression. Clearing his throat, he shakes his head. "I'm sorry. That... that was someone from the hospital closest to the palace. My father was taken in yesterday. It took them a full day to get in contact with me."

My eyes widen. I step closer to him, reaching out and touching his inner arm. He looks at me, still scowling.

"Is your father okay? What happened?"

He pulls a face. "Apparently my father had a heart attack."

It takes me a second to fully absorb that fact. "Heart attack... how bad?"

He frowns. "I don't know. The doctors can't really tell me much. Apparently, my dad is awake, and he is clamoring to leave the hospital already. I thought... I thought that I was going to have to rush to get on the plane and fly back to Copenhagen. You know, to be with him. But as it turns out, he doesn't want to see me. In fact, he forbade the doctors from contacting me. I just got lucky that there was a rebellious nurse on my dad's case. I guess she felt like someone should know where to find him."

I'm at a loss for words. I know that we don't have a language worked out between us for how we comfort each other. But now seems like a good time to start figuring that out.

I hug him, using my lightest touch and looping my arms around his waist. I rest my head against his chest, feeling a little overwhelmed by his news.

"I'm sorry," I murmur.

I feel his arms come around my back, holding me a little closer. His lips find the back of my head and he takes a deep breath. When he lets it out, I look up at him. His expression is nothing short of tortured.

"We should go to the airport. If we leave now, we can be back in Copenhagen this afternoon."

He flinches. "My father doesn't want me to come to the hospital. He told the doctors and nurses that he is fine. Which is just not true, obviously, but..."

I rock back and forth ever so slightly as I hold him, because that feels like a comforting gesture. "Do you want to be there?"

His expression turns bitter. "I don't know. I would like to be able to make that choice. I mean, I would like for once to just be a normal kid with a normal parent. But I guess I should've given up on that a long time ago."

I bite my lip, frowning. "If you want to go, or you want to at least be in Copenhagen right now, we should go. No matter what your father's mental status might be... we should go. If your father isn't giving you what you need, you have to take it. Sometimes, you just have to take what you deserve."

He pulls back an inch, looking down at me with the most intense expression. He scans my face. "How did you become so wise?"

I suddenly feel awkward. Shrugging a shoulder, I give my head a tiny shake. "I don't know. It doesn't really matter, does it? We can be at the airport in twenty minutes and be in the air in forty. That's enough for me."

He frowns, looking pensive. "You know what I just figured out? I just realized that there is a lot more to you than meets the eye. You're way, way deeper than you want people to think."

I give him a sad little smile. "Maybe."

He takes a deep breath and closes his eyes ever so briefly. Then he drops a kiss on my lips and steps back, turning toward where he left his phone.

Before I know it, we are bundled into the back of the limo, heading for the private airport. I keep looking at Erik, needing to reassure myself or maybe comfort him. But he just looks worried, not paying any attention to me. We pull up to the tarmac and he slides me a look, giving me a brief smile. Then he squeezes my hand and opens the door.

He slides out before I can even think of what to say. And I follow him after a second, reminding myself that his needs come first right now.

Chapter Twenty-Six

ERIK

I LOOK out over the city lights of Copenhagen, standing on the penthouse balcony of this building that is near the hospital where my father is staying. I have always known that this place was owned by the royal family, but it's Annika's first time here. She's somewhere behind me, through the open patio doors and in the lavish luxury loft. If you can call this place a loft…

After all, it may be only one room, but it's also the entire floor. At some point, you reach a place where it's just ridiculous to call any place like this something so silly as a loft.

I suck in a breath and shake my head. I picked this place because of its proximity to Copenhagen's best hospital. But my father is still refusing to see me. I flew back to Copenhagen and put Nika at risk of the paparazzi finding out that she is in town. I did all that for no reason, as it turns out.

Why is my father such a bastard?

"Erik?"

I turn to find Nika just steps behind me, looking concerned. She beckons me inside. "Come on. You haven't eaten all day. Let me make you a sandwich or something, at least."

My eyebrows raise. Lured by her offer and no little amount of curiosity, I step inside and close the doors behind me. The walls of the loft are all glass. Everything inside is sleek and light colored and modern. The over-large living room area that is to my left, the dining room table set up to my right, and straight ahead is a truly luxurious kitchen that any chef would die to have.

I follow Annika toward it, noting the stainless steel appliances and the huge marble island. She walks to the refrigerator and opens it, biting her lip as she frowns at the contents.

"Oh, I thought… I assumed that there would be… like sandwich things or something." She flushes, looking up at me. "It looks like we are out of luck unless we want some expensive wine and cheese."

I exaggerate my eye roll for her benefit. "Move over, Princess. I'll make something very simple for us. You need to eat as much as I do."

I catch a tiny frown on her face, but it's gone as quickly as it appeared. She relinquishes her space at the fridge. I quickly assemble a platter of the expensive cheeses, bread, sliced fruits, and cucumbers. I add a couple glasses of sparkling wine, sliding it all onto the marble countertop.

Nika cants her head at me. "We should eat in the living room. Come on."

She picks up the platter of food and her champagne flute and makes her way to the living room. I snag the bowl of bread and my own drink, following her. I would never think to eat on the expensive looking white fabric couches that line the corner of the penthouse. But Princess Annika does it without thinking about it. She and I are just fundamentally different, I suppose.

She throws herself down on the couch, putting the wooden platter of food down beside herself. I take my own seat on the other side of her with more caution, settling the bread down between us. She glances at me, tucking her fair hair back behind her shoulder. She raises her glass, biting her lip.

"Is it tacky to toast right now?" That same little frown appears on her face.

I shake my head. "I don't think so, no. Cheers."

We clink our classes together and then I lift my flute to my lips, taking a long pull of the wine. It's extremely sweet but there is a certain satisfaction that I feel, a poor man toasting with the most expensive champagne in all of Denmark. That's nothing to sneeze at.

I sip my wine and look out at the dark landscape of Copenhagen. There are a million thoughts playing over and over again.

How my father is a bastard.

How I feel like I've done something to let him down, even though a part of me knows that that's not the truth.

How I'm sitting in this penthouse, surrounded by all of this obscene wealth and yet I know that none of it is mine.

So, I brood. I drink my champagne and nibble on a piece of cheese. And I think over all the things that have been bothering me ever since I got the fateful call this morning.

Nika sets her glass down and looks at me carefully. "I can see that you have a lot of things on your mind. Do you want to talk about it?"

I squint at her, finishing the last of my wine before setting my glass aside. "You don't really want to hear it. It's all just noise."

She bites her lip, a wrinkle appearing in her brow. "Yes, I do. I want to hear whatever you are thinking."

I arch my eyebrows at her and tilt my head. "Really?"

She rolls her eyes at me. "Yes, really. I'm here for you. I'm listening."

She adjusts her position on the couch, pulling her short white skirt down an inch and looking at me quite seriously. I shrug my shoulders, looking away over her shoulder at the darkened city skyline.

"I don't know. I was just thinking that…" I pause, trying to think of how to word what I am feeling. "I know that this emergency isn't about me. But I'm just so mad at my father. He is such a bastard. *Of course* he doesn't want the nurses fussing over him. He just wants… He just wants to go back to his little cottage and drink himself to death."

Nika frowns. "That has to be frustrating. It's hard to care for people that don't care about themselves."

I inhale a deep breath and nod. "My father makes it next to impossible. One minute he curses me for how invested I am in the royal family. He says that I am too uppity, and I need to learn my place. He seems to think that I belong back with him, working in the stables. And the next moment, he pushes me away, saying I'm a lost cause. It's definitely hard to be around him."

Her brows rise and she scoots forward, frowning at the platter of food between us. She gets up and moves to the other side of me, settling herself on the couch, one knee overlapping my own. She presses herself close, leaning her head against the couch.

I find myself grabbing her hand, twining our fingers. She gives me a squeeze, shooting me a comforting look. "I'm sorry that you have to deal with this. It isn't fair."

I squint off into the distance, uncomfortable just now with meeting her gaze. "I mean, it is what it is. Everybody has their things. If the royal family has taught me nothing else, it's that everyone's life is hard, no matter how glamorous it might seem from the outside."

The ghost of a smile crosses her lips. "That's very true. It doesn't lessen the burden for you, though."

I glance at her, scanning her face. "Ah, shit. I wish I hadn't told you any of it. I don't want to seem… I don't know. Weak, I guess."

Her eyebrows fly up. She leans close to me, her hand clutching my own. "Erik, look at me."

I still, my gaze latching onto hers. She looks so perfect and so untouchable in that moment. She grips my hand.

"When you are vulnerable with me, it makes me trust you more. It makes me feel like you're letting me in. It makes me feel so special. It's important to me that you understand that."

My eyes widen the little. I cocked my head, not quite knowing how to respond to that. I end up chuckling. "Okay… That sounds a little crazy but…"

"But nothing. It's how I feel. And that is the only true thing that I know." She leans in and offers her mouth up to me for a kiss.

I press my lips to hers, my thoughts in a mess. Her mouth feels so damn good beneath my lips, like honey and cinnamon and something utterly unique. She draws back after a second, her eyes shining with tears.

I didn't expect her to cry. That's the last thing in the world that I want right now.

I cup her face, using my thumbs to brush away the tears glittering in the corners of her eyes.

"Hey, hey. I thought we were getting along. What's the deal with the tears?"

She gives me a slow smile. "We are. I just… I guess I'm overwhelmed."

I take a moment to kiss her lips again and then whisper gently against them. "Is that a bad thing?"

She's shakes her head, putting her hands on my shoulders. "No. I think it's just a part of us growing closer. I think it's pretty natural to experience some wild emotions when you're… I mean… you know, whatever we are."

I trace my hands down her neck to her shoulders and then continue down until my hands grip her waist. I look at her, her beautiful, powder blue eyes seeming like they know my innermost thoughts. "And what are we, exactly?"

A hint of surprise shows on her features. "What do you mean?"

I bite my lip and smirk at her just a little. "Is this a relationship? Or are you going to leave me the second you get your freedom back?'

She closes her eyes for a brief second. I was only kidding, but now her hesitation has me sucking in a breath. When she opens her eyes again, there are wet with a fresh batch of tears.

When she speaks, it sounds like a threadbare whisper. "Are you asking me to be your girlfriend?"

My gaze tightens on her face. Am I asking that? I take a few seconds and exhale.

"I don't know. I mean… I know we aren't going to last forever. But it would be nice to pretend for a little while, wouldn't it?"

She launches herself into my arms, hugging me with such force that I can't breathe for a moment. She giggles and pushes me backwards on the couch, kissing me soundly. It's strange to feel her taking control for a moment. So, I wrested the control from her hands and flipped the script on her.

I reach up and grab her face, fisting both my hands in her hair and kissing her so hard that I swear I can almost taste blood. She doesn't lose an ounce of her eagerness, either.

She moans under my touch, writhing against my body like a heathen.

I pick her up and carry her into the first bedroom I find, stripping myself bare and then doing the same to her. And then I proceed to fuck her until we are both unable to move, hours and hours of skin to skin and clutched sheets and sultry moans.

In the dark, many hours later, we lie in bed together, me on my back and her on her side, pressed against me. Whatever anguish I was feeling before over my father's hospitalization, I feel empty now. I fucked it all out of my system, apparently. I lie on my back, sweat cooling, and think of absolutely nothing.

She's pulled the sheets up, very insistent on that fact. And I let it go because there isn't a damn thing I care about outside of this bedroom.

She surprises me by bringing up the same topic that we were talking about hours before.

"Can I tell you something?" she asks, her voice a frail thing.

My voice has gone to gravel. I clear my throat. "You can tell me anything, princess."

In the dark, I can just make out her shy smile. "I was just thinking about you and your father. And I realize that we have something in common."

I turned my head to look at her. "Oh yeah?"

She nods. "I think we both longed for approval as kids. Right?"

I shrug. "I guess so."

She makes a face. "We looked around for the people that were supposed to love us, namely our parents. And they weren't there. I know we had very different childhoods, but I think we have more in common than we think."

I give her a surprised look. "That's some pretty heavy thinking that you been doing."

She ducks her head. "After I read through that book on body positivity and self-love, I picked up a dozen more self-help books. It's slow going, but I'm finding out new things on every single page."

I stare at her for a beat. "I didn't realize that you were interested in all that. I mean, more than the radical self-love stuff."

She looks away for a moment. I imagine that her cheeks are glowing red by now. "Well, I am."

I reach out, turning her face back towards me. I place a gentle kiss on her lips and then look at her meaningfully. "I think it's great. I have almost no interest in that, but I support you being curious."

She bites her lip. "Do you think I'm right though? About how we had similar childhoods?"

I think about that for a second. "I don't know. I mean, I guess so. My father was never around because he was busy working the stables or passed out drunk. My mom left when I was very young. She never came back. And when your father offered to take me off my father's hands, my father jumped at the opportunity."

She rubs circles on my chest, nodding. "Yes."

"And your family obviously had their own set of issues. I mean… Not to speak badly of them, but they didn't give a fuck about anyone other than themselves."

Nika scrunches her nose. "I know. They really were just not around almost all of my childhood. I had mom. And I had all my brothers… But I never really had a family. I mean, not in the traditional sense of the word. It's funny to think of the King of Denmark having such a mess of a family."

I reached my arm around her, squeezing her waist. "I'm sorry that your parents missed out on you, Nika. You're pretty wonderful for having essentially raised yourself."

That same shy smile comes over her face again. "You too, Erik."

I kiss her one more time, then close my eyes and let my breathing even out. It's nice, laying here with my… well, my girlfriend. It's the first time for that, at least.

I settle in, opening my eyes a crack. Just to check on her before I fall asleep. But to my surprise, I find her wide eyed and frowning, as she lies on my chest.

"Hey. Whatever you're worried about, it can wait until tomorrow."

She raises her eyes to me, her frown deepening. "I guess so."

I sigh and open my eyes a little bit more, continuing our talk even though I'm basically exhausted. "What's on your mind?"

I can feel the hesitancy rolling off of her in waves. She sighs, bringing both her hands up to cover her face. "I don't mean to be a bummer."

I groan and raise myself up on my arm, frowning down on her. "Well now you have to tell me. What are you thinking about that has you all worked up?"

She lowers her hands and looks at me. "Our relationship."

"I'm going to need a little bit more to go on than that."

She scrunches up her face. "People won't understand. The world will judge us. And… I don't even want to think about what my brother will think?"

Stellan.

Thinking about him is like a punch to the gut. I can just imagine his face when he finds out that I am dating his little sister. Some combination of fury and outrage will run across his features, I'm sure.

Still, that doesn't change the fact that I have feelings for Nika. If anything, it makes my feelings more pronounced.

I glance at her. "Does that make a difference to you?"

She bites her lip, hesitating again. My heart starts to pound. And then she shakes her head, tucking her platinum hair behind her ear. "It doesn't. It should, but it doesn't."

I gather her up in my arms, shifting onto my side and kissing the top of her head. "Good."

She places her small hand on my upper arm and buries her head against my bare chest. If she continues to have doubts, she doesn't say anything about them. Soon her breathing slows and evens out, letting me know that she is near sleep.

But she has unintentionally infected me with her worries. Because now I can't get Stellan's enraged face out of my head. And even as I close my eyes, he follows me into sleep...

Chapter Twenty-Seven

ANNIKA

JUST A COUPLE DAYS LATER, I am sitting at the kitchen island, sneaking a look at my iPad. I haven't had any contact with the outside world other than a phone call with Kal. And so far, I've been pretty much happy. But some part of me, some self-destructive little voice in the back of my head, is screaming at me to check my social media accounts.

I bite my lip and open twitter, my heartbeat already pounding in my ears before the page even loads.

Is Annika drying out somewhere?

Maybe she is on a permanent vacation where she can just eat and booze all day and all night...

Good riddance. Denmark is better without her.

What will we do without our very own Princess Piggie?

Each snide comment is captioned on a different unflattering picture from the red carpet event. I look like a hot mess in those photos, drunk and a little too thin and completely out of the loop. My artfully done make up is marred by my tears. And of course, there is a picture of me in full break-down mode, being scooped off my feet and into Erik's arms.

Ugh, I hate myself so much. Why did I even look at Twitter?

I turn off my iPad and leave my head down on my arms. The cool marble countertop receives my tears, the stone unflinching. I don't even remember my eyes welling up. I just feel like everything in the world is piling on top of me, forcing me down, caging me in.

I struggle to draw in a breath. Shit, it's happening again.

One glance at social media and I'm in a tailspin, having a panic attack.

What should I do?

I feel my chest tightening and I'm aware of my hands turned numb.

Shit. Shit. If Erik sees this, he will probably freak out.

I push myself to my feet, looking around the house. My vision is wonky, going black at the edges. I try to stagger to the couch, but I don't make it all the way. Instead I tumble to the ground in the middle of the room, crying and sobbing and gasping for breath. I curl up in a ball, praying like hell that this will pass.

It feels like I'm dying, though.

And this exact moment is when Erik decides to come back in from taking a shower. He is clad in only a towel and his wet hair is slicked back. He takes one look at me and breaks into a run, scurrying over to my side and dropping to his knees.

"Nika? Nika, what's going on? You have to tell me. Are you okay?"

He sounds frantic. I can barely nod. I can't speak. I can't move. I am struggling for breath and there's nothing that Erik can do to help.

Erik scoops me up in his arms, groaning as he climbs to his feet. He carries me into the bedroom that we've claimed as our own and carefully places me on the bed. He sits right beside me, worry etched on his face. "Is this a panic attack? Are you having another one? Because if you're not, I have to call someone. Just nod if you are having a panic attack."

I nod frantically. He blows out a breath and looks down at me, his hand coming up to my back. He rubs small circles into my flesh, seeming to think about what to do. "I read that panic attacks only last five or ten minutes at most. And I'm going to stay right here. I'm not going anywhere, Nika. You're going to be okay. You're going to be fine."

A sense of doom claws its way up from my chest and I close my eyes, sucking in breath after breath. In the back of my mind, I am embarrassed that Erik has to see me this way again. But that feeling is shoved to the side by more immediate concerns.

Erik doesn't even hesitate. He just keeps up his calming touches and reassuring words. "Everything is fine. Everyone is fine. This will pass. Everything is fine. Everyone is fine. This will pass…"

I tremble and sweat drips off my body. Squeezing my eyes closed seems to help, in some small way. So, I do that, eventually reaching up and grabbing Erik's free hand, twining his fingers with my own.

I'm okay. I know that I'm okay. I feel like I'm going to fucking die but I'm okay...

I repeat those words to myself like a mantra, waiting for the panic attack to subside. After a few minutes, it seems a little easier to breathe. I don't feel the sense of approaching doom anymore. I take a deep breath and blow out a breath, opening my eyes.

Erik is looming over me, his green-brown eyes deeply concerned. "Nika? How are you feeling?"

Not trusting myself to speak just yet, I nod. I'm thirsty, maybe thirstier that I've ever been before. I manage to squeak out the word. "Water?"

Erik looks beyond relieved. He lets my hand go and stand up. "I'll be right back with a glass of water."

I close my eyes and only reopen them when he sits down beside me again on the bed, pressing a cool glass into my palm. I sip from a glass very gratefully, my heart still pounding. It takes another minute for me to regain full use of my voice.

"Thank you, Erik. I'm starting to feel a little bit more normal now."

He looks down at me, his expression somber. He starts stroking my back again, looking worried as ever. "You scared the shit out of me, Nika. I know you didn't mean to. But what set this whole thing off?"

I look at my glass, avoiding his eyes. I shrug a shoulder. "I might have... gone online and checked Twitter."

His expression turns sour immediately. "What would make you do that? Why would you do this to yourself?"

I push out my cheek with my tongue. "I don't know. I guess... I was just feeling like things were good. You know, things between us, things with the royal palace..." I make a helpless gesture. "I'm not used to things feeling fine. Maybe I just... needed to dip my toe back in reality for a moment. And the quickest way that I knew how to do that was to check Twitter and see what people were saying about me."

His brows rise. "I thought you were dying. I felt helpless. I don't like feeling that way. You have to find some other way of dealing with this, Nika. If that's what really set you off..."

He looks a little angry and pretty disappointed. My cheeks flush.

I exhale loudly. "I know. I think… I mean, I didn't know that it would cause a panic attack. But I am not used to being so… happy."

He takes my hand, placing it against his heart and pressing it close. "I'm glad that you're happy. But this self-destructive little habit of yours? It won't work. I can't deal with it. I won't."

Pushing myself to a seat, I reach up and touch Erik's face. "I'm sorry. Really, I am. I'll try to figure out another way to deal with it, I guess."

He frowns. "For the record, I'm happy too. And my father is resting at the cottage, although apparently, he has turned several nurses away at the door. And so, I am just taking it as it comes, trying to keep my mind off of it. And because I need the distraction, I am extra happy that I'm here with you."

I turned my face up to him, seeking a kiss. He brushes his lips against mine very briefly. Then he pulls back, brushing back a few strands of my hair. "I don't want to see you hurt like that, Nika. I think you should see someone professionally. For the panic attacks, I mean."

I screw my face up. "I did talk to a psychotherapist. For a little while, anyway. When I was a preteen, I started to realize how distorted the mirror that the press holds up to the royal family really is. And the press almost always had something to say about me. How much I did or didn't eat. How I looked in jeans. One time, they wrote that a dress I wore made me look 'extremely plump'."

His eyebrows shoot up. "They called you fat?"

I nod. "Yeah. Can you imagine calling a twelve-year-old 'extremely plump'? I still remember how miserable I was. I used to eat chocolate and…" I pause, not sure how much to tell him. Glancing up, I take a deep breath. "I binged on foods and then threw them up. At times, I grew tired of that, so I restricted my food intake very severely."

Erik's eyes narrow on my face. "Are you saying you had bulimia?"

I look down, embarrassed. "Not had. Have. I don't believe that kind of disordered thinking about food ever goes away completely. If you think that I don't know exactly how many calories I've had today and how many we've burned off fucking, you're *nuts*." I frown. "My point is, I talked to a therapist trusted by the royal family then."

He's silent for a second. I glance up at him, feeling a nervous shiver slide down my spine. He looks somber. "I'm glad you told me."

Feeling awkward, I shrug. "Whatever."

"Nika," he says, shaking his head. "I hope you realize that there is more to you than just a pretty face."

I roll my eyes. "Yeah, yeah."

He gives me a little shake. "You're intelligent. You're deep. You're compassionate. If anyone ever so much as breathes a word to the contrary, I'll fucking kill them."

He looks dead serious when he says it. My eyes widen a little bit.

Erik nudges me. "I mean it. And I meant what I said about you seeing a professional." His face crinkles. "Maybe you could see someone that has nothing to do with the palace."

I arch a brow. "You are so quick to turn your back on the royal press office."

He smirks. "They'll be glad to see the back of me."

"What, are you leaving?"

His smile vanishes. "Eventually."

My brow hunches. "Do you want to tell me your plans?"

He stretches, looking down. "Maybe later. What I really want is to get dressed and then make us some breakfast."

He presses a final kiss to my lips then gets up, heading to dress. I collapse on the bed, thinking to myself that telling him about my eating disorder wasn't at all terrible. He just makes the past seem…

I don't know, far away and out of focus.

And that's a good thing, so far as I can tell…

Making a mental note to look up therapists, I close my eyes for a few minutes and wait until Erik calls me to breakfast.

Chapter Twenty-Eight

ANNIKA

TODAY IS A SPECIAL DAY. Not only does the day mark the one month anniversary of Erik and I officially dating. But it also happens to be my birthday.

I know, I know. It's definitely passé and gauche to make a big deal out of what is essentially just another day on the calendar. Especially my twentieth birthday… I don't even get any special privileges for turning twenty. But even before I open my eyes, a shiver of excitement runs through me.

I can't help it. I just love celebrating holidays and my birthday definitely counts as one of those.

I open my eyes to find the space beside me in bed empty. I reach out my hand, touching Erik's side of the bed. He has obviously been gone a while because his side isn't even warm anymore.

I sit up, looking around sleepily. From the sun slanting in the windows of the loft, I would guess that it's still early, probably only eight or nine in the morning.

I hear some vague banging in the main area of the loft. Pushing off the heavy satin coverlet, I get up and pull one of Erik's black T-shirts on over my head. Then I pad barefoot over the cool stone floors, my eyes widening when I realize that Erik is already in the kitchen.

He looks up at me from spreading preserves on toast, his face lighting up a little. God, the way that he looks at me just now, his warm green-brown eyes and his cool yellow hair against the backdrop of his big muscular body... I feel lucky suddenly.

I have warm shivers all over my body and I beam at him.

"Hey," I say, shoving a hand through my thick sinuous hair. I look at him, trying to decide whether or not to tell him that it is my birthday. It feels a little ridiculous to make a big deal out of it but there's a part of me that definitely wants to.

"Hey. I thought I would surprise you with a little breakfast in bed. After all, it is your birthday."

My eyes widen. "How did you even know that?"

He finishes coating the toast with some kind of glossy fruit preserves and smiles up at me, bringing a plate full of eggs and toast over to me. Then he presents me with a little white vase with a single white rose inside of it, placing it beside my breakfast with a flourish. "I'm a mind reader, that's how."

I roll my eyes a little, but I can't keep the stupid grin off my face. "Well... Thanks. Not to be ungrateful, but is there coffee?"

He nods. "There is. Sit down and I'll pour you a cup."

I noticed that there are mylar balloons and several gift boxes on the far counter. I nod at them as he delivers a fresh cup of coffee. "What are those?"

He smiles lately. "I think they are all gifts and notes from your family. Kal made a special gift too, and I had it all delivered here."

I arch my brow. "Nothing from you?"

He rolls his eyes. "I didn't get you anything so tame. You can't unwrap my present. Hope it wasn't crazy, not getting you designer jewelry for your birthday."

Shaking my head, I shoot him a shy smile. "You're not wrong."

I pick up a piece of toast, biting into it. It's crispy and buttery and sweet. I close my eyes, enraptured for a moment.

I don't know how I'm going to tally that in my calories for the day but damn if I'm not glad that I tasted it.

When I open my eyes, Erik is staring at me. His expression is intent. "What?" I ask.

He shrugs. "You're just beautiful when you enjoy yourself, that's all."

He pushes off the counter and starts heading toward the bedroom. "You should open Kalindi's present first. Then hurry up with your breakfast because we have a lot to do."

I shoot him a questioning look, but he is already gone, vanished into the hall where the bedrooms are. I stuff another half piece of toast in my mouth, crunching happily, and I stand up to head to the presents.

True to form, Kal's present is perfectly decorated. It's the one with the mylar balloons attached, balloons that probably are supposed to be for a younger girl's birthday. But they are the right shade of hot pink with big white bubble letters that say happy birthday. I pick up the hot pink and pale green polka-dotted box that the balloons are attached to. Untying the perfectly knotted green ribbon, I find an assortment of toffees and other sugar free sweets. Under that, there is a picture of me and Kal at age 11, attached to a very heartfelt poem.

It makes me smile. My best friend has my best interests at heart, no matter whether we see each other on our birthdays or not. Something about that makes me very happy.

All the other gifts are from Momse and my parents and other palace officials.

A matching diamond tennis bracelet and diamond necklace. That would be from Momse. I sigh and shove it to the side, rifling through the remainder of the presents. Everything else is neatly wrapped and obviously a luxury item, but there is little evidence that any thought was put into it aside from 'would a twenty year old girl like this?'.

It's not surprising. And I am grateful. But I soon move on, finishing up my toast and eating a couple bites of the eggs. I slurp down half the coffee and then put my dishes in the sink, heading back towards the bedroom.

I'm surprised to find Erik fully dressed and in dark jeans and a dark T-shirt, laying out clothes for me. He chooses something casual, a pink flouncy baby doll dress and a pair of white flats. I cock my head, narrowing my eyes at him.

"What is this?"

He winks at me. "Get dressed. I'm not saying that you need to wear this outfit exactly, but you don't need to go overboard on getting dressed up. We are not going to see anyone else today. We're just going to your birthday surprise."

"Well." I wiggle my eyebrows. "Whatever I can do to make that happen, I guess..."

In a matter of minutes, I'm dressed. Other than swapping out his practical white flats for just a strappy black heel, I take his suggestions to heart.

He holds out a length of white silk, just big enough for me to make a blindfold. He nods at the silk. "I'm going to need you to wear a blindfold. Then we can go. We are not going very far."

Crinkling my brow, I allow him to tie the blindfold on me. I can't see anything, but I can make out my surroundings and tons of sunlight pours in through the blindfold.

Then he guides me out of the apartment, down the elevator, and out onto the street. I assume that we will get in a car of some sort, but Erik surprises me by just walking a very short distance, maybe three blocks or less.

I grin as he directs me, holding me by the waist every step of the way.

"Watch the door, there's a step there..."

He leads me into a building and up another elevator. Then we step off the elevator and he comes around behind me, steering me to the exact place that I need to be. I can't see much but the place Erik guides me to is filled with sunlight, at least.

"Okay," he says. His hands are still on my shoulders, his big body behind mine. "You can look now."

I reach up and push the blindfold up, pulling it off entirely. My eyes widen as I take in the scene before me.

I'm in a bedroom, standing right in front of a huge fourposter bed. The bed is draped with colorful hanging curtains and covered in soft white comforter. All around tiny twinkling lights are strung around the ceiling. They are mirrored by the candles that are lit on every surface: the dresser, the side tables, the low white satin chaise in the corner.

The room screams cozy and then whispers *expensive*.

The walls are covered with fairy lights and pieces of stiff linen paper, each one with a photograph attached. I'm drawn to the closest one, a photograph of me looking happy on the beach. Frowning, I turn to see another picture. This one is from the arcade, it's me and Erik, clinging to each other and looking breathlessly happy. I step back and look at more pictures... Pictures from our recent trip to the Greek Isles, pictures from our everyday lives at the palace, pictures from the Greta von Grissel fashion show. There are even a few pictures from the last few days. I turn my head and look at the next wall, which has the same pieces of linen paper but instead of the photographs, they have words.

Kindness. Compassion. Humor. Fun. Style. Intelligence. Snark.

Each one has a different word, but they all contain something positive.

Frowning, I look at Erik. "What are these? What is this place?"

He takes a deep breath, meeting my eye. "It's my house. Newly acquired, I guess you could say. And someday, I hope that you could live here too. I think for now it could be a good place to hide out from the press. I… I want you to love it."

He draws my attention to a jar of my favorite toffees and a door that obviously leads into a closet that is empty.

My heart starts pounding. "Is this all for me?"

He gives me a funny look. "Of course. Who else would it be for? It's the very beginning of your personal hideaway, I hope." He scrunches up his face. "I paid cash for it so if you don't like it, please say something now."

My eyebrows fly up. "What, you're kidding? This place must have cost you a fortune! How… How can you afford this?"

He rolls his eyes little. "Let's just say that I have been known to play the stock market and win big."

I absorb all of that for a second. Nodding my head, I look around in awe. I didn't even notice that there are the same linen pieces of paper up on the third wall, listing facts about me.

Loves coffee.

Hates waiting in line.

Graduated at the top of her class.

Would choose the ocean over mountains anytime.

I raise my hand, walking over to touch one of the cards. For some reason, this is the most touching thing that I've seen yet. My eyes mist over as I read the facts printed on each card.

"So?"

I blot at my eyes, turning with a question on my face. "What?"

He looks down for a moment. And when he looks back up, his gaze is smoldering, threatening to burn me alive. "I know we haven't been together for that long. But… I was just thinking about your rooms at the palace and how happy you've been for the last month, since I took you away from there. I want you to know that you will always have another place that you can live. You don't have to be a trained seal for the royal family, Nika."

My heart pounds.

My mouth is dry.

I don't know quite what to say.

"This place… it's for me?" I say again, wide eyed. It's just so hard to wrap my head around.

I am officially swept off my feet. I put a hand over my heart, my mouth crumpling.

"No one has ever done anything like this for me," I whisper. It's the hardest thing not to just break down in tears of gratitude right now.

Erik shrugs a shoulder. "Well, I see us living here, eventually. Assuming you don't get tired of me first. I… I like spending time with you."

I stare at him for a second, not sure I'm hearing him right.

No one has ever asked for me to spend more time with them before. No one has ever cared enough about me, not even my family. My mouth opens, but no words come out.

Erik makes a face, coming over and wrapping his arms around my waist. "I need you to say something, princess."

I bob my head, burying my face against the solid wall of his chest. "Yes. Yes! I would love to live with you, Erik. I mean… more permanently than I do at the moment."

He tips my chin up with a finger, kissing my lips. I kiss him back fiercely, really moved that he did all of this for me. He smiles against my lips.

"I'm glad you like it," he whispers.

I break into a grin. "I love it… I really…. I love you, Erik."

He freezes for a second. His expression is one of complete surprise. His hands tighten around my waist. "Oh, Annika…"

I bite my lip and blush. "I'm sorry. That kind of slipped out."

He shakes his head. "Don't apologize. I care about you too, Nika. More deeply than I can say."

I bite my lower lip. "Yeah?"

He shakes his head and kisses me tenderly. "I do."

I take a deep breath, feeling a little off-center. Does that mean that he loves me and just can't say it aloud? Or am I being optimistic to think so?

Erik takes my hand, guiding me back to the bed. I sit down, enjoying how squishy that mattress is.

"I'll be right back," he says.

He returns with a huge silver tray and sets it between us on the bed. It's been made up with a silver ice bucket with champagne chilling, a platter of French macarons and handmade chocolates, and two champagne flutes. And right in the center of all of it is a single pink cupcake with a candle, just waiting to be lit.

I grin as he sits down on the other side of the tray.

Erik pops the bottle of champagne and pours us each a glass. I pick up a pink macaron, nibbling it delicately. It's sweet and light, made of almond flour and raspberry cream.

He holds up his glass to me. I pick mine up and clink it against his. He smiles.

"Happy birthday, Nika."

I wiggle my eyebrows at him as I taste the champagne. "Thank you for doing all of this, Erik."

His lips twitch. "It was nothing." He takes a sip of his drink then looks at me. "Isn't this the part where you tell me your goals, birthday girl?"

I shoot him a smirk. "My goals?"

"Yep." He reaches over to the platter and touches the edge of the cupcake, taking just a little frosting off of it. Then he pops his finger in his mouth, smacking his lips appreciatively.

My lips twist. I sigh, tilting my head and leaning back on the bed. "I'm not sure. I…" Pausing, I bite my full lower lip. "If I weren't a princess… if I could break away from the royal family, I would live a very different life."

His eyebrows rise. He sets his glass on the floor and runs a couple of his fingers along the outside of my arm. "What would you do?"

I push out my cheek with my tongue. "I would probably focus on charity work? Maybe something with fashion… or maybe raise awareness for people with eating disorders? I don't know. I would just be excited to go out without the paparazzi following me everywhere."

His lips quirk. "Like this morning?"

I nod. "Exactly."

He screws up his face for a second. "We could break away from the palace, you know."

I give him a funny look. "What?"

He shrugs, looking down at the platter. "I'm just saying. You can do anything you want to do, if you are willing to pay the price."

I give a half-hearted chuckle. "What about you? Where are you in this scenario? Because I don't see you being Stellan's secretary if you encourage his little sister to run off and become a *former* royal."

He looks up at me suddenly, spearing me with his deep, serious gaze. "I don't plan on being his secretary for much longer. Before all of this, I was trying to find the right time to tell him that I wanted to leave. Now, I have even more motivation to leave."

I stare at him. My heart pounds. "Are you saying you would go with me if I made the jump?"

He nods. "I would. In a heartbeat."

I frown. "And what would our future look like together? How would we live?" I scrunch up my nose. "I imagine that I would receive some sort of stipend from the royal family but— "

"We don't have to worry about money," he says, tilting his head at me. "I have enough. I mean, it's nothing like the kind of money that the royal family has. But it'll do. I can take care of you for the rest of our lives, Nika."

I narrow my gaze. "I don't want you to feel like you have to take care of me."

He shrugs. "It's just money. I would rather spend it on making a life with you than anything else."

I bite my lip and frown at him for a few seconds, taking it all in. My heart lurches in my chest. "You're serious? You would break off from my family if I agreed to go?"

He trails his touch along my arm, nodding. "Yes."

I scoot around to be close enough to kiss his gorgeous lips. For a minute, we just explore each other's mouths, languorously kissing. When I finally open my eyes and look into his face, my heart is so full that I can't help but grin.

He smirks. "How should I read that? Is that a yes?"

I nod, biting my lip. "I would be a fool to say no. I'm not promising anything, but… I will leave if you're propping me up."

"I can't think of anything better." Erik pauses, his brow wrinkling. "We should wait until after Stellan's wedding to make any announcements. Right?"

"Yes. That would be the polite thing to do." Reaching up to his side-burn, I run my fingers through the short hair that I find there. "It would be even more polite to wait until after he gets back from his honeymoon."

He pulls a face. "It would be polite, yes. But I don't want to wait that long. Do you?"

My lips twitch. I kiss his lip for a second before shaking my head. "No."

Erik moves closer, kissing me more deeply. We get lost in the moment and I sigh breathily as he starts to brush his lips against my collarbone…

Chapter Twenty-Nine

ERIK

ANNIKA IS LOOKING at me like a fucking angel. I can't not touch her. I put the tray of food on the floor and pull her closer. She moans with this breathy little voice that makes me wild and crazy.

Shaken to my very core, I drag my thumb across her lower lip, then follow the caress with the press of my lips against hers. She responds immediately, ravenous for my touch.

Fuck.

Echoing her sentiment with an appetite all my own, I bend her backward, trailing kisses down her neck. I grab her by the waist and bring her down to the floor, spreading her thighs and bringing us together. My mouth descends upon hers, hungry and demanding.

She opens her mouth and her thighs for me, drawing me in without a second of hesitation. Her hands slip around my neck, fingernails lightly scoring the flesh of my shoulders. I palm one of her breasts, then pinch her nipple, drawing a cry from her lips.

I trail kisses down her jaw, skipping over her neck, and bend down to nuzzle the space between her breasts. I feel her legs wrap around me, her heels digging into the backs of my legs, pulling me as close as possible.

I reach down and hike her pretty dress up, finding her bare underneath. I groan as I rip off her dress, kissing her exposed breasts. I know I'm not being delicate with her, but I'm too entranced to care.

She doesn't seem to mind, her head thrown back. She's making these little oh sounds that are killing me, every second I'm not inside her.

Fuck. I need to have her, right this second.

She kisses me, and I bite her lower lip. She grabs my head and bites me on the neck, which I swear makes my cock pulse.

"Talk dirty to me again," she whispers. Her words are another turn on.

"Fuck!" I grit out. "You are such a bad girl, princess."

I squeeze one of her breasts hard, and she gasps.

"Bad enough to get punished?" she whispers.

"Ohhh fuck," I say, pushing her down against the floor. I look at her for a second, searching her face. "You don't really want that."

She struggles under me, trying to push me off. "Maybe I do."

I bring my hand up to her neck, fitting my fingers around the slim white column of her neck. I apply just a little bit of pressure, making her gasp and writhe beneath me. When I release her, she tries to pull me closer for a kiss. I allow it for a moment, but then I pull back. There is much more I want to do to her.

I move back, kneeling on the ground. I strip off my own jeans and T-shirt.

Her eyes are immediately drawn to my cock, which jumps at the attention she pays it. She looks up at me, biting her lip.

"Can I taste you?" she asks quietly, seeming unsure.

God, could Nika be any sexier? I reach down and stroke my cock with one hand, nodding. Her eyes twinkle a bit, and she pushes herself up on the bed. "I have been dreaming about your taste..."

She reaches out, brushing her hand along my length. I grit my teeth as pre-cum leaks from the tip of my cock.

"If you insist," I say, amused. She presses her free hand against my chest, turning me onto my back. I go willingly, trying not to flutter my eyes closed as she moves down, kissing as she goes.

When Nika circles her wet tongue around the head of my cock, I can't breathe for a second.

"Like this?" she asks, looking up at me. She shifts so that she's on her knees.

"That's... perfect. Jesus, you're hot when you're on your knees like that."

Swallowing, I look down at her heart-shaped face. Her pouty lips part as

I guide my cock to her mouth. The second I touch my cock to her lips, the sensitive head probing the wet heat of her mouth, I have to close my eyes for a moment.

My dick twitches, and it takes everything in me not to just bury myself in her hot mouth. I imagine how I would do it. How good it would feel just to put my hand in her hair, to let go and fuck her mouth and throat.

But no. I open my eyes again, breathing hard. She's looking up at me, her lips on the very tip of my dick, her eyes telling me that she trusts me. I have to remember that.

"Open your mouth a little, and stick out your tongue," I encourage her, pressing the blunt head against her lips.

She does, rolling out the velvety tip of her tongue. It caresses the head of my cock and sends tiny lightning bolts of electricity down to my feet. My toes curl.

"*Fuuuuuuck,*" I whisper. She nudges my hand out of the way, closing her little fist around my cock. I put my hand into her hair as she sinks her mouth down on my dick.

She starts to work her head forward and back, fucking me oh so slowly. I groan as she picks up the pace a little, closing my eyes and leaning my head back.

Usually when I'm fucking a girl's pussy, I'm in a position of complete control. I can stop or slow down as often as I want, which helps me to keep from blowing my load before I'm ready. Even with throat-fucking, I am in control more than I am now.

And control is something I desperately need to have, especially now. Especially with Nika.

I can't scare her off of going down by grabbing her and fucking her throat. And as much as I'd like to cum in her mouth, I know that I can't. It's too much.

"Fuckkkk," I hiss. Her mouth feels incredible, it's going to be hard to restrain myself. "Okay, okay. You have to stop, otherwise I'm going to finish in your mouth."

I gently grab her face and push her back. She sits back on her heels, wiping at her mouth with the back of her hand.

"You taste good," she says, her eyes scanning my face. She licks her lips. For a second, my eyes are on her mouth, watching her tongue.

Yeah, I would've finished there without a problem.

"Your mouth is incredible." I pin her onto her back. "I just didn't want to come in there, when there are so many other places that call my name."

She giggles for a second. I grab her knees and force them apart, leaning down to kiss her breasts. Then I go straight for her pussy, spreading it with two fingers, and licking her clit.

Nika cries out and buries her hands in my hair, her back bowing. I trace figure eights around her clit and dip my tongue into her pussy, loving the scent and taste of her. Just as she gets worked up, her juices flowing, I press her knees up and lick my way around the tiny pucker of her ass.

"Oooh!" she cries, startled.

I kiss and lick it for a second, penetrating her ass with the tip of my tongue. Then I break away, kissing her inner thighs, kissing and biting her breasts.

"I want you to touch yourself again," I whisper in her ear. "While I'm taking you from behind, I want you to make yourself come."

She nods eagerly, and I flip her over. She braces herself on her knees and elbows, showing her pretty pussy and ass to me. I grasp my cock, pressing the head to her entrance.

"Touch yourself," I order. She reaches under her body and starts to play with her clit.

I plunge inside her and hear her gasp. She feels so hot and so tight that I have to go slow, otherwise I'll come right away.

"Oh my god," she gasps. "Erik, your cock feels so good."

I grab her hips and use them as leverage while I fuck her, working my cock in and out of her pussy. She begins to tighten her innermost muscles even more as she plays with her clit. I focus, closing my eyes, and try to hit her g-spot every time I thrust.

Finally, she bursts, coming with a shout. I speed up as soon as I feel her begin to spasm, letting myself pound into her like a jackhammer. She cries out my name, which has never sounded better.

I feel my cock start to twitch and pulse as I drive home again and again. I feel like I'm coming like a fucking fountain, her pussy milking my cock for everything it's worth.

"Fuck!" I shout. "God damn, Nika."

We collapse in a sweaty, laughing pile. I kiss the side of her face and she beams at me. "You know what I want now?"

"I hope it's a cupcake," I say, still catching my breath.

She looks at me for a long second. "That's exactly right, Erik."

I laugh and roll over to grab the cupcake from the floor. And we enjoy it together, savoring the moment.

Chapter Thirty

ERIK

"WE ARE ALMOST THERE. Just a little further."

With my hands over Nika's eyes I walk behind her a few more steps. I look up at the soaring factory ceiling above me, wetting my lips. It's bright in here, everything is painted white. The stainless steel machinery in the center of the room makes surprisingly little noise. Just a gentle whirring sound, mostly.

"Are we there yet? I'm dying to know where you brought me. My birthday was a week ago…" she reminds me.

I nibble at her ear and laugh. "Okay, okay. You can look now."

I pull my hands away, dropping them to her shoulders. She looks around with wide eyes, inhaling fragrant wafts of toffee-scented air. She looks at me with a surprised little grin. "Are we at the factory where they make toffee?"

I give her a slow grin. "Yup. We're here to see how the toffee is made and to try some of their test flavors. I called ahead a few weeks ago and they said that today would be the perfect day to come and visit."

She squeals, hugging me hard. "Oh my God. I had no idea that you had this plan! Thank you, thank you, thank you…"

She hugs me one more time then pulls away, grabbing my dark green plaid button up shirt by the hem and towing me along. We are all alone on the factory floor, walking to the left of machines that make the toffee. Just in front of us is the one that stirs the melted sugary goodness. As we walk down the catwalk a little further, I can see that the candy is poured into little molds and cooled down by yet another machine. We keep heading around the outside of the factory line. We look through a clear plexiglass windows at a spot where the candy is freed from the molds and dropped straight into the shiny gold wrappers. Annika looks up at me, taking my hand and squeezing it hard.

"I can't believe you did this for me."

I smile. "It wasn't that big of a deal. I only had to name drop the royal palace once."

Nika grins. "Still. I wouldn't have even thought of this. I didn't realize that I wanted to come here but now that I've been, I don't know if I ever want to leave. Why go anywhere else?"

I slide an arm around her, pulling her closer as we continue walking. Spotting a gray-haired gentleman in a hairnet and a white laboratory jacket, I nod towards him. "I think that man is waiting for us."

Nika looks like I've just told her that she's going to get to fly to the moon or something. "Is this the part where we get to taste the weird flavors of toffee?"

I grin at her. "I think so."

She makes a little fist, pumping it in the air. "Yes..."

We head down to meet the man waiting for us, who introduces himself as Noah, the factory manager. We might be here on a lark, but Noah is all business right now. He has a face like a weathered apple and if he has ever felt joy, it isn't readily apparent.

"If you will just follow me this way, I can show you to the room where I have all the samples laid out for you to try."

He hustles us into a brightly lit room with a giant metal table. On the table are two dozen samples, laid out neatly and labeled. I follow Nika's lead and wait patiently as she tries different flavors of toffee out.

Banana, coffee, butter rum, maple, vanilla, raspberry... So on and so forth.

I drift along in her wake as she samples each flavor, excitedly offering half of whatever she has just tasted to me.

I'll admit it right now, I don't like toffee at all. I don't like caramels or anything that is sticky and sweet. But I keep trying them because I don't want to ruin Nika's excitement. So, I make pleasured sounds whenever I put them in my mouth even though I want nothing more than to spit them out.

"The coffee and butter rum flavors are my favorite. Where do you get them?" she asks Noah.

He clears his throat and looks dour. "I prepared a goodie bag for your highness to take with you. Unfortunately, it's impossible to purchase many of these toffees here in Denmark. There are flavors that are more popular internationally."

Nika's eyebrows go up but she just nods. "Wow. Well, thank you."

Noah bows. "There is one more thing, if you don't mind. We have a very special flavor that we would like your highness to try. It's brand-new."

Nika's eyes widened and she looks at me, her excitement evident on her face. "We would love to. Thank you!"

Noah bows again and produces a final sample, a brownish toffee on a white plate. She goes ahead and picks it up, biting half of it off and offering me the other half. I shake my head gently. "It's for you."

"Mm. Oh my God, I love it. What is it? Chocolate and… some kind of pecan?"

Noah nods. "You nailed it exactly, Your Royal Highness. If you like it, the candy company would like to offer you your very own flavor. You could name it as you like, but we were thinking of just calling it princess's blend."

Annika's eyes widen with excitement. She tosses her hair and looks at me, a goofy grin on her face. "This is the best birthday present anybody could've ever gotten for me. I don't know how anyone could ever top this."

She steps closer and hugs me, while responding to Noah's question. "I love it. Noah, I would be extremely proud to have my name on your product."

Noah smiles briefly, his face creasing for only a moment. "Thank you, your highness. We are happy to oblige. I know I speak for everybody in the company when I say how thrilled we all are that you are a fan of toffees. I know they are a bit stuffy and boring."

"No, no. I don't feel that way at all. Can I ask, is there any chance of you making this toffee low calorie or sugar free?"

Noah smiles again. Bowing his head, he answers her. "It already is sugar free. The fact that you can't taste it is a good sign, I think."

Nika grins at both of us. "I would say so. Thank you for helping us out today, Noah. Can I sign anything for you? I'm sure that you have some little girls in your family that would like an autograph."

He bows his head. "Thank you, Princess. My niece would love your autograph."

I shoot Noah a little glare, but Annika doesn't seem to mind signing a couple of company brochures. She carefully scrawls Noah's niece's name, signs a few more brochures, and then hands them all over to him.

I gather up the bags of samples that we are taking with us and Noah sees us out of the factory. He is very diligent but still quite grateful.

As we leave, heading down the stairs and out into the parking lot, Nika slides her arm around my waist and gives me a hug. "Thank you for doing that. It was really a once-in-a-lifetime treatment."

I smiled down at her, kissing her lips for a moment. "You're welcome. Admittedly, I didn't come up with the idea of naming a flavor after you. When I called to make the arrangements for a factory tour, the company was very gracious. I didn't do much of anything, really."

Nika chuckles. "You knew me. You knew how much this would mean to me. That's really the essence of why I am so blown away. That's it."

Tugging her to a stop, I leaned down and brush my lips over hers. "I'm glad you got what you wanted."

She pulls back, looking at me. For second, I feel her gaze as it rakes up and down my face and shoulders. "You know, I think that I got a lot more in the bargain than I asked for. And I'm not talking about the candy."

The corners of my mouth turn up a little. "No?"

She's shakes her head. "No. I'm talking about you."

I don't really know how to accept her complement straight on. So, I just grab her hand, kiss her on the lips, and pull her toward the car.

Chapter Thirty-One

ERIK

IT'S BEEN ten days since Nika agreed to move in with me. Ten days of delirious happiness. Ten raunchy, dirty nights.

Every time I look at her, all the good chemicals in my brain start listening, trying to convince me that I love her.

The sound of her laughter.

The way she presses her face against my chest, burying her head.

The feeling of completeness I have at the end of the day, holding her in my arms.

Is it love? I have no idea.

But I know that I'm not ready to say anything to her, lest she be let down by my inevitable flip-flopping.

Still, I think that everything is going pretty well for us. I make an early morning run to the palace, scooping up a few of Nika's things and checking in on Stellan. I don't even get the chance to talk to the king.

So, after I stop for some fresh bread and nice piece of salmon, I head back upstairs to the penthouse loft that I own. When I get inside the door, I am aggravated for about the twelfth time by a loose floorboard that's sticks up a quarter of an inch.

I grit my teeth and remind myself that I just have to call someone to fix it. Living in the new loft is a little weird because it's the first time that I've ever had to think about things like that. I've never owned anything before, certainly not pieces of property with such obvious flaws.

Carrying the groceries with me into the kitchen, I make a mental note to call someone to fix it today, before Nika notices that it's a problem. For some reason, the idea of her noticing such a tiny flaw really kills me. I had the same realization this morning when I noticed tiny, hairline cracks in the porcelain of the bathroom sink.

I set the paper sacks of groceries on the counter in the kitchen, absently wondering where Nika is. "I'm home!" I call.

She emerges from the bedroom, wearing nothing but one of my gray T-shirts. She holds her iPad, which I didn't even realize she had here. I raise an eyebrow.

She stops me before I can say anything. "I wasn't looking up myself. Kal texted me a link to some press about Stellan and Margot. Here, have a look."

She saunters over to the kitchen counter, setting her iPad in front of me.

I squint down at the tablet, taking in the headline and the matching photo. In the picture, Stellan and Margot are at a market and they look extremely unhappy. Stellan is raising his hand to point at something, shouting. Margot has her arms crossed across her chest and looks extremely pissed off. The caption reads, "Are King Stellan and his new Queen already on the rocks?"

I scan the first few lines of the article, the corners of my mouth turning down. As far as I know, there is no trouble in paradise. But then again, what do I know? I've been isolated from Stellan and the whole royal family for almost two months now. Still, it doesn't seem like something I should have to worry about.

Stellan is completely in control at all times. I doubt that that has changed much since I was last his secretary.

I push the iPad away. Glancing up at Nika, I shrug a shoulder. "I don't see a problem. It's just the press making things up. You should know about that, shouldn't you?"

She puts her blonde hair in a long, messy ponytail and winces a little. "Apparently Stellan and Margot have been the talk of the Royal Palace lately. Wedding planning is really getting to them, it seems."

I roll my eyes a little. Turning toward the refrigerator, I fish out a bottle of sparkling water. "Do you want a glass?"

She frowns at me. "No. What I want is to know whether you're going to call Stellan or not. This is a pretty big deal, if it's true. And I think that it is. I mean, Kal did send it to me for a reason."

Cracking open the bottle, I take a long pull. Then I shrug. "It sounds like the press is trying to sow the seeds of discontent between the two of them. And you, who should know better and who should have their back no matter what, are falling for the press's tricks."

Her eyebrows go up. "You're not going to talk to my brother about this? I mean, no one is saying that you have to flourish this article in front of his face. I just mean… I'm sure he needs someone to talk to."

I tried to set the bottle of sparkling water down, but I am a little too forceful and I manage to shatter the bottom of the glass. "Shit. I can't believe I did this."

Nika frowns and heads over to the nearby closet, opening it and handing me the broom and dust pan. I sweep up every last piece of glass, mindful of the fact that she has no shoes on and probably will walk in here in short order.

When I'm done cleaning, I look up to find her staring me down. "What?"

She shrugs. "So, you're just going to abandon my brother?"

I glare at her. "Your brother isn't taking my calls. Or at least I imagine so. I tried to say hello to him just a few minutes ago and he was mysteriously absent. No one seemed to know where he is. So no, I'm not abandoning my best friend. He abandoned me."

Nika folds her arms across her chest and cocks her hip. She levels her gaze at me. "What if it were us?"

Her question stops me dead. "What?"

She jerks her head toward the iPad. "It could just as easily be us that the press is picking on. I would hope that in that position, Stellan would pick up the phone and call you."

I snort. "I don't even think that he has noticed that I'm missing from the palace. And anyway, it's not like we are in the exact same position as Stellan and Margot. They are engaged. They have real problems."

She frowns and rubs her palms together. "What is that supposed to mean? I thought that you and I were moving forward."

It's everything I can do not to roll my eyes. "Forget I said anything. We are moving forward. Let's just… move on with our day."

She stalks a few steps closer to me, staring me down. "What do you mean they have real problems?"

I rub the back of my neck. "I don't know, Annika. I'm just saying that they have married people problems and we don't. We don't have any idea of what the king and the future queen will have to deal with. That's all I was saying."

"Do you not think that we will face similar challenges? I mean… This is all because Stellan is King of Denmark and Margot is a commoner. If that doesn't ring any bells for us, I don't know what would."

A commoner. That's the line that makes me lose my cool. I don't know why exactly, since I've said it a thousand times myself. But the way she says it, it sounds… dirty. And not the sexy kind of dirty, either.

I grit my teeth. "Well, maybe they are crazy to be getting married. Hell, maybe we're crazy too! Maybe we are living in a bubble and not being practical. Have you thought of that?"

Her brow hunches. "What is that supposed to mean?"

"It means that I have no illusions about our future together. You are going to marry a real royal and I am going to be cut loose, eventually. It's just what people do. People who aren't Stellan, that is."

Her eyes widen. "What? You can't possibly think that I'm going to just leave you. I'm not a different person than I was five minutes ago or five hours ago or five days ago."

I shake my head. "We shouldn't be arguing. Let's just enjoy what we have while we have it."

I turned away, taking the dustpan to the glass recycling. When I turn around, she is right there, glaring up at me.

"Are you saying that you don't think that we can make our relationship work in the long term?"

I glare at her, moving her aside. "Let's not talk about it right now."

She makes a frustrated growl. "You are so stubborn. Just… I could strangle you right now."

She turns away, she storms out of the room. I call after her. "Annika… Annika?"

I clench my fists. I didn't mean to start a fight or whatever the hell just happened. That was definitely not my intention. But it seems like I have really put my foot in it.

I head back to the kitchen counter, spotting her iPad. I turn it on and read a little more of the article, which is obviously full of hot air. It's just more royal headlines to earn the paper more clicks.

It's not worth calling Stellan about, that's for sure.

Nika comes storming out of the bedroom, tucking her gray T-shirt into a pair of sleek black jeans. She shoulders her purse, looking pretty angry. As she starts heading to the apartment's front door, I called after her.

"Where you going?"

"Out for a drink."

Before I can say another word, the front door slams, leaving me alone in the apartment.

Chapter Thirty-Two

ANNIKA

IT'S dark outside by the time I stumble out of the elevator and into Erik's loft. It's cool and quiet up here right now, the lights dimmed. Maybe Erik has gone out as well…

It's been a full day since I walked out this morning. A whole day that I have just been trying to disguise my appearance, flitting from bar to bar.

I know, it's beyond old news that I shouldn't drink and play over the scene from this morning in my head, again and again. I just can't get my head around the fact that he said that he doesn't expect us to ever be engaged. It boils down to the fact he doesn't believe in the potential for longevity of our relationship.

Which I knew, I swear I did. But hearing him say it?

It killed me.

I lean against the front door and take my shoes off, sighing with relief. I'm more than a little drunk and still revved up from the argument. I head to the fridge, opening it and helping myself to a pint of fresh berries and a bottle of sparkling water. When I close the fridge door, I'm surprised to see Erik standing not two feet away from me, a glower on his face.

"So, you're alive."

I rolled my eyes at him. "Yup."

"What were you thinking, Annika? You know you can't just go out alone."

I pop one of the berries into my mouth and make a face at him. "I can do whatever I want."

Sliding the berries across the counter and in front of a chair, I sit down and pull the top off of the sparkling water. I take a big gulp and eye him. His face is tense.

"What's your problem? I thought we were getting along."

I shrug a shoulder. "Who says we aren't getting along? For right now, anyway. Who knows what will happen tomorrow?"

He glares at me, making a disapproving sound. "What is that supposed to mean?"

I pick up a strawberry, biting into its succulent fruit. "Why did you even ask me to move in here with you?"

Apparently, my question was unexpected. He tilts his head, trying to puzzle out what I mean. "Why? I don't know. I guess I felt like we were spending all our time together anyway… So why not?"

I snort. "How utterly unromantic. Here I was, feeling like it was a sign that things are going well between us."

He holds his arms across his chest. "They are."

I arch a brow at him. "For how long? Because if we are not building something that can last… I'm not interested. I am trying to shape my future here."

He pushes his cheek out with his tongue. "Let's not get ahead of ourselves here. That's all I am trying to say."

I glare at him. "What do you see for us in the future? A year from now. Or five years from now. Do you see us getting married someday? Starting a family?"

He frowns and looks pensive. I'm forced to wait for a full minute while he thinks about my questions. I take another sip of water as he considers what to say.

"I don't know, exactly." He shrugs. "I try not to think too much about what will happen in the future. It's easier just to focus on what is right in front of me."

I toyed with the cap of the water, unable to look at him. "I'm asking if you think that we will be together. That's it."

There's a note of hesitation on his face. "What do you want me to say? I don't know. I feel like there are so many factors working against us. If I had to make a wager, I would probably bet against us in the long term."

My heart sinks. I knew that he felt that way. That's a big reason why I disappeared all day to mope on my own.

But it's a whole different thing to say it out loud.

I can't meet his eye anymore. "You're getting in your own head. That's what this is about, isn't it? This morning, when I said that you needed to talk to Stellan, it shook you. And now you're not even sure that we should be together. Do I have all that right?"

A muscle in his jaw tenses. "Why are you so worried about the future? Why can't you just be happy with what we have right now?"

I put my hands on the counter, pushing up from my seat. "Because that isn't good enough for me. What woman wants to hear that you like her right now, but you don't know about what the future holds? That's how relationships fail."

He arches a brow at me. "And you're the expert, are you? Admit it. You don't have any idea of how relationships work."

"Neither do you. Obviously."

His gaze narrows on my face. "So, what, then? Where do we go from here?"

I give a humorless laugh. "I don't see how we do anything together at this point. If you don't believe that we will be together for the foreseeable future, I think I would rather just call it what it is right now. Because if you think that something is going to die, it usually does."

He squints at me. "I'm not saying that we will not last."

I shake my head and roll my eyes. "That's not good enough, Erik. Either you believe in us or you don't. And it sounds an awful lot like you don't."

He flexes his fingers and tightens his fists.

"You know just as well as I do that when the press gets ahold of the existence of our relationship, we're done for. That's not even talking about what Stellan will feel when he finds out that I'm banging his little sister. And your grandmother? God, I can just see the expression on her face right now."

I level a gaze at him. Crossing my arms, I walk to the hallway, pausing. "It's funny. Your worries are all related to how you feel that people will perceive us. I thought that I was supposed to be the one that was so worried about appearances. I guess that was all wrong, too."

With a heavy heart, I head into the hallway, planning to grab a bag full of my stuff. Erik follows me, glowering at me the entire way.

"Where are you going?" he demands.

I huff at him. Pulling a tote bag out of the closet, I start stuffing it with necessities. "Where do you think? It's not like I have many other places to go to."

He leans in the doorway, folding his arms across his chest and frowning. "You're being crazy, Nika. Why don't you just take a while to cool off and then we can approach this more logically."

My eyes mist over. Even though part of me very much wants to stay, to spend as much time with him as he will allow me to, I know I have to go. And that breaks my God damned heart.

Blotting at my eyes, I pick up the tote bag and turn to face Erik. "The thing is. You either believe in us. You believe wholeheartedly that we can make it… Or you don't. It's just that simple. So, tell me. Do you believe? Or are you still caught up in what other people think about us that you can't see the forest for the trees?"

He pushes out his cheek with his tongue. "Nika… Don't. Please. I'm asking you to stay. Isn't that good enough?"

Sucking in a breath, I shake my head slowly. "No, Erik. I don't think it is."

I walk towards him, waiting for him to move, to get out of my way. But he doesn't. He just stands there, an immovable brick wall of smoldering anger.

"You're making a mistake." His voice is rough, gone to gravel. "If you walk away, that's it. We're through."

A tear breaks free from my eye, running down my cheek. I step up to him, a hair's breadth away. Peering up at his face, I utter the words that will echo in my head for a long, long time.

"So be it. I would rather be alone than be with someone that doesn't believe in me."

Erik shakes his head, pushing himself off the doorway and backing out of the way. I push past him into the hallway as tears begin to run down my face freely.

I raise my head and stalk out of the apartment, reminding myself that I am a princess. No matter that I can't see because I am blinded by my own tears and my own weak heart.

The last thing I see before the elevator doors close is Erik, his face tortured, his big body looming just outside the elevator door.

I open my mouth to say something to him but the doors close before I can get it out. Pushing the button to take me to the ground floor, I promise myself I won't break down until I am out of the building.

# Chapter Thirty-Three

ERIK

"ARE you sure you're ready for this?" I whisper to Stellan. He adjusts his tux, giving me a hard look. Behind him, a whole cathedral full of dressed up wedding guests sit, chatting and laughing, their voices low like ambient noise.

Stellan runs his tongue over his teeth, wiping his hands on his expensive tuxedo pants. "I'm as ready as I'll ever be. I'm very excited to have this part over and done with so that Margot and I can rule the country. That, and we have a hell of a honeymoon awaiting us."

I smile at him. "It sounds like you have your priorities in order. You have any second thoughts?"

He clears his throat, looking behind me at his brothers. He will always be the oldest son, the one in charge. There's no getting around that.

"None whatsoever. We've already done a private ceremony with just the family. This is just an elaborate show for the public."

I nod, casting an eye over the church. "Fair enough."

Behind me, the organist begins playing a hymn. I look around, as if the person that I'm the most anxious to see will be in the crowd. But I know for a fact that Nika will be marching down the aisle with the other bridesmaids. Just thinking about her, my palms begin to grow sweaty.

Lars edges over to me and leans in close. "You look like shit. When is the last time you even slept?"

I probably haven't slept for four whole hours at a time ever since Nika left me. I toss and turn every single night, trying to piece together what happened and figure out if there is a way back for the two of us.

There has to be, right? That is very much on my mind at the moment.

I wince. "I haven't slept much this week."

Lars raises an eyebrow. "That bad, huh? Our little Annika seems to have you wrapped around her little finger..."

I shoot him a glare as the first bridesmaid makes her way down the aisle. It's a random brunette woman that Margot and Pippa know from New York. Pretty enough in her own way, she swishes down the aisle looking like a cupcake. She winks at me, hinting that she is available. Although that's the last thing on my mind right now.

I turn away, clearing my throat and keeping my eyes on Stellan.

Next is Pippa, looking breathtaking as usual in a pretty pink gown. When I glance over at Lars, I see him watching her with a crackling gaze that seems almost electric.

Those two are definitely going to get together. The question is when.

I forget all about Pippa and Lars and their weird friendship that is on the verge of breaking into a full-blown lust. Because Annika steps out into the cathedral at that moment, literally stealing the breath out of my lungs. I can't look away from her: her hair is piled atop her head, her makeup subdued, her body looking unbelievable in her strappy pale pink dress.

I school my expression. No one else here needs to know that I have been turning myself inside out every day and every night since she left. No one else here knows that we were even a thing.

But when Nika looks at me, pinning me in place with her frost-tinted eyes, I forget all of that. I can only focus on how amazing she looks and how much I want her to run straight to me.

When our gazes meet, her cheeks turn pink and she looks away immediately. She walks up the aisle towards me, avoiding my gaze. At the last moment she turns right and climbs the stairs to stand beside Pippa.

I keep my expression blank, but I can't help the fact that my gaze is drawn to her over and over again throughout the ceremony. In her barely-there strappy sleek dress, she displays miles of bare, glowing skin. Skin that I know, every single inch of it.

I swear, I can feel her skin against mine, her warm body pressing against my flesh.

When Margot comes in and the music changes, I have to rip my eyes away from Nika. Margot does look beautiful, wearing a gorgeous white gown and a long, glamorous veil and train that are carried by two young men.

No one walks her up the aisle, which is a little odd. But when I look over at Stellan, he has tears in his eyes. I'm reminded of his engagement party, of the fact that Margot and Stellan look at each other like they are the only two important planets in their tiny universe.

What they have is truly special. Even I can admit that.

Margot walks up the stairs, bowing slightly so that Stellan can peel back her veil. She's all smiles today, already in tears. Her cupcake pink hair has never seemed so coiffed.

And yet, my eyes keep wandering over to Nika. I listen as the ceremony proceeds, but I keep darting my gaze over to her again and again.

I have to do something. I can't let her walk away again. Not this time.

Stellan leans back towards me, looking at me clinically. "The rings," he prompts.

I pat my pocket before reaching in and producing both of the rings. Stellan doesn't seem to mind the fact that I wasn't paying a bit of attention. Then again, he seems to be wholly caught up in his own world.

Before I even realize it, the wedding ceremony is almost over. There is a moment where Stellan and Margot kiss.

My gaze finds Nika. And to my surprise, she is looking right at me. She blushes and looks away, but I have the satisfaction of having caught her.

The priest announces the new couple and they head down the stairs, walking down the aisle like they are floating on air. I follow them out, heading down the aisle, Lars at my side. I give him a look and he shrugs.

"Weddings give girls ideas that we actually want to marry them," he jokes.

I roll my eyes at him. "Can you not just be happy for your brother? Besides, we all know who you are going to end up walking down the aisle with. There is no suspense or mystery to be had there."

He glares at me. "I'm going to tell you this for the one billionth time. Pippa and I are just friends. That's all we will ever be. Should just take your lamentations about dating someone in this family and shove them up your ass."

I shoot him a look. It's better to avoid the entire subject of dating someone in his family, I think. "I'll race you to the reception."

He smirks and elbows his way past a group of older women who have just gotten up from the pews. "You're on."

Rolling my eyes, I hurry after him. For the next two hours, the wedding takes precedence over anything I want to do. There's the receiving line, walking to the reception at a very posh hotel, and then there are speeches and the first dance between Margot and Stellan. I see Annika several times throughout the preceding events, but she always looks away and pretends to be busy with someone else.

Honestly, it makes me grit my teeth. It's not until after I deliver my rousing best man's speech that I can slip away unnoticed.

I corner Annika in a quiet hallway, just off the main room. As I approached, she looks up at me, her eyes going wide. Her gaze slides around the hallway. She bites her lip.

"Erik…" Her voice sounds like a shaky warning. "Today isn't about us. You would do well to remember that."

I pace over to where she stands, looking at her amazing body in that perfect little pale pink dress. I breathe in, catching a whiff of her natural scent.

It's maddening.

"Your brother is happily involved with his new bride. Now I have all the time in the world." I reach out, brushing my fingers along her upper arm. She shivers and swallows, her wide, innocent eyes seeming to spear me.

"Have you changed your mind, then?"

I smirk at her. "You still think I'm the one that was in the wrong?"

Her gaze hardens. "Yes. I thought I was pretty clear."

Sliding my big hand around her tiny waist, I pull her flush against my body. I hear her sudden exhalation of breath. She feels so good in my arms. I'm sure that there is not a single woman on earth that I would rather be with right now then Nika.

I lean my head down, brushing my lips over hers. I whisper against her mouth. "You want me. I can tell. It's written all over your face."

Her hands come up to push at my chest, but I kiss her again and they relax a little, her nails digging into my skin through my tux. I bend her back and kiss her properly, not even thinking about the fact that we are in a public space.

No, I'm only thinking about the girl in my arms, about how much I have missed her. When Stellan himself comes rushing over, I take too long to pull back from her lips.

And that second of hesitation allows him to land the first punch, nearly a knockout blow. I stumble backwards, still holding Nika in my arms. She pushes me away and stumbles backward, her wide eyes on her big brother.

Stellan is furious with me. "You fucking asshole. You're… what, you're sleeping with her? You stole something from my family. What the hell?"

I raise my hands, only now aware of the crowd forming behind Stellan. I definitely don't want to get into a fist fight with him, not today of all days.

"Just go back to your wedding, man. Look, Margot's waiting for you." I nod to her, feeling my jaw where he punched it. It's achy.

Stellan doesn't look satisfied with that. He rounds on Nika, pointing his finger at her. "You should've known better. You should have stayed out of his bed. I don't want to see you anymore today. Just go." He looks at me, his fury evident. "As for you, consider yourself fired from the royal family service. Good riddance to bad garbage." He spits on the floor, his face going red.

My hands bunch into fists. He called me garbage. Nobody does that to me as an adult and gets away with it.

Nika scowls at her brother. "Don't call him that. He may have ruined my life but he's not garbage."

Stellan raises his head and sniffs. "I said what I said."

"You're wrong," Nika says, facing him down. "You've never seen him for the prize that he really is. That's been clear to me from the jump."

He sneers at me. "Are you just going to let my little sister fight all your battles?"

I take a step towards him, baring my teeth. But Nika raises her hand to block me, looking at Stellan. "We will go. We don't want to make trouble, honestly."

He squints at both of us. Then he relents a little bit, or so I think. "Nika, you can stay. But Erik, I want you gone. I won't have someone that would stab me in the back so eagerly hanging around. That's what you've done your whole life. You hung around. Now it's over. So I want you gone. From this event. From the palace. From my life. Just go."

Stellan cuts me to the core, skewering me with his words. And because he is the king, I'm pretty sure that he can follow up on his threats.

Just like that, I have lost the life I've built over so many years. I look to Annika, wordless and beseeching.

She presses her lips into a thin line and looks like she is about to die of embarrassment. Then Stellan turns around, storming off toward where he left Margot on the dance floor. Nika looks at me, swallowing tensely. She shakes her head at me, like she doesn't even know me. When I try to reach out to her, she just shrugs out of my touch.

"Don't. Don't touch me. I think you should leave now."

As she says it, two blue jacketed guards approach me. They both have serious looks on their faces, like they are ready to throw down. I try to protest but one of the guards grabs me by the elbow and shoves me toward the exit door, taking me to the stairs at the back instead of through the crowd of people gathered and watching.

Just before the door swings closed on me, I look back and catch a glimpse of Annika, her expression nothing short of tortured.

And then I am being pulled down the stairs, telling the guards to take it easy.

I turn forward and stumble along, feeling so overwhelmed that I can't process any of it at all.

Chapter Thirty-Four

ANNIKA

I STAND at the very corner of the ballroom, looking out the huge plate glass windows. The wedding reception is still going on behind me although it is winding down by now. I look out the window to the sun setting on the Copenhagen skyline and try not to cry.

There are so many thoughts and feelings going on in my head right now.

But this is not the time or place to air them out… Especially not when my big brother is brooding and twirling his new bride on the dance floor. I turn and eye the ballroom, trying to guess when I can slip away and not be noticed.

My misery is complete, the source of it has been escorted from the premises. And yet, I am more alone than ever.

I spot Kal coming towards me, looking chic as always in her lavender gown. She arches a brow at me as she approaches, handing me a flute of champagne. I accept it, giving her a sad smile.

She lifts her glass, clinking it against the rim of mine. "To Stellan's wedding, I suppose."

My mouth lifts a little, but I repress an eye roll and take a sip of the wine. "I'm sure that Stellan probably hates me right now. I interrupted his wedding with my personal drama. How perfect."

Kal wrinkles her nose and looks around. "What do you say we get out of here? Just for a little while. I think I saw a sign that said you could get to the roof from here."

I sigh. In the normal course of events, I would say no. But today, I have royally screwed up. No pun intended.

So, I just nod. "I think that sounds great."

Kal leads me to the same stairwell that Erik was escorted out of just a little while ago. She opens the door, waving me inside.

"Wait!" A woman's voice calls. Kal and I both turn and find Pippa making her way towards us. She flashes us a gentle smile and follows us through the door into the stairwell.

"Wherever you guys are going, I want to go to. I am tired of having Margot and Stellan's love rubbed in my face. It's enough for one day at least."

Kal's lips twitch. "We were just going up to the rooftop. Come on."

She leads the way up the staircase, opening the door that leads onto the roof. It's surprisingly peaceful up here, the rooftop bar and patio area set up but empty. It's balmy outside, the late Copenhagen summer evening still nice. Pippa leads the way to an empty table, pulling up a chair to it.

When we both sit down, Pippa looks around at both of us. "So? Spill the beans. Dish the dirt. What happened with you and Erik?"

I take my seat and lean my elbows against the table, pressing my hands against my face. "I don't even know where to begin, honestly."

"I didn't even realize that you guys had broken up!" Kal protests. I sigh heavily and drop my hands, putting my arms on the table. "

I screw up my face. "Yeah. I mean… It got a lot bigger than just sleeping together and it happened fast. I…" I stopped speaking, my eyes misting over. I swallow. "Sorry…"

Kal gets up and leans down to hug me, which is exactly what I needed just now. I turn towards her, my hand resting on her shoulder as I fall apart against her collarbone.

She shushes me, murmuring that everything will be all right. She has no way of knowing that, of course, but it's still comforting to hear.

Pippa frowns. "I'm sorry to see you so sad over this. Do you want to tell us about it?"

I suck in a breath and shake my head. "Not really."

Kal gives me a squeeze and pulls her chair next to mine, sitting down. She looks at me, her mahogany eyes piercing. "Let me just ask one thing, then. How far did things progress? I mean, did you guys say those three little words, or are we talking about something less?"

Pulling away from her chest, I waved at my eyes. "I told him I loved him. He didn't say it back, though."

Kalindi and Pippa both look surprised at that. My cheeks heat and I look down at the table, embarrassed. Pippa reaches out and takes my hand, squeezing it.

"I'm so sorry. That isn't very fair."

Blotting my eyes, I sniff. "Thanks. You are nice to say it."

Kal frowns and leans back in her seat. She seems unsatisfied with that answer. "What did he think he was going to gain by kissing you today?"

I slowly shake my head. "I don't know. He seems to want me to take him back. But he doesn't believe that there is a long-term relationship in the cards for us. Why would I do that?"

Tilting her head, Pippa pulls a face. "I can tell you one thing. Men suck. Maybe you're better off without him."

A door opens up behind me. I turn and look to see who it is and am surprised to see Margot and her beautiful white wedding gown. She blushes a little as she comes outside, looking between all of us. "Is there room for one more?"

Pippa is the first to grin and wave her over. "Today, you get whatever you want. Come sit down by me."

Margot walks over, showing off a champagne bottle that she brought up from the wedding. "I come in peace and I bring gifts."

Kal smiles at her, getting up and grabbing for champagne flutes from behind the empty bar. Margot sits down and Kal puts the flutes down in front of her. Margot pours a little champagne into each glass, looking at me with a small smile.

"I gather that things aren't good between you and Erik."

Taking the glass that she offers me, I exhale loudly and take a sip of the champagne. Rolling it around in my mouth, I savor the sweetness of the wine. "You could say that. Of all the things that I intended for today, telling Stellan was the least among them. I'm very sorry that Erik and I made a scene."

Margot scrunches her nose up and tucks a strand of her pink hair behind her ear. "He'll be just fine, believe me. I'm sorry that he reacted so poorly. He feels bad about punching Erik in the face. Or at least I think he does."

Kal tilts her head questioningly. "Has anyone heard from Erik?"

Pippa shakes her head and Margot just sighs. "Not that I know of. It's better if he and Stellan have a cooling off period from each other, anyway."

I look at her for several long seconds, finishing off the glass of champagne in one long pull. "Go ahead. Say it."

Margot's brows delicately rise. "Say what?"

I look down at the table, dropping her gaze. "Whatever my brother sent you out here to say to me… What is it? Is it about how Erik betrayed him? Is it about how Erik is way too old for me? Or maybe it's the fact that I am seen as just a baby, and he thinks that Erik somehow took advantage of me? What is it?"

Margot waits for me to finish, sipping her champagne. She takes a full breath. "Stellan has a few issues with you and Erik hooking up, not the least of which is the fact that he worries that you are being naïve. He said that he's worried about the appearances of it, that people will think that Erik is using you for a title or some kind of money somehow. But I don't run errands for my husband. I just came out because I know that you are very important to Stellan and would like for us to be close too. I wanted to make sure that you were okay. That's all."

I glance up at her a little sheepishly. "Oh. Well… Sorry. I think I am just still a little confused and defensive."

Pippa interjects. "Margot, Annika was just telling us that Erik doesn't seem to know what he wants. Apparently, she told him that she loved him and that sent him into a tailspin somehow."

"Really? You love him?"

Margot appears thoroughly surprised. I nod, unhappy. "I do. Or I did. Whichever way makes me sound less pathetic."

She gives me the soft smile. "I think I know one way to make you feel a little bit less miserable." She reaches underneath the table and then shows me her palm, a heavy skeleton key sitting in the middle of it. She picks it up and offers it to me.

I take it, frowning. It's made of ancient wrought iron and inscribed with old, worn letters. "What is this for?"

She wiggles her eyebrows. "A Tuscan Villa. We were supposed to stop there during our month-long honeymoon, but we changed our minds at the last minute. So, I'm presenting it to you now. For a little recovery time… or maybe you end up liking it and want to stay. Either way."

I close my hand around the key, gripping it and looking her in the eye. "Thank you. As it turns out, I will be needing a new place to stay."

Margot smiles and pats my hand. "Us girls have to look out for each other, don't we?"

Nodding slowly, I give her a pathetic little smile. "Yes, we do."

She takes another sip out of her glass and then pushes herself to her feet, brushing her hands down her hand beaded wedding dress. "You know, we don't know each other very well. Which I hope someday will change. But I do know one thing. Whatever you decide to do, it's the right thing. Stay with Erik. Don't stay with Erik. I just want you to know that either way, you have my enthusiastic backing. That is just automatic."

My eyes fill with tears. Standing up, I walk over and hug her, careful not to cry on her wedding dress. She hugs me tightly, making me realize how small she actually is. She is a tiny person, almost pocket-size.

"Thank you," I whisper.

She beams at me. "That's what sisters-in-law are for. Now if you'll excuse me, I have a wedding party to get back to. Pippa, will you accompany me?"

Pippa rises to her feet, looking graceful. "Coming, Margot." She starts walking towards the rooftop entrance, looking back at me. "Stay in touch, will you?"

I nod and she winks at me. Then she and Margot head downstairs, leaving me and Kal by ourselves. I breathe in a shaky breath and look at my best friend. "So, what now?"

She tips up her glass of champagne, drinking it all down and then looking at me. "Now? Now we dance. Come on."

Standing up, she holds her hand out to me, and I walk over and take it, grasping it gladly. I may not have Erik in my corner, but I will always be cared for.

Taking a deep breath, I head downstairs to the wedding.

Chapter Thirty-Five

ERIK

I DRAIN the last few drops of expensive whiskey from the bottle and then chuck the empty vessel off the end of the dock. I'm good and soused... and I feel like absolute hell.

Laying back on the dock, I put my feet into the cool water and stare up at the sky. Nika really did a number on me. And having Stellan kick me out of his own wedding was a humiliation that I wasn't expecting.

Granted, if I kept dating Nika, I would've had to have told him at some point. But I left Copenhagen in a cloud of shame, without either of the people that I claimed to care about.

Nika is nowhere to be found and Stellan is supposedly off on his honeymoon.

And me? I'm renting a house not far from the beach house that the royal family owns. I'm alone and I've been drunk for approximately four days straight. Or is it five days?

I'm not actually sure.

I close my eyes and throw my arm over my face. This is about as bad as I get. I've never moped like this for so long over anyone or anything.

And the kicker is that moping isn't making me feel any better. It's just a little salve on the wound that's sure to bleed me dry soon enough.

I hear footsteps on the dock. Odd, since I don't remember inviting anybody else out to this misery fest. A shadow falls over my face.

I move my arm and find Lars Løve staring me down, lifting his glasses up from his eyes.

"You look like shit." I squint and glance down at what I am wearing. I have on the same T-shirt and shorts that I've had on for three days, black on black. I also notice that I am sunburned beyond reckoning.

I guess that's what I get for getting drunk and falling asleep in this very position for days on end.

I sit up or at least try to. I fall back and laugh a little. "Yeah, well. Apparently, this is what I look like when I've been dumped."

He frowns down at me. "Okay. It's time to get you up and get you sober. Come on." He grabs my hand and hauls me to my feet, helping me down the little dock and up the slanted hill to the magnificent beach house.

I look at Lars, frowning as we walk into the house. "What are you doing here? "Shouldn't you be ignoring me? There's some sort of royal decree against me, I know it."

He grunts. "Shower first. I'll make some coffee. And then we can talk." He wrinkles his nose. "You smell even worse than you look."

I pull a face at him, especially when he walks me into the downstairs bathroom and turns on the taps to the shower. "You're so high and mighty right now. I can't even talk to you."

He just shakes his head and leaves the bathroom, slamming the door as he goes. I take a second to smell myself, inhaling a deep, long pull. I splutter and cough, overwhelmed by my own scent. Lars is right about one thing. I definitely do need a shower.

I strip down and hop in the shower, the warm water doing wonders to sober me up. I'm still a little drunk as I groom myself and get dressed, pulling on a fresh pair of black jeans and a white T-shirt.

When I appear in the kitchen, Lars is just pouring two cups full of coffee. He looks me up and down, judging. "Here." He thrusts the coffee mug in my hand. He points to a seat at the bar. "Sit down and drink this coffee. Then we can really get down to why I am here."

I frown at him, but I move towards the bar, sitting and drinking the fragrant coffee. I realize then that I probably haven't actually eaten anything other than an uncooked cheese sandwich last night. My stomach growls and I try to think what is in the house that I can eat.

"How are you feeling?" Lars asks. "That is to say, are you feeling more sober?"

I squint at him. Now that I am a little less drunk, the world seems harshly lit and missing the buzzy warmth of the world had when I was intoxicated.

I nod at him. "I think I just realized that I'm hungry."

He stands up, padding over to the refrigerator and cracking it open. To my surprise, he has a takeout container filled with a roast chicken and a side of sweet potatoes. He offers it to me with a fork on the side, not saying anything. I give him a questioning look and dig into the food, which is pretty tasty even though it's not brand-new.

After I power through most of the food and two more cups of coffee, I officially have the start of a mean hangover. I beckon to Lars, heading into the cool theater room and lying down. He looks around, completely unimpressed by what he sees, but then again he's an actual Danish prince so…

I cover my face up with my arm again, sighing. "Well, if your goal was to make me more miserable, you have succeeded. Now I'm just suffering from a hell of a headache and some serious dehydration."

He sits across from me, pulling his legs under his body. "Tough shit. I'm here because no one has heard from you in a week. It was actually pretty hard to track you down since you left your cell phone at the palace. So thanks for that, by the way."

I give him a humorless chuckle. "What are you doing here, Lars?"

He goes quiet for a minute. It's long enough to make me look up at him. When I do, I catch his gaze. He looks a little concerned.

"I expected to find you moping about your breakup with Nika. What I didn't expect was that you would be completely tanked. That's not like you." He scowls for a moment. "From what I've heard, it sounds like your father. Is that what you intended?"

Angered by his words, I sit up. But I take it a little too fast and I have vertigo for a moment. Wincing, I rub my temple.

"Are you just here to rub it in more or what? I know that if it was up to your brother, I would be banished from the kingdom altogether. I get that he thinks what I did was wrong."

Lars squints at me. "Leave Stellan out of it. As far as you're concerned, Stellan doesn't even exist right now. What does exist is the rest of the whole entire world. I know that it seems like hiding out here is a good idea, but I came to make sure that you have a better plan than that. Because I think you need one. It seems like you are… floundering a little bit."

I shake my head and shrug. "How am I supposed to just go back to living normally? What am I supposed to do with myself? I can't… I don't know how to do it. Annika won't have me. Stellan can't stand the sight of me. I really screwed up." My eyes mist over, making me more miserable than ever.

No way am I about to fucking cry in front of Lars, friend or not.

"Okay, okay. Let's just slow things down for a minute. What happened with Nika?"

I swallow, looking off into the darkness. "I don't know. I mean… I obviously screwed things up big time with her. She told me…" I pause. "She said some things that indicated that she was getting pretty serious about our relationship. And I freaked out. I did what I always do, which is push people away. And now I've managed to not only alienate her, but alienate her brother, who is basically like a brother to me."

My voice breaks on the last word. I swallow again and avoid looking at Lars. He sits forward, putting his feet on the floor and bracing his elbows on his knees. "I didn't realize that things had gotten so serious between you two."

I manage a stiff nod. "It went fast. Like, it was so quick that I was just…" I blow out of breath. "I guess I was scared. That's what it comes down to."

I sit back, covering my eyes again. Lars is quiet for a full minute. I'm just sitting here, thinking of all the things I said to Annika that were wrong. If I had any power, I would go back in time and fix every single flaw that I see so well in hindsight.

Lars rises from his seat wordlessly. "Come on."

I groan and follow him into the kitchen, where he grabs several bottles of water from the refrigerator. He turns and sets them down on the counter in front of me. "Get hydrated."

I look at the water, feeling how dry my lips are. I grab a bottle and chug it down, then do the same with another. The third bottle I take more slowly, as the water splashes and sloshes around in my stomach.

Lars leans on the counter, crossing his arms and watching me carefully. "Would you do anything differently if you were given a second chance with Nika?"

I glance up at him, surprised. "Of course. I would do almost everything differently. I would not chase her off by talking about how I don't believe in the idea of having a relationship forever, first of all."

His blue gaze burns into my face. "What about the other thing, the thing where she told you she loved you and you just..." He makes a small explosion noise. "What would you do about that?"

I finish off the third bottle of water, wincing. "I would tell her that I needed a little more time, but that I felt that way too..."

He squares off with me. "Do you love her?"

Looking down at the fourth bottle of water, I slowly nod my head. "Yeah, man. I love her. I can't believe I was stupid enough to run her off like I did."

He studies me for a long second. Then he cocks his head at me. "Would it help if I told you where she was going to be in two days?"

My eyes widen. I look up at him, trying to tell if he is serious or not. "What? How could you know? I thought she was hiding out or whatever."

He rolls his eyes. "My sister is not good at deception. She told Pippa where she is going to be the day after tomorrow. And it just so happens that it's very close. As in three beach houses down, kind of close."

The possibility of being able to talk to Annika again makes my heartbeat speed up. "Are you serious right now? You're not fucking with me?"

He shakes his head. "I'm serious as a heart attack. That's her itinerary, as far as I know. What you do with the information that I just gave you, that's up to you. But this?" He waves his hand over the recycling bin and steps on the latch that pops the lid up. I am embarrassed to say that I'm a responsible drunk and every one of the bottles that I emptied this week is right there, plain to see. My neck heats. He looks at me, dead serious. "This isn't how you deal with bad news. I need you to promise me that you understand that before you try to go win back my little sister."

I swallow, my jaw tensing. "Of course. I mean... Thanks. I don't really know what else to say."

He steps off the latch, looking at me. "Don't say it to me. Say it to Annika. She's the one that you seem to have massively ticked off somehow."

I take a deep breath, sucking it into my lungs. Running a hand over my face, I try to figure out what I could say to her.

"Where do I even start? What does Nika need me to say? Because I will say anything if it means she'll take me back." For keeps this time.

His lips twitch. "I would start with that. And telling her that you love her can never steer you wrong."

He picks up a set of keys from the counter by the fridge, holding them out to me. "It sounds like you have a ton of stuff to work out. I have to head back to the city but I'm glad that you are going to meet Nika at the house."

Bowing my head gratefully, I grab the keys and walk him to the front door. "Thanks man. Really."

We hug briefly and then Lars leaves me alone with a million thoughts crowding in on each other.

Chapter Thirty-Six

ANNIKA

AS WE PULL up to the big beach house just north of Copenhagen, I look up at the modern structure with a silent sigh. I don't want to be here. I'm a hundred percent sure that all I will think about the entire time I am at this particular house will be Erik.

How nearly three months ago to the day, I kissed him clumsily for the first time. Little did I know, it would spark something so consuming and burn for so long.

I climb out of the car, pressing my lips into a thin line and shouldering my bag. It's a little cooler outside now then it was that day three months ago. But despite the changing weather, everything else is the same. I glanced up at this cloudless sky and wish like hell that Kal and Pippa had just let me stay in Tuscany.

Kal glances at me, leading the way up to the door. "Are you okay with this?"

I shrug even though my heart aches. "We are here already. There's no point in going back, is there?"

Pippa heads up the end of our little party of three. She just joined me and Kalindi in Copenhagen and she smiles at me carefully, like I'm fragile and going to shatter at any moment.

Granted, I did well up at least twice on the ride here so…

Kal opens the door, standing back to let Pippa and me through. From here, I head straight to the stairs. Pippa stops me with a gentle hand on my elbow.

"Don't you want to check out the downstairs? I think there is some new furniture outside…"

I frown at her. "I just want to go lie down. I'm sorry that I'm not psyched up for this mini vacation. I just feel like I am better off being by myself. You can't make anybody depressed if you don't hang out with them."

Kal comes up behind me, putting her arm around my shoulders. She pushes the bag off my shoulder and gives me a little squeeze. "Come outside. Just for a minute. And then you can go upstairs and hide if you really want to."

I roll my eyes but put my bag to the side near the wall. "Okay, okay. Five minutes. Then I can hang out by myself all I want to. Deal?"

Kal shakes her head at me. "Deal, I guess."

Pippa and Kal put their bags beside mine and we all trail toward the back of the house, making our way to the back door. From here, I can see through the plate glass windows that a white tent has been erected over the whole patio area. I squint at it, seeing a flash of movement inside the tent.

I look suspiciously at Pippa. "What is this? Please tell me that you guys didn't do anything foolish. There isn't a party out there, is there?"

Pivot shoots me a sneaky grin. "Nope. Come on, we want to see your face when you see what is in store for you."

Rolling my eyes like it's going out of style, I open the sliding door and step outside. It's only about forty paces from the back door of the house to the back of the tent. Glancing over my shoulder at Kal, I shake my head and take a deep breath. Then I plunge inside.

My eyes widen. My jaw drops.

I look around at the scene before me, disbelieving. It's noisy in here, lots of electronic beeping sounds. The walls and ceiling are painted to look like an arcade, complete with brick façade and glowing neon electric signs. On the floor around me I see tons of machines, the cabinets of video games, an air hockey table, and a whole bank of nothing but Skee-Ball machines.

At the far end of the tent, there is a whole bar set up, bar taps and everything. Behind it, a whole tower of shelves holding liquor bottles sits, lit by glowing neon lights from beneath each shelf.

I take a few steps forward, looking at a small table that has been placed amongst the machines. It has several kinds of junk food, pizza rolls and popcorn and dishes of sugar free toffees. I look around and realize that there are several such tables sprinkled throughout the machines, all throughout the place.

Everywhere I look, it is bright color and flashing lights. The Skee-Ball machines make a raucous dinging.

I turn to look at Pippa and Kal, extremely surprised. This is my private fantasy, not exactly something that the public knows about. It's a dirty little secret of mine. "How did you guys know that I loved the arcade? I can't ever remember sharing that with either of you…"

Kal steps forward, gently turning me around. "You didn't tell us. You told Erik."

I look up and see Erik himself, wearing dark jeans and a white T-shirt. He has an anxious expression on his face, like he is not sure whether I would want to see him or not.

Instantly, my heartbeat starts pounding in my ears. I catch his eye and swallow, not sure what is happening. I feel Kal and Pippa take couple of steps back, receding into the background.

There is only Erik in this room as far as I am concerned. But do I even want to see him?

He runs his fingers through his hair and swallows. I take a step forward, uncertain. He beckons to me, inviting me to come closer.

Taking a deep breath, I take five steps towards him. When I am close enough almost to touch, I stop and look up at him, licking my lips nervously. "What are you doing here, Erik?"

He smiles at me, a dimple flashing in his cheek. "You said to me once that if you could stay in the arcade forever, you would. So, I thought that bringing the arcade to you wouldn't hurt anything." He reaches out, taking my hand. The feel of his hot fingers against my cool ones makes me shiver.

I gaze up at him, not really understanding what's happening. "That doesn't really answer my question, does it?"

He smiles again and shakes his head. "I was trying to think of the best way to beg you to come back to me. And I figured that using a place that we were so happy once could only help my circumstances.' He tugs me closer, using his free hand to brush a lock of my hair back and cup my cheek. My eyes fill with tears as I scan his face. He seems so earnest.

"What about the future?" I whisper.

He pulls me against his big body. I lean my head back, not sure that this is even real. Ever so slowly, he starts talking. "I have realized a few things since you left. I realize I don't have any control over what may happen. I can't predict the future. But one thing I can do is be with you, be whatever you need, for as long as you will let me. And I realized how foolish I've been to push you away for something that's completely out of your control. I'm sorry, Annika."

I bite my lip. "That doesn't really solve any of the things you were really worried about though, does it?"

He laces our fingers together, his eyes burning into mine. "None of that really matters though. Does it? I mean, there is an income disparity between us. There is no denying that. And you are much too young for me. But I can't help the way I feel."

He hesitates. "I love you, Annika. So much that it hurts. And if you are willing to set aside all of these shortcomings that I have, I will promise that you will have me for as long as you want me."

My breath leaves my lungs. It takes a second to get my bearings. "What are you saying, Erik?"

He smiles at me softly, that dimple flashing in his cheek again. "If you're asking whether I brought a ring with me, the answer is yes. I don't know if you want that though." He tilts his head, his gaze dropping to my lips. "I love you, Nika. I'm crazy about you. And I'll do whatever I have to do to have you by my side. Even if that means appearing at public functions as nothing more than your boyfriend."

My brow furrows. "Oh, Erik. I was so destroyed when we broke up. I don't know if I can do that again. I don't know that I will survive."

He meets my eye again, stepping back for a second. Then he pulls a ring box out of his pocket, dropping to one knee. My hands fly up, covering my mouth. My eyes widen. "You're going to do this right now?"

He opens the ring box. I'm expecting a gorgeous, dazzling platinum and diamond ring. But instead of that, the ring he won me at the arcade sits nestled amongst the velvet. I start crying at that, the fact that he managed to keep that ring.

It means more to me than I can say.

"See, Annika? I do know you," he says, grinning. "And I would gladly pledge my life to you rather than see you walk away from me again. Give me your hand."

I hesitate for a moment, wiping my eyes. Then I take a deep breath and extend my shaking hand towards him.

His fingers are warm when he takes my hand.

"Ready?"

I manage a nod. "Yes, Erik. You have to know that my answer is yes."

He grins. "Let me get through my speech, woman."

Shaking my head, I grin. "Okay."

He takes a deep breath. Looking at me, his gaze fears me. "Nika, you are wise and funny and brave and extremely compassionate. I would be lucky to spend my life with you. Will you do me the honor of becoming my bride?"

Tears overwhelm me, making it almost impossible to speak. I nod enthusiastically, forcing out the word. "Yes..."

He slides the ring up my fourth finger, a grin on his lips. "I'm a lucky man."

He stands up and pulls me close, bending me back before kissing me so totally and completely that I am left breathless. I raise my hand to his cheek, cupping his face and feeling so overjoyed that I can't even speak.

That's when Kal and Pippa stepped back into my line of sight, both of them looking pleased as punch. Kal reaches out a hand, touching my arm gently. "We're so happy for you. And I will just assume that you forgive us for our little deception..."

I sniffle. "I think so, this time."

I hug Kal and Pippa, struggling just to breathe. Erik stands back and lets us have a moment. Then he pulls at my hand.

"Come on. I got four Skee-Ball machines. I think that this calls for some champagne and an epic Skee-Ball showdown."

I grin at him, kissing him on the lips. I swear, my heart is so full just from looking at him that I'm on the cusp of crying again. "That sounds perfect."

He grabs me by the waist and lifts me in the air. "I love you, Nika."

Tears gather at the corners of my eyes. "I love you too, Erik."

He squeezes my hand then starts toward the back corner of the tent, a smile on his lips.

Chapter Thirty-Seven

ERIK

MY GRIP TIGHTENS on Nika's waist as I look around the crowded room. She's in her finest, wearing a gown of gold lamé that looks like it was painted on. And I am hovering beside her, an anxious man in a tux. I feel like at any moment, I could be replaced by any decent looking man my age.

Annika reaches over and takes my hand, squeezing it as she looks at me. "We are almost done. Really. This is a pretty fair exchange for stepping away from royal duty."

I look down into her beautiful face and I can't help but smile. "I know. The royal family has to make a big deal over our engagement. I get that. I just… I haven't seen Stellan and I am sort of…" I trail off, shrugging.

My gaze wanders up, taking in everyone in the ballroom again. Nika gets drawn into yet another conversation about her ring. We did the proper thing and went to an actual jeweler, spending a fuck ton of money to nab the perfect princess cut platinum and diamond ring.

She still wears the other ring on a little chain around her neck, refusing to take it off. And I have to say, part of me loves her for that.

I fidget with the coins in my pants pockets, resisting the urge to check my watch for the five millionth time. Nika is right; this is a small price to pay for the relative anonymity that we asked for. In exchange, we've worked out a much stepped down plan with the royal press office. They get her one weekend a month.

The rest of the time, Annika and I can roll around like two happy clams at the royal beach house. Since I purchased the house outright, I will never have to worry about following the royal rules. With the purchase of my second property, my stable of homes has begun to look quite comfortable.

I spot Mr. Earl, his rumpled tux and his graying hair unmistakable. He's one of King Stellan's advisors and he corners me, clapping me on the shoulder and wishing me good luck. "I have to say, we will miss you around here. I know that the rumors about you stealing off with our own Princess Annika are rampant around here… But I still think you are a great fellow."

"Thank you. I have already branched out and started my own venture capital firm. I think Princess Annika and I will be just fine."

Mr. Earl looks puzzled. "Venture capital? Isn't that a little out of your wheelhouse? I would think that you would just apply for a similar position with another high profile person."

I struggle to maintain a blank expression. "Yeah, well. I'm going to miss working at the palace. But I am sure you will be glad to know that I will be working to make the princess happy. And what makes her happy is not being in the spotlight." A little lie, but this is politics, after all. If Mr. Earl were being truthful with me or anyone else here, he would have come out of the closet a long time ago.

Mr. Earl smiles. "So, there's no truth to the fact that you were unceremoniously fired, then?"

I arch a brow. "Nope. I don't know where you heard that."

I see Nika moving away, turning her head back for just a second to make sure that I'm okay. I bow to Mr. Earl, excusing myself.

One of the palace employees manages to step between me and Nika, bringing me up short. I looked down into his dark features with a frown. He smiles nervously.

"If you don't mind, there is a phone call for you, sir."

I take a deep breath and nod. "Lead the way."

I touch Nika shoulder as I go by her, smiling faintly. The employee leads me out of the grand ballroom and across the hall to an empty office. There's nothing in the room except for a desk and an old, gold-plated telephone. I look at the landline, a little surprised. But the palace employee merely bows, letting himself out of the room and closing the door. I sigh, picking up the phone.

"Hello?"

"It's your father."

He coughs loudly, clearing his throat. I narrow my eyes at the phone.

"So… what, now we are in fact related? Because I can definitely give you the name of at least five nurses that will swear up and down that we are not blood relations, according to you."

He coughs again. "You think that you can just get married to one of them royals without even so much as telling your father about it? You're spoiled. That's one of the reasons why I didn't need you or anyone else hanging about my bedside, wringing your hands."

I pinch the bridge of my nose. If I had been told that my father was the one on the phone, I might have just skipped this conversation altogether. "Have you called to wish your son congratulations, then?"

He guffaws. "You think you're so great and so smart. You'll see. You're not any better than me. When the little princess figures out that you are just a haircut in a suit, she will be done with you. And when that happens, don't come crying…"

I grit my teeth. "Shut up! I should've said that to you years ago. Just shut up! If you have anything else to say about Annika or our relationship, about which you know nothing at all, you can just keep it to yourself. You're a hateful old man. And I fully expect an apology the next time that you decide to call me. Otherwise? Don't call me."

I slam the phone down, running my hands down my sleeves and pulling out my cuffs. I'm furious, of course.

But it feels good to have said what I wanted to say for so long to my father. There are some people that just can't change or be helped. I guess my father is just one of them. And I will do my best to do better than he did, if Annika and I ever have kids.

That's years down the road, anyway.

I take a deep, calming breath and center myself. And then I pull the door open, striding out into the hallway.

A tall, dark-haired man dressed in a tuxedo stands by the doorway to the ballroom, looking on quietly. When I get closer, he turns his head and I see that it is Stellan.

I feel like he punches me in the gut just by looking at me. I don't see Margot anywhere. He clenches his fists when he sees me, his gaze narrowing.

My expression hardens. I guess it's going to be one of those days where I get a lot of things off my chest, all at once. So be it.

I stalk up to him, keeping an imperious expression on my face. He watches me warily, holding a hand up to preempt me.

"I come in peace," he says, frowning.

I fold my arms across my chest, unamused. "What are you doing here? I thought you were supposed to be on your honeymoon."

He jerks his head inside the ballroom. I look inside and see a tiny woman with pink hair hugging my fiancée. Margot looks like a pixie, beaming up at Annika. The hard knot in my stomach unclenches just a tiny bit.

Stellan sighs. "I didn't realize that you two were in love," he comments. He looks over at me, pursing his lips. "It seems awfully fast though."

I arch a brow at him. "I think my courtship with Nika actually lasted longer than yours. How long did you and Margot make it before your engagement was announced?"

His lips thin. "Don't."

I just shrug. "I won't apologize for doing exactly what you did."

"The difference is my baby sister. Why did you have to choose her, of all the fucking women in the world?"

My gaze narrows on his face. "It wasn't a choice. You don't fall in love because you want to, in my experience. It just happened. And I'm fucking lucky that I fell for Nika." My lips twitch and my gaze is pulled back to her. "You might not know this, but she's the best person I know. While you guys weren't looking, she was growing one hell of a feisty, funny personality."

Stellan is silent for half a minute. "It's nice to hear someone stick up for her."

I slide him a careful look. "I told you. I love Annika."

He drags in a deep breath, pinning me with that eerie gaze of his. That look wouldn't have been out of place on Nika's face.

"I'm not just going to forgive you."

"Did I ask for your forgiveness?"

He purses his lips. "No."

Brushing the front of my suit jacket off, I give him a look. "As far as I'm concerned, we aren't even friends anymore. You called me garbage. Friends don't do that, especially not when they know that word has been used against me by my father."

Stellan appears taken aback by that. "Ah." He scrunches up his face. "I'm sorry. I was angry."

"You were a douche."

He gives me a flat look. "You slept with my little sister!"

I roll my eyes. "Your friendship has been very important to me, Stellan. When you kicked me out of your wedding and Nika wouldn't talk to me, I realized how much my life and yours were intertwined." I frown a little. "But I think I have to draw a line in the sand. If I have to choose between you or Annika, I choose her. I would choose her a thousand times over."

One corner of his mouth lifts briefly. "As much as it pains me to say this, I understand. If I were put in the same position, I would choose my wife over you." He scrunches up his face. "I don't want to have to choose, though."

"Well, neither do I."

We look at each other for a long moment. Then he glances away.

"We have extended our honeymoon for two more weeks. After we get back, maybe we should talk. We can even talk about you coming back to work for the family."

I hesitate. "I would like to figure things out between us. But… I won't be returning to the palace as an employee. I've devoted my life to you and the royal family. Now it's time to do something different."

Stellan gives me a long look. "You're a part of the royal family now, don't forget."

I smirk. "I have better things to focus on." I nod to the ballroom, where Margot and Annika are making their way over to us. "I have a feeling you do too."

Stellan stretches, putting his arms over his head. "Yeah. I guess I do."

He smiles as Annika comes over, hugging me as she looks at him shyly. I slide my arm around her waist and pull her close.

"Congrats, little sister."

She beams at him. "Thanks, Stellan."

Margot grabs his hand and looks at Nika and me. "We have a plane to catch. But let me just tell you one more time: I couldn't be happier for the both of you."

I look down at Nika, my grip tightening on her waist. "Thanks."

Leaning down, I kiss her lips and smile. Stellan rolls his eyes. "Okay. We're late. But… when we get back, we should all celebrate privately."

I give Annika a squeeze. She smiles at her brother. "That sounds lovely."

Margot and Stellan say their goodbyes. And I can breathe a little easier, knowing that my biological father might be in the wind, but my adopted family still stands strong.

Chapter Thirty-Eight

ANNIKA

"UGH," I sigh, dropping the final box I've packed on top of a stack of boxes. Stretching out my back, I look around the living room area of the room I called my own.

Erik comes in, a little sweaty from moving boxes around in my former bedroom. I bite my lip and eye him. He smiles at me, sipping water from a bottle.

"Can you believe we're leaving the palace?" he asks.

I shake my head. "No. I really can't. But at the same time, I'm very excited to go. Now that the seasons are changing, I have a wild hair to go up to a little chalet somewhere. It'll be all cold and snowy. And we can hang out by the fire, just the two of us..."

He arches a brow at me. "Naked, I assume. Because that is how I plan to see you the first four months of us living together."

I bite my lip, smiling. He sets his water down and comes over to give me a hug and pat my butt. I lean my head back and look up at him, offering my mouth up for a kiss.

He brushes his lips over my own but then he pulls back with a sigh. "You are a temptation, that's for sure. But if we don't get on the road soon, we won't make it up to the beach house by dark."

I scrunch up my face. "You need to start calling it *our* house. We own it.

And no one else does. It's just a big, beautiful house that happens to be by the beach."

He makes a fake sound of aggravation, a little *grrr*. Then he kisses me on the lips again and starts to head out to the car, picking up a box of my necessities as he goes. He calls over his shoulder. "I'll be right back. When I come back with help, that should speed things along."

I cock my head to the side and watch him walk away, admiring his ass as he goes. Damn. I am still over the moon that I get to see him naked for the rest of my life… What a lucky girl I am.

Sitting down on the pair of couches, I pull out my phone and scroll through my private Instagram. It's mostly pictures of cute animals and feeds from close friends. This way I can still use social media and yet not get overwhelmed by the public.

I see an email from Dr. Baker, my new psychologist. She asks if Tuesday afternoon works for my schedule and I happily reply that I have nothing planned.

That's a weird feeling. Not having to run every single thing by the royal press office is exhilarating.

A knock at the doorway draws my attention up. I look to find Momse standing outside the door, her steel gray skirt suit perfectly complementing her silver updo. When I take too long to invite her in, she narrows her gaze and clears her throat.

"Come in, come in," I say, standing up awkwardly. I probably look like a mess. I've been moving all day and I feel like I look a little squirrely.

Momse walks in, her sharp blue eyes absorbing every detail of the room and my outfit, which is just a pair of black leggings and an old white T-shirt.

"Hello, Annika. I see you have indeed gone through with your little move." One corner of her mouth turns down. "Where is Erik?"

I sweep my hand over the couch, gesturing for her to sit. She perches on it, looking unhappy. Though now that I think about it, when has Momse ever looked happy?

"He's here. He's done almost everything, actually. I've just been directing, mostly."

She crosses her ankles and smooths out her skirts. "Well, that's as it should be. Not only are you the woman of the two of you, you are a princess and he is a commoner. I know you are moving away but there's no cause to forget that."

I repress a sigh. "Are you here to tell me something in particular, Momse? Because I really have a lot left to do today."

That's not true exactly, but it's a coping strategy that Dr. Baker and I came up with.

She tilts her head, looking at me. "Well. Since you are moving out and you will not be under my watch any longer, I thought I would just take a moment to…" She pauses.

My breath catches. For second, as sure that she's about to say something terrible to me. I brace myself for it, blinking my eyes carefully.

But she surprises me.

"I want to say that I was the youngest child in my family. I had seven older brothers and two older sisters. I felt like I spent most of my life being passed over and not made a priority. When I got the chance to marry your grandfather, the king… I jumped at it."

My eyes widen. I lean back, clearing my throat. "Whoa. I didn't know that you came from such a large family."

She gives me a cold little smile. "Yes, well. Family planning wasn't practiced with any regularity back then. Anyway, I wanted to say… I know that being the youngest child can have its disadvantages. And believe it or not, I struggled with being in the public eye when I first married the king."

My brows rise. "Wait, you did? You seem so… poised."

She gives me a smile. "Yes, it would seem that way now. But back in the beginning, my family name was often questioned. It was a lot of strangers, picking over whether my name was good enough for the new king. It was a load of bullshit, if I am perfectly honest about it."

"I had no idea," I tell Momse.

Momse leans closer to me, smiling that cool smile again. "I'm just saying that I have been where you are. Sure, the details are a little different. But I wanted you to know that I do care about you. Things just coincided oddly. Stellan ended up needing so much of my time…" She looks away out the window, frowning. "I suppose I thought that you would be all right here by yourself."

I bite my lip, shifting in my seat uncomfortably. When Momse looks up again, her gaze spears me.

"I'm afraid that I haven't done a very good job with you. Honestly, I don't have the relationship that I would like to have with any of you aside from Stellan. It's… regrettable, to say the least."

If I wasn't working to actively keep my expression straight, my jaw would probably drop. Is this a Momse's way of telling me that she is sorry?

"I… I mean, everything turned out fine." I mumble. "Thanks for coming to me and telling me how you feel, though."

Momse smiles tightly, inhaling deeply. Then she uncrosses her legs and stands up. I hurry to stand up to.

She extends her hand, and I step forward, thinking that we are going to exchange some kind of awkward handshake or something.

Momse surprises me again by pulling me close for a quick, tight hug. Then she steps back, tears in the corners of her eyes. She looks at me.

"Be well, Annika. Please come back to visit regularly."

I open my mouth to answer. She turns, quickly walking out of the room. I stare after her, unsure of what just happened.

Just as Momse leaves, Erik comes through the door. He does a double take, frowning at Momse as she hustles out.

"What was that all about?"

I squint after her. "I think she came in here to apologize. I'm not entirely sure though." I laugh a little, confused.

Erik walks up to me, pulling me down onto the couch again. He seems tired but also, he sounds pretty content. "That's good, I think. We can use all of the royals on our side that we can get."

Burying myself against the wall of his chest, I find comfort in his arms. He kisses the crown of my head absently.

I relax into his hold, feeling like I finally found the person that can make me feel at home.

He picks up my left hand, admiring the engagement ring that sparkles there. "I love you. You know that, right?"

I look up at him, a slow grin spreading across my face. "I do know that. Thanks. And I love you too, if that weren't painfully obvious by now."

He toys with my ring, unable to stop himself from smiling. "It is painfully obvious. But it goes both ways."

I hug him tightly, feeling my heart swell three sizes. I'm not sure what the future holds for either of us, but I know we will face it together.

And with Erik by my side, I could not feel better about the future.

Chapter Thirty-Nine

PIPPA

I'M STANDING in my little apartment in Copenhagen, staring blankly at the peeling bright yellow paint on the kitchen wall. I reach out and trace my fingertips along a seam above the stove, a silent sigh on my lips.

It was a long day at *Politiken*, the newspaper where I work. I feel like I've been wrung out and all my mental energy has been drained away. Now I'm just waiting for my little microwave burrito to be heated through so I can eat and pass out.

My phone chimes, stirring me. I look at it. Lars's photo pops up, a dark haired devil with a cocksure grin. Lars is the king of Denmark's younger brother, one of family of five. He's actual living, breathing royalty and I…

I am a fool for even thinking about what spending a night in his bed would be like. Being underneath his big body as he growls commands and pulls moans from my lips…

It's forbidden. And yet still, my heart squeezes at the very mention of his name.

I know he's my best friend.

I know I should cherish what we already have.

I know I shouldn't long for him to touch me.

And yet, even getting a text from him excites me beyond reason.

I shiver as I check the text.

I'm coming upstairs.

Goosebumps break out over my skin. I close my eyes and hold my cell-phone close to my now rapidly-beating heart.

A few second later, I hear the slide of a key being turned in the lock on the front door. I'm much too tired for any visitors tonight. But Lars has always done exactly what he wanted, exactly when he wants.

This is no exception.

Screwing up my face, I press the pause button on the microwave. Lars walks into my shoddy little apartment, ducking his dark head slightly as he enters. He's so tall that my building's prewar design is really at odds with his height. When he straightens up, he looks at me with his trademark devastating smirk.

I cast a look over his tuxedo, which makes him look ridiculously fetching.

"Hello, Pippa," he purrs.

I swallow, my eyes widening. "Lars." Pushing back several strands of my long, fiery copper hair, I watch as he closes the door behind himself. I spread my hands down the skirt of my gray silk dress, drawing a breath. "It's awfully late. Shouldn't you be on a date with some unnamed mystery blonde?"

His smirk deepens, his aquamarine eyes sparkling. "I was in the middle of a date when I was summoned unceremoniously to the palace."

I fidget. "Why are you here, Lars?"

He wanders toward the living room of my cramped flat, leaving me to follow. He looks around the tiny couch and the ancient television that is stacked atop several light blue milk crates.

Every surface is covered with reading material, books and magazines and newspaper clippings. Piles spill into piles; the television screen is actually blocked by a towering stack of literature. I admit that I'm a bit of a mess and I'm ashamed to say that there is nowhere to sit.

Wrinkling my nose, I automatically start to clear off the sofa, my cheeks burning. I gather an armful of books, but I'm not sure where to put them.

"Let me just find a place for these…" I murmur, casting my gaze around the small space. I find a spot on the very top of another pile of books, biting my lower lip hard as I turn around.

"Pippa, I don't need to sit down," he says, grabbing my hand. His touch is electric. When I glance up at him, his blue gaze sears me through.

I raise an eyebrow. "What do you need?"

He smirks a bit, pulling me a little closer, making me look up into his face. From this distance, a hair's breadth away from our bodies touching, I feel adrenaline coursing through my veins.

"I need a favor."

My forehead creases. My mouth turns down just a bit at the corners. This is what he does, what he has always done. He uses his charm, knowing quite well how smoothly hypnotic his presence can be. I've seen him do it to hundreds of women in the years that I've known him.

Usually he doesn't use it on *me*, though.

I pull out of his grasp, moving back a half step. "What is it?"

His expression grows intense. "I need you to pretend that I have asked you to marry me and you have said yes."

I swear, I don't mean to laugh. But it bubbles up from deep within my chest and bursts out of my lips, a snort of disbelief and a surprised chuckle all at once.

"What?" I ask, the word coming out strangled.

He squints at me. "I slept with the wrong diplomat's daughter."

I fold my arms across my chest, trying to slow my racing heart. "Again? How many times do you have to get caught before someone banishes you from the whole country of Denmark?"

His gaze tightens on my face. "It's really not funny. And now unless I have a really good excuse, I'm going to have to join the navy. Obviously, I don't want that. I mean, have you seen the inside of a submarine? That would seriously cramp my style."

A low throb starts at my temple. I rub it with one hand, staring at Lars. "And this has what to do with me, exactly?"

He steps closer, snagging my free hand and bringing it to rest against the hard wall of his chest. "I need a fake fiancée. Momse told me today that unless I settle down and get married, I'm going to have to join the military."

I push my cheek out with my tongue. "What is stopping you from finding the right girl?"

Someone royal. Or at least someone without the… let's call them *complications* that my history presents. I know very well the list of reasons why I can't be tied to someone like me.

I'm a fraud.

I'm a fake and a liar.

I'm not who I say I am.

And that's only the *beginning* of my troubles if anyone finds out.

He gives me a wicked little grin. "You're saying I should sign my death warrant, then? Because that is what being told that I have to get married feels like. I don't want to be tied down. I don't want to be smothered. I just want to keep living like I do now."

I shake my head. "Lars, really—"

He slides his hands down my back and pulls my hips against his. My breath catches in my chest as I gaze up into those pretty blue eyes of his.

I'm *this close* to pushing up on my tiptoes and pressing my lips against his.

Arching a brow, he utters the magic word. "I really need this. Please, Pips? Do it for me?"

And just like that, all my defenses melt away.

Of course I will do it for him.

How can I not?

Lars sees the expression of my face change and knows my answer before I even say it.

"Okay," I whisper.

He's already folding his strong arms around me, pulling me into the shelter of his body. "Ahh, thanks, Pips. I knew you would come through."

I sink into the bear hug, my eyes fluttering closed. He's sinfully warm. His smell, pure and clean and masculine, is driving me wild right now.

I inhale of lungful of his scent, feeling like a fool. "That's me. Reliable old Pippa saves the day again."

Lars pulls back. I look up at him with a dreamy-eyed expression and he grins. "Should we wake the jewelers at Tiffany's up right now? Shit, I should've stopped on the way here and gotten you a ring—"

I push him away, eyeing him firmly. "There will have to be rules. A firm time limit, for instance. And… no physical contact."

He gives me a funny look. "It's going to take a little hugging and kissing to convince my family, don't you think?"

I squint at him. "I mean when we are alone."

He rolls his eyes. "Yeah, sure. I will behave like a proper gentleman, if that's what you want."

I shake my head, crossing my arms. "No one has ever thought to call you a proper gentleman, I'm fairly certain."

Lars grins at me, his eyes glittering. "If that's what it takes, I'm willing to try."

I shoot him a look. "I'm regretting this already."

He tilts his head, considering me. "Should we go for a drink to celebrate?"

Stepping closer to him, I turn him around and begin marching him toward the door. "We can figure it all out tomorrow. For now, I want to eat something before I pass out."

He chuckles, opening the front door. He catches my hand and gives me a squeeze. "You really are the best, Pippa. You know that, right?"

The corners of my mouth tighten. "Do me a favor. Don't sleep with anyone, okay? If this little deception is going to work, you'll have to play along and not be your usual man-whore self for a while."

Lars smirks at me. "You got it, love of my life."

For a second, I can't even wrap my head around that. My heartbeat speeds up. If he had any idea of how long I've waited to hear those words…

But then he turns, showing me his black-clad back as he disappears down the hall.

"Goodnight, Pippa…" he calls over his shoulder.

I watch him disappear, slumping against the doorframe when I hear the downstairs front door open and close.

I am in so much trouble.

I know that.

If anyone does the slightest bit of digging, I could be exposed.

My life would cease to be my own at that point.

But I can still feel my heart racing, feel the heat of his body pressed against mine. I can sense the excited energy that follows Lars in his wake, everywhere he goes.

Deep in my soul, I know that I shouldn't have agreed to be his fake fiancée.

Oh god.

What have I gotten myself into?

Turning, I close my door and head back to my sad microwave dinner.

You can pre-order Royal Fake Fiancé here.

Chapter Forty

THERE'S a little bit more of Erik and Annika, just waiting for you! Get the bonus chapters — once the beginning of the story — right now when you sign up for Vivian's mailing list! Head to https://BookHip.com/LMWGNK for more info.

Thank you for reading His Forbidden Princess! I know if you liked this book, you will LOVE Lars and Pippa's story, ***Royal Fake Fiancé***! Look for it in Winter 2020.

You can get it right now!

Sign up HERE for my mailing list to get the FIRST *Royal Fake Fiancé* news and to hear about freebies first!

Sinful Princess Bonus Epilogue

Chapter One

"COME." Momse, my rather severe grandmother, pulls me out of the ballroom where the soiree is in full swing. The sound of the string quartet and the gentle murmur of the crowd of people follows us out into the hall. My grandmother's sleek black evening gown rustles a bit as she turns, handing me a glossy tabloid magazine.

She narrows her eyes at me. "The Princess Annika Problem has surfaced again."

I glance down at the tabloid. I scowl, plucking at the skirt of my strapless silk ballgown. "I hate when you use that phrase, Momse."

She arches a brow. "If you would behave yourself, the phrase would not exist."

I'm sitting here in heavy shadow, wishing like hell I were anywhere else but here.

Anywhere but trapped in this room, being lectured by the Queen Mother on how I should work harder at being the princess that the Danish people truly desire.

It makes me want to scream.

Looking down at the tabloid, I scan the headline. ROYAL BLUES: NEW KING'S BABY SISTER IS OUT ALL NIGHT AGAIN!!

Below that, there is a photo of me from a couple months ago, being dragged out of a club in the wee hours of the morning. I'm young, blonde, exceedingly thin, and wearing an expensive dress. Mostly importantly, I look barely conscious, my ice blue eyes barely open as two bodyguards push me into a car.

My eyes immediately travel to my arms, which the bodyguard has in his grasp; his hold makes the part of my arms above where his hands are look like they are fatter than they really are.

I take the photo in without saying a word, but I definitely flinch. I circle my upper arm with my fingers and try to keep my breathing even. The paparazzi always focus on my weight or my so-called partying. According to them I'm either starving myself, pigging out, drying out, or liquored up.

This is why I hate the press.

"Annika!" Momse says.

I raise my chin and swallow. "This picture was not my best moment, I'll admit. Especially since the paparazzi apparently only have this one picture and they splash it across the pages of their magazines anytime it's a slow news day."

Momse's eyes narrow. She shakes her head and paces a little, winding up for a lecture. When she speaks, her voice is low.

"Annika, be serious for once in your life. You cannot do anything to encourage the revitalization of The Princess Annika Problem. Since you've returned from boarding school in Switzerland you've been walking a tightrope—"

Heaven forbid we draw any attention to ourselves. My mouth twists.

"I've learned to leave nightclubs through the service doors, if that's what this entire thing is about," I bite off.

My grandmother doesn't roll her eyes. She merely looks away toward the shadows. She walks farther away from the ballroom, expecting me to follow her down the hallway.

I was raised by her; I'm not fooled by her aloofness. She's seriously ticked off by me and my behavior. Just like always.

"I don't think you were capable of leaving that club at all," she says.

I stop in the middle of the hallway, bunching my hands in my dress. That last barb really *stung*.

"Annika!" Momse scolds. "You are ruining your dress! Stand up straight. You were raised to be elegant. I know that you know to be better behaved."

I open my mouth to fire back a retort, but I'm interrupted by the arrival of my brother Stellan and his new fiancee Margot. He's at the other end of the hall but he's headed this way with a furious expression.

"I have a problem," he declares.

I squint at him, but he has locked in on my grandmother. I see the change in Momse as Stellan approaches; her posture straightens a fraction, her eyes light up.

It's her favorite grandchild, the king of Denmark. It takes everything in me not to pull a face.

Stellan has only recently become the king. But he has the swagger of a man who knows he owns everything in sight; he's always been imperious and lordly, even before he had the title to match his attitude.

He stalks down the hallway, tall, dark, and commanding. There is an angry expression on his face that makes my gut roil.

"Momse—" he starts, then spots me. "Annika. How fortuitous. I was just coming to talk to Momse about you."

Well that can't be good. I wrinkle my nose. "Lucky me."

Margot trails after Stellan, looking for all the world like a tiny cupcake with her pink hair, small frame, and short pink cotton dress. Everything about her is petite and yet she never seems to diet; I would hate her for that alone, but she's actually pretty sweet.

Margot's cautious expression is out of place on her normally expressive face; I can bet that it is the result of too many run-ins with Momse. She scans the hallway, bows to Momse, and then makes the wise decision to head for me.

"*Haj*," I mouth to her. Her eyes sparkle for a second and she winks at me, but otherwise doesn't call any attention to herself.

That's wise, considering the mood of everyone else that's present. Stellan paces the floor, looking mad.

My grandmother walks over and pats his cheek. "Hello, darling. It's good to see you, even if you are only visiting to talk about your sister."

I narrow my eyes at the exchange. Momse has a special place in her heart for my brother, now the king; always has, always will. I've never had that kind of relationship with our grandmother.

If I was forced to put my feelings into words, I would say that I'm definitely jealous. As the baby of the family and last of five children, I always get the leftover dregs of affection and attention. Whatever heedfulness and warmth doesn't go to Stellan or one of my older brothers, whatever sunlight filters down through the trees to my on the forest floor.

The same rule rule applied to my mother and father too. It seems like they just… can't be bothered with me.

I hate to say that I'm desperate for any attention paid to me, but there it is.

Stellan accepts her touch for a moment before pulling away. His face flushes and he clears his throat. "Annika, this morning when I woke up, I found a note waiting for me. It was a blackmail demand from a reporter looking for an interview. Do you know what he plans to use as leverage?"

I scrunch up my face. They could be using anything as blackmail. I can think of five or six stories that I wouldn't want getting out…. but it's best not to let my brother know that.

"No," I say, keeping it simple.

He points to the *Ekstra Bladet* in my hands, glaring at me. "There are apparently a whole new set of photos to accompany the current one they have."

I shoot him a look. "That's not fair. It was was so long ago!"

"It was two months ago," Stellan corrects me.

My grandmother tuts. "The truth hardly matters. The reporters don't care," she says, her tone sharp. "Margot, you used to be a reporter… Tell my granddaughter that your former colleagues don't care, my dear."

Margot's face flushes. I look at her, raising a brow. She wrinkles her nose.

"Sorry, Annika. They really don't care. Even when a reporter is on your side, they are still working some kind of angle."

I repress an eye roll. I like Margot, but she's still kissing my grandmother's ass.

Momse smiles coolly at us. "See? I told you."

It's impossible not to roll my eyes. "I get it, okay? I don't what I'm supposed to do about it though. If I could turn back time I would make a different choice. But I can't. And lecturing me about it doesn't really do either of us any good."

"Annika, this is very serious," Stellan snaps, narrowing his eyes at me. "Margot and I have enough gossip and innuendo to deal with. The day after tomorrow is our engagement announcement; we'll be trying to defend ourselves every moment from then until the wedding. Margot being…

Margot… is going to be enough of a challenge without you adding anything to our load."

I wave the tabloid at him. "I didn't do anything to warrant this story being printed today. What would you have me do differently? Do I just need to spend the next few months banished to Antartica? How can I possibly bend over backward *more* to make it easier for *you two* to deal with the press?"

He rolls his eyes. "I'm really not asking very much. Just cool it until the official wedding ceremony. That's only three months from now."

Momse straightens. "Actually, it would be better if Annika kept a low profile indefinitely."

My brow lowers. "Why don't I just fuck off and live somewhere without the internet or telephones? That's what would suit you the best."

My grandmother doesn't bat an eyelash. "Language, young lady. And are you offering? Because we can gas up a private jet at a moment's notice."

Stellan shoots her a cutting look. "You aren't helping right now, Momse."

She shrugs elegantly. "I'm only being practical."

Margot speaks up. "There must be something we can do to appease both sides. A compromise can be found, surely."

Momse glares at her, making her face go red. Stellan has more patience with his bride to be.

"I'm sure that there is some middle ground," he agrees, looking at Margot with a soft smile.

"Do you two need us to leave?" I ask.

Margot and Stellan both give me hard looks.

"Don't be bitter. It doesn't suit you," Stellan snaps.

I favor him with a frown. "It is not my fault that the newspapers find every single thing I do newsworthy. I can't go anywhere or do anything without it being recorded." I wave the tabloid paper at him again. "This photo was taken in Switzerland after a friend's birthday party. I had too much to drink, yes. But what you don't see pictured here are other the seven drunk girls being carted out of the club." I toss the tabloid onto the floor, disgusted. "That's because there aren't any photos of them. Everyone else gets to live their lives in relative anonymity if that's what they choose."

"We are the royal family," my grandmother says, raising her chin. "We were born into it. We did not choose it. And yet, there will always be eyes on us. Watching. Waiting for us to fail. It goes with the territory, Annika."

I just shake my head. "What do you want me to do, exactly?"

"We are just asking for you to be extra vigilant," Stellan says. "Keep your head down. If you can't do that, I'll have to assign you a babysitter."

I chuckle. "I'm sorry, what?"

Margot shoots Stellan a look. "That would be extreme."

"It would be fitting," Momse says. "Stellan, why don't we just put two-man security team on Annika until your wedding?"

My fists ball up.

"Umm, hello. The last time I checked, this was not a fascist state. You don't need to restrict my movements by weighing me down with a bunch of uptight bodyguards!" I protest.

"Oh, they're not that bad," Momse says dismissively. "You would get used to them. After a while, you'd forget that they were even there."

Stellan makes eye contact with me. He squints; I get the distinct feeling that I'm being measured right now. Finally he sighs.

"Just stay under the radar, okay? I don't want you to feel punished. I just want everything to go smoothly."

My grandmother sniffs but she doesn't say a word. Of course not; Stellan is her favorite grandchild. What he says goes.

I swallow and nod. "*Ja*, okay."

"Good." He looks at his watch. "And now if you will excuse us, I think we are overdue to talk to the Prime Minster. Margot?"

Margot takes the arm he offers. She smiles at me. "We should get together, just you and me. You can give me all of the dirt on Stellan. Okay?"

I nod and smile. She squeezes me shoulder as she follows Stellan out of the room. Then I'm left with Momse once more.

"Satisfied?" I ask her.

She gives me an icy smile. "Almost never, my dear."

I roll my eyes and head down the hallway, heading to rejoin the party. I have almost reached the wide double doors when Momse calls my name.

"Annika."

I turn back, raising a brow. "Yes?"

"Be a good girl."

I scowl at her advice. What does that even mean?

I bob my head and then push myself into the gala, quickly fading into the background of rich people sipping champagne and dancing.

Chapter Two

"AND THEN I said that I'm really only asking her to cool it until the wedding." Stellan shakes his head, looking down at his tie. "Is this thing straight?"

I run a hand down my own tie, peering at his. "It's definitely crooked. Here."

I pull him over to an ancient-looking standing mirror, showing him. We are reflected in the surface. Stellan is tall and dark haired, his expensive dark suit clinging to his shoulders. I have blond hair, hazel eyes, and an ever so slightly taller frame. In this particular suit, I look like the grave digger someone brought in out of the cold and shoved into an expensive garment.

I have always felt like the awkward wraith clinging to the shadows whenever Stellan is around, even when we were very little.

"Shit." He makes a face, trying to fix it. I step in and straighten it, frowning a little. When I'm finished, I step back and he claps me on the back. "You are still the best royal chaperone that anyone could hope for, Erik."

He chuckles. I merely grunt, looking behind us. We are standing in the wings of the Royal Danish Theater, waiting for the ancient windbags before us to finish talking about how important the ballet is. As the new king,

Stellan is tasked with opening the ballet season. But he's also due for four other speaking engagements today and time is running short.

I frown at my expensive watch. "We are supposed to be back in the limo in half an hour," I sigh. "If these guys would hurry the fuck up, we can still make it to the next appointment on time."

Stellan looks at me, his lips quirking. "You always say that. You're a control freak."

I shoot him a glare. "If everyone would respect our time, there wouldn't be an issue." I pause. "Maybe four engagements is too many. Sine you've become the king, everyone wants more time with you."

He shrugs a shoulder. "I seem to recall you having the exact same complaints before I was king. It's probably the very first thing that you ever complained about, back when we were kids."

That makes me smile ruefully. "Well, I don't like to be told where to go and what to do. Which makes me ill-suited to be your personal secretary, I guess. Because there are always people trying control you… and where you go, I go."

A small sigh escapes his lips. "It's just part of the contract I have with the Danish people."

I'm more than aware of that. Just like I'm aware of being a hybrid between the royal family and the staff. As a kid, when we would pack up and head to the Greek Isles for summer vacation, I could always sense the ambivalence of the adults around me.

He's just the son of the stable master. Do we really need to accommodate him on the royal yacht?

In the end, Stellan would throw an absolute fit if I wasn't right beside him at all times. That cut both ways though… it was shelter, yes. But it was also another person holding me in place…

Telling me what to do. I don't like being told what to do by anyone, not even Stellan.

"They could really hurry things up," he says with another sigh. He cranes his neck, checking on the progress of the parade of people on stage. "What was I telling you? I interrupted myself."

I squint. "Something about your little sister, I think."

Stellan's face lights up. "Ah! You should've seen the look on her face when I told her that she has to be on her best behavior. Annika was ready to murder me."

My lips curve up as I imagine it: the sultry blond Annika, all dressed up, her perfect red lips forming a pout, her powder blue eyes narrowing just slightly. It's definitely a look I've seen on her face plenty of times since she came back to Copenhagen last year.

"I bet," I reply, looking at my watch.

Stellan gives me a look. "I'm not boring you, am I?"

I shake my head. "I'm just annoyed with everyone that planned this event. More than usual, it feels like."

A plump older woman comes rushing up to us, dressed in a black velvet gown that is about four sizes too small. "Your royal highness," she says, curtsying. "We are ready for you onstage."

Stellan smiles and allows her to usher him toward the waiting crowd. He calls back. "I'll try to keep it short!"

I pull out my phone and look at the calendar for today. We are definitely not going to make it to the next engagement, which is supposed to take place on the other side of the city. I fire off a quick text message to the royal press office to let them know.

What they do with that information, I don't know. I'm too busy focusing on whatever comes next.

I pace a little, wandering away from the stage and into the ill-lit back hallway. Colorful props and black velvet draped backdrops line both sides of the hallway, but I am too sucked into my phone to really pay much attention.

I thumb through the pages of my phone's calendar, trying to see if it truly will be possible to cut down our engagements. It isn't until someone clears their throat. I look up to find a whip-thin man in a tuxedo staring at me expectantly.

"You're not where you're supposed to be," he scolds me.

I squint a little. "Excuse me?"

"The wait staff are supposed to be in the kitchen," he sniffs. "Run along please."

I glance down at the multi-thousand pound bespoke suit I'm wearing. Sure, it's a black suit and I'm wearing a white shirt and dark blue tie. But it's well made.

Stellan has three just like it in his closet.

I narrow my eyes. "I don't work here."

He gives me a suspicious look. "Oh?"

"I'm Prince—" I halt, catching myself just in time. "King Stellan's private secretary."

He doesn't look convinced. "All the staff should be in the back area. You're right be the stage right now… wander the wrong way and someone might see you."

I glare at him. "I'm fine where I am, thank you."

"How did you get such a position? I've met most of the former king's private secretaries and they have all been much older than him."

I raise an eyebrow. "The king and I were raised together."

He coughs, turning red. "What's that, you say?"

"I said that I've known Stellan since I was four years old."

He coughs again, producing a handkerchief out of his pocket. "You come from noble stock?" He scans me briefly.

I feel my neck heat. "No. I didn't say that. Not that's any of your business anyway."

He sneers. "I didn't think so. Your accent says that you were educated, though."

My hands curl into fists. I start looking around for a way out of this conversation. "Yes. King Stellan and I were playmates. We were raised side by side and educated together. Now if you don't mind, I should really place a call."

Slipping my phone out of my pocket, I ignore the old man and start messing with the phone's screen.

His eyes tighten on my face. Then he shrugs, wandering off, muttering about uppity staff. He's clearly a fossil from a bygone era but he managed to put me in a foul mood.

An alert pops up on my screen and I select it. The stock market app on my phone notifies me that I have five stocks currently rising quickly in value; one of them is a little known tech stock that I predicted last week would triple in market price.

It looks like I was right. Which is good, since I bought ten thousand pounds worth of shares. Scrolling down, I estimate that I've earned eighty thousand pounds in four days.

That puts a smile on my face. Not a bad days' work.

"Erik," Stellan calls.

I glance up, shutting my phone screen off. Not that I am hiding it from Stellan, exactly. I just prefer to keep my many stock market gains private.

"*Ja.* Are you ready?" I ask.

He approaches me, trying to feign illness. "I have a headache all of the sudden."

I narrow my eyes. I smell bullshit. "What, did Margot just send you a naked photo or something? Or do I need to call a doctor?"

Stellan glares at me. "Just cancel the rest of my engagements for the day, okay?"

My lips quirk. "Of course."

Stellan is infatuated with his fiancee, an awkward American girl named Margot. Since becoming king, I thought that his passion for her would fade... but I have yet to see their love flag.

Maybe they are just the luckiest people ever. Personally, I don't believe in love. I'm too logical for something so... foolish. Being struck down by cupid's arrow is just not something that will ever happen to me.

I get on my phone and start sending texts, cancelling our plans so that he Stellan can spend a few extra hours with his bride to be. We walk down a few flights of steps where we are met by a pair of bodyguards, who hustle us into the backseat of a royal limousine.

Putting my phone on silent to ignore the flood of angry text messages I'm about to get, I sigh. Copenhagen passes by the window at a dizzying pace. I sit back and watch it slide by as I think about what I'm going to do with my day now.

"Do you think I should assign Annika a babysitter?" Stellan asks.

When I turn to look at him, he's staring out his window thoughtfully. I shift, my size making even the limo seem too small to ride in comfortably.

I screw up my face. "If that will make you and Margot feel more relaxed, I say do it."

He chuckles. "There is almost nothing that will make me relax until the official wedding ceremony is over."

I nod. "I can see that. I think you are too worried about what everyone will think, but... I'm not the one with a fiancée to protect."

He looks at me, a wrinkle of worry appearing between his brows. "Is everything ready for the engagement announcement tomorrow?"

"*Ja.* I know I've said this a hundred times already, but try to relax. Have a glass of wine, get laid. Take your mind off the whole thing."

He smirks. "That's your answer for everything. I should be giving you that advice. Erik, relax. Erik, don't worry about it."

My lips curve upwards. "It's my job to worry. It's your job to lead."

He snorts. "Like I could lead anyone anywhere without you there to remind me which direction is north."

I roll my eyes. "I am glad that I'm not in charge. Let's leave it at that."

I turn and stare out the window, thinking.

One day, I will need to tell Stellan that I'm leaving. I know I need to do it. But… it's complicated. Almost everything I am today, I owe to Stellan and his family. Without him, I would still be living in relative poverty, trying to scrape by.

Unwilling to think about the matter any more, I close my eyes and lean my head back as we are driven home.

Pretend Princess

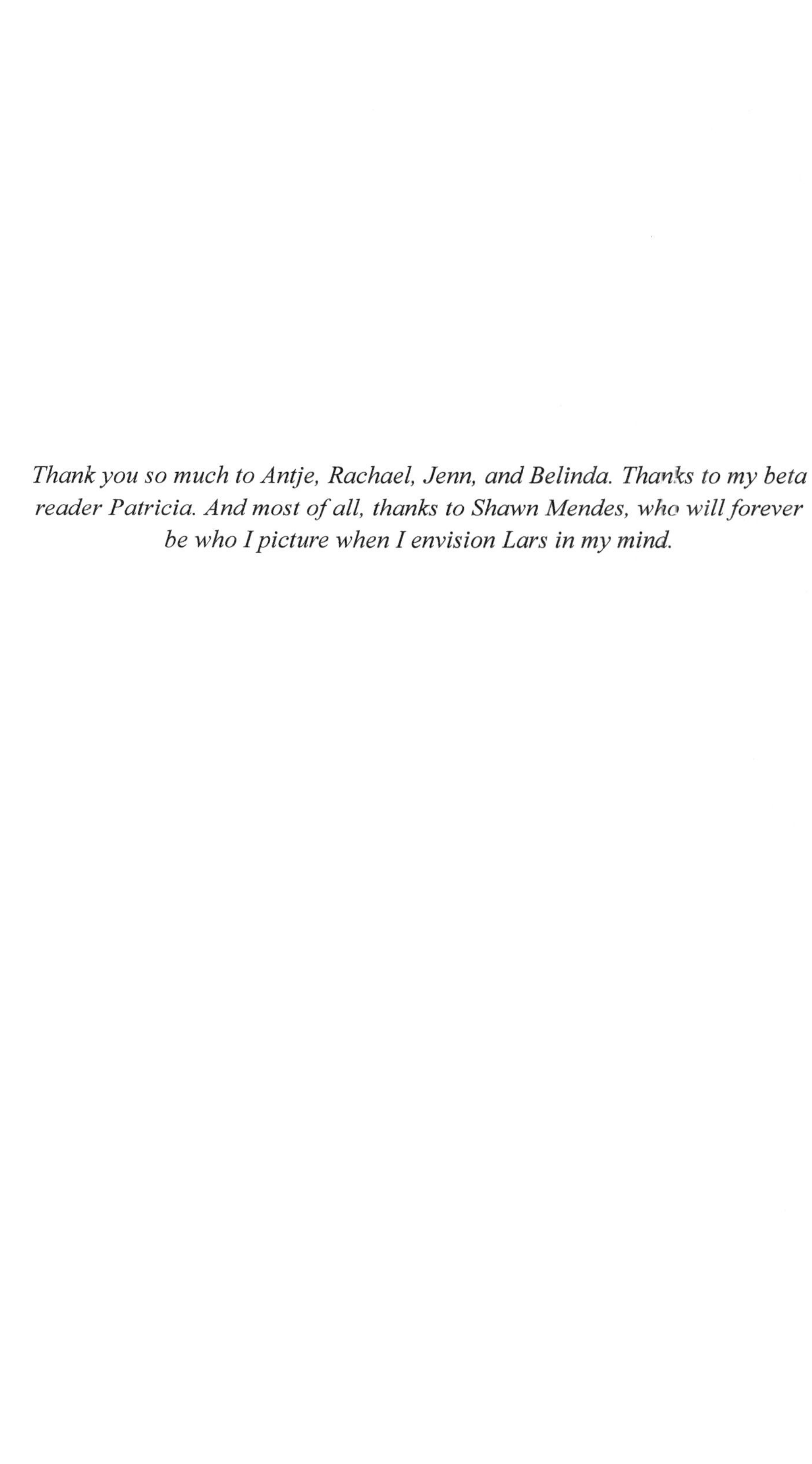

Thank you so much to Antje, Rachael, Jenn, and Belinda. Thanks to my beta reader Patricia. And most of all, thanks to Shawn Mendes, who will forever be who I picture when I envision Lars in my mind.

CHAPTER 1

Lars

FIFTEEN YEARS Earlier

Standing on the highest balcony at the school, I shiver. My eyes trace the jaw dropping beauty of the Swiss Alps. The scene is set dramatically with two nearly vertical cliff faces. Each is snow-capped and soars impossibly high, chilling the dark stone foundations of the school I'm standing on. A waterfall crashes down nearby, providing a perfect frame for the backdrop of more snowy, white peaks.

I sniffle as the wind picks up, bringing with it the season's first fat flakes of snow. The balcony I'm on is barely three feet deep and a dozen feet long, easily accessible through a thick wooden door. It's one of a dozen small balconies clinging to the castle's upper floors; in medieval times, this was probably meant for archers to be able to pop out and fire rapidly.

We've been studying castles and the feudal system during history and the castle itself has been rather illustrious.

Too bad that I hate it here.

Bracing myself against the cold, I will myself to stop crying.

Princes don't cry.

It's just that this boarding school is very far away from home. I was sent here last month after being kicked out of yet another prep school back in Copenhagen. And it hasn't been an easy adjustment.

St. Matthew's is housed in an old castle, drafty in the winter and dark all the time. Back home, I slept in adjoining rooms with my older brother Stellan; here I feel alone nearly all the time.

Not to mention the fact that the kids that attend St. Matthew's are the dictionary definition of a clique. So far, I only seem to be able to piss off the boys and make the girls turn up their noses.

It really hasn't been a very good start to the second half of my seventh grade year.

I stare out at the mountains in the distance, I wish I were like their dark, rocky surfaces. Hard, impenetrable, cold. I'm very much not those things. Instead, I'm slipping away from my pre-algebra class to sneak outside for privacy and bawl like a little baby. If anybody in school found out that I did this regularly, I would be humiliated.

As I grapple with my runaway emotions, the heavy wood door creaks open. One of my classmates sticks her head of bright copper curls out, checking to see if anyone is here.

God, please don't let her come out here. Please don't let her see me like this. I wipe my face, waiting for a second.

Then she steps out, looking away toward the majestic waterfall. I suck in a breath and slip away from her, pressing against the building facade. Thank god the building turns ever so slightly and hides my presence.

I watch as the girl steps out, letting the door close behind her and leaning on the dark stone balcony railing. She's slender and willowy, her skin as fair as cream. She has light colored eyes and an upturned button nose. Her crown of curls spirals down her shoulders, falling almost to her waist. She's only wearing her uniform: a white button up shirt, a heavy black sweater with the school logo stitched into it, a pleated gray plaid skirt, and thick black tights. I'm wearing my heaviest coat and I'm still freezing. She has to be crazy.

Tilting my head, I try to put a name with her face. Unfortunately I haven't really learned everyone yet, especially not the people who aren't popular. My eyes slide over her again, head to toe.

I'm a little surprised at not recognizing this girl, because she is really pretty.

No, pretty isn't right.

As she raises her eyes to the sky, her lips moving silently, she makes my heart skip a beat. She's beautiful.

I'm not expecting her to start weeping, though. She murmurs something that I can't quite hear, dropping her head low. Her face contorts. Her eyes shimmer with tears.

I straighten my head, looking away. She's clearly expecting privacy. I try to give it to her, although there isn't much room on the balcony to move.

I inch away from her, shivering. There is a small pebble on the floor, something that I thoughtlessly kick out of my way. She suddenly looks up, her eyes wide.

When she speaks, her breath condenses in the air. "Is someone there?"

Her accent is foreign, perhaps British. Her voice is smooth and light, melodic to my ears.

I freeze. Before I can decide whether or not to call out, she takes a step closer, coming around the sharp point in the facade. Her eyes go wide with alarm.

"What are you doing here?"

She wraps her arms around herself, her words sounding like an accusation.

I straighten my spine, my head cocking. "I could ask you the same question. I was just out here, minding my own business. You are intruding into my space, technically."

Her eyes narrow as she takes me in. I'm dark haired and scrawny, probably only emphasized by the fact that I'm wearing a huge coat.

"Who are you?" she asks.

My neck heats. "My name is Lars."

I see the moment that she realizes who I am; something clicks and there is a second of acknowledgement in her clear blue eyes.

"Ah. You're the prince."

My expression sours. "Yes. Go ahead, make your jokes."

Her eyebrows rise. "I'm sorry?"

I turn away, looking out toward the mountains. "You heard me. That's what I've heard from everyone in this school so far. So go ahead, question my lineage. Talk about how my parents planned well when they decided to have me. My brother is the heir, I'm just the spare."

I spit on the ground, bracing for whatever she is about to say. My angry breath leaves me mouth in distinct huffs. I'm certain that she's about to tear into me, tell me I barely qualify to be a prince.

"It's my second week here."

My eyebrows rise; I look over at her, thrown off by her words. "What?"

She shivers, wiping her nose on her sleeve. "I'm new here. If the other children tease you, they certainly don't share it with me." Her mouth twists. "Haven't you heard? I'm a scholarship student. A charity case. In the pecking order, you definitely come above me."

My mouth opens. I'm not quite sure what to make of this little spitfire. She huffs a laugh, turning away.

"Great, now you too. Everybody at this school looks down on me because I am not a titled heir with a huge fortune. Even the teachers look at me with pity."

She says it with such anger and conviction, her hands balling into fists.

I pull a face. "I wasn't thinking that."

She frowns. "You weren't?"

I shake my head. "I wasn't. I was just wondering two things."

She looks uncertain. "What?"

I exhale, feeling a little shaky. "First, I was wondering if you were ever going to tell me your name."

Two spots of bright pink appear in the apples of her cheeks. "I'm Pippa. Pippa Welch."

I step forward, holding out my hand. She looks at me for a second, as if she's trying to decide whether I'm serious or not. Then she takes a couple of steps, taking my hand. I shiver as electricity washes over my skin.

From this close, I can make out the freckles that span the bridge of her nose.

I give her the tiniest smile. "It's nice to meet you, Pippa."

She sniffs, taking her hand back and shivering again. "What was the other thing that you were wondering?"

My smile broadens. "I was wondering if you wanted to head inside." I pause, scrunching up one side of my face. "I have a hot plate and some cocoa in my room. It's contraband, obviously—"

She cuts in. "I'm freezing. So yes, cocoa sounds nice." She turns around, moving toward the door. "Where is your room?"

I blush. It just now occurs to me that I have invited her to my room and… well, she's a girl.

A pretty girl.

"It's in the east wing," I say, following her.

She looks back at me, wrinkling her nose as she pulls the heavy wooden door open. "I've never snuck into a boy's room, much less a prince."

Just now, I have a funny feeling in the pit of my stomach. Pippa's eyes sparkle mischievously. I clear my throat, trying to come up with a proper response to that.

"I won't tell if you won't," I end up saying.

She wrinkles her nose, amused, and tosses her upper curls as she heads inside. And I follow her, feeling my whole world shift on its axis.

It takes me a few hours to realize what the feeling fluttering around my stomach is: stupid, blind, complete love.

God help me.

CHAPTER 2

Lars

MODERN TIMES

I sit at the far end of a dimly lit, crowded cocktail bar, drumming my fingers on the counter and looking at my watch. It's getting late, well past midnight.

Pippa was supposed to meet me here at exactly twelve.

The bar is noisy. The patrons are talking and laughing over the sophisticated notes of jazz in the background.

Any minute, I expect to see Pippa: tall, lithe, and redheaded. From this distance, I'll be able to see the two spots in the apples of her cheeks as she rushes toward me, dressed in some sort of a flowy designer gown. Her eyes are this almost electric shade of teal. When she looks at you, her gaze seems to pin you in place.

But only if she's here, of course. I glance at my watch again with a sigh.

We've been best friends for long enough that I expect her usual tardiness. Pippa is exceptionally late though, even by her standards.

I look down at my whiskey and soda in its glass tumbler. I'm up at the crack of dawn every single day to train for the one thing I've wanted since I was seven years old: to be a member of the National Space Institute's next class of astronauts.

I know it's a crazy goal. You have to be the best of the best and the brightest of bright to be accepted to the program. You have to have a ridiculous, impossible to maintain physique and your mind must be sharp enough to cut.

I've got that part down. The only thing that might hold me back, funnily enough, is my title. See, I'm not the heir… but I am supposed to be waiting in the wings in case anything happens to King Stellan.

I'm not much of the wait and see what happens type, but that's neither here nor there.

At any rate, I try not to drink too much while I'm still training.

Draining the last drops of whiskey, I push my glass away. When the bartender comes by, asking if I want another drink, I shake my head. He nods and replaces my drink with a glass of water. I sigh, looking around the bar again.

That's when I notice a couple of girls looking my way. As a member of Denmark's royal family, I'm used to getting those stares. The ones people give you when they can't quite place you at first…

If I were my brother Stellan, the King of Denmark, I would be too famous to even lurk in this dark corner of the bar. But as second in line to the throne, people are much slower to recognize me.

I glance over at the girls again, trying to decide if they recognize me as Prince Lars or the just think I'm some guy in the bar that's attractive. They bow their heads together, giggling softly. I really hope that it is the latter of the two and that the girls are just flirting with me.

That would be optimal, because I'm seriously done with being royal at this moment.

After a moment, both girls approach me. I cast my gaze over them, my stomach starting to sink. Normally if there are girls that think I'm attractive in a bar, they don't come right up to me and tell me about it. No, I'm pretty sure that their approach means that they have figured out who I am.

I raise my hand to the bartender, signaling that I do want another whiskey soda. I'll hurt tomorrow because of it, but so be it.

One of the girls is a pretty ash blonde. She leads the way over to me while her friend slinks behind her, a more timid brunette. The blonde smiles as she tucks her hair behind her ear, gesturing to show that she means no harm.

"Excuse me, you wouldn't happen to be Prince Lars, would you?"

I exhale slowly, looking her up and down. She is very young, probably only eighteen, but her tiny black dress shows off her cleavage and her supermodel legs. I spin in my chair, favoring her and her friend with a smirk. "Who is asking?"

Both of the girls blush an enchanting pink. The blonde speaks for both of them. "I'm Anya and this is Katya."

I toy with the rim of my glass, looking at them. So young, so sweet, so innocent…

It happens in the same manner that it *always* happens.

The rational, thinking half of my brain switches off. And the base, impulsive half of my brain turns on instead. One minute, I'm thinking of Greene's latest article on string theory. The next minute, I'm thinking of the way this pretty blonde's tongue will feel as she uses it to tease my cock.

It happens so quickly, between breaths. There's nothing I can do to stop it, not that I particularly want to.

Biting my lip, I lean forward with an inviting smirk.

"You've found me out," I say. I tilt my head to the side, eyeing both of the girls up and down. "Aren't you two clever?"

Both of them flush an alluring dark pink. The blonde ducks her head. "We were wondering why you are here at the bar all alone. Do you want some company?"

My smirk deepens. I know just how good looking I am. I know that I'm a prince. I hold all the cards here.

"I wouldn't say no to that offer."

The seats on either side of me are unoccupied and the girls slide onto the leather stools, the blonde on my left and the brunette on my right. This isn't the first time that this exact thing has happened. I sit back, raising my hand to signal the bartender.

"Let me get you both a drink," I say.

The blonde smiles widely at me while her brunette friend looks on, still red as a beet. While the bartender makes them a couple of fruity cocktails, I sit back and take in the blonde's cleavage and short, tight skirt.

"Are you two in school somewhere?" I ask.

The blonde is in the middle of sipping her drink so the brunette clears her throat. "We're in our first semester at the Copenhagen Academy of Fashion. Do you know it?"

I dip my head in a nod. "*Ja.* My friend Pippa went there for a year."

The blonde arches a brow. "Your *friend* probably dropped out because it's hard."

I frown at the way she used the word friend to mean… something else. I sip my water, feeling myself check out of the conversation. Looking bored, I shrug. "She left to pursue journalism, if that's what you mean."

The brunette cuts in, giving her friend a sharp glance. "I'm sure that Anya didn't mean anything by that. We are both having the damnedest time with our course loads, that's all."

Anya shoots her friend an irritated glance. "Thanks, Katya. But really, who wants to talk about our boring lives? You're a real, live prince. What is that like?"

I find myself checking my watch, wondering when Pippa will be here. "What part, exactly?"

My eyes are already roving the bar, looking for something more interesting than these two can offer. I know exactly how the rest of this conversation will go, down to the moment when the blonde leans in and whispers that we should leave together. I'm not against it, and certainly I have no problem with women expressing their sexuality.

Quite the opposite, actually.

It would just be nice if one of these women did something surprising for a change. Something more stimulating than batting their eyelashes and subtly toying with their hair.

It's nice. It's just been done so many times before.

"Ummm, what is King Stellan like? Ohh, and Queen Margot! You must love spending time with them."

My gaze wanders to Anya again. I put zero thought into how I'm going to answer that question.

"Stellan is the same asshole he's always been. And Margot is as sweet as sugar for putting up with him."

She laughs, leaning in and putting her hand on my forearm. "That's amazing. Tell me, how is it that you are still single? I mean, you're very handsome and very eligible…"

My gaze slides over to the brunette, who has pulled out her phone and isn't paying attention anymore. I take another sip of my water. "I don't know. I'm only twenty five. That leaves me plenty of time to settle down, I think. Besides, I'm incredibly choosy about the girls I sleep with."

That's just a bald-faced lie, but it slips past my lips unchecked and unheeded. Anya laughs again, gripping my arm.

God, I'm so tired of how meaningless this conversation is. So deeply, deeply exhausted.

I open my mouth to excuse myself, looking out across the bar. And that's the moment when I see Pippa.

She's wearing a billowy beige lace dress with a dramatic slash of cleavage in the front, an enormous black faux-fur coat, and black high heels. Her beautiful copper hair is wound in braids around her head; her blue-green eyes stand out even from this distance; her delicate pink mouth is twisted in an almost-grimace as she heads straight toward me.

For a moment, my stomach flip flops. The two girls I was talking to are all but forgotten as I rise, sure that my height will call Pippa's attention more than my black leather jacket, black cotton t-shirt, or dark jeans ever could.

I would wave, but I'm certain that I would look like a complete fool. So I just stand for a second, a head above the next tallest person here.

It does the trick. She looks my way. Our eyes clash.

She gives me the most sheepish smile, biting her lower lip as she rushes over to me. Warmth splashes through my insides like warm water, filling me to the brim.

Thank god.

"Sorry! I'm so, so late!" Pippa exclaims, elbowing two guys out of her way. Her accent is British, her o's short and her a's choppy.

She stops short, hugging herself nervously as her eyes dance over me. There has always been an unspoken rule between us, ever since we were kids.

No hugging.

No touching.

Trust me, it's been a savior for me, time and time again.

I shrug, pointing to a booth. "Want to go sit down?"

I can see hesitance on her heart shaped face. "What about your, uh… friends?"

I turn my head, only at this moment remembering that the other girls are still at the bar. The blonde is currently looking at Pippa with judgmental, jealous eyes.

"Oh. You girls don't mind if I go talk to my friend, do you?" I paste on my fakest, most charming smirk. "I'll be back in a bit, if you're still here."

It's not really a question. I'm not interested in their input, really.

I lean in, brushing against the blonde and wink as I scoop up my glass of water. Then I make eye contact with the bartender, holding up two fingers and pointing to the booth where I'll be at. He nods and I walk away, swaggering over to the dark little booth where Pippa is making herself at home.

I slide into the other side of the cracked black leather booth, peeling off my jacket. Pippa pushes her coat off, spreading her palms flat against the dark wood of the table. She sighs, craning her neck.

I let my eyes wander down her pale, graceful neck and slip down to her pronounced collarbones. I don't look at her slash of exposed cleavage; that's another unspoken rule.

Don't touch her. Don't even look at her.

And if you do look, don't get caught staring.

"It has been the longest day ever," she declares, running her hand over her face. "When did other people become so bothersome?"

My laugh leaves my chest in a rumble. I tilt my head at her. "I've always thought they were pretty awful."

She wrinkles her nose. "Some of them are."

The bartender brings us two fresh drinks. We come here quite a bit, enough for him to know what we drink. A fizzy cocktail for Pippa, a whiskey soda for me.

"Thanks," I say, lifting the glass at him.

Pippa's lips curve and she raises her glass, clinking it against mine. "Here's to people being the worst."

I smile as I take a sip, the honeyed sweetness of the whiskey balanced by the bubbles and sharp tang of alcohol. Rolling it around in my mouth for a moment, I sit back.

She makes a satisfied sound. "That's a nice cocktail. Speaking of which, I thought you were laying off the liquor for the next few months."

"Thanks, *mor*. I am bending my own rules a little, *ja*. But I will be the one who pays the price when my alarm goes off at five. Besides, I wouldn't even still be here if you weren't so late."

Her cheeks color a little. "I said I was sorry. And anyway, you seemed to have found your own company, as usual."

She arches a brow and gestures to where I left the girls sitting at the bar. The corners of my mouth curl upward. "You left me to fend for myself. What can I say?"

She sighs, shaking her head. "You are a womanizer, through and through."

I shrug, sipping my drink. "I think we can both agree that I'm not the best choice for anyone. Fathers, lock up your daughters!"

I chuckle to myself. Pippa rolls her eyes.

"Yes, yes. You're a big, brooding bad boy. I get it, okay? Trust me, everybody gets that it's your *thing*."

I laugh at her dismissiveness. "*Ja, ja*. I just tell it like it is."

Her lips quirk. "I think you're just afraid to let yourself get comfortable. Every night, a new bed. Every day, you're doing some harebrained, daredevil stunt for the sake of… I don't know… adrenaline, I guess?"

She shudders.

"Hey, don't act like I haven't grown up in the… what, fourteen years you've known me?" I smirk at her.

"Fifteem years," she says, toying with the rim of her glass. "Okay, example one. You're still a pilot in the Royal Air Force. Example two, I know about you applying for the Danish Space Institute, or whatever. The royal family may think that you've matured, but I am not fooled so easily." Her eyes sparkle as she sips her cocktail.

I lean in, liking the feistiness of her words. "I'll have you know that I only race expensive yachts and go base jumping on weeks when I'm not scheduled to fly in the RAF."

She rolls her eyes. "You are so irresponsible. Perpetually, I fear."

"You wound me." I smirk again, belying my own words.

Her slow smile tells me everything I need to know. She shakes her head. "Hey, speaking of which. Did you get the invitation for St. Matthew's winter celebration?"

I snort. "No. Maybe our alma mater realizes I live here in Denmark and have no interest in flying back to the Swiss Alps in this weather."

"I am wholly certain that they sent it to you and you just didn't read it. It's okay though, because I'm pretty sure that they're just asking alumnus to come back as a fancy way to open our checkbooks."

I nod slowly. "It is always about the money with them. In any case, I'm sure that the royal family just writes them a big fat check every year. The next time that they donate, I should just have them add your name to the roster."

Pippa glances down into her drink, frowning for a split second. I realize

I've accidentally tripped over my own tongue. Pippa and I both went to an elite boarding school, but we went under very different circumstances.

Pippa is an orphan who attended the school thanks to a mysterious benefactor.

And me?

I attended because I was such a bad kid at ten years old that I had been kicked out of every notable prep school in Denmark.

I clear my throat, changing the subject to cover my gaffe. "You're coming to the palace tomorrow, *ja?*"

She smiles softly at me. "If you want me to be there, I will."

"I always want you," I say. The words just tumble out of my mouth, unchecked.

When Pippa's cheeks go pink, my neck heats. I look down at my drink, shaking my head. "You know what I meant. Just come, please. Save me from my own family like you do every year."

She smiles. For a moment, I can't tell if her expression is genuine or not. "I will come. Thanks, Froggy."

Her use of my childhood nickname draws a laugh from my lips. "Anything for you, little witch."

She looks up, catching my gaze for just a second. She bites one of her soft, full lips.

Those kissable, perfectly plump lips. So close and yet…

So very, very off limits.

I swallow. Just now, I know a moment of pure want.

God, I could just reach across the table right now, drag Pippa over here, and plunder those sexy fucking lips.

Then she breaks the spell by tipping up her glass, finishing the last drops, and grabbing her voluminous coat. "All right. I should get home. And you should too, though somehow I don't think you will find yourself there anytime soon…"

She tips her head toward the bar. I look over and see the blonde from earlier still waiting there. I squint, looking back to Pippa with a shrug.

"Let me drive you home," I say, yawning. "I'm tired anyway."

Pippa stands up, shaking her head. "No. You stay. Have a good time!" She gives me a quick grin, touching my shoulder as she passes me. "I'll see you tomorrow, Lars."

I move my hand up my chest to touch hers as it lands against my skin.

I'm too slow, though. She's gone before I can do anything else, leaving my heart aching just a bit.

Isn't that always the way of things? Pippa slipping away, while I'm still trying to tamp down my more dangerous emotions around her.

Quaffing the rest of my drink, I stand up, turning to watch Pippa's elegant form disappearing through the crowd. Taking my wallet out of my pants pocket, I toss a wad of cash on the table. Then I make eye contact with the simpering blonde from earlier.

I only have to cock a brow and jerk my head toward the exit. She positively beams at me, nodding her head enthusiastically. I grab my leather jacket, putting it on.

There is something wrong though.

I know it even as I head for the door.

The blonde's smile doesn't light me up inside the way Pippa's does.

No one else even comes close.

As I push the heavy door open and try to put that thought out of my mind as I escort the blonde out to my waiting chauffeured car.

CHAPTER 3

Pippa

GOD, how beautiful the world is right now. I blink up into the winter sky, thankful that it's actually clear and sunny. It's still cold as all get out though. Huge snow drifts are everywhere I look. As I hurry down the cobbled streets of Copenhagen, a hushed sort of wonderland is all around me.

Most of the cars are still snowed in from last night. Lights twinkle nearly everywhere I look. This is the fanciest part of town, full of lavish window displays and signs proclaiming *Jul* cheer. Every window I pass has cute gingerbread men or simple red and white paper hearts pressed against the glass. All the shops and businesses are closed for *Julaften*, the Danish version of Christmas Eve.

When I turn the corner, I see Amalienborg palace rising just at the end of the street. The snow has been all but vanquished here, shoveled away by unseen hands. There are four massive beige brick buildings all huddled in a circle, all saluting a rather large statue of a man on a horse. With their white-trimmed windows, dark roofs covered by snow drifts, and guards dressed in scarlet, the palaces definitely proudly exude *money*.

I check my slender silver wristwatch as I scurry up to the palace, stopping at the newly-installed guard station. It's made entirely of plastic sheeting and PVC piping, looking like a strong enough gust of wind might blow it away entirely.

I try not to voice my frustrations out loud; the palace has been implementing more stringent rules lately because of *elevated threat levels*, whatever that means.

Two scarlet-clad guards are standing between me and the palace door. I can't help but start to feel nervous as I clear my throat, reaching into my bag and fishing out my identification.

The new checkpoint has nothing to do with you, I remind myself calmly.

"*Haj*," I greet the guards. "*Glædelig jul!*" I say brightly. Roughly translated, it means Merry Christmas.

The guard is all business. He holds out his hand, expectant. I can't help but notice my hand is trembling ever so slightly as I offer them my driver's license. "Here you go."

"*Taak.* One moment." One of the guards bows his head, takes my ID, and then disappears into the little tent.

Breathe, I reprimand myself. *You are not of any interest to these guards. No one is going around, digging up fifteen year old secrets. They are just doing their job.*

The guard is taking his time with my ID, though. I can feel a few droplets of sweat start to break out on the back of my neck. I clench and unclench my fists, trying not to seem agitated.

The guard that is waiting outside with me shoots me a polite smile. "It will just be another minute, I'm sure."

I shiver, wrapping my coat more snugly around myself. The guard in the booth emerges at last, my identification card pinches between two fingers. His gaze narrows on my face.

My stomach drops as he stalks over to me.

"I'm sorry, frøken, but the system doesn't recognize your ID. It says your records don't exist. I can't let you into the palace without the proper clearance."

My eyes go wide. I stammer out, "What?"

They can't know. It's *impossible*. My identification card is real. Pippa Welch might not have existed when I took the name at eleven, but definitely exists now.

"Pippa!"

I glance up to find Lars bursting out of the heavy double doors on the other side of the guard booth. With his dark hair, his intense blue eyes, and his ruddy complexion, he looks like he just walked off a damn runway. His black cable knit sweater and casual black jeans fit him like a glove.

And he's about to find out that his best friend in the entire world is a liar.

Oh god, this is the last thing I want.

He can't find out like this.

I open my mouth, trying to explain away the guards. But Lars just storms up to the guards, taking them to task.

"What is the problem here?" he snarls at the guard closest to him. He snatches my ID card out of the man's hand, his eyes flickering with anger.

Lars has a fiery temper, to put it lightly. Usually I would step in and defend the poor guard, but in this case… I just lick my lips nervously and say nothing.

"Your highness, I am just following protocol…" the guard says, turning pink.

"It's Julaften," Lars says, tilting his head. "In the spirit of the holiday, I'm going to restrain myself." He steps closer to the guard, making him step back. "Pippa Welch is here as my guest. She is *always* welcome. If you've got a list of names somewhere, you'd better write hers down. I don't want to have this conversation again."

The guard swallows, nodding. "Yes, your highness."

Lars shakes his head, turning to me. He beckons to me, his voice still curt. "Come on, Pippa."

I walk toward the heavy wood double doors, my heart pounding, my palms still a bit damp. Lifting my chin, I stride through the doors as they are opened for me. I don't even give the guard stand a second glance.

As we walk inside, I feel Lars put his hand on the small of my back. My stride breaks for a moment.

Cool down, I tell myself. *Be a lady, for god's sake.*

I exhale and shed my coat, handing it off to a servant. Lars eyes me as we start climbing the white marble stairs that lead up into the palace proper. I feel his gaze on my slinky gold dress, judging me like I'm a prize heifer.

"Stop staring," I scold him, not even looking over to see if it's true or not. "I'm wearing a perfectly presentable dress, if that's what you are worried about."

I hear the smile in his voice. "I wasn't thinking about that."

"Then why are you looking at me?"

I turn, shooting him a glare. He shrugs, his little smirk maddening. "You look nice, that's all."

Wrinkling up my face at him, I huff. "Well, quit it. I'm not some blonde at the bar. You can't chat me up and take me back to someplace dark for a bit of fun. We're best friends, not fuck buddies."

Lars chuckles. "Fair enough, little witch."

I shoot him an irritated look and pick up the hem of my dress, holding it up as we keep climbing.

We make it up the steep stairs and I stop, my eyes widening. The palace is always something to behold. Gray marble floors, gray marble columns flanking both sides of the hallway, an incredible arched and carved white marble ceiling.

I've never seen it decorated quite so thoroughly, though.

Towering trees stand between each column. Each one is festively decorated with delicate red paper hearts, crisp white paper snowflakes, and shimmering gold tinsel. There is a cheerful red runner on the floor and garlands of tiny red and white flags strung overhead. At the far end of the hall, I can just make out the shapes of gingerbread men and toy soldiers plastered against the floor to ceiling window.

"Whoa," I say.

Lars rolls his eyes at the decorations, pulling at my hand. "Margot went a little nuts with the decorating. Come on, the sooner we get into the sitting room, the sooner we can leave."

A laugh bubbles to my lips as I let him lead me toward the party. "Where have you got to be? Everyone you know is here."

He gives his head a shake, not interested in explaining. There is only one door open in the grand hallway. Light spills out and as I get closer, I can hear laughter.

A chill runs down my spine. This is far from my first Julaften, but I swear I will never tire of how much this family enjoys being around each other. Lars goes through the doorway just ahead of me. When I step through, it's exactly as I would have hoped it would be. A beautifully decorated sitting room, with a full decorated tree in one corner and a whole buffet of delicious-smelling foods up against one wall. All of Lars's extended family is clustered together around the fireplace, sitting near their partners.

Dark-haired Stellan is standing closest to the fire, beaming down at his pink-haired pixie of a wife Margot. On the couch beside Margot is Lars's lovely blonde sister Annika, and her enormous blond fiancé Erik.

Lars's parents, Mor and Dar, are sitting on a couch on the other side of the fireplace. His brothers Finn and Anders have pulled up chairs just beside them. And there is an empty loveseat facing the fireplace, obviously meant for Lars and me to occupy it.

Margot lays eyes on me and pops up out of her seat, her eyes shining with genuine joy. "Pippa!"

My lips curl upward. Margot is one of my oldest friends. It just so happens that she fell head over heels for Stellan this spring after I introduced them. So I always look forward to seeing her, especially now during the holidays. I throw my hands wide, greeting the room.

"Glædelig jul!" I declare, wishing her a merry Christmas.

Margot runs over to me and I embrace her, setting an arm around her small body. She is dainty and delicate like a child, but I know the rebel heart that beats in her chest. "Merry Christmas," I murmur in her ear.

She pulls back, tears glimmering in her eyes. Margot didn't exactly have an easy childhood. Looking at all the over the top decorations that the palace doesn't usually have this time of year, it's obvious that this Christmas is her way of living out her childhood fantasies.

"Here, here," she says. She ushers me over to the loveseat, pushing on my shoulder. "Sit down. Let me get you a mug of cocoa."

I pull a face but she isn't listening to me.

"Margot's too wrapped up in all the Christmas cheer, it seems." Lars sits down beside me, taking up most of the room on the loveseat. I shoot him a look and he shrugs innocently.

Nika leans forward, looking elegant as always. "Hello, Pippa. Merry Christmas."

I cast a gaze over her. She and Erik are sitting with their hands clasped. I smile because three months ago, that would've been a really big deal.

"You too. How's the charity work?"

She beams, excited. "It's good. Remind me to catch you later and bend your ear about my latest project. It's inspired, if I do say so myself."

Margot has moved over to the buffet that is laid out for our gathering. Stellan shakes his head, calling over to her. "Margot, let Lars make Pippa I drink. You don't have to do everything for everybody, darling."

I notice Lars's parents have been unusually quiet. On any normal day, I expect them to be making everyone pay attention to them and dote on them. That definitely seems like the commonality between his parents. But it seems that I have missed their antics today. His mother drains her glass of champagne while his father just looks extremely tired.

Lars's mother and father stand up, his father yawning a little. She looks at him, putting her arm in his quite tenderly. "I think that we should say good night now. Your father isn't feeling too well. It was nice to see you all, though."

Lars looks a little concerned but he lets it pass unremarked. Instead, he gets up and kisses his mother on the cheek and claps his father on the back. I watch the exchange warily; we've known for a while that Lars's father is terminally ill.

Margot carries my drink over to me as Stellan's parents exit. I take the mug from her thankfully, clutching it as I look around the room. Margot settles in where Lars's mother just was and Stellan joins her, his arm going around her shoulders. I look at that small gesture of intimacy with no small amount of longing.

I want that. I have the familiarity with Lars part down, but I don't see how we will ever get to be as close as Margot and Stellan are. It's the only sort of limitation placed on my friendship with Lars.

We follow the unspoken rule that there is just absolutely no touching for *any* reason.

I clear my throat and swing my gaze over to Annika, only to find her whispering something in Erik's ear.

Ugh. This place is full of people who have fallen deeply and irrevocably in love with each other… And it's really killing my buzz.

Lars must feel the same way, because he pipes up. "Could you guys please save it for the bedroom? Some of us are just trying to live our lives over here, you know?"

As my lips curl up, I notice that my knee brushes Lars's. I shrink myself back from him a few inches, wishing like hell that we were sitting on anything but this loveseat. Lars doesn't even seem to notice. He clears his throat.

"Stellan, now that our parents are gone, do you think that we could add some booze to this party?"

Stellan grins. "I thought you would never asked."

For the next couple of minutes, the room is a flurry of motion. Stellan gets a bottle of champagne and look pops it; champagne flutes are filled and handed out. I raise my eyebrow at Margot, making sure that she sees my expression.

She flushes just a little bit. I know her big secret… she is pregnant. I'm not even sure why Stellan would pour her a glass of champagne, honestly.

She holds up one finger, which I take to mean that I need to wait just a minute.

Anders raises his glass. "What should we toast to? Just Merry Christmas?"

Stellan's smile widens. He puts his free hand on Margot's me. "Actually, we have some news. We're not telling people yet, obviously. But we're expecting."

Margot looks slightly embarrassed, tucking her bright pink hair behind her ear. I beam as I look at her. She looks like she is truly, enviably happy. And she found that happy ending with the king of Denmark, no less. As she takes Stellan's hand, I feel a strange pinch. I want the kind of love that they have.

"Hear, hear!" I say, raising my glass.

Everyone else cheers, congratulating the couple.

Even though I knew about the pregnancy news ahead of time, my eyes still fill with tears of happiness. I beam at Margot. She's basically living my most basic bitch dreams.

Not that I would ever tell anyone, but all I have ever wanted is to end up living in a big house with a white picket fence. Two point five children, scruffy little dog, and a husband that loves me to the ends of the earth.

My life has never resembled a Norman Rockwell painting, but a voice inside tells me that I really should expect it still.

I know, it's stupid. It goes hand in hand with my idiotic longing for Lars.

I try to ignore it as best I can.

Margot wipes her eyes. "Thanks, guys."

Lars interjects. "When are you due?"

I arched my brow at him, wondering how he knows to even ask that question. He meets my gaze and shrugs.

Margot smiles prettily at us. "In the middle of May."

Stellan clears his throat. "We're both very excited. It goes without saying that the news doesn't leave this room. I don't even want my parents to know, much less anyone that would leak the information to the press. Sorry, Pippa."

I blush. He's referring to my job at *Politiken*, the Copenhagen daily newspaper.

I'm quick to assure him that I won't tell anyone. "It's not my news to share. I think you should keep it secret as long as you can, honestly."

He grins down at Margot, squeezing her in a side hug. "I'm going to try."

Lars moves to get more comfortable, squishing me in the process. He's arranged himself so that his thigh presses against mine. I sigh, shooting him a look.

We have established some age-old boundaries with each other, not the least of which is that we expend effort to avoid casually touching each other. He glances at me, his eyebrow arching.

"What?" he asks.

I shake my head, pushing his knee away and starting to get up. Too late though, I realize that Finn and Anders have started to reenact a skit of some sort in the middle of the semicircle of seats.

So I'm forced to sit back. Lars looks at me, his eyes twinkling, and throws his arm around my shoulders. It's too much; he's touching my thigh, my hip, and my shoulders. Everywhere he is touching me vaguely tingles. I think that the sensation of knowing I shouldn't be so close to the guy secretly I'm in love with is too intense to handle.

I immediately start to squirm out of his hold. He grips my shoulder to keep me in place.

"Oh, little witch," he teases me. "I know you hate being touched, but just deal with it for a minute. Come on. You secretly like it, I think."

My cheeks flood with heat and I look down. It's not that I dislike being touched.

Not, it's the opposite.

I crave it.

I want him to do it more.

But Lars and I don't have that kind of intimacy. We can't, not without it turning into something more.

And I won't be one of those nameless, faceless girls that he never sees again.

I couldn't handle that.

Pushing myself up and out of his grasp, I stand up, straightening my dress. I shoot him a purposeful look as I walk around the circle, crouching down next to Margot.

She's delighted to see me and starts chattering away.

But I still feel his eyes on me.

Watching.

Waiting.

For what, I don't know.

Lars

THERE IS nothing so exhilarating as flying this fucking jet. My eyes are as wide as can be, scanning the horizon. My mind is almost blank as I pilot the jet, making a thousand tiny alterations to my speed and altitude and direction. My heart pounds.

There is something zen about having so much to focus on at once. It's very much like running a marathon in the way that every single resource you have is pulled into doing it; mentally, physically, you have to give it your all.

Or else…

Well, I would fall from the sky.

I look out my window, glancing at the ground. Up here, the world is carved into little blocks of dull gray, dark brown, and black. I can see the block of runway that I'm heading for; from the distance, it just looks like a long Tetris block of heather gray. If I really stare hard enough, I could probably make out the bright yellow runway markings.

"Tower, looking for permission to land," I say into my headset.

There's a second of silence. My heartbeat pounds in my ears.

A crackle informs me that my request has been heard. "This is tower one. Permission granted."

"Coming in now," I say into my headset.

I point myself down and find that same state of electric zen-ness as I hurtle toward the ground. The world rushes by, but I barely notice. It's all just muscle memory at this point.

As I smoothly taxi my little jet down the RDAF runway, I feel the surge of adrenaline rushing through my system. As I glide into the parking bay, I look around. I push the brake to stop the jet and unbuckle my helmet. I push the button to stop the engine and open the cockpit.

A rush of cool air prickles across my scalp, raising the hairs on the back of my neck. I undo my seat belt and use the jets outside steps to get down to the ground, jumping down the last step. When I hit the ground, I look up to find Erik standing there, waiting for me. Erik and I are old friends, going back to the first days of his unofficial adoption into the palace.

I flash him a grin. We are closer probably even than he and Stellan are, but don't tell either of them that.

He is also an officer in the Royal Air Force, although he has since retired. Arching a brow, I stride toward him. He looks me up and down, smirking a little at my jumpsuit.

"So just an average morning for you then?"

I grin at him. "Yup. Hey, I'm just finishing here. Do you want to go grab a drink?"

He looks at his watch, squinting. "It's not five yet."

I clapped him on his shoulder. "It's five somewhere. Come on."

He follows me for a second. "Actually, I have something to drop off to a friend. Go ahead and change and I'll meet you in the canteen."

I shake my head, continuing through the space and into the men's locker rooms. I shower and change with my usual efficiency, putting on a pair of dark jeans and a dark gray sweater. By the time I head out to the canteen, one of the only places for people to gather and socialize on the base, Erik is sitting at a table already.

He is dressed in a white button down shirts and dark blue trousers, looking for all the world like he belongs on the cover of GQ or something. If I didn't know better, I would think he had gotten quite lost on the way here.

I sit down at the little gray aluminum table, just as Erik is pouring amber beer out of a pitcher into two pint glasses. The Royal Air Force canteen is not exactly known for having a great beer selection on tap. In fact, they only have the shittiest beer and the most bargain-basement labels of hard alcohol.

Given the choice, I think Erik made the right decision.

I raise my pint glass toward him. He clinks his glass against the rim of mine and we both take a long sip. It's cheap and it tastes like water. But hey, a drink's a drink, I guess.

Erik looks at me, quirking his lips. "So… I hear you are training to be an astronaut."

I look up at him, a frown on my face. "Who told you that?"

He shrugs. "A friendly face here on the base. He told me in confidence, if it makes you feel any better."

I pull a face. "It doesn't really. No one is supposed to know that I'm even training for it. It's all very hush-hush."

"My source says that it's a bit of a long shot. Add in the fact that you, as a member of the royal family, are considered one of the country's important resources… It puts you pretty solidly in the 'will not happen' category."

I roll my eyes. "I've heard that. But I've also asked command if my being second in line to the throne puts me out of the running entirely. And no one has said yet that I won't get the mission just because of who I am. That's pretty much against the code of the Royal Air Force. So I'm just going to keep running for it as long as I can."

Erik sips his beer, watching me over the rim of his pint glass. When he is done, he licks a bit of foam from his lips and continues asking questions. "If you're pretty sure that you're not going to get it, why do you keep going? What motivates that kind of thinking?"

I shrug a shoulder. "It's a chance to go to space, man. If I did that… If I actually made it to space, I would be…" I trail after second and then shake my head. "I don't want to go down in history as the second in line to the throne. I want my name to mean something to somebody. I want to be remembered."

His brows shoot up in surprise. "Really?"

I nod, feeling a bit sheepish. But he purses his lips again, seeming pensive.

"That's a hell of a way to start a legacy. Most people just get married and have kids."

I chuckled dryly, shaking my head. "Not me, man. I can't even meet a girl that I like, much less one that I want to marry."

Erik huffs out a laugh. "I think that Pippa would disagree about that."

I rock back in my chair. "Besides Pippa, I mean. She doesn't count, obviously."

"No? What's wrong with Pippa?"

I fixed him with a stare. "We've already been over this 100 times. She's my best friend, not a potential mate. Girls are so flighty. They're really only after my title. Pippa isn't like that. But that's just because we been friends for well over fifteen years. I don't want to rock the boat and risk losing my oldest, closest friend." I set my beer down with a smirk. "Besides, Pippa is so busy with her life that I don't even know where I would fit in."

I say the last line as a joke, but the rest of it I really mean. I spent hours agonizing over how to tell Pippa how I feel, only to realize that this imagined love may only run one way. I would rather risk never finding someone to love me then to risk what I have with Pippa.

It's just not worth it.

Erik leans his elbows on the table. "But what if she loves you just like you love her?"

I roll my eyes, tipping up my pint glass to drain the contents in a few swallows when I'm done, I grab the pitcher and refill my glass. "I don't want to talk about her anymore. Let's change the subject. How about we poke around in your private business with Nika?"

That earns me a scowl. I slide the beer pitcher over to him and he accepts it with a frown. "That's not very funny."

I huff a laugh. "And yet, it's more entertaining than talking about why Pippa and I aren't an item. I think at this point, I have to admit to myself that I don't think I'm cut out for love. Being in love, believing in love, the whole thing is just very…" I wrinkle my face up.

Erik takes a few moments to fill his glass and take a sip. He looks up at me after he's done, his keen eyes pinning me in place. "It's funny you say that, because not that long ago, I was saying that too. And then… there was Annika. Your sister hit me like a hurricane and I had no choice but to fall in love with her." He smiles into his beer. "She's very lovable."

I give him a smarmy smile. "You two would have never gotten together if it hadn't been for Stellan and my grandmother sticking their big fat noses in where they didn't along. It created a tension, a sense of taboo, where there wasn't one before. I blame that entirely on you and Nika. '

Erik fans his hand out. "Maybe. I think there is more to love than the sense of forbidden longing though."

I purse my lips. "Maybe that is why I haven't ever been in love. I don't even think I'm capable of it."

He frowns. "I'm sure that's not true."

"It really is. And that's okay. Someone has to stand out among all the rest."

He rolls his eyes. "I wouldn't word it like that."

"Look, I know that I'm not the safest of choices. But I will still be a handsome retired Royal Air Force pilot and a prince when I am seventy years old. Hell, I might have even been to space! I have difficulty believing that I will never be able to walk into a bar and get any girl that catches my eye. That's not something that most people can say."

He laughs a little at that. "I think that's your age talking. When you are fifty years old, you will be watching Pippa and whatever guy she settles down with. And you'll feel sorry that you ever thought that you would always be able to get all the pussy you want."

I roll my eyes. "For the longest time, Pippa and I have been facing questions about our friendship. The fact that we've managed to keep close but separate is honestly a miracle."

He gives me a look and shakes his head. "I guess it is whatever makes you happy."

My lips curve upward. "Exactly. Pippa isn't your average girl. She is exceptional in every way. And that includes the fact that I'm not interested in her in that way."

He arches a brow. "So you don't think Pippa is hot?"

I shoot him a little smile. "All my friends are hot."

He shakes his head again. "You're crazy." He stands up, quaffing the rest of his drink. "I think I need some fries to go with this beer. You want anything?"

"Hah. The RDAF has some of the worst food on the planet. So I'll stick to their watery beer for now."

He nods a little as he heads to the canteen counter. I watch him go, sighing. He's told me a hundred times before that he doesn't understand my relationship with Pippa.

She's right there. You're both attractive. You like each other enough. Just go for it.

Each and every time he brings it up, I rebuff him. It's a tale as old as time, to be perfectly frank. And not to mention that it's boring as fuck, feeling like I have to explain to Erik and everyone else.

Why won't people just mind their own business?

Taking a sip of my beer, I mull it over again in my head.

Pippa is wonderful. She's sweet. She's smart. She's playful. She knows my history.

Hell, she's been there for a lot of it.

Plus there is the fact that she's absolutely fucking smoking hot.

But there is an edge to her. There is a point at which she grows uncomfortable with closeness, pushes everyone away, including me. I have the vague sense that there is just more to her that I can't quite touch. She is a lake whose depths are yet-unknown to anyone. And as you delve deeper, the water gets cold as ice.

I don't know for sure, but I get the feeling that at the bottom is a solid, frozen wall.

So yes, I may have a thing for her.

But there is definitely no way that I'm about to take it further. Even if I could, I'm not sure I would want to.

A bird in the hand is worth two in the bush. I have Pippa's friendship. Asking for more than that seems… greedy, somehow. It's better to have the closest friendship than to have no Pippa at all.

I stare down at my empty glass, trying to reassure myself.

CHAPTER 5

Pippa

SYLVIE MARTIN. That was the name that I was born with.

Sitting on my couch in my tiny apartment, I open my laptop and type the name in. Swallowing quickly, I hit return.

A million results are returned in my search box. I guess Sylvie Martin is a pretty common name. But I keep scrolling down, looking for old mentions of myself. Clicking next on every page of links that don't have anything to do with me, I finally find a link to an old newspaper article on the sixth page.

The old newspaper article is in French, though it's only the work of a minute to translate it with Google. It reads, *Ansel Martin sentenced to thirty life sentences this week. The terrorist that bombed French Parliament is survived by his daughters Sylvie and Stella. The two girls have gone to live with a close family friend, although authorities will not release that guardian's name. It is believed that they will be placed in witness protection and start new lives under new names...*

I swallow, closing the page. I want more than anything to know exactly what happened to my little sister Stella. She disappeared from my life around the same time that I went to a Swiss boarding school and changed my name to Pippa Welch.

That's my biggest regret: I have no real idea what happened to Stella. By the time that I reached out to the family friend who got me accepted to

St. Matthew's boarding school, the family friend and my little sister had disappeared without a trace.

In retrospect, I should've asked a lot more questions. But at the time, it seemed like I just had to get away from my old life. I let Stella go as part of the deal.

Biting my lip, I figure a little digital snooping won't hurt anyone. I type *in what happened to Ansel Martin's daughters?* and *Paris* into the search bar and get a million fresh results. After reading a few articles about where weirdos on the internet think we might be, I finally find a name.

Sylvie Martin.

God, could my sister actually be living under her given name?

I quickly type her name into Facebook. Scrolling through a few pages, I see a list of Facebook profiles.

I've looked for Stella online before... but I've never tried looking on Facebook. I click the link and cruise through four pages of results before I find someone I recognize. Her face is fuller and rounder, her eyes more grown up than I remember. Her red hair is unmistakable though, a nest of fiery copper curls.

My heart seizes up as I click on her profile. Her page is set to private so there is almost no information to be found... except for her location.

She lives in Nantes, a little more than three hours from Paris.

A million questions enter my mind.

How long has she lived there?

What is she like now?

Is there any room in her life for her surely long-forgotten sister?

I bite my lip, my finger hovering over the button that will add her as a friend. Is that something she would want? If I were her, would I want a big sister reappearing in my life, fifteen years after the fact?

In the end, I bookmark her Facebook profile, unable to bring myself to click on the *add as a friend* button. I stare off into the distance, thinking about the past.

If I could do it all over again, given what I know today, I would do everything differently. Then again, what if doing anything differently resulted in not knowing Lars quite as well as I do now?

That thought haunts me.

I get a text message, which pops up on my computer screen and chimes. I startle a little as I shake my head and check the message. It's from Margot.

Hey, are you still planning on meeting me at the baby store later? I know that I shouldn't be planning already, but I'm in full baby crazy mode. Help!

My lips curve up slightly. I text her back.

It's funny to see you like this, because you were never the baby crazy one of the two of us. I always figured that I would already be married with a bunch of kids by now. You would be the fun aunt and you would spoil my whole brood. And yet... Here we are.

She texts back.

I know, right? I never expected it either. But now that I'm expecting, I can't help it. I spent an hour this morning watching Tik-Tok videos of cute babies and sobbing uncontrollably. There's no helping me.

I chuckle. *I'll be there. Just let me know which store you decide on. And be ready for me to buy you every cute onesie that I see.*

She just replies with the *100* emoticon. I set my laptop aside and stand up, stretching. I looked down at my current outfit, a black sweatshirt and a pair of pink tie-dyed leggings. I'm definitely going to have to reconsider my outfit choice if I'm going to actually go into *Politiken* today.

The very thought of going into the actual office makes my stomach sink a little. I usually love my job, but lately it's been a lot less fun. Mostly because I have this new editor that is all over me, constantly asking what I'm working on and why I am not focusing more on my *insider knowledge* of the palace.

My phone starts ringing, shaking me out of my thoughts. I frown and walk over to answer it, seeing that my editor is calling as though I summoned her.

I take a deep breath and answer. "Freja. To what do I owe the pleasure?"

Her high-pitched voice grates on my ears. "Pippa! I was just wondering when we would see you in the office. I have some story ideas that I would very much like to run by you."

I grit my teeth. "Well, why don't you just run them by me right now? I'm probably not going to be in the office today…" I don't know why the lie just slips past my lips, but there's something about Freja that just gets on my nerves.

She clears her throat. "Well, all right. I guess it couldn't hurt. I have three ideas that are really good. The first one is about you and Margot and how you went to college together…"

I shake my head a little. Who would've guessed that Freja would present such a terrible idea to me? I try to keep this sigh from my answer. "Uh-huh. I don't think that the Queen would really like me taking advantage of our mutual past like that."

"Oh, I'm sure that's not true. Queen Margot seems like a cool person. I think she would—"

I interrupt her. "Let's not get into what she would or would not do and what you personally think would or would not be okay with her. You said you had three ideas. So what are the other two?"

There's a few seconds of awkward silence on the line. I hear the sound of pages flipping as she clears her throat again. "Well, okay. I've got another idea that is about you and Lars and how your relationship first started almost fifteen years ago in boarding school."

I grimace. "Again, I think you are asking me to trade on my personal relationships in order to give an inside look into the personal lives of the royals. And I don't think that Lars would appreciate it any more than Margot would. I think that's one of the reasons that they both respect me is that I may be a journalist, but I'm not always asking annoying personal questions *on the record* when I'm hanging out with them. We're friends first. I'm a journalist second. Does that make sense to you?"

I can just imagine her pinched face, her look of disappointment complete. "I don't think that you are really getting a full picture of what I am asking you for. It's nothing that couldn't be gleaned from reading the papers…"

I clench my jaw. "I think I've already answered your question. What is the third idea?"

She blows out a breath. "Well, this one is a little more personal and a little more out there, but I was thinking that you could take a vacation with Lars or Margot and record little short video clips of reminiscing on your friendship—"

I make an aggravated noise. "Ja, no. I'm not going to do that. It seems like all of your story ideas center around my friendship with the royal family. None of the other editors have any problem with assigning me stories that are not directly related to my friends. I don't quite understand what the issue is that you seem to have."

"I don't have an issue with you, Pippa. You seem to be the one that has an issue with this newspaper. And to be frank, I don't see how we can keep employing someone that clearly has interests other than the paper at heart. So I would think long and hard about the three stories I presented. I would plan to do one of them. Because until you do, I don't think that you can be assigned another story."

My lips thin and my eyes narrow. "Have you talked to upper management about this? Because David certainly wouldn't like you poking your nose into the royal family any more than I like being asked to do it."

Freja sounds a little happy to deliver the news. "Didn't you hear? David left the paper. We are all undergoing a radical shift right now and reconsidering the terms of employment for all of our writers. So I put it to you instead… Do you think that you can be useful to us? Because if not…"

My mouth opens but no words come out. I am just utterly aghast. "Are you saying that either I do the story that you seem to want or I find another job?"

I can hear her smiling through the phone. "Yes, honestly. I think you have to do some serious consideration of exactly where your priorities lie. I suggest that you take the long weekend and think about whether or not you really want this job."

That's when I hang up the phone on her. I didn't exactly mean to do it, I am just so put off by everything she had to say and how she had to say it. I couldn't listen to another word.

I'm left staring at my phone screen, agog.

Was I just fired from the paper? It certainly feels that way.

I get a notification on my phone that Freja just shared a document with me. I open it up, biting my lower lip. It's a breakdown of each story she has asked me to pursue and how she sees each one ending up. Essentially she has already all but written the articles that she is demanding. I'm just supposed to write down some words and sign my name to this… this *fiction*.

I just can't believe it. As if everything else in my life is just going fine and dandy…. No, it's definitely not. I don't need any additional stress and finding a job as a journalist right now is definitely beyond harrowing.

With my heart still heavy, I start to get dressed to meet Margot as we have agreed. I shower quickly and then I put on a peach silk dress, layering it with a long white cardigan and chunky black heels.

I'm still fuming as I finish getting dressed. How dare Freja even make such demands of me? Someone in the royal press office needs to hear about this in the morning. I kind of hate to fight dirty, but they can exert pressure on the owners of *Politken* when I may or may not have any say in the matter.

I can't be bothered with my hair so I up throw it up in a messy bun and put on just enough mascara and blush to make myself presentable.

Then I look at the time and realize that I am definitely going to be late to meet Margot, even if I hurry. Pulling on my warm winter coat, I grabbed my purse and head downstairs. The cool winter air of the late afternoon catches me by surprise.

It's not that I don't know that it's cold outside, I just didn't expect it to be *this* cold. I pull my jacket tight around myself, thinking that maybe I should catch a cab. I only have to go about ten blocks, but if I catch a cab, I will not only be warm but I will get there faster.

In my haste, I rush by a chic blonde woman in a dark trench coat, bumping her shoulder carelessly. I turn to apologize, my mouth flying open. But when I turn, she is standing still, a tiny smirk on her face.

"Careful, Sylvie."

My eyes widen. My pulse starts racing.

How does she know that name?

"I'm sorry?" I say, pretending that she has the wrong person.

Hell, for all I know, she does.

She arches a delicate brow. She takes off her glove and extends her hand to me, staring at me. "We haven't had the pleasure yet, Sylvie. You can call me Ms. Olson."

Frozen in place, I don't move to shake her hand. "You must have me mistaken for someone else."

I start to turn away, clearing my throat. Ms. Olson steps forward and grabs my elbow, turning me back around. This close, her gray eyes seem like they are filled with a laughing sort of mockery. "Oh, I don't think so. I think you are Sylvie Martin. And I think that you've been masquerading as Pippa Welch for years. Have I got it right, Sylvie?"

Trembling, I jerk out of her grasp. "I don't know who you think I am, but you had better leave me alone."

Her eyes sparkle maliciously. "Unless you want me to tell Prince Lars your secret, you will listen to me."

I shake my head, beginning to walk away. I called back, pointing a finger skyward. "Leave me alone. I mean it."

She calls after me. "You're going to get the opportunity to make yourself a bigger part of Lars's life soon. If you're smart, you'll position yourself to be his future spouse. And when that happens? I'll be in contact."

I stop, glancing back at her. "You're crazy. You don't even know me. You definitely don't know that there's going to be any kind of quote on quote *'opportunity coming down the line'*." I pause, dragging in a breath. "Shit. Why am I even talking you again?"

I start walking away, shaking my head. My hands are shaking with a mixture of fear and anger.

Who is this stranger? And how does this woman know who I am?

I turn the corner, but I can't miss the words that are shouted at my back. "I'll see you again very soon, Sylvie…"

I start to run.

CHAPTER 6

Lars

I'M SITTING at the end of a long, polished conference table, trying not to feel like I'm about to be punished. I lean back in the chair I was given, pushing my cheek out with my tongue.

It's well past eight in the evening. The shadows here in Stellan's study have lengthened. I try not to fidget or show that this little charade of calling me here so late has made me quite nervous.

Inside though, I am drawing a big blank where it comes to guessing what the purpose of this little meeting could be. At the other end of the conference room table, Stellan sits with our very nosy grandmother, Queen Ida, and an older cabinet minister.

Jorgenson. No, Svenson.

Shit, I've forgotten his name.

Stellan looks a little uncomfortable. Momse, as we call the former Queen, looks as pert and pulled together as always. Her sleek gray hair pulled back in a chignon and her dove gray silk dress hiding her too-demure smile.

It just makes me think of how I've never really gotten on with my grandmother like everyone else does. Momse is controlling and manipulative, always behind the scenes trying to pull everyone's strings like a puppeteer. She was always more interested in Stellan, as he was going to take the throne someday.

I try not think about it too much.

The older cabinet member is short and gray-haired, his piercing black eyes focused on me. He is outright glaring at me, held in check I'm sure by whatever machinations my grandmother has in place. I have no idea exactly why I've been summoned here, but I know that it isn't good. I'm trying not to show it on the outside, though.

Stellan leans forward, running a hand to his dark hair. He shakes his head a little as he looks at me. "I think you have really done it this time, Lars."

My heart beats a little faster. I'm not sure exactly what I've done or how I can be punished for it, but seeing my grandmother here is definitely not a good sign. Still, I try to play it cool.

"You're gonna have to be more specific about what I have done wrong this time." I say it casually, as if I'm just tossing off the first response it comes my head. But underneath the table, my hands are clasped together in my lap, knuckles turning white.

My grandmother tucks an unseen hair behind her ear and smiles a little flatly. "As expected, as I have warned you not to do on multiple occasions, you have violated the wrong young woman."

I squint at the three of them. "Violated? Who are we talking about, here? I definitely never done anything to anyone who wasn't a willing participant."

Stellan and my grandmother both arch their brows, reminding me only now that they are definitely related.

The minister shoots to his feet, pointing at me and unleashing a torrent of invective. "You are lucky that there is still a chance to redeem yourself, you complete waste of space. I for one would have you drawn and quartered for the way that you treated my granddaughter. Ever since you sweet-talked your way into her bedroom, she's been inconsolable. Won't eat, can't sleep, doesn't seem to enjoy anything."

I squint. "It sounds like something your granddaughter has more serious problems than me not calling her after we…" I pause, searching for the right term. "Were together."

He looks like he's about to blow a gasket. "It's only recently that she has admitted that she is sad because you didn't call her! You're just lucky that your grandmother jumped in and offered that you should marry her."

I freeze. "I'm sorry, what?"

He leans close, jabbing his finger at me and roaring. "You are going to marry my granddaughter or I will personally see to it that you are skinned alive. That's a promise!"

I put my hands flat on the table, looking at Stellan. "Please tell me that you don't support any of this nonsense."

He sighs, gesturing to the minister. "Well, did you sleep with his granddaughter?"

I push my cheek out with my tongue. "I have no idea. Probably. This isn't nineteen fifty though. Not everybody that sleeps together has to get married. I definitely am not just going to agree to marry some girl that I barely know. I mean, I'm almost afraid to ask which girl this guy's granddaughter is, honestly."

My grandmother pushes to her feet, running a hand down her dress. "I would think that you would be more interested in knowing the name of your bride to be. Her name is Anna, if you are curious."

I narrow my eyes at her. "Ja, I'm not Stellan. I'm not interested in letting you manipulate me. There's nothing in it for me. What are you guys going to do? What leverage you have? None, that's what."

The old man's face turns bright red. "I'll kill you, you bastard!"

Stellan looks at me flatly. "I'll kick you out of the RAF, for a start. And then I will disinherit you. What will you do then, Lars?"

I look away, at the fireplace crackling on one side of the room. My jaw clenches. The idea that Stellan could take away what I have worked for, the very program that may just send me to space one day… It isn't fair.

Not that I would ever tell him that. With my grandmother and the minister watching, I just say the first thing that floats up to the top of my mind.

"Well, that's going to be pretty hard, since I'm already engaged."

The lie comes to me both spontaneously and smoothly. Before I can even think it over, it's out of my mouth. My words give Stellan, Momse, and the minster pause.

I look back at the three of them at the other end of the conference table and they are all stunned. Well, stunned and disbelieving. Which is totally fair because I am absolutely full of shit.

My grandmother puts her hands on the table and leans in, her gaze frosty. "To whom?"

My heart rate speeds up.

Who?

Uhh…

I say it with only the slightest hesitation. The only person that I know for a fact will back me up no matter what, my best friend in the entire world. "Pippa."

Stellan's eyebrows go up. The minister looks livid. He turns to Stellan, pounding his fist on the table. "He can't do this." He looks at my grandmother, dead serious. "You promised me that my granddaughter would marry a royal! That's the only reason I even walked in here. If Lars doesn't marry my Anna, I'm walking out of this room. And my vote for the treasurer goes with me."

My grandmother fixes him with a glare. "If Lars says he is already engaged, he's already engaged. What do you expect me to do about it?"

The minister actually snarls at my grandmother, making Stellan rise to this feet. He quickly steps between them, looking down on the minister.

When he speaks, his voice is eerily flat. "I think you should leave. Don't make me ask security to escort you out."

The minister seems to shrink back at that, realizing that he has displeased the King of Denmark. He points at me, grimacing, and backs out of the room slowly.

I didn't actually know if my hasty ploy would work, but it seems to have stirred some real emotion in the room. Stellan looks at me, his gaze uncertain. "If what you say is true and you are in fact engaged, then I think the only thing I can say to you is congratulations. But please know that I'm definitely watching you, Lars."

With that, he turns and heads out of the room, leaving me alone with my grandmother.

She folds her arms, pacing over toward the window. "Well, now you have done it."

I push up out of my chair, regarding her as I walk over to the bar. It's just a little mini bar and it only has scotch and champagne for some reason, but I'll take whatever I can get. I pour myself a glass of scotch, probably a little too much, and sigh.

"What have I done, exactly?"

She turns to consider me. "If this engagement is not real, you are going to face some real trouble from me. You had better be serious."

I take a slug of scotch, covering my nervous reaction. "It's real. Everyone has always said that I might as well just marry Pippa because that makes sense for some reason. We got to talking about it yesterday and we just decided to make a go of it."

My grandmother arches a brow. "That's not very romantic. I thought that one of the reasons that you were so against being paired up was that you were waiting for romance."

I lift a shoulder and shrug. "What can I say? Pippa and I have always been in love. A platonic sort of love. We've decided that we should make it more formal, that's all."

I feel her ice blue eyes narrowing on my face. "Have you set a date, then?"

I am halfway through another sip of the scotch and I sputter a little bit, wiping at my mouth. "What?"

My grandmother paces across the room, coming over to me. There is a knowing look on her face. "A date for the wedding."

I feel the back of my neck start to heat. "Oh… no. We just… We got so swept up in the moment…"

She looks like she's amused. "You know, for your sake, I hope that you are really engaged and not just trying to weasel your way out of this situation. Because if you fuck around, if you get caught in the arms of another woman, that's it. You've always been a wild child, never listening to me or anyone else. And now I finally have a chance to have some positive sway over your life. But somehow, you manage to wriggle out of it. If I find out that you are not really engaged, I'll make sure that Stellan kicks you out of the RDAF *and* the royal family."

It's surprising to me how easily I lie right to her face. "You're being too serious about this whole thing. Pippa and I are engaged. I would've told you all eventually, it just so happened that--"

She interrupts me, cutting me off. "You have a month. One month to set a date and plan the engagement party. If not, I'll be all over you. I will use Stellan to bring catastrophe for you. That's a promise."

I open my mouth to respond, but she just takes the glass of scotch out of my hand, throws it back into her mouth, and slams it on the bar as she stalks out of the room. The gauntlet has been thrown down, that much is for certain.

Now all that remains is just the little matter of actually telling my fake fiancé that we are getting married.

I swallow thickly, tightening up my tie.

CHAPTER 7

Pippa

I'M STANDING in my little apartment in Copenhagen, staring blankly at the peeling bright yellow paint on the kitchen wall. I reach out and trace my fingertips along a seam above the stove, a silent sigh on my lips.

It was a long day at *Politiken*, a day full of finding out with some disappointment that all of the big bosses have been fired. There is no one left to stand up for me. I feel like I've been wrung out and all my mental energy has been drained away. Now I'm just waiting for my little microwave burrito to be heated through so I can eat and pass out.

My phone chimes, stirring me. I look at it. Lars's photo pops up, a dark haired devil with a cocksure grin. It bite my lip.

I am a fool for even thinking about what spending a night in his bed would be like. Being underneath his big body as he growls commands and pulls moans from my lips…

It's forbidden. And yet still, my heart squeezes at the very mention of his name.

I know he's my best friend.

I know I should cherish what we already have.

I know I shouldn't long for him to touch me.

And yet, even getting a text from him excites me beyond reason.

I shiver as I check the text.

I'm coming upstairs.

Goosebumps break out over my skin. I close my eyes and hold my cellphone close to my now rapidly-beating heart.

A few second later, I hear the slide of a key being turned in the lock on the front door. I'm much too tired for any visitors tonight. But Lars has always done exactly what he wanted, exactly when he wants.

This is no exception.

Screwing up my face, I press the pause button on the microwave. Lars walks into my shoddy little apartment, ducking his dark head slightly as he enters. He's so tall that my building's prewar design is really at odds with his height. When he straightens up, he looks at me with his trademark devastating smirk.

I cast a look over his tuxedo, which makes him look ridiculously fetching.

"Hello, Pippa," he purrs.

I swallow, my eyes widening. "Lars." Pushing back several strands of my long, curly copper hair, I watch as he closes the door behind himself. I spread my hands down the skirt of my gray silk dress, drawing a breath. "It's awfully late. Shouldn't you be on a date with some unnamed mystery blonde?"

His smirk deepens, his aquamarine eyes sparkling. "I was in the middle of a date when I was summoned unceremoniously to the palace."

I fidget. "Why are you here, Lars?"

He wanders toward the living room of my cramped flat, leaving me to follow. He looks around the tiny couch and the ancient television that is stacked atop several light blue milk crates.

Every surface is covered with reading material, books and magazines and newspaper clippings. Piles spill into piles; the television screen is actually blocked by a towering stack of literature. I admit that I'm a bit of a mess and I'm ashamed to say that there is nowhere for him to sit.

Wrinkling my nose, I automatically start to clear off the sofa, my cheeks burning. I gather an armful of books, but I'm not sure where to put them.

"Let me just find a place for these…" I murmur, casting my gaze around the small space. I find a spot on the very top of another pile of books, biting my lower lip hard as I turn around.

"Pippa, I don't need to sit down," he says, grabbing my hand. His touch is electric. When I glance up at him, his blue gaze sears me through.

I raise an eyebrow. "What do you need?"

He smirks a bit, pulling me a little closer, making me look up into his face. From this distance, a hair's breadth away from our bodies touching, I feel adrenaline coursing through my veins.

"I need a favor."

My forehead creases. My mouth turns down just a bit at the corners. This is what he does, what he has always done. He uses his charm, knowing quite well how smoothly hypnotic his presence can be. I've seen him do it to hundreds of women in the years that I've known him.

Usually he doesn't use it on *me*, though.

I pull out of his grasp, moving back a half step. My frown grows deeper. "What is it?"

His expression grows intense. "I need you to pretend that I have asked you to marry me and you have said yes."

I swear, I don't mean to laugh. But it bubbles up from deep within my chest and bursts out of my lips, a snort of disbelief and a surprised chuckle all at once.

"What?" I ask, the word coming out strangled.

He squints at me. "I slept with the wrong diplomat's daughter."

I fold my arms across my chest, trying to slow my racing heart. "Again? How many times do you have to get caught before someone banishes you from the whole country of Denmark?"

His gaze tightens on my face. "It's really not funny. Stellan has threatened to strip me of my title and have me kicked out of the RAF. Obviously, I don't want that."

A low throb starts at my temple. I rub it with one hand, staring at Lars. "And this has what to do with me, exactly?"

He steps closer, snagging my free hand and bringing it to rest against the hard wall of his chest. "I need a fake fiancée. Momse told me today that unless I settle down and get married, I'm going to be kicked out of the royal family."

My breath freezes in my lungs. My mind races, immediately going to what the creepy, trench-coated Ms. Olson said.

If you're smart, you'll position yourself to be his future spouse.

Lars leans in, almost close enough to my face for me to think he's about to kiss me. At the last moment, he turns his head, whispering in my ear.

"Breathe, little witch. Don't look so scared."

His breath is warm against my ear, fanning against my overheated skin.

I won't melt against him. *I won't.*

I push my cheek out with my tongue, forcing my brain to quit pining. Shaking my head, I push myself back and look at him.

"What is stopping you from finding the right girl?"

Someone royal. Or at least someone without the… let's call them *complications* that my history presents. I know very well the list of reasons why Lars can't be tied to someone like me.

I'm a fraud.

I'm a fake and a liar.

I'm not who I say I am.

And someone is already coercing me over an opportunity just like this one.

And that's only the *beginning* of my troubles if anyone finds out.

He gives me a wicked little grin. "You're saying I should sign my death warrant, then? Because that's what being told that I have to get married feels like. I don't want to be tied down. I don't want to be smothered. I just want to keep living like I do now."

I shake my head. "Lars, really—"

He wiggles his brows. "What if I told you that I would bankroll whatever project you asked me to? I know that your work has been a drag lately. So do this: be my fake fiancée for a little while. And in exchange, I'll pump as much money into you starting your own magazine or whatever you want."

My eyes widen. Lars grins at my expression. "You know you want to, Pippa."

I bite my lip. "I don't think it's a good idea, Lars."

He slides his hands down my back and pulls my hips against his. My breath catches in my chest as I gaze up into those pretty blue eyes of his.

This. This feeling, this energy crackling between us?

It's the reason we don't normally allow ourselves to touch, even casually.

I'm *this close* to pushing up on my tiptoes and pressing my lips against his.

Arching a brow, he utters the magic words. "I really need this. *Please*, Pippa? Do it for me?"

And just like that, all my defenses melt away. All the reasons that I can't do it suddenly seem very far away.

Of course I will do it for him.

How can I not?

Lars sees the expression of my face change and knows my answer before I even say it.

"Okay," I whisper. "I will do it. But not forever."

He's already folding his strong arms around me, pulling me into the shelter of his body. "Ahh, thanks, Pips. I knew you would come through."

I sink into the bear hug, my eyes fluttering closed. He's sinfully warm. His smell, pure and clean and masculine, is driving me wild right now.

I inhale a lungful of his scent, feeling like a fool. "That's me. Reliable old Pippa saves the day again."

Lars pulls back. "What do you think about six months?"

I crinkle my nose. "I was thinking a single month would be sufficient."

He gives me a look. "Four months."

I narrow my eyes at him. "Two."

His gaze turns speculative, watching my face intently. "Three months. Surely you can play my fake fiancée for three months."

I look up at him, crinkling my entire face. "Okay. I think I can handle three months."

He grins. "Thanks, Pips. Should we wake the jewelers at Tiffany's up right now? Shit, I should've stopped on the way here and gotten you a ring—"

I push him away, eyeing him firmly. "There will have to be rules. No physical contact, for instance."

He gives me a funny look. "It's going to take a little hugging and kissing to convince my family, don't you think?"

I squint at him. "I meant when we are alone."

He rolls his eyes. "*Ja*, sure. I will behave like a proper gentleman, if that's what you want."

I shake my head, crossing my arms. "No one has ever thought to call you a proper gentleman, I'm fairly certain."

Lars grins at me, his eyes glittering. "If that's what it takes, I'm willing to try."

I shoot him a look. "I'm regretting this already."

He tilts his head, considering me. "Should we go for a drink to celebrate?"

Stepping closer to him, I turn him around and begin marching him toward the door. "We can figure it all out tomorrow. For now, I want to eat something before I pass out."

He chuckles, opening the front door. He catches my hand and gives me a squeeze. "You really are the best, Pippa. You know that, right?"

The corners of my mouth tighten. "Do me a favor. Don't…" I hesitate. "Don't sleep with anyone while I pretend to be your fake fiancée, okay? If this little deception is going to work, you'll have to play along and not be your usual man-whore self for a while."

Lars smirks at me. "You got it, love of my life."

For a second, I can't even wrap my head around that. My heartbeat speeds up. If he had any idea of how long I've waited to hear those words…

But then he turns, showing me his black-clad back as he disappears down the hall. He didn't mean it.

Not like I want him to, anyway.

"Goodnight, little witch…" he calls over his shoulder.

I watch him disappear, slumping against the doorframe when I hear the downstairs front door open and close.

I am in so much trouble.

I know that. I have lied to Lars since the first moment I met him.

If anyone does the slightest bit of digging, I could be exposed.

My life would cease to be my own at that point.

But I can still feel my heart racing, feel the heat of his body pressed against mine. I can sense the excited energy that follows Lars in his wake, everywhere he goes.

Deep in my soul, I know that I shouldn't have agreed to be his fake fiancée.

Oh god.

What have I gotten myself into?

Turning, I close my door and head back to my sad microwave dinner.

CHAPTER 8

Pippa

I WAKE the next morning to the insistent buzzing of my phone. Squinting into the early morning light, I groggily reach out across my bed to snag my phone from the nightstand. It's too early for me to really process anything.

I rub my eyes as I read the first text, which happens to be from Margot. *Pippa! What the hell? When were you going to tell me about this?*

For a solid seconds I can't actually connect the dots. I narrow my eyes.

What is she talking about?

I sit up, scrolling through the numerous calls and texts. It's only when I read the words *you're engaged?* from Annika that I put it all together.

The story about my supposed relationship with Lars must be out, then. I assume that Lars himself leaked it, because the whole situation is fake as anything.

He works fast, I guess.

I text Lars immediately. *A warning shot would've been nice.*

He texts back. *And ruin the surprise?*

I shake my head, pushing my copper curls out of my face. Pushing back the covers with a groan, I shower and start getting dressed. When my cell phone vibrates again, I check it and find a message from Lars.

I hope you're ready to go ring shopping. I'll be at your door in five minutes. And just in case you were wondering, I have a horde of reporters on my tail.

Good lord. If I'm going to be on camera, I have to dress for it.

In my black lace bra and slip, I run into my spare bedroom where I keep my racks and racks of clothes. I hunt through the racks, looking for the garment that floats nebulously in the back of my head.

A one piece pantsuit. Lighter in color, maybe pink or tan. Coupled with a long white mohair coat…

I frown as I dig through my clothes.

Admittedly, I am something of a clotheshorse. There is something exciting and elegant about a new designer dress and a great pair of heels.

Add that to the fact that I'm tall and thin, naturally looking as if I just rolled off of a runway…

Designers like the way their clothes look on my body.

I'll admit it. When I first moved here to Copenhagen, my photo was often snapped when I was hanging out with Lars and Stellan. And I used that exposure to convince up and coming designers to lend me elegant clothes.

At this point though, I'm something of a designer darling. I have ten boxes of unopened clothes in my living room, sent unsolicited from the top fashion houses.

I flip through another half-dozen garments before I come to a stop on what is possibly the perfect dress for the occasion. Long sleeves, floor-length, and cut out of this lovely off-white satin. There are little hand stitched magenta roses on it, cascading and multiplying as they spill downward to the dress's hem. The body of it is perfectly fitted and elegant.

It's a dress fit for a princess, I think. Annika and Margot would definitely fight me for it, anyway.

Slipping it on, I add pink rosette earrings, simple black heels, and a gray muslin coat. I'm putting on a coat of dark pink lipstick when the door buzzes. I cast a final look in the mirror, tilting my head at my own reflection.

Somehow, going ring shopping in this outfit *feels* right.

The door buzzes again, making me roll my eyes and stomp to the front door. I press the button and buzz Lars up without even looking to make sure its him.

I'm just gathering my purse when he opens the door, poking his head in. For a second, I falter as I lay eyes on him. He's very tall, impeccably dressed in his steel blue suit, and so handsome that he takes my breath away. He's had a recent haircut; his dark hair is longer and tousled on top and close cropped on the sides.

He swings that sparkling blue gaze my way. When he sees me, his face lights up in a grin.

It's heart stopping, being the object of his attentions.

Well, *fake* attentions. I'll have to get used to that, I guess.

"We are going to have to talk about your building's security," he says casually. His eyes sweep the living room, his mouth turning down at one corner. "Actually, maybe we should move you to a bigger place."

Swallowing, I arch a brow. "That sounds like you would be doing me a very expensive favor. What is my rule about that?"

He rolls his eyes, jerking his head toward the doorway. "I know, I know. That's not allowed. Come on, we can talk about it on the way to the jeweler."

I wrinkle my nose, sighing as I follow him. "All right. But you owe me coffee. Actually, you owe me coffee every single day for eternity. And I mean the fancy kind, too."

Heading downstairs, I emerge from my building.

I'm not expecting the sea of photographers and reporters waiting there, shouting my name. My eyes widen and I freeze.

But Lars smoothly puts his arm around my waist and pulls me onward. He leans in, shouting in my ear to be heard above all the hubbub. "It won't always be like this."

I look up at him, trying to parse what he means. He grins at me. "How about a kiss for the cameras?"

Without skipping a beat, he puts his hands on my waist, pulls me close, and kisses me full on the mouth. His lips feel hot and pliable against mine; his grasp on my waist feels so intimate that I blush furiously. I blink, trying to wrap my head around the fact that this is even happening.

Lars Love is kissing me.

It's only something I've imagined a thousand times over. It's better than the fantasy though.

So, so much better.

Inside, I start to melt.

It takes me a solid fifteen seconds to realize I need to kiss him back. So I reach up timidly, wrap my arms around his shoulders, and open my mouth to him.

As soon as I do, though, he pulls back with a quizzical gaze. I bite my lower lip, feeling embarrassed that I got so wrapped up in everything.

Lars clears his throat, steps back from me, and takes my hand. Only then do I realize that there are still reporters shouting our names and flash bulbs going off.

He pulls me along the street. I shiver, waiting for a break in the reporters shouting at us. But no, as we move along, the crowd's yammer never dies down. I look at Lars, making a face at him. But he just shrugs and continues down the early-morning Copenhagen street.

By the time we reach the jeweler on High Street, I've gone from feeling overwhelmed by the noise of the reporters to being irritated by it. I know I signed myself up for this, but… I'm already over it.

Lars stops at a glass storefront, looking up. It's a high-end jeweler with a few tasteful pieces of jewelry displayed at the front window, diamonds and sapphires, gleaming white gold and titanium.

Lars surprises me by opening the door for me. He never does that; I've actually only seen him open doors for the girls he dates. I arch a brow at him as I step through.

A sarcastic comment is on the tip of my tongue. But it is swept away when a short, balding man dressed in head to toe black approaches us.

"Your royal highness," he says, bowing low. He has a French accent. "Welcome to my shop. I am Etienne."

I curtsy. "Bonjour, Etienne."

Lars just nods and gives a curt smile. "The royal press office said that you were the jeweler to come see."

"Oui, monsieur. Please, come right this way…"

Lars puts his hand on my lower back, gently nudging me forward. My eyes widen at his touch.

He usually doesn't touch me, even casually. Etienne shows us into a back room, which is well-appointed with a pair of heavy, dark wood couches and several tall, thin mahogany chests of drawers.

"Please, make yourselves comfortable," Etienne waves to the couches. "Would you like something to drink? Water, coffee, a latte…"

"No, thank you." My answer is automatic.

Lars slides me a look. "You don't want coffee?"

My cheeks turn pink. I do want coffee, but I don't want to put Etienne out. So I shake my head. "I'm fine."

Etienne purses his lips. "Very well. If you'll both have a seat, we can get started."

Running a hand over my dress, I find a seat on the couch. Lars does too, unbuttoning his suit jacket and leaning back, throwing his arm over the back. He looks like he owns the place, which makes my mouth turn down just a hair.

Etienne picks up a black velvet-lined tray, walking over to us and displaying his wares. I'm not sure what I expected to see. Maybe a selection of new and untouched rings in the latest styles or something.

But instead, Etienne holds a tray of gleaming antique-looking rings, varying in precious metal and stone. They are, on the whole, not especially stunning. When I think of a jaw-dropping engagement ring, I think of some huge, sparkly diamond.

These are much smaller stones, much less glittery than I had imagined. My surprise must be written on my face when I look up, because Etienne offers me a smile.

"Her royal highness, the former Queen Ida, suggested that you might like to choose a ring that is already in the family."

I lick my lips, darting a glance at Lars.

"I see." I don't know quite what else to say.

Lars frowns at the selection of rings. "These are all hideous. Do you have something…" He squints.

"A little more modern, perhaps," I suggest.

Etienne bows his head. "But of course."

With that, he takes the tray back to the dresser, swapping it out. When he presents the new selection, I arch a brow. These may be a little newer, but not much.

I glance at Lars, taking a deep breath. He pulls a face. "Can I see the tray that Stellan and Margot chose their ring from?"

"That won't work," I say. "If I recall correctly, Stellan already had the ring. Margot didn't get to choose."

Lars sighs. "Oh. Well… can we start with the newest rings and work our way back?" He pauses. "You know, Pippa, if we don't find anything you like, we can always keep looking."

I shoot him a look, willing him to remember for a second that this is all fake. There is no need for a fancy ring. After all, I'll only have to wear it for three months.

Etienne steps back. "Yes, your royal highness. Allow me to try again."

As soon as Etienne's back is turned, I mouth *be nice* to Lars. Lars just smirks, shrugging one shoulder. I scowl at him.

When Etienne returns, he holds out a black velvet tray filled with twenty four of the biggest, shiniest rings I think I've ever seen. My jaw drops as I take in the array of white gold, rose gold, and platinum settings. There is no way that these rings aren't worth half a million pounds or more.

"Oh. I think we've gone too big," I say quickly. One ring in particular catches my eye, an enormous square cut diamond with two smaller sapphires on each side, all set in white gold. My fingers itch to touch it.

Lars reads my expression and nods to the tray. "Which one? You want to try it, I can tell."

I shake my head, looking at Etienne. "These are… they're beautiful, but they are too much. I want something simpler."

Lars shoots me a glare. Etienne bows his head, disappearing and reappearing with yet another tray.

This one has rings that are more affordable, that's for sure. As I will only be wearing it temporarily, I point out the first ring that I see that just seems… reasonable.

"May I see that one?" I ask.

Etienne smiles a bit. "I do apologize, mademoiselle. His royal highness may pick up any of the pieces that he chooses…"

Lars shoots me a smug smile as he leans over and plucks the ring off the tray. "Your hand please, my dear, sweet Pippa."

I wrinkle my nose, turning to Etienne. "Would you excuse us? I promise, we are not going to steal any of these rings or anything."

Etienne ducks his head, smoothing a hand down his tie. "Of course, mademoiselle. His royal highness does own them, ma'am."

He has a point. He leaves, shutting the heavy door behind him. I turn to Lars.

"Quit it," I warn.

He gives me an innocent look. "What?"

"Behave."

"Make me," he says, grinning.

I roll my eyes, holding my hand out. He takes my fingers ever so gently, which makes my pulse pick up. I swallow as he looks me dead in the eye, slips the ring on my finger, and gives me the cockiest grin ever.

"Now you're mine," he tells me.

My face heats, my heart beating embarrassingly fast. "No, I'm doing you an immense favor because you asked me very nicely. And by the way, I meant it about our fake relationship only lasting for three months."

A dimple flashes in his cheek. "I was thinking of pushing it out to a year."

I pull my hand from his grasp, putting a little more space between us. "And I was thinking of changing my mind and saying that I couldn't possibly be bothered for longer than a month."

"Six months," he fires back.

My eyes narrow on his face. "Three."

He looks me up and down, as if considering my offer. "Four months. And you let me move you into my place temporarily."

I open my mouth to argue, but he stops me with a gesture. "There is no more haggling. It's four months. And at the end, you will have your magazine funded. Yes?"

I frown. Four months isn't a breeze, but it seems doable. I don't like that he sees my terms as being flexible, though. Alas, that is very typical of Lars.

I clench my jaw. "Fine."

"Great." His eyes twinkle. "Now are you sure about this ring?"

I look down at the ring, my mouth twisting. It's two sizes too large and not the right shape at all. If this little deception was real, if I had to wear this ring forever, then no way. But it's just a prop.

A very expensive prop, but fake nonetheless.

I nod, taking a breath. "*Ja*, I'm sure."

He grins at me, dazzling me with his smile. "Good. Now come on, wife to be. I think we should tell Etienne together."

Getting up, he offers me his arm. I rise, taking his arm, a sigh on my lips. "Lead the way."

CHAPTER 9

Lars

I'M WAITING ANXIOUSLY at the swankiest hotel in Copenhagen, trying not to freeze my ass off while I wait by the front doors. Pippa's my New Year's Eve date. Actually, we have had this planned out for weeks.

It just so happens that now I have just added a ton of weird pressure by making it our debut as a couple. And royal couple at that.

I'm genuinely a little worried. Pippa was pretty grumpy all of yesterday, fueled in part at least by our brand new arrangement.

And I get it. She is doing me a huge, immense favor, getting me out of a less than savory situation.

So she gets to be a little grouchy, I guess.

When her limo pulls up and she emerges, I'm beyond relieved to see her look for me and then smile.

Then I allow myself to breathe a little… and to take her in. She's wearing a huge fuzzy floor length white coat, which she sheds the second she walks in the door. What she reveals actually makes my mouth water. She's wearing a floor length, long sleeve gown made of what looks like molten silver. It hugs every tantalizing curve and only enhances her fiery copper curls, which trail down her back.

She turns for a second, handing her coat off to a waiting attendant, and I see that the dress is cut very low in the back, emphasizing her amazing skin.

Looking at her right now is making my tuxedo pants a little tight. I feel like ripping off my bowtie. I'm stifled, looking at her silver-coated curves.

She floats over to me, a smile curving her lips. "Don't you look dashing."

I drag my gaze away from her, refusing to be thirsty. "I was just thinking the same thing about you."

She touches my arm, looking up at the hotel's second story. I follow her gaze up to see several people taking pictures of us surreptitiously.

But when Pippa leans over and kisses my lips ever so carefully, it still takes me by surprise. Worse than that, when she pulls away again, I'm left aching.

God, this is going to be a long night.

A long four months, really.

I shouldn't have chosen the girl I'm in love with to fake an engagement. I'm kicking myself over the choice now.

I clear my throat. "Shall we?"

Pippa smiles, seeming in good spirits. "Lead the way, your highness."

"Don't start with that shit," I say, rolling my eyes.

I usher her to the escalator and we ride up to the second floor. I spend the whole time looking at Pippa's ass and speculating whether or not she's wearing any panties.

My guess is no.

On the way off the escalator, I stop and look around. Tonight, my favorite hipster bar has taken over this floor and they've really gone all out. The doors to the grand ballroom are thrown open, revealing some extremely hip black and white decor. To our right, there is a bar set up, the stylish bartenders in their black shirts and denim aprons busy mixing drinks. And to top it all off, there are uniformed waiters walking around with trays of drinks and appetizers.

Pippa pulls away, heading for one of the waiters. I follow, noticing that people are looking at me oddly.

Pippa hands me a glass of champagne, nodding subtlety to a group of girls who are gawking at me. "What do you think is going on there?"

I lift a shoulder in a shrug. "If I had to place odds, I would wager we are watching my pool of dating prospects drying up."

Her eyes twinkle as she takes a sip of her champagne. "How will you ever survive?" She laughs. "Just remember, you were the one who pushed for four months of faking your engagement."

Before I can come up with a good comeback, Margot peeks her head out of the ballroom. "There you two are!" she says, beaming. "Come on, we have a table waiting."

Pippa throws a look at me over her shoulder, heading into the ballroom. I follow her, entering the dimly-lit space. Electronic music courses through the whole place. The ballroom's high ceilings and classic parquet floors are enhanced by the white tables and futuristic white decorations hanging from the ceiling. Margot waves us over to a corner where Stellan is sandwiched in with Erik and Annika. I repress a sigh, pulling up a seat at the end of the table.

Stellan shoots me a look, like I've already done something wrong. Then I look up and realize that Pippa hasn't sat down yet. I don't like my brother reminding me of social customs, but he's right. I stand, pulling Pippa's chair out and deftly moving it right beside my own.

Pippa smirks at my gesture. "Thanks," she says, taking her seat. Turning to Annika, she smiles. "I love this dress. Actually, I love Margot's dress too. A part of me is definitely envious."

Ja, I could definitely use a drink. One of the reasons that we chose this party, of all the parties going on tonight, was that it promised the liquor would be flowing. The other was that I felt that there would be plenty of ladies around, looking for their next one night stand.

I guess that isn't in the cards tonight, though.

Looking around, I spy a waiter and signal him to come over. I don't even have to ask Pippa what she wants to drink.

"A French 75 and a whiskey neat. If I don't ever see the bottom of either glass, there will be something extra for you, okay?" I tell the waiter.

He rushes off like his life is at stake. I smirk and watch as Pippa catches up with Margot and Nika.

I cast a gaze over to Erik, who is giving me a funny look. "What?" I ask.

He slides a look to Stellan. "You just cost me a hundred pounds. I bet Stellan that you would never settle down. Especially after telling me just a few days ago that Pippa is basically your sister—"

I glare at him. "Shut up."

He shrugs, looking elegant in his tuxedo. "I'm just wondering why you completely flipped your story, that's all."

I casually put my arm around Pippa's shoulders, arching a brow. She blushes, pulled away from the conversation. "What now?"

I lean over to kiss her full on the mouth, adding a little tongue in for good measure. She freezes up, resisting at first. Then she seems to remember that she agreed to this, relaxing in my grip.

Her mouth is hot and her lips plump. Her eyes close a little. Then she opens her mouth for me the barest inch…

My eyes close involuntarily as I gently slip my tongue into her mouth. Damn, she tastes good. I've imagined this moment a thousand times over, my very first time French kissing Pippa.

But it's so much better and deeper and more complex than I'd imagined. She makes a soft sound, curling her fist against my lapel, pulling me closer.

God, I can smell her delicate floral perfume, taste her minty mouthwash overlaid with a splash of sweet champagne fizz.

"All right, all right!" Erik shouts. "We get it, you guys are in love…"

Pippa pulls back, her eyes a little wide. It looks like I'm not the only one who got a tiny bit carried away. Pulling from my grasp, Pippa flushes and turns to the rest of the table.

"Sorry," she apologizes. "You know how it is, I would guess."

Annika leans in and covers Pippa's hand, giving her a secretive smile. "I promise, we all do. Congrats on finally deciding to sleep together."

I grin. "Actually, I don't know if you saw Pippa's hand, but we are engaged."

"I know!" Margot says. "Let me see the ring!"

Pippa lifts her hand to Margot, her cheeks burning bright red.

I smirk as my gaze slides to Stellan. His eyes narrow on my face, suspicious as ever. Of course, he has every right to be suspicious; there is no relationship between myself and Pippa except friendship.

Really good friendship.

The kind of friendship that is a once in a lifetime find. Not worth risking, not for any price.

I drop my gaze, reminding myself of that very important fact. The waiter delivers me a fresh whiskey and I pound it, not even pretending like I'm too classy. Getting drunk is more important.

Several drinks later, Pippa is red-cheeked and grinning around the table.

That's Pippa's drunk face, which is sort of the opposite of mine. I generally get more scowl-y the more I drink.

Annika stands up, drunker than I have ever seen her, and pulls Erik out to the dance floor. Margot and Stellan are right on their heels, Margot grinning and laughing even though she's dead sober.

Pippa glances at me, biting her lip. "I know you don't dance, but I think you should make an exception. Come on."

She stands up, pulling me along with her as she heads out to the dance floor. The music slows down a good bit, changing tempo to something nice and easy to dance to.

I can actually ballroom dance. It's just the whole dancing alone and looking like a fool thing I'm not good at.

I beckon to Pippa, putting my hand out. She takes it, an uncertain smile on her lips.

Then I pull her into my arms and dip her. When I pull her back up, she's laughing. "Lars! I didn't know you could dance."

I tuck her snugly against my body, feeling cheeky. "I can slow dance."

I slide my hands down the sides of her body, making her shiver. As I suspected, she isn't wearing a bra. Bracketed in my big hands, her waist seems impossibly slim. I wonder if I were to let my hands wander down further if they would find a thong or not.

God damn, this woman in my arms is so hot.

"Hey!" Pippa's voice breaks through my reverie. "Do you mind?"

…and I realize that I'm staring right at her tits. I look up at her, my neck heating. "Sorry," I say with a shrug. "They were just right there…"

Pippa shoots me a glare and tries to pull away. Because I'm so much bigger than her, I just hold her a little tighter. She scowls at me, leaning close.

"Let me go," she whispers, looking fierce.

I bite my lower lip, my eyes sinking to her lips. "I don't want to."

She grips my forearms. "Seriously, Lars? You're drunk."

I scoff a little. "You're drunk too. Stop being melodramatic. We are supposed to be engaged. I'm just acting like an engaged guy who is super horny for his fiancée." I cock my head. "Hell, maybe we should just sleep together. Call it an experiment."

Her face turns red. In a second, all the teasing vanishes from her tone and body language. "Get off of me."

Shit, I crossed a line. I immediately let go, stepping back. "I was just kidding," I add lamely.

Pippa takes a deep breath in, looking me dead in the eyes. "Tomorrow, we are establishing better boundaries."

Then she turns, zeroes in on a waiter carrying a tray of champagne flutes, and grabs two. She upends both of them, poring them down her gullet, and then wipes her mouth.

"Take it easy with the booze," I say. "You throw up pretty easily."

Her mouth twists. "Don't worry about me."

My brows rise. That's impossible. I've always been looking out for Pippa's best interests, even when she doesn't know what they are.

Pippa makes a show of dancing with Margot and Nika, getting more and more drunk. With a sigh, I slow down my intake of alcohol.

One of us has to be sober enough to get us both home.

When the DJ turns the music down and tells us it's almost midnight, I pluck two champagne flutes off a waiter's tray and wade over to find Pippa. She is really drunk now and she screams with excitement when she sees me, throwing her arms up.

"Dance with me!" she says, bouncing up and down.

I roll my eyes. "You have had a lot of wine, haven't you?"

She just laughs and hugs me, snagging one of the champagne flutes that I brought over. "You want to know something?"

I crack a smile. "What is that, drunk Pippa?"

She beams at me. "You look really handsome in that tux. Like... really. You know how to... to... work it. If you were anyone else, I would have already tried to come onto you."

I roll my eyes at her drunk compliment, but I can't help grinning. "Thank you. You look quite sexy in that dress."

She opens her mouth. Before she can respond, the DJ comes over the mic. "All right, everyone! It's fifteen seconds now until the new year. Let's all count... ten! Nine! Eight!"

Pippa grins up at me, counting along. "Seven! Six! Five! Four!"

I squeeze her tightly. "Three! Two! One!"

Everyone shouts happy new year. That, I was prepared for.

But the hot, wet, drunken kiss that Pippa lays on me... the one that has me pulling her closer, and her grabbing my face... the one that goes for almost half a minute...

This is unexpected.

When she pulls away, my cock is hard, my breathing coming out in pants. I look down into her eyes, trying to make sense of that kiss.

What was that supposed to be for? She holds my gaze for a second, gazing back up at me. I press her body closer and try to read her expression.

"Do you—" I start.

Which is when she turns away, delicately putting the back of her hand against her lips and dry heaving.

Aww, shit. I hustle her toward a bathroom, grabbing an empty ice bucket as we go. She immediately throws up in the bucket.

I switch from party mode into medic mode, getting her into the bathroom and helping her kneel down before the toilet.

Then I try not to get too grossed out for the next twenty minutes as she wretches, throwing up over and over again. All I can do is hold her hair and feel bad.

After all, I'm pretty sure that she wouldn't have gotten so drunk if I hadn't come on so strong earlier.

I end my night by calling for a royal limousine and bundling her inside. Erik, Stellan, and their respective women are nowhere to be seen.

"Just take us to my apartment, please," I tell the driver.

I sit back, letting Pippa lie in my lap, and feel very tired all the sudden.

CHAPTER 10

Pippa

I WAKE up in the early hours of the morning, before the sun has even thought about rising. Opening my eyes a crack, I realize a couple of things pretty quickly. First, I am so completely and utterly hungover, it's ridiculous. I think I remember being sick… but when I think too much about it my head really starts throbbing.

And second, I am in Lars's bed. I have no memory of coming here. In fact, the last thing I remember was…

Ah. Getting absolutely plastered at New Year's Eve. That tracks.

I'm not wearing the slinky silver dress from earlier. Somehow that has been replaced by one of Lars's plain white tees. I can't help but sniff it and rub it against my chin. It's old and soft, washed so often that it almost feels fragile. I stick my hand down the covers, hoping against hope that I'm still wearing my little black thong.

Somehow I am. Thank god for that.

God, I'm so thirsty and I really, really have to pee.

I throw my heavy blankets off and stand up. My mind is still foggy as I stumble to the en-suite bathroom. Lights seem too bright for the moment. So I just close the door and use the light from the window as I try to put things right.

I pee, use a little toothpaste to do a quick rinse of my mouth, and halfheartedly try to tame my curls. There is no point in the last one; with my mane of red curls I look like a lioness, and not in a good way.

This is one of many reasons I don't spend any nights over here at Lars's place. No frigging hair products and nothing to even comb my hair with other than my fingers.

I feel vaguely silly when I drink straight from Lars's elegant tap but the water tastes pure and so, so good.

At last I yawn, leaving the bathroom. My brow furrows as I take in the spectacular view of downtown Copenhagen. Lars showed me this view once when he first moved into this place. How many bedrooms have such a spectacular view?

Wait a second…

My eyes widen. I glance over at the bed, where Lars himself is stretched out on the bed. It looks like I stole most of his heavy comforter for myself some time during the night… leaving him with the barest edge to cover himself with. My jaw drops.

He's perfect. At first all I can stare at are his abs, which seem like they are carved from frigging stone. Then I notice his long arms and legs are splayed out, covered in a fine layer of soft, sparse fuzz. His dark head is resting on a fluffy white pillow. And as I tilt my head to one side, considering how he's only covered his thighs, one of his eyes cracks open.

"Pips?" he asks. He pats the expanse of bed beside him. "Come on, come back to sleep."

My cheeks heat. I tug down the hem of his old tee shirt, conscious of my bareness. "I… uh… I didn't think I was in your bedroom."

He eyes close briefly. "I didn't exactly put you in here. You found your own way."

Lars pulls at the comforter, covering himself more. I'm at once terribly glad that he did and also sort of sad. It's not very often that I get to admire… well, so much of Lars. Visions of him will populate my fantasies for years, I'm sure.

"Pippa!" he snaps.

My eyes widen. "What?"

"Will you please stop being so fucking weird? Get back in the bed. We're adults. We can share a bed for a night, surely."

I lick my lips. Do I say no?

Or should I—

"Get the fuck back in bed," he growls. "And try not to snore this time."

Reacting to his tone, I tiptoe over to the bed and avert my eyes as I lie down. Lars throws the covers back on top of me. I freeze, unable to look over at him. He's naked under the comforter and… well, I just don't trust my hands not to… wander.

Haven't I dreamed of just exactly this moment happening? I'm absolutely sure of it.

I look up at the high ceiling, swallowing. For a few seconds, I wonder if he has just gone back to sleep. Curling my hands into fists, I will my heartbeat to slow down.

He sighs and adjusts next to me. "I can actually feel your brain growing hot from too much thinking."

I bite my lip, turning my head toward him. "How did I get out of my dress?"

He makes a vaguely amused sound. "I don't know. I brought you back here to my apartment. You made a beeline for my bathroom. A few minutes later, you said you needed a tee shirt. I didn't think it wise to ask any questions."

"Oh god." I cover my eyes, blushing furiously. "Did I really snore?"

I peek at him. He chuckles, nodding. "Yes you did, little witch."

I groan, which makes my head throb more insistently. "Happy engagement."

That pulls a genuine laugh out of him. He turns over on his side toward me, tucking a bit of the blanket in around his hips. I only let my gaze drop there for a second before the internal red light starts going off.

Danger! Danger! Not a good idea! Do something else with your eyes!

So I drag up gaze upward, up his flat stomach, past his amazing abs, above his stellar pecs. I look at his face, which is mostly obscured by shadow.

Lars is staring right at me when I get to his eyes, startling me. I don't say anything but my eyebrows do fly up.

He finds it funny, letting out a rumble of laughter. "You are something else, you know that?"

I feel my face grow hot. "Am I?"

"Yes," he affirms.

I cock a brow. "At least I wear clothes when I sleep."

"Pfft." He rolls his eyes. "As if that is worth bragging about."

I turn on my side, facing him, and stick my tongue out at him. "One of us has to be the adult here."

His laugh rumbles again. "Would it truly be so terrible if we were both naked?"

I frown. "Well… yes."

He shakes his head. "Why would that be bad? Hmm? As I said, we're both adults."

I squint at him. "That's probably the line that you use to get girls to play strip poker or something. And it won't work on me."

He shifts forward, so that I can see more of his face. He's smirking, which makes me want to hit him.

"First off, you *wish* I was asking you to play strip poker. And second, you would one hundred percent fall for a line."

I scrunch my nose up. "I would not."

"You would," he says, grinning. "You definitely would. Here, let me try out a line on you."

I snort. "Go right ahead."

Lars looks thoughtful. Then he pulls his comforter up, wrapping a corner of it around his body like a toga. He lifts his chin, smirking at me with a knowing look. He reaches over the side of the bed and pulls his shirt onto his stomach. Then he looks at me, his eyes sparkling with mischief.

"Feel my shirt."

I crinkle my entire face. "What? We just established that you are all but naked."

"Come on, play along. Feel my shirt."

Shaking my head, I reach out, smoothing my hand against the hardness of his chest through the thick comforter. "Feels… um… nice?"

He covers my hand with his, trapping it at the same time he pins me with his gaze. "Ja? You know what it's made of?"

It feels like someone has sucked all the air out of the room. Lars's skin against mine is hot. I lick my lips, shaking my head a little.

"No, what?" I ask. My voice sounds a little breathy; I blame it on the late hour, though.

Or is it early? It's hard to tell.

He meets my eyes, grinning broadly. "It's made of boyfriend material, sweetheart."

It's impossible not to crack up at that. For some reason, that strikes me as the funniest thing I've ever heard. "That's terrible!"

He smirks at me, wiggling his eyebrows. "You doubt me, but it's true."

I can't stop laughing. I ball up my fist, hitting him lightly. He acts like I've just killed him, groaning and turning onto his back, using my hand to pull me nearer. He wrangles my hand so I'm all but toppling across his chest.

"You murdered me! I'm dying!" he cries, trying not to laugh. "You've done it now, little witch."

I grin at him, biting my lower lip. "You deserve it for that terrible pun."

"Hmm," he says, flashing that wicked grin again. "It made you forget about being awkward, though."

I realize then that Lars has pulled me so that I am pressed up against him. Only the thick blanket separates our bodies. My breath leaves me in a huff. A shiver of anticipation skitters down my spine.

I look up, right into Lars's deep blue eyes. I swallow, my tongue darting out to wet my bottom lip. My gaze slides to his mouth.

Lars's eyelids close halfway as he moves in toward my mouth.

I can feel the kiss before it even happens. He moves closer. I close my eyes, my lips parting ever so slightly. His breath against the sensitive skin of my lips makes me shiver.

There is no room for softness in this kiss. Lars cups the back of my head and brings my mouth against his, searing me through. His lips are hot against mine. I open my mouth more and he takes full advantage, growling low in his chest. He moves his tongue against mine in a rhythm as old as the ages. I can barely help myself, curling my hand around the warm back of his neck and pulling myself closer. He tastes of clean mint and smells like aftershave; it is beyond me how he can smell so good while he's asleep.

His free hand comes down to the notch in my waist. I feel small compared to his much bigger body, almost dainty.

That's a new sensation for me. I may be slender but I am still tall.

When his hand slides up to cup my breast, all the breath leaves my lungs in a rush. I suck in a breath and a moan escapes my lips.

Yes.

God, yes.

Lars is touching me.

I nip at his full bottom lip. He slides his hand down my waist and hip to my knee, pulling my leg onto his hard, hot body. I can feel my body tightening, my breasts growing heavy, my pussy growing wet. I lean into him, rocking my lower body against his. I want him to touch me everywhere, but my clit is actually so hot it's almost achy.

I'm on fire for him.

Only him.

He stops kissing me for a second and rolls away, opening his bedside table. My brain takes a second to process the crinkling sound. But he holds a condom up in the air.

"Got it," he says.

My face contorts. It feels like I've suddenly been drenched with a bucket of ice water. I wasn't expecting to actually have sex with him…

"Umm… hold on." I murmur. Sitting up, I pull the blankets up over my chest.

Lars looks a little puzzled. "You don't use protection?"

I frown. "We were just kissing. I mean…" My face grows hot. "I think I'm still drunk, Lars. I don't want to… do more than that."

The words spill from my lips, unbidden. Lars frowns and looks away. "Oh." He clears his throat awkwardly. "I mean… of course."

Oh god, I can tell from his facial expression that I've hurt him. He clears his throat, trying to pretend away his awkwardness.

I reach out, my fingertips falling on his forearm. "I'm sorry, Lars."

He tosses the condom off the bed, shaking his head. "No, it's… I mean, I shouldn't have… assumed…"

I drop my hand. "We shouldn't… I mean, what we have is already so special."

He takes a deep breath, pinning me with his aquiline gaze. "Seriously, it was just… a lapse. I was on autopilot or something."

My eyes widen a bit that. The fact that his autopilot involves condoms is just…

It hurts my soul.

Before he can puzzle out my wounded expression, I turn onto my back and pull the covers up to my neck. "It's for the best. Like I said, I'm still drunk." I bite my lower lip, desperate to change the conversation. "I can't believe you let me drink so much."

I feel him roll onto his back beside me, sighing. "I didn't let you do anything, little witch."

Silence stretches between us for half a minute. "Can we just not talk about this ever again?"

"Sure," he says, a little too quickly.

I roll away from him, facing the Copenhagen skyline instead. "Um. Night, Lars."

He just grunts, shifting a few times. Then I assume he just goes right to sleep.

Not me.

No, I lay here and go over things again and again in my mind. Like how amazing the kiss was. How into it I was.

And how he definitely ruined my mood by completely assuming that I would just fuck him. Like it was that easy.

Like it wouldn't have effects on our friendship.

My mouth twists.

If I thought there was the remotest possibility of that, Lars and I would have gotten naked and sweaty together ages ago.

At some point, my eyelids drift closed. I don't remember falling asleep. But when I wake up, it's mid-morning.

I roll over to find Lars's side of the bed has been made. And a hand-written note on the pillow.

P —

Had to work out early.
There's coffee in the kitchen.
See you later.

— L

Groaning at how casual his note sounds, I pull the blankets over my head. I definitely learned one lesson for the fiftieth time in our friendship. It sucks to be in love your best friend.

I roll over, squeezing my eyes shut, and try to pretend last night didn't happen.

CHAPTER 11

Pippa

THE NEXT COUPLE of days are hellish. Lars seems to handle me with kid gloves, being very courteous while at the same time keeping me at arm's length. Nika is angry at me for some slight I made when I was drunk.

And to top it all off, I have a lingering remnant of a headache that just won't go away. I blame the champagne for it.

Actually, I blame the alcohol for a lot of things. Like French kissing my best friend, for instance.

After running all my errands Friday evening, I finally arrive home. I have to be careful when I carry my grocery bags upstairs because my entryway is absolutely bursting with thousands of dollars' worth of clothing. I skirt the boxes and let myself into my flat, only to nearly drop the bags when I get the door open.

A small, dark-haired figure in a belted trench coat stands at the window. She turns and quirks an eyebrow at me.

Ms. Olsen is here, in my fucking flat.

I drop my bags unceremoniously, backing out the door. I trip on the boxes behind my feet, trying to get my cell phone out of my purse.

"Pippa, dear," Ms. Olsen lets out the tiniest smirk. "I let myself in. I hope you don't mind."

"Of course I bloody mind!" I yell, looking at my phone screen. "Listen, whoever you are. I'm dialing the authorities right now!"

She steps forward, her lips quirking. "You can, if you wish. But I wouldn't."

I shake my head, pressing the call button. "You're insane. You know that? Just totally daft."

The phone starts ringing. Ms. Olsen smiles coolly. "Do you not care about Lars's wellbeing, then?"

I glare at her. The operator picks up. "Emergency services. What is your emergency?"

I flush. "Yes, hi. I just came home to my apartment and there is an intruder," I say quickly.

"What is your address, please?" the operator asks.

Ms. Olsen arches a brow. "We will tell him your secret." She pulls out her phone, showing me a flash of a photo. In the photo is the same girl that I found on Facebook, my little sister Stella. "And we will hurt your sister, if we have to."

I open my mouth, but that gives me some pause. My eyes slide over to Ms. Olsen's face, which is both smug and superior.

Is she serious?

I cover the microphone. "You should leave."

Ms. Olsen tilts her head. "You should hang up the phone, my dear."

"Excuse me, what address?" prompts the operator.

Ms. Olson scrolls through six or seven pictures of my sister, obviously taken when she was leaving the grocery store. I automatically reach for the screen, curious. She yanks the phone away from me, her tone threatening.

"Hang. Up." Ms. Olsen looks serious now.

"Uhh… never mind. I thought it was an intruder, but I… was mistaken?"

The operator replies. "Are you sure?"

Ms. Olsen checks the elegant silver wristwatch she wears.

"Yep!" I blurt. "Sorry."

I hang up the phone, a scowl on my face. I don't know how to even approach this subject. How should one act when being blackmailed?

"What do you want?" I ask at last.

Ms. Olsen's expression lightens. "For now? Not a thing."

"Why are you here? Why are you waving these… these creepy photos around?" I ask, gesturing wildly.

She shrugs a single shoulder. "Those are questions that I do not have the answers to. I'm just here to ascertain if we believe that you can be loyal or not."

I ball up my face. "What are you talking about?" I shout, exasperated. "Can you leave my flat?"

Ms. Olsen gives me another cool smile as she looks me up and down. "I think I'll tell my bosses that they had better keep Lars and Stella under observation for now."

I shake my head in disbelief. "Just wait until he hears about this."

She gives a tiny yap of laughter. "If you tell him, if you tell anyone, we will expose you. No one will even remember the story you tell because they will all be focused on the story of Sylvie Martin. And oh, what a story it is…"

I lift my chin. "I don't know what you are talking about. Please, leave my apartment!"

She purses her lips. "We both know that isn't true, Sylvie."

Tears prick my eyes. "I mean it. I will call emergency services back."

She sticks her hands in her pockets, moving forward slowly. I can't step back so I stand my ground. Her eyes twinkle for a moment as she pulls one of her hands out, revealing a basic flip phone. She reaches out to me as she comes to stand in front of me.

"We will be in touch. Take care of Lars, Sylvie."

My beat beats like a jackhammer in my chest. "I don't want your phone."

Ms. Olsen navigates around me, heading down the stairs. "Keep it close."

As I look over my shoulder, she raises down the stairs and out the front entrance of my building. Glancing down at the black phone in my hand, I realize that I am shaking.

Who is Ms. Olsen?

What does she want?

Staring at the phone, I can't come up with a single answer that makes sense.

CHAPTER 12

Lars

"TRY NOT to look as though the car in front of you has done something to personally offend you," I whisper into Pippa's ear.

She blinks a few times, blushing as she looks at me. She clears her throat and runs a hand down her light pink dress, licking her lips. "Sorry," she whispers back.

"And this car is the very first automobile to have rubberized wheels!" the older man leading our tour says. "You might think that the wheels look the same as they did in the last model, but I assure you they are not."

Pippa looks around the massive white tent where we have been learning about Denmark's part in the automotive boom. I check out Pippa while she isn't looking, finding the way that pink fabric clings to her ass much more interesting than the history of cars.

We've been extremely awkward since she spent the night in my bed last week. I've been kicking myself for blowing my one chance with the woman of my dreams.

And Pippa has seemed wrapped up in something else altogether. I guess it's better that way.

"Now if we move on to the next car, you will see that the shape looks a bit different..."

Pippa glances at me. I raise a brow. She leans close. "Please don't make me listen to any more. I'm begging you, Lars."

I can't help but smile. "What, you're not riveted to our guide's dissertation on how some old cars were made of wood and…" I pretend to fall asleep, snoring mid-sentence.

She rolls her eyes. "Come on. If anybody asks, I'll tell them I am not feeling well."

My lips curve upward. "You deceptive little minx. Lead the way."

One corner of Pippa's mouth tugs down but she just sighs silently. Turning on her heel, she spins and makes her way toward the tent's exit. I follow her as she weaves her way around half a dozen more old cars, then duck out of the tent into the bright sunshine. There are even more cars parked here, rows upon rows.

And these cars are much newer, much sexier, and much sportier than anything parked inside. Pippa glances back at me, arching a brow. "Isn't this one of the cars that James Bond drove in the 1960s?"

I wander towards the baby blue Aston Martin, feeling cooler just by being near it. I run my hand along the door, whistling. "Yes, I believe it is."

She wrinkles her nose. "You boys and your toys." She steps closer to me, bringing her hand up to my neck to straighten my tie. "At least you look the part."

My stomach sort of flip flops when she touches me. I play it cool, not reacting outwardly. "What? Devastatingly handsome?"

Her snort of good humor warms a little of the frost I've been feeling coming from her direction. "I just meant you were wearing a suit."

I put my hands behind my back, twisting my spine to survey the other cars. "Bond is known for wearing a tuxedo, if I'm not mistaken."

Her lips tip upward. "Tell me about this James Bond. I'm afraid I'm not familiar with him, seeing as how he is only my country's most famous fictional spy and all."

There it is. The banter that I've so greatly missed for the past week seems to have returned. I roll my eyes, taking a deep breath. "Who do you imagine I have to charm and dazzle to get the keys to one of these cars?"

Pippa pulls the ends of her pink cardigan closer, shivering. "Maybe that gentleman?"

She points behind me. I turn and spot a blond man in a dark winter coat approaching. He doesn't seem to recognize me until he's only a few feet away. Then he slows his pace, his gaze sliding between me and Pippa.

We've been splashed across the front page of every tabloid for a few days. His expression grows tense as he approaches.

"Your royal highness," he greets me. "Do you have a question about one of the cars, sir?"

Taking a step toward Pippa, I grab her around the waist. "My fiancée here was wondering if we might test drive one."

Pippa shoots me a flat look, elbowing me in the ribcage. I grin at her.

"Oh, I'm not sure… I mean…" The man grows red-faced. "Let me ask."

I nudge Pippa. "See?"

She shakes her head at me. "You are so spoiled. You know that, right?"

I wink at her, enjoying holding her close for a moment. "If you don't complain about it, I will let you drive a bit."

She wrinkles her nose. "I can't drive."

Nodding to the returning employee, I disagree. "He's got the keys right there."

"No, I mean—"

I cut her off, raising a hand to the dark-jacketed man. "Toss them!"

He looks vaguely nervous but he does toss a set of keys high in the air. "Here you go, your royal highness. I didn't realize that this car collection belonged to your father, sir."

Pippa glances at me, her eyebrows rising. "Wait, really?"

I shrug. "It's okay. Tell me, which car do these belong to?"

He gives a tiny bow. "The lime green Porsche, sir."

My eyes land on it, a few rows away. There is certainly no mistaking it for anything else. I grin. "Oh, that'll do nicely."

Jerking my head toward the car, I wiggle my brows at Pippa. She scrunches up her face as she follows me over to it. I go to the passenger side door, getting in.

"Lars!" I hear Pippa complain. "Seriously, I can't drive. I don't know how."

"And I heard you the first time. Get in. There is no time to learn like the present."

I pat the leather seat beside me. She huffs but reluctantly climbs in the car, sitting in the injection-molded seat. She glances around, the keys still clutched in one hand.

"Are you sure that this is okay?"

I point to the ignition. "Yes. Put the key in."

Scrunching up her face, she does. She turns the key, as if expecting the car to start up.

"It's a manual transmission, little witch," I tell her. "Look at the gas pedal."

She bites her lip, looking down. "I see three pedals."

I lean over, touching her leg. It's very little contact, but still enough to make my pulse race. "Look, the one closest to me is the clutch. The gas is in the middle. The brake is on the far side."

She arches a brow. "Why don't they make it simpler?"

I smirk a little at her. "Why ruin the fun?"

"Okay." She wrinkles her nose. "What now?"

"Push down on the clutch and hold it down. The one near me. Ja. Now the key should turn."

She does it a bit clunky, pressing down the clutch and the brake all the way to the floor. When the engine turns on, she looks at me. "Did I do it right?"

"*Ja, ja.* I mean. You got the thing running, at least. Ease up on the clutch. It only takes a light touch…"

She lets up completely and the car dies. She looks at me, panicked. "Oh god!"

I wave my hand. "No big deal. Do it again. Only don't stomp all the way to the floor. And don't let up on the clutch completely."

Her brow furrows as she does it with a tiny bit more grace this time. Then she looks over at me, awaiting instruction.

"The next part is tricky," I say, moving a bit closer. "You have to press the brake a little, keep pressure on the clutch, and shift into first."

I tap the gear shift. To my great surprise, she does it right the very first time, as if she has been doing it forever.

"Is that it?" she asks.

"Yep. Now comes the hard part. You have to press the gas pedal while you ease completely off the clutch. It's a smooth, even transfer, like this." I mime the pedals switching positions.

"Okay…"

Pippa lets go of the clutch too fast and the engine dies. She howls with frustration, hitting the steering wheel. "Stupid car."

"Come on, come on. Try it again. After you manage this, you can drive."

She makes a little grr sound but she does try again. And again... and again.

On the fourth try, she nails it. The car lurches forward a few feet. Pippa is so surprised that she takes her foot off the gas.

The engine dies.

I expect her to groan but she doesn't. Instead she turns to me, eyes shining with excitement, and throws her hands up. "I drove!"

She hugs me, doing a little dance. I freeze for a second, only relaxing when I force a laugh out. "You did. Well done."

She pulls back, her expression radiant.

Ah. That face she is making, the way her eyes are shining, the cheerful glow in the apples of her cheeks...

I live for that expression.

It doesn't last long, though. She sighs, rolling her head on her shoulders. "I think that's rather enough for one day, don't you?"

I look at her, completely serious. "It's whatever you want Pippa. We only go on your word."

A flush rises in her cheeks. She gives me an odd look. "Well, I think I'm done. I'm also freezing. Come on, I think I saw hot cider being poured in the refreshment tent."

She hops out of the car. I lean over and pluck the keys from the ignition, then follow her.

As I head toward the tent once more, I repress a sigh. For the millionth time, I am reminded of just how deeply in love with Pippa I am.

But at the same time, how much she means to me as a friend. If anything were to happen to our friendship, I would be...

Well, it wouldn't be good, at least.

Pippa turns, tucking a bit of her red hair behind her ear. "Are you coming?"

I nod. "I am."

Wishing I had found anyone else in the world to have a fake relationship with, I head into the tent.

CHAPTER 13

Pippa

I GLANCE AT LARS NERVOUSLY, sucking my full bottom lip into my mouth and abrading it with my teeth. He stands stiffly beside me, his eyes turned forward to the open balcony doors. I slip my hand to his elbow and rest it on his heavy black jacketed arm. He doesn't seem to notice.

I draw a breath and smooth a hand down my frost blue heavy winter coat. Lars looks over at me, his expression lightening a bit. "I can tell you are stressing too much," he says. He reaches over and fusses with the white lily that is pinned to my coat. "We are just pretty background decoration, I promise. We won't be expected to speak." He rolls his eyes. "This is Stellan's show."

I wrinkle my nose. "I just assumed I would watch the King's speech from the massive audience gathered outside."

He tilts his head to the side. "That's Pippa Welch talking. You have to forget about yourself and remember your role. What the palace is expecting is the future Duchess of Marion. I find it is easier to deal with it all if I know to put Lars Love away and bring out Prince Lars of Denmark."

I nod, pensive. "I suppose so."

Two of Lars' brothers, this and that, make their appearance. They stand just behind us in line, coming after Lars in line for the throne. I peer around them to Nika and Erik, who currently have their heads close together, whispering about something.

Behind them are Lars's silvering father, his mother in royal blue, and his scary but always elegant grandmother.

The whole family is just waiting on the King and Queen now.

There is a commotion behind us. I turn my head and see Stellan and Margot arriving with a flock of secretaries and assistants. I must say, they do look rather royal. Stellan is outfitted in a dark suit and a dark overcoat similar to Lars. Margot is wearing her signature light pink color in her coat and dark heels.

If I didn't know them as people, I would still think that they made a stunning King and Queen of Denmark.

Margot shoos away one woman who is trying to put a final touch on her hair. She stops for a second to squeeze my forearm and wiggle her eyebrows. "We'll talk after the speech."

My lips curve up. "Sure."

But even as I answer, she is hustled past me to stand at Stellan's side. The balcony doors are swept open by two footmen. The audience begins cheering as Stellan and Margot step outside, smiling and waving.

"Your royal highness," a palace secretary says, beckoning Lars forward.

Lars clasps my hand in the crook of his elbow and steps forward. I fall into step almost automatically, wincing a little as the sheer wave of sound overtakes me. I step forward and look out at thousands upon thousands of people, cheering and holding signs. It's freezing outside, but the Danish people don't seem to care.

"Wave and smile," Lars shouts in my ear. "And don't forget to breathe."

I lift a hand, plastering a smile on my face. He guides me to our prominent position beside Stellan and Margot. We continue smiling and waving as the rest of the family finds their places. The crowd continues to cheer, especially when Annika steps out with Erik.

She's always been the people's favorite princess, so no surprise there. Stellan takes the microphone and coughs into it; the noise dies down as he begins his speech.

"Welcome," he welcomes the crowd. "As you undoubtedly already know, on this day in 1953…"

My brain blanked out whatever he is saying. Not that it's not important. But I'm too fascinated by looking around at everyone clustered on the balcony on this cold, bright morning.

I look up at Lars, biting my lower lip. He's focused on a spot in the crowd. I follow his gaze to find that several young girls are holding posters with my picture pasted on them. They say "Pippa + Lars 4Ever" and "Team Pippa!"

I have to admit, I don't even know who I am playing against in whatever team sport that young girl is so pumped about. I glance at Lars again and he looks at me, giving me a secretive smile. He nods towards Stellan, reminding me that the King is still speaking.

I yank my gaze to Stellan, who speaks for some length of time about the country's values and how proud he is to be Danish. I smile and sort of check out for a while, coming around when the crowd starts to cheer once more. I applaud, looking around at Lars's brothers.

Everyone seems to politely clap. No one has even a note of boredom on their faces.

Interesting. I know that Annika has not even the vaguest hint of interest in what Stellan was talking about. Yet I look at her pretty blonde features and she looks engaged.

That must be something learned over time, I guess. I've watched a thousand royal events as a member of the audience; it wasn't until today that I really got to see the other side of things.

"Pippa," Lars says, putting his hand on my lower back. He guides me back inside, following Stellan and Margot. As soon as we step inside, we are enveloped by warmth and the sound of cheering is immediately dampened.

I take a deep breath as Lars leads me down the stairs in the procession to the formal dining room. The dark wood room has a single long table in the middle with an elaborate and decorative place setting. As we step through the doors, footmen wait for our coats. Lars has his off in a flash, revealing his suave black suit beneath. He smiles at me as he helps me take my coat off, his chilly bare fingers touching my nape for long enough to raise goosebumps.

A server approaches with a tray of champagne. Lars picks up two glasses, just assuming that I want one.

I accept it from him and look around at everyone milling about near the window. "So now what?"

Lars shrugs a shoulder and sips his drink. "Stellan will probably give another speech about how we are all lucky. Then we'll have dinner."

I raise my brows. "Is that it?"

"Pretty much, ja." I see him wrinkle his nose slightly. "Fuck. My grand-mother is looking at me like she expects something."

His hand instinctively finds mine. I blush as his grandmother comes marching over, leading several aunts and uncles in her wake. It's very diffi-cult not to fidget as his grandmother looks me up and down. Her mouth turns down at the corner.

It's hard not to take that personally. Nevertheless, I greet her formally, curtsying. "Your royal highness."

Those bright blue eyes of hers pierce me. She's wearing a blue skirt and a cream top that make her eyes seem to pop. "Pippa, I presume."

"Momse," Lars cuts in. "You promised to be nice when I let you meet Pippa."

She touches the back of her silver hair. "Did I?"

He lets go of my hand. Before I can do anything else, he slides his arm around my waist and tugs me into his side. "Do we have to do this fifth degree business? Can't you just be happy for us, Momse?"

Momse raises her chin. "How are we to know that she is really the girl for you, Lars? If she's really your fiancée, that is."

Lars bristles. "She is what I say she is."

I cut in, trying to lessen the tension. "We went to the palace jeweler and got a nice ring." I lift my left hand, showing the ring off.

The expressions mirrored back to me are confused. One tall, gray haired gentleman clears his throat.

"It's very… nice. Very tame," he allows.

I frown. This man, who probably has never worked a full day in his entire life, thinks my ring is too small?

"The diamond costs what a new car would cost. I don't need or want anything larger."

Lars's grandmother shoots us an unreadable smile. "Very sensible of you."

Lars squeezes me close. "Pippa is nothing if not sensible."

Momse narrows her gaze on us, not impressed. "So it's to be a marriage between friends then, is it?"

My eyebrows fly up. "What?"

"No, we… we love each other," Lars declares, his hand on my waist flexing.

I know suddenly what I must do. Turning to Lars, I smile sweetly.

"They want to see us kiss, darling," I say.

There is a flash of puzzlement across his face before it's replaced with resolution.

"Ah." He smirks at the crowd. "You want a show?"

Without warning, he dips me backward, pulling me into position for a kiss. My hands come up to his chest and I am about to protest.

But before I can utter a word, Lars zooms in and presses his lips against mine. For a second, I am lost in the sensation of the kiss.

His lips are hot. My whole body tightens at that. When he opens his mouth to me and I do the same to him, he tastes like clean mint and a hint of champagne.

My hands curl in his lapels. My eyes drift shut. I wish it were possible to get closer to him; if we were alone, I would definitely quantify the feeling I have as distinctly horny.

Lars slides his hands down from my waist to my ass, making me giggle. I open my eyes, staring deep into his…

He grins at me, a smile that promises naughty things to come.

For a relationship that is fake, this is starting to feel dangerously real. Every time he so much as touches me, it's the kindling to my body, lighting the match to my soul. Even while I know in my gut that it's not fucking real, it feels too good to be fake.

I stare into his eyes, trying to find a similar emotion in those cool blue depths. What does he feel?

Someone across the ballroom drops a glass, making me cringe. And that's when I remember that the rest of the world still exists. I redden, looking at the people watching with wide eyes. Momse clears her throat and shifts her stance.

"Yes, all right," she says, waving a hand. "I'm satisfied for now, Lars."

He is quick to physically separate us, laughing a little. It sounds fake to me, but then again, I'm in on his big secret.

The sound of a glass being gently rung with a knife cuts through all the noise. "Everyone!" Stellan calls out. "If you would find your places at the table, I'd like to say a few words."

Momse shoots Lars a last look before turning away and moving toward the head of the table. I exhale a shaky breath. Lars grabs my hand, giving it a squeeze.

"What do you say we try to sit far away from my grandmother?" he asks.

I nod, moving away from that end of the table. "She's very direct and intense."

His lips quirk. "Indeed."

We find two seats at the end, far away from his grandmother, and listen to Stellan talking about how lucky the people gathered here should feel.

And I do feel lucky, more so than most of the royals. But I watch Lars out of the corner of my eye, wondering.

Was that kiss merely for show?

It didn't feel like I was faking anything.

Then again, I'm really in love with him, so... maybe that's why it convinces people.

Blowing out a breath, I drag my gaze away from Lars, trying to focus on literally anything else.

CHAPTER 14

Lars

PIPPA LOOKS over at me from her seat in the chauffeured limousine, giving an aggravated groan. "Three days! It's been three days of nonstop royal visits and parading ourselves around to prove that we are really engaged. Does the palace just assume that we have nothing better to do with our time?"

I straighten my tie, sighing as I adjust my seat. "Yes. Traditionally, we are in positions that put us at the palace's beck and call."

She scrunches up her face. "I'm so unbelievably done with being a fake royal right now."

"Oh Ja?" I ask, raising a brow. "Try doing it twenty four hours a day, seven days a week for twenty five years."

Pippa picks at a bit of lint, flicking it off of her slinky black dress. "I honestly had no idea. No wonder you loved going to boarding school so much."

One corner of my mouth turns up. "I did love St. Matthew's. I was all but forgotten while I attended. I don't know if you remember, but I campaigned to be allowed to remain at school through winter and summer breaks."

She smiles a little at the memory, tucking a bright copper stand of her hair back. "Of course I remember. You were upset because the school refused. So you invited me home for the winter break as a sort of rebellion."

I chuckle. "I did. Of course, my mother and father barely noticed. If I hoped to grab their attention by bringing home an orphaned scholarship student, I failed miserably."

"Ja, sure." Pippa's cheeks warm and she looks away. That's usually her reaction to hearing herself described as either orphaned or disadvantaged.

A muscle in her jaw flexes. She looks out the window, her brow furrowing. "If you'd told me then that I would be here now, faking an engagement with the prince of Denmark, I wouldn't have believed you."

My lips twitch. "Same."

Out my window, I see the familiar-looking gates of the Air Base Karup looming. The whole base is ancient, a repurposed medieval fortress with a load of airplane hangars and landing strips surrounding it. All of it is neatly encircled by enormous iron gates.

"Is that the place we are going to?" Pippa asks, leaning over to look out my window. She's let her hair down today and the magnificent copper mass looks amazing. One particular curl seems to stand apart from the others; my fingers itch to smooth it down.

I swallow. "Ja. Ja, this is our last stop for the day."

She straightens, huffing a sigh. "At least you will know the people here." Her brow wrinkles. "Or does that make it harder? Since, you know… we are lying."

The limousine driver pulls up to the base's gates, rolling down the window. I watch him talk to the guard, distracted.

"I hadn't given it that much thought," I say, shrugging a shoulder. "We won't be the starring attraction anyway. There is some sort of show being put on today that a lot of the soldiers have been talking about. It's like a tame form of burlesque, I think."

She nods, looking ahead. The limo is waved through the gates and soon we pull up to the fortress. I run my hand over my uniform one final time, preparing myself.

"Ready?" I asks Pippa.

She nods. "After your grandmother's questioning, I feel like the military will be a breeze."

I grin as I get out of the car and escort Pippa into the actual building. It's gloomy inside the formal reception area. As soon as we step inside, a group of high ranking brass marches through, on their way from one area of the building to another. I pull Pippa toward the wall and salute them; one of the generals gives me a stiff nod as they pass.

Pippa cranes her neck to watch them go. "It's crazy that in the palace this morning, everyone was bowing and scraping and calling you royal highness. Yet here, that doesn't seem to matter at all."

I nod to the receptionist and pull Pippa along, resting her hand on my inner elbow. "The RDAF runs on their own rules. Everything here is decided by rank and merit."

Pippa smirks a little. "I see. You aren't seen as a prince here. I can tell by your tone that you like that."

I nod to another group of lower ranking cadets who stop and salute me. "Yes, I've been allowed to thrive here. It's a lot like St. Matthew's, in a way. Whatever you are outside these walls, once you step inside, it all falls away."

A jet takes off outside as we continue down the corridor. Pippa looks around, taking it all in. "I expected that the Royal Air Force would have done more remodeling. It basically looks in here as I imagine it looked a thousand years ago. There's absolutely zero soundproofing in here. Plus it is so…" Her mouth twists. "Well, it's a bit dank."

I smile at her. "That it is, Pippa. We like it like this." I turn a corner, pulling her to a stop. There is a line of uniformed men slowly filing into the fortress's big auditorium.

I pull her along, going with the flow as we squeeze through the double doors. The space we step into is truly awe inspiring, with a very high ceiling and smooth concrete underfoot, reminiscent of an airplane hangar. There is a ton of light in here from skylights cut into the ceiling; at the far end of the room, a stage has been assembled, a microphone stand the only decoration.

Pippa takes it all in with wide eyes. "What a space," she breathes.

"Come on," I say, taking her by the hand. "Let's get a place up front. We will be accepting some award or the other on behalf of the palace, but I assume that will be after the main show."

As I lead her forward, elbowing my way through the crowd toward the stage, a uniformed officer taps the microphone. "Good afternoon, Royal Air Force Base Karup!"

There is an immediate wave of loud applause and wolf whistles. The officer refers to a piece of paper. "Please welcome the Dusseldorf Dance Troupe!"

Loud rap music starts booming over the sound system. I manage to squeeze myself and Pippa up near the left side of the stage. Ten people parade out wearing a very bastardized, hot pants version of the same dress blues the Royal Air Force is known for. There are seven women and five men dancing. My eyebrows rise as I watch the spectacle. They separate into two rows, one moving forward and going down to their knees. They move quite deftly to the rap music, as I suppose you would expect a dance troupe to move.

I am deciding whether or not to be offended by their take on our uniforms. Everyone around me whistles and cheers, though. They don't seem to mind.

I frown.

Pippa leans in close with a secretive grin. "What do you think?"

I shoot her a glare and lean my head closer. "I think they are very close to mocking us with those uniforms—" I stop mid-sentence, because several of the dancers shed their uniforms for bikinis or speedos. My jaw drops.

One of the dancers edges near the area of the stage where I stand. She casts her gaze around and makes eye contact with me. All the while, she gyrates and grinds, shooting me naughty expressions.

I tilt my head, trying to decide if the blonde is sexy or if I'm still offended. Pippa squeezes my arm.

I glance at her. She doesn't look entirely pleased with me.

"What?" I ask.

Pippa leans her head in close. "At least act like you're in public with your fiancée," she hisses. "That is part of the deal. No making me look bad."

I roll my eyes. "Calm down. I'm not doing anything but looking."

Her cheeks flush. She pulls away from me and gives her head a little shake. Then she turns and starts threading her way through the crowd, heading toward the exit.

Fuck. I didn't mean to make her mad.

I glance back at the stage, guessing that I have plenty of time before I have to be onstage. Elbowing my way through the crowd, I heave a sigh.

If I wanted to deal with stuff like this, I would've just proposed to the minister's granddaughter. I push open the heavy double doors, spotting Pippa as she hurries down the hallway.

"Pippa!" I call.

She stops, turning with a frown. "What?"

"You're being ridiculous," I say, walking over to her. It's only when I get up close that I can smell her rose perfume and see the unshed tears in her eyes.

"You promised me that you wouldn't sleep with anyone else while I am pretending to be your fiancée," she whispers. "You could at least try to hide it a little better."

I reach out for her arm, tugging her closer. "I didn't do anything, Pippa. I was just standing there."

A tear breaks away from one of her eyes. She wipes it away angrily. "I saw your face. Everyone could see you making eyes at that dancer."

I shake my head. "Honestly, I wasn't. I was trying to decide if I was offended by her uniform." I take a deep breath, looking down into her face. "I think you might be overreacting a little bit."

She pulls out of my grasp. "Stop telling me that. Stop telling me what I'm supposed to feel. I hate that!"

I raise my hands up, backing up half a step. "Whoa. Okay."

She wipes at her face again, looking miserable. "You asked me to be your fake fiancée. Which is a lot. It's fine, but… a lot to ask another person. And all I asked in exchange is that you don't make a fool out of me by fooling around behind my back." She grows tearful. "It's not a lot to ask, Lars."

I don't know what else to do, so I enfold her in a hug. "I know, Pippa. I know." I murmur into her hair. "I'm sorry if it seemed like I was…" I pause. "Whatever you thought was going on. I assure you, there is no reason to feel jealous."

She looks up at me, her face contorting. "I'm not jealous. I'm just… I'm trying to tell you how other people perceive you!"

I narrow my eyes on her face. I could challenge her, but I want to calm her down. And that isn't the way, knowing Pippa as I do.

She is the only person in my entire life that demands so much of me and doesn't treat me as if I am special; but at the same time, she doesn't hold herself apart from me, either.

There's no way I'm about to risk that over something so small and dumb.

"I'm sorry," I tell her. "Really, I am."

She hangs her head with a sigh. "Okay."

My mouth twists. "You know that I will eventually have to go back to living my life though, right? You can't be all up in arms about me making eye contact with other girls forever."

She shoots me a glare. "I know that, thank you. I'm just trying to preserve some small amount of dignity. In two months, you can eye fuck anyone else that you want."

I repress an eye roll. "Fine. We'll deal with that when we get to it. For now, can we go back in the auditorium?"

She sniffs. "Fine."

I wave a hand toward the doors. "Fine. Lead the way."

As I follow her though, I can't help but turn the whole situation over and over again in my mind.

CHAPTER 15

Pippa

"OKAY. Wait here for just a second. Don't look!" Lars says.

I keep my eyes covered and shiver against the cold air. Lars has brought me somewhere an hour and a half north of Copenhagen, saying we need a break from everything. I listen as his boots crunch across the snowy ground.

"Where the hell are we?" I ask.

"You'll know in about thirty seconds," he says with a laugh.

Wrinkling my nose, I kick at the ground beneath my feet. I can tell it's been freshly shoveled, but I don't dare peek out from behind my hands just yet.

I hear something scraping the ground. Lars comes back and leads me forward a few steps, standing right behind me.

"Okay. You can look."

I drop my hands and see an enormous modern cabin before us, the door open wide, the heat escaping it in clouds. I look at Lars, extremely surprised.

"Where are we?" I ask again.

He grins and grabs my hand, leading me up the front steps and into the foyer. "I rented us a cabin for the next few days. It's sort of my way of saying I'm sorry for dragging you to three days of royal events."

I look around the cabin, if it can even be called that. One of the walls is made entirely of glass. Just outside, the landscape drops dramatically away, making for a breathtakingly snowy vista.

A living room is set up immediately in front of me, all the cozy white furniture arranged around a wrought iron fireplace with a chimney going up to the ceiling. The kitchen gleams from across the space, all dark stone and stainless appliances. Between the two is a charming cedar table set for six.

"Well?" Lars prompts me. "What do you think?"

I turn to him with a slow smile. I point out the skis hanging on the wall in the entryway. "It's amazing. But why here? As far as I know, we've never skied or done anything remotely woodsy."

He shrugs, closing the door behind him. "Well, maybe it's time we tried. Hmm?" He shoves him dark hair back off of his forehead. "I think I've put us in a high pressure situation. So this is me trying to release some steam that has been building up."

My lips quirk. "Ah. You're talking about how I lost my cool at the Air Base Karup, I'm guessing."

He shrugs. "I mentioned to Erik that we needed a break. He suggested a cabin in this area. Now here we are."

I turn around, giving him a soft hug. "Thank you. It's very thoughtful. Maybe I could use a break, now that you mention it."

The hug lingers for a second too long before he steps back, clearing his throat. "Want to try skiing? Or better yet, we can snowboard."

I laugh. "Sure. Let me just change into more layers. Then we'll try whichever you want." I pause, tilting my head. "As long as I make myself clear. I think that too much exercise is for people who secretly hate themselves."

He grins. "Come on, get dressed."

The next few hours are fun, if not productive. Lars trying to snowboard and failing. Me trying to ski and ending up on my ass, over and over. Both of us laughing as we hold hands and sled down the huge hill behind our house on a big double raft.

By the time the sun starts to dip behind the trees, I'm completely done for. I wave a hand, stuck in a snow drift with my skis askew.

"I give up!" I laugh. "I am not any better at skiing than I was a few hours ago."

Lars frees himself from his snowboard, which he's actually annoying okay at. He walks over and grabs my hands, helping me up.

"Ja, I'm ready to call it a day. I'm also so hungry at this point that I could eat a bear."

I follow him to the cabin, my eyes dropping to the spot on his ass where he's landed enough times to make his pants damp. "Mm," is all I have to add to the conversation.

We head inside the cabin, shedding our clothing before the snow that clings to it melts. I head into my bedroom, just upstairs. Digging fresh clothing out of my suitcase, I change into a loose, flowy white dress.

I guess I don't fully understand that our bedrooms are connected by a bathroom. Because I step into the bathroom, my mind on my hair. And I see Lars with no shirt on, just buttoning a pair of dark, low slung jeans.

He turns around and catches me looking at him. He smirks as my cheeks grow red.

"Don't let me stop you," he jokes. "By all means, little witch. Take all the time you want. Stare away."

I shoot him a glare. "Ha ha." I clear my throat and drag my gaze to the big mirror in the shared bathroom. He pulls a white tee shirt on as I try to futz with my halo of insane curls. I try not to notice that he fills up almost the entire doorway with his sheer height.

Lars leans in the doorway, his biceps gently bunching as he crosses his arms. I won't let myself notice.

Just because he's unspeakably hot and I have wanted him forever doesn't change anything at all. First, I am a fucking liar. I have been since the week we met.

And there is the fact that our friendship is more important than anything else. We can't forget that, can we?

"What are you thinking about?" he wonders.

I blush, looking at his reflection in the mirror. Ja, I'm not answering that one.

"What's for dinner?" I ask instead.

He smiles slowly, pushing off the doorway. "The oven is heating up for a frozen pizza. I also think there is a salad."

I turn. "I'm starving. Let's go raid the fridge while we wait."

We eat pizza and talk about inane things for the next hour. Up here, in his jeans and tee shirt, Lars is imperceptibly more laid back. His smiles are more frequent, his jokes are mostly terrible. There is none of the posturing and bravado that usually follows him around. He's just… happier.

I realize that he probably needed a break from everything almost as much as I did. That thought comforts me a little bit.

Lars eventually opens a bottle of wine and pours us each a glass. I swirl the contents of my glass gently, looking at him as he settles on the couch. He quirks an eyebrow at me.

My lips quirk. "Yes?"

He spreads out on the couch and shrugs. "Nothing."

I narrow my eyes. "I know you too well for that. What is it?"

He takes his time sipping his wine before he answers. "I was just wondering what it would be like if we lived very different lives."

I tilt my head. "In an alternate universe? We wouldn't know each other, probably." "Maybe. But I was more thinking of a world where we knew each other. I wonder what would have happened if we had just met in our twenties."

My brows rise. "Oh?"

"Ja. Imagine if we had not been largely ignored by our respective families growing up. If we were both just normal, well-adjusted adults when we met."

I wrinkle my nose. "I can't picture it, honestly. We wouldn't have any history."

He chuckles a little. "No. I wonder if we wouldn't just date each other."

My heartbeat instantly speeds up. I lick my lips. "You think we would be an item?"

He shrugs a shoulder, picking up my feet and putting them in his lap. I bury my toes under his thigh, enjoying his warmth. He shoots me a secretive smile.

"Maybe. I mean, you are definitely not my type. But maybe in this alternate world, you would be."

Oh god. I blush a little bit.

"I've seen your blonde supermodels come and go like a revolving door," I answer crisply. "I'm really not interested in being your type, I think."

That's a lie. It feels false even as I say it.

He finishes his glass of wine and sets it aside, rubbing one of my bare feet with both of his thumbs. He goes right to a spot that feels so good, digging into the pad of my foot.

"Oh, little witch," he sighs. "There is no denying that we have both found each other attractive."

My brow descends. "Ja. It's all the other pieces about you that I find problematic. For instance, the fact that you've slept with half the pretty, young blonde girls in the city."

He smirks. "What if I was well-behaved? Hmm? Would that make you happy?"

One corner of my mouth bends downward. "Hypothetically?"

He pins with his sapphire gaze. "I don't know, Pippa. Do you want us to be discussing things hypothetically?"

No.

God, the way he is looking at me just now. The way he is smirking at me. The way he touches my feet.

My hormones want him to stop talking and kiss me. Hell, they wouldn't mind if I jumped him.

I lick my lips again, taking in the expression on his face. "Are you actually suggesting that we sleep together, Lars?"

He pauses, pushing his cheek out with his tongue. "I could be. I mean, you think I'm hot. I think you're hot. We could just… take it to the next level."

I frown. While I obviously want him more than anything, I don't want to destroy what we already have.

"I… I don't know, Lars. We are best friends. And to me, that is more important than some little fling."

He bites his lower lip. "So we'll just… keep it casual."

I shake my head. "I don't think that's a very good idea."

Lars narrows his eyes on my face. "Kiss me."

I shoot him a look. "What?"

"Kiss me," he says, moving closer. "Just one time. Kiss me for real. And then if you still feel like it's a risk to our friendship…" He reaches up to my face, brushing back a curl. "Then we can pretend it never happened."

I swallow. My eyes are on his, trying to gauge how serious he is. I suck in sips of air and notice how his eyes slip down to my neckline. My nipples pebble at the very thought of his lips touching my overheated skin.

God, my heartbeat is so loud in my own ears that I am afraid he will hear it.

He puts my feet down, moving so he's only a few inches from my face.

He licks his lower lip, reaching out slowly to cup my jaw with his elegant fingers.

"Pippa?" he murmurs.

I can barely breathe. "Yes, Lars?"

He brings his face closer, feathering a kiss over the corner of my mouth. I open my mouth, sighing silently. I can feel a storm gathering inside me.

Lars kisses my cheek, grazes his lips over my earlobe. "All you have to say is yes," he whispers.

A dam breaks in me. I move my head, catching his lips with my own. He is surprised for a split second. Then he takes control of the kiss, cupping my jaw and teasing my lips apart.

He's sweet and salty and earthy, his tongue working against mine. My hands come up to grab his shirt, forming fists as I drag him closer.

He pulls back and nips at my lower lip. I can't help it. I let out a little moan.

"Is that a yes, little witch?" he whispers.

I nod, struggling to draw a breath. "Yes." He moves in to kiss me again, but I pull back.

"There have to be rules," I say, looking in his eyes. "To protect us both."

He looks puzzled. "Like what?"

I draw in a long breath. "We are friends first. Okay? We just… we don't do anything that would hurt that." I reach out, grabbing his hand and pulling it over my heart. "Promise me."

He frowns. "Of course, Pippa."

I lick my lips. "Okay. There are probably more rules—"

He cuts me off with a kiss so dominating that all thoughts of rules are driven from my mind. My hand fists in his shirt. He moves effortlessly to scoop me up off the couch, not breaking the kiss.

And then he starts carrying me upstairs.

CHAPTER 16

Pippa

LARS PRESSES his lips to mine, bending me backward. My hands touch his face and then creep around his strong neck. He picks me up. My legs go around his waist naturally. I moan as he walks us both backward, toward the bed.

God, is this really happening right now?

As he lays me back on the bed, I shiver. He breaks off the kiss only to move his mouth lower, to my jaw and my neck. Scorching a path to my pulse point, he buries himself there. I feel the sting of his teeth for a second before he kisses the sensation away.

I had no idea that his mouth could be so *hot*. His lips against the pale column of my neck causes my breasts to tighten and lift. I realize that he is already pressing himself between my legs, falling there naturally when he moved us both on the bed. I am suddenly aware of the place between my thighs where I ache, the feeling more and more insistent the longer I'm with Lars.

His hand trails down to cup my breast through my shirt, pinching my nipple through my bra. Everything he does feels amazing, like a fire burning through a drought-parched land. He pinches my nipple again, sending shivers of electricity down my spine. I gasp at how connected my breasts seem to be to the slit between my legs, the slit that is growing damp now.

I have some ideas for what would feel good right now, most of them centered on the bulge in Lars's jeans. Pressing my hips up against his, I make a sound of pure need.

Lars pulls back, desire flaring high in his eyes as he meets my gaze. When he speaks, his voice is rough as gravel.

"Tell me what you want," he murmurs. "Tell me that you want me half as badly as I want you, little witch. Make me believe it."

I suck in a breath. Do I want him? With every single molecule of my being, with every breath in my body.

"I want you, Lars," I whisper, looking into his eyes.

He smirks. "Are you sure, Pippa? Because I want you so damn much it hurts."

I bite my lip and nod, my eagerness overcoming my shyness. He kisses me again, his hands drawing my tee shirt dress up and over my head. Just like that I am bare before him, wearing nothing but my bra and leggings.

Lars looks at me hungrily, his eyes dipping down to my breasts. He takes a second to unlace his boots.

I watch him, my heart beating in my throat. Then he strips off his shirt, leaving me half-drooling at his hard muscles. His abs. His pecs. His biceps…

Everywhere I look is ridged with muscle. The exercise regimen that he's been on is no joke, it seems.

He returns to me, unbuttoning his jeans. He leaves them zipped, cradling my face as he kisses me. My heart is a humming bird, fluttering in my chest. A moan emerges from my mouth as he takes me back onto the bed, trailing his hot kisses down my neck and across my chest.

He kisses his way down to my breast, pulling one strap of my bra down and baring my nipple.

The breath seizes in my lungs. Then he fastens his wicked mouth on my nipple. I cry out at the almost electric sensation. It makes the ache between my legs spread a little wider.

He releases my breast, his face utterly dark as he reaches behind me to unclasp my bra. I take a little bit of initiative and draw my bra off, tossing it aside. Then I'm bared before him, my hard nipples jutting proudly between us.

I hear his harsh intake of breath. It makes me flush.

"You are so goddamned beautiful to me," he whispers, reaching out to cup one of my breasts. "It's killing me, I swear."

My cheeks flood with heat. Reaching out a hand of my own, I touch his neck and trail my fingers down his arm. "You're a Greek god, in case anyone was keeping score."

That makes him chuckle, his eyes crinkling. His humor is infectious and I find myself smiling softly.

"What?" I say.

"I never know what you're about to say, that's all. I find you surprising, continually." His eyes wander down my body.

He runs his hands down my sides, finding the fullness of my hips between his two hands. He kisses me again, firmly and passionately, making me gasp with want. I hardly realize that he's stripping off my leggings until they are gone, until I am left with a skimpy pair of black lace panties as my last layer.

He leans down and presses his face close to my mons, inhaling. "Fuck, you smell so good. It should be illegal to smell like this."

He starts to touch the tiny triangle of damp fabric between my legs, running his fingers down from the hem to the vee of my thighs. I let my eyelids flutter closed as his clever fingers begin trailing closer and closer to my aching slit. God, even this much friction is incredible.

He kisses me, his lips and tongue every bit as clever as his fingers. I'm shamelessly excited by him, by what lies ahead. I know nothing except how those fingers and that tongue make me feel.

Soon my panties too are gone, slid down my legs by his hasty hands. I look up at him as he spreads my thighs wide.

"Fuck," he says, running his hands down my inner thighs. "You're shaved smooth. Fuck!" He swallow, his eyes dark with excitement. "You have the prettiest pussy I've ever seen, little witch."

He brushes his fingers along my slit. I groan, trying to stay still.

"Ah, fuck," he murmurs.

I'm wet for him, excited beyond measure, unsure that this is really happening. He traces the line of my slit, gathering the evidence of my excitement of his fingertips. When he draws his fingers to his mouth, glistening with my wetness, my mouth falls open.

He closes his eyes briefly, moaning a little. Has anything ever been sexier than watching Lars lick my juices off of his own fingers?

Then he lifts himself up, his fingers going to his waistband. I watch, wide eyed, as he begins to unzip his pants. His cock springs free almost immediately, unencumbered by any underwear. My eyes zero in on it. It's long, thick, and perfectly pink.

My mouth starts to water.

He's going to fucking stretch me out with that perfect cock of his.

I shouldn't be surprised to find out that Lars is well endowed, but my jaw does drop a little anyway. He shoves his pants down and steps out of them completely. Now he's naked before me, his thighs and hips as taut with muscle as the rest of him.

There is even that little vee of muscle at his hip bone. I shiver when I see that. My fingers reach out to touch that vee, without my ever having consciously thought about it. He moves closer, allowing my inspection.

And why not? He's certainly got nothing to hide.

My heart in my throat, I know that this is it. I'm going to lose my heart to Lars, right here and now. Once he has sex with me, spends the night making me call out his name, that will be it for me.

I'm already in love with him. By touching me, by exciting me, by fucking me… he's going to ruin me for everyone else on the planet. He's going to shred my heart.

And yet, I can't stop. I won't. I grip his hip, looking at him with a pleading gaze.

"Touch me," I whisper. "I'm on fire for you, Lars."

When he finds my pussy with his fingers again, stroking up and down the slit in rhythmic caresses, his gaze latches onto mine.

In his clear blue eyes, I see an expression of pure want. As his hand works a little faster, I make tiny mms and ohhhs of pleasure.

He leans down, his cock pressing against me intimately. My mouth opens to kiss him when he gets closer, but he surprises me by murmuring in my ear.

"I want you so badly, little witch. You've cast a spell over me, I think," he breathes, his words tickling my ear.

I flush. My mouth is suddenly dry. I lick my lips, unable to move my body away from his clever fingers. "Yes," I say. "I want you, Lars. I need you to fuck me."

"Are you on birth control?"

I just nod again. His mouth curls into a grin. He kisses a spot on my neck, sucking it hard enough to pull a moan from my lips. "I'm going to rock your fucking world, Pips."

He surprises me yet again by pulling away and sinking to his knees. I sit up partway, alarmed, but he pushes me onto my back with steady hands against my stomach.

"I've been waiting a lifetime to do this to you," he whispers, bringing his hand up to part my pussy lips. "Your pussy smells so good. I am going to make you come apart with just my tongue, little witch."

Then he touches the tip of his tongue against my exposed clit, the part of my that has been throbbing for so long. It feels like a lightning bolt, straight to the pleasure center of my brain. The breath leaves my lungs for a minute as his tongue works around it in steady circles.

Soon I'm burying my hands in his hair and moving in time with the rhythm he sets. It's so good that my whole body is on fire. He seals his lips around my clit and sucks. I'm on a precipice, holding onto my connection with reality by a thread.

Then he groans into my flesh, sending a tidal wave straight to the heart of me. With a shudder and a low moan I come apart, gripping at his hair. He's so good that I tremble and groan, calling out his name softly.

He continues to lick and kiss my clit gently until I stop him with my fingers.

I pull him back up to my head, kissing him hard. He tastes like ozone and something a little sweet. With a start, I realize that that's my unique flavor that I'm tasting on his lips and tongue.

He pulls me under him, kissing me soundly. I groan as his hard cock brushes the sensitive folds of my pussy. I'm still feeling the aftershocks when he fists his cock, bringing the head to my entrance. I'm slick from what he just did with his mouth, but when he starts to push his cock inside, even the smallest amount stretches me out. My body is resistant even though I want him.

He's just so fucking *big*.

There is a moment of genuine pain, bringing tears to my eyes. And then he is thrusting all the way in, making me forget the pain. Our bodies merge. I cling to him, my mouth open, my eyes closing. I'm enraptured.

I relax into the thrust of his big cock. I start to feel something building, a vague pressure from far away. It is different than the burning desire I felt before, more like a spring slowly tightening.

"Open your eyes, Pippa," he grits out.

So I do. I stare up into his gaze, feeling the coil of my desire tightening, inch by inch. Raking my nails down his back and meeting his thrusts with my own, I feel I have never been closer to another person than I am to Lars right now.

"Fuck," he mutters. His expression says he is either in pain or ecstatic, one of the two. "You are so goddamn beautiful."

Watched by those dark blue eyes, I start to shatter once more, spasming as I come. He is right behind me, fucking me frantically, finding my hand and gripping it so hard that I am honestly afraid that it will break.

He comes with a shudder, pounding into me relentlessly. I can actually feel his cum inside me, but in the next second I forget that I was even thinking about it because he kisses me, long and with tongue. For several seconds, it's just me and him, no one else even existing in the entire world. My heart beats erratically, in time with Lars's, and it just feels so *right*.

Everything that I was worried about… how he's a player and out of my league… it just melts away. All that is important is the here and now, his body against mine.

Eventually of course he does roll away. He turns onto his side and takes me with him. Kissing me again, slowly and meaningfully, he sighs against my lips.

"I need ten minutes to recharge, sweetheart," he says, kissing his way to my ear. "Then I can make us both come again." I shiver as he nips my ear. "But while I'm waiting…"

His hand slips down my belly, tracing its way between my thighs, teasing. I open my mouth and a gasp comes out as he parts my lower lips and finds my clit.

"Oh, little witch," he murmurs. "You're already wet for me…"

I kiss his lips, desperately wanting this moment to go on forever.

CHAPTER 17

Lars

I FUCK Pippa twice more before we fall asleep, sweaty and exhausted. The last thing I remember before falling asleep is the sound of her steady breathing and the feel of her lying on my chest.

I open my eyes to find myself alone in my bed. Pippa's clothes are gone from my floor. Her side of the bed has been straightened. There is no sign that Pippa was even here other than the wrinkled sheets.

It's early in the morning but I can hear her moving around downstairs.

After a quick shower, I head down to see what she's up to. Clattering down the stairs, I find Pippa in the kitchen, cooking eggs in a loose light blue dress. She turns to me, blushing a little, and points to the French press on the counter.

"Coffee."

I pad over to the French press and find a mug. As I take a sip of the steaming brew, I eye her. She is using a spatula to stir the eggs and making a concerted effort not to look my way.

"You're being weird," I say.

She sets the spatula down and pushes back her copper curls. She turns, wrapping her arms around herself and resting her hip against the counter. "I feel pretty weird," she admits. "I just spent the night in my best friend's bed. I'm not sure where to go from there."

I take a deep breath, tilting my head. "Do you want things to change drastically?"

She looks down, frowning a little. "Not really."

I shrug a shoulder. "Then they won't. We'll just be friends who occasionally fuck each other's brains out."

She bites her lower lip. "Won't that complicate our fake relationship?"

"Why would it?" I nod at the pan of eggs. "Those are going to burn if you don't stir them."

Two spots of color appear in her cheeks. She stirs the eggs then pushes some toast in the toaster. Her expression is unreadable.

"You're overthinking things," I say, taking another sip. Her expression remains puzzled.

"It doesn't seem like we should just be able to do this," she says, shaking her head.

The toast pops up. She dishes the eggs out into plates and adds the toast.

I stop her as she's about to pick up the plates. Turning her around, I put my hands on her shoulders and look down at her.

"We can do whatever we want," I say, looking intently at her expression.

There is a little fear in her blue eyes. "I don't want anything to come between us and ruin our friendship. You're basically the only family I have, Lars."

My heat thumps in my chest. "I promise that won't happen."

She looks at me, her expression almost begging. "You swear?"

My lips tip upward. "On my life, Pippa. And I will abide by your rules — that is, not seeing anyone else while we're… choosing to be intimate."

She chews on her bottom lip. "Are you sure?"

I huff a laugh. "Ja, I'm quite sure."

She exhales a deep breath. "Okay."

I pull her into the shelter of my arms, kissing the top of her head. She smells faintly of vanilla.

"One thing that will probably make it easier is the fact that we have a planned escape hatch," she murmurs.

Pulling back, I raise a brow. "Oh?"

She smiles lightly and moves away, picking up the plates. "Ja. I mean, we are supposed to break up in a couple of months anyway. So that will be a good time to think about… ending things."

I grab our coffee mugs and follow her to the table. "You already have that planned out, huh?"

She sits down, shooting me a little glare. "Look, some of us don't live like you do. We don't base jump or race yachts just because we like the rush of adrenaline. Some of us are plotters and planners."

I pull a plate of eggs over to me, digging in. "You had better eat fast."

Her brows rise. "Why?"

"Because," I say, picking up my toast and taking a bite. "After this, I will be sufficiently recharged."

Her expression is questioning. "Are you talking about skiing again?"

I pin her with a heated gaze. "No, Pippa. As soon as I'm done eating, I'm going to drag you over to the couch and fuck you senseless. So hurry the hell up."

Her eyes widen. She blushes furiously. "Oh!"

I notice that she doesn't exactly protest, though. Instead she just wolfs down her breakfast, finishing it with sips of coffee.

CHAPTER 18

Pippa

WE FUCK.

We nap.

Then we fuck some more.

"Like what you see, little witch?" His voice is still groggy, but oh so beautiful.

"Yes. I suppose that I shouldn't be staring while you're asleep though, huh?"

He reaches a hand up to my face, brushing my hair from my eyes and tucking it gently behind my ear, fixing me in place with his piercing eyes.

"It's okay. I like you looking at me. Like seeing you looking at me more."

"Even then, it's rude to stare at a sleeping person." I avert my gaze and focus on my knee instead.

"Pippa, you can stare at me all you want. As long as it's me you're staring at like that, I'm happy. Fucking ecstatic, actually." He cups my chin so that our eyes meet, still not moving to hide any part of himself.

"It's okay to be curious. Hell, I'm fucking honored to be the one who gets to indulge your curiosity." The way he is looking at me, practically naked, eyes hooded and dark with desire, relaxed about his exposed body… it had to be the single most erotic thing I'd ever seen.

My breath hitches at his words, but I wasn't feeling shame anymore at being caught. It is amazing how comfortable he made me feel, how at home, how wanted.

He is still looking at me with desire, waiting for my reply. I have no words as I start tracing the lines of his chest, then the ones on his arm and all the way to his hand. Next, I trace the muscled lines of his stomach down to his hips. His breath hitches. His cock twitches, begging for my attentions.

I trace my fingers down his stomach and toward the elastic of his boxer briefs, it jumps again. "I'm really trying to let you do your thing here, little witch. But you're really fucking killing me."

I am killing him? That seemed impossible, but yet, the evidence is right in front of me. A shiver of excitement runs up my spine and I can feel dampness seeping from my slit.

"Fuck," he breathes as I run my hands over the outline of his hard cock over his boxer briefs. "I can't fucking wait to get inside of you."

He flips me onto my back and presses his body to mine, kissing me deeply and tracing the neckline of my tank top as he runs his other hand up and down my thigh. I moan as he reaches the edge of my shorts and grasps at the fabric. He rolls my shorts over my ass, down my legs and then kicks them off the bed without breaking the kiss.

"Pippa," he said softly. "Look into my eyes for a second." I open my eyes and he drinks me in, running one hand up and down my side, leaving goosebumps in his wake.

"I'm trying to go slow here, little witch. But you're making it very, very hard for me." He reaches for my hand, pulling it to the bulge in his boxer briefs. "See what you do to me?"

I look into his eyes and slowly nod.

He kisses my neck. "I need to hear you say it, Pippa."

"I see," I breathe softly. I shape his cock inside his boxer briefs and he lets out a soft moan.

"Oh, little witch. You are such trouble." He kisses down my neck, planting soft kisses and nips between his words. "I can't wait to taste you again."

He looks up at me, one hand tracing my nipple through my shirt. I bite my lip, unable to form words because of the sensations he is eliciting in my body.

He is still teasing my nipples, planting soft kisses on the exposed skin on my stomach.

I barely manage a nod. My skin is on fire everywhere he touches me, aching for more. Each stroke on my nipples causes my pussy to clench and I am pretty sure that by now, my panties are drenched. I would be embarrassed, if I could bring myself to think that far, but all my thoughts are completely wrapped in what he is making me feel.

His hands slide my panties down and my tank top disappears over my head. I am now completely naked in front of the most gorgeous man on the planet.

If this were anyone else, I would be trying to cover up. But the way that Lars is looking at me, his blue eyes dark with lust, makes me feel sexy, desirable and beautiful.

He drinks me in with his eyes, growling softly as his fingers stroke my dripping slit.

"God, Pippa. You're so fucking wet." He brings his glistening fingers to his lips and licks my juices off the tips of his fingers. He closes his eyes and lets out a low moan as he tastes me on his skin. "Fucking delicious, little witch. So sweet. I can't wait to taste you."

All I can focus on is his fingers that are now playing with my clit, teasing my seam.

He kisses me deeply, hungrily. I can feel his rock hard cock digging into my hip. I moan loudly, still unable to form any words.

"Fuck, Pippa. I've never cum from just sounds before, but if you keep that up, that might change. Breathe, little witch…" His voice is husky, low.

I follow his advice, taking a deep breath to clear my ridiculously, pathetically aroused mind enough to whimper, "For fuck's sake, Lars. You're killing me. Taste me! Or fuck me! Do something, anything…" I beg.

He lifts me as if I weigh nothing at all, moving me up the bed. Then he drops his whole body down low, kissing his way across my stomach and making me writhe.

He licks slowly but hungrily along my seam. Up and down, sucking in my lips, darting his tongue into my pussy, before starting all over again. He let out a low moan again. "So fucking sweet, Pippa." He groans before taking my sensitive clit in his mouth, sucking lightly, his tongue flicking against my bud.

His tongue reduces me to a shivering, moaning maniac. I try to buck my hips against him, unable to contain myself any longer, but his strong hands on my hips keep me in place. He licks and sucks until I see nothing but stars and fireworks, feeling like I am about to fly away if it wasn't for him anchoring me down.

Far too soon, the pressure that had been building up inside me releases into a ball of light, my mind shattering in every different direction possible. I scream his name, digging my fingers into his shoulders and tugging at his hair.

He keeps licking until he wrings every last drop of pleasure from my body. He crawls up and kisses me as he slips his boxer briefs off. I can feel the tip of his cock against my entrance, positioned perfectly to slide into me. He doesn't though, he kisses me hard and I can taste myself on his lips. Somehow, it just arouses me even more. I moan into his mouth and hear a low sound at the back of his throat.

"I want you inside of me," I say, my voice coming out in a breathy whine. "Please, Lars."

He lets out a low growl, but doesn't say any more. I can feel his hard cock gently pushing against my entrance. He slides in slowly, watching my every facial expression, seemingly gauging my every move.

"Fuck, so tight," he breathed as he edged in, still very slowly. He's so fucking big but the delicious fullness and pleasure of having him inside my outweighs the discomfort. I cling to him and run my hands through his hair and down his back.

When he is all the way in, he stops, driving me crazy. His muscles are taut, eyes blazing with need, but he doesn't act on it. He is huge, but I need to feel him move already.

"Okay there, little witch?"

"I'm fine, Lars. I need to feel you!" I manage, my voice breathy. "Fuck me, Lars."

At that, it is as if his resolve breaks and he starts moving.

Slowly at first, but it is the most incredible feeling I have ever experienced. Pleasure fills my body, taking over every inch of me. The entire world has disappeared and all that exists is the feeling of him in me, his body on mine, breathing deeply and softly growling and moaning into my ear, kissing me and whispering to me.

He rocks into me with perfect rhythm, with just the right amount of depth. I can feel the pressure building again. His breathing is ragged now and I can feel his muscles start to shake as he thrust into me more forcefully, but still taking care not to hurt me. He is nearly there, and I am right there with him.

A final thrust and my world is shattered into a million pieces again as the knot that has been building inside me releases. All those things I'd ever heard and read about mind-blowing orgasms could not compare to this. To him.

He nips at my bottom lip as his eyes roll back, his muscled shoulders flexing and thighs quivering as he fills me. I feel his orgasm pour into me, his cock twitching deep inside of my body. And it is the most exquisite thing that I've ever felt.

He presses his lips against mine and pulls me into a long, deep kiss.

CHAPTER 19

Lars

ONCE I CONVINCED Pippa to fuck me, she was insatiable. We would fuck for hours and hours, catching a quick nap or a bite to eat before tearing into each other again. It felt like something that had been brewing between us ever since I laid eyes on her.

For as long as I have known Pippa, I've been half in love with her. And now I had her in my sights. Hell, I had her in my bed, screaming my name.

I was not eager to let her go again.

The only thing that came close to marring our time together was Pippa's mysterious, unspoken boundaries. If I held her for too long after sex, she would squeeze out of my hold and act skittish about it.

But when I dangled the carrot of fucking in front of her again, she was on board. On board… and hungry for more.

For three days, I canceled my royal duties and just focused on Pippa. Even I am pushed to my limit, operating on almost no sleep.

I'm still sad to leave that little cabin, though. Even for this tour of the European Space Agency's facilities here in Denmark, which is pretty exciting.

As I place a hand on Pippa's lower back and rush her up to the European Space Agency building, she glances at my dark blue uniform. I shoot her a questioning look.

"What?" I ask.

She wrinkles her nose, plucking at the hem of her dark dress. "You look handsome in your uniform. That's all."

I grin. "You're having lustful thoughts about me while walking into what is sure to be a big boring meeting?"

Pippa sticks out her tongue at me. I laugh and hold the door open for her. Inside the building, everything is steel and glass, ultramodern in style. We are greeted right away in the lobby by a young woman who bows her head. "Your royal highness."

I nod. "We are here for a tour of where your astronauts work and train."

The dark-haired young woman blushes. "Yes, your highness. I'm Ingrid and I'll be showing you around today." She curtsies to Pippa, who squeezes my hand hard. She smiles at Pippa. "Ms. Welch. It's my pleasure to show the future princess around our facilities. If you two will just follow me?"

She turns and opens a door. Pippa and I follow her. Pippa shoots me a wide eyed look.

"The future princess?" she mouths silently. "Oh my god."

I shake my head, smothering a yawn. Pippa sees me do it and is immediately triggered into a yawn of her own. Ingrid looks back, catching Pippa's yawn.

"Would you like some refreshment, ma'am? Perhaps some coffee or water?"

She swipes her identification badge and unlocks a set of doors. Pippa smiles at her. "No, thank you."

Ingrid ushers us deeper into the building, showing us several pristine laboratories and a room devoted to 3D goggles.

"The young woman training in there right now is in a space simulator of the international space station's tiny food prep area. It's one of many such exercises that we have our astronauts-in-training run through."

I nod. "I imagine you have a simulation for almost every scenario."

Ingrid blushes, seeming uncertain what to do with her hands. "Yes, your royal highness."

I chuckle. "Please, call me Lars."

Pippa rolls her eyes. Ingrid tucks her hair behind her ear and gives me a shy smile.

"If you both will follow me, we'll go down to the spacewalk tank. I believe we should see someone using it…"

I wiggle my eyebrows at Pippa. She shoots me a filthy look.

"What?" I whisper, following Ingrid.

Pippa brushes back her hair, shaking her head. "You just can't turn it off, can you? Just let the poor girl do her job."

I smirk. "I don't know what you mean."

She drops her voice to a whisper. *"Oh Ingrid, please, call me Lars. I'm so charming and elegant and royal."*

I grin at her. "Is that jealousy I hear?"

Pippa looks irritated. "What? No."

"Are you sure about that, little witch?" I ask.

She shoots me a glare and pushes her shoulders back, hurrying after Ingrid. I press my cheek with my tongue, trying to decide just what to make of that.

Is Pippa really acting jealous? I mean, we did have four amazing nights together. But… she knows that it's going to come to an end.

…right?

We meander through the rest of the tour. I keep a close eye on Pippa, but she just seems irritable for most of the time. After the tour is complete, I shake hands with several generals and scientists that oversee the space program. Everyone is smiling, but I can sense an edge to Pippa's cool smile.

She also pulls out of any embrace I initiate after a few seconds.

By the time we finally get out of the building and into the chauffeured limo, I level her with a look. "You are pissed off at me?"

She licks her lips and looks out her window. "No. It's not… I'm just tired."

"I've known you for more than half my life, Pippa. I've seen you tired. I have never seen… whatever that was back there."

She puts her hands over her face and sinks lower in her seat. "Sorry."

I grab her elbow, slowly pulling one of her hands away from her face. "If we were trying to put on a happy front to the world today, we failed."

She squints. *"Ja. Ja,* I'm sorry. You, uh… you hit a nerve, I guess."

My eyebrows lift a little. "Wait, I did?"

"Oh god. This is so embarrassing." She sinks lower in her seat, her cheeks burning bright red. "You called me jealous. And a little voice in the back of my head knew you were right. God, how much of a child am I?"

She closes her eyes, shaking her head.

I pull at her hand, easing her onto my lap. "So… you got jealous. You didn't feel that way on purpose, did you?"

Her light blue eyes open just a slit. "No."

I run my fingers down her arm, enjoying how pale her skin is against mine. "It didn't hurt anyone, did it?"

She wrinkles her nose. "No. But… that's such a ridiculous thing to feel. I mean, we just basically hooked up one time. Like… that doesn't give me the right to feel jealous. Especially not just because you were flirting with some tour guide."

She lets out an exaggerated exhale.

My lips curve up. "I have to say, I didn't really expect jealousy from you. But as it turns out, green looks pretty damn good on you."

She eyes me. "I embarrassed you."

I let out a sharp bark of laughter. "Hah! No. I can't be embarrassed. I have an immunity."

She sighs again, sitting up. "I'm sorry, Lars."

I am tired of this conversation. So I change it by kissing her full, lush lips.

And she doesn't exactly seem to mind or protest…

CHAPTER 20

Pippa

I SWALLOW as I watch the palace grow closer and closer out the window of my limousine. Momse, Lars's grandmother, called me and personally invited me to a soiree she is throwing to celebrate our coming nuptials.

She barely let me get a word in edgewise about the party tonight. She just spent most of our brief time talking about what I would wear. At the end of the call, she said she'd just 'send some dresses over'.

Which is how I came to be wearing a very expensive, very fine strapless ballgown made of ivory silk. The dress itself is absolutely gorgeous. But as I try to adjust it while the limousine pulls around to the grand entrance, I remember all too well that the dress is very heavy.

Keeping that in mind, I touch the back of my hair, which has been piled up on my head. The car comes to a stop. I take a deep breath as the car door is opened for me.

Then I smile and get out of the back seat, only wobbling a little bit. This dress almost forces me to have perfect posture as it trails behind me. I hug my wrap, made of the same silk, and smile at the palace guards as I head inside.

A red carpet leads me up the stairs. My heart races thinking of all the people that I am going to lie to tonight.

At least no one would dare stop me and ask for my identification now. I'm a princess-to-be.

Or that's what everyone thinks, at least.

As I climb the stairs in my extravagant dress, I feel a few beads of sweat break out across my forehead. This dress may look like a fairytale, but it is hot and heavy.

As I come to the last stair, I see Lars waiting rather impatiently for me. He looks so dashing in his tuxedo that it actually takes my breath away.

He turns his head and spots me. A huge smile appears on his face. He walks towards me, his eyes taking me in. "Fuck, Pips. You look..." He shakes his head, biting his lip.

I flush a little. "Like the topper for a wedding cake, maybe?"

He offers me his arm, arching a brow. "I was going to say hot, but that's not quite it. Maybe... beautiful? Radiant?"

My neck heats. "Thanks. I'm glad that you find this dress acceptable. I think you're hot too, obviously."

He nods toward the ballroom. "Ready?"

I nod. "Why would I not be eager to enter a ballroom full of people that I plan on deceiving? Let's go."

He walks me in, a smirk on his face. I can hear the murmur of the crowd from here. When we step through the double doors, everyone immediately turns and ceases their conversations. All eyes are on us.

I can't help but swallow nervously. Lars is great and all, but at this exact moment I'm wishing that I had never agreed to his little plan.

"Lars!" His grandmother says. "I thought perhaps you two were not coming. After all, it is quite late..."

Lars rolls his eyes. "We're here, Momse."

His grandmother rushes up to us, taking our elbows and wedging herself in between us. She beams out at the crowd, which is relatively packed. "Every dignitary in Denmark is here right now, every military general and every polished socialite."

They are all looking at us, judging for themselves how Lars and I fit together.

I hate it.

Lars's grandmother clears her throat. "It is my pleasure to announce that Lars and Pippa have set a date for their wedding. It will be held in June, at the Royal Palace. Isn't that wonderful?"

I blink rapidly, my gaze going straight to Lars. His expression is questioning too.

Not only did we not set that date, it's also actually the first time I've ever even heard it and mentioned at all. Everyone in the audience applauds politely as Lars and I shower the room in our confused smiles.

Momse moves forward, glancing at both of us. She doesn't seem worried that she just announced a random date that we are supposed to get married on. "I'm so happy for both of you. Come, I have some people for you to meet."

Behind me, Lars finds my hand and gives it a squeeze.

For the next hour, I plaster on my smile and murmur *thank you* in response to everyone's well wishes. At one point, Lars is so antsy and ready to leave Momse's company that he keeps sighing. I look at him, my eyes begging him to take me with him. So he does the unthinkable: he just tells Momse flat out that we want to mingle alone.

"Pippa and I are going to take a turn around the room by ourselves, Momse. I'm sure you have a lot of people to talk to. Don't let us get in the way of that." He grabs my elbow, pulling me close.

Her eyes narrow. "Surely you can allow me this one night to celebrate you both."

He smiles lightly. "You got your hour on the arm of the new Prince and Princess. You've declared a wedding date. I think you've done enough."

Momse's eyes open quite wide. "I don't appreciate how you're talking to me right now, Lars."

He removes her hand from his arm, shaking off her grip. "Ja, I'm not Stellan. I'm not interested in politics or in whatever weird power play you're trying to pull right now. So Pippa and I are going to go over there and talk to our friends. And when we are tired, we're gonna leave. So…" He shrugs. "There you go."

With that, he takes my arm and pulls me away toward Stellan and Margot. I glance at him, my eyes wide. "What was that?"

He rolls his eyes. "Momse has some idea that we are going to dance to her feet now that we are supposedly engaged. It's better for both of us if we just don't let her boss us around, not even a little. Because if she is given an inch, she'll take a mile. Trust me on this."

He rakes his gaze over me, smiling a little sadly. I don't know what exactly he is talking about, but I lift my hand to touch his cheek, the gesture intimate enough to let him know that I hear what he's saying.

He slows down, turning to face me. Then he truly totally surprises me by sliding one hand around my waist and cupping my jaw with the other. He bends me back a little and kisses me so deeply and firmly that I forget everything else in the world.

For just a few seconds, it's just Lars and me. Just two bodies, all alone in the universe. His taste is on my lips, his scent in my nose, his hot hands on my sensitive skin...

I almost forget that we are not actually in a relationship, that we are not the real Prince and Princess. When he breaks away, I look up into his handsome face, my heart beating fast, my breath all but gone. Lars looks at me, a smile tugging at the corner of his mouth.

"Should we go talk to our friends, then?"

At this moment, he is irresistible to me. I nod slowly, grinning at him still.

Lars takes me by the hand and pulls me along toward Stellan and Margot. Stellan looks like a much more uptight version of Lars, all dark and tall and buttoned up and brooding. Margot still looks like a little pixie, although she has only recently stopped bleaching her hair. Instead, I see that she has had her hair professionally dyed, and it falls around her shoulders and face just so. She looks at me with genuine delight, raising her arms to embrace me.

I let go of Lars's hand, hurrying into Margot's embrace. I hug her hard, inhaling her cotton candy sent. "I have missed you so much. Where have you been?"

She pulls back, looking at me. "Where have I have been? Where have you been? I've been right here, trying to get the king to relax a little during the holiday."

Stellan frowns at us both. "Someone has to do the work around here. Keep the lights on, that sort of thing."

Lars beckons to Stellan, drawing him away. I have no idea what Lars is telling his brother, but I am glad for a little alone time with my bestie.

"What are you drinking?" I ask Margot.

She sighs, hooking her arm in mine. She lifts her cup, showing me the contents. "It's some blend of ciders or something. I asked for something hot and something nonalcoholic and this is all that they could come up with other than coffee." She wrinkles her nose. "One of the less amazing things about being… in the condition I am in."

I smirk. "Are you two still not telling people?"

"No, we decided to wait another month. Well, I decided. Luckily my husband is willing to bend on the issue at hand."

"Well, you let me know the second you can go shopping for baby necessities without causing a national crisis. Because I will be there with all the bells and whistles that I can carry."

She smiles up at me. "I'm really very glad that we are friends, Pippa. I mean, looking back five years, would you have imagined that we would be standing right here, with these men as our partners?"

A flash of guilt runs through me. I look away, frowning at an imagined sight on the other side of the ballroom. "Is that Annika?"

I feel bad for lying, especially to her. But I am completely certain that she wouldn't be able to conceal the truth from Stellan, and Stellan would come down hard on Lars. So I have to lie to her, for everyone's sake.

Her brow wrinkles as she searches the crowd. "I thought Annika and Erik were on some tropical vacation or something. I think you might've seen someone else."

I nod. "It's entirely possible."

Margot sighs. "I think I have to pee again. Will you excuse me?"

I look around as she slips away through the crowd, sucking in a deep breath. To my left, I can see Lars's grandmother talking to a group of people and sizing me up. I definitely don't want to be trapped talking to her, especially not after what Lars said to her earlier. So I take a sharp right turn, almost plowing into a gorgeous, very thin blonde in a hot pink, skintight dress.

"Oh! I'm so sorry," I apologize.

She laughs daintily, as if I have just told a funny joke. When she answers, her accent is clearly German or Austrian. "Oh, excuse me. I am so clumsy sometimes." She sticks out a hand. "I am Gretchen."

I grip her palm, shaking my head at the same time as I shake her hand. "It was all my doing. I'm Pippa, by the way."

She arches a brow. "Oh, I know who you are. I think everybody in this room knows who you are. It's nice to meet you, Pippa."

I blush. "Yes, I keep forgetting that I am engaged to the second most famous man here. It's all pretty new still."

"What's new?" Lars asks, coming up from behind me. His hands land on my waist and he pulls me a little closer to him, kissing the top of my head. I blush again, feeling like that gesture is something intimate and private, usually just kept between the two of us.

I look up at him, shooting him in a look. "Our engagement. I was just telling Gretchen here that I keep forgetting why everyone knows who I am already even though I don't know them."

He squeezes me a little. "*Ja*, it's true. She is still pretty starstruck by being engaged to me."

Without thinking about it, I actually glare at him and hit him on the shoulder. Gretchen titters at us.

"Look at the two of you. Aren't you just made for each other?"

Gretchen beams at both of us. I slide my glance over to Lars, expecting… Well, I'm not exactly sure what I was expecting.

Perhaps he would be looking at her in a certain way that indicated interest. Or laughing at what she just said even though it wasn't really a joke. Or if my own experiences being true of his style, he might even touch her wrist or slide his arm around her waist.

But instead, I look at him and find him staring directly at the dark and space between my breasts. He isn't even remotely listening to Gretchen. He isn't staring at her, even though she is tall and blonde and extremely thin and gorgeous. Not to mention she is wearing a dress that would shame the devil.

Lars doesn't even seem to notice her. He looks up at me, cocking a grin, and my cheeks flame scarlet. I can't do anything but give him a secretive smile. His intention is just so all-encompassing that I sink into his eyes for a long moment, forgetting that Gretchen even exists.

I bite my lower lip. He pulls me in closer, smirking a little. His fingers tighten on my waist.

I know that he is not actually mine. And I know that just because he's paying attention to me right now doesn't mean he will be in the future. But it feels so good to be looked at in this way, by this man, at this moment.

"Well, I can see you two are busy… If you will excuse me, I have to find the ladies room…" Gretchen says, smiling and wandering off.

I look up at Lars, wrinkling my nose. "Was that rude? It felt rude."

He shrugs a shoulder. "I couldn't care less. If I had to make a list of all the people who I was rude to in a day, I would never do anything else."

I quirk my lips. "As long as you're not rude to me, I suppose I don't have anything to say about that."

He draws me close, raising my chin with his finger. The press of his lips against mine is brief and not nearly deep enough for my liking. But we are in a ballroom full of people and we should probably be on our best behavior.

Lars sighs. "I have to catch Stellan again before we leave," he says. He frowns a little. "I think I actually know something that will help him in negotiations with the minister of Belgium. Do you mind if I just…?"

I smile. "Of course not. I'm actually going to step outside for a minute and just get some cool air. You wouldn't believe how hot this dress is."

Lars looks me up and down, a grin spreading across his face. "Oh, I believe it. You know where it's gonna look even better than it looks on you right now?"

I pull away from him, rolling my eyes and smiling. "If you say on your floor, I am going to revolt. And you should take that seriously, Prince Lars."

I waggle my finger at him, heading away toward the big balcony doors that open up into the night. A few people cast questioning glances at me as I pull open the door and let myself out into the chilly night. I shiver even as I sigh with relief. Hopefully no one is able to tell that I am as hot as I am. Under the full skirts of this dress, I'm wearing a lacy slip and a thong and both are plastered to my skin. I walk a few feet away from the doors toward the balcony, glancing down.

"Hello, Sylvie."

I freeze at the sound of Ms. Olson's voice. Turning my head, I find her looking in the shadows, talked away behind a stone pillar. My heartbeat races as I glance behind me nervously. "What are you doing here?"

Ms. Olson emerges from the shadows, showing off her slim figure in a bright red ball down. She gives me a cold little smile. "Visiting you, of course. I see that you took my advice and accepted Lars's proposal. Clever girl."

I gather my skirts, fisting the fabric. "You can't be here. You just… I don't even know who you are, but you need to leave. You are bothering me."

Ms. Olson gives a bark of laughter. "Bothering you? You should be thanking me. My organization made you and Lars happen."

I pause. Part of me wants to scream at her, tell her that there is no *me and Lars*. But the other, smarter part makes me fold my arms across my chest. "What is it that you want? I'm very close to calling a security guard, so I would make it quick if I were you."

She smirks at me. "Oh really? I don't think you're going to do any such thing, Sylvie. Not if you want to keep that precious sister of yours a secret, anyway."

I shake my head, turning to go inside. "This is crazy. You're crazy."

"All I'm asking is for a few questions to be answered. Surely that is worth your secret being kept, no? Because otherwise, I will go straight to Queen Margot and tell her who you really are."

I slow. "I don't know what you think I can do for you. I don't know anything. Lars is not the head of state or anything. He's just…"

"Just the brother of the king. And that's fine. I just have a couple of questions. Specifically, I would like to know what Lars's position in the Danish Royal Air Force is and whether or not he has much contact with Colonel Ahmad."

I cock a hip and cross my arms, turning to glare at her. "I don't know the answer to that. How would I even go about finding out the answer to that question?"

Her smile is staid. "I also want to know if the younger Løve brothers have girlfriends or boyfriends. Is there anyone on the horizon for either of them?"

I scrunch up my face, disbelieving. "What? I don't know."

"Well, I would make it your business to find out. When you do, you can dial my number in the prepaid phone I gave you. I won't answer, but you can give the message to whoever picks up the phone." She smiles again. "That's all I really require at the moment."

I shake my head. "You're insane. Just… Don't contact me again. I don't care what you threaten me with. It can't be worse than thinking I am plotting against the country of Denmark."

"Oh, Sylvie. Do me a favor before you go telling anybody about these little meetings of ours. I would check my phone first." She whirls on her heel, heading back into the shadows. I shiver against the cool breeze that picks up, turning toward the balcony doors again.

I slip inside and immediately start searching the room for Lars. The need to be near him, to be protected by him, is intense right now. Or maybe it's the other way around and I feel like I'm protecting him? Either way, I have to find him.

After looking around for him for a few minutes, I finally find him talking to Stellan just outside the ballroom doors. When he looks up and sees me heading his way, his eyebrow rises. "What's going on?" he asks.

I smile at Stellan, putting my hand on Lars's arm. "Do you mind if I just borrow him for a second?"

"Be my guest," Stellan says, waving his arm.

Looking both ways up and down the hall, I lick my lips and pull Lars toward the first room that seems unoccupied.

CHAPTER 21

Pippa

I FLUSH, looking over my shoulder as Lars hustles me out of the room. He's right; his grandmother is glaring at me now.

I turn around and hurry after Lars. I glimpse Stellan talking very intently with two of the palace staff just outside the doors. Lars quickly heads the other way, trying not to draw attention as he opens another door.

He hurries me inside what looks like an ill used study. Light pours in the window, spilling across several large pieces of furniture that have been draped with protective white cloth.

Lars looks around, one brow raised. "I don't think I've ever even been in this room before."

I walk over to a cloth-draped desk, lifting the corner to peek at the massive oak shape below. "We are honestly just lucky that you chose this room and not a mop closet."

"You are right about that," he agrees. He looks around the room and then shrugs. Taking a seat on the cloth-covered couch, he coughs a little from the dust released.

I wrinkle my nose and plop down beside him. A plume of dust rises, landing in a fine sheet over both of us.

Lars shakes his head at that, sipping his champagne. "Now you've done it. We are both ruined. If we go back to the dinner, we'll both look like we rolled around in a pile of ashes."

I scrunch my face up. "Maybe that's what I was going for."

He flashes me a smirk. Slipping a finger under his necktie, he loosens it. "Might as well get comfortable, then. Once everybody has had a few glasses of wine, they are less likely to notice a pair of sewer rats in their number."

I laugh at that. Lars grins; he's always trying to make me laugh and only sometimes succeeding.

"Okay. Well, I'm taking off my heels. They are absolutely killing my feet."

I stand up and take my shoes off, letting them fall on the ground. When I sit back down, I realize that I am close enough to Lars that our knees knock together. Instantly I start to get up again, thinking to give him some space.

But Lars grabs my wrist. "Where are you going now?"

Heat sizzles along my skin. I look up at him, blushing.

"Nowhere, really."

He leans closer to me, giving me a delicate sniff. "You smell good. I mean, you always smell good. You smell of roses right now, though."

I give an awkward titter. "And what do you smell like?" I sniff his chest. "You smell like pine trees and…" I give another sniff. "What is that called? Like right after it rains?"

He throws me another smirk. "Petrichor."

I nod, leaning back. "Of course you know the name for that smell."

He grins. "Well, Ja. It is a natural phenomenon."

I pull a face, sipping my wine. "Sure."

He seems amused. "I see you're back on the champagne then. I could swear you avowed never to drink again after New Year's Eve."

I squint down at my glass, shrugging. "Well, I definitely thought that I was going to die on New Year's day. Which, by the way, you conveniently disappeared for."

He smiles. "I thought I would just do us both a favor and get dressed. And then I had time to think about how I should work out…"

"You didn't just want to avoid me, then?"

He shoots me an innocent look. "No. Why would I?"

I blow out a breath. "Because… we made out the night before?"

He rolls his eyes. "I make out with a lot of girls, Pippa. It's perfectly natural."

I tilt my head at him. "Is it?"

He arches a brow. "For two people who are as close as we are and as attractive as we are to kiss? I would say so, yes."

My cheeks redden. I bite my lip, playfully eyeing him. "You think I'm attractive?"

He scoffs. "Oh, please. It goes both ways. Don't think I don't notice you staring when I take my shirt off."

I squint at him. "Do not."

He sets his glass aside, leveling me with a look. "Look. It was just a kiss. I can kiss you right now. It doesn't mean anything."

Before I know it, he's grabbing me around the waist. My heartbeat skyrockets. I try to bring my hands up to block him, but he captures both of them and brings his lips down on mine.

He tugs at my waist, pulling me into the kiss. I soften against him, under the heat of his lips pressed firmly against mine.

My cheeks feel hot as I let my eyelids slide closed.

CHAPTER 22

Pippa

LARS LEANS DOWN, cupping one breast and pulling the nipple to his mouth. I immediately groan at the sensation of his hot, wet mouth on my flesh. He rolls it around with his tongue, then bites it very carefully, almost like he's testing me.

"Ahh!" I gasp. "God, that feels so good."

He smirks, looking up at me. "Everything I do to your body should feel that good."

Then he elbows me aside, lying down. I look at him a little quizzically, but in the next second he lifts me onto his body, so that I'm straddling him. He angles me so that he's planted face first between my breasts, and my bare ass is in the air. I'm a little shocked at how easily he picked me up, but he clearly has other things on his mind.

He licks the skin between my breasts with his tongue, then pulls one nipple into his mouth. I moan as he bites it and sucks it, alternating pain and pleasure for me. His hands wander down to my hips. He runs his hands over my ass, groaning as he shapes my body.

He releases my breast with a wet pop, looking up at me. "*Fuck.* Do you know how turned on I am?"

I blush, slowly shaking my head. "Uh uh."

He pushes my hips down until my pussy is pressed directly against his cock through his unbuttoned jeans. We both groan as he bucks up against me. He runs his hand through my hair, fisting it, and uses his hand on my hip to guide me just where he wants me.

I gasp silently as he lifts his hips and bears down on me, his denim-clad cock almost touching my clit. He starts kissing and licking my neck. He sucks the spot where my neck meets my shoulder, bucking his hips up, and my eyes roll back into my head.

"Fuck!" I cry. "Lars—"

He's not satisfied with that, though. He releases me, pushing me off of his lap. I'm left breathing hard. He gets up and starts to peel his jeans off.

I'm taken aback for a moment by the image of Lars, completely naked. He's all muscle, his cock juts proudly out… and right now, he's looking at me like he's going to consume me.

He climbs onto the bed, dragging me down to lie beneath him, and he starts kissing my neck again. I wrap my arms and legs around him, pulling him closer. I can feel his hardness against my thigh, long and hot and throbbing. He sucks at my neck, my breasts, and then he moves lower.

I don't know if I can even handle his mouth on my clit, but he passionately kisses my thighs and my knees. His five o'clock shadow tickles me in the best way. I open my legs wide for him, spreading my thighs. He makes a growling sound as he kisses my clit, and my whole body is suddenly alive with electric sensation.

"Oh my god!" I cry out, my hands burying in his hair.

Already, I'm bucking my hips against his mouth, desperate for more. He closes his mouth around my clit and sucks on it in long pulls, each one sending ripples of sensation up my spine. My toes curl as he brings his hand up to my pussy and introduces one thick finger. He ever so slowly pushes his finger inside as he circles my clit with his tongue.

I come suddenly, clenching and crying out. His tongue slows, helping me ride out my orgasm. Soon though, he climbs up my body, kissing me hard. I taste the faint flavor of my own juices on his tongue and shudder.

He pulls back a little bit, grasping his cock and positioning himself just so. The blunt tip of his cock presses against my pussy, and I still for just a second. I'm busy looking at his cock, biting my lip with anticipation of how he's about to stretch me out. He pushes inside the barest inch.

I gasp, feeling so full of his hot cock.

Lars glances down at me, biting his lip. "You're so tight, Pippa."

I'm honestly not sure if that's a good thing or not, judging by his face alone. He looks like he's trying to defuse a bomb or something. I wrap my legs around his hips, pulling at him a little, urging him onward.

He closes his eyes and pushes himself inside, inch by slow inch. I feel like he's stretching me out, little by little, filling me up and touching every single part of me. It's uncomfortable, even though I'm wet, but I push for more. When he is finally inside me to the hilt, he opens his eyes, staring down at me with the most intense aquiline gaze I've ever experienced.

I look him right in the eye, remembering that I'm in love with him. I don't care that his dick is so big that it hurts a little; I'm too busy being stupidly, dumbly in love with Lars.

I reach up to pull his mouth down to mine, tenderly kissing him. He kisses me back, starting to move his body, withdrawing his cock and then thrusting back in.

"Ahhh, that's so good," he mutters, raising himself up so that he can see our bodies joined together. "Fuck, Pippa. God, you're so damned beautiful."

He grabs my wrists and pulls them up above my head, working his thick cock in and out of my pussy. I dig my heels into his upper back as he starts kissing and biting my neck again. I start to forget the discomfort, focusing instead on the pleasure of his lips on my skin, the wonderful weight of his body against mine.

I moan as he releases my hands in order to palm my breasts. It feels natural to wrap my arms around him, to lightly rake my fingernails down his back.

Lars suddenly withdraws from me, flipping me over. He guides me to my hands and knees, positioning his cock at my entrance before he plunges back inside.

"Ohhh!" I cry out, feeling my innermost muscles clench.

"Your pussy feels so good," he grits out. He takes my hand and guides it down to my clit, rubbing it in gentle circles. "I want you to come. Show me what a good girl you are. Make yourself come for me."

His words send a shudder of pleasure down my spine. He lets go of my hand and grabs my hips, thrusting his cock into me again and again, as hard as he can. I call out, an insensible sound, as I start to touch myself.

The way he is fucking me now is rougher, coarser than before… but for some reason I like it more. A lot more. I close my eyes, rubbing my clit, and feeling the brutal way he handles me, ramming into me over and over again.

An invisible spring tightens deep inside me with every thrust, feeding my craving. My fingers help me along, but it's really Lars's cock that makes little ripples of pleasure swell and burst across my body.

He's touching some spot deep inside me, a spot that I seem to be able to angle my body just so to encourage him to hit over and over again.

"Yes," I groan desperately. "Yes, right there… I…"

And then I'm calling out his name, screaming it, as I go over the edge, falling into a deep ocean of pleasure. He stiffens and growls, filling me with three single, brutal thrusts. I can feel him pulsing inside my pussy.

He slows at last, half-collapsing on the bed with me. He turns me over, kissing me tenderly.

I curl up against his chest, completely satisfied, and feel like a warm glove has been wrapped around my body.

CHAPTER 23

Lars

"MOVE that stack of boxes right over here by the door," I say. "Be careful."

"Sir." The mover hauls the last of Pippa's boxes into the huge main room of my loft apartment and sets them down.

I smile at him, passing him a fat wad of cash as a tip. "Thank you. And remember, Pippa and I are really not telling anyone that we are moving in together yet. So if by chance someone tells the newspapers about us living together, I'm going to blame you. I'm going to blame your company. You don't want to know what kind of legal headaches that will entail for you guys. Okay?"

He swallows, nodding. "Yes, sir."

He hurries off down the hall, pressing the elevator button insistently. As soon as he is in the elevator and the doors are closed, I turn around and look at my messy apartment. There are boxes on every surface and I've given up two entire closets to Pippa's enormous clothes collection. But I did actually convince her to move in… At least for the time being.

Pippa sticks her head out of the bedroom, brushing back her magnificent curls. "Is that the last of the boxes?"

"It was," I say, smirking a little as I sauntered towards her. "You're officially a resident now."

She rolls her eyes, a little flush rising in her cheeks. "I'm not officially anything and you know it. This whole moving in business is just to further your little deception. Let's not forget that."

I sidle up to her in the doorway of my bedroom, leaning against the frame and leaving only a few inches between us. "I hear you talking, but I don't see your point." I look down at her loose black tank top and black leggings, running a finger down her shoulder and into her cleavage. She giggles, embarrassed, and smacks my hand away.

"I am busy unpacking!" she protests. She can't help but grin as she says it though. "Look, I'll make you a deal. We will unpack a whole room and then after we're done with that, we will take a break together. Does that sound okay?"

I pull a face. "You're no fun. Didn't I offer to have people sent here from the royal palace to unpack your things for you?"

She shoots me a look. "This is what normal couples do. They move in together and they are messy and they don't have servants to attend to their every need. People all over the world do this exact same thing. Whether they're in a real relationship or not."

I groan and roll my eyes. "*Ja*, whatever. Just promise me that when we finally get naked, you will let me do that thing I brought up last night."

She glances at me, wide-eyed. "Are you talking about… *anal?*"

I wink at her. "I may be. Have I ever done anything to you that you didn't like?"

She gives her head a tiny shake. "No."

"Then start unpacking somewhere. Pick a room." I frown. "A *small* room. Let's get this show on the road."

She looks around with a sigh. Pursing her lips, she heads toward the second bedroom. "I might as well start in the closet. I can't think of the last time that I even looked in your spare bedroom…"

She pads down my hallway and disappears inside the second bedroom. I follow her with a frown. It's not that I don't trust her, per se. It's just that there are several boxes tucked away in the walk in closet that are full of my personal things.

Childhood mementos, long distance use sportswear items, and some heavy jackets that have been long forgotten about. Blowing out a breath, I turn and head out of my second bedroom and start grabbing the heavier boxes. Pippa may be mostly disorganized, but she is on top of her packing and moving game. Every box has a tag with specific components that can be found within the boxes contents. *Dress shirts, summer*. Or *books, not for rereading*.

I sort through the boxes, starting with the heaviest ones, and figure that I should bring her the clothes into the closet she'll be using first. It turns out that Pippa has a million different boxes of clothes, at least forty percent of what she owns.

So for a little while, it's just a lot of moving boxes into the spare bedroom. I stack them all neatly by the wall and figure that she will just find the ones that she needs. After I move things for a while though, I get curious about what Pippa is up to.

I stick my head into the walk in closet, finding Pippa up on her knees, sifting through a box of my stuff. A knot forms in my stomach. She wasn't supposed to be looking at any of my old stuff. She's just supposed to be making room for hers.

But when she turns her head and looks at me with the biggest, brightest grin, the knot loosens a little.

She raises a picture of all of the Løve siblings, taken when I was probably four years old. We are wearing matching naval uniforms and all looking bored. "I didn't mean to find this," she swears. "But look at how serious you were as a child. Look at your face!"

I sigh. "*Ja*, I like the fact that we are all wearing matching outfits. Somebody thought that was a good idea, apparently."

She wrinkles her nose. "I think it's kind of cute actually." She takes the picture back from me, sticking it back in the box full of mementos. Just underneath it is a plastic binder that I vaguely recognize. I step in the closet and reach down, pulling the binder loose.

My lips curl up. "Ah. So, I remember this well. My English tutor as a kid was a failed poet. So we all had to learn about poetry." I laugh a little, flipping through the pages. "Here's the very cutesy poem that I did about a ladybug."

Pippa gets to her feet, coming over and peering over my arm. "The ladybug has tons of spots, which should go on and on, red and black…"

She looks at me, touching my arm. "You're adorable. I mean, you were adorable. But also, that you are now."

I hand her the sheaf of papers, clearing my throat. "I'll have you know that I did the best out of all my siblings on this specific subject, according to the would-be poet. So there you go."

She grins, returning the paper to the box and tucking it inside before closing the flaps. "You mind moving this over there?" She points. "I'm trying to make space."

I grunt and move the box for her. She sort of sighs. "It figures you would be good at that. You're good at everything. When we were in school together, I was often jealous of the fact that you were just effortlessly talented at everything."

I cock a brow. "It is hard to be in the presence of perfection, I can only assume."

She shakes her head, continuing as if I hadn't spoken. "God, remember how we both got really into photography for a while there? You were so good at it. It drove me nuts."

My lips twitch. "Ja, I think when we were around fifteen years old. I had a dark room installed in the royal palace, as I remember. I spent many hours there for about three months and then…" I shrug.

Her lips curl up. "I think that was right around the age that you discovered how to drive. Another thing that you are just so stupidly good at. Ugh, was there anything that you weren't naturally good at?"

I roll my eyes. "Well, it helps that I came in second to Stellan at basically everything. Not only at being the crown prince, but almost everything else as well. I only look good to you because you aren't witnessing how badly I was beaten in every competition on a regular basis."

Her eyes narrowed a little on my face. "What? What competitions were you and Stellan part of?"

I turn around, shaking my head. Walking out of the door, I yell back at her. "Anything and everything. Stellan was groomed to be the king from an early age. And I was always kept as his backup. It was fucked up, looking back at it. I didn't know that at the time, though."

I walk out into the main area of my apartment, pursing my lips. My eyes roam around, trying to decide which box to pick up next.

Pippa follows me out of the bedroom, a frown on her face. "Give me an example."

I shrug. "I don't know. When we were in school together, before I was sent to St. Matthews, we would often go head to head over spelling or naming the world capitals. Or really *any* subject. And it seemed like Stellan, for only being a year older than me, easily had the answers to everything. It wasn't fair, or didn't seem that way at the time."

Her lips press into a thin line. "That sucks. I'm sorry."

"My entire life growing up I was compared to Stellan, told that I was the second choice. You know, until Stellan reached eighteen, I wasn't allowed to do anything fun. Nothing dangerous, nothing risky, nothing that could possibly put me in harm's way."

Pippa tilts her head a little. "I remember there being a long list of things you were supposed to do, yes. I also remember that you and I did most of them anyway." She smiles a little. "Remember when we climbed up that mountain and all the teachers at St. Matthew's were looking for us for hours? God, we caused much trouble."

I smile at that. "I remember that we both forgot to wear sunscreen on that trip and we got back to the school and had the worst sunburn ever. I just remember that I couldn't sleep because I was so sunburned."

Pippa sidles up to me, catching my wrist and pulling me closer. I grab her around her waist and lift her up, my lips lifting as well. "I thought we are supposed to be unpacking things."

She wrinkles her nose and presses a kiss to my lips. Maybe I was hasty, deciding not to take advantage of the helpers that you offered. I forgot that unpacking things is just so boring."

A deep rumble slips from my chest. "You know what's not boring?"

Her eyebrows raise a little bit. "What?"

I wiggle my eyes brows at her. "I'm so glad you asked."

I carry her into my bedroom, kicking the door closed behind me, and she giggles with glee.

CHAPTER 24

Lars

"JUST KEEP GOING," I say aloud to myself. "No matter what, just keep going."

I'm jogging on a treadmill hooked up to the space agency's many machines, measuring my heart rate, pulls, oxygen level, and of course speed. I've been running for almost twenty minutes now and I'm starting to feel some serious fatigue.

That really is the point of this test; what happens when I feel fatigue?

Sweat rolls down my brow, soaking my shirt. I'm aware of a tiny bit twinge in my left foot, just above the heel. But I don't let myself be distracted by it. Instead, I look straight ahead and count to myself. Someone a long time ago told me that counting to thirty would give me the purpose needed to run any length of time. And I have kept it going since then. I just count to thirty then start over again.

The clock to the right of my field of vision hits twenty minutes, blinking in bright red letters. I slow my pace on the treadmill, breathing hard. I'm used to running ten miles every day as a regular course of affairs, but I'm rarely running flat out as I am now.

I spend about half a minute slowing my pace, coming to a halt finally. I'm winded, sucking in deep long pulls of air, leaning on the treadmills arms as I press the stop button.

"Very good," the older doctor says, stepping in front of me. He smiles at me kindly, motioning for me to get down off the treadmill. "Please, come down. We can remove all your guide wires now."

I breathe out. "How did I do?"

The doctor smiles lightly. "You did well, I'm very sure."

"*Ja?* How did I do in comparison with the other candidates?"

He gives me a cool little smile. "I'm sure you did well."

He removes the guide wires and the bits of plastic stuck to my chest then steps back. "That's all we need right now. Have a good day, your royal highness."

He motions toward the locker room, bowing again.

"Thanks." I pick up my water bottle and drink from it as I walk out into the locker room. It's late in the day, past six o'clock. Still light outside, but because it's the weekend there is almost no one else in this locker room.

I power through showering and changing, heading outside to the cool stone corridor of the Royal Air Force Base. The second I step outside of the locker room, I see Erik leaning against the wall, obviously waiting for me. I arch a brow.

"How did you know that I would be here??

He gives me a little smirk. "The secretary at the royal press office was feeling especially chatty today. She said that you were doing an endurance test for the space program. I figured you might want to grab a bite to eat when you got out of the test."

I run my hand through my dark, damp hair, nodding. "Ja. As it happens, Pippa is eating dinner with Margot and Nika tonight."

He rolls his eyes, smiling. "I know that. That's why I came to find you."

I squint. "Oh. Maybe I need to eat more than I thought I did. It's proving hard to think right now."

He claps me on the shoulder and turns me toward the base's exit. "Come on, I want to go get a steak. Have some real manly food." He will wiggles his brows, teasing

I let him drive me to a place not far from the base, a little hole in the wall that serves steak and potatoes and cold beer. We walk into the dimly lit restaurant, looking around at the four plastic tables surrounded by a clutter of chairs. Two of the tables are occupied so we take the farthest one back. I laugh a little as Erik chooses between two small chairs, which is only funny because Erik is the only person that I know that is taller than me.

We sit down, my stomach rumbling. One waitress comes out of the back with a platter of sizzling steaks, rushing towards one of the other tables. I groan a little bit. When the waitress drops off the steaks and comes by, I make sure to order a steak and two potatoes and a giant glass of cold beer. Erik orders the same, but he adds an order of cheesy bread as well. I cock a brow at him, but he just shrugs.

"I ran ten miles this morning. I can carbo load all I want."

The waitress comes back quickly with our beers and an order of bread and we dig in. The beer is nice and frothy, the bread hot and cheese melty. I nod, voicing my appreciation.

"You're right. This is pretty much heaven after exercising so much."

His lips twitch. "I'm glad. It seems like it's been a really long time since we have had a chance to catch up. It's been what, almost six weeks?"

I nod. "*Ja*. At the same time though, it seems like it's only been a week or something. It's funny how life becomes so busy."

He slides me a sly glance. "Ja, I bet it has. I heard that you moved in with your new fiancée."

My head bobs. "She moved in this week. It's been… Well, a lot of fucking, frankly."

He snorts into his beer. "That I am sure of. Things are going well for you two otherwise, I guess? I mean, at least neither of you has Queen Ida on your back. I'll tell you this right now, she really caused a lot of tension in the early days of me and Nika."

"Truth be told, I don't think that I would've asked Pippa to marry me if it wasn't for my grandmother butting her nose in. It was that or I would probably be engaged to some older minister's granddaughter. Take your pick."

That seems to have been the wrong thing to say. Erik shoots me a look that isn't happy. "Wait, you asked Pippa to marry you because your grandmother put pressure on you? That isn't very romantic."

I purse my lips. Taking a second to have a swig of my beer. I shrug one shoulder. "My reason for the engagement really has nothing to do with my relationship with Pippa. The engagement is really just for show."

His eyes narrow on my face. "Are you trying to tell me that you and Pippa are not an item?"

I shake my head. "No, we are an item. Or… we are something. But we definitely got engaged just to pacify my grandmother. Without Momse, we would probably still just be two very attractive people, not looking to settle down at all."

He squints at me. "I thought you had been in love with Pippa for a thousand years or something."

I shoot him a glare. "It's a lot more complicated than that. Besides, I've never said that I was in love with anybody at any point."

Erik pulls off another piece of bread, pointing it at me. "No, you'd never admitted it. But if you think I didn't know what was going on, you're crazy. That's why I kept bugging you about getting together with her."

I roll my eyes. Looking around, I wave the waitress down. "Two more beers?"

I turn back to the conversation, sighing aloud. "I'll admit to you, Erik. I'm as unlikely now as I was then to listen to you tell me about how perfect Pippa is for me."

He raises his brows. "Really? Name one way in which she is lacking."

I shoot him a glare. "Don't say it like that. She's not lacking. It's just… You know, I'm supposed to go to space at some point…" I purse my lips. "And there's… There's this wall that she has…"

He tilts his head. "You're gonna have to be more specific. You mean like Hadrian's Wall or the Great Wall of China or…"

I wave off his silly answers. "No, no. Like there is this wall between me and her. This like wall that blocks off a certain part of her from… I don't know, being intimate I guess."

He frowns. "How does that happen exactly?"

I suck in a breath, finishing the last of my beer. "Well, it's like… We will be lying in bed, just after we finished fucking. And will be like… looking in each other's eyes or whatever. And then I suddenly will see a little bit of fear run across her face. And then I just like come up against this wall. It's like one second she's there, the next second she's rolling over and burying her head under the pillows. She just doesn't want to be that close to me, I guess."

He looks thoughtful. "I see. I mean, I don't really see? But I can imagine. I've never gotten that close to Pippa, honestly. But I can see that you are frustrated."

The waitress brings a fresh round of beers and I take a sip of the refreshing brew. I nod my head a little bit. "Ja. So between that and the whole *I might be going to space* thing… It's not perfect, is what I'm getting at."

He picks up his beer, regarding me over the rim. After a long swallow, he sets his glass down. "It sounds like she knows about you going to space, right?"

I nod.

"Then it sounds like she's sticking around for the long haul. So I would definitely bear that in mind."

I push out my cheek with my tongue. "Ja, she has already set a deadline on this whole wedding business. We're supposed to pull the escape latch when it's been four months."

He frowns. "Pull the escape latch? What, from your relationship? Are you serious? How are you gonna do that?"

My neck heats and I give him sheepish look. "I hadn't thought that far, honestly."

"She's crazy, if that's really what she intends to do. Because I will bet you more money than either of us has that she loves you as much as you love her. It's obvious enough if you spend two minutes with the two of you."

I roll my eyes. "She doesn't love me. She's just playing along because I begged her to do this as a favor for me."

He looks unimpressed. "I say that she's doing it for love. Those are the facts, man. She loves you. She's known you for half of your life and yet she still loves you like crazy."

"If she does love me, which I doubt, she has a funny way of showing it. I'm telling you, this wall of hers is impenetrable. There is no getting through it. And when her wall is up? It's useless trying to get around it."

One corner of Erik's mouth curls up. "I think that's your challenge, my friend. No one said that love was going to be easy, did they?"

I exhale a long breath. "I think there is a difference between loving someone from a distance and really falling in love with a girl. Right? I mean, I've loved the person that Pippa is for a long time. But it's almost easier in a way to love someone as a friend because all those little imperfections and quirks… You can just let those go. That can be okay because you are friends. But loving someone in a deeper, more meaningful way?" I shake my head and take a sip of my beer. "That isn't for everyone."

Our steaks arrive, sizzling and smelling absolutely amazing. We dig in, the conversation naturally sliding onto easier topics. But Erik's words ring through my head for hours afterward.

Could Pippa really love me? Or more to the point, could I really be in love with her?

That idea unsettles me as much as it excites me and I can't get the thought out of my head.

CHAPTER 25

Lars

FINN TAKES off his shirt and cracks his neck, standing up straight. He passes his gaze around the small locker room, biting his lip. "Thanks for inviting me here, big brother. Ever since I got back from climbing Mount Kilimanjaro in Kenya, I've felt like my whole system is out of whack or something. I think what I need is really a good long soak."

I shed my T-shirt, standing up. "No problem. After all, how often do we get the chance for a little bonding time? You're always out of the country."

Finn smiles, pushing his hand through his dark wavy hair. At the moment, he is letting his hair grow out a little, so it is hanging down in his eyes in the front. Not my style exactly, but it does let me know what I would look like if I ever decided to grow out my military style haircut. His eyes twinkle a little mischievously.

"I can't believe I asked Kalindi and she actually agreed to come. I figured that she would say that she was too busy or something."

I cock a brow at him. "*Ja?* I always thought that she kind of liked you, at least the few times that Nika has brought her around. I figured that she just had better things to do than to waste time with either of us. I mean… We're not even the *good* royals."

Finn cracks a smile at that. "You are right about that. We are the second and third string of the royal family, for sure." He wrinkles his nose. "I don't know, I kind of like it this way though. I mean, Stellan is so consumed with being king. I am not consumed with any particular thing except for what-ever passing fancy I might have. It's pretty great, I'm not gonna lie."

I shake my head. "You won't hear any argument from me. Come on, let's go out to meet the girls."

I slip on my sandals and head out to the natural hot spring, shivering at the cold air. We're outside here, surrounded by several natural steaming pools and steely gray skies above.

I look around and don't see Pippa or Kalindi, so I take a spring at random, dipping my toe in. I'm satisfied with how hot it is, so I walk to the bench and slip off my shoes, noting that there are fresh towels hanging on a towel warmer above the bench.

I turn around and check what Finn is doing but he is off looking into the distance, doing whatever it is that Finn does. So I climb into the hot spring, making a funny face at the incredibly hot water as I slide in.

I breathe out for a minute, circulating a little. The water is a little higher than my bellybutton, with some stone benches on one side of the little pool that I'm in. Finn joins me soon after, making the same face that I did when he gets in.

"Woo, this is really *hot*."

"That it is, little brother. I'm starting to like it though. Especially if you duck down and sit so that the water covers your shoulders? That's pretty much where it's at, as far as I'm concerned."

I swim over to the other side of the pool and sit on the stone bench, breathing a sigh of relaxation. That's a moment at which I hear Pippa talk-ing, laughing a little as she coaxes Kalindi outside.

"Come on. Seriously, there's no one out here…" Pippa steps out, gesturing to a hidden person. My eyes dip down from Pippa's curtain of glorious hair to her barely there bikini. I can see practically everything, her boobs, her hips, her ass…

When she turns to face me, I can see her nipples standing out from the tiny black triangles of fabric over her to it. I bite my lip appreciatively. She sees me and sees the look on my face. She makes eye contact with me and reddens, laughing.

She turns back toward Kalindi. "Okay, you may want to bring a towel out or something. Granted, it's only our men that can see us but…"

Finn settles then on the other end of the bench, about ten feet away from me. Pippa finally manages to coax Kalindi out of the changing room.

Kalindi is small and dark-haired, a young British girl of Middle Eastern descent. Her arms and legs are shapely, I'll give her that. But if there is more to see, I have no idea. Because she shuffles out to the pool, clambering in and removing her towel inch by inch as she does.

Not my Pippa though. She kicks her shoes off and smoothly descends into the water, her smile bright. "Oh, this is nice. How have I never been here before?"

She wades over to where I'm sitting, taking a seat beside me. Kalindi looks a little lost and out of place, her gaze starting from the empty seat between Pippa and then to the empty pools around us.

"Are you sure that we are not each supposed to get our own pool?"

"You are welcome to get another pool if you want. But that will require getting out of this pool, which I assume will be freezing cold. So make your choice carefully." Pippa winks at her.

Kalindi eventually settles into the last seat on the bench, glancing at Finn like he is about the most attractive thing in the world. I roll my eyes. Finn is a daredevil like I am, but he also loves to travel and seems very worldly. He attracts a certain kind of girl, and apparently Kalindi is one of those. Not that I particularly care, because I have a hard time paying attention to anyone that isn't Pippa.

"This is so nice," Pippa sighs. I can't wait to get my hands on her. So I beckon her over.

"Wait until you have been massaged while you are in the water." Turning her around with gentle hands, I start rubbing her neck and her shoulders. Pippa makes the most contented sort of sounds. That in itself really fills up some missing part of me that is been empty for too long. I'm not getting any gratification from this exchange other than the amazing feeling of a very wet Pippa under my hands. But it still gives me an unadulterated kind of joy when she tips her head back and lets out a breathy little moan.

We hang out for a little bit, Finn and Kalindi talking, Pippa and I mostly just enjoying touching each other innocently. There is a moment when Pippa puts her hand on my knee. I can't help but get excited whenever she so much as touches me like that. She gives me a naughty smile as she caresses my inner thigh, teasing me a little.

That's when I start to get hard under the water. At the same time, Kalindi and Finn are getting a little too hot to stay in the spring anymore.

Finn turns to me, standing up. "We're gonna go ahead and go inside and get changed for the next little while. I think that this place offers food so we are going to try to grab a little smorgasbord to bring outside. Okay?"

"*Ja.* Thanks. I think we will stay outside for a little while longer." My eyes slide to Pippa. I cock a brow. "Right?"

Her face is already quite flushed from the heat of the pool but she turns even redder under my gaze. She nods. "That sounds great."

Kalindi seems to struggle to get out of the other end of the pool. Finn splashes over and jumps out, pulling her out of the water with both hands. For second, my gaze is riveted on Kalindi's body.

For being such a slight person, she has a huge ass. And her jiggly breasts are just incredible. Even buried in the rather modest black bikini she is wearing, she's definitely worth looking at.

Apparently I stare a second too long because Pippa smacks me on the arm, sounding a little angry when she calls my name. "Lars! Seriously?"

I look over at her and she is wearing a look of anger and disappointment, her curly red hair slicked back and her cheeks rosy. "You don't have anything to say for yourself?"

Not really knowing what else to do, I get defensive without really thinking about it. "What, I can't look at another girl?"

Pippa levels me with a glare. "Not like that you can't. You're just lucky that she wasn't looking. If she had been, she probably would have been horrified. At the very least, it's embarrassing. To her, but also to you."

I narrow my eyes at her. "I'll be the judge of what I find embarrassing, okay?"

Pippa smacks me on the arm again. "I want you to apologize."

"To whom? You just said that Kalindi didn't see me."

She makes an aggravated sound. "To me, you... you *caveman*. As if I didn't already have enough to worry about."

I give her a puzzled look. "What? What do you mean?"

She pushes a hand through her damp red curls. "Lars, I live in a world where I worry all the time about whether or not you will still find me attractive if I gain a pound or get a little older. I worry about that all the time. And for you to stare at Kalindi like that, so openly, just... It undermines all the work that I've done to reassure myself. I tell myself that I am being crazy worrying about these things, but this doesn't help me feel that it's true.

My mouth opens, but no words come out. Usually I don't hear Pippa say things like this out loud and to hear them now, said in anger, is just a little shocking.

Before I can say anything or disagree, she pushes away from me, making a disgusted sound. She starts to climb out of the pool. But I'm not about to just let her run away from me after lobbing a grenade like that.

"Oh no you don't," I say, grabbing her by the waist and pulling her back into the water. "We need to talk about this."

She spins in my arms, looking up at me with anxious eyes. "Maybe I was a little too honest there," she says very softly.

I pull her against me gently, wrapping one arm around her lower back. She looks so lovely right now, so open and honest, so alluring. I touch her bottom lip, cup her jaw, slide my fingers into the mass of her hair.

"I don't want you to think that I am some shallow young princeling," I utter, scanning her face. "If it wasn't already obvious, I like you for a lot more than your looks."

Her eyebrows go up just a little. "Really? You're not just..." She swallows. "You're not just sleeping with me?"

"Oh, little witch..." I sigh. "I am very much in this for more than just your body. Okay? I mean, don't get me wrong. I fucking love your body. Every inch of you is absolutely incredible. But I like you for more than the sum of your parts. The fact that you didn't know that already makes me think that I am doing something wrong."

She puffs out her cheeks for a moment. "Are you going to apologize for staring at Kalindi?"

I nod very slowly. "I apologize. Especially for making you feel less than you are. Because you are incredible. That's an absolute fact.

She gives me a tiny smile then presses up on her tiptoes, catching my lips with her own. I respond in kind, dominating the kiss, grinding my lower body against hers. Backing her against the wall of the spring, I trap her and enjoy her soft sighs of pleasure. And before I know it, we are lost in each other for some time, forgetting the entire world exists.

CHAPTER 26

Pippa

"AND SO I TOLD HIM, why don't you just buy both houses? I know it's the most basic rich girl thing to say, but honestly. I was just tired of hearing about it. Lake house, ski lodge, who cares?"

Nika throws her arms up in the air, looking frazzled. I walk down the sidewalk beside her, peering at Margot to see her reaction. Margot does in fact look a little bit puzzled, even though she's by far the richest one among the three of us.

Her face wrinkles. "I assume that Erik set you straight. Normal people don't go around buying houses left and right, you know."

Nika shoots her a look. "He said something similar, as a matter fact. I told him that it didn't matter to me which house he bought or whether he bought any house at all. We can live on an abandoned oil freighter for all I care."

I snort. "I don't think that Erik took you very seriously, Nika. Of the three of us, you are the one who was raised with unimaginable wealth."

Nika sighs. "I know, I know. I just couldn't hear one more word about where we were going to vacation. It's like… rent a house, buy a house. I really don't care. Just don't bother me with it." She pulls a face. "Anyway, thanks for letting me vent. I know it's silly."

Margot leans over and brushes a fleck of dust off of Nika's long wool jacket. Her breath fogs a little in the air.

"It's quite all right. We all need to vent about the man in our lives now and then. Don't we?"

The last it is definitely directed at me, which she lets me know by pointedly staring at me. My cheeks flush and I look ahead on the street, not really wanting the conversation that Margot is seeking from me. "Um…"

"Oooh! Look!" Margot pulls her attention away from the conversation, pointing across the street. Where she points there is a large shop with a beautiful glass display case, filled with wedding dresses of every style imaginable. My eyes widen but Margot already has her begging face on.

"Oh, please, please! I know that you'll probably get your wedding dress designed by someone famous, but please say you'll let us pick out a silhouette together? It's basically like the perfect moment to do it, and I do still love playing dress-up."

I open my mouth to say no, my mind reeling. The last thing I want is to be plied with gorgeous white dresses right now. After all, the girls still don't know that the whole engagement is completely fake. But before I can say a word, Margot yanks me across the street, a determined look on her face.

"That's what we have to do," she mutters. "We have to make sure that Pippa falls in love with the dress and the wedding as much as anything else. That's how you can trick someone who's both a clothes horse and a commitment-phobe into planning their wedding with you."

"I really don't think…" I tried to butt in. But the two women shushed me, pulling me into the fancy shop.

A bell tingles as we walk into the store. My eyes widen as I take the shop in at a glance. I have there are ten mannequins all done up in their wedding dresses and gorgeous veils and pretty stands of pearls. I'm attracted to the first one I lay eyes on, a skintight lace number that feels good underneath my fingertips. My lips twitch. It's not the dress for me, but I could definitely see myself wearing it somewhere else.

Then again, where else you need a full length lace wedding dress?

A plump blonde woman looks up from sewing the hem on a dress mannequin. It only takes a second for her to recognize Margot, the Queen of Denmark. Her dark eyes dart over Princess Annika… then they land on me. She quickly realizes that I must be the one marrying into the royal family. A look of pure, unadulterated joy comes over her face.

"Ladies!" She curtsies awkwardly. "Or should I say your highnesses?

I'm Brigid. Welcome to my shop. Please, come in and make yourself comfortable. Tell me what I can do for you."

Nika and Margaret obviously each have their own dresses in mind, because they start talking at once, at full volume.

"I was thinking something like strappy top and full at the bottom…"

"I think Pippa needs something simple, something with no sequins or anything shiny…"

I roll my eyes. Brigid seems unfazed by the girls talking over each other. She hustles us to a large fitting room area, with several seats surrounding a runway of sorts with a three way mirror at the other end.

"Please, sit. Would you like some champagne?"

"Sure," I say, relieved to at last be presented with something that I can say yes to. Nika and Margot immediately decline, causing me to raise my eyebrows.

When Brigid is off getting my champagne, I look at Nika. "Is there reason you're not drinking?"

Nika flushes. "Nothing so exciting as that, I'm afraid. I just have a dress fitting next week and I am trying to maintain my figure, that's all."

I look at Nika's perfect, petite body and I pull a face. "Well, all right then. I guess I will drink alone."

Bridgid returns with my champagne and askes for what I am looking for exactly in a dress. I wrinkle my nose delicately.

It's not as if I have not dreamt of exactly what my dress would look like. I'm a very girly girl and I'm into fashion already. But it just seems wrong to even talk about that when I know that I won't be wearing any dress.

She sees the hesitation on my face. She leans over, pats me on the shoulder, and says, "Should I just pick some things out for you? We can go from there."

My cheeks flush. I nod a little. "That would be great, thank you."

I sit back, sipping my champagne and looking at Nika and Margot. Margot is eyeing me, trying to figure out what I'm feeling so weird about. She peels off her white woolen coat and straightens the hem of her pink skirt.

"What's going on with you and Lars? I sense that there is something that you aren't telling us."

I take another sip of champagne as I decide how to answer that. "What do you mean?" I finally settle on.

Margot leans forward. "I've seen you two together. It's obvious that you are both in love with each other. But you aren't excited about trying on wedding dresses? That's not the Pippa I know."

Nika shoots me a smirk. "Wasn't it just yesterday that we were sitting together at a fashion show? Surely you should be inspired by the dresses, at least."

I suck in a breath, trying to figure out how to thread this very thorny needle. I don't want to lie to my friends. But I also don't want to tell either of them the truth. I would hate for them to know that I am just playing a part.

Then again, I have been playing a part for so many years now that it's hard for me to tell the difference.

I opt for changing the subject very slightly. "Lars is fine. I just haven't slept much in last month. You know how that is, surely." I raise a frank brow at both of them.

"That we do," Margot agrees.

"So, it's easy dating Lars, then?" Nika asked. "I always imagine that it would be sort of a nightmare. Seeing him settle down with you instead of running around with a new blonde supermodel every week is just sort of… gratifying, yes. But also somewhat mystifying. I genuinely thought he would never get it together."

Margot sits down beside me, shooting Nika a glare. "I'm sure what she means is that we're very glad for both of you. I just want to make sure that you know that you have us to talk to, no matter what."

"Seriously, just knowing that I have you two to vent to does worlds of wonder." Nika says.

"Thank you, girls." Trying to hide my discomfort, I smile and take another sip of my champagne.

Brigid returns with a rolling rack full of dresses, smiling brightly. "Do you want to come look, ladies? Er… Your highnesses, I mean."

Margot and Nika bound to their feet, eager to look at the dresses. I am slower to move as I follow them, wistfully touching the first dress on the rack, an off-shoulder cream number with full skirts. I run my hand down the satin, my mouth twisting sourly. "This dress is lovely. Actually, all the dresses I've seen today have been."

Margot peeks her head out from behind a rack, her eyes bright. "Pippa, tell Brigid your size. Let's start trying on some dresses."

I set my champagne aside and give Brigid a little smile. "Do you have a restroom that I can use?"

She smiles back at me. "Of course! If you go out this door, it's all the way at the end of the hall. Will be waiting for you when you come back."

I press my lips into a smile and rush out the door that she pointed to, my face heating. I'm not a very good liar, not in the average proceeding of things anyway. I rush down the hallway to the ladies room. When I find it, it's quite nice, all granite inside with a large mirror over the sink and a beautiful looking antique chair separate from the stall. Walking over to the mirror, I run a little bit of water and what a paper towel, pressing it against my face. I look in the mirror, my eyes scanning my own expression.

"This is too much," I say to my reflection. "No one ever said that I was going to end up lying to Margot and Nika. What do I do about it?"

I sigh, steeling myself. If I can just get through this little part of my girls day out, I think I will be happier.

I turn and march to the door, opening it.

And I come face-to-face with Ms. Olson, her arms crossed across her chest. She arches a brow.

"I haven't heard from you in some time, Sylvie. Did you forget about me?"

My skin flushes hot. I begin to tremble. "What are you doing here?" I drop my voice to a whisper, peeking out into the hallway where she's standing. "It's almost like you want be caught by the royal family."

Ms. Wilson smirks at me. "I thought it would be better if you were motivated to give me what I want so I can leave."

Shooting her a glare, I reach out and grab her arm, pulling her roughly into the bathroom with me. I close the door, rounding on her. "This has to stop. I don't know anything. I don't want to be your spy. If you don't leave me alone right now, I'll call the authorities. I'm not joking."

She gives me a cool little smile. "Aren't you going to ask me how Stella is doing?"

Her question catches me off guard. I frown. "I… I don't know…" I shake my head. "Just because I'm curious about this girl that you keep talking about doesn't mean anything. You think that you know who I am but you don't."

Ms. Olson clicks her tongue at me. She shakes her head. "I'm not here to listen to your lies, Sylvie." She looks at her watch. "I do have to be running along. But I came here for reason. Your fiancé is going to get some very precious news at work today. And I need you to find out exactly what that news is. It's too sensitive to just talk over the phone, so I will be dropping in on you again, Sylvie."

I ball my fist up. Stepping closer to the middle aged woman, I show her my teeth. "I don't want to see you again. If you leave right now and don't come back, I can forget that all of this ever happened."

Ms. Olson doesn't even blink. "Oh, Sylvie. You need a display of force? Really? Something to show you that I'm not full of hot air?"

She pulls out his cell phone and types of brief message. I give her a look, turning to open the door. This woman is unbalanced and I should have already reported her to the police. There's nothing stopping me from doing that right now.

I yank open the door, sticking my head out. "Nika, Margot? Will someone please call the police? I think I have a stalker…"

Ms. Olson gives a little sniff as she pushes past me, turning right and heading to the exit. Just before she gets there though, she stops and turns around. "I would check my bank accounts if I were you. When you find your money missing, call me. You'll know I am serious and I'll know that you are going to be a good girl."

She whirls and pushes out of the back door just as Margot and Pippa arrive in the hallway, Brigid at their heels.

"What's going on? Who was that?" Margot demand.

I turn to her, my eyes filling with tears. "I don't know," I tell her honestly. "It isn't the first time I have seen her though…"

Margot rushes to my side, hugging me hard. And I hug her back, taking a small matter comfort in her gesture. But I feel a strange pull to check my bank account, even though I'm pretty sure that Ms. Olson is full of crap.

When I finally go home, I do just that. And sure enough, one of my accounts is overdrawn, missing thousands of dollars. I bite my lip, trying to decide what to do.

Should I just tell the bank that my money was stolen?

Maybe I should tell Lars what's going on.

I sit down on my couch, unable to decide. My phone chimes, alerting me to a new text. I check it, finding several photos of me and Lars in bed together. We obviously don't realize we are on camera, because we are smiling and laughing in a few of the photos.

Another text comes in. *Are you sure you want to ruin this?*

My heartbeat races. I'm not sure. I'm paralyzed.

So I do nothing for now, although this situation clearly needs some kind of resolution… I am just too scared to make the wrong move and put Lars in jeopardy.

CHAPTER 27

Lars

THE NEXT WEEK is made up of seven days of nonstop royal visits. I drag Pippa along to open factories, speak at schools, see various cultural exhibitions, and just generally just try to represent the royal family as well as we can. Pippa, for her part, seems very distracted. She's right there by my side, holding the giant ribbon cutting scissors for me or tasting the newest wine. Always with a smile plastered on her face.

But she's not really there, not completely.

After a week of touring, I surprise her with a getaway to Monte Carlo, feeling like the only cure for whatever Pippa is experiencing is somewhere out there in the white sand beaches and yacht parties.

"Whoa," Pippa says, staring out the window as we arrive at the palatial beachside mansion I've rented. It's three stories high, beautifully made, and looks like the home of a tech billionaire. She turns her eyes to me, almost disbelieving. "Is this ours?"

I grin at her. "Permanently? No. But for the weekend, it is."

Her phone chirps and she looks down at the screen, frowning. I reach over into her lap and take her phone, turning it off and then pocketing it. She glances up at me, her expression mildly alarmed.

"Hey, I might need that. There are a lot of things still happening in Copenhagen even though we are not there."

I shoot her a coy smile. "It can wait until you get back. Can't it?"

She bites her lip, her frown increasing. But she does nod. "I guess it can."

Our car stops outside the big entrance to the house. We slide out of the car and I slip my arm around her waist, hugging her body against mine. She looks up at me, her expression unreadable. But instead of pulling away as I thought she might do, she leans up, puts her hand on my cheek, and kisses me firmly on the lips.

Her kiss is the kiss of a desperate woman, hungry for my touch, demanding my attentions. I sink into that kiss a little, letting it go on for too long. When the limo driver clears his throat beside us, indicating that he is ready to leave, I finally pull back from her in brace.

I nod towards the house. "Let's go inside. We should technically make it into the house before we start fucking."

Her lips quirk at that. "If we must."

I hustle her inside. I wait until the door closes, then rip off her clothes and have her right then and there, on the cold hardwood floor in the foyer. There's a desperation to our sex, a unspoken worry underlying every moan. I bury myself in her curves, worshiping her, the very act of being inside her feeling like some sort of sacred ritual.

"Faster," she whispers. "Please, Lars. Harder. I need you. I need this."

I thrust into her, my hips moving as fast as I can go, every single thrust like a prayer. The whole time, I restrained myself from saying what I really want to say.

That I love her.

That I need her.

That being with her, being inside her, completes me in a way that nothing else can.

We come together, her breath drawn ragged, our cries rising to the high ceiling. After we catch our breath, I help her up and pull her along to the main bedroom, touching her and kissing her as we both get in the shower.

We're both spent by then. She stands under the water with me, pressed against me. Her eyes are closed as she enjoys the simplicity of my touch and the heat from the shower.

I kiss her, not knowing quite what is going on in her head. When I cup her cheek and raise her face towards me, she opens her eyes a slit.

"This is nice," she murmurs. "I didn't think I would be glad that we came away for the weekend… But I think I really needed it." She pauses. "I think I really need you most of all."

My heart beats faster at her words. I band down and kiss her mouth, taking all of the love I feel but can't say out loud and putting it into my kiss.

We fuck again, exhausted, falling into the tangled sheets. At some point, I lose track of time. The sun goes down as I lie on my side, breathing heavily. Pippa falls asleep on my chest, curled against me.

I do daydream a little bit, letting my mind drift. I get the feeling that I am in a fast moving stream, the water swelling as it reaches a low point before dropping away down a waterfall. That's how I feel about my current relationship with Pippa. I'm worried that if I don't go along with it and ease into the flow, I will miss something. But I already know that the date of our break up is looming up ahead.

In two months, I'm supposed to give her up. And I don't know how I'm going to do it.

I'm not sure what I am supposed to do about it, exactly. All I can think of is that I have to just muster the courage to tell her how I really feel.

I think that she wouldn't dismiss it out of hand. She would at least give me a chance.

But I'm not sure. And my uncertainty about her reaction causes me to feel dread.

The idea of Pippa not being present in my life anymore looms large. If I somehow cause that, I would not know what to do with myself.

Somehow I managed to fall asleep and I wake up a few hours later, finding Pippa beside me still. We seem to wake at the same time, our eyes meeting. She smiles at me.

"So much for seeing the sights in Monte Carlo," she says shyly.

I kiss her lips briefly, savoring her taste. Then I sit up with a sigh. "This is Monte Carlo. Some of the best spots are only to be viewed at night. That is, as long as you're willing to take a little risk."

Her eyebrows raise a little. "Oh? You mean go out right now?"

I cast my gaze down her naked body, pursing my lips. "That is, unless you have other plans…"

She chuckles, rolling her eyes. "Even I have limits on my libido. Give it a couple of hours and I'm sure it will be back in full force."

I grin. "Well, I say we hit the strip, then. Downtown Monte Carlo it's basically a bunch of large hotels and casinos, all spaced out by shops and restaurants. We can get something to eat or grab a drink…"

She brightens. "Does that mean we should dress up?"

I smirk at her. "Monte Carlo demands nothing less of us."

Just like that, she's climbing on the bed, rushing to her suitcases. She unzips a white garment bag, rifling through its contents excitedly. To my delight, she dresses herself in a simple but stunning black gown. It has high slits on each side and the satiny material is soft to the touch. I watch her get dressed, opting for a pair of dark dress pants and a white button up with the sleeves rolled up in the collar undone.

Then we hit the strip on foot. Out to our left is the dazzling sea. Up ahead, the city lights gleam from gorgeous Mediterranean style buildings, the sandstone facades and the red copper roofs flickering against the night sky.

We walk for a ways, Pippa clinging to my arm. We talk about nothing, laugh at everything. I look down at Pippa as we hit the crowded part of Monte Carlo, my heart so full that I can't even speak. She looks at me, grinning, and pulls me into the first crowded bar she sees.

The party is in full swing already, judging by the intensely loud music and the insane crowds once we get in the door. As I make it up the last couple of steps, I can actually feel the floor vibrating.

At the top I stop and stare. The doors are thrown open and the party is so packed that it's spilling out into the hall. Men in tuxes yell into the ears of ladies in ballgowns. There are people lined up for drinks from the bartenders at the bar set up just outside the doors.

The liquor is flowing freely too, from the looks of it. We grab a couple of drinks and then head into the dance floor, shuffling and maneuvering to get past the crowd at the door. Inside, the electronica music is bright and sounds vaguely distorted, but I suppose that's probably on purpose. The lights are lower here by the door and brighter over across the dance floor, centering on a small, tightly packed dance floor.

Everywhere I can see, there are people dancing and chatting and drinking. Pippa dances against me and I try to keep up with her. I finish my drink quite quickly, ready for another. I don't see any waiters, so I guess I'll have to head back to the line outside.

"I'm going to get another drink for both of us," I shout into her ear.

She sways to the music, giving me a thumbs up. I head out to the bar line, standing in it for what seems like forever and being sure that the bartenders make my drinks doubles. The music throbs as I wait.

I'm annoyed by the loud, persistent booming. I want to move on from this bar, to continue down the strip, to go back to laughing and talking like we were doing before.

And that's when I see my fiancée and another guy.

Without question, I know it's Pippa. She is wearing a simple black dress, fitted and full length with thick straps. She pushes a strand of her curly red hair back as she stands by the wall, talking to a man in a tux. Her expression is unreadable, but I can tell by her body language that the man is hitting on her.

I can tell she doesn't like it.

As I start to push my way through the crowd towards her, I see the man grab her arm, lean in, and try to kiss her. She makes a face and turns her head slightly, avoiding direct contact between their mouths.

That's when I start seeing red.

Fuck anyone who touches her against her will.

Fuck any guy that touches her and isn't *me*.

As I start plowing my way through the crowd, I see her protest as the guy tries to pull her closer.

"Stop!" she yelps. "Seriously, you don't even know me—"

"If you would just—"

That's all the guy manages to say before I get close enough to yank him off of her. Pippa's eyes widen when she sees me and takes in my expression.

"Lars, don't—"

"*Foutre le camp!*" the guy says. It's clear to me that he's very drunk, but that doesn't excuse his behavior.

I punch him right in the nose, knocking him down to the floor. The crowd instantly parts, He makes a startled sound and holds his face; bright red blood starts to bloom on his face.

"Lars!" Pippa says, looking tense. She rushes to my side, tugging at my arm.

I glance at her, then back to the guy on the floor, who is just now getting surly.

"Who the fuck are you?" he yells.

I step closer, ignoring Pippa's hand on my arm. "You don't fucking touch her," I tell him. "You don't touch anybody unless they ask you to, you fucking asshole."

"I didn't do anything!" he cries, holding his nose.

"Bullshit," I tell him. "I saw it all. And if you think that I'm the only one who would've stepped in, you're wrong. You can't just step all over a girl nowadays and expect that no one will stop you."

Pippa makes a frustrated noise. "Seriously, Lars—"

"Okay! Okay." I take a step back, gripping Pippa's waist. My gaze meets hers. "I'll go if you go with me."

"Yes," she says, tugging me toward the door of the club. "I'm going with you."

I let her pull me away with one last glare at the man, who is just now getting to his feet. Then he's gone, obscured by the dancers and people talking that stand in between me and the wall. Turning toward the doorway, I step in front of her to make a path.

Soon we are out of the bar. I don't stop there on the landing, though. I grab Pippa by the waist and halfway carry her down the stairs, not stopping until we hit the front door. There are a few people who drunkenly watch as I carry my fiancée a little ways, finally putting her down in front of a white sandstone building. I grab her and pin her against the wall, my eyes fiery.

"Fuck that guy," I grit out.

She looks up at me, her eyes slitted. "I think you showed him who's in charge," she says.

I roughly kiss her, forcing my lips down on hers. She sinks against me. Burying her hands in my hair, she opens her mouth to me, letting my tongue slide against hers. When she finally breaks away, pulling back, I can see the desire written in her blue eyes.

"Take me home," she asks quietly. "Show me just what went through your mind when you saw him trying to kiss me."

I pull away from the wall, grabbing her hand, and rush toward our rented home.

CHAPTER 28

Lars

IN THE LATE MORNING, I look at Pippa gathering her things.

"Are you thinking of heading up to the beach?" I ask.

"Err… yes." She colors, lifting the tote bag that is on her shoulder. "I brought a book and a towel."

"And sunblock, I hope," I tease her. "I'll come with you."

I feel her gaze slide down my chest. She bites her lip, turns even redder, and then nods. "Okay."

She turns and starts walking away, leaving me to grab my water and catch up. As we walk, I keep an eye trained on her.

Pippa has never said anything even remotely romantic to me. I mean, we've shared our bodies with each other. That's for sure. But nothing about her feelings.

Certainly nothing about wanting to make our relationship real.

Still, gazes like the one she's giving me now speak volumes in their own way.

She thinks I'm hot. She thinks I'm funny. She thinks I'm worth knowing.

I just have to find the right moment to pop the question, as it were.

Will you make our fake relationship real, little witch?

I sigh. She casts an eye over me, squeezing my biceps. "Did you run too hard this morning or something? I saw you get up to work out."

I smirk at her. "I like running. It's just me time. Besides, I have to keep it tight for you." I say the last with a wink.

She shakes her head. "You know, you're lucky you're hot."

I grin. She's not wrong. I am hot. I work my body hard to maintain it.

"So, um…" She ducks her head as we walk, tucking her hair behind her ears. "I've been thinking about what I want you to fund. You know, after we… break up."

My heart speeds up. "*Ja?*"

"Mmhm. I've narrowed it down to three ideas. Tell me what you think." She ticks off the numbers on her fingers as she goes. "One, I think maybe some kind of newspaper for women my age. Good reporting, a mixture of fun stuff and serious stuff."

I nod. "That sounds good."

"I also was thinking about taking a year off, writing a book, and launching myself as a brand."

I cock my head, thoughtful. "What would you write?"

She blushes. "I guess I would have to figure it out."

"What's the third thing?"

"Some sort of publishing house for punk rock and feminist writers. I haven't really defined that idea very well."

Blowing out a long stream of breath, I nod slowly. "Cool. I mean… what if I just gave you the money now? We could still carry on the fake engagement and everything. It's not like you're about to ghost me."

Pippa looks at me, surprised. "If that would make you happy, I guess." She frowns. "You're still happy with our arrangement, right?"

I shrug. "I guess. We do have the four month mark coming up, creeping closer and closer. I feel like we'll have to decide what we want to do then."

Her lips quirk. "What do you mean?"

The back of my neck heats. I clear my throat. "I mean, do we keep fucking? Do we… stay engaged for longer? Do we stop everything all at once?"

Her eyes widen. She looks out at the beach, biting her lower lip. All I get from her is a grudging, "I have no idea," mumbled quickly out of the side of her mouth.

Before us, the road gives way to the sloping beach. It's rocky after we cross the road. The ocean glides gently up toward us and then back again, leaving a sandy beach in its wake.

Pippa picks a spot, laying her tote bag down. "God. It's beautiful out here." She shivers. "It's unexpectedly chilly. I guess there isn't anything to keep the wind off of us."

I toss my shirt down next to her bag. "It's nearly brisk. I like it. But I don't think that I want to get in the water, though. It's not the right time of year for that, I'm afraid."

A smile tugs at her mouth. "I suppose not. Maybe I'll just sit here and read."

She purses her lips and sits down in the pebble-strewn sand, well away from the water. Normally I would just look at the sea for a minute and then head back to the shelter of the house. But since Pippa seems intent on staying, I sit down next to her.

She is pretty quiet, dragging her book out. It's big and thick, not beach reading at all. My knee accidentally brushes hers as I settle in, and my touch leaves traces of crimson in her cheeks. Then she apologizes, as if she had done something bad.

"Oops, sorry!" she says, scooting herself another inch away from me.

As if we didn't start this morning with amazing, steamy shower sex. As if I didn't cup her tits, pull her hair, and fucking come inside her gorgeous body mere hours ago.

My first instinct is to drag her a little closer, put my calloused palms against her smooth skin. Just to see how she would react.

I blow out a breath. "I hate to be one of those people, but what are you reading?"

She wrinkles her nose, showing me the cover. The cover is hot pink and designed to look very 1990s. "It's a look back at how music and feminism shaped millennials."

I look at the sand in front of me, reach out two fingers to trace a figure eight. "I think it's been a while since I've read anything more complicated than a Wired article."

"Oh," she says carefully, gripping her book to her chest with both hands. "I think my brain needs to be fed a steady diet of new and thought provoking material." She wrinkles her nose. "All I ever did as a kid was read." Her cheeks stain again. "Actually, my childhood wasn't that different from my life right now in that regard. I'm still a giant nerd." She crinkles her face up and huffs out a laugh.

I smile a little. I've known her since she was thirteen. And for the most part, she's right. When I picture her, her nose is always stuck in a book. "I wished I was a nerd sometimes. I wished I was basically anything but a prince." My mouth flattens. "I think that sometimes the royal family is sort of trapped. They are set in their ways, always performing the same ceremonies, fragile beings kept under glass."

She straightens her spine and frowns. "I can see why you feel that way." Her mouth twists. "Do you ever dream of escaping this life? Just starting over somewhere that no one will know you?"

I push myself onto my back, laying out against the sand. "*Ja*. Of course. When I was little, I would spend hours studying maps, trying to chart a course for a great ship to take me away. "

Pippa pushes her hair behind her ears, her expression a little sad. She reaches out and touches my arm ever so gently, causing goosebumps to raise all over my body. "I'm glad you didn't sail away. Is that selfish? I'm so glad I met you, especially when I did."

Her words are so earnest, making the back of my neck heat. It's a little weird that she has such complete faith in me when I've never really done anything to earn it.

"Well, me too. I guess I could wish that so many things had turned out differently. But if they did, I might not be here right now," I say, tilting my head. "And I would hate to miss out on this."

Pippa leans over and kisses my lips, a small smile on her face. I feel myself growing sentimental, so I change course. "We should be talking about something more interesting. Like…" I grasp for straws, eager to talk about easier things. What am I good at?

Sex. How do I work that into the conversation?

"Okay…" I say. "Ah! Who was your first crush?"

Her cheeks color. "I don't know…" she hedges.

I'm enjoying her embarrassment too much. "Mine was Star Wright. I don't think you knew her, but when I was a kid, she was a super popular singer. Tall, sexy, and she always wore these bright colors. Oh, and she had really great hair." I wrinkle my nose at Pippa. "I guess you two have that in common."

Pippa looks at the ground. "I had a crush on all of the Beastie Boys," she mumbles. "I liked how they all dressed. They had a lot of style."

"Oh *man*," I say, cracking up. "You liked how they dressed. Of *course* that's your answer." I laugh about that for second, my eye on Pippa. "All right. How about a tougher one?"

She gives me a look that says she couldn't imagine anything she would rather be talking about less. I grin, my shoulders feeling looser.

"How about… are you a boobs girl or a butt girl? Or… what's the female equivalent? Hot arms or strong back muscles?"

She scrunches up her face. "I would rather crawl under a rock than answer that."

I bump her with my shoulder. "Relax. I'm not going to tell anybody. Me, I'm a butt guy, all the way. Boobs are great, but I like an ass. Gives you something to hold onto when you're fucking."

Pippa pinches her eyes closed. "I hate you."

"Just tell me. Which do you fantasize about? Arms or back? Oooh, or abs maybe?"

She grabs her book, holding it in front of her face. "I like the adonis belt, I guess…"

That gives me pause. "The fuck lines, eh? That's pretty raunchy, little witch."

She moves her book to the side and shoots me a glare. "You are seriously the worst. *The. Worst.*"

My grin widens. "What's the hottest sex you've had? Hmm?"

She goes bright red in an instant, glancing away. She drops the book, but she won't look anywhere near me. "Ummm…"

I grin. Reaching out to touch her bare knee, I rib her a little. "Come on, you can tell me."

She looks back at me, her blue eyes full of mortification. "You're going to make fun of me."

"Me? No." I shake my head. "I would never."

Pippa shakes her head. "Would it be too dorky to say the first time we had sex? I feel like I wanted it for a long time before it happened."

My heart thuds in my chest. "Really?"

She pins me with a look. "Yes. Well, it would be a tie. The sex we had on the plane ride here was pretty hot too."

"It really was," I say, my imagination kicking into high gear. I let my gaze slide down her body, biting my lip.

"What was your best sex experience?" she asks, frowning just a little.

I smirk at her, pulling her against my body. Leaning down and cupping her face, I kiss her, deep and with tongue. By the time I pull back, I'm breathless.

I lean my forehead against hers. "How about we work on making some new memories instead of talking about the past?"

Her lips curve up. "I think that sounds like a great plan."

Helping her up, I hustle her toward our lavish rental house, feeling exactly like the desperate man that I am.

CHAPTER 29

Pippa

IT'S a race to the bedroom, both of us giddy and laughing as we strip off our sandy clothes. Lars looks at me as he takes off his shirt, his eyes glinting.

"Take it all off," he says, pointing at the clothes I've already shed. "I want you naked and ready."

With shaking hands, I unhook my bikini top and let it drop. Then I push my bottoms down my legs, making eye contact with Lars the entire time. He watches me, his eyes slitted, biting his lip.

I'm left bare, no bra or panties. Lars buries his face in the space between my breasts, pushing them both toward his mouth. He takes his time with each one, kissing and licking it, running his tongue over the nipple. He even uses his teeth, setting me on edge and making me ridiculously horny.

All the while, my hands roam over his body, feeling different muscle groups flex. I wrap my legs around him, pressing my pussy against the outline of his cock through his jeans.

He knows just how to make me crazy. He makes this sound deep in his chest, while his mouth is on my breasts. It's a rumble, or a growl maybe. I just can't get enough of it.

He pulls back. "I want you to ride my mouth, Pippa."

I turn red all over. "I don't know, Lars…"

"Yes. Come on, try it. I think you'll like it," he says. I look in his eyes, blue as the sea in the morning, burning with lust.

"I'm embarrassed," I admit.

"Don't be," he says. Your hair tossed back, your breasts thrusting out, a book of pleasure on your face… I can't think of anything hotter."

I pull my lower lip between my teeth, but he's already getting off of me and laying down on the bed. *I guess I'm doing this, then.*

One thing I know is that Lars will never laugh at me or make me feel awkward on purpose. As we spend more and more time together, that becomes readily apparent.

I move up the bed to the wall, kneeling beside his head.

"Ready?" I ask hesitantly.

He nods, caressing my thigh with a smirk. "Extremely ready."

I maneuver myself over his face, straddling him. It's a balancing act and I'm glad that the wall is right there to lean on for a second. I have never felt so awkward in my life, but Lars's hands come up to the tops of my thighs, gently pushing me down.

I spread my knees a little wider, biting my lip. I feel the warmth of his breath just before he kisses the inside of my thighs. I close my eyes, forcing myself to breathe.

I can feel my pussy growing wet as he kisses upward toward my mound. It makes me squeamish, but at the same time, I bite my lip and think of how hot he'll look after I come. Wiping my juices from his face?

Ja, that makes me fucking hot.

He presses the tops of my thighs down further until I fully rest on his face. At the same time he kisses my aching clit, ever so lightly. I moan.

"Oh god," I say as he kisses it again, increasing the pressure a little.

I bite my lip, unsure what to do with my hands. I run my hands over my body, ending up enjoying the sensation of cupping my own breasts. I lean my head to the side, groaning at the stimulation of Lars slowly licking my clit.

I pull on both my nipples at once, and buck against his wicked tongue a couple of times. I keep imagining him after I come all over his face, which makes me crazy.

He shifts for a second, moving his arm. His big hand splays out over one ass cheek, then he coaxes me back down to his mouth. Lars does figure eights with his tongue over my clit, the hand on my ass trailing lower and lower, teasing the cleft of my ass.

He closes his lips over my clit and sucks, which makes me cry out. At the same time, he slips a probing fingertip just to the pucker of my ass. I immediately moan so loud that I embarrass myself. The sensation of him playing with my ass like that just makes me fucking wild. I freeze up, even though Lars sucks harder on my clit. I feel myself blossoming like a flower, a feeling of fullness growing low in my body.

He feels me lock up, and pulls back. "Easy, Pippa. What's going on?"

I go red as a beet. "I like it. I like it too much, if that's possible. But I feel like you should get off, too."

He kisses my inner thigh. "I can, if you want to turn around. You can suck my cock and ride my face at the same time."

How… dirty.

I nod, awkwardly repositioning myself. When I am facing his cock though, I have something to do. My fingers unbutton his jeans, pushing down his boxer briefs to reveal his long, hard, perfect cock.

As Lars closes his lips over my clit again, I take his cock in my fist. He groans, which is eminently satisfying. I strain to wrap my lips around his tip, which is too far away for much else.

I *mmmmm* at the male taste of him, salty and bitter earthy in my mouth.

I try to concentrate on his cock, wetting my lips and covering my teeth with my lips. I try not to worry about what Lars is doing, try not to focus on every single stroke of his tongue.

It's very difficult, though. I run my tongue around his cock and carefully pump my fist up and down his length. I can feel my inner spring winding up, becoming taut. I am aware of his clever finger slipping down to my ass again, penetrating it with just the tip.

Fuck, I think, *it feels good so damn good.* I moan against the tip of his cock. He works his whole finger inside my ass, and I am suddenly aware of the sensation of fullness. The knowledge that I'm going to come soon pops into my mind, and it makes it very difficult to try to pay attention to sucking his cock.

I pause and raise my head, eliciting a groan from him. "I'm close," I whisper.

He moans and doubles down on my clit. I sigh as I sink my mouth down on his cock again, moving my hand in time with my tongue. His taste changes a little, grows saltier as I moan around his cock.

"Oh god," I whisper. What he's doing with his mouth and his naught finger up my ass feels so good. I can't take it anymore. "Oh god, I'm—"

Suddenly I erupt, going over the precipice into a world of pleasure. He starts to come right after me, emptying lash after lash of his salty cum into my mouth, getting a lot of it on my face.

When we finally slow, I slide off his face, pushing myself upright. I finally get that moment I've been waiting for, watching him lick and wipe away the moisture from his mouth and chin.

I lean over and kiss him deeply, loving that I can taste myself on his lips and tongue. He starts chuckling, high on endorphins. I giggle sheepishly, laying down beside him.

He grins and holds me close, his breathing still ragged. No words pass between us, but none are really needed. I've never been achingly aware of the fact that I love someone before, but I would definitely say that's what I'm feeling just now.

We just lie there, basking in each other's afterglow. I curl up on my side, laying my head against his chest, and try my best to breathe through my feelings.

CHAPTER 30

Pippa

THE WEEKEND GOES TOO FAST. One minute, I am in Monte Carlo, buried in Lars's arms. The next moment I blink and everything is changed. Suddenly I am looking at a sea of people in the royal palace, blinking as Lars steps close to me, sliding his arm around me. I barely remember getting dressed for this event, but here I am, wearing a shimmering pink floor length gown, blinking into a photographer's flashes. Lars is just beside me, wearing his tux. He leans close, whispering in my ear.

"Are you okay?"

I lick my lips, looking up at him. He looks back down at me, his eyes concerned. I want to do nothing but smooth those worry lines from the corners of his eyes. I smile instead, though it feels a little forced.

"I'm fine," I say. "I was just wondering how our weekend away went so fast."

A slow smile spreads over his face. "I can think of a couple of ways how a whole day or two might slip away…"

I give him and knowing look. "I bet you can."

The photographer who is shooting our pictures calls for our attention. "Your highness? If you could just look over here for another minute…"

I look forward, repressing a sigh. We are off to one side of the ballroom that we're in, having our official engagement photos taken. Just outside the thin screens set up by the photographer, the crowd mills around. People laugh, I hear the clinking of glasses together. It's the same as it ever has been, the same as the last five parties that we attended here as an engaged couple.

I glance at Lars, wondering how he doesn't lose his mind with boredom. I thought that I knew exactly what his life entailed, but I had no idea that he was sheltering me from so many boring royal events.

One of the camera flashes catches me off guard and I wrinkle my whole face up. "Can we be done?" I asked the photographer. "Please, you've gotten at least fifty good photos of us together. Surely that's enough."

I feel Lars's fingers tighten on my waist. The photographer looks shocked; Lars quickly steps in, smoothing the situation over.

"We just got off a plane," he said quickly. "Jet lag, you know?"

The photographer seems a little worried but agrees to let us go. Of course, there is no stopping Lars if he doesn't want to have his picture taken anymore… But whether or not that privilege extends to me, I don't know.

Lars steers me out of the little portrait studio, immediately taking a hard right turn toward the ballroom doors. I glance up at him, a little anxious. "Where are we going?"

His expression is unreadable as the moves me out of the room. "We need a break. Or I do, anyway."

Just as we make it to the doors though, a servant stops Lars. "Your highness? The king wishes to speak with you. Do you mind?"

Lars is gaze hardens. He doesn't roll his eyes exactly, but he doesn't look pleased either. He turns to me, apologetic.

"I'm sorry. I'll be right back. I think I saw Nika over by the refreshment table, if it helps."

My lips twist. "Go. You are a prince, after all. If the king summons you, what choice do you have?"

He gives my arm squeeze and then disappears from the ballroom, following the servant that was sent to summon him. I suck in a deep breath and turn around, eyeing the crowd.

I don't want to be here. I am experiencing something like burnout. Worse, I'm doing it publicly.

How do the royals do it this day after day for their whole lives? I've only been doing it officially for two and a half months and I feel so fragile and brittle that I am about to break.

I clear my throat, looking around the room for Nika's small frame. As I am searching for her, Queen Ida spots me from across the way. Petite but elegant, with eyes of steel and sleek silver hair, she zooms in on me. I see her coming, her chic black dress looking as expensive as ever. She arches a brow as she advances.

"There you are, Pippa. I was just wondering if I was going to see you here or not. I have something to show you." She steps forward and takes my arm, towing me along as she makes a beeline for the exit. I don't know what to say so I just clear my throat nervously.

When I let myself be pulled outside the ballroom, I frown. Queen Ida murmurs hello to a passing servant as she toes me along. I finally get up the nerve to speak.

"I don't want Lars to miss me…" I say, glancing back at the rapidly disappearing ballroom behind me. Around me, the soaring white hallways ceilings and majestic red carpeting go on and on seemingly endlessly.

"You'll love this," she says confidently. "I have just had it flown in from being tailored in Milan."

My brows rise a little. "Milan?"

She sneaks me a look. "Yes, dear. That's what I said. Come on, it's in here."

She pulls open a random palace door, ushering me inside. I swallow and step through into a small office. The only thing worth seeing is hanging on a dress hanger in the middle of the room. It's a wedding dress, and an old one at that. It's entirely the wrong size and shape for me, a tall and slender person. This dress is made of crepe and lace, so short and wide that… Well, I would call it serviceable if I were being nice about it. I squint at the dress, as if the garment has answers for me.

"Well, what do you think?" Momse asks.

Careful to keep my face perfectly blank, I turn and face her. "I'm not sure what I am looking at," I admit.

Her eyebrows fly up. "Why, your wedding dress, of course. I thought you would want to get married in the traditional wedding dress that all the second son's wives have shared." She pauses, arching a brow. "Are you not pleased?"

I flush, though I'm not exactly sure why. I lick my lips. "No one said anything to me about already having a dress." I frown. "It's not really my style."

"Nonsense." She moves around me, touching the sleeve of the wedding dress with two fingers. "It's perfectly functional. Just like your engagement ring. I took one look at you and I already knew that I would send for this dress."

I blink rapidly. This has to be some kind of joke. "You have to be testing me or something. Margot didn't wear a proscribed gown. Why would I have to?"

She huffs. "A lot of women would kill for the opportunity that you are turning your nose up at. Lars is my grandson, and he's strong stock. I know that I didn't have much of a choice over this engagement, but I'll be damned if I will be cut out of planning the wedding."

My mouth opens. I don't quite know what to say. "I was under the impression that you were planning the wedding entirely, and I was only expected to pick out what I'm wearing. I didn't even get a say on what day my wedding date will be."

I can feel my face growing hot, feel something like rage creeping up in my tone. Queen Ida looks at me, gives another little half smirk, and looks back at the gown. "You'll wear the dress. And while we're on the topic of things you need to do, I think that you and I should sit down and talk about how it is appropriate to comport one's self when you're representing the royal family. Because I for one don't want to be embarrassed any further."

My hands curl into this. I narrow my eyes at Queen Ida, feeling myself start to shake. "Does Lars even know that you are talking to me right now?"

"Should he?" she shoots back.

It takes everything in me to keep from lashing out. Instead, I press my fingernails into the palm of each hand, speaking slowly and clearly. "I'm not sure what kind of game you're playing. I'm not even sure if you are playing on the same field as I am. But this need for control that you have, this bizarre compulsion that you feel, it won't go on. Not with me. I won't have it."

My voice rises until I'm almost but not quite yelling by the end of the sentence. An elegant little smirk appears on her face. "I think you will do just exactly what I ask you to do."

I turn, elbowing my way past her and heading for the door. "This is outrageous. I'm just going to pretend like this little tete-a-tete never happened. You would be wise to do the same."

Momse clears her throat. "Where are you going?"

I don't even look back at her. "I'm going to find my fiancé and tell him that I'm not feeling well." I fling the door open, taking a step outside.

That's when she drops the bomb.

"I wouldn't do that if I were you, Sylvie."

I freeze mid-step. Turning around slowly, my brow hunches I squint at her. "What?"

She gives me a smirk. "You heard me. What, did you think that I didn't know who you really are?" She laughs. "Like I would just let *anybody* be friends with one of my grandsons. Fat chance."

My face is so hot, I'm sure that I must be flushed all over. I take a step back towards her, dropping my voice. "I don't know what you think you know, but I'm sure that you are mistaken."

She rolls her eyes. Please. "Maybe you haven't been listening for all these months. Apparently my envoy wasn't clear enough for you."

I give her a puzzled look. "What?"

She folds her arms across her chest. "Ms. Olson said that you had the nerve to kick her out of a wedding dress shop last week. And I am here to tell you personally, that won't do. You are going to smile and play along and marry my grandson. You're going to have his kids and go on vacations and do all the royal handwaving that I ask of you. And you do it without being asked. Because I know your dirty little secret, *Sylvie*."

She looks a little proud of herself as she says it. "I also know all about Stella."

At this point, I'm so dumbstruck that I don't even know what I could possibly say. Anything that floats to the top of my mind seems like a bad idea because I would have to acknowledge that I am in fact Sylvie Martin. And something tells me that I definitely don't want to show this woman my belly.

"Pippa?" I turn my head to see Lars zooming over to me, concern for me weighing his brow. Are you okay?

I turn away from Queen Ida, automatically pulled toward the one person I feel the safest with in the world. I tried to force a smile on my lips but I know I have failed by looking at his puzzled expression.

"I'm not feeling well," I tell him. "Will you take me home?"

He looks surprised, striding up to me and taking one of my hands. It's only then that I realized my fists is still balled up. He looks down at my hand and then catches sight of his grandmother in the office. She inclines her head but otherwise says nothing.

Lars slides his gaze back to me, trying to figure it out. But I don't give him that kind of time.

"Can we go please?" I ask him softly. "Please, Lars."

He gives his grandmother one last glance and then puts his arm around me, pushing me toward the exit. "Of course," he says.

I've never been so glad to leave the royal palace as I am at that moment.

CHAPTER 31

Lars

I SIT IN MY KITCHEN, brooding as I stare out at the early morning light falling onto the city of Copenhagen. The city is quiet right now, in my view is breathtaking. But I'm in no mood for the dazzling panoramic views. I sip my coffee, sighing silently.

Behind me, I hear Pippa's bare feet padding into the kitchen. I turn, casting and eye over her form. She has bed head and wears nothing but one of my overlarge t-shirts. She nods to me quietly and then goes to pour herself a cup of coffee.

"Are you feeling any better today?" I ask.

She turns to me, a steaming cup of coffee in her hand. "Yes," she says quietly. She looks down at the floor as she answers, making me wonder if I'm getting the entire truth. I hate that feeling, sloshing around in my stomach like acid. Still, I try to make conversation. "Do you want to talk about what happened with between you and my grandmother?"

She sips her coffee, shaking her head a little. "I'd rather not. It was just a petty disagreement about my wedding dress. Nothing to be worried about."

I walk over to the kitchen counter, setting my coffee down. I straighten my tie, trying to read the expression on her face. She glances at me, her blue eyes pinning me in place for a moment.

Something electric shivers through the air, bouncing back and forth between us. I don't understand exactly why she is so morose and with-drawn, but I'm willing to bet that it has something to do with Momse.

"If there is something wrong, you would tell me, wouldn't you?"

She ducked her head and drops her gaze again, nodding. "Sure."

"Pippa," I say. "Look at me."

She looks up, her eyes flashing with emotion. If I didn't know better, I would think that she was feeling guilty about something. But what could she possibly be guilty for?

She sets her mug down too hard on the counter, sloshing coffee over the edge. She mumbles a curse and turns around to get a wad of paper towels, mopping up the mess. I watch as she moves around the kitchen, that strange acid washing around in my stomach again.

The feeling that she's not being truthful. I hate that.

I clear my throat. "I have to go and meet one of my commanders for coffee this morning. Will you be okay here by yourself?"

She nods, swallowing. "I'm fine. I'll be fine. I just need some self-care, I guess." She frowns. "When you get back, we should talk about your royal schedule. I think… I think it's just too demanding for me." She looks up at me, tugging the hem of her oversized T-shirt down.

My eyebrows rise. "That's what you're upset about? Jesus, Pippa. You had me worried. Of course we can talk about paring my schedule back."

She blows out of breath, nodding. "That would be great."

I walk over to where she's standing, reaching out and sliding an arm around her waist. She comes easily to my side and I place a kiss on the crown of her head, my nose probing her coppery curls. "I have to go," I say. "Be good."

She looks up at me, a small smile appearing on her sweetly shaped face. "Should I plan for you to be back by lunch?"

I can't help but smile when I looking at her. "I think you should," I say.

She wrinkles her nose. "Okay. I'll miss you."

I pull her in for a final kiss, loving the way she fills all my senses. Her scent tickles my nose, she feels so good under my hands, she tastes even better than she smells. I open my eyes, gaze deep into hers, and then it just pops out of my mouth.

"I love you."

The second I say it, my eyes widen. Pippa gives me a shocked expression, as though she couldn't possibly imagine why I would say such a thing to someone like her. My neck heats.

"Lars I…" She bites her lip.

I can't stand here and have her tell me that she doesn't love me back. My heart thunders in my chest. I released her from my hold suddenly, clumsily, and straighten my neck tie. I look in any direction that isn't right at her face. "I uh, I have to go. I… I'll be back."

"Lars, wait…" she says in a pleading tone.

I look back at her, biting my lower lip. She blushes, dropping her gaze to the floor. "I love you too. You know that, don't you?"

On the last word, she looks up and pins me with that blue gaze. I'm a little dumbfounded. She loves me?

Like really loves me?

The thought breaks over me like the sea over a boat's stern. I stand there for a few seconds, staring at her almost blankly. She gets that weird guilty look on her face again, dropping her gaze. "I know you have to go," she says. "I know that. But when you get back, we should really talk. There are things that you don't know about me, things that you probably have every right to know…"

I stop her in her tracks, putting my hand on her upper arm and pulling her towards me. I still don't have the words to communicate what I feel exactly. But when my lips seek hers, my kiss hungry and searching, I pour all those feelings into the kiss. She responds immediately, raising up on her tiptoes and curling her hands into my lapel. She makes a soft sound of want against my lips. I slide my hands around her and take her up, needing her to feel how much I love her.

A moment later, she gently breaks off the kiss, looking me deep in my eyes. "You have to go. You don't want to be late."

I groan a little, not wanting to put her down. "I don't want to though."

She gives me a small sad smile. Running her hand through my hair, she kisses my lips ever so briefly. "I'll still be here when you get back. I'm not going anywhere. I promise."

I kiss her one final time before I put her down, checking the time on my watch. Fuck. If I don't hurry, I'm going to be late. And there is nothing that I want less then to show up late to a meeting with my commanding officer when I'm trying to prove that I'm an outstanding member of the Royal Air Force.

Letting my eyes travel down her body, I step back. "Do me a favor. Don't change clothes. I want you to be in this exact outfit when I get home. I want to tear it off your body." I arched a brow. "Okay?"

She blushes, smiling a little bit. "Okay, okay. Now go. You're going to be late."

Luckily as I hurry out the door and into the waiting car, I only have to go a couple of miles. The second the car pulls to a stop outside the coffee shop, I burst out the door and run into the shop. I'm looking at my watch as I hurry through to the door. I am exactly 1 minute late.

My commanding officer, Gen. Ted, is sitting at a corner booth, drumming his fingers on the table. I push my hand through my hair as I stride over to the table, saluting the general.

"Sir. Sorry I'm late, sir. It will not happen again."

"Capt. Løve," the general greets me with a nod. "Please, sit down."

I slide into the booth, my eyes scanning the general's face for any signs. I don't know why I was called here exactly, but I have a feeling that it's either very good news or very bad news. I sit up straight and try not to appear nervous.

The general frowns at the cup of coffee sitting before him. His expression is unreadable. "I called you here today because you applied for a promotion to our space force." He glances up at me. "I'm sorry to say that you have not been chosen. Not because of any shortcomings about you as a person, soldier. But because of your royal rank."

My heart freezes in my chest. I stare at the general's lips, willing him to not tell me what he came here to tell me. But he just continues anyway.

"Are you listening, soldier?"

I look up, but you my bottom lip. "Sir. Yes, sir."

He puts his elbows on the table, steepling his fingers. "After talking to Royal Air Force high command, it was decided that you were simply more valuable down here on earth then you would be as a potential astronaut. This is a reflection of your value as a royal prince. It's not a reflection of your performance or any inability on your part. You understand that?"

I feel numb as I nod. "Sir. Yes, sir."

He clears his throat. "I believe that if you are still interested in moving up the ladder, there is a position available for you. That is, if you decide to continue with the Royal Air Force. I knew a lot of men in your position that probably would not."

I glance at him, meeting his gaze had on. "Because I am a prince?"

He just inclines his head.

I shake my head, trying to pretend like he didn't just smash all my dreams. "I'm not so spoiled and materialistic as to want to leave the Royal Air Force, sir."

He smiles coolly. "No, I suppose you are not." He checks his watch, clearing his throat. "I have to be on my way now. I suppose I will see you on the base later?"

I slide of the booth, my body immediately stiffening into a salute. "Sir. Yes, sir. Thank you, sir."

He slowly climbs out of the booth and slaps my back, walking away. I turn and watch him walk out the doors, my heart pounding in my chest.

After a moment of staring, I walked to the door, heading out to the street. It's not so busy here, it's far from downtown and the middle of the work day. I don't know what I'm supposed to do or feel, so I just stare blankly down the street, trying to wrap my head around the fact that I will not be an astronaut.

I clench my fist. I've been lying to myself for a long time. I thought that if I was smart enough, if I was fit enough, if I devoted my life to being the best that I could be, I would escape my family somehow. That I would be chosen to train as an astronaut because I had made myself worthy, not because of some stupid title from of a made up hierarchy. But no, now I see all too clearly.

I am still worth more as the spare to Stellan's heir then I am as me, just a person trying to rise through the ranks. It stings like hell, that thought stated plainly.

Looking down, I start walking back to my apartment, ambling slowly while I turn my thoughts over in my head.

CHAPTER 32

Pippa

AFTER LARS LEAVES, I sit at the kitchen counter, looking listlessly out at the Copenhagen skyline. I'm going to have to come clean to him when he gets back. I know it.

After fifteen years of lies, I'm finally about to tell him that I was born someone else. That thought makes me shiver.

As I finish my cup of coffee, I head to the sink to put the mug down. I hear a bell chime and I cock my head. That's certainly a new sound that I haven't heard before.

I wander into the hallway, where it the chime sounds again, louder this time. I think somehow it's a doorbell, though I don't know exactly where or how to address it.

I run into the bedroom and grab one of Lars's robes, pulling it around myself before I head down to the very end of the hallway near the elevator. A panel of lights is illuminated there, where normally it would blend in with the beige colored walls. I reach out a hand and touch it as the bell chimes again, revealing a screen.

Ms. Olson stares up into the camera lens, her mouth set in a grim line. My whole body runs cold. What is she doing here?

I look around for a second, wondering if I can just claim that I wasn't at home. Then again, now that I know that Ms. Olson works for Queen Ida, it probably goes along that Ms. Olson will know exactly where I am.

Exhaling a long breath, I press the button at the bottom of the screen labeled *admit*.

Ms. Olson quickly appears as the elevator doors open, a little smirk on her face. "Hello, Sylvie."

She doesn't ask, she just barges in, her shoulder bumping mine.

"Excuse me," I say. "This is the prince's house. You can't just come in whenever you feel like it."

She throws a smirk over her shoulder, heading toward the kitchen. "I can do whatever I please, Sylvie. The sooner that you hear my demands, the sooner I will be out of your hair. So let's hurry it up."

I trail after her, my eyes widening. "Are you serious right now?" I ask as I walk into the kitchen. "Did they have to pick someone who was such a bitch to deal with me? Because I am not inclined to work with you. Actually, scratch that. I'm not inclined to work with anyone. I wish that you spies would all talk to each other and get your stories straight."

She checks her silver watch, looking bored. "We have your sister, Sylvie."

I look up at her, my expression puzzled. "What do you mean you have her?"

Ms. Olson pulls a phone from her pocket, showing me this screen. A video starts playing of a younger version of myself, standing in front of the Royal Palace. The cameraman says something inaudible to Stella. Stella smiles right into the camera and says, "Bonjour! My name is Stella and I am here in Copenhagen, on the first leg of my European tour…"

Ms. Olson turns the phone off, looking at me pointedly. "We have her here. She doesn't know that you even exist. She thinks that she has won a songwriting contest and is now on the tour to represent France."

My heart beats loudly. I stare at the phone though the screen is powered off, not quite able to put it all together. "And what are you going to do with my sister, exactly?"

"That's up to you. If you do what you are supposed to do, Stella will continue on her European tour and nothing will happen to her. But if you don't, the man that filmed this video will hurt her. You understand that? Stella's life is in danger."

I stare at her face, trying to weed her expression. But she is solemn and there is nothing more to read there.

I lick my lips. "And what is it that you want from me?"

She smirks a little. "We want you to behave yourself. That means that you'll accede to any and every demand that is put to you by the royal family. You will wear the wedding dress that has been picked out for you, dance to the song that has been selected for you, and generally be a perfect princess all through the wedding. And then, the real work starts. You will keep track of Lars's movements and report everything back to me. Oh, and you will absolutely have Lars is children. That's not in question."

My heart dies. My first inclination is just to laugh in her face. But my gaze is drawn down to the phone again. I don't know that the video that she showed me is even really Stella, although they did find a young woman that looked remarkably like the photo I saw on the internet. If she's an actress, she's a good one.

I must take too long think to think about it because Ms. Olson claps her hands at me, startling me. "You are taking too long to respond. I'm not here to offer you a plethora of decisions. I'm here to tell you exactly what is going to happen from here on out."

I squint at her. "How do I even know that this the woman that you have on video is really my sister?" I give my head a tiny shake. "I mean, for all you know, that may not be the way to control me. I may be heartless. I may not care."

Her lips twist into a cool smile. "I think we've already established the fact that you do care for Stella."

I narrow my gaze at her. "You're threatening me with the harm of someone that I am not even sure is actually my sister. I'm trying to tell you now that I could very easily just tell you to shove off."

Her eyebrows rise. "Is that so?" She reaches down to the phone, turning it on and dialing a number. She puts the phone on speaker.

A man answers. "Hello?"

"Kill the girl," Ms. Olson says. "Make sure you capture her death on film."

"Are you sure?" the man asks.

Ms. Lowe's and looks at me, raising a brow. "I don't know. Am I sure, Pippa?"

I stare her down for a good five seconds before slowly shaking my head. "No," I mutter.

She smiles at me and tells the man on the other end of the line not to worry about it.

As she hangs up, I swallow nervously. There's no way of knowing whether she's serious or not about killing the girl. There's no honest way of telling whether or not Stella is in fact my sister. But one thing is very clear to me: it's obvious that I am bringing danger and pain into Lars's world by continuing to pretend to be his fiancée.

So, Ms. Olson says, folding her arms across her chest. "Dc we have an understanding then?"

I nod. I would've said just about anything to get her to call off her dogs. And knowing that, I realize what must be done.

I have to break up with Lars. I can't risk being an enemy to him while I was supposed to be engages to him. I would never put him in any peril. And I fear that by remaining his fiancée, I'm putting him in danger.

So I have to break off the engagement. And the sooner it's done, the better.

That realization makes my eyes well up with tears. My heart breaks, thinking about the conversation that I'm going to have to have with Lars.

He is my heart, love of my life, but in the grand scheme of things I would rather know that he is safe then to risk putting him in danger over and over again just him with my presence.

Ms. Olson looks pleased with herself. "Well then, "she says. "I've already made an appointment for you with the royal tailor. He will fit the royal wedding dress on you. And don't feel the need to respond to any wedding planning invitations, because everything has already been dealt with. There will be no detail left unattended."

I nod a bit glumly. Ms. Olson looks satisfied with herself and picks up the phone, putting it in her pocket. Under normal circumstances, I would ask her more questions about where my sister was and what she intended to do with her. But today, I don't.

If she finds the lack of questions unusual, she doesn't say anything about it. In the back of my mind, I am trying to figure out what the best plan to save Stella would be.

"Sylvie?" I look up, wiping at my eyes.

She starts walking towards his door, smiling her particular little smile. "I think you will see that you made the right choice. I think you will be satisfied. After all, isn't it every little girl's fantasy to marry a real life prince?"

I don't say a word. I just cross my arms across my chest and look at her blankly. She smiles at me, gives me a head to toe glance, and then shrugs. "I'm sure we'll see each other soon," she tosses over her shoulder as she heads out of the room.

After she's gone, I sit and stare off into space. I don't know how I will find the strength to do this. But I'm going to have to break up with him, no matter how much it tears my heart into pieces. Worse than that, I know that my secret, the one held closest to my heart for so many years, is going to get out one way or the other. I have a choice I suppose.

I can take my story to a newspaper and hope that they don't sensationalize who I am and what my father did. Or I can wait until someone else slips the paper this information.

God, if I could do everything all over again, I would tell Lars the whole and unvarnished truth on the day that we met. It might've changed the course of our friendship… But I wouldn't be staring down the barrel of this terrible decision right now.

It occurs to me that maybe Lars won't care about who I used to be. It's possible. But if I tell him, layout the whole tragic truth, there is always the possibility that he won't understand.

In any event, I will have to break off our engagement. No way will the royal palace let him marry someone who has lied about who she was for so many years. The daughter of an anti-monarchist terrorist?

Ja, I'm definitely not going to be welcome at any kind of family event.

I hear Lars in the hall and I suck in a breath. Do I have to do it right now?

On the other hand, can I stand to wait?

When Lars finally comes around the corner from the hallway, I can see the sadness written all over his face and in his slumped shoulders. My heart wrenches.

"What happened?" I ask him softly.

He looks up at me, shaking his head. "I didn't get into the space program," he says. "My commander said it is because they need a prince more than they need me as an astronaut. The palace probably shot down the idea."

He walks over to me, ripping off his tie. His eyes are so full of pain that I don't quite know where to start.

I open my arms to him and he steps into them, hugging me hard. He lays his head on my shoulder.

I close my eyes and suck in a deep lungful of his unique scent, thinking only that I can't possibly break up with him right now. Not when he's just gotten such terrible news.

When he straightens and cups my jaw, I lift my face to his and let my eyes flutter closed. His mouth finds mine, his tongue teasing my own. And I think that just for now, just for today at least, this is enough.

CHAPTER 33

Pippa

I SHIVER and invite him to come closer. His lips find a pulse point at my neck, his big body coming down on top of mine. My breath stops when he grinds his cock against my pubic bone.

Ohh. Yes, I had almost forgotten how delicious every single touch could be. Addictive, almost.

Lars's lips touch my collarbone, trailing down to my breast. I gasp and arch into his kisses, making him chuckle.

"You missed me," he says, pulling back. His expression is amused, but his bright blue eyes are hungry.

"Maybe," I tease.

He kisses me, making me lose my breath as his tongue slides against mine. Then he pulls away again, standing up fully.

"I want you naked and in my bed before I'm out of the shower. I hope you don't have anything planned because I'm going to fuck you so hard that you won't be able to walk straight tomorrow."

My cheeks turn scarlet as my eyes widen. With that, he turns and bounds up the stairs. I can hear him as he goes, taking the stairs two at a time.

It feels more naughty than usual, being left to prepare myself for him. For the specific purpose of readying myself for his needs. I climb the stairs slowly, heading into his bedroom and stripping down to nothing.

I lie on his bed, arranging and rearranging myself, trying to figure out which way to present myself to him.

When Lars steps out of his bathroom, drying himself with a towel, he is the only thing I can concentrate on. My eyes travel down his form, taking in his muscled, toned body. He ambles over to me, his eyes still ravenous, and he drops the towel on the floor.

I look at him, six and a half feet of perfect olive skin and well-toned muscle. He's all arms and abs, pecs and muscular thighs. And his face, with those angular cheekbones, icy blue eyes, and his dark eyebrows.

Not to mention, he has the nicest cock. I don't have much to compare it to, but when he fills me up with his cock, I almost implode every single time.

All in all, the perfect package. He comes over to the bed, grabbing me by the ankle and pulling me to the edge of the bed. But that doesn't shut me up. As he nuzzles my neck, the question bubbles up to my lips.

Lars's big hand slides around the front of my throat, squeezing. My hands come up to pull his hand away, but he growls so loudly I can feel it where our bodies touch. The sound vibrates over my naked skin, sending out goosebumps.

"Oh, little witch." He leans close, inhaling the sudden scent of my fear. Knotting his fingers in my hair, he seems almost amused. "I'm going to fucking ruin you tonight."

Yes. God, yes.

His fingers tighten in my hair, making me moan. He smashes his mouth to mine, as much kissing me as showing his dominance. He pulls on my hair again, making me gasp, and then uses that moment to invade my mouth. He licks and rolls his tongue around the entirety of my mouth, biting my lower lip until I groan.

When he pulls his mouth away, I gasp for breath. He doesn't let up on his grip on my hair. Instead, he sits down on the bed, forcing my head down to his lap. I can barely open my mouth before he's shoving his cock in it, pushing my head down onto his long, thick dick.

Lars moans a little. He keeps his thrusts shallow, his cock coming just to the point of making me gag, then pulling back.

"Christ," he mutters, keeping my head moving steadily. "Pippa, holy fuck. I love watching you. Fuck, I love knowing I'm giving you exactly what you need."

The whole time, he just bobs my head up and down on his massive cock. He groans and leans back a little, watching my mouth traveling up and down his cock intently. There is so much saliva that it starts to drip down to the base of his dick.

For some reason, that is the thing that flips a switch for me, turning me on. I close my eyes, loving the feel of his slick flesh in my mouth. But before I can really do anything crazy, he stops me.

"Enough," he grates, pulling me off of his cock. My mouth makes a satisfying *pop* sound as he pushes me off.

I can't go far though, because he moves to flip me over onto my knees. He leans down and spreads my legs, pushing my head down. As he strokes my clit from behind, I can feel myself grow wet.

Fuck, with Lars teasing me just like this, I can't help but give in. He's dominating me, giving me pleasure while exerting control. And I love it.

I can feel his clever fingers skating over my pussy. I shiver.

He surprises me by pushing his face against my pussy forcefully. He presses his hand on my lower back and puts his mouth to my pussy, his tongue finding my clit without fail.

He circles my swollen clit a few times, then traces his tongue to my aching entrance. He delves inside. I let out a moan, pushing back against his face.

Then he moves again, pushing me down on the bed. I feel him settle against the back of my legs, his big cock nudges my entrance. I moan.

"Yes," I whisper, closing my eyes.

He thrusts into my pussy without a second's hesitation, filling me to the hilt, stretching my pussy out in the best way possible. We both make a sound as he drives his cock all the way home.

Lars grips my hips, slamming himself into me, heedless of me. His touch is brutal, the swing of his hips frenzied. I can just barely hang on, riding the waves of pleasure building inside me.

When I come, it's sudden and unexpected and bright, a burst of magnificent color and melodious sound. Lars is right behind me, groaning his release.

CHAPTER 34

Lars

WHEN I WAKE in the morning, Pippa is still asleep beside me. She faces away from me, scrunched into a ball. Her amazing curls look like nothing so much as a bright fire. I sweep them off her neck, placing a kiss at the place where her collarbone and her neck meet.

She awakens sleepily, yawning and stretching as she rolls over. Then she sees me and her whole face falls. I frown, reaching my hand up and touching her hip.

"What is that about? Don't make that face at me."

She bites her lip and swallows. "I have to tell you something." Her eyes fill with tears. "It's serious."

Propping myself up on my hands, I look at her with mock seriousness. "Okay. I'm ready."

She wipes away her own tears, shaking her head a little "Don't joke right now. Please."

She pins me with that blue gaze of hers. A little wrinkle of worry appears in her forehead, right between her brows.

I push my cheek out with my tongue, exhaling along breath. "You can tell me anything, Pippa." I catch her hands, squeezing her fingers together. "Don't you know that by now?"

A shudder runs through her. She squeezes my fingers, releasing them. She looks so damn guilty that I don't even know what to say about that.

"A story is going to come out about me in the press. A really bad story."

I squint at her. "A story about what? Not that it matters. You know I don't care about what's in the press."

She looks at me, her gaze scanning my face. "I'm afraid to tell you what I have to tell you because I don't want you to stop looking at me the way that you do. I don't want you to stop loving me."

I frown, reaching out for her. I pull her close, shaking my head. "Just tell me. It can't be that bad, whatever it is."

A fresh round of tears fills her eyes and she wipes at her face, not stopping them in the least. "You may not care... At least I hope you don't. But I think it will keep me from ever being able to marry you."

My eyebrows shoot up. "Tell me. What could possibly be that bad?"

She looks down for a beat, her eyelids fluttering closed. Then she looks back at me, her eyes filled with pain. "I'm not Pippa Welch. Pippa Welch is a complete fabrication."

I blink a few times. "What?"

She licks her lips, her hand finding mine. She clenches my fingers. "I'm not Pippa Welch. I was born under a different name. I've been lying for most of my life."

I know that she is looking at me and saying these words, but I shake my head in disbelief. "No, that's not right. I mean, you were Pippa Welch when I met you. We have known each other for ages."

She grips my fingers so hard that it's almost painful. "I'm telling you the truth, Lars. I was brought to St. Matthews after being smuggled out of France. My father was Ansel Martin, the terrorist who bombed French Parliament. He *killed* people."

I squint, trying to make sense of her story. "So what? So your father was a terrorist? I don't understand why that qualifies you to change your name and move to another country..."

She swallows heavily. "I was just a little girl. I was only twelve when it happened. A family friend took my sister and I in for a while. She thought that eventually we would stop being harassed by everyone that we met... But after a year, she made the decision to split us up and change my identity." She shakes her head. "I agreed to it. I agreed to be separated from my sister and to go live a new life under a new name. None of this would ever have come out except..." She bites her lip, her eyes steady on mine. "Except for you are a prince."

She falls silent then, tears overwhelming her once more. I sit up, shaking my hand a little. She lets go of it and I make a fist to regain blood flow. "So you're… you're not Pippa Welch." I look at her, frowning. "Are you even from England?"

Her cheeks burn red. "My mother was. She died a few years before my father… killed all those people." She dropped my gaze, looking down at the sheets.

"What's your real name?" I ask.

"Sylvie. Sylvie Martin," she whispers.

I crack my knuckles, shaking my head a little. "I guess I am in shock of some kind. Why didn't you just tell me? Literally you could've told me anytime in the past fifteen years. You could've told me before we got engaged, for Christ's sake. I think it would be nice to know that you are not really who you say you are."

She sits up, pulling up the sheet with her, and touches my arm imploringly. "That name… that girl is dead. She died on the way to St. Matthews. I am Pippa. I've only ever been Pippa since I met you."

I blow out a long breath. "Why are you telling me this now?"

She looks down again. "Because your grandmother found out somehow. And she's been blackmailing me for months." Pippa glances up at me, tucking her hair behind her ear. "It's a long story, but essentially she has known since before we were engaged. And she's been… trying to get information on you, I guess."

I stare at her, feeling like for the second time in as many minutes she's speaking a language other than my own. "What? We…" I shake my head angrily. "My grandmother has been blackmailing you?"

Pippa's face grows anguished. "Yes," she answers simply. "I didn't know at first that she was behind the person blackmailing me. But it turns out that she expected me to play along with her and her schemes. Your grandmother had a woman name Ms. Olson come visit me. She wanted to know everything that you said to me." She bites her lip. "She had pictures of my little sister. She had photographs of you and I in a compromising position. And she threatened me that if I didn't obey her rules, she would hurt you or my sister."

I squint at her. "Momse threatened you? Seriously?"

Her cheeks turn bright red. She nods. "Ms. Olson threatened me first but when I didn't comply with her, your grandmother quite openly said that she would deal with me and I wouldn't like it."

"And what does the press have to do with this little story of yours exactly?" I ask.

Pippa dashes away her tears. "The story is out there now. If Ms. Olson knows, chances are that other people know. And while you may not care about who I am, the royal press office is going to have a lot to say about me and how I can't be trusted. The story will get out one way or another. It would be better if I were the one to tell it to a friendly journalist."

I stand up, feeling like the world is shifting beneath my feet. "Maybe you can't be trusted. I mean, for all I know, you're not Pippa or Sylvie or… whoever."

She looks down on her the hands in her lap. "I'm sorry, Lars. Really I am. The only reason I didn't tell you before because it just seems… easier to forget who I used to be, I guess."

Reminding myself to breathe, I walk to the huge glass window, looking out at the dark and city skyline. I have a million questions, I feel like. I try to go through them methodically, to sort out what I absolutely need to know right now. One thing that sticks out in my mind though.

I turn to her, a frown on my face. "You said my grandmother asked you about what I said and did?"

She swallows. "Well, mostly Ms. Olson asked me. But yes, she asked me for reports on you. I refused, but she wouldn't let me go that easily. I told her as little as I felt I could."

"Did you tell my grandmother about me trying to be an astronaut?"

Look of surprise on her face is complete. "Well, *ja*. I did. I thought that was kind of an open secret."

"And did you tell her about any of my other job details? Any of my confidential conversations that I had with Royal Air Force personnel?"

Her cheeks flush. "I… I don't know. I don't I don't think so but… I could have. Is that important?"

My lips twist. "I don't know Pippa. I don't know about that. I just…" I shake my head. I need to think. I need to… run or something."

Heading to my closet, I grab a t-shirt, a pair of running pants, and a light windbreaker. I change quickly, my mind racing. When I leave my closet and return to my room, Pippa is sitting on my bed, tears in her eyes. She looks so sorrowful that I desperately want to wrap my arms around her.

But I don't. I can't yet. I'm going on a run.

I just walk right by her, stalking out of the apartment, needing to clear my mind and digest all the information that I have just received. I head onto the darkened Copenhagen streets and push myself, running as fast and as far as I can handle for almost two hours. By the time I am jogging back into my apartment lobby, the sun has risen.

I'm fucking exhausted. I'm still not sure what I'm going to say to Pippa, but I am a lot more centered than I was two hours ago.

But when I get into my apartment, it's still and silent.

"Pippa," I call. No response. "Pippa?"

But she is nowhere to be found. I grab my phone and try to call her but there is no answer there either.

Pippa Welch or Sylvie Martin or whoever she is… She's definitely not in this apartment anymore.

Fuck.

CHAPTER 35

Pippa

I'M STANDING OUTSIDE in the freezing cold, looking out over the frosty majesty of landscape. I don't know what exactly drew me to this skiing cabin again. When I left Lars's house, tears streaming from my face, I had no place to go. I suppose that I came here because I only have good memories associated with this cabin.

But those good memories have driven me out onto the balcony, away from the memories of everything that happened in that bedroom, on the couch, on the dining room table…

I sniffle and blot at my eyes with my mittens, feeling like I've lost everything that I ever held dear. I turned off my phone the second that I left Lars's place. The thing is that I know him pretty well and I think that he would have forgiven me eventually.

But I can't be a part of his life.

Not if my part in it is to be a marionette, my strings being pulled by his grandmother. Not in exchange for my sister being tied up in all of this.

I'm not even sure what I'm going to do now. Maybe I will go back to France. Or England, I guess.

There's no way that I can stay in Copenhagen and not see Lars every single place that we've ever been, or at least the memory of him.

I shiver and pull the edges of my coat closer around me. I have no job. I have no boyfriend or fiancé. My best friends are both entangled with the royal family.

There's nothing left here for me.

Inhaling a shaky breath, I blow it out in a long stream. It clouds in the air, hanging for a moment. I hear the crunch of gravel.

Whirling, I watched as a huge black SUV comes climbing up the snowy driveway. My heart starts racing. Could it be that Lars has tracked me down?

I push down the hope that rises in my chest. Even if he does get out of the car, even if I do see his face, even if I want him so badly I don't know what to do with myself...

That doesn't fix or solve anything at all. It would only prolong our mutual sadness.

The car comes to a stop. I head across the porch to watch as the back doors open on both sides of the car. And then I see Margot's face.

The Queen of Denmark is here to see me. My eyes fill with tears. I cover my mouth with my hands, almost missing that little blonde Nika follows Margot up the last few feet of the driveway. They both look chilled to the bone despite wearing layers and layers of clothing.

Margot locks eyes with me and sees that I am crying. She burst into a run, trotting up the steps to where I am standing. She doesn't ask questions, she doesn't say anything. She just barrels into me, wrapping her arms around me.

A ragged sob leaves my lips, unable to be controlled the longer. I've been so miserable these past four days and seeing her is bittersweet. After all, she essentially is the royal palace personified.

But mostly, I look at her and see the same girl that I met when I was a freshman in college, figuring out my roommate situation. She looks almost the same as she did then, only now she pulls back, brushes back my hair, and looks at me sternly.

"Where have you been?" she lectures. "Do you know that I had to pull all kinds of strings and track your credit card to find you? I'm not even sure what I did was technically legal."

Nika comes to stand next to me, throwing an arm around me. She smiles brightly at me. "You got her all riled up. You should've heard her talking about you in the car. She was pissed."

I wipe my eyes, apologetic. "I'm so sorry, Margot. Both of you. I just… I don't have a good reason. I'm just pathetic right now."

Nika shivers. "Let's go inside. We can talk about how wrong you are until we're blue in the face but I personally do not want to be out here for a second longer."

I huff out a watery laugh. "Of course." I lead the way into the house, holding the door open for Margot and Nika. I feel like a fool as I usher them in, taking their coats and telling them to make themselves welcome. I rush to take off my coat and I am a little bit self-conscious because my normally carefully chosen outfits are still in Lars's closet. I'm wearing what I could pick up from the ski lodge's store: a long sleeve T-shirt and a pair of ski pants. I see Nika look at my outfit was some surprise but luckily she is a good friend that she doesn't say anything.

I flush as I hurry into the kitchen. "Do you want tea?" I call. "You guys like tea, right?"

Nika settles in on the couch, her expression disapproving. "We want answers. That's what we want." Margot turns to her and gives her a look. She stands up, putting her hand over her belly. I realize that she has actually started to show.

For some reason, that actually makes me cry all over again. I have a mini breakdown over the sink, crying as I fill the kettle. Margot comes up behind me and hugs me, slipping her arms around my rib cage. She rests her cheek against my back.

I can't help but love her. It seems so unfair that among all the things that I am about to miss, I'm going to miss out on Margot and Stellan's first child. I may get a picture now and then, but I won't really know him or her. It won't be the same.

"Do you want to tell us what happened?" Margot murmurs. "Lars just said that you got into an argument with his grandmother. Which let me say, I have been there personally."

Nika calls out. "Margot's too nice to say that she's a bitch, but my grandmother is definitely a bitch."

I wrinkle my nose. "I hate that word. Let's just say that she is… a monster."

I wipe my eyes and sniff a little. Margot steps back and I turn around, drawing in a shaky breath.

"What else did Lars tell you?" I ask, my eyes going from Margot to Nika.

"He said something about how you said you weren't who you claim to be or something? Honestly, it was pretty hard to follow. At the time that he was telling me, he was technically on a run and he was pretty out of breath."

"*Ja*, it's been hard to get him on the phone even." Margot wrinkles her nose. "He's been very distraught since you disappeared from his apartment. So?"

"*Ja*, spill the beans. Tell us everything."

Margot takes the tea kettle from my hand, setting it aside and guiding me back to the living room. I sit down on the couch and suck in a breath. "I don't even know where to start. It's all so confusing and sort of fucked up and…"

Nika leans forward, putting her hand on my knee. "I'm gonna need you to stop talking like that. I feel like you are editorializing a lot and making yourself look as bad as possible when I just want the facts. Okay?"

My cheeks turn pink. "Sorry."

Margot sits down on the other side of me and sighs. "I'm also going to need you to stop apologizing. Weren't you the one that told me that when I first met you? You told me that I apologize too much. I want you to take some advice from yourself."

I run a hand over my face. "*Ja. Ja*, okay. It just… It involves some deception. Of Lars, but of you guys too. So be prepared for that, I guess."

I tell the story of the fake engagement, of Ms. Olson and her demands, and of Lars's grandmother in as few words as possible. I try not to editorialize, as Nika called my derogatory view of things.

When I'm done, I look at Nika and Margot, trying to read their expressions. Nika just looks vaguely confused. Margot on the other hand looks furious. I don't really know how to deal with furious Margot, so I steel myself.

"Are you telling me that Stellan's grandmother knew who you were the entire time? That she threatened you, Lars, and your sister because of some… some *gossip?*"

I pause, not sure how to answer that for a second. I wasn't really expecting her to be angry with anyone but me in this scenario. "Um? *Ja*, I guess I am telling you that."

Nika up pipes up. "That is so fucked up. I can't believe that Momse would do that." She scrunches her face up. "Well, I can believe it, I just don't want to. That makes me *so* mad."

Margot shakes her head. "My question is, where does Lars fit into this picture? Because I don't think that he is so upset with you that he is never going to speak to you again. I think that he would really like to know where you are and to be allowed to come here."

I sit back on the couch, shaking my head. "I know. He's way too forgiving for his own good."

"Lars?" Nika asks. "I don't think that forgiving is among the top fifty adjectives that you would use to describe my brother. I do however think that he is more understanding than you give him credit for. You didn't even really talk about it. You just like told him what happened and then he was super confused and he went for a run and…" She makes a gesture. "You were gone."

Margot touches Nika's arm, letting her know that she's said enough about that.

Margot looks at me. "Why did you run away?"

I swallow against the lump in my throat. "Because I know that the royal family can't forgive what I did. They can't forgive me not telling them the truth about my identity. They can't forgive my father or what he did."

Margot squints at me. "I think it would be a mistake to equate everyone's personal feelings with the amount of forgiveness that you receive from the royal family. Also, I think that you overestimate Stellan's grandmother's power. Whether she likes it or not, Stellan and I have been making decisions mostly on our own. She's losing a lot of her steam these days."

I bite my lip, glancing between Nika and Margot. "If you are here to talk me into going back, you are mistaken. Lars is better off without me. He's better off finding a girl that he can settle down with that will not create as much political drama as I will. As soon as that story comes out…"

Nika cuts me off. "It's been out for three days."

I don't quite know what to say to that. I flush and cover my eyes with my hand, shaking my head. "Of course it has. Because the royal press office has absolutely zero chill."

"I just talked to Stellan this morning about how I was going to try to find you and make you come back with me. He didn't seem opposed to it. I think that you spent fifteen years waiting for the other shoe to drop, thinking that you did something terribly wrong. And you didn't. I mean… Maybe it wasn't on the up and up, but it really wasn't that bad." Margot scrunches her face up.

"And you were a child," Nika adds. "You didn't have that much of a say in whether or not you started a new life or not."

Margot nods. "*Ja.* Everybody is on your side. Everybody that is not Stellan's grandmother, of course."

"Who sucks, by the way," Nika says.

I give my head a tiny shake. "I'm so glad that you guys came up here. I am glad that Lars is okay. But I'm not going back. I can't."

Margot and Annika look at each other, Margot sighing. She cast an eye over my outfit, looking me up and down. "Do you have any more comfy clothes?"

"Well, I have the ski shop right down the street," I hedge.

Margot looks at me, dead serious. "I will need to go hit that store up. Because I'm not coming back without you. So if I have to get comfortable, that's what I'll do."

Nika pulls out her cell phone and starts scrolling through this screen. "I'm ordering new clothes for all of us as we speak. One of my assistants is going to drive them here. No arguments."

I cross my arms, frowning at both of them, and get ready to make my case.

CHAPTER 36

Lars

I AM GLOWERING as I stare down the length of the polished dining room table, pushing my cheek out with my tongue. At the other end of the table is Momse, looking quite tense. I make a gesture, ready for her to start explaining herself.

"So? The papers have got Pippa's story. I believe that you have been working behind the scenes and pulling the strings, whatever you need to do to make Pippa look bad. How can you defend yourself?"

She looks affronted. "Lars, I think if you just put aside your attachment to Pippa, you'll see that she was never the right girl for you anyway…"

I slam my hand down on the table, my eye twitching. Momse looks at me, her eyes widening just a little bit. "There's no call for that, is there?"

I ignore that. "So you essentially have no justification for your actions. Blackmailing my fiancée, bullying her, driving her out of Copenhagen… This is all part of your plan?" I shake my head, disgusted. "The only reason I even agreed to this meeting today was to give you one last chance to explain yourself."

My grandmother stands up from her chair, walking over to the window. "I know that it seems like I'm intruding. But really, I have to make sure that my grandchildren have the best chances for continuing the royal bloodline. I went wrong with Stellan. Annika got away from me too. So you are my third attempt at trying for the best outcome."

She shrugged, turning and looking at me innocently. "You can't blame me for wanting to make sure that everything goes right. And I knew the second that you said that you were engaged to Pippa that she couldn't make you happy. Not really, not in the long run."

I raise for my chair, sighing. "Well, it doesn't matter now."

A little smile crosses her mouth. "No, I suppose it doesn't. With Pippa gone, we can focus on finding you a more suitable girl."

I shake my head. "No, you misunderstand me. It doesn't matter anymore because you are kicked out of the royal family. I'm not sure exactly how I'm going to do it or by what means, but you have meddled with not just one, not just two, but three serious relationships. Luckily your grandchildren are stronger than you think and we all see what you done… But you have caused so much chaos and turmoil between the Løve siblings and those that we are partnered with. It's time that you retire from royal life and go live out your remaining years in solitude. Somewhere far away from Copenhagen."

She lifts her chin and scoffs. "You don't have the authority to do anything like that."

I give her a cool little smile. "Enjoy the last days of your royal reign. Because I have Stellan on my side and now it's just a matter of figuring out how to strip you of your title and remove you from our ranks."

She narrows her eyes at me. "You wouldn't."

I make my way toward the door, my hands still punched into fists. "I've already done it. This is just a courtesy, letting you know that it's already been done. So with that, I feel like we have nothing left to say to each other. Goodbye, Momse."

I pull the door open, stepping outside. I hear Momse's plaintive voice, trying to pull me back in.

"Lars… Lars! You can't do this…"

I march down the palace halls, heading for Stellan's office. I knock on his door.

"Come in," he calls.

I enter his little study, finding him and Erik sitting on the long couches that bracket the fireplace. Stellan raises a brow at me.

"Was it good? Do you feel remotely better now that you finally told Momse to fuck off?"

I walk to the same couch as Stellan, collapsing on it with a sigh. "I think it would've felt good if I didn't have so much else to worry about. Is there any word about Pippa's location?"

Erik squints toward the window. "I think if you really wanted to find her, you probably could. There are ways. But the question is, does she want to be found?"

"And what are you going to do with her once you find her?" Stellan chimes in.

I blow out of breath. "That's a good question. All the papers have pictures of Pippa plastered across the covers, with headlines that call her a liar and a fallen princess. I think that she was at least partially right in the fact that she shouldn't hold her breath, waiting for the royal family to forgive her for her sins."

"Can I make a suggestion? Retire from public life." His gaze slides to Stellan. "I know that you like having Pippa around to do some handwaving, but I think if you allow him to retire from public life, he can still get married eventually."

Stellan grunts. "I think he is right. As much as it pains me to say it, I don't think that we can have you being married to Pippa and still be a member of the royal family. You'll still receive your inheritance, I think. But you would not represent us anymore."

He shrugs. Erik nods his head.

I take a deep breath, sighing loudly. "I hate that I have to be worried about what I feel is something too advanced for our relationship. Like, I think that in the normal course of things, we wouldn't even mention marriage. But I got the ball rolling by fake proposing to her…"

"I'm still mad at you about that, as an aside." Stellan jabs his finger at me.

"Get in line. There's nothing that you can say that I probably haven't thought myself."

"What are you going to do to win her back?" Erik asks again. "You need to figure out the grand gesture. Something that will make her realize how much she needs you in her life. Because I guarantee you right now, she is doing the math and sorting out whether you are worth it."

I shoot him a glare. "I hadn't really thought about it. I'm just focused on finding her.

Stellan fishes his phone out of his pocket, frowning at the screen. "Well, it looks like the girls found Pippa. I don't know how, but I'm glad that Pippa is safe and sound."

I blow out a breath. "She's all right? Where is she?"

Stellan looks up at me. "Margot says that the three of them are talking things through. So if I tell you, I need you to promise that you are not going to just immediately rush over there. I know it's been a few days, but Pippa needs some reinforcement from her lady friends."

I give him a droll look. "I promise."

"She's up at a ski cabin about an hour north of here. Margot said that you would know which one."

My eyebrows rise with surprise. "That's where she went?"

"Maybe she felt like getting her exercise in every day," Erik jokes.

I shoot him a cool look. "That's the place we were staying when we first hooked up."

Stellan quirks a brow. "Wait, was that not just a couple of months ago?"

My neck heats. "*Ja*, we might've lied about some stuff. We didn't start fucking until we were already fake engaged."

Stellan shakes his head. "You really are a bastard, do you know that?"

"Wait, wait," Erik cuts in. "That doesn't really answer the question of what you're going to do to prove to Pippa that you are the only choice for her."

Eager to get away from talking about my past deceptions, I latch onto that question.

"I should propose again. I mean, for real this time."

Erik shakes his head at me. "That's obvious enough. But how should you do it?"

"Yeah, what does she like?" Stellan adds.

"Hmm", I say thoughtfully. "A lot of things, obviously."

"Duh," Erik says. "Name some stuff, Get the juices flowing. There are no bad ideas."

I purse my lips. "She likes dressing up and being elegant. She loves parties. She loves people. She likes…" I chuckle. "Pippa loves getting me to dance."

Stellan lifts a brow. "It sounds like you need to throw a huge party, with everyone she knows in attendance."

A light bulb goes off for me. "Actually…" I glance at both of them with a sly expression on my face, biting my lip. "I think I have the perfect idea. I will just need a shit ton of help…"

758

CHAPTER 37

Pippa

IT TAKES the better part of two whole days for Margot and Nika to convince me to return to Copenhagen. When we are about to leave, Margot pulls me aside and shows me a garment bag. My eyebrows lift a little as I unzip the bag.

Inside is the most gorgeous dress I have probably ever seen. It is made of sheer lace with light pink and purple splashes all over it and an elegant train that trails behind it.

I look up at Margot, arching my brow. "What is this?"

She gives me a secretive smile. "Just put it on. I'll see you out in the car."

I change into the dress and pin my hair up, wondering what exactly Margot has planned. I don't know and that fact gives me a lot of anxiety.

The ride to Copenhagen is practically silent. Margot and Nika are on their phones, probably checking in on all the things that they have willingly missed in order to talk some sense into me. I bite my lip and look out the window, thinking about how I will show up at Lars's house, apologetic that I ran away.

Will that be enough for him to take me back? That's the real question.

When we get into downtown Copenhagen, we don't go to either the palace or Lars's apartment. Instead, we pull up beside a row of shops on a busy street in downtown Copenhagen, not far from the palace. I arch my brow at Margot. She's quick to reassure me.

"I thought that you could do you with a little bit of shopping before your big reunion with Lars. You know, let off some steam, get your ducks in a row."

I squint at her. "Are you sure I shouldn't just go straight to wherever Lars is?"

Nika opens the car door, ready to get out. "This sounds fine. Let's do it. We can go back to the mission at hand once we are through."

"Yeah, it will be half an hour or an hour at most. Besides, this bakery over here has these éclairs that I am currently fetishizing." Margot pulls a face. "Do it for my poor, pregnant self."

My lips quirk but I give in fairly easily. "All right. I mean, I do love to shop…"

We slide out of the back of the SUV, shielding our faces against the bright morning light. I see the pastry shop that Margot mentioned. Looking across the street, I start heading there.

As I cross the street, there is a young woman dressed as a ballet dancer, dancing for the public. My gaze snags on her, on her delicate light pink dress and elegant form. Suddenly music starts playing. The strains of The Cure's "Friday I'm In Love" start to rise into the air. I look around but don't see where the music is coming from. It's loud enough that it's obviously part of the dancer's performance, as she doesn't bat an eyelash at the loud sound.

She waves her hand at the audience and five people emerge from the crowd, all lining up equally distant from the ballerina. They are all wearing full-face white masks, making me frown as I study them.

They all start to dance, their moves smooth and organized, sort of a hip-hop style. Instantly there are plenty of crowd members, curious about the music and what other people are looking at. The ballerina joins the line of dancers, dancing along with the same moves.

I can't help but smile. Nika and Margot come stand by me, urging me forward a few steps to get closer to the performers. I study their faces, but I can't see much other than their blank white masks.

Margot leans in with a whisper. "They're quite good, aren't they?"

I don't take my eyes off the dancers, but I whisper back to her. "They are good. I don't know about the bloke at the end, he seems like he might not be a professional dancer like the rest of them. But they're all pretty decent."

The ballerina gestures to the crowd again and six more people join them, white masks and street clothes on. My eye keeps wandering down to the guy at the end, who is honestly trying to do all the moves but seems to be partially failing.

Nika grasps my elbow, smiling at the dancers. "Doesn't this just lift your spirits?"

I give her a rueful smile. "It does, actually. Do you think that these dancers work on an hourly basis? And I just hire them to come and cheer me up whenever I'm feeling blue?"

Margot shushes me unexpectedly, nodding toward the ballerina. The ballerina heads toward us, a beatific smile on her face. Margot squeezes my forearm, earning a look from me. She has tears in her eyes and I wonder if being pregnant has made her a little bit more prone to cry or if she knows something that I don't.

The ballerina dances up to us, bowing elegantly and looking me straight in the eyes. She doesn't say anything, but she does hold out a hand. My cheeks burn bright red as I accept the invitation to dance. She pulls me toward the center of the wide circle of people.

The music rises, reaching a crescendo. The dancers all move into a triangle position and I dance along beside them despite not knowing the steps at all. All the dancers but one suddenly kneel.

One of the dancers is left standing, the awkward dancer. That one person walks over to me, reaching out and taking my hand.

Then he takes a knee, pushing his white mask up. My eyes widen as I realize that Lars is kneeling before me, looking more nervous than I think I've ever seen him. He pulls out a ring box.

"Oh god," I gasp. "Lars, you planned all of this?"

My hands fly to my mouth, my heart beats so loud that I almost can't hear anything else. He cracks the box open and takes my hand.

Lars has to almost shout over the sound of the music, but he makes himself known. "Pippa, I did this for you because it's something that you like. I hate dancing but for you I will go anywhere, do anything. I did it because I love you, more than I can possibly say."

I try to interject. "But what about my history and the royal family…"

Lars shakes his head. "What about it? I would rather be with you than to be part of any institution that wouldn't welcome you with open arms. I talked to Stellan and I think that we can work something out."

My chin wobbles, my eyes brim with tears. I just nod, too overwhelmed for a long speech. "I love you too," I say.

Lars doubles down on his proposition, as it were. "I know you've been my fake fiancé for too long, but I'm hoping that you will make it real. Would you do me the honor of being my wife?"

My eyes fill with tears as I nod. "Yes. Yes, Lars."

He frees the ring from its box, sliding it onto my finger beside my old engagement ring. I recognize it; it is the ring that I looked at for so long when we were at the jeweler's, a large princess cut diamond with sapphires around it.

He stands up and embraces me, his demeanor quite emotional. I press up onto my tiptoes, seeking his mouth. His lips brush mine and I can't help my tears as I kiss him.

The music ends, the dancers fade away back into the audience. But Lars and I stay in that spot, holding each other and kissing for what feels like a lifetime. When at last he steps back, beaming down at me, I am almost too emotional to speak.

Erik and Stellan appear suddenly, clapping Lars on the back. Margot and Nika grin and congratulate me. The audience seems to get the biggest kick out of their royal family acting out their lives where the public can see.

No one says anything to me about who my father was or anything else; they are just seem to focus on the fact that I am a princess and I am here, within their reach.

To my delight, the music starts again, playing something slower this time. Lars grins and takes my hand, pulling me into a slow dance against his body. I look up at him, feeling so overwhelmed.

He looks down at me, wrinkling his face. "What?"

"I just… when I think about you and me and how we finally got together, it makes me smile. But I also know that there will be critics." I pull a face. "Your grandmother is a prime example."

Lars cocks his head, smiling. "My grandmother is no longer a part of the royal family. She has had it coming for a while now, but this was the nail in her coffin."

I blink up at him, unsure that I heard him right. "What?"

He shrugs. "I told Stellan about how horribly Momse treated you, how she blackmailed and threatened you. And he agreed that we don't want to give her a chance to get her hooks into our children. So she's not banished from Denmark, but she is forbidden from all of the palaces and all the family events." His lips quirk. "To tell you the truth, I really never cared for her much anyway. Momse was one misstep away from me just deciding not to talk to her anymore. And you were a hell of a misstep, Pippa."

Tears threaten to overtake me again. "Thank you, Lars."

He shakes his head. "Don't thank me. I'm the reason that such a poisonous person was ever in your life. I don't think we will miss her one single bit. Do you?"

I lean my face against the firm wall of his chest, shaking my head. "I don't think so."

For half a minute, we just dance like that, totally wrapped up in each other. Eventually he dips me, kisses me, and makes me laugh again.

"God, I fucking love you," I say, breathless from laughter.

"And I love you, little witch," he says, squeezing my body tightly against his. "I've loved you since the first second I laid eyes on you back in school. And if I am lucky, I will love you for the rest of my long, long life."

I wipe my eyes and feel incredibly lucky. My friends surround me, Lars holds me close, and though I know that there will be some more things to figure out, I am just so glad that my best friend has become my fiancé for real this time.

CHAPTER 38

Lars

I MARRY my best friend two months later on a cool early spring day. After much discussion, it's decided that we should just keep it private, only invite people that we actually want there.

So now I am standing in the nave of a church, anxiety pumping through my veins, as my family and friends look on. I'm wearing a dark pair of dress pants and a white button up; Pippa didn't want anything too fancy or fussy. And I am willing to give her whatever she wants.

Stellan and Margot, Nika and Erik, and my parents stare up at me from the pews. That's the entire group that will see us get married today. That's it.

The door opens at the other end of the markedly somber church, revealing my bride. She enters in a rose-colored lace gown, simple and elegant. I grin at her as she glides down the aisle toward me.

This is the moment that I have been slowly building to for fifteen years. Of course, I didn't know that this exact thing was what I wanted, but I think if you'd have told me that I would end up marrying beautiful redheaded Pippa, I would have been okay with it.

And standing here today, as Pippa climbs the steps and takes my hand, I feel like all my dreams are coming true. I lift the delicate veil off her face, pushing it back a little. Pippa looks up at me, tears shining in her eyes, and she just looks so fucking beautiful. It takes my breath away.

The minister keeps our ceremony short and simple. We hold hands and recite our vows to each other. The minister pronounces us husband and wife and suggests that I kiss my bride.

I grab Pippa's waist, pulling her in and dipping her back for a dramatic kiss. I can feel her smile.

It matches my own, I am certain.

I offer Pippa my arm, cocking a brow. "Are you ready, Ms. Løve?"

Her cheeks go pink but she beams up at me, ridiculously happy. "Yes, your highness."

I grin at that. "You know, you are now the Duchess of Marion. And your children will be titled too," I remind her.

She looks me dead in the eyes and utters the words I most need to hear. "I couldn't really care less about the title, Lars. You're the only one I care about."

I kiss her on the lips, jubilant. She takes my arm and I lead her down the steps, the following a procession made of my family.

Afterward, we toast our vows at an upscale brunch. Pippa insisted on picking a restaurant for the reception, such as it is. So soon I am pushing in her chair at a white linen table set for eight, looking around the brightly lit space. Pippa beams at me as I take my seat beside her, incredibly excited about everything.

"So? What do you think?"

Finding her hand under the table, I give it a squeeze. "You have to be more specific, love."

She wrinkles her nose at me. "I know that you didn't want this small of a ceremony…"

I chuckle. "No, I didn't have any feelings about even having a ceremony. Honestly, I thought that I would never get married. Obviously, I was wrong."

She wiggles her eyebrows at me. "You were. I forgive you, though."

All the family that we invited finds their seats around us, chatting amongst each other for a moment. Everyone gets a flute full of champagne or sparkling cider. The food has already been ordered so we all just sit back and relax.

Stellan stands up, bringing a knife to the rim of his glass, calling for a toast. He raises his champagne flute. "To the bride and groom! May you live a long and happy life together."

"Hear, hear!" everyone agrees.

Margot pushes up out of her chair, cupping her pregnant belly. She also raises her glass, looking at Pippa and I. Tears shimmer in her eyes as she smiles broadly at us. "It was a long time coming. But that doesn't make it any less special. I'm glad that you two found your happily ever after. I wish you all the best."

Pippa wipes at her eyes, blowing Margot a kiss. I glance at the faces around the table, faces of the people that I hold dearest, and I feel like the luckiest man on earth.

CHAPTER 39

Pippa

I REACH behind my body as I step out of the airport's cargo terminal, needing reassurance. Luckily Lars is right there, grabbing my hand and giving it a kiss. He is always right beside me when I need him, a solid presence. Today of all days, I cling to him.

"I know you're anxious, little witch," he says. "But you've got no reason to be nervous. The doctor said that you being stressed is bad for the baby. So just breathe."

I wrinkle my nose. "I know. I'm just not sure I'm ready for this, you know?"

Lars pulls me close, kissing the top of my head. "It will be okay. You'll see."

Holding my hand, he leads me over to the waiting SUV, putting me in the back seat. As we pull out of the airport, I look at the city of Paris looming in the distance. Against a steel gray sky, it is a dark shape, taking up more and more of the horizon as we approach it.

This was where my little sister Stella finally agreed to meet me. I press my palm against the window, frowning at the darkening sky. It starts to rain a little, giant fat drops from above. I do my best to breathe instead of tensing up my entire body, but I know that my blood pressure is higher than the doctor would like.

As we make our way into the city, turning down dark gray streets, I reach across the seat and take Lars's hand again. He doesn't say anything, but he does wrap my small hand in his big one, squeezing and reassuring me. We get out of the car at the address that Stella gave me.

It's in a nondescript part of the outskirts of Paris, on a block where there are a few little shops on the side. Lars points to the shop that obviously has a giant coffee cup on the window. I think that's the spot we're looking for.

I stand in the street, staring at the coffee shop for a few seconds. Someone on a Vespa honks their horn at me, startling me into motion. Lars leads the way across the street and into the shop.

From outside, I can see Stella perched by the window. Her halo of red curls is on full display as we walk in the door. The coffee shop she's chosen is very small and she's essentially the only customer. She is sitting with a cup of coffee, nervously jiggling her crossed legs. She looks up and our gazes connect.

The fact that I ever doubted that she might be my sister is immediately erased from my mind. She has the same blue eyes that she did when we were kids, the same earnest stare. She stands up, nervously running her hands over her light blue sweater and tucking her hair behind her ear.

Lars steps forward, stretching his hand out to Stella. "Bonjour," he says. "I'm Lars."

He uses a hand on the small of my back to propel me forward, so I stick my hand out too, still nervous that my little sister might judge me poorly. She grips my hand and blushes, obviously fairly nervous herself.

When she lets go, she motions to the service counter. "Would you like something to drink?"

The fact that she just offered to buy two of Europe's richest people coffee is not missed by me. I blush and turn to Lars, that he is already waving me down. "I'll get it. You just sit down."

Stella takes her seat back, leaving three padded chairs facing her in a loose semi-circle to choose from.

I take the closest one, feeling like I have so many questions and so many apologies to make that I don't even know where to begin. Stella pulls out a pair of wire-rimmed glasses and perches them on her nose, wrinkling her face daintily.

"So…" I start, clearing my throat.

She surprises me by leaning over, touching my hand, and looking at me very directly. "You don't have to be nervous. You don't have to explain anything or apologize for anything. I just want to know what's going on in your life, that's all. I hope that's okay."

I'm instantly overwhelmed, my eyes filling with tears. I glance at her as I wipe away tears from my face, trying to find the words for exactly what I need to say to her.

"I know you said that you don't need me to apologize. But I am sorry. I'm sorry that I ever let you go."

She smiles a little bit, but her eyes are emotional. "I wish that we had never been separated. I wish that our father hadn't done what he did. But that's not really important, is it? All we can do is try to be better moving forward."

She glances down at my hand, raising a brow. "Are you married now?"

I nod a little. "Lars and I got married two months ago in a private cere-mony. Just friends and family, you know. I wish… I wish that you had been there. But I understand why you said no to my invitation."

Her cheeks go pink. "It was just bad timing. I have my big move from Nantes to Paris and I was literally in the middle of that. And let's be honest, I was nervous, too. I'm sorry about it, for what it's worth."

I clench her fingers, smiling. "I'm glad to see you in person. There's so much I want to get off my chest and clear my head before the baby comes."

Her brows shoot up. "You're expecting?"

I nod. "Yes. I'm due in about five months. It's going to be a girl."

She bites her lower lip. "Can I… Would it be okay if I were a part of you and the baby's life?"

Tears brim in my eyes again. I'm hoarse as I answer. "Of course. I would love that."

She bites her lower lip. "I want to hug you."

I nod vigorously and throw my arms open wide. She comes in and hugs me, her body feeling so strange and yet so familiar all at once.

"We have so much catching up to do," I whisper into her hair.

She pulls back, wiping her eyes, and nods. "I'm going to go get another cup of coffee and then we can really drill down on everything that we've missed. Okay?"

"Okay," I answer. "I can't wait."

As she leaves, Lars steps into the circle, holding two steaming cups. He glances backward over his shoulder at Stella. "Is everything okay?"

After he sets the steaming cups down, I grab his shirt and pull him in for a kiss. He goes along with that, clearly not about to resist me. When he pulls away, he cocks a single brow.

"What was that for?"

"Just a way of saying thank you. Thank you for pushing me to do this. I'm so happy to see my sister and I know that without you, I would've been too afraid."

He crouches down next to me, cupping my jaw in his hand. "You are very welcome, little witch. And remember…" He looks at me, his eyes scanning my face. "I love you."

I grin, kissing him, knowing that I always have him at my back and on my side. No matter what, forever.

THE END

The King's Wicked Christmas

Chapter One

"IT'S NEARLY CHRISTMAS," I murmur, looking out the window of the chauffeured car. The sky is the cool gray of stainless steel, bright but lined with clouds that will mean more snow. It's my first Christmas in Copenhagen. My first Christmas married.

My first Christmas as Queen of Denmark.

I'm excited and nervous and a little overwhelmed. After all, I have no warm and fuzzy memories of Christmas from my crummy childhood in New York. How am I supposed to be a cheerful Queen during the holidays here in Denmark?

The limo pulls up to the red brick walls and wrought iron gates surrounding the skating rink. I lean closer to the window, my breath fogging it a little.

An excited crowd stands in front of the entrance gates, waiting for us to arrive. The whole place is decorated with twinkling lights and festive red and white paper hearts, a Danish tradition. Just above the audience's heads is draped a lovely white banner with red lettering. *Welcome King Stellan and Queen Margot!*

I swallow at that, fidgeting with my dazzling diamond wedding ring. I desperately want not to let anyone down, especially not my new husband.

Stellan clears his throat and I turn from the window, biting my lip as I look at him.

He's extremely tall and exceedingly handsome, with short dark hair and sparkling blue eyes. He arches a brow at me, a hint of a smirk on his face.

I find myself blushing as I take him in. I'll be damned if Stellan needs to know that he's so handsome that just a glance in his direction makes me a little breathless. He literally looks like a caricature of Prince Charming.

That's the thing. He was my Prince Charming. Now we're married and we're living in the happily ever after. The moment after Cinderella marries her Prince and they ride away in the carriage?

That's me right now.

I bite my lip, trying to suppress a grin. Stellan's lips twitch. "What?"

I reach out and grab his black coat lapel, drawing him closer. Turning up my mouth as an offering, I pause only a hair's breadth away from his lips.

He makes a soft sound as he kisses me, a quiet rumble of satisfaction. His mouth is hot and demanding. His hand comes up to cup my cheek as he takes his time to explore my mouth. He only releases me with great reluctance when the car door is opened.

Stellan gives my lips a final kiss and then turns toward the door. I wait as he gets out first, waving to the gathered crowd. Flashes go off as I follow him a few seconds later, putting on my most brilliant smile.

The press is here in full force, shouting questions to Stellan. I have recently learned to ignore them, which hurts the little reporter's heart beating in my chest. Until I agreed to marry Stellan, I would have been out there with the press, elbowing to get a spot in the front of the crowd.

But it was necessary to adapt to Stellan's lifestyle to be with him; honestly, ignoring the press is less stressful than some of the other expectations placed on my shoulders.

Shivering against the cold morning air, I raise my hand and wave to the excited crowd.

Stellan takes my hand and we head toward the skating rink, smiling and greeting people that press in from both sides. I cling to his fingers as people call our names and titles out. King Stellan! Queen Margot!

We pass the crowd, the royal bodyguards pushing ahead and clearing a path. Before us is the skating rink, a dozen clusters of people already out moving smoothly around the ice. We stop by a bench and Karl, Stellan's new secretary, steps up with two pairs of ice skates. "Here you go." He bobs his blond head to us and we accept the skates. After sitting and lacing them up, I look up at Stellan, biting my lip. He stands, graceful as ever.

He grins and offers me his hands. "Come on. I can't believe that you've never been ice skating before."

I exhale, my breath leaving me in a clouded puff. I wrinkle my nose, taking his hands and standing. "Be nice to me. Some of us weren't raised by the royal family here in Copenhagen."

He wiggles his dark brows, pulling a face. "*Ja, ja.* I know. I'm rich and snooty. Just remember, you are too now, by extension."

I glare at him, making him laugh. He pulls me closer, placing a kiss on my lips. "Listen… you are going to be great."

I shake my head, nervous to even be walking on the cement surrounding the frosty white oval of ice. "I am only sure of one thing: I'm going to slip and fall about a hundred times…"

Stellan winks at me, pulling my body against his. "I've got you, skatter. Never doubt that for a moment."

A slow smile spreads over my face as I stare up at him. My heart beats in double time, reminding me of just how stupidly, blindly, head-over-heels in love with him I am.

In that moment, everything else fades away. The press, the crowd, the glitz and glamour of royal life. It all just vanishes.

It's just the two of us, Stellan and I, gazing at each other intently. I beam up at him and he squeezes my hand.

I'm a total sucker for my dapper Prince Charming. And knowing that feels good, if not a little self-indulgent.

"Ready?" he says.

I nod, biting my lip. I draw in a breath. "Yes."

He guides me up to the rim of the rink, stepping down and finding his balance. Then he reaches for me, putting his hands on my waist as I carefully make the first step onto the ice.

"Ahh!" A terrified sound escapes my mouth as I falter. But Stellan is right there, holding me steady. I grip his hands as they rest on my waist.

"Relax," he says, clearly trying not to laugh.

I narrow my eyes at him. "Don't you dare find amusement in my flailing."

He pulls a face. "I wouldn't dare. I'll hold onto you, no matter what. I promise."

I shake my head a little, rolling my eyes at the predicament we are in. It certainly wasn't my idea to come to this skating rink. Nor was it my idea to invite the press. Of course, the press wouldn't have been Stellan's doing. He would ban the press altogether from the entire country, given the choice.

I suck in a deep breath and try to move a little. Stellan holds me loosely in his grasp, his eye on my form. He frowns.

"Okay, I can see that you will need to shift your posture a little. Put your hands out like this and lean forward a little. Bend your knees..." He lets go of me for just a second to mimic the posture he means. I do my best to follow his instructions.

He takes my waist again. "That's good. Now you're ready to take a few steps and let your body sort of glide across the ice. Ready?"

I glance up at him, feeling his blue eyes upon me. I shove a hand through my hair and nod. "Whenever you are."

He smiles encouragingly but lets me lead the way. I venture out further on to the rink, feeling like a little kid learning to walk. True to his word, Stellan is right there beside me, his hands never leaving my waist. After a few moments of floundering, I find that I'm able to glide just as he instructed me to do.

My eyes are fastened on the ice in front of me, not really looking much ahead. The press has been mostly unintrusive so far, although if I look up into the lenses of the cameras that they hold, the flashes can almost blind me. Stellan moves a little closer, pulling me against his body.

"Just let me move us both," he says, whispering in my ear. "See how freeing it can be?"

My back hits the front of his chest as he glides forward, carrying me with him. And he is exactly right. It is nice, being able to go a little faster. I look up to him with a grin, feeling very silly.

He looks down at me, his expression intense, his hands on my waist tightening even more. "God, you're so beautiful. I can't get over it."

My cheeks flush. I can't help but beam at him. "You are such a flatterer."

He huffs out a little laugh, "Guilty as charged."

I'm so swept up in the moment that we are having that I'm not looking where I'm going. I just let Stellan be my guide, while I stare up at him, wondering exactly what I did to end up married to such a wonderful man.

There is a flurry of motion in front of me that pulls my gaze away from

Stellan. I jerked my eyes forward just in time to see a photographer kneeling directly in front of me, zooming his camera lens in on me and Stellan. The photographer doesn't seem concerned with my trajectory right towards him. He seems more concerned with making sure he gets his shot. I freak out, my whole body locking out and I feel myself begin to lose my balance.

In the next second, I tumbled to the left side, not sure where I'm going or what I'm doing except that I don't want to run over the photographer. Stellan is right behind me, trying to manage my fall as best as he can. My knees hit the ice hard, my body hits the ground and the breath is knocked out of my body. It's a minor fall, even I can tell that. But that doesn't seem to matter to Stellan.

As I tumble to the ground, Stellan is already growling at the other man." What are you doing? Are you blind or stupid? Get away from here. I mean it. I don't want to see you again." His mood is black, mercurial as ever. He looks at the photographer with a dead eyed glare. The photographer backs up and holds up his hands, skating away.

"Stellan," I say, pulling on his hand. "Help me up. Come on, don't worry about him."

He helps me gain my feet again, holding onto my hand like a lifeline. Then he turns to the small crowd of press members, pointing at them. "If any of you pull any shit like that again, that will be the end of your press credentials. I'll see to it personally."

I shake my head out at that. "Hey. Stellan. Look at me."

He turns back to me, his expression concerned. "I'm sorry about that."

I repress a sigh. "Don't look at them. Look at all the other people enjoying this beautiful day. Look at that family over there with the kids just learning to skate. Focus on that."

He grimaces but doesn't say anything. I look at the family again, two men with their little boy and girl, the girl probably only three years old. She is blonde and blue eyed, looking exceptionally Scandinavian at the moment. She's wearing a snowsuit with a lot of obvious padding. I elbow Stellan and point her out. "See, that's what I should've worn. I thought I was being fancy by trying to be cute. But I think that family has it right. She could fall and probably not even feel it."

Stellan's lips twitch. "That is pretty cute," he said. He takes in her whole family, pulling me closer and starting to glide across the ice once more. "It feels funny to look at that family and sort of… I don't know, long for what they have, I guess."

My eyes light up. I turned to him, a smile spreading over my face. "Yeah? Are you talking about how they have kids?"

Stellan nods. "*Ja*. I am. I know that that's kind of silly."

I squeeze his hand. "It's not silly at all. When I think about our future, I definitely see us chasing around a bunch of kids. Most of them look exactly like you, the little devils."

He snorts. "We would make very pretty children."

I glanced down at my feet, trying to make sure that I'm not about to trip. "That's very true. I have to admit, I'm a little bit baby crazy even though we've only been married a short period of time. I don't know why."

His lips lift at the corners. "I didn't realize that you had such strong maternal instincts."

I wrinkle my nose. "I didn't either. I don't know where it comes from. God knows that I didn't exactly have the most stable mother growing up…"

He pulls me close, hugging me around the waist. "I didn't either. But I think that we will make better choices for our children when the time comes. That much I do know."

I shoot him a grin, biting my lip. "Yeah?"

He looks amused. "*Ja*. I think that you will make an excellent mother. That's just my gut feeling."

I blush. "Let's deal with that when we get to it. One day at a time."

Squeezing me around the waist, he cocks a brow. "Whatever you say, *skatter*."

We continue to skate around the ring, me clinging to Stellan's touch. After a while, my legs are like Jell-O and I beg him to let me stop.

"Okay, I have to quit for today. That was a good first experience, though."

He helps me over to the side of the ring and I strip off my skates with glee. I'm ready to leave but Stellan looks up, spotting the bright red cable car, rising into the air on its thin wires. One leaves every ten minutes or so and there are a queue of people waiting to get into one of the heated cars.

He gets a mischievous twinkle in his eye. "How do you feel about resting in one of those?"

I blow out a breath. "You're gonna get tired of hearing me say this, but I've never been in one."

He flashes me a devilish grin. "Oh, I think it's beyond time. Come on."

I shove my feet into my shoes and hurry along after Stellan, up the little incline and into the line. Stellan is impatient sending a pair of his bodyguards ahead to check out the little sky bucket that we eventually climb into. It's nice, a little box that is closed around our heads. We can see out but it's difficult to see in. I sit down as the sky tram starts, pulling us up into the sky.

Chapter Two

AS SOON AS we take off, Stellan double checks the lock on the door. In the next second, he's all over me, kissing my neck. I look at the ground falling away beneath us, biting my lip.

"Stellan," I murmur. "The king of Denmark can't be caught fucking the Queen so publicly."

"Shhh," he says, sucking at a tender spot on my neck. "Forget our titles. Forget everything. Right now, in this moment, it's just you and me. Focus on that."

I close my eyes as he kisses my ear, gently nibbling on the lobe and tracing the shell with his tongue. I draw in a shuddering breath and my eyes roll up in my head. My toes curl. My whole body aches in the sweetest way whenever he does this to me. He puts his tongue inside my ear, making me moan.

God, Stellan makes me weak.

"Fuck," he mutters, sliding his gaze up to meet my own. "Do you realize how fucking beautiful you are, *skatter*?"

My cheeks turn pink. He used my nickname again, one that only he could give me. He called me skatter in the dirty underground club in New York. It means *my heart*. He's never stopped calling me that and I don't ever want him to. Under his relentless gaze, I feel so *seen*, the opposite of invisible.

"No," I breathe. "I only feel that way when you're looking at me, my love."

His look is so direct and frank, so honest. It sears me from the inside out.

When he speaks again, it's as much a worshipful promise as it is a compliment.

"I do." He sucks in a ragged breath. "I've always thought you were beautiful. From the very start, the first moment I saw you. I think I always knew that I loved you, even though I thought I hated you."

In the next second, Stellan buries his face in the space between my breasts. He strips away the thick fleece I'm wearing and pulls my white t-shirt up and over my head. He growls as he pushes aside the flimsy material of my pink bra and exposes both my breasts. He shoves it off roughly so that my breasts are bare before him.

"Fuck," he mutters again, looking at my tits. My hard pink nipples demand attention. My whole body tingles in anticipation of his mouth on my skin.

He puts his hands on my breasts, pushing them together, licking and kissing them both. My back bows, thrusting my nipples out and pushing my head back. I feel that familiar connection in my body, between my neck and my breasts, my nipples and my pussy. I roll my hips against his, my mouth opening to release a soft moan.

This is everything. This moment, these sensations, that passionate expression on his face. They are what I was missing, without even knowing it. I suddenly feel like I am on the threshold of being a whole person.

I push eagerly onward, rolling my hips again. Stellan has whatever I lack. He's going to fill a chasm deep inside of me that I never even knew was there.

Burying my fingers in the short hair at his nape, I gasp at his attention.

He groans, looking at me, his blue eyes saying all the things he wants to do to me. He reaches for my waistband, pushing my black leggings down my hips.

"It's not enough, Margot. I want you naked, wet, and ready for me," he grits out.

His gaze is direct and scorching. He is a ravenous fire, threatening to burn me alive. And I am the kindling, stacked and ready, welcoming his spark to my dry tinder. We are so very close to combusting.

"I'm ready," I whisper, helping him find the hidden zipper to my skirt. "I need you, Stellan."

His fingers rip at my leggings in his hurry to get me naked. At the same time, I pull up his shirt, exposing his abs and then his chest. He stops and tears his shirt over his head, pressing his kiss down on me like he's drowning and I'm the only oxygen in the world.

I work at the zipper on his jeans, undoing it and then sliding my hands around to his ass. I slip my hands down the strong muscles I find there, pulling him against my body again. He shucks my leggings down my legs as I slip his jeans down his hips, pushing up on my tiptoes to kiss him again. Our tongues dance for several beats.

He frames my breasts with his touch, then slips one of his hands down my ribs, down my belly, to the fine thatch of hair that grows between my legs. I close my eyes and moan as he probes the folds of my pussy. It's all I can do not to spread my legs and beg for him to touch me like a bitch in heat.

In the next second though, he nips at my earlobe and takes that away from me.

"Scoot back," he urges, voice gone to gravel. "Open your legs for me, Margot. Let me see your creamy pussy."

Dropping my head and moving a couple of inches further back on the bed, I moan as his clever fingers find my clit.

"That's it," he coaxes, looking down. He puts a little space between our bodies, urging me onward. "Spread your knees wide for me, honey."

Feeling a weird combination of shameless and embarrassed, I spread my legs as far as they will go. If anybody else saw me like this, so naked and utterly desperate, I would die. But I look at Stellan and the desire in his expression emboldens me.

I want to be wanton with him, to show him how hungry I am for whatever he will give me. I've waited for this my whole life, so I might as well be brazen right now.

Stellan puts two fingers in his mouth, then drops those fingers down to massage my clit. I am not a choir girl, I've definitely rubbed my clit before. But when he does it, it feels wholly different. It feels so damned good, like I'm stretching and reaching for something explosive that is just outside of my grasp. He looks deep in my eyes and controls me with his touch, so that I'm spread open and wet, my heart pounding.

He grabs my breast with his newly freed hand, swapping the two. I lean back a little, biting my lip and staring at him like he's a whole damned meal and I'm starving.

Stellan gets this little smirk on his lips as he looks at me.

"What?" I ask, flushing at his probing gaze.

His smile widens just a bit. His fingers dip from my clit to my core, circling and teasing.

"I'm just watching you. Waiting to see you come apart." He slides one finger into my core, lighting up a whole part of my body that I didn't even realize felt good.

I shiver against the sensation. "What if I don't?"

God, what if I can't? I never thought about it, but that *is* possible.

Now he grins, leaning down to kiss my collarbone. When he speaks, the sound of it reverberates against my flesh. "You will."

He sinks down to his knees. My thighs tense and my knees start to close, but he tuts at me. "Stop."

Putting both hands out to push my knees wide again, Stellan starts kissing the inside of my thigh, making a clear path to my pussy. I squirm as I ache for what I know is coming.

I've seen enough movies to know that he is about to eat me out. I can feel the excitement building, feel myself growing hotter and wetter every second. His nose tickles the inside of my thigh.

I can't help the moan that escapes my lips when he parts my pussy lips with two fingers, blowing delicately on the too-needy flesh he finds there.

Stellan glances at me, still smirking. "If you like what I'm doing, if you want more of something, I expect you to tell me. Moan, use words, whatever feels right."

I don't know what else to do but nod. As he slowly kisses my pussy, I hold my breath and bury my fingers in his hair. When his tongue circles my clit, a moan bursts from my throat. It feels natural, so I just go for it.

He sets up a rhythm, licking and sucking, making me as hot as fire. It feels good to rock my hips against his mouth, to whisper *yes* when he hits the right spot, to throw my head back and let soft sounds leave my throat.

All the while, he keeps leading me down a path, driving me wilder and wilder with desire, until…

I climax suddenly, violently. Choking, I feel the vibrations deep within my body ripple out to my breasts, my collarbone, my legs, my fingertips, my toes. Stellan is already kissing his way up my body, getting to his feet. I turn my flushed face up to him, offering him my mouth.

He takes it greedily, his breath tasting deep and earthy and charged, the flavor a little like putting my tongue on a battery. It's my taste, I realize with a start. I have a flavor of my very own.

His hands are everywhere, sliding from my shoulders down to grab my ass, then back up to my breasts. Although I just orgasmed, already I can feel my body preparing for more. I still want him.

I cling to his shoulders with one arm, smoothing my fingers down his back to his bare ass. Now I've lost some of my shyness, exploring the shape of his ass boldly. It's dense muscle, lean and smooth just like every other place on his body that I've touched.

Stellan moves back an inch, pushing his jeans down to reveal his cock. Thick and long and nothing short of glorious, his cock jumps at my touch. I reach out and feel the weight of his hard desire in my palm.

He bites his lower lip and allows my inquisitive touch for a moment. When I curl my fingers around his cock and give it an experimental stroke though, he hisses and stops my hand.

"Not this time, Margot," he manages, looking a little strangled.

The next second Stellan puts those thoughts out of my mind by leaning down and kissing me passionately. He pushes me back, then takes his cock from my grip and presses the blunt tip against the inside of my thigh. I pull him in with my legs, making him readjust a little until he settles the tip of his length against my slippery core. We both groan in unison as he pushes inside, stretching me out with each inch.

I grip his shoulders, my nails digging into his flesh. His brow furrows in concentration as he works his length all the way in. I wince as I adjust to the size of his cock. Having so much weight crushed against me and being so intimately stretched out is painful and exquisite in equal measure.

I clutch at his shoulders, moaning and sucking in a breath.

"God *damn*," he murmurs. "You are so fucking tight, Margot."

The reverent look on his face excites me.

"Keep going," I whisper.

He looks up at me, a sheen of sweat beginning to break across his forehead. He moves then, slowly pumping his cock in and out of me. I start to feel ripples of pleasure, tentative at first, then more and more certain.

Stellan takes my breast in one hand, plucking at the nipple. I start to move in time with him, rolling my hips. Little licks of flames start to unfurl themselves deep inside of me, stealing my breath away.

"Ohh," I moan. Tossing my head back, I meet his cautious thrusts. He's being careful with me, but I don't want that. "I want... *more*. Fuck me harder, Stellan."

He stiffens for just a moment, then grabs my hips and pulls me up a few inches. He forgets his hesitant rhythm and starts hammering himself in and out of my pussy. My eyes widen for a second. He starts sweating in earnest, his sweat mixing with my own every single place that my fingers touch.

Looking at his fierce expression, I'm unsure what I've unleashed in him, more beast than man. But at the same time, the ripples of my inner pond are growing in size, becoming chaotic.

It feels unbelievably good to move my hips in time with each thrust. I focus on that, letting my eyes drift closed, my fingers reaching for my own nipple. Stellan groans and pushes my hand aside, slipping his hand down between us.

He brushes my clit, the sensation like a live wire. I suddenly feel electrified, moaning and clutching at his shoulders. He punctuates each thrust by stroking my clit.

"Come for me," he whispers, his words a plea and a command at once.

I clench my eyes shut, stretching, reaching for some unknown goal. "Stellan... I..."

I reach a sudden cliff, running up one side and launching myself off. Suddenly I am falling down a deep, dark crevasse, seizing up, my whole body shaking and clamping down. Feeling a million tiny jolts of sensation overwhelming my entire system, all at once.

I cry out his name, my eyes closing, every muscle awake and firing.

Stellan doesn't need to ask if I climaxed. I open my eyes and keep my hips moving, trying desperately to breathe. He hammers his cock home at a blistering pace, his movements freeze as he approaches his own peak.

"God damn," he whispers, pumping his hips madly. "Fuck, *skatter*, you're making me come..."

Then he roars, thrusting hard and ragged, a half dozen times or more. I feel him coming, feel his semen fill me in hot pulses. I can only turn my lips up to his once more.

I feel so complete, so full, so utterly shattered and at the same time so fucking loved. My eyes fill with tears and I kiss his shoulder, his neck, the corner of his face.

Stellan leans down and cups my jaw, kissing me slowly, tenderly. I smile as I kiss him back, feeling at once complete and yet already yearning.

Chapter Three

"NO, NO," I say, shaking my head. I turn to one of the palace servants, pointing to the fire in the middle of the room. "You have to make sure that the fire is just high enough, but not too high. We don't want to start a fire in the middle of all this paper. Can you take care of it?"

The young woman bows low. "At once, your highness."

I suck in a deep breath, looking around the palace's ballroom. It's important to me that everything is just right for this evening in particular. It will be Margot's first introduction to a Denmark style *Jul*, or Christmas. I really want her to fall in love with the season in the ways that I have.

Maybe I went a little overboard, hiring special decorators to come into the palace and create this wonderful scene. But I can't be held accountable for being too enthusiastic, can I? I chew on my bottom lip as I survey the scene set before me.

There are a dozen towering pine trees set as the backdrop for my *Jul* scene, each one decorated with beautiful hand crafted red and white Christmas decorations and lit candles. Fake snow is piled everywhere, laying prettily on the landscape. At the bottom of the trees a mountain of gifts spills out, all the packages wrapped in red and white paper and tied with gleaming bows. On the far left side of the ballroom stand six full-size reindeer that are harnessed to a sleigh, with another heap of presents piled high in the back.

On the far right side, I have had the palace caterers set up a long white cloth table covered with steaming plates of my favorite foods: fried blodpølse, meatballs in sauce, pork roast, and the sweet rice pudding with cherry sauce. At the end of the table, a whole pyramid of champagne flutes is stacked high, just waiting for a palace servant to begin pouring.

And in the middle, I had the designers set up a homey little room. Rugs on the floor, white couches and dark wood furniture on top of that. A freestanding brazier of hot coals sits beside the furniture, making it warm and adding to the cozy feeling. When I look at the elaborate scene I have set up, I know that Margot is going to be equal parts impressed and appalled at the lengths I went to put this scene together.

I pace, anxiously looking at the furniture. I desperately want to make this holiday meaningful to Margot. I want to start some traditions for her, here and now. She didn't grow up with much of anything so it's going to be new, no matter what.

"King Stellan?" my secretary calls. I turn toward the door, arching my brow. He bows a little. "You wanted to know when Queen Margot was on her way. She just left your private chambers and is heading here now."

I run my hand down my black cable knit sweater, heading toward the door to wait for her.

My secretary wrinkles his nose sympathetically. "The last few weeks have been a bit of a challenge, your highness. It's nice of you to put this together for her."

My mouth creases. "*Ja*. Margot's coronation was a big deal and I'm still a little stressed about it. The press has always been very interested in our relationship in general but they've been whipped into an absolute frenzy lately."

He nods. "That sort of interest can cause an undue amount of stress on any relationship, but especially one as new as the one you have formed with Queen Margot."

I shoot him a cool smile. "We've only been married just over a month and Margot has only been Queen for half that time. It's been a whirlwind. I just want to make sure that we are rock solid as a couple going into this holiday season."

He bows deeply. "I understand. I will be in my office if you have any need for me later tonight."

"Thank you." I nod my head in response. "That will be all. You should go home and enjoy your evening."

He bows again. "Thank you, your highness."

I wait outside the door, looking down the long, navy carpeted hallway. The hall that leads to the ballroom that I'm standing in is especially majestic. All white marble underfoot and gold fixtures overhead, understated Navy tones with huge gilded mirrors on the walls.

Margot appears coming down the staircase, still wearing her gold lamé gown with her pink hair piled up in a ritzy updo. When she sees me, her whole heart shaped face lights up, a dazzling smile appearing on her mouth.

Just looking at her expression makes my heart skip a beat. I can't help but mirror her grin. When she is close enough to touch, I reach out a hand and grab her by the waist, pulling her close to my body. In her gold gown, she is as slender as a young girl, as delicate as a fresh flower.

I looked down into her eyes, growling just a little as I pull her hips against mine. "You look ravishing. Where have you come from?"

Her lips twitch. "From the gala for people experiencing homelessness. What have you been up to?"

I give her a kiss on the lips and then pull back, tugging her toward the ballroom. "Come see. I set up a little early Jul celebration just for the two of us..."

Leading her inside the ballroom, I watch her face as she takes the scene I had the servants lay out. Her eyes go wide and her mouth opens, but no words come out. For a long second, I wait with baited breath. She just looks around, trying to take in the reindeer and the couches and the food.

She looks at me, her eyes unexpectedly filling with tears. 'You set this up for me?"

She crumples, burrowing into my arms and hiding her face against my chest. I don't know what to do exactly so I just enfold her in my grasp and rub her back in little circles. She cries for a few minutes, her tears wetting my sweater. When she has cried herself out, she wipes at her face and looks up at me, her gaze imploring.

"Stellan, I had no idea that you were going to do anything so grand. I just... I don't even know where to begin. Thank you so much."

She pins me with her gaze and I breathe a sigh of relief. "Of course. I feel like this is my way of inviting you to enjoy the Jul season with me. I know it's a little over-the-top..."

She laughs. "Are you serious? You brought real reindeer into the palace. You arranged this entire ballroom to be full of Christmas-themed things…" She sweeps her hand around, indicating the landscape. "I would definitely say that you went above and beyond."

Lacing my fingers with hers, I lead her further into the ballroom, heading toward the long white table filled with silver platters of food. "I went all out, that's true. Over here, you can see that all of the traditional *Jul* foods are here… Roast goose, *Jul* ham, some sweets. Would you like something?"

She wrinkles her nose. "Are those molasses cookies? Because I will have one of those. And a glass of champagne wouldn't hurt anybody either. I'm sorry to say that I am still full from the gala."

I give her a little smirk. "That can be arranged. Here, you go sit down and I'll bring us each a glass of champagne and a plate of cookies. Sound good?"

Her lips twitch. "It does indeed."

A few minutes later, Margot is settled on the couch, holding a glass of champagne and nibbling on a gingersnap cookie. I sip my own glass of champagne, smiling as I give her a look.

She glances up at me, her cheeks flushing. "What?"

I reach out and trace the line of her arm, smiling. "Nothing. I'm just enjoying you while you luxuriate in all of this."

She looks around, eyeing the reindeer. "I imagine that it was very difficult to get them up the stairs."

I shrug. "I'll admit, I wouldn't know. I had a lot of help setting all of this up."

"Still." She takes another bite of her cookie and her gaze slides over to the trees, and the massive piles of presents underneath. "Please tell me that those boxes are just decoration."

I chuckle. "Actually, they are all real. But they're not for you. We have a tradition here in the palace that all of the staff can bring their children in and their children can open one present."

Margot presses a hand to her heart. "I love that. Do you know what the presents are?"

I shake my head. "No, not at all. Last year, I think the children received money and a toy of some kind. I assume that they get the same sort of thing this year. But I don't know. Why, do you want to open one of the presents?"

Margot rolls her eyes but smiles. "No. I'm just curious."

Looking at all the presents, I cock my head. "I'm thinking about leaving the trees up and letting the children come in and grab a present. What do you think?"

She sucks in a breath and looks at me. "I think that sounds wonderful. If I had received that treatment as a child, I would have been very grateful."

My lips quirk. "Of that, I have no doubt. I just want to make sure that you get all the *Jul* love that you deserve. I have a feeling that you didn't get enough when you were growing up. And I can't do much about the past… but I can try to give you the *Jul* you deserve now."

Margot sets her glass aside, scooting closer to me on the couch. I move the plate of cookies and she puts her legs over mine, moving her arms over my chest to cling to my body.

I feel very loved and very seen right now, which makes me feel a little emotional. Dropping my head to the crown of her head, I inhale her feminine scent and think of how lucky I am.

As if she can read my thoughts, she says them out loud. "We are very lucky. You know that? Not everybody finds what we have found in each other. And that's not even beginning to address the wealth that you were born into."

I nod. "I know. I was just thinking about that, sort of."

She pulls back, glancing up at my face, her soulful eyes pinning me. "We should share the wealth. It is a holiday after all."

For a second, I narrow my gaze on her face. "Are you talking about starting a family?"

She pulls a face. "No. I mean… I do want to start a family. But I mean that we should be more charitable. I have been trying to figure out exactly how lately. Something that will help children and people experiencing homelessness… That would be a good start…"

I nod slowly. "What you are saying makes sense. Do you have any ideas about how we go about that?"

She looks away, her cheeks flushing. "Nothing more than minor ramblings. I do think that we could be doing so much more for the children of Denmark, though."

Eyeing her for a long moment, I sigh silently. "You just let me know when you are ready to tackle that subject. I may not be the most active person in the world when it comes to charity, but I have an almost endless supply of money. And I trust you to spend it wisely. Okay?"

She looks at me, screwing up her face. "You trust me, huh?"

My laugh is barely more than a rumble in my chest. "*Ja*, I do. You've only ever been very up front with me. I hope that you trust me in the same way."

I reach out and brush a strand of her hair back, tucking it behind her ear. She reaches out and puts her hand over mine, nuzzling her face against my fingers. "I do. I don't trust easily. I think that was whipped into me when I was pretty young. But when I do trust someone the way I trust you, I always feel secure whenever they are around. And since you're around me all the time, I always feel safe."

A warm feeling spreads through my chest at her words. "I'm glad."

She scrunches up her face. Looking around, she heaves an exaggerated sigh. "I feel like I should've brought something for you to unwrap. It seems silly to be in such a festive setting and have no present for you."

I wiggle my eyebrows. "You know how you were just telling me that you want to start a family?"

Margot looks at me, a little surprised. "Well… Yeah. I wanted to start the ball rolling, at least."

"Here in Copenhagen, or at least amongst the royal family, it's traditional to wait for a year between the wedding and having your first baby. I know that we haven't done anything that's traditional yet, but I feel like that's not an unreasonable time frame to set out."

Her expression darkens just a little bit. She bites her lower lip, seeming hesitant. "What if it just happens? I mean… It could. It's not like I'm on birth control or anything. If we are talking about family planning, we should really be considering all our options. Like using condoms, at the very least."

I give her a wry smile. "Let's not go too far with that. We are a married couple. We are in the financial place to take care of any children. And we are not averse to the idea of having kids. Besides, it feels so much better to fuck you without anything between us, even such a thin layer of latex." I shoot her a smirk. "I'm willing to take the risk if you are."

She shakes her head at me, a knowing smile on her lips. "Somehow, I knew that was going to be your answer."

I bite my lip, arching my eyebrows. "Are you going to give me grief about this? Or can I have one of the servants bring your first present in?"

Her eyes widen and she sits up a little bit. "What? Wait, really?"

I grin at her. "I'll take that as a yes, then."

Moving her legs aside, I stand up and head out into the hallway. The palace servant that I asked to be there is right where I expect him to be. I glance at him briefly, smiling tightly. "Bring the present in, please."

He fiddles with his phone and I head back into the room, beckoning to Margot. "Come on. Come over here and let me cover your eyes."

She bounds up off the couch, her excitement and curiosity almost getting the better of her. I pull her over, putting her in front of my body and covering her eyes. The puppy wrangler, for lack of a better term, pokes her head in the doorway. I nod to her, a smile spreading across my face.

When she guides the puppy in, leading it into the ballroom, I can almost feel my excitement growing. The puppy is dark eyed with a dark brown head and a dark brown splash across her back. What makes her special is the white markings on the rest of her body, complete with small brown spots dappling her legs and stomach. She's the dictionary definition of an old Danish pointer, and I can't wait until Margot sees her.

I wait until the puppy and the handler are only a few steps in front of us before I hold up my hand, signaling to the handler to wait. Then I whisper in Margot's ear. "Open your eyes."

Stepping aside, I look at Margot's face. Her reaction is amazing: first she is wide-eyed, then she's excited, and then she immediately burst into tears. "Is that…" she chokes out. She looks at me, tears staining her cheeks. "Is that for me?"

I grin, nodding. "Yup." Looking at the handler, I thank her. "We'll take it from here. Margot, you can grab her. She's an old Danish pointer, the same royal line that has always been in my family…"

Stepping closer, I take the leash from the handler, leading the puppy towards Margot. Margot kneels down, her hands already out. And the puppy runs straight to Margot, not showing the least bit of concern that Margot might be a danger.

I watch as she hugs the puppy to her chest, laughing as it licks her face and struggles to get free of her hold. Margot lets her go, her tears almost overwhelming her. "Are you a good girl? I bet you are. Are you growing up too fast?" She looks up at me, wiping her tears away. "What's her name?"

My mouth turns up at the corners. "That's for you to decide."

She shakes her head a little bit. "Come here. I don't want to move too far from the puppy but I need to hug you right now."

I smile as I drop the puppy's leash, going to sit beside my wife. My breath gets a little knocked out of me by how forcefully Margot hugs me, her pink up do starting to fall. I hug her back, putting out my hand to pet the wiggly puppy as she ventures over to sniff me.

Her wet tongue on my hand feels like a reward of its own.

Margot pulls back, looking up at me, tears still shining in her eyes. "Thank you, Stellan. This is the best gift that anyone could've ever gotten me. I've never even considered owning a dog but I am more glad than I can say that this was your gift."

I chuckle. "You are very welcome, *skatter*."

She leans close, offering her lips up to me. And I give her a little growl, kissing her as I pull her closer. The puppy begs our attention in the next moment, running up between us and putting her paws on both of us with a tiny bark. We break apart with a laugh, but my gaze never leaves Margot's face.

"I love you, wife. Never forget that."

Margot gives the puppy her hand to lick, grinning at me. "I'm the luckiest woman in the world, Stellan. I love you more than I can say."

A fresh batch of tears shines in her eyes. I smile and slip an arm around her waist, content.

Chapter Four

CLIMBING the steps that lead to the second floor of the palace, I feel more tired than I can ever remember feeling. Pippa is right behind me, climbing stairs elegantly as always. I make it to the landing and push myself onward, casting a glance at her. She looks absolutely amazing, from her elegant red tresses that flow down her back to her white haute couture down. Head to toe, Pippa always looks absolutely impeccable.

I feel as if I've been wrung out to dry even though I'm also wearing a frilly pink designer gown. Even under normal circumstances, I can't compete with gorgeous, glowing Pippa. I heave a sigh. Her brow hunches a little as she looks me up and down. When she speaks, it's with a posh English accent.

"And what's the matter with you?"

We walk down the hallway towards my chambers. I draw myself up and sigh. "It just seemed like that gala we were at was going to go on forever. No one told me that being Queen meant an endless number of galas." I roll my eyes, emphasizing that what I'm saying is silly.

Pippa smiles. "I imagine that you are pretty ready to take those heels off. I noticed that you have made more of an effort to wear high heels recently."

I finally reach the doorway to my chambers and push it open, running inside and kicking my shoes off. I sigh with relief and stretch my arms up over my head. "God, yes. I'm trying to be more royal. But a lifetime of wearing Converse hasn't properly prepared me for such fancy footwear. Not to mention, I've been feeling run down for like two weeks. I'm so tired that I might go to bed before ten p.m. tonight." I wrinkle my nose. "Is it ten yet?"

Pippa arches a brow. "It's only eight p.m. It just seems later because the sun goes down by four. That's Denmark in December for you…" She passes a glance around the living area and then heads over to one of the herring-bone-covered couches, collapsing on it and pulling off her shoes.

I reach behind myself and find my zipper at the very top of my shoulders, then pull it down. I sigh as a great deal of pressure is released from my rib cage. When I look up, I see Pippa arching a brow at me again.

"What?" I ask.

I shimmy out of the fancy dress, leaving me only in a white shift. I don't feel at all self-conscious in front of Pippa, who was my first college roommate and has been a longtime friend.

Pippa is the reason that I'm the Queen of Denmark, essentially. She introduced Stellan and I at a sketchy club in New York… And the rest is history, I guess.

Pippa's lips twitch. "Nothing. I'm just getting used to seeing you as the Queen of Denmark and then seeing you… Well, as yourself. Two different people, that's all."

I carefully hang my dress over the back of a chair and then join her on the couch. "It's taking some getting used to from my side, too. Believe me."

She scrunches up her nose and sighs. "I don't suppose you want to drink, do you?"

I pull a face. "No, not really. I just have been feeling like I've had the flu for a couple of weeks. Well… not the flu exactly? It's like the flu except that I have no respiratory symptoms. What is that, you think?"

Pippa purses her lips. "Have your breasts been tender?"

I give her an odd look. "What? Why?"

She holds up her hand, ticking things off as she makes a list. "You've been feeling really run down. You want to sleep all the time. You have an aversion to alcohol…"

I interrupt. "I wouldn't say that. I don't have an aversion. I just am too tired to drink. I think it's just being on royal duty all the time."

She sits up, eyeing me. "Or you could be pregnant."

I freeze. Scowling at her, I shake my head a little. "I'm sure it's nothing.

Just a little cold or something. You know, the cold without the sneezing and coughing or being congested."

Pippa favors me with a look. "Have you and Stellan been trying to prevent pregnancy in any way?"

My cheeks redden. I look away from her, mumbling my response. "No. But it hasn't been that long since I've had my period. I mean..." I squint, trying to count the weeks. "It's been... Four weeks? No, that's not right. It's been..."

Her lips quirk. "If you can't remember, that's not a good sign. Or maybe it is, depending on whether or not you want a baby. Either way, you would think that the king and queen of Denmark would have this under greater control. It's a little bit funny."

I shoot her a glare. "It is not funny. And anyway, it takes people ages to get pregnant. Right?"

She rolls her eyes. "Wrong. It takes *some* people a long time to get pregnant. But not everyone. If you guys aren't using condoms and you're not taking the pill, you had to have thought this out already..."

I shake my head. "No, I'm sure I'm not. My mom always tells me stories about how she never thought she was going to get pregnant. In fact, she thought that she couldn't get pregnant until me. But I was relatively late in her life, I think. She was pushing forty by the time she had me."

Pippa looks at me for a long moment. "Have you taken a pregnancy test?"

I give her a funny look. "Never."

She gets up off the couch and starts putting her feet back in your shoes. I watch her, frowning. When she starts heading out of the room, I call out to her.

"Where are you going?"

She just waves a hand at me, rushing out of the room. She's gone for some time before I decide that I ought to get more comfortable. Heading through the door to my private chamber, I change into more comfortable pajamas and wash my face.

Pippa stands in the doorway when I finish my beauty routine. I arch a brow at her. "Did you find whatever you were looking for?"

To my complete surprise, Pippa holds up a little box, long and rectangular and with Danish scrawled all over it. Even though I can't read the words, I can guess from the picture just what it is. She's clutching a pregnancy test.

I turn to her, rolling my eyes. "I hardly think that's necessary. I'm telling you, it took my mother forever to conceive me."

She looks at me flatly, holding out the test to me. "Take the test. That way you know for sure. And by the way, the housemaids are stocked to the gills with these things. Just for future notice."

My eyes widen. I take the test from her. "You asked one of the housemaids for this? You know that they are all terrible gossips. Every single one of them is on the payroll of somebody that I probably don't want to know my personal news."

She wrinkles her nose. "I know. That's why I told them it was for me."

I bust out laughing at that. "Wait, really? Oh, the housemaids are probably all atwitter right now, trying to figure out if you and Lars are going to be getting married."

Lars is Stellan's brother and he has also been Pippa's best male friend since they were preteens. She shakes her head at me and starts closing the bathroom door. "You pee on the stick. I'll be right here, waiting with baited breath."

Rolling my eyes, I quickly follow the instructions on the box.

The whole time I keep thinking: there's no way that I could be pregnant. It's just not something that I have planned for or in any way prepared myself for. I mean, I know that what Pippa said is right? It's not that. It's just…

I set the test down on the sink, washing my hands. The entire time, I'm trying to think of when the last time I had my period was. The longer I think about it, the more anxious I get. I am completely certain that I have no idea what I'm even panicking about at this point.

Pippa knocks on the door. "Are you done?"

I let out a long exhale. "Yes. Come in."

Staring down at the pregnancy test, I feel chills throughout my entire body. Pippa opens the door and comes into the bathroom, staring at the test over my shoulder. I look up into the mirror, taking us both in. I am short and I have cupcake pink hair. She's tall and glamorous, with fire red locks.

I currently look like a dead person, all the blood drained from my face. She takes one look at me and points to the bathtub. "Take a seat. We don't want you passing out."

I do as she says, feeling immense relief at the very act of sitting. I remember faintly some piece of information floating through my head, something about how you should lower your head between your knees and try to breathe.

Oh my God

Oh my God.

Stellan and I just talked about this not two days ago. I said that I wanted to start a family. And he countered with the fact that he wants to wait a full year. Simple as that.

I close my eyes and suck in a breath.

What if…

"Um, Margot? This test says that you're pregnant."

At the sound of Pippa's voice, I set up ramrod straight and my eyes fly open. "That's not possible! How… Why…"

My eyes fill with tears. Pippa takes one look at me, sets the pregnancy test down on the sink, and flies to my side. "Whoa, whoa. I didn't realize that you would get upset about this. I thought you wanted kids!"

I sniffle, unable to meet her gaze. "Stellan and I talked about having children and he said that he wanted to wait a year…" My voice breaks on the last word and I bite back a sob.

Pippa pulls me into her arms, shushing me. "It's okay, Margot. It's all gonna be okay. So what if you can't wait a year…"

I hiccup. "He said that it is the tradition in the royal family."

She rocks me gently back and forth. "So? You guys haven't done anything according to tradition. You are the entirely wrong kind of girl for that. First of all, you're American. You are the opposite of privileged. You were a fricking journalist when you guys met. And yet you won Stellan's heart just by being yourself. Do you think that he will not be out of his mind with excitement when you tell him? Because I think that he is going to be elated."

I wipe at my eyes. Looking up at her, I shake my head. "I don't know…"

Pippa grabs both my hands, looking me directly in the eye. "But I do. I've known Stellan since I was a kid. And I am telling you that he loves you and he will be excited. You were planning on doing this anyway, eventually. It's just a little sooner than you planned."

I suck in a shaky breath, shaking my head to clear it. "Are you sure you read the test right?"

She squints at me. "Yes. But just to be on the safe side, you should go see a doctor tomorrow morning. I can make the arrangement for you if you like. Then you can be sure."

My heart races. I looked down at my body, at my flat stomach. Frowning a little, I manage to center myself somewhat.

A baby.

I know that it's what I wanted anyway, but it's just so much sooner than I had expected…

Pippa draws me to my feet, snapping me out of my thoughts. She looks at me, pulling my hands together. "Tell me you're excited."

I bite my lip. Am I excited?

My pulse is racing. I'm mostly overwhelmed. But underneath all of that, a little spark of joy has been lit.

Slowly, I nod my head. "I think I am. It just… just took me by surprise, that's all."

Her lips twitch. She hugs me then, quick and hard. And I hug her right back, glad that she is my best friend.

"Thank you for making me take that test." My voice breaks on the last word and I start sobbing again. Pippa pulls me against her chest, rocking her body from side to side. "Come on. Let's get you in bed. Then we can talk about tomorrow and the doctor and everything that comes after that. It will be great, just you wait and see."

I take a deep breath and nod, leaning on Pippa as we head out of the bathroom. I feel so overwhelmed and so stunned by the news, but under it all, I feel joyous…

Chapter Five

IT'S OFFICIALLY CHRISTMAS EVE, or *Jul* as we Danes call it.
Normal families gather around the *Jul* tree and have elite lunch together.
But seeing as how I'm not remotely normal, I have to attend the royal
banquet during the afternoon hours. Everyone is dressed to the nines,
completely glamorous in their tuxes and ball gowns. The scene is every bit
as glamorous, the grand ballroom set up with long tables decorated in white
and red, snowflakes hanging from the high ceiling.

Everyone who's anyone is here today, a ton of Denmark's finest families
stuffed in one room.

Margot is right beside me, her white crinoline dress and pink hair
making quite a statement next to my traditional black tux. I shake everyone's hand and smile until I'm sure that my face will never be the same
again.

At the end of it all, I grab Margot and duck out of the ballroom, ripping
my bow tie off. I glance at Margot, who has been very quiet all day. She
looks at me, her smile cool. "I take that as a sign that you are done?"

I slip my hand around her waist, pulling her to my side. "Beyond done. I
don't think that anyone could possibly have asked for more from me. Nor
you, I suppose."

A sigh leaves her lips. "What's next on the day's agenda?"

I pull her toward the grand staircase, eager to get to our private chambers. "We have this family gathering later this evening… but there are a few hours of downtime penciled in to our schedule. And I plan to take full advantage of them. Just you and me, exchanging gifts. How does that sound?"

Her brows rise as she hits the staircase, climbing the steps. "Really? It's been a while since we've just spent a couple hours on our own. No press, no family members…"

My lips quirk. As we hit the end of the stairs and head down the hall, I hug her to my side. "I know. You should've heard the fight that I had with the royal press office to get this little reprieve today."

She grins up at me, her heart-shaped face making my heart grow two sizes in my chest. "I'm glad that you did. I've been trying to find the time to give you your presents."

We make it to the door and I swing it open, holding the door for her. She gathers up her skirts and hurries into the living room with an excited murmur. I follow right behind her, a little smirk on my lips. I'm thinking of what I got for her for Christmas and how surprised she is going to be.

Margot goes right over to the little crate where we are keeping our new puppy. She lets her out and looks back at me with a soft smile. "I've been thinking about what we should name her. I was looking at some popular names and Luna stuck out at me. What do you think?"

She scoops the puppy up in her arms, giving her a kiss on the nose. The puppy gives a sharp bark and licks Margot's face, making her laugh.

Closing the door behind me, I follow her footsteps, unable to resist my wife holding the puppy as she cradles her in her arms. I'm not thinking about the name that Margot proposed in the least.

No, I'm thinking instead of how amazing Margot will be as a mother. I don't know why exactly, but watching Margot and this puppy together is pushing a lot of buttons for me.

God, my cock is halfway hard. I bite my lower lip and nudge Margot's hip with my lower body. She looks at me with a laugh.

"You're not even listening," she accuses. She doesn't look cross, though.

"I was! You suggested that we call her Luna." I wrinkle my nose as I look down at them both. "That sounds perfect."

Luna wiggles and demands to be put down. Margot complies, a smile on her lips. She watches as the newly named Luna runs around the room, sniffing the couches. Margot arches a brow at me. "Are you ready for presents, then?"

I give her a grin. "Very."

Margot smiles wickedly and heads over to the tall *Jul* tree that we have set up in the room, looking down at all the gold-wrapped presents. She picks up two small presents, one in a small box the size of maybe two lemons and one in a wide flat package. She hands them over to me, wiggling her brows.

I accept the presents, looking suspiciously at them. Neither one weighs much of anything. I shake them gently, wondering what they could be.

Wrinkling my nose, I set the packages on the couch and then retrieve Margot's presents. One is a large flat box and one is a gift wrapped set of papers. She throws herself on the couch and holds her hand out to me, beckoning for her presents. I hand them to her, taking a seat beside her and watching her.

She looks at me, biting her lip. "Who goes first?"

I give her a tiny grin. "I think you do, by virtue of being more excited about them than I am."

She flushes. "When you come from a disadvantaged background like I did, you tend to get excited about every little thing. Don't shame me."

I laugh. "No shame intended. I just enjoy watching you, that's all. It's secondhand excitement, you might say."

She scrunches up her face and picks up the larger of the two presents, shaking the box a little. She looks at me with a mischievous smile and then starts tearing the gold wrapping paper off the box. In seconds, the whole box is shredded, and she is pulling out the most inexpensive of my presents. I watch the look on her face as she holds up a particularly naughty garment. It's a black and pink négligée, reminiscent of the one she wore the very first night she and I met.

Her cheeks turn red and she gives me an embarrassed grin. "You know my taste, apparently."

I grin at her. "And mine too, if that's not patently obvious by now."

"I'll have to model that for you later." She gives me a wicked grin. She sets the entire thing aside, picking up the sheaf of papers. They are loosely held together by a gold wrapped manila envelope. It takes her a minute to rip off the wrapping paper and undo the twine but then she is looking at the papers, her brow puckering in concentration.

I know exactly what she's looking at: a trust that I've started or a children's charity in her name.

When she looks up at me, her eyes glitter with tears. "Ten million dollars? You started a charity for me for ten million dollars?"

I begin to nod but in the next second I am knocked nearly breathless by her sudden lunge towards me. She wraps her arms around me and buries her face against my chest. "Oh Stellan, I don't know what to say. Thank you. Thank you so much."

I am surprised at her reaction, though by now I suppose I shouldn't be. Of course her favorite thing that I got her was not even really for her. I put my arms around her, rubbing circles on her back. "Of course. To be clear, you don't need my permission to do anything like this. I just figured that I would get you started."

She looks up at me, tearful. "It's exactly what I wanted. You got it exactly right."

She kisses me then, her lips sweet as wine. I cup her jaw and deepen the kiss, amazed at how giving and generous she is. It seems that there are few boundaries that Margot will not cross for the sake of children. And I find myself feeling exceptionally lucky that I fell in love with her.

I may have had to move heaven and earth to keep her at my side, but by god, it was worth it.

She breaks away, pushing me back a few inches. She dashes tears from her eyes. "You still have to open my presents."

I splay my hands. "If that's what you want, sure."

She tucks a strand of hair behind her ear and reaches around me. She pulls the small box and the wrapped piece of paper onto my lap. I look at her as I unwrap the box first, smiling lightly as I produce a kiwi fruit. Raising a brow, I cock my head.

"Are you saying I don't eat enough odd fruits?" I tease.

She blushes. "It's the only thing I could think of to represent the present I got you. I figured since your father has been ill, you two might like to spend some time together. So I booked you both a trip to New Zealand in the New Year." She bites her lower lip. "I've already told him about it, so I hope you are excited."

Opening my mouth, I freeze. My heart beats loud in my ears. I look at her, speechless.

"Of course I am. I… I love that you thought of me," I eventually say, reaching over and squeezing her thigh. I shake my head, shocked. "I'm really surprised. I haven't really thought of spending time with *dar*."

She beams at me. "I know. But I feel like one day, you will thank me."

Pulling her close, I kiss her lips. "I'm grateful now. Really, I am."

She sighs. "Oh, good. I'm glad."

Wiggling my eyebrows at her, I take a bite of the kiwi. Margot pulls a face.

"I'm not sure you're supposed to eat the whole thing like that."

I shrug, grinning. "We will see, won't we?"

I turn to her second present, unwrapping what seems to be a single thick piece of paper. I glance at her and find her biting her lip, looking very anxious.

I pull the paper away and find a grainy black and white photo of…

I squint.

It looks like a wall of grainy gray with a perfect black bubble on the left side. Inside the black bubble, there is… a bean?

I slide Margot a look. "You're going to have to help me out here. What am I looking at?"

She surprises me by pulling the kiwi away from me and lacing our fingers together. "It's a baby, Stellan. Our baby."

For a few solid seconds, I am not sure I heard her right. "Come again?"

An unsure expression ripples across her face. "I'm pregnant, Stellan."

My eyes tear up as I look back at the photo. "You're… you… this is our baby?"

She nods, wiping away a tear. "Yes," she answers softly.

"I'm going to be a dad?"

She nods again. "Yes, Stellan."

Moving so suddenly that Margot's breath leaves her lungs, I hug her hard. "Oh my god."

I bury my face against her neck, out of breath. I gulp, my emotions almost overwhelming me.

I can't believe that I'm going to be a father.

Pulling back, I cup Margot's face and kiss her lovely lips so sweetly. She kisses me back, her lips curving under my own. I grin and shake my head, disbelieving. "Fuck, *skatter*." I lean back, shouting to the sky. "I'm going to be a dad!"

I hug her again and she laughs as I pull her down onto the couch, kissing her.

"Does that mean you are happy?"

I nod, grinning and wiping at my eyes. "*Ja, skatter*. I am very happy."

Then I find her lips again, deepening the kiss, so happy I could explode.

$$Chapter\ Six$$

"GET NAKED," he rasps, his voice nothing short of an order.

It causes goosebumps to break out across my skin. I make a needy noise. He's already out of patience, his hands rending the front of the fancy dress I'm wearing.

"Stellan!" I laugh, pushing at his hands.

His lips twitch. "I need you bare and writhing, begging for me to fuck you. Now *get naked.*"

Shaking my head, I wriggle out of the dress, wrinkling my nose before casting it to the ground. Stellan turns me around, roughly ripping my panties and bra off.

There is something so primal about his touch, about how badly he needs me, that just adds to my usual arousal. I lean into his kiss before I am even certain what is happening. His hand cups my chin and controls my head. With my head lifted towards him, his lips are on mine. I can taste nothing but the flavor of him, clean and masculine and raw.

He sits down on the couch, drawing me with him.

When his tongue slips between my lips, I let out a moan, meeting it with my own. My back arches, my chest presses up against him. He explores the stretch of silky skin at my hip, and slowly moves lower, lower. He drags out every moment, an exquisite torture.

He grabs my thigh and drapes it across his lap, leaving me exposed. His hand travels up toward my center, kneading and squeezing my thigh as he goes.

When his fingers brush my core, he finds me already wet.

"This?" he says, his voice gone to gravel. He teases my crevice again with the lightest of touches. "This is mine."

I can do nothing but gasp and nod.

He grins and squeezes my ass as he pulls me on top of his lap. As I straddle him, I can feel his cock between my legs, wrapped in his jeans. I'm already wet, but can't help grinding against him. Even through his pants, I feel his hardened cock.

I've never been so ready for him before. I'm ready for him to tear off the rest of his clothes and fuck me right this second.

It's never that easy or fast with Stellan, though. He likes to take it slow, to tease and torture me.

His mouth moves from my lips to my jaw and travels to my neck. A part of me feels suddenly shy, even though this was far from our first time together. He tweaks my nipple, drawing a gasp from my lips.

Stellan smirks at my shyness. "You know that you are probably the most beautiful girl I've ever seen?"

He shifts me, raising me up above him so my nipples meet his mouth. I feel his fingers digging into my ass cheeks, dangerously close to my pussy, as the warmth of his mouth consumes one nipple, and then the other.

I whimper as I feel my nipples harden against his tongue. I want desperately to be lower, to be able to rub myself against his cock again, but he keeps me firmly poised inches above his lap.

I squirm and his hands that clutch my bare ass shift closer to my center. His fingers slowly, slowly spread me apart. The ache of emptiness is unbearable.

"Fuck, you're wet," he tells me between sucks on my nipples.

"Stop teasing me," I say, frustrated.

"Is this what you want?" he asks as he lowers me back down.

Instead of letting me go completely, he slides a finger inside my pussy and pushes his thumb against my clit. I shudder at the surprise of it—and the pleasure of having some part of him inside me.

I can't bring myself to reply, but I move against his hand eagerly. His hands are deft, with practiced flicks against my G-spot and just enough pressure on my clit to get me halfway to orgasm.

But no closer. He knows exactly what he's doing and it's driving me insane.

I kiss him deeply, my eyes squeezing shut. All I want is to come.

"Slow down," he tells me. "Enjoy the ride, *skatter*."

There is a part of me that thought maybe he'll just stop. Maybe it is all just a game, a power trip. I ride his hand harder, lifting my head, and offer my breasts to his lips again. He spanks me once on my ass, hard.

"I said slow down," he growls.

The slap surprises me, but even as the sting fades and I feel my ass turning red, I also feel a new gush of wetness between my thighs. My pussy is on fire, and I need him like I've never needed him before.

He slips his finger out of my pussy and flips me onto my back. The coolness of the couch is a shock to my skin. He kneels and spreads my legs wide.

"You really are ravishing," he tells me. "And I'm about to ravage you."

I smile and let my head fall back as he kisses his way down my thighs. When he reaches my mound, he kisses his way across it, trailing his tongue against my sweat-slicked skin. He comes so close to tasting me, really tasting my pussy, and yet he pulls back.

I shake my head back and forth, ready to burst.

"Fuck! Stellan, come on!" I cry, pounding my fists.

"What do you want?" he asks me, smirking.

"Stellan, *please*," I say, arching my back as far as I can.

"You're going to have to tell me," he says tauntingly.

I bite my lip just as he blows lightly on my clit.

"I want you to eat my… eat my pussy," I say, going red as I say the words.

"Good girl." He grins before he lowers himself to my flesh.

His tongue runs across my clit, firm and slow, before it dips down into the deepest of my folds. I cry out and dig my fingers into his hair to hold him closer to me.

"Oh god. Oh, Stellan!!" As he works his tongue faster, I can't stop calling out his name. When he slides a finger into me again, I reach for my breasts and pinch my nipples.

I don't want to come, not like this. Not without giving him a taste of his own medicine.

"I want to taste you," I say, breathless. He pulls his finger from my body and leaves a flutter of kisses on my clit.

"What about you? Don't you want to come?" he asks, even as he unbuckles his trousers.

I have to grin at his eagerness.

"I want you to feel good first… and then I want us to come together," I say.

When he unzips and shows me his cock, I bite my lip. I know I've seen it all before, but his cock is so perfect, so thick and long, so perfectly pink. That ache that is throbbing deep inside of me doesn't have a chance of stopping.

I reach for him, but he stops me. He straddles my chest and takes my hands in his.

"Press your tits together," he encourages me. "God, you are already so fucking hot, you know that?"

I blush, eagerly pressing my breasts together. As soon as I do, he slides his cock between my breasts, the tip reaching to my mouth. I lick and suck at him like a starving creature. The heat of his length between my breasts blended with his own taste in a way that is intoxicating.

He keeps one hand loosely on my head and caresses my cheek while he watches me take him deeper and deeper into my mouth. He rises up, brushes my hands away from my breasts, leans down and kisses me.

"Every part of you tastes so good," he whispers. I want to tell him the same, but my jaw aches and my lips are numb from sucking on just the couple of inches he gave me.

Standing up, he stretches briefly.

I laugh. "What are you doing?"

"I want to fuck you properly," he says. "I have got to stay flexible, *ja*?"

His grin is infectious. I grin right back at him, crooking a finger. "Come here."

Stellan cocks his head and then scoops me up, carrying me toward our bedroom. I kiss his neck as he makes his way in, tossing me on the bed. He climbs on the bed, looming over me.

"I want you so fucking bad," he swears. "Fuck, *skatter*. How do you do this to me?"

I beckon to him and he spreads my thighs, his big body pressing down on me. When he penetrates me, I feel shockingly tight. It feels so fucking good. I feel every single inch of him as he thrusts his long, proud cock inside my body.

I must be making an odd face, because he slows, watching me closely.

"Are you okay?" he asks me. "I don't want to hurt the baby…"

"Yes, yes," I breathe into his ear. "Please… I want you to fuck me. *Please*, Stellan."

He buries his face in my neck and breathes me in. He takes his time, sliding in and out of my pussy oh so slowly.

When he teases me, lingering with barely his tip inside me, I struggle and demand that he go deep. Every time he slides against my g-spot, I scratch at his back and call out his name.

"Stellan, yes! Oh, please don't stop."

I am so wet it is almost unbelievable. He kisses me, slowing even though I just told him not to.

"Not so fast, *skatter*. I want you to slow it down. Get on top," he tells me. "I want to watch you."

I bite my lip, and he switches our positions. On his back, he watches me straddle him. My hair has come undone and hangs in knotted waves over my breasts. He reaches up, pushes the hair aside, and pulls my nipples. I look down and grasp his cock to bring him to my opening.

He moves his hands to my hips.

"Slowly," he tells me. "Remember what I said."

I let my weight fall onto him, but he holds me up. I blush again. He seems to want to watch me take his cock into my pussy.

"Please," I whisper when he is halfway in. He pulls me down hard, a sudden lurch. I throw my head back and call out.

My nails dig into his chest and he clutches my ass as I ride him. It's perfect, the two of us moving as one, our breathing harsh. My breasts bounce wildly. Every part of his skin feels like silk underneath my fingertips. My wetness is so intense it drips down between his thighs.

My eyes close tight and I grind hard against him.

"Look at me," he tells me.

I open my eyes and he can tell I am close.

"I love you. I love you so fucking much," he says, his blue eyes practically glowing.

"I love you too," I whisper, my breath coming in gasps.

He pushes himself up and I wrap my legs around his back. From here, he is in complete control — and my nipples are once again aligned with his face.

He lifts me and lowers me onto his cock, while he covers my chest in marks that I know would darken to hickeys by the next day. I score his back with my nails, marking him in my own way.

My legs are locked around him, his cock soaked with my juices.

"I—" I gasp out. "I'm going to come…"

He can feel my orgasm start to wash over me as the heat of my insides clench. It is enough to push him over the edge and he comes with me. When he explodes inside of me, I scream out loud. "Oh my GOD!"

"Fuck! Margot, fuck," he whispers.

I shudder against him as I ride out the last of my orgasm. He kisses my neck gently and makes his way to my lips.

Stellan lies beside me, lining our bodies up and holding me close as I struggle for breath. He's breathing hard too, but he kisses my neck, my shoulder, the curve of my breast. Each kiss is a burning brand, causing a shudder to ripple across my exhausted body.

I want to beg him to stop, but I also want to have him again, right now. There's something about him that just makes me insatiable. He looks up at me, then presses a kiss to my lips.

"Fuck," he says softly, making eye contact with me.

I can't help but laugh a little. "What?"

He kisses me, long and slow. "God, Margot. I just can't get enough of you."

I grin at him. "You won't run out of me, Stellan."

He sucks in a breath, pulling my hips against his body. "I can't believe we are adding to our family. Just…" He slides his fingers over the smoothness of my abdomen. "I just can't believe it."

I bite my lip, tipping his chin up so that he has to meet my eyes.

"You swear you're not mad?" I ask, holding my breath.

He looks at me so seriously, it almost takes my breath away. "I swear, Margot. We've never done anything traditionally in our whole relationship… so I can't be surprised that we didn't do this the traditional way, either. Besides, it's not like you got yourself pregnant, is it?"

My mouth curves up. "No, I don't think I did."

He kisses me again, his fingers pressing into my belly. "When can we start telling people?"

I huff a laugh. "At least a month, my love."

He smirks. "Well… in the meantime…" He presses his cock against me, its growing hardness impressive. "We have a couple more hours until we are due at the Jul celebration. What do you say that I see how many times I can satisfy us both?"

I slip my arms around his neck, luxuriating in him. "That sounds like one hell of a plan, Stellan."

He kisses me and we sink into oblivion, ridiculously happy.

Chapter Seven

THERE IS a razor thin edge between love and hate.

As the crown prince of Denmark, duty and honor come first.

So when I meet a fiesty pink haired girl from the wrong side of the tracks, I keep mum about my royal birth. That way I can have one earth shattering night together with her.

Proud, rebellious, gorgeous -- Margot is my weakness.

Sleeping with her is the best thing I can't ever do again... until I realize that she's a journalist. Reporters like her have made my life a living hell. And when she shows up again in Copenhagen again? She's tasked with doing a story about me and the future of the royal line.

So Margot and I are shackled together. She hates my guts because I ditched her without a word back in New York. And my teeth are set on edge by her endless barrage of questions and snapping photos.

I don't want to find her attractive. I want to be repulsed. But...

Now that we're forced together, my resolve starts to crumble. Every time our hands brush, every damn time she bites her lip... Eventually, even my strong will can't overcome temptation. Though it's wrong, even though I might lose everything, I can't resist her.

* * *

Want to find out what happened between Margot and Stellan? Get THE WICKED PRINCE right now!

You can also join my email list for upcoming releases.

About Vivian Wood

Vivian likes to write about troubled, deeply flawed alpha males and the fiery, kick-ass women who bring them to their knees.

Vivian's lasting motto in romance is a quote from a favorite song: "Soulmates never die."

Be sure to join her email list to keep up with all the awesome giveaways, author videos, ARC opportunities, and more!

Vivian's Works

Wildflower Lane
Small Town Romantic Comedy
The Accidental Honeymoon

Cape Simon Billionaires
Small Town Billionaire Romance

The Grumpy Boss Agreement
The Fake Fiancée Proposition
The Playboy Rival Arrangement

Billionaires Ever After
Steamy Bad Boy Romance
His Best Friend's Little Sister
Claiming Her Innocence
His Fiancé To Keep
His Lovely Virgin

Sinfully Rich
Steamy Billionaire Romance
Sinful Fling
Sinful Enemy
Sinful Boss
Sinful Chance
Forbidden Professor

Ruined Castle Trilogy
Forbidden Billionaire Romance
The Single Dad
The Nanny
The Caress

Broken Slipper Trilogy
Forbidden Billionaire Romance
The Patron
The Dancer
The Embrace
Possessive

Married At Midnight
Forbidden Billionaire Romance
Deal With The Devil
Wed to the Devil
Vow to the Devil

Dirty Royals
Forbidden Royal Romance
Cruel Heir
Sinful Princess
Pretend Princess

King's Capture Duet
Dark Billionaire Romance
King's Capture
Queen's Sacrifice

Fifth Avenue Villains
Fifth Avenue Devil
Fifth Avenue Romeo

Hush Hush Club
Forbidden Billionaire Romantic Suspense
Such A Good Girl
Such A Spoiled Brat

Addiction Duet
Angsty Dark Romance
Addiction
Obsession

Other books
Wild Hearts

For more information….
vivian-wood.com
info@vivian-wood.com